# the host

# *the host*

## A NOVEL

## STEPHENIE MEYER

**BACK BAY BOOKS**
Little, Brown and Company
**NEW YORK   BOSTON   LONDON**

The author is grateful for permission to reprint the poem "Question" from *Nature: Poems Old and New,* by May Swenson. Copyright © 1994 by The Literary Estate of May Swenson. Reprinted by permission of Houghton Mifflin Company. All rights reserved.

Back Bay / Little, Brown and Company
Hachette Book Group
237 Park Avenue
New York, NY 10017
Visit our Web site at www.HachetteBookGroup.com.

Printed in the United States of America

Originally published in hardcover by Little, Brown and Company, May 2008
First Back Bay international mass market edition, July 2009

10 9 8 7 6 5 4 3 2 1

**ATTENTION CORPORATIONS AND ORGANIZATIONS:**
Most HACHETTE BOOK GROUP books are available at quantity discounts with bulk purchase for educational, business, or sales promotional use. For information, please call or write:
**Special Markets Department, Hachette Book Group**
**237 Park Avenue, New York, NY 10017**
**Telephone: 1-800-222-6747 Fax: 1-800-477-5925**

# *the host*

---

*To my mother, Candy,*
*who taught me that love is the best part of any story*

---

# QUESTION

Body my house
my horse my hound
what will I do
when you are fallen

Where will I sleep
How will I ride
What will I hunt

Where can I go
without my mount
all eager and quick
How will I know
in thicket ahead
is danger or treasure
When Body my good
bright dog is dead

How will it be
to lie in the sky
without roof or door
and wind for an eye

with cloud for a shift
how will I hide?

—May Swenson

# Inserted

The Healer's name was Fords Deep Waters.

Because he was a soul, by nature he was all things good: compassionate, patient, honest, virtuous, and full of love. Anxiety was an unusual emotion for Fords Deep Waters.

Irritation was even rarer. However, because Fords Deep Waters lived inside a human body, irritation was sometimes inescapable.

As the whispers of the Healing students buzzed in the far corner of the operating room, his lips pressed together into a tight line. The expression felt out of place on a mouth more often given to smiling.

Darren, his regular assistant, saw the grimace and patted his shoulder.

"They're just curious, Fords," he said quietly.

"An insertion is hardly an interesting or challenging

procedure. Any soul on the street could perform it in an emergency. There's nothing for them to learn by observing today." Fords was surprised to hear the sharp edge marring his normally soothing voice.

"They've never seen a grown human before," Darren said.

Fords raised one eyebrow. "Are they blind to each other's faces? Do they not have mirrors?"

"You know what I mean — a wild human. Still soulless. One of the insurgents."

Fords looked at the girl's unconscious body, laid out facedown on the operating table. Pity swelled in his heart as he remembered the condition her poor, broken body had been in when the Seekers had brought her to the Healing facility. Such pain she'd endured. . . .

Of course she was perfect now — completely healed. Fords had seen to that.

"She looks the same as any of us," Fords murmured to Darren. "We all have human faces. And when she wakes up, she will be one of us, too."

"It's just exciting for them, that's all."

"The soul we implant today deserves more respect than to have her host body gawked at this way. She'll already have far too much to deal with as she acclimates. It's not fair to put her through this." By *this,* he did not mean the gawking. Fords heard the sharp edge return to his voice.

Darren patted him again. "It will be fine. The Seeker needs information and —"

At the word *Seeker,* Fords gave Darren a look that could only be described as a glare. Darren blinked in shock.

"I'm sorry," Fords apologized at once. "I didn't mean to react so negatively. It's just that I fear for this soul."

His eyes moved to the cryotank on its stand beside the table. The light was a steady, dull red, indicating that it was occupied and in hibernation mode.

"This soul was specially picked for the assignment," Darren said soothingly. "She is exceptional among our kind — braver than most. Her lives speak for themselves. I think she would volunteer, if it were possible to ask her."

"Who among us would not volunteer if asked to do something for the greater good? But is that really the case here? Is the greater good served by this? The question is not her willingness, but what it is right to ask any soul to bear."

The Healing students were discussing the hibernating soul as well. Fords could hear the whispers clearly; their voices were rising now, getting louder with their excitement.

"She's lived on six planets."

"I heard seven."

"I heard she's never lived two terms as the same host species."

"Is that possible?"

"She's been almost everything. A Flower, a Bear, a Spider —"

"A See Weed, a Bat —"

"Even a Dragon!"

"I don't believe it — not seven planets."

"At least seven. She started on the Origin."

"Really? The Origin?"

"Quiet, please!" Fords interrupted. "If you cannot

observe professionally and silently, then I will have to ask you to remove yourselves."

Abashed, the six students fell silent and edged away from one another.

"Let's get on with this, Darren."

Everything was prepared. The appropriate medicines were laid out beside the human girl. Her long dark hair was secured beneath a surgical cap, exposing her slender neck. Deeply sedated, she breathed slowly in and out. Her sun-browned skin had barely a mark to show for her . . . accident.

"Begin thaw sequence now, please, Darren."

The gray-haired assistant was already waiting beside the cryotank, his hand resting on the dial. He flipped the safety back and spun down on the dial. The red light atop the small gray cylinder began to pulse, flashing faster as the seconds passed, changing color.

Fords concentrated on the unconscious body; he edged the scalpel through the skin at the base of the subject's skull with small, precise movements, and then sprayed on the medication that stilled the excess flow of blood before he widened the fissure. Fords delved delicately beneath the neck muscles, careful not to injure them, exposing the pale bones at the top of the spinal column.

"The soul is ready, Fords," Darren informed him.

"So am I. Bring her."

Fords felt Darren at his elbow and knew without looking that his assistant would be prepared, his hand stretched out and waiting; they had worked together for many years now. Fords held the gap open.

"Send her home," he whispered.

Darren's hand moved into view, the silver gleam of an awaking soul in his cupped palm.

Fords never saw an exposed soul without being struck by the beauty of it.

The soul shone in the brilliant lights of the operating room, brighter than the reflective silver instrument in his hand. Like a living ribbon, she twisted and rippled, stretching, happy to be free of the cryotank. Her thin, feathery attachments, nearly a thousand of them, billowed softly like pale silver hair. Though they were all lovely, this one seemed particularly graceful to Fords Deep Waters.

He was not alone in his reaction. He heard Darren's soft sigh, heard the admiring murmurs of the students.

Gently, Darren placed the small glistening creature inside the opening Fords had made in the human's neck. The soul slid smoothly into the offered space, weaving herself into the alien anatomy. Fords admired the skill with which she possessed her new home. Her attachments wound tightly into place around the nerve centers, some elongating and reaching deeper to where he couldn't see, under and up into the brain, the optic nerves, the ear canals. She was very quick, very firm in her movements. Soon, only one small segment of her glistening body was visible.

"Well done," he whispered to her, knowing that she could not hear him. The human girl was the one with ears, and she still slept soundly.

It was a routine matter to finish the job. He cleaned and healed the wound, applied the salve that sealed the incision closed behind the soul, and then brushed the scar-softening powder across the line left on her neck.

"Perfect, as usual," said the assistant, who, for some reason unfathomable to Fords, had never made a change from his human host's name, Darren.

Fords sighed. "I regret this day's work."

"You're only doing your duty as a Healer."

"This is the rare occasion when Healing creates an injury."

Darren began to clean up the workstation. He didn't seem to know how to answer. Fords was filling his Calling. That was enough for Darren.

But not enough for Fords Deep Waters, who was a true Healer to the core of his being. He gazed anxiously at the human female's body, peaceful in slumber, knowing that this peace would be shattered as soon as she awoke. All the horror of this young woman's end would be borne by the innocent soul he'd just placed inside her.

As he leaned over the human and whispered in her ear, Fords wished fervently that the soul inside could hear him now.

"Good luck, little wanderer, good luck. How I wish you didn't need it."

# CHAPTER 1

# *Remembered*

I knew it would begin with the end, and the end would look like death to these eyes. I had been warned.

Not *these* eyes. *My* eyes. Mine. This was *me* now.

The language I found myself using was odd, but it made sense. Choppy, boxy, blind, and linear. Impossibly crippled in comparison to many I'd used, yet still it managed to find fluidity and expression. Sometimes beauty. My language now. My native tongue.

With the truest instinct of my kind, I'd bound myself securely into the body's center of thought, twined myself inescapably into its every breath and reflex until it was no longer a separate entity. It was me.

Not *the* body, *my* body.

I felt the sedation wearing off and lucidity taking its place. I braced myself for the onslaught of the first memory, which would really be the last memory — the last moments this body had experienced, the memory of the end. I had been warned thoroughly of what would happen now. These human emotions would be stronger, more vital than the feelings of any other species I had been. I had tried to prepare myself.

The memory came. And, as I'd been warned, it was not something that could ever be prepared for.

It seared with sharp color and ringing sound. Cold on her skin, pain gripping her limbs, burning them. The taste was fiercely metallic in her mouth. And there was the new sense, the fifth sense I'd never had, that took the particles from the air and transformed them into strange messages and pleasures and warnings in her brain — scents. They were distracting, confusing to me, but not to her memory. The memory had no time for the novelties of smell. The memory was only fear.

Fear locked her in a vise, goading the blunt, clumsy limbs forward but hampering them at the same time. To flee, to run — it was all she could do.

*I've failed.*

The memory that was not mine was so frighteningly strong and clear that it sliced through my control — overwhelmed the detachment, the knowledge that this was just a memory and not me. Sucked into the hell that was the last minute of her life, I was she, and we were running.

It's so dark. I can't see. I can't see the floor. I can't see my hands stretched out in front of me. I run blind and try to hear the pursuit I can feel behind me, but the pulse is so loud behind my ears it drowns everything else out.

It's cold. It shouldn't matter now, but it hurts. I'm so cold.

The air in her nose was uncomfortable. Bad. A bad smell. For one second, that discomfort pulled me free of the memory. But it was only a second, and then I was dragged in again, and my eyes filled with horrified tears.

I'm lost, we're lost. It's over.

They're right behind me now, loud and close. There are so many footsteps! I am alone. I've failed.

The Seekers are calling. The sound of their voices twists my stomach. I'm going to be sick.

"It's fine, it's fine," one lies, trying to calm me, to slow me. Her voice is disturbed by the effort of her breathing.

"Be careful!" another shouts in warning.

"Don't hurt yourself," one of them pleads. A deep voice, full of concern.

Concern!

Heat shot through my veins, and a violent hatred nearly choked me.

I had never felt such an emotion as this in all my lives. For another second, my revulsion pulled me away from the memory. A high, shrill keening pierced my ears and pulsed in my head. The sound scraped through my airways. There was a weak pain in my throat.

*Screaming,* my body explained. *You're screaming.*

I froze in shock, and the sound broke off abruptly.

This was not a memory.

My body — she was *thinking! Speaking* to me!

But the memory was stronger, in that moment, than my astonishment.

"Please!" they cry. "There is danger ahead!"

*The danger is behind!* I scream back in my mind. But I see what they mean. A feeble stream of light, coming from who knows where, shines on the end of the hall. It is not the flat wall or the locked door, the dead end I feared and expected. It is a black hole.

An elevator shaft. Abandoned, empty, and condemned, like this building. Once a hiding place, now a tomb.

A surge of relief floods through me as I race forward. There is a way. No way to survive, but perhaps a way to win.

*No, no, no!* This thought was all mine, and I fought to pull myself away from her, but we were together. And we sprinted for the edge of death.

"Please!" The shouts are more desperate.

I feel like laughing when I know that I am fast enough. I imagine their hands clutching for me just inches behind my back. But I am as fast as I need to be. I don't even pause at the end of the floor. The hole rises up to meet me midstride.

The emptiness swallows me. My legs flail, useless. My hands grip the air, claw through it, searching for anything solid. Cold blows past me like tornado winds.

I hear the thud before I feel it. . . . The wind is gone. . . . And then pain is everywhere. . . . Pain is everything.

Make it stop.

*Not high enough,* I whisper to myself through the pain. When will the pain end? When . . . ?

The blackness swallowed up the agony, and I was weak with gratitude that the memory had come to this most final of conclusions. The blackness took all, and I was free. I took a breath to steady myself, as was this body's habit. *My* body.

But then the color rushed back, the memory reared up and engulfed me again.

*No!* I panicked, fearing the cold and the pain and the very fear itself.

But this was not the same memory. This was a memory within a memory — a final memory, like a last gasp of air — yet, somehow, even stronger than the first.

The blackness took all but this: a face.

The face was as alien to me as the faceless serpentine tentacles of my last host body would be to this new body. I'd seen this kind of face in the images I had been given to prepare for this world. It was hard to tell them apart, to see the tiny variations in color and shape that were the only markers of the individual. So much the same, all of them. Noses centered in the middle of the sphere, eyes above and mouths below, ears around the sides. A collection of senses, all but touch, concentrated in one place. Skin over bones, hair growing on the crown and in strange furry lines above the eyes. Some had more fur lower down on the jaw; those were always males. The colors ranged through the brown scale from pale cream to a deep almost-black. Aside from that, how to know one from the other?

This face I would have known among millions.

This face was a hard rectangle, the shape of the bones strong under the skin. In color it was a light golden brown. The hair was just a few shades darker than the skin, except where flaxen streaks lightened it, and it covered only the head and the odd fur stripes above the eyes. The circular irises in the white eyeballs were darker than the hair but, like the hair, flecked with light. There were small lines around the eyes, and her memories told me the lines were from smiling and squinting into sunlight.

I knew nothing of what passed for beauty among these strangers, and yet I knew that this face was beautiful. I wanted to keep looking at it. As soon as I realized this, it disappeared.

*Mine,* spoke the alien thought that should not have existed.

Again, I was frozen, stunned. There should have been no one here but me. And yet this thought was so strong and so aware!

Impossible. How was she still here? This was me now.

*Mine,* I rebuked her, the power and authority that belonged to me alone flowing through the word. *Everything is mine.*

*So why am I talking back to her?* I wondered as the voices interrupted my thoughts.

# *Overheard*

The voices were soft and close and, though I was only now aware of them, apparently in the middle of a murmured conversation.

"I'm afraid it's too much for her," one said. The voice was soft but deep, male. "Too much for anyone. Such violence!" The tone spoke of revulsion.

"She screamed only once," said a higher, reedy, female voice, pointing this out with a hint of glee, as if she were winning an argument.

"I know," the man admitted. "She is very strong. Others have had much more trauma, with much less cause."

"I'm sure she'll be fine, just as I told you."

"Maybe you missed your Calling." There was an edge to the man's voice. Sarcasm, my memory named it. "Perhaps you were meant to be a Healer, like me."

The woman made a sound of amusement. Laughter.

"I doubt that. We Seekers prefer a different sort of diagnosis."

My body knew this word, this title: *Seeker.* It sent a shudder of fear down my spine. A leftover reaction. Of course, *I* had no reason to fear Seekers.

"I sometimes wonder if the infection of humanity touches those in your profession," the man mused, his voice still sour with annoyance. "Violence is part of your life choice. Does enough of your body's native temperament linger to give you enjoyment of the horror?"

I was surprised at his accusation, at his tone. This discussion was almost like . . . an argument. Something my host was familiar with but that I'd never experienced.

The woman was defensive. "We do not choose violence. We face it when we must. And it's a good thing for the rest of you that some of us are strong enough for the unpleasantness. Your peace would be shattered without our work."

"Once upon a time. Your vocation will soon be obsolete, I think."

"The error of that statement lies on the bed there."

"One human girl, alone and unarmed! Yes, quite a threat to our peace."

The woman breathed out heavily. A sigh. "But where did she come from? How did she appear in the middle of Chicago, a city long since civilized, hundreds of miles from any trace of rebel activity? Did she manage it alone?"

She listed the questions without seeming to seek an answer, as if she had already voiced them many times.

"That's your problem, not mine," the man said. "My job is to help this soul adapt herself to her new host without unnecessary pain or trauma. And you are here to interfere with my job."

Still slowly surfacing, acclimating myself to this new world of senses, I understood only now that I was the subject of the conversation. I was the soul they spoke of. It was a new connotation to the word, a word that had meant many other things to my host. On every planet we took a different name. *Soul.* I suppose it was an apt description. The unseen force that guides the body.

"The answers to my questions matter as much as your responsibilities to the soul."

"That's debatable."

There was the sound of movement, and her voice was suddenly a whisper. "When will she become responsive? The sedation must be about to wear off."

"When she's ready. Leave her be. She deserves to handle the situation however she finds most comfortable. Imagine the shock of her awakening — inside a rebel host injured to the point of death in the escape attempt! No one should have to endure such trauma in times of peace!" His voice rose with the increase of emotion.

"She is strong." The woman's tone was reassuring now. "See how well she did with the first memory, the worst memory. Whatever she expected, she handled this."

"Why should she have to?" the man muttered, but he didn't seem to expect an answer.

The woman answered anyway. "If we're to get the information we need —"

"*Need* being your word. I would choose the term *want.*"

"Then someone must take on the unpleasantness," she

continued as if he had not interrupted. "And I think, from all I know of this one, she would accept the challenge if there had been any way to ask her. What do you call her?"

The man didn't speak for a long moment. The woman waited.

"Wanderer," he finally and unwillingly answered.

"Fitting," she said. "I don't have any official statistics, but she has to be one of the very few, if not the only one, who has wandered so far. Yes, *Wanderer* will suit her well until she chooses a new name for herself."

He said nothing.

"Of course, she may assume the host's name. . . . We found no matches on record for the fingerprints or retinal scan. I can't tell you what that name was."

"She won't take the human name," the man muttered.

Her response was conciliatory. "Everyone finds comfort their own way."

"This Wanderer will need more comfort than most, thanks to your style of Seeking."

There were sharp sounds — footsteps, staccato against a hard floor. When she spoke again, the woman's voice was across the room from the man.

"You would have reacted poorly to the early days of this occupation," she said.

"Perhaps you react poorly to peace."

The woman laughed, but the sound was false — there was no real amusement. My mind seemed well adapted to inferring the true meanings from tones and inflections.

"You do not have a clear perception of what my Calling entails. Long hours hunched over files and maps.

Mostly desk work. Not very often the conflict or violence you seem to think it is."

"Ten days ago you were armed with killing weapons, running this body down."

"The exception, I assure you, not the rule. Do not forget, the weapons that disgust you are turned on our kind wherever we Seekers have not been vigilant enough. The humans kill us happily whenever they have the ability to do so. Those whose lives have been touched by the hostility see us as heroes."

"You speak as if a war were raging."

"To the remains of the human race, one is."

These words were strong in my ears. My body reacted to them; I felt my breathing speed, heard the sound of my heart pumping louder than was usual. Beside the bed I lay on, a machine registered the increases with a muted beeping. The Healer and the Seeker were too involved in their disagreement to notice.

"But one that even they must realize is long lost. They are outnumbered by what? A million to one? I imagine you would know."

"We estimate the odds are quite a bit higher in our favor," she admitted grudgingly.

The Healer appeared to be content to let his side of the disagreement rest with that information. It was quiet for a moment.

I used the empty time to evaluate my situation. Much was obvious.

I was in a Healing facility, recovering from an unusually traumatic insertion. I was sure the body that hosted me had been fully healed before it was given to me. A damaged host would have been disposed of.

I considered the conflicting opinions of the Healer and the Seeker. According to the information I had been given before making the choice to come here, the Healer had the right of it. Hostilities with the few remaining pockets of humans were all but over. The planet called Earth was as peaceful and serene as it looked from space, invitingly green and blue, wreathed in its harmless white vapors. As was the way of the soul, harmony was universal now.

The verbal dissension between the Healer and the Seeker was out of character. Strangely aggressive for our kind. It made me wonder. Could they be true, the whispered rumors that had undulated like waves through the thoughts of the . . . of the . . .

I was distracted, trying to find the name for my last host species. We'd had a name, I knew that. But, no longer connected to that host, I could not remember the word. We'd used much simpler language than this, a silent language of thought that connected us all into one great mind. A necessary convenience when one was rooted forever into the wet black soil.

I could describe that species in my new human language. We lived on the floor of the great ocean that covered the entire surface of our world — a world that had a name, too, but that was also gone. We each had a hundred arms and on each arm a thousand eyes, so that, with our thoughts connected, not one sight in the vast waters went unseen. There was no need for sound, so there was no way to hear it. We tasted the waters, and, with our sight, that told us all we needed to know. We tasted the suns, so many leagues above the water, and turned their taste into the food we needed.

I could describe us, but I could not name us. I sighed

for the lost knowledge, and then returned my ponderings to what I'd overheard.

Souls did not, as a rule, speak anything but the truth. Seekers, of course, had the requirements of their Calling, but between souls there was never reason for a lie. With my last species' language of thought, it would have been impossible to lie, even had we wanted to. However, anchored as we were, we told ourselves stories to alleviate the boredom. Storytelling was the most honored of all talents, for it benefited everyone.

Sometimes, fact mixed with fiction so thoroughly that, though no lies were told, it was hard to remember what was strictly true.

When we thought of the new planet — Earth, so dry, so varied, and filled with such violent, destructive denizens we could barely imagine them — our horror was sometimes overshadowed by our excitement. Stories spun themselves quickly around the thrilling new subject. The wars — wars! our kind having to fight! — were first reported accurately and then embellished and fictionalized. When the stories conflicted with the official information I sought out, I naturally believed the first reports.

But there were whispers of this: of human hosts so strong that the souls were forced to abandon them. Hosts whose minds could not be completely suppressed. Souls who took on the personality of the body, rather than the other way around. Stories. Wild rumors. Madness.

But that seemed almost to be the Healer's accusation. . . .

I dismissed the thought. The more likely meaning of his censure was the distaste most of us felt for the Seeker's Calling. Who would choose a life of conflict and pursuit? Who would be attracted to the chore of tracking down unwilling hosts and capturing them? Who would have the stomach to face the violence of this particular species, the hostile humans who killed so easily, so thoughtlessly? Here, on this planet, the Seekers had become practically a . . . militia — my new brain supplied the term for the unfamiliar concept. Most believed that only the least civilized souls, the least evolved, the lesser among us, would be drawn to the path of Seeker.

Still, on Earth the Seekers had gained new status. Never before had an occupation gone so awry. Never before had it turned into a fierce and bloody battle. Never before had the lives of so many souls been sacrificed. The Seekers stood as a mighty shield, and the souls of this world were thrice-over indebted to them: for the safety they had carved out of the mayhem, for the risk of the final death that they faced willingly every day, and for the new bodies they continued to provide.

Now that the danger was virtually past, it appeared the gratitude was fading. And, for this Seeker at least, the change was not a pleasant one.

It was easy to imagine what her questions for me would be. Though the Healer was trying to buy me time to adjust to my new body, I knew I would do my best to help the Seeker. Good citizenship was quintessential to every soul.

So I took a deep breath to prepare myself. The monitor registered the movement. I knew I was stalling a bit. I hated to admit it, but I was afraid. To get the information the Seeker needed, I would have to explore the violent memories that had made me scream in horror. More than that, I was afraid of the voice I'd heard so loudly in my head. But she was silent now, as was right. She was just a memory, too.

I should not have been afraid. After all, I was called Wanderer now. And I'd earned the name.

With another deep breath, I delved into the memories that frightened me, faced them head-on with my teeth locked together.

I could skip past the end — it didn't overwhelm me now. In fast-forward, I ran through the dark again, wincing, trying not to feel. It was over quickly.

Once I was through that barrier, it wasn't hard to float through less-alarming things and places, skimming for the information I wanted. I saw how she'd come to this cold city, driving by night in a stolen car chosen for its nondescript appearance. She'd walked through the streets of Chicago in darkness, shivering beneath her coat.

She was doing her own seeking. There were others like her here, or so she hoped. One in particular. A friend . . . no, family. Not a sister . . . a cousin.

The words came slower and slower, and at first I did not understand why. Was this forgotten? Lost in the trauma of an almost death? Was I still sluggish from unconsciousness? I struggled to think clearly. This sensation was unfamiliar. Was my body still sedated? I felt alert enough, but my mind labored unsuccessfully for the answers I wanted.

I tried another avenue of searching, hoping for clearer responses. What was her goal? She would find . . . Sharon — I fished out the name — and they would . . .

I hit a wall.

It was a blank, a nothing. I tried to circle around it, but

I couldn't find the edges of the void. It was as if the information I sought had been erased.

As if this brain had been damaged.

Anger flashed through me, hot and wild. I gasped in surprise at the unexpected reaction. I'd heard of the emotional instability of these human bodies, but this was beyond my ability to anticipate. In eight full lives, I'd never had an emotion touch me with such force.

I felt the blood pulse through my neck, pounding behind my ears. My hands tightened into fists.

The machines beside me reported the acceleration of my heartbeats. There was a reaction in the room: the sharp tap of the Seeker's shoes approached me, mingled with a quieter shuffle that must have been the Healer.

"Welcome to Earth, Wanderer," the female voice said.

# CHAPTER 3

# Resisted

S he won't recognize the new name," the Healer murmured.

A new sensation distracted me. Something pleasant, a change in the air as the Seeker stood at my side. A scent, I realized. Something different than the sterile, odorless room. Perfume, my new mind told me. Floral, lush . . .

"Can you hear me?" the Seeker asked, interrupting my analysis. "Are you aware?"

"Take your time," the Healer urged in a softer voice than the one he had used before.

I did not open my eyes. I didn't want to be distracted. My mind gave me the words I needed, and the tone that would convey what I couldn't say without using many words.

"Have I been placed in a damaged host in order to gain the information you need, Seeker?"

There was a gasp — surprise and outrage mingled — and something warm touched my skin, covered my hand.

"Of course not, Wanderer," the man said reassuringly. "Even a Seeker would stop at some things."

The Seeker gasped again. Hissed, my memory corrected.

"Then why doesn't this mind function correctly?"

There was a pause.

"The scans were perfect," the Seeker said. Her words not reassuring but argumentative. Did she mean to quarrel with me? "The body was entirely healed."

"From a suicide attempt that was perilously close to succeeding." My tone was stiff, still angry. I wasn't used to anger. It was hard to contain it.

"Everything was in perfect order —"

The Healer cut her off. "What is missing?" he asked. "Clearly, you've accessed speech."

"Memory. I was trying to find what the Seeker wants."

Though there was no sound, there was a change. The atmosphere, which had gone tense at my accusation, relaxed. I wondered how I knew this. I had a strange sensation that I was somehow receiving more than my five senses were giving me — almost a feeling that there was *another* sense, on the fringes, not quite harnessed. Intuition? That was almost the right word. As if any creature needed more than five senses.

The Seeker cleared her throat, but it was the Healer who answered.

"Ah," he said. "Don't make yourself anxious about some partial memory . . . difficulties. That's, well, not to be *expected,* exactly, but not surprising, considering."

"I don't understand your meaning."

"This host was part of the human resistance." There was a hint of excitement in the Seeker's voice now. "Those humans who were aware of us before insertion are more difficult to subdue. This one still resists."

There was a moment of silence while they waited for my response.

Resisting? The host was blocking my access? Again, the heat of my anger surprised me.

"Am I correctly bound?" I asked, my voice distorted because it came through my teeth.

"Yes," the Healer said. "All eight hundred twenty-seven points are latched securely in the optimum positions."

This mind used more of my faculties than any host before, leaving me only one hundred eighty-one spare attachments. Perhaps the numerous bindings were the reason the emotions were so vivid.

I decided to open my eyes. I felt the need to double-check the Healer's promises and make sure the rest of me worked.

Light. Bright, painful. I closed my eyes again. The last light I had seen had been filtered through a hundred ocean fathoms. But these eyes had seen brighter and could handle it. I opened them narrowly, keeping my eyelashes feathered over the breach.

"Would you like me to turn down the lights?"

"No, Healer. My eyes will adjust."

"Very good," he said, and I understood that his approval was meant for my casual use of the possessive.

Both waited quietly while my eyes slowly widened.

My mind recognized this as an average room in a medical facility. A hospital. The ceiling tiles were white with darker speckles. The lights were rectangular and the same size as the tiles, replacing them at regular intervals. The walls were light green — a calming color, but also the color of sickness. A poor choice, in my quickly formed opinion.

The people facing me were more interesting than the room. The word *doctor* sounded in my mind as soon as my eyes fastened on the Healer. He wore loose-fitting blue green clothes that left his arms bare. Scrubs. He had hair on his face, a strange color that my memory called red.

Red! It had been three worlds since I had seen the color or any of its relatives. Even this gingery gold filled me with nostalgia.

His face was generically human to me, but the knowledge in my memory applied the word *kind*.

An impatient breath pulled my attention to the Seeker.

She was very small. If she had remained still, it would have taken me longer to notice her there beside the Healer. She didn't draw the eye, a darkness in the bright room. She wore black from chin to wrists — a conservative suit with a silk turtleneck underneath. Her hair was black, too. It grew to her chin and was pushed back behind her ears. Her skin was darker than the Healer's. Olive toned.

The tiny changes in humans' expressions were so minimal they were very hard to read. My memory could name the look on this woman's face, though. The black brows, slanted down over the slightly bulging eyes, created a familiar design. Not quite anger. Intensity. Irritation.

"How often does this happen?" I asked, looking at the Healer again.

"Not often," the Healer admitted. "We have so few full-grown hosts available anymore. The immature hosts are entirely pliable. But you indicated that you preferred to begin as an adult. . . ."

"Yes."

"Most requests are the opposite. The human life span is much shorter than you're used to."

"I'm well versed in all the facts, Healer. Have you dealt with this . . . resistance before yourself?"

"Only once, myself."

"Tell me the facts of the case." I paused. "Please," I added, feeling a lack of courtesy in my command.

The Healer sighed.

The Seeker began tapping her fingers against her arm. A sign of impatience. She did not care to wait for what she wanted.

"This occurred four years ago," the Healer began. "The soul involved had requested an adult male host. The first one to be available was a human who had been living in a pocket of resistance since the early years of the occupation. The human . . . knew what would happen when he was caught."

"Just as my host did."

"Um, yes." He cleared his throat. "This was only the soul's second life. He came from Blind World."

"Blind World?" I asked, cocking my head to the side reflexively.

"Oh, sorry, you wouldn't know our nicknames. This was one of yours, though, was it not?" He pulled a device from his pocket, a computer, and scanned quickly. "Yes, your seventh planet. In the eighty-first sector."

"*Blind* World?" I said again, my voice now disapproving.

"Yes, well, some who have lived there prefer to call it the Singing World."

I nodded slowly. I liked that better.

"And some who've never been there call it Planet of the Bats," the Seeker muttered.

I turned my eyes to her, feeling them narrow as my mind dredged up the appropriate image of the ugly flying rodent she referred to.

"I assume you are one who has never lived there, Seeker," the Healer said lightly. "We called this soul Racing Song at first — it was a loose translation of his name on . . . the Singing World. But he soon opted to take the name of his host, Kevin. Though he was slated for a Calling in Musical Performance, given his background, he said he felt more comfortable continuing in the host's previous line of work, which was mechanical.

"These signs were somewhat worrisome to his assigned Comforter, but they were well within normal bounds.

"Then Kevin started to complain that he was blacking out for periods of time. They brought him back to me, and we ran extensive tests to make sure there was no hidden flaw in the host's brain. During the testing, several Healers noted marked differences in his behavior and personality. When we questioned him about this, he claimed to have no memory of certain statements and actions. We continued to observe him, along with his Comforter, and eventually discovered that the host was periodically taking control of Kevin's body."

"Taking control?" My eyes strained wide. "With the soul unaware? The host took the body back?"

"Sadly, yes. Kevin was not strong enough to suppress this host."

Not strong enough.

Would they think me weak as well? *Was* I weak, that I could not force this mind to answer my questions? Weaker still, because her living thoughts had existed in my head where there should be nothing but memory? I'd always thought of myself as strong. This idea of weakness made me flinch. Made me feel shame.

The Healer continued. "Certain events occurred, and it was decided —"

"What events?"

The Healer looked down without answering.

*"What events?"* I demanded again. "I believe I have a right to know."

The Healer sighed. "You do. Kevin . . . physically attacked a Healer while not . . . himself." He winced. "He knocked the Healer unconscious with a blow from his fist and then found a scalpel on her person. We found him insensible. The host had tried to cut the soul out of his body."

It took me a moment before I could speak. Even then, my voice was just a breath. "What happened to them?"

"Luckily, the host was unable to stay conscious long enough to inflict real damage. Kevin was relocated, into an immature host this time. The troublesome host was in poor repair, and it was decided there wasn't much point in saving him.

"Kevin is seven human years old now and perfectly normal . . . aside from the fact that he kept the name

Kevin, that is. His guardians are taking great care that he is heavily exposed to music, and that is coming along well. . . ." The last was added as if it were good news — news that could somehow cancel out the rest.

"Why?" I cleared my throat so that my voice could gain some volume. "Why have these risks not been shared?"

"Actually," the Seeker broke in, "it is very clearly stated in all recruitment propaganda that assimilating the remaining adult human hosts is much more challenging than assimilating a child. An immature host is highly recommended."

"The word *challenging* does not quite cover Kevin's story," I whispered.

"Yes, well, you preferred to ignore the recommendation." She held up her hands in a peacemaking gesture when my body tensed, causing the stiff fabric on the narrow bed to crackle softly. "Not that I blame you. Childhood is extraordinarily tedious. And you are clearly not the average soul. I have every confidence that this is well within your abilities to handle. This is just another host. I'm sure you will have full access and control shortly."

By this point in my observations of the Seeker, I was surprised that she'd had the patience to wait for any delay, even my personal acclimatization. I sensed her disappointment in my lack of information, and it brought back some of the unfamiliar feelings of anger.

"Did it not occur to you that you could get the answers you seek by being inserted into this body yourself?" I asked.

She stiffened. "I'm no skipper."

My eyebrows pulled up automatically.

"Another nickname," the Healer explained. "For those who do not complete a life term in their host."

I nodded in understanding. We'd had a name for it on my other worlds. On no world was it smiled upon. So I quit quizzing the Seeker and gave her what I could.

"Her name was Melanie Stryder. She was born in Albuquerque, New Mexico. She was in Los Angeles when the occupation became known to her, and she hid in the wilderness for a few years before finding . . . Hmmm. Sorry, I'll try that one again later. The body has seen twenty years. She drove to Chicago from . . ." I shook my head. "There were several stages, not all of them alone. The vehicle was stolen. She was searching for a cousin named Sharon, whom she had reason to hope was still human. She neither found nor contacted anyone before she was spotted. But . . ." I struggled, fighting against another blank wall. "I think . . . I can't be sure . . . I think she left a note . . . somewhere."

"So she expected someone would look for her?" the Seeker asked eagerly.

"Yes. She will be . . . missed. If she does not rendezvous with . . ." I gritted my teeth, truly fighting now. The wall was black, and I could not tell how thick it was. I battered against it, sweat beading on my forehead. The Seeker and the Healer were very quiet, allowing me to concentrate.

I tried thinking of something else — the loud, unfamiliar noises the engine of the car had made, the jittery rush of adrenaline every time the lights of another vehicle drew near on the road. I already had this, and nothing fought me. I let the memory carry me along, let it skip over the cold hike through the city under the sheltering darkness of night, let it wind its way to the building where they'd found me.

Not me, *her*. My body shuddered.

"Don't overextend —" the Healer began.

The Seeker shushed him.

I let my mind dwell on the horror of discovery, the burning hatred of the Seekers that overpowered almost everything else. The hatred was evil; it was pain. I could hardly bear to feel it. But I let it run its course, hoping it would distract the resistance, weaken the defenses.

I watched carefully as she tried to hide and then knew she could not. A note, scratched on a piece of debris with a broken pencil. Shoved hastily under a door. Not just any door.

"The pattern is the fifth door along the fifth hall on the fifth floor. Her communication is there."

The Seeker had a small phone in her hand; she murmured rapidly into it.

"The building was supposed to be safe," I continued. "They knew it was condemned. She doesn't know how she was discovered. Did they find Sharon?"

A chill of horror raised goose bumps on my arms.

The question was not mine.

The question wasn't mine, but it flowed naturally through my lips as if it were. The Seeker did not notice anything amiss.

"The cousin? No, they found no other human," she answered, and my body relaxed in response. "This host was spotted entering the building. Since the building was known to be condemned, the citizen who observed her was concerned. He called us, and we watched the building to see if we could catch more than one, and then moved in when that seemed unlikely. Can you find the rendezvous point?"

I tried.

So many memories, all of them so colorful and sharp. I saw a hundred places I'd never been, heard their names for the first time. A house in Los Angeles, lined with tall fronded trees. A meadow in a forest, with a tent and a fire, outside Winslow, Arizona. A deserted rocky beach in Mexico. A cave, the entrance guarded by sheeting rain, somewhere in Oregon. Tents, huts, rude shelters. As time went on, the names grew less specific. She did not know where she was, nor did she care.

My name was now Wanderer, yet her memories fit it just as well as my own. Except that my wandering was by choice. These flashes of memory were always tinged with the fear of the hunted. Not wandering, but running.

I tried not to feel pity. Instead, I worked to focus the memories. I didn't need to see where she'd been, only where she was going. I sorted through the pictures that tied to the word *Chicago,* but none seemed to be anything more than random images. I widened my net. What was outside Chicago? Cold, I thought. It was cold, and there was some worry about that.

Where? I pushed, and the wall came back.

I exhaled in a gust. "Outside the city — in the wilderness . . . a state park, away from any habitations. It's not somewhere she'd been before, but she knew how to get there."

"How soon?" the Seeker asked.

"Soon." The answer came automatically. "How long have I been here?"

"We let the host heal for nine days, just to be absolutely sure she was recovered," the Healer told me. "Insertion was today, the tenth day."

Ten days. My body felt a staggering wave of relief.

"Too late," I said. "For the rendezvous point . . . or even the note." I could feel the host's reaction to this — could feel it much too strongly. The host was almost . . . *smug*. I allowed the words she thought to be spoken, so that I could learn from them. "He won't be there."

"He?" The Seeker pounced on the pronoun. "Who?"

The black wall slammed down with more force than she'd used before. She was the tiniest fraction of a second too late.

Again, the face filled my mind. The beautiful face with the golden tan skin and the light-flecked eyes. The face that stirred a strange, deep pleasure within me while I viewed it so clearly in my mind.

Though the wall slapped into place with an accompanying sensation of vicious resentment, it was not fast enough.

"Jared," I answered. As quickly as if it had come from me, the thought that was not mine followed the name through my lips. "Jared is safe."

# CHAPTER 4

# *Dreamed*

It is too dark to be so hot, or maybe too hot to be so dark. One of the two is out of place.

I crouch in the darkness behind the weak protection of a scrubby creosote bush, sweating out all the water left in my body. It's been fifteen minutes since the car left the garage. No lights have come on. The arcadia door is open two inches, letting the swamp cooler do its job. I can imagine the feel of the moist, cool air blowing through the screen. I wish it could reach me here.

My stomach gurgles, and I clench my abdominal muscles to stifle the sound. It is quiet enough that the murmur carries.

I am so hungry.

There is another need that is stronger — another hungry stomach hidden safely far away in the darkness, waiting alone in the rough cave that is our temporary home. A

..e, jagged with volcanic rock. What will he do if I......back? All the pressure of motherhood with none of the ...wledge or experience. I feel so hideously helpless. Jamie is hungry.

There are no other houses close to this one. I've been watching since the sun was still white hot in the sky, and I don't think there is a dog, either.

I ease up from my crouch, my calves screaming in protest, but keep hunched at the waist, trying to be smaller than the bush. The way up the wash is smooth sand, a pale pathway in the light of the stars. There are no sounds of cars on the road.

I know what they will realize when they return, the monsters who look like a nice couple in their early fifties. They will know exactly what I am, and the search will begin at once. I need to be far away. I really hope they are going out for a night on the town. I think it's Friday. They keep our habits so perfectly, it's hard to see any difference. Which is how they won in the first place.

The fence around the yard is only waist high. I get over easily, noiselessly. The yard is gravel, though, and I have to walk carefully to keep my weight from shifting it. I make it to the patio slab.

The blinds are open. The starlight is enough to see that the rooms are empty of movement. This couple goes for a spartan look, and I'm grateful. It makes it harder for someone to hide. Of course, that leaves no place for me to hide, either, but if it comes to hiding for me, it's too late anyway.

I ease the screen door open first, and then the glass door. Both glide silently. I place my feet carefully on the tile, but this is just out of habit. No one is waiting for me here.

The cool air feels like heaven.

The kitchen is to my left. I can see the gleam of granite counters.

I pull the canvas bag from my shoulder and start with the refrigerator. There is a moment of anxiety as the light comes on when the door opens, but I find the button and hold it down with my toe. My eyes are blind. I don't have time to let them adjust. I go by feel.

Milk, cheese slices, leftovers in a plastic bowl. I hope it's the chicken-and-rice thing I watched him cooking for dinner. We'll eat this tonight.

Juice, a bag of apples. Baby carrots. These will stay good till morning.

I hurry to the pantry. I need things that will keep longer.

I can see better as I gather as much as I can carry. Mmm, chocolate chip cookies. I'm dying to open the bag right now, but I grit my teeth and ignore the twist of my empty stomach.

The bag gets heavy too quickly. This will last us only a week, even if we're careful with it. And I don't feel like being careful; I feel like gorging. I shove granola bars into my pockets.

One more thing. I hurry to the sink and refill my canteen. Then I put my head under the flow and gulp straight from the stream. The water makes odd noises when it hits my hollow stomach.

I start to feel panicked now that my job is done. I want to be out of here. Civilization is deadly.

I watch the floor on my way out, worried about tripping with my heavy bag, which is why I don't see the silhouetted black figure on the patio until my hand is on the door.

I hear his mumbled oath at the same time that a stupid squeak of fear escapes my mouth. I spin to sprint for the front door, hoping the locks are not latched, or at least not difficult.

I don't even get two steps before rough, hard hands grab my shoulders and wrench me back against his body. Too big, too strong to be a woman. The bass voice proves me right.

"One sound and you die," he threatens gruffly. I am shocked to feel a thin, sharp edge pushing into the skin under my jaw.

I don't understand. I shouldn't be given a choice. Who is this monster? I've never heard of one who would break rules. I answer the only way I can.

"Do it," I spit through my teeth. "Just do it. I don't want to be a filthy parasite!"

I wait for the knife, and my heart is aching. Each beat has a name. Jamie, Jamie, Jamie. What will happen to you now?

"Clever," the man mutters, and it doesn't sound like he's speaking to me. "Must be a Seeker. And that means a trap. How did they know?" The steel disappears from my throat, only to be replaced by a hand as hard as iron.

I can barely breathe under his grip.

"Where are the rest of them?" he demands, squeezing.

"It's just me!" I rasp. I can't lead him to Jamie. What will Jamie do when I don't come back? Jamie is hungry!

I throw my elbow into his gut — and this really hurts. His stomach muscles are as iron hard as the hand. Which is very strange. Muscles like that are the product of hard living or obsession, and the parasites have neither.

He doesn't even suck in a breath at my blow. Desperate, I jab my heel into his instep. This catches him off guard, and he wobbles. I wrench away, but he grabs hold of my bag, yanking me back into his body. His hand clamps down on my throat again.

"Feisty for a peace-loving body snatcher, aren't you?"

His words are nonsensical. I thought the aliens were all the same. I guess they have their nut jobs, too, after all.

I twist and claw, trying to break his hold. My nails catch his arm, but this just makes him tighten his hold on my throat.

"I *will* kill you, you worthless body thief. I'm not bluffing."

"Do it, then!"

Suddenly he gasps, and I wonder if any of my flailing limbs have made contact. I don't feel any new bruises.

He lets go of my arm and grabs my hair. This must be it. He's going to cut my throat. I brace for the slice of the knife.

But the hand on my throat eases up, and then his fingers are fumbling on the back of my neck, rough and warm on my skin.

"Impossible," he breathes.

Something hits the floor with a thud. He's dropped the knife? I try to think of a way to get it. Maybe if I fall. The hand on my neck isn't tight enough to keep me from yanking free. I think I heard where the blade landed.

He spins me around suddenly. There is a click, and light blinds my left eye. I gasp and automatically try to twist away from it. His hand tightens in my hair. The light flickers to my right eye.

"I can't believe it," he whispers. "You're still human."

His hands grab my face from both sides, and before I can pull free, his lips come down hard on mine.

I'm frozen for half a second. No one has ever kissed me in my life. Not a real kiss. Just my parents' pecks on the cheek or forehead, so many years ago. This is something I thought I would never feel. I'm not sure exactly what it feels like, though. There's too much panic, too much terror, too much adrenaline.

I jerk my knee up in a sharp thrust.

He chokes out a wheezing sound, and I'm free. Instead of running for the front of the house again like he expects, I duck under his arm and leap through the open door. I think I can outrun him, even with my load. I've got a head start, and he's still making pained noises. I know where I'm going — I won't leave a path he can see in the dark. I never dropped the food, and that's good. I think the granola bars are a loss, though.

"Wait!" he yells.

*Shut up,* I think, but I don't yell back.

He's running after me. I can hear his voice getting closer. "I'm not one of them!"

*Sure.* I keep my eyes on the sand and sprint. My dad used to say I ran like a cheetah. I was the fastest on my track team, state champion, back before the end of the world.

"Listen to me!" He's still yelling at full volume. "Look! I'll prove it. Just stop and look at me!"

*Not likely.* I pivot off the wash and flit through the mesquites.

"I didn't think there was anyone left! Please, I need to talk to you!"

His voice surprises me — it is too close.

"I'm sorry I kissed you! That was stupid! I've just been alone so long!"

"Shut *up!*" I don't say it loudly, but I know he hears. He's getting even closer. I've never been outrun before. I push my legs harder.

There's a low grunt to his breathing as he speeds up, too.

Something big flies into my back, and I go down. I taste dirt in my mouth, and I'm pinned by something so heavy I can hardly breathe.

"Wait. A. Minute," he huffs.

He shifts his weight and rolls me over. He straddles my chest, trapping my arms under his legs. He is squishing my food. I growl and try to squirm out from under him.

"Look, look, look!" he says. He pulls a small cylinder from his hip pocket and twists the top. A beam of light shoots out the end.

He turns the flashlight on his face.

The light makes his skin yellow. It shows prominent cheekbones beside a long thin nose and a sharply squared-off jaw. His lips are stretched into a grin, but I can see that they are full, for a man. His eyebrows and lashes are bleached out from sun.

But that's not what he is showing me.

His eyes, clear liquid sienna in the illumination, shine with no more than human reflection. He bounces the light between left and right.

"See? See? I'm just like you."

"Let me see your neck." Suspicion is thick in my voice. I don't let myself believe that this is more than a trick. I don't understand the point of the charade, but I'm sure there is one. There is no hope anymore.

His lips twist. "Well . . . That won't exactly help anything. Aren't the eyes enough? You know I'm not one of them."

"Why won't you show me your neck?"

"Because I have a scar there," he admits.

I try to squirm out from under him again, and his hand pins my shoulder.

"It's self-inflicted," he explains. "I think I did a pretty good job, though it hurt like hell. *I* don't have all that pretty hair to cover *my* neck. The scar helps me blend in."

"Get off me."

He hesitates, then gets to his feet in one easy move, not needing to use his hands. He holds one out, palm up, to me.

"Please don't run away. And, um, I'd rather you didn't kick me again, either."

I don't move. I know he can catch me if I try to run.

"Who are you?" I whisper.

He smiles wide. "My name is Jared Howe. I haven't spoken to another human being in more than two years, so I'm sure I must seem . . . a little crazy to you. Please, forgive that and tell me your name, anyway."

"Melanie," I whisper.

"Melanie," he repeats. "I can't tell you how delighted I am to meet you."

I grip my bag tightly, keeping my eyes on him. He reaches his hand down toward me slowly.

And I take it.

It isn't until I see my hand curl voluntarily around his that I realize I believe him.

He helps me to my feet and doesn't release my hand when I'm up.

"What now?" I ask guardedly.

"Well, we can't stay here for long. Will you come back with me to the house? I left my bag. You beat me to the fridge."

I shake my head.

He seems to realize how brittle I am, how close to breaking.

"Will you wait for me here, then?" he asks in a gentle voice. "I'll be very quick. Let me get us some more food."

"Us?"

"Do you really think I'm going to let you disappear? I'll follow you even if you tell me not to."

I don't want to disappear from him.

"I . . ." How can I not trust another human completely? We're family — both part of the brotherhood of extinction. "I don't have time. I have so far to go and . . . Jamie is waiting."

"You're not alone," he realizes. His expression shows uncertainty for the first time.

"My brother. He's just nine, and he's so frightened when I'm away. It will take me half the night to get back to him. He won't know if I've been caught. He's so *hungry.*" As if to make my point, my stomach growls loudly.

Jared's smile is back, brighter than before. "Will it help if I give you a ride?"

"A ride?" I echo.

"I'll make you a deal. You wait here while I gather more food, and I'll take you anywhere you want to go in my jeep. It's faster than running — even faster than *you* running."

"You have a car?"

"Of course. Do you think I walked out here?"

I think of the six hours it took me to walk here, and my forehead furrows.

"We'll be back to your brother in no time," he promises. "Don't move from this spot, okay?"

I nod.

"And eat something, please. I don't want your stomach to give us away." He grins, and his eyes crinkle up, fanning lines out of the corners. My heart gives one hard thump, and I know I will wait here if it takes him all night.

He is still holding my hand. He lets go slowly, his eyes not leaving mine. He takes a step backward, then pauses.

"Please don't kick me," he pleads, leaning forward and grabbing my chin. He kisses me again, and this time I feel it. His lips are softer than his hands, and hot, even in the warm desert night. A flock of butterflies riots in my stomach and steals my breath. My hands reach for him instinctively. I touch the warm skin of his cheek, the rough hair on his neck. My fingers skim over a line of puckered skin, a raised ridge right beneath the hairline.

I scream.

I woke up covered in sweat. Even before I was all the way awake, my fingers were on the back of my neck, tracing the short line left from the insertion. I could barely detect the faint pink blemish with my fingertips. The medicines the Healer had used had done their job.

Jared's poorly healed scar had never been much of a disguise.

I flicked on the light beside my bed, waiting for my breathing to slow, veins full of adrenaline from the realistic dream.

A new dream, but in essence so much the same as the many others that had plagued me in the past months.

No, not a dream. Surely a memory.

I could still feel the heat of Jared's lips on mine. My hands reached out without my permission, searching across the rumpled sheet, looking for something they did not find. My heart ached when they gave up, falling to the bed limp and empty.

I blinked away the unwelcome moisture in my eyes. I didn't know how much more of this I could stand. How did anyone survive this world, with these bodies whose memories wouldn't stay in the past where they should? With these emotions that were so strong I couldn't tell what *I* felt anymore?

I was going to be exhausted tomorrow, but I felt so far from sleep that I knew it would be hours before I could relax. I might as well do my duty and get it over with. Maybe it would help me take my mind off things I'd rather not think about.

I rolled off the bed and stumbled to the computer on the otherwise empty desk. It took a few seconds for the screen to glow to life, and another few seconds to open my mail program. It wasn't hard to find the Seeker's address; I only had four contacts: the Seeker, the Healer, my new employer, and his wife, my Comforter.

> There was another human with my host, Melanie Stryder.

I typed, not bothering with a greeting.

> His name is Jamie Stryder; he is her brother.

For a panicked moment, I wondered at her control. All this time, and I'd never even guessed at the boy's existence — not because he didn't matter to her, but because she protected him more fiercely than other secrets I'd unraveled. Did she have more secrets this big, this important? So sacred that she kept them even from my dreams? Was she that strong? My fingers trembled as I keyed the rest of the information.

I think he's a young adolescent now. Perhaps thirteen. They were living in a temporary camp, and I believe it was north of the town of Cave Creek, in Arizona. That was several years ago, though. Still, you could compare a map to the lines I remembered before. As always, I'll tell you if I get anything more.

I sent it off. As soon as it was gone, terror washed through me.

*Not Jamie!*

Her voice in my head was as clear as my own spoken aloud. I shuddered in horror.

Even as I struggled with the fear of what was happening, I was gripped with the insane desire to e-mail the Seeker again and apologize for sending her my crazy dreams. To tell her I was half asleep and to pay no attention to the silly message I'd sent.

The desire was not my own.

I shut off the computer.

*I hate you,* the voice snarled in my head.

"Then maybe you should leave," I snapped. The sound of my voice, answering her aloud, made me shudder again.

She hadn't spoken to me since the first moments I'd been here. There was no doubt that she was getting stronger. Just like the dreams.

And there was no question about it; I was going to have to visit my Comforter tomorrow. Tears of disappointment and humiliation welled in my eyes at the thought.

I went back to bed, put a pillow over my face, and tried to think of nothing at all.

# CHAPTER 5

# *Uncomforted*

Hello there, Wanderer! Won't you take a seat and make yourself at home?"

I hesitated on the threshold of the Comforter's office, one foot in and one foot out.

She smiled, just a tiny movement at the corners of her mouth. It was much easier to read facial expressions now; the little muscle twitches and shifts had become familiar through months of exposure. I could see that the Comforter found my reluctance a bit amusing. At the same time, I could sense her frustration that I was still uneasy coming to her.

With a quiet sigh of resignation, I walked into the small brightly colored room and took my usual seat — the puffy red one, the one farthest from where she sat.

Her lips pursed.

To avoid her gaze, I stared through the open windows

at the clouds scuttling past the sun. The faint tang of ocean brine blew softly through the room.

"So, Wanderer. It's been a while since you've come to see me."

I met her eyes guiltily. "I did leave a message about that last appointment. I had a student who requested some of my time. . . ."

"Yes, I know." She smiled the tiny smile again. "I got your message."

She was attractive for an older woman, as humans went. She'd let her hair stay a natural gray — it was soft, tending toward white rather than silver, and she wore it long, pulled back in a loose ponytail. Her eyes were an interesting green color I'd never seen on anyone else.

"I'm sorry," I said, since she seemed to be waiting for a response.

"That's all right. I understand. It's difficult for you to come here. You wish so much that it wasn't necessary. It's never been necessary for you before. This frightens you."

I stared down at the wooden floor. "Yes, Comforter."

"I know I've asked you to call me Kathy."

"Yes . . . Kathy."

She laughed lightly. "You are not at ease with human names yet, are you, Wanderer?"

"No. To be honest, it seems . . . like a surrender."

I looked up to see her nod slowly. "Well, I can understand why you, especially, would feel that way."

I swallowed loudly when she said that, and stared again at the floor.

"Let's talk about something easier for a moment," Kathy suggested. "Do you continue to enjoy your Calling?"

"I do." This *was* easier. "I've begun a new semester. I wondered if it would get tiresome, repeating the same material, but so far it doesn't. Having new ears makes the stories new again."

"I hear good things about you from Curt. He says your class is among the most requested at the university."

My cheeks warmed a bit at this praise. "That's nice to hear. How is your partner?"

"Curt is wonderful, thank you. Our hosts are in excellent shape for their ages. We have many years ahead of us, I think."

I was curious if she would stay on this world, if she would move to another human host when the time came, or if she would leave. But I didn't want to ask any questions that might move us into the more difficult areas of discussion.

"I enjoy teaching," I said instead. "It's somewhat related to my Calling with the See Weeds, so that makes it easier than something unfamiliar. I'm indebted to Curt for requesting me."

"They're lucky to have you." Kathy smiled warmly. "Do you know how rare it is for a Professor of History to have experienced even two planets in the curriculum? Yet you've lived a term on almost all of them. And the Origin, to boot! There isn't a school on this planet that wouldn't love to steal you away from us. Curt plots ways to keep you busy so you have no time to consider moving."

"*Honorary* Professor," I corrected her.

Kathy smiled and then took a deep breath, her smile fading. "You haven't been to see me in so long, I was wondering if your problems were resolving themselves. But then it occurred to me that perhaps the reason for your absence was that they were getting worse."

I stared down at my hands and said nothing.

My hands were light brown — a tan that never faded whether I spent time in the sun or not. One dark freckle marked the skin just above my left wrist. My nails were cut short. I disliked the feeling of long nails. They were unpleasant when they brushed the skin wrong. And my fingers were so long and thin — the added length of fingernails made them look strange. Even for a human.

She cleared her throat after a minute. "I'm guessing my intuition was right."

"Kathy." I said her name slowly. Stalling. "Why did you keep your human name? Did it make you feel . . . more at one? With your host, I mean?" I would have liked to know about Curt's choice as well, but it was such a personal question. It would have been wrong to ask anyone besides Curt for the answer, even his partner. I worried that I'd already been too impolite, but she laughed.

"Heavens, no, Wanderer. Haven't I told you this? Hmm. Maybe not, since it's not my job to talk, but to listen. Most of the souls I speak with don't need as much encouragement as you do. Did you know I came to Earth in one of the very first placements, before the humans had any idea we were here? I had human neighbors on both sides. Curt and I had to pretend to be our hosts for several years. Even after we'd settled the immediate area, you never knew when a human might be near. So *Kathy* just became who I was. Besides, the translation of my former name was fourteen words long and did not shorten prettily." She grinned. The sunlight slanting through the window caught her eyes and sent their silver green reflection dancing on the wall. For a moment, the emerald irises glowed iridescent.

I'd had no idea that this soft, cozy woman had been a part of the front line. It took me a minute to process that. I stared at her, surprised and suddenly more respectful. I'd never taken Comforters very seriously — never had a need before now. They were for those who struggled, for the weak, and it shamed me to be here. Knowing Kathy's history made me feel slightly less awkward with her. She understood strength.

"Did it bother you?" I asked. "Pretending to be one of them?"

"No, not really. You see, this host was a lot to get used to — there was so much that was new. Sensory overload. Following the set pattern was quite as much as I could handle at first."

"And Curt . . . You chose to stay with your host's spouse? After it was over?"

This question was more pointed, and Kathy grasped that at once. She shifted in her seat, pulling her legs up and folding them under her. She gazed thoughtfully at a spot just over my head as she answered.

"Yes, I chose Curt — and he chose me. At first, of course, it was random chance, an assignment. We bonded, naturally, from spending so much time together, sharing the danger of our mission. As the university's president, Curt had many contacts, you see. Our house was an insertion facility. We would entertain often. Humans would come through our door and our kind would leave. It all had to be very quick and quiet — you know the violence these hosts are prone to. We lived every day with the knowledge that we could meet a final end at any moment. There was constant excitement and frequent fear.

"All very good reasons why Curt and I might have formed an attachment and decided to stay together when secrecy was no longer necessary. And I could lie to you, assuage your fears, by telling you that these were the reasons. But . . ." She shook her head and then seemed to settle deeper into her chair, her eyes boring into me. "In so many millennia, the humans never did figure *love* out. How much is physical, how much in the mind? How much accident and how much fate? Why did perfect matches crumble and impossible couples thrive? I don't know the answers any better than they did. Love simply is where it is. My host loved Curt's host, and that love did not die when the ownership of the minds changed."

She watched me carefully, reacting with a slight frown when I slumped in my seat.

"Melanie still grieves for Jared," she stated.

I felt my head nod without willing the action.

"*You* grieve for him."

I closed my eyes.

"The dreams continue?"

"Every night," I mumbled.

"Tell me about them." Her voice was soft, persuasive.

"I don't like to think about them."

"I know. Try. It might help."

"How? How will it help to tell you that I see his face every time I close my eyes? That I wake up and cry when he's not there? That the memories are so strong I can't separate hers from mine anymore?"

I stopped abruptly, clenching my teeth.

Kathy pulled a white handkerchief from her pocket

and offered it to me. When I didn't move, she got up, walked over to me, and dropped it in my lap. She sat on the arm of my chair and waited.

I held on stubbornly for half a minute. Then I snatched the little square of fabric angrily and wiped my eyes.

"I hate this."

"Everybody cries their first year. These emotions are so impossible. We're all children for a bit, whether we intended that or not. I used to tear up every time I saw a pretty sunset. The taste of peanut butter would sometimes do that, too." She patted the top of my head, then trailed her fingers gently through the lock of hair I always kept tucked behind my ear.

"Such pretty, shiny hair," she noted. "Every time I see you it's shorter. Why do you keep it that way?"

Already in tears, I didn't feel like I had much dignity to defend. Why claim that it was easier to care for, as I usually did? After all, I'd come here to confess and get help — I might as well get on with it.

"It bothers *her*. She likes it long."

She didn't gasp, as I half expected she would. Kathy was good at her job. Her response was only a second late and only slightly incoherent.

"You . . . She . . . she's still that . . . *present?*"

The appalling truth tumbled from my lips. "When she wants to be. Our history bores her. She's more dormant while I'm working. But she's there, all right. Sometimes I feel like she's as present as I am." My voice was only a whisper by the time I was done.

"Wanderer!" Kathy exclaimed, horrified. "Why didn't you tell me it was that bad? How long has it been this way?"

"It's getting worse. Instead of fading, she seems to be growing stronger. It's not as bad as the Healer's case yet — we spoke of Kevin, do you remember? She hasn't taken control. She won't. I won't let that happen!" The pitch of my voice climbed.

"Of course it won't happen," she assured me. "Of course not. But if you're this . . . unhappy, you should have told me earlier. We need to get you to a Healer."

It took me a moment, emotionally distracted as I was, to understand.

"A Healer? You want me to *skip?*"

"No one would think badly of that choice, Wanderer. It's understood, if a host is defective —"

"*Defective?* She's not defective. *I* am. I'm too weak for this world!" My head fell into my hands as the humiliation washed through me. Fresh tears welled in my eyes.

Kathy's arm settled around my shoulders. I was struggling so hard to control my wild emotions that I didn't pull away, though it felt too intimate.

It bothered Melanie, too. She didn't like being hugged by an alien.

Of course Melanie was very much present in this moment, and unbearably smug as I finally admitted to her power. She was gleeful. It was always harder to control her when I was distracted by emotion like this.

I tried to calm myself so that I would be able to put her in her place.

*You are in my place.* Her thought was faint but intelligible. How much worse it was getting; she was strong enough to speak to me now whenever she wished. It was as bad as that first minute of consciousness.

*Go away. It's my place now.*

*Never.*

"Wanderer, dear, no. You are not weak, and we both know that."

"Hmph."

"Listen to me. You are strong. Surprisingly strong. Our kind are always so much the same, but *you* exceed the norm. You're so brave it astonishes me. Your past lives are a testament to that."

My past lives maybe, but this life? Where was my strength now?

"But humans are more individualized than we are," Kathy went on. "There's quite a range, and some of them are much stronger than others. I truly believe that if anyone else had been put into this host, Melanie would have crushed them in days. Maybe it's an accident, maybe it's fate, but it appears to me that the strongest of our kind is being hosted by the strongest of theirs."

"Doesn't say much for our kind, does it?"

She heard the implication behind my words. "She's not winning, Wanderer. *You* are this lovely person beside me. She's just a shadow in the corner of your mind."

"She speaks to me, Kathy. She still thinks her own thoughts. She still keeps her secrets."

"But she doesn't speak for you, does she? I doubt I would be able to say as much in your place."

I didn't respond. I was feeling too miserable.

"I think you should consider reimplantation."

"Kathy, you just said that she would crush a different soul. I don't know if I believe that — you're probably just trying to do your job and comfort me. But if she *is* so strong, it wouldn't be fair to hand her off to someone else because I can't subdue her. Who would you choose to take her on?"

"I didn't say that to comfort you, dear."

"Then what —"

"I don't think this host would be considered for re-use."

"Oh!"

A shiver of horror jolted down my spine. And I wasn't the only one who was staggered by the idea.

I was immediately repulsed. I was no quitter. Through the long revolutions around the suns of my last planet — the world of the See Weeds, as they were known here — I had waited. Though the permanence of being rooted began to wear long before I'd thought it would, though the lives of the See Weeds would measure in centuries on this planet, I had not skipped out on the life term of my host. To do so was wasteful, wrong, ungrateful. It mocked the very essence of who we were as souls. We made our worlds better places; that was absolutely essential or we did not deserve them.

But we were *not* wasteful. We did make whatever we took better, more peaceful and beautiful. And the humans *were* brutish and ungovernable. They had killed one another so frequently that murder had been an accepted part of life. The various tortures they'd devised over the few millennia they'd lasted had been too much for me; I hadn't been able to bear even the dry official overviews. Wars had raged over the face of nearly every continent. Sanctioned murder, ordered and viciously effective. Those who lived in peaceful nations had looked the other way as members of their own species starved on their doorstep. There was no equality to the distribution of the planet's bounteous resources. Most vile yet, their offspring — the next generation, which my kind nearly worshipped for their promise — had all too often been victims of heinous crimes. And not just at the hands of strangers, but at the hands of the caretakers they were entrusted to. Even the huge sphere of the planet had been put into jeopardy through their careless and greedy mistakes. No one could compare what had been and what was now and not admit that Earth was a better place thanks to us.

*You murder an entire species and then pat yourselves on the back.*

My hands balled up into fists.

*I could have you disposed of,* I reminded her.

*Go ahead. Make my murder official.*

I was bluffing, but so was Melanie.

Oh, she thought she wanted to die. She'd thrown herself into the elevator shaft, after all. But that was in a moment of panic and defeat. To consider it calmly from a comfortable chair was something else altogether. I could feel the adrenaline — adrenaline called into being by her fear — shoot through my limbs as I contemplated switching to a more pliant body.

It would be nice to be alone again. To have my mind to myself. This world was very pleasant in so many novel ways, and it would be wonderful to be able to appreciate it without the distractions of an angry, displaced nonentity who should have had better sense than to linger unwanted this way.

Melanie squirmed, figuratively, in the recesses of my head as I tried to consider it rationally. Maybe I should give up. . . .

The words themselves made me flinch. I, Wanderer,

give up? Quit? Admit failure and try again with a weak, spineless host who wouldn't give me any trouble?

I shook my head. I could barely stand to think of it.

And . . . this was *my* body. I was used to the feel of it. I liked the way the muscles moved over the bones, the bend of the joints and the pull of the tendons. I knew the reflection in the mirror. The sun-browned skin, the high, sharp bones of my face, the short silk cap of mahogany hair, the muddy green brown hazel of my eyes — this was me.

I wanted myself. I wouldn't let what was mine be destroyed.

# CHAPTER 6

# Followed

The light was finally fading outside the windows. The day, hot for March, had lingered on and on, as if reluctant to end and set me free.

I sniffled and twisted the wet handkerchief into another knot. "Kathy, you must have other obligations. Curt will be wondering where you are."

"He'll understand."

"I can't stay here forever. And we're no closer to an answer than before."

"Quick fixes aren't my specialty. You are decided against a new host —"

"Yes."

"So dealing with this will probably take some time."

I clenched my teeth in frustration.

"And it will go faster and more smoothly if you have some help."

"I'll be better with making my appointments, I promise."

"That's not exactly what I mean, though I hope you will."

"You mean help . . . other than you?" I cringed at the thought of having to relive today's misery with a stranger. "I'm sure you're just as qualified as any Comforter — more so."

"I didn't mean another Comforter." She shifted her weight in the chair and stretched stiffly. "How many *friends* do you have, Wanderer?"

"You mean people at work? I see a few other teachers almost every day. There are several students I speak to in the halls. . . ."

"Outside of the school?"

I stared at her blankly.

"Human hosts need interaction. You're not used to solitude, dear. You shared an entire planet's thoughts —"

"We didn't go out much." My attempt at humor fell flat.

She smiled slightly and went on. "You're struggling so hard with your problem that it's all you can concentrate on. Maybe one answer is to not concentrate quite so hard. You said Melanie grows bored during your working hours . . . that she is more dormant. Perhaps if you developed some peer relationships, those would bore her also."

I pursed my lips thoughtfully. Melanie, sluggish from the long day of attempted comfort, did seem rather unenthused by the idea.

Kathy nodded. "Get involved with life rather than with her."

"That makes sense."

"And then there are the physical drives these bodies have. I've never seen or heard of their equal. One of the most difficult things we of the first wave had to conquer was the mating instinct. Believe me, the humans noticed when you didn't." She grinned and rolled her eyes at some memory. When I didn't react as she'd expected, she sighed and crossed her arms impatiently. "Oh, come now, Wanderer. You must have noticed."

"Well, of course," I mumbled. Melanie stirred restlessly. "Obviously. I've told you about the dreams. . . ."

"No, I didn't mean just memories. Haven't you come across anyone that your body has responded to in the present — on strictly a chemical level?"

I thought her question through carefully. "I don't think so. Not so I've noticed."

"Trust me," Kathy said dryly. "You'd notice." She shook her head. "Perhaps you should open your eyes and look around for that specifically. It might do you a lot of good."

My body recoiled from the thought. I registered Melanie's disgust, mirrored by my own.

Kathy read my expression. "Don't let her control how you interact with your kind, Wanderer. Don't let her control you."

My nostrils flared. I waited a moment to answer, reining in the anger that I'd never quite gotten used to.

"She does not control me."

Kathy raised an eyebrow.

The anger tightened my throat. "You did not look too far afield for your current partner. Was that choice controlled?"

She ignored my anger and considered the question thoughtfully.

"Perhaps," she finally said. "It's hard to know. But you've made your point." She picked at a string in the hem of her shirt, and then, as if realizing that she was avoiding my gaze, folded her hands resolutely and squared her shoulders. "Who knows how much comes from any given host on any given planet? As I said before, I think time is probably your answer. Whether she grows apathetic and silent gradually, allowing you to make another choice besides this Jared, or . . . well, the Seekers are very good. They're already looking for him, and maybe you'll remember something that helps."

I didn't move as her meaning sank in. She didn't seem to notice that I was frozen in place.

"Perhaps they'll find Melanie's love, and then you can be together. If his feelings are as fervent as hers, the new soul will probably be amenable."

"No!" I wasn't sure who had shouted. It *could* have been me. I was full of horror, too.

I was on my feet, shaking. The tears that came so easily were, for once, absent, and my hands trembled in tight fists.

"Wanderer?"

But I turned and ran for the door, fighting the words that could not come out of my mouth. Words that could not be my words. Words that made no sense unless they were hers, but they *felt* like mine. They couldn't be mine. They couldn't be spoken.

*That's killing him! That's making him cease to be! I don't want someone else. I want* Jared, *not a stranger in his body! The body means nothing without him.*

I heard Kathy calling my name behind me as I ran into the road.

I didn't live far from the Comforter's office, but the darkness in the street disoriented me. I'd gone two blocks before I realized I was running in the wrong direction.

People were looking at me. I wasn't dressed for exercise, and I wasn't jogging, I was fleeing. But no one bothered me; they politely averted their eyes. They would guess that I was new to this host. Acting out the way a child would.

I slowed to a walk, turning north so that I could loop around without passing Kathy's office again.

My walk was only slightly slower than a run. I heard my feet hitting the sidewalk too quickly, as though they were trying to match the tempo of a dance song. *Slap, slap, slap* against the concrete. No, it wasn't like a drumbeat, it was too angry. Like violence. *Slap, slap, slap.* Someone hitting someone else. I shuddered away from the horrible image.

I could see the lamp on over my apartment door. It hadn't taken me long to cover the distance. I didn't cross the road, though.

I felt sick. I remembered what it felt like to vomit, though I never had. The cold wetness dewed on my forehead, the hollow sound rang in my ears. I was pretty sure I was about to have that experience for my own.

There was a bank of grass beside the walk. Around a streetlamp there was a well-trimmed hedge. I had no time to look for a better place. I stumbled to the light and caught the post to hold myself up. The nausea was making me dizzy.

Yes, I was definitely going to experience throwing up.

"Wanderer, is that you? Wanderer, are you ill?"

The vaguely familiar voice was impossible to concentrate on. But it made things worse, knowing I had an audience as I leaned my face close to the bush and violently choked up my most recent meal.

"Who's your Healer here?" the voice asked. It sounded far away through the buzzing in my ears. A hand touched my arched back. "Do you need an ambulance?"

I coughed twice and shook my head. I was sure it was over; my stomach was empty.

"I'm not ill," I said I as pulled myself upright using the lamppost for support. I looked over to see who was watching my moment of disgrace.

The Seeker from Chicago had her cell phone in her hand, trying to decide which authority to call. I took one good look at her and bent over the leaves again. Empty stomach or no, she was the last person I needed to see right now.

But, as my stomach heaved uselessly, I realized that there would be a reason for her presence.

*Oh, no! Oh, no no no no no no!*

"Why?" I gasped, panic and sickness stealing the volume from my voice. "Why are you here? What's happened?" The Comforter's very uncomforting words pounded in my head.

I stared at the hands gripping the collar of the Seeker's black suit for two seconds before I realized they were mine.

"Stop!" she said, and there was outrage on her face. Her voice rattled.

I was shaking her.

My hands jerked open and landed against my face.

"Excuse me!" I huffed. "I'm sorry. I don't know what I was doing."

The Seeker scowled at me and smoothed the front of her outfit. "You're not well, and I suppose I startled you."

"I wasn't expecting to see you," I whispered. "Why are you here?"

"Let's get you to a Healing facility before we speak. If you have a flu, you should get it healed. There's no point in letting it wear your body down."

"I don't have a flu. I'm not ill."

"Did you eat bad food? You must report where you got it."

Her prying was very annoying. "I did not eat bad food, either. I'm healthy."

"Why don't you have a Healer check? A quick scan — you shouldn't neglect your host. That's irresponsible. Especially when health care is so easy and effective."

I took a deep breath and resisted the urge to shake her again. She was a full head shorter than I was. It was a fight I would win.

A fight? I turned away from her and walked swiftly toward my home. I was dangerously emotional. I needed to calm down before I did something inexcusable.

"Wanderer? Wait! The Healer —"

"I need no Healer," I said without turning. "That was just . . . an emotional imbalance. I'm fine now."

The Seeker didn't answer. I wondered what she made of my response. I could hear her shoes — high heels — tapping after me, so I left the door open, knowing she would follow me in. I went to the sink and filled a glass with water. She waited silently while I rinsed my mouth and spat. When I was through, I leaned against the counter, staring into the basin.

She was soon bored.

"So, Wanderer . . . or do you still go by that name? I don't mean to be rude in calling you that."

I didn't look at her. "I still go by Wanderer."

"Interesting. I pegged you for one that would choose her own."

"I *did* choose. I chose Wanderer."

It had long been clear to me that the mild spat I'd overheard the first day I woke in the Healing facility was the Seeker's fault. The Seeker was the most confrontational soul I'd come across in nine lives. My first Healer, Fords Deep Waters, had been calm, kind, and wise, even for a soul. Yet he had not been able to help reacting to her. That made me feel better about my own response.

I turned around to face her. She was on my small couch, nestled in comfortably as if for a long visit. Her expression was self-satisfied, the bulging eyes amused. I controlled the desire to scowl.

"Why are you here?" I asked again. My voice was a monotone. Restrained. I would not lose control again in front of this woman.

"It's been a while since I heard anything from you, so I thought I would check in personally. We've still made no headway in your case."

My hands clamped down on the edge of the counter behind me, but I kept the wild relief from my voice.

"That seems . . . overzealous. Besides, I sent you a message last night."

Her eyebrows came together in that way she had, a way that made her look angry and annoyed at the same time, as if you, not she, were responsible for her anger. She pulled out her palm computer and touched the screen a few times.

"Oh," she said stiffly. "I haven't checked my mail today."

She was quiet as she scanned through what I had written.

"I sent it very early in the morning," I said. "I was half asleep at the time. I'm not sure how much of what I wrote was memory or dream, or sleep-typing, maybe."

I went along with the words — Melanie's words — as they flowed easily from my mouth; I even added my own lighthearted laugh at the end. It was dishonest of me. Shameful behavior. But I would not let the Seeker know that I was weaker than my host.

For once, Melanie was not smug at having bested me. She was too relieved, too grateful that I had not, for my own petty reasons, given her away.

"Interesting," the Seeker murmured. "Another one on the loose." She shook her head. "Peace continues to elude us." She did not seem dismayed by the idea of a fragile peace — rather, it seemed to please her.

I bit my lip hard. Melanie wanted so badly to make another denial, to claim the boy was just part of a dream. *Don't be stupid,* I told her. *That would be so obvious.* It said much for the repellent nature of the Seeker that she could put Melanie and me on the same side of an argument.

*I hate her.* Melanie's whisper was sharp, painful like a cut.

*I know, I know.* I wished I could deny that I felt . . .

similarly. Hate was an unforgivable emotion. But the Seeker was . . . very difficult to like. Impossible.

The Seeker interrupted my internal conversation. "So, other than the new location to review, you have no more help for me on the road maps?"

I felt my body react to her critical tone. "I never said they were lines on a road map. That's your assumption. And no, I have nothing else."

She clicked her tongue quickly three times. "But you said they were directions."

"That's what I think they are. I'm not getting anything more."

"Why not? Haven't you subdued the human yet?" She laughed loudly. Laughing at me.

I turned my back to her and concentrated on calming myself. I tried to pretend that she wasn't there. That I was all alone in my austere kitchen, staring out the window into the little patch of night sky, at the three bright stars I could see through it.

Well, as alone as I ever was.

While I stared at the tiny points of light in the blackness, the lines that I'd seen over and over again — in my dreams and in my broken memories, cropping up at strange, unrelated moments — flashed through my head.

The first: a slow, rough curve, then a sharp turn north, another sharp turn back the other way, twisting back to the north for a longer stretch, and then the abrupt southern decline that flattened out into another shallow curve.

The second: a ragged zigzag, four tight switchbacks, the fifth point strangely blunt, like it was broken . . .

The third: a smooth wave, interrupted by a sudden

spur that swung a thin, long finger out to the north and back.

Incomprehensible, seemingly meaningless. But I knew this was important to Melanie. From the very beginning I'd known that. She protected this secret more fiercely than any other, next to the boy, her brother. I'd had no idea of his existence before the dream last night. I wondered what it was that had broken her. Maybe as she grew louder in my head, she would lose more of her secrets to me.

Maybe she would slip up, and I would see what these strange lines meant. I knew they meant something. That they led somewhere.

And at that moment, with the echo of the Seeker's laugh still hanging in the air, I suddenly realized why they were so important.

They led back to Jared, of course. Back to both of them, Jared and Jamie. Where else? What other location could possibly hold any meaning for her? Only now I saw that it was not *back,* because none of them had ever followed these lines before. Lines that had been as much of a mystery to her as they were to me, until . . .

The wall was slow to block me. She was distracted, paying more attention to the Seeker than I was. She fluttered in my head at a sound behind me, and that was the first I was aware of the Seeker's approach.

The Seeker sighed. "I expected more of you. Your track record seemed so promising."

"It's a pity you weren't free for the assignment yourself. I'm sure if you'd had to deal with a resistant host, it would have been child's play." I didn't turn to look at her. My voice stayed level.

She sniffed. "The early waves were challenging enough even without a resistant host."

"Yes. I've experienced a few settlings myself."

The Seeker snorted. "Were the See Weeds very difficult to tame? Did they flee?"

I kept my voice calm. "We had no trouble in the South Pole. Of course, the North was another matter. It was badly mishandled. We lost the entire forest." The sadness of that time echoed behind my words. A thousand sentient beings, closing their eyes forever rather than accept us. They'd curled their leaves from the suns and starved.

*Good for them,* Melanie whispered. There was no venom attached to the thought, only approval as she saluted the tragedy in my memory.

*It was such a waste.* I let the agony of the knowledge, the feel of the dying thoughts that had racked us with our sister forest's pain, wash through my head.

*It was death either way.*

The Seeker spoke, and I tried to concentrate on just one conversation.

"Yes." Her voice was uncomfortable. "That was poorly executed."

"You can never be too careful when it comes to doling out power. Some aren't as careful as they should be."

She didn't answer, and I heard her move a few steps back. Everyone knew that the misstep behind the mass suicide belonged to the Seekers, who, because the See Weeds couldn't *flee,* had underestimated their ability to *escape.* They'd proceeded recklessly, beginning the first settlement before we had adequate numbers in place for a full-scale assimilation. By the time they realized what the See Weeds were capable of, were willing to do, it was too late. The next shipment of hibernating souls was too far away, and before they'd arrived, the northern forest was lost.

I faced the Seeker now, curious to judge the impact of my words. She was impassive, staring at the white nothingness of the bare wall across the room.

"I'm sorry I can't help you further." I said the words firmly, trying to make the dismissal clear. I was ready to have my house to myself again. *To ourselves,* Melanie inserted spitefully. I sighed. She was so full of herself now. "You really shouldn't have troubled yourself to come so far."

"It's the job," the Seeker said, shrugging. "You're my only assignment. Until I find the rest of them, I may as well stick close to you and hope I get lucky."

# CHAPTER 7

# Confronted

Yes, Faces Sunward?" I asked, grateful to the raised hand for interrupting my lecture. I did not feel as comfortable behind the lectern as I usually did. My biggest strength, my only real credential — for my host body had had little in the way of a formal education, on the run since her early adolescence — was the personal experience I usually taught from. This was the first world's history I'd presented this semester for which I had no memories to draw upon. I was sure my students were suffering the difference.

"I'm sorry to interrupt, but . . ." The white-haired man paused, struggling to word his question. "I'm not sure I understand. The Fire-Tasters actually . . . *ingest* the smoke from burning the Walking Flowers? Like food?" He tried to suppress the horror in his tone. It was not a soul's place to judge another soul. But I was not surprised, given his background on the Planet of the Flowers, at his strong reaction to the fate of a similar life-form on another world.

It was always amazing to me how some souls buried themselves in the affairs of whichever world they inhabited and ignored the rest of the universe. But, to be fair, perhaps Faces Sunward had been in hibernation when Fire World became notorious.

"Yes, they receive essential nutrients from this smoke. And therein lies the fundamental dilemma and the controversy of Fire World — and the reason the planet has not been closed, though there has certainly been adequate time to populate it fully. There is also a high relocation percentage.

"When Fire World was discovered, it was at first thought that the dominant species, the Fire-Tasters, were the only intelligent life-forms present. The Fire-Tasters did not consider the Walking Flowers to be their equals — a cultural prejudice — so it was a while, even after the first wave of settling, before the souls realized they were murdering intelligent creatures. Since then, Fire World scientists have focused their efforts on finding a replacement for the dietary needs of the Fire-Tasters. Spiders are being transported there to help, but the planets are hundreds of light-years apart. When this obstacle is overcome, as it will be soon, I'm sure, there is hope that the Walking Flowers might also be assimilated. In the meantime, much of the brutality has been removed from the equation. The, ah, burning-alive portion, of course, and other aspects as well."

"How can they . . ." Faces Sunward trailed off, unable to finish.

Another voice completed Faces Sunward's thought. "It seems like a very cruel ecosystem. Why was the planet not abandoned?"

"That has been debated, naturally, Robert. But we do not abandon planets lightly. There are many souls for whom Fire World is home. They will not be uprooted against their will." I looked away, back at my notes, in an attempt to end the side discussion.

"But it's barbaric!"

Robert was physically younger than most of the other students — closer to my age, in fact, than any other. And truly a child in a more important way. Earth was his first world — the Mother in this case had actually been an Earth-dweller, too, before she'd given herself — and he didn't seem to have as much perspective as older, better-traveled souls. I wondered what it would be like to be born into the overwhelming sensation and emotion of these hosts with no prior experience for balance. It would be difficult to find objectivity. I tried to remember that and be especially patient as I answered him.

"Every world is a unique experience. Unless one has lived on that world, it's impossible to truly understand the —"

"But you never lived on Fire World," he interrupted me. "You must have felt the same way. . . . Unless you had some other reason for skipping that planet? You've been almost everywhere else."

"Choosing a planet is a very personal and private decision, Robert, as you may someday experience." My tone closed the subject absolutely.

*Why not tell them? You* do *think it's barbaric — and cruel and wrong. Which is pretty ironic if you ask me —*

*not that you ever do. What's the problem? Are you ashamed that you agree with Robert? Because he's more human than the others?*

Melanie, having found her voice, was becoming downright unbearable. How was I supposed to concentrate on my work with her opinions sounding off in my head all the time?

In the seat behind Robert, a dark shadow moved.

The Seeker, clad in her usual black, leaned forward, intent for the first time on the subject of discussion.

I resisted the urge to scowl at her. I didn't want Robert, already looking embarrassed, to mistake the expression as meant for him. Melanie grumbled. *She* wished I wouldn't resist. Having the Seeker stalk our every footstep had been educational for Melanie; she used to think she couldn't hate anything or anyone more than she hated me.

"Our time is almost up," I announced with relief. "I'm pleased to inform you that we will have a guest speaker next Tuesday who will be able to make up for my ignorance on this topic. Flame Tender, a recent addition to our planet, will be here to give us a more personal account of the settling of Fire World. I know that you will give him all the courtesy you accord me, and be respectful of the very young age of his host. Thank you for your time."

The class filed out slowly, many of the students taking a minute to chat with one another as they gathered their things. What Kathy had said about friendships ran through my head, but I felt no desire to join any of them. They were strangers.

Was that the way I felt? Or the way Melanie felt? It was hard to tell. Maybe I was naturally antisocial. My personal history supported that theory, I supposed. I'd never formed an attachment strong enough to keep me on any planet for more than one life.

I noticed Robert and Faces Sunward lingering at the classroom door, locked in a discussion that seemed intense. I could guess the subject.

"Fire World stories ruffle feathers."

I started slightly.

The Seeker was standing at my elbow. The woman usually announced her approach with the quick tap of her hard shoes. I looked down now to see that she was wearing sneakers for once — black, of course. She was even tinier without the extra inches.

"It's not my favorite subject," I said in a bland voice. "I prefer to have firsthand experience to share."

"Strong reactions from the class."

"Yes."

She looked at me expectantly, as if waiting for more. I gathered my notes and turned to put them in my bag.

"You seemed to react as well."

I placed my papers in the bag carefully, not turning.

"I wondered why you didn't answer the question."

There was a pause while she waited for me to respond. I didn't.

"So . . . why didn't you answer the question?"

I turned around, not concealing the impatience on my face. "Because it wasn't pertinent to the lesson, because Robert needs to learn some manners, and because it's no one else's business."

I swung my bag to my shoulder and headed for the door. She stayed right beside me, rushing to keep up with my longer legs. We walked down the hallway in silence. It wasn't until we were outside, where the afternoon sun lit the dust motes in the salty air, that she spoke again.

"Do you think you'll ever settle, Wanderer? On this planet, maybe? You seem to have an affinity for their . . . feelings."

I bridled at the implied insult in her tone. I wasn't even sure how she meant to insult me, but it was clear that she did. Melanie stirred resentfully.

"I'm not sure what you mean."

"Tell me something, Wanderer. Do you pity them?"

"Who?" I asked blankly. "The Walking Flowers?"

"No, the humans."

I stopped walking, and she skidded to a halt beside me. We were only a few blocks from my apartment, and I'd been hurrying in hopes of getting away from her, though likely as not, she'd invite herself in. But her question caught me off guard.

"The humans?"

"Yes. Do you pity them?"

"Don't you?"

"No. They were quite the brutal race. They were lucky to survive each other as long as they did."

"Not every one of them was bad."

"It was a predilection of their genetics. Brutality was part of their species. But *you* pity them, it seems."

"It's a lot to lose, don't you think?" I gestured around us. We stood in a parklike space between two ivy-covered dormitories. The deep green of the ivy was pleasing to the eye, especially in contrast to the faded red of the old bricks. The air was golden and soft, and the smell of the ocean gave a briny edge to the honey sweet fragrance of the flowers in the bushes. The breeze caressed the bare skin of my arms. "In your other lives, you can't have felt anything so vivid. Wouldn't you pity anyone who had this taken from them?" Her expression stayed flat, unmoved. I made an attempt to draw her in, to make her consider another viewpoint. "Which other worlds have you lived on?"

She hesitated, then squared her shoulders. "None. I've only lived on Earth."

That surprised me. She was as much a child as Robert. "Only one planet? And you chose to be a Seeker in your first life?"

She nodded once, her chin set.

"Well. Well, that's your business." I started walking again. Maybe if I respected her privacy, she would return the favor.

"I spoke to your Comforter."

*And maybe not,* Melanie thought sourly.

"What?" I gasped.

"I gather you've been having more trouble than just accessing the information I need. Have you considered trying another, more pliable host? She suggested that, did she not?"

"Kathy wouldn't tell *you* anything!"

The Seeker's face was smug. "She didn't have to answer. I'm very good at reading human expressions. I could tell when my questions struck a nerve."

"How dare you? The relationship between a soul and her Comforter —"

"Is sacrosanct, yes; I know the theory. But the acceptable means of investigation don't seem to be working with your case. I have to get creative."

"You think I'm keeping something from you?" I demanded, too angry to control the disgust in my voice. "You think I confided that to my Comforter?"

My anger didn't faze her. Perhaps, given her strange personality, she was used to such reactions.

"No. I think you're telling me what you know. . . . But I don't think you're looking as hard as you could. I've seen it before. You're growing sympathetic to your host. You're letting her memories unconsciously direct your own desires. It's probably too late at this point. I think you'd be more comfortable moving on, and maybe someone else will have better luck with her."

"Hah!" I shouted. "Melanie would eat them alive!"

Her expression froze in place.

She'd had no idea, no matter what she thought she'd discerned from Kathy. She'd thought Melanie's influence was from memories, that it was unconscious.

"I find it very interesting that you speak of her in the present tense."

I ignored that, trying to pretend I hadn't made a slip. "If you think someone else would have better luck breaking into her secrets, you're wrong."

"Only one way to find out."

"Did you have someone in mind?" I asked, my voice frigid with aversion.

She grinned. "*I've* gotten permission to give it a try. Shouldn't take long. They're going to hold my host for me."

I had to breathe deeply. I was shaking, and Melanie was so full of hate that she was past words. The idea of having the Seeker inside me, even though I knew that I would not be here, was so repugnant that I felt a return of last week's nausea.

"It's too bad for your investigation that I'm not a skipper."

The Seeker's eyes narrowed. "Well, it does certainly make this assignment drag on. History was never of much interest to me, but it looks like I'm in for a full course now."

"You just said that it was probably too late to get any more from her memories," I reminded her, struggling to make my voice calm. "Why don't you go back to wherever you belong?"

She shrugged and smiled a tight smile. "I'm sure it *is* too late . . . for voluntary information. But if you don't cooperate, she might just lead me to them yet."

"*Lead* you?"

"When she takes full control, and you're no better than that weakling, once Racing Song, now Kevin. Remember him? The one who attacked the Healer?"

I stared at her, eyes wide, nostrils flared.

"Yes, it's probably just a matter of time. Your Comforter didn't tell you the statistics, did she? Well, even if she did, she wouldn't have the latest information that *we* have access to. The long-term success rate for situations such as yours — once a human host begins to resist — is under twenty percent. Did you have any idea it was so bad? They're changing the information they give potential settlers. There will be no more adult hosts offered. The risks are too great. We're losing souls. It won't be long before she's talking to you, talking through you, controlling your decisions."

I hadn't moved an inch or relaxed a muscle. The Seeker leaned in, stretched up on her toes to put her face closer to mine. Her voice turned low and smooth in an attempt to sound persuasive.

"Is that what you want, Wanderer? To lose? To fade away, erased by another awareness? To be no better than a host body?"

I couldn't breathe.

"It only gets worse. You won't be *you* anymore. She'll beat you, and you'll disappear. Maybe someone will intervene. . . . Maybe they'll move you like they did Kevin. And you'll become some child named Melanie who likes to tinker with cars rather than compose music. Or whatever it is she does."

"The success rate is under twenty percent?" I whispered.

She nodded, trying to suppress a smile. "You're losing yourself, Wanderer. All the worlds you've seen, all the experiences you've collected — they'll be for nothing. I saw in your file that you have the potential for Motherhood. If you gave yourself to be a Mother, at least all that would not be entirely wasted. Why throw yourself away? Have you considered Motherhood?"

I jerked away from her, my face flushing.

"I'm sorry," she muttered, her face darkening, too. "That was impolite. Forget I said that."

"I'm going home. Don't follow."

"I have to, Wanderer. It's my job."

"Why do you care so much about a few spare humans? Why? How do you justify your *job* anymore? We've won! It's time for you to join society and do something productive!"

My questions, my implied accusations, did not ruffle her.

"Wherever the fringes of their world touch ours there

is death." She spoke the words peacefully, and for a moment I glimpsed a different person in her face. It surprised me to realize that she deeply believed in what she did. Part of me had supposed that she only chose to seek because she illicitly craved the violence. "If even one soul is lost to your Jared or your Jamie, that is one soul too many. Until there is total peace on this planet, my job will be justified. As long as there are Jareds surviving, I am needed to protect our kind. As long as there are Melanies leading souls around by the nose . . ."

I turned my back on her and headed for my apartment with long strides that would force her to run if she wanted to keep up.

"Don't lose yourself, Wanderer!" she called after me. "Time is running out for you!" She paused, then shouted more loudly. "Inform me when I'm to start calling you Melanie!"

Her voice faded as the space between us grew. I knew she would follow at her own pace. This last uncomfortable week — seeing her face in the back of every class, hearing her footsteps behind me on the sidewalk every day — was nothing compared to what was coming. She was going to make my life a misery.

It felt as if Melanie were bouncing violently against the inner walls of my skull.

*Let's get her canned. Tell her higher-ups that she did something unacceptable. Assaulted us. It's our word against hers —*

*In a human world,* I reminded her, almost sad that I didn't have access to that sort of recourse. *There are no higher-ups, in that sense. Everyone works together as equals. There are those whom many report to, in order to keep the information organized, and councils who make decisions about that information, but they won't remove her from an assignment she wants. You see, it works like —*

*Who cares how it works if it doesn't help us? I know — let's kill her!* A gratuitous image of my hands tightening around the Seeker's neck filled my head.

*That sort of thing is* exactly *why my kind is better left in charge of this place.*

*Get off your high horse. You'd enjoy it as much as I would.* The image returned, the Seeker's face turning blue in our imagination, but this time it was accompanied by a fierce wave of pleasure.

*That's you, not me.* My statement was true; the image sickened me. But it was also perilously close to false — in that I would very much enjoy never seeing the Seeker again.

*What do we do now? I'm not giving up. You're not giving up. And that wretched Seeker is sure as hell not giving up!*

I didn't answer her. I didn't have a ready answer.

It was quiet in my head for a brief moment. That was nice. I wished the silence could last. But there was only one way to buy my peace. Was I willing to pay the price? Did I have a choice anymore?

Melanie slowly calmed. By the time I was through the front door, locking behind me the bolts that I had never before turned — human artifacts that had no place in a peaceful world — her thoughts were contemplative.

*I'd never thought about how you all carry on your species. I didn't know it was like that.*

*We take it very seriously, as you can imagine. Thanks*

*for your concern.* She wasn't bothered by the thick edge of irony in the thought.

She was still musing over this discovery while I turned on my computer and began to look for shuttle flights. It was a moment before she was aware of what I was doing.

*Where are we going?* The thought held a flicker of panic. I felt her awareness begin to rifle through my head, her touch like the soft brush of feathers, searching for anything I might be keeping from her.

I decided to save her the search. *I'm going to Chicago.*

The panic was more than a flicker now. *Why?*

*I'm going to see the Healer. I don't trust* her. *I want to talk to him before I make my decision.*

There was a brief silence before she spoke again.

*The decision to kill me?*

*Yes, that one.*

# CHAPTER 8

# *Loved*

"*You're* afraid to fly?" The Seeker's voice was full of disbelief edging toward mockery. "You've traveled through deep space eight times and you're afraid to take a shuttle to Tucson, Arizona?"

"First of all, I'm not afraid. Second, when I traveled through deep space I wasn't exactly aware of where I was, what with being stored in a hibernation chamber. And third, this host gets motion sickness on shuttles."

The Seeker rolled her eyes in disgust. "So take medication! What would you have done if Healer Fords hadn't relocated to Saint Mary's? Would you be driving to Chicago?"

"No. But since the option of driving is now reasonable, I will take it. It will be nice to see a bit more of this world. The desert can be stunning —"

"The desert is dead boring."

"— and I'm not in any hurry. I have many things to think through, and I will appreciate some time *alone*." I looked pointedly at her as I emphasized the last word.

"I don't understand the point of visiting your old Healer anyway. There are many competent Healers here."

"I'm comfortable with Healer Fords. He has experience with this, and I don't trust that I have all the information I need." I gave her another significant look.

"You don't have time to *not* hurry, Wanderer. I recognize the signs."

"Forgive me if I don't consider your information impartial. I know enough of human behavior to recognize the signs of manipulation."

She glowered at me.

I was packing my rental car with the few things I planned to take with me. I had enough clothes to go a week between washing, and the basic hygiene necessities. Though I wasn't bringing much, I was leaving even less behind. I'd accumulated very little in the way of personal belongings. After all these months in my small apartment, the walls were still bare, the shelves empty. Perhaps I'd never meant to settle here.

The Seeker was planted on the sidewalk next to my open trunk, assailing me with snide questions and comments whenever I was in hearing distance. At least I was secure in the belief that she was far too impatient to follow me on the road. She would take a shuttle to Tucson, just as she was hoping to shame me into doing. It was a huge relief. I imagined her joining me every time I stopped to eat, hovering outside gas station bathrooms, her inexhaustible inquisitions waiting for me whenever my vehicle paused at a light. I shuddered at the thought. If a new body meant freeing myself of the Seeker . . . well, that was quite an inducement.

I had another choice, too. I could abandon this entire world as a failure and move on to a tenth planet. I could work to forget this whole experience. Earth could be just a short blip in my otherwise spotless record.

But where would I go? A planet I'd already experienced? The Singing World had been one of my favorites, but to give up sight for blindness? The Planet of the Flowers was lovely. . . . Yet chlorophyll-based life-forms had so little range of emotion. It would feel unbearably slow after the tempo of this human place.

A new planet? There *was* a recent acquisition — here on Earth, they were calling the new hosts Dolphins for lack of a better comparison, though they resembled dragonflies more than marine mammals. A highly developed species, and certainly mobile, but after my long stay with the See Weeds, the thought of another water planet was repugnant to me.

No, there was still so much to *this* planet that I hadn't experienced. Nowhere else in the known universe called to me as strongly as this shady little green yard on this quiet street. Or held the lure of the empty desert sky, which I'd seen only in Melanie's memories.

Melanie did not share her opinion on my options. She had been very quiet since my decision to find Fords Deep Waters, my first Healer. I wasn't sure what the detachment meant. Was she trying to seem less dangerous, less of a burden? Was she preparing herself for the invasion of the Seeker? For death? Or was she preparing to fight me? To try to take over?

Whatever her plan, she kept herself distant. She was just a faint, watchful presence in the back of my head.

I made my last trip inside, searching for anything forgotten. The apartment looked empty. There were only the basic furnishings that had been left by the last tenant. The same plates were still in the cupboards, the pillows on the bed, the lamps on the tables; if I didn't come back, there would be little for the next tenant to clear out.

The phone rang as I was stepping out the door, and I turned back to get it, but I was too late. I'd already set the message system to answer on the first ring. I knew what the caller would hear: my vague explanation that I would be out the rest of the semester, and that my classes would be canceled until a replacement could be found. No reason given. I looked at the clock on top of the television. It was barely past eight in the morning. I was sure it must be Curt on the phone, having just received the only slightly more detailed e-mail I'd sent him late last night. I felt guilty about not finishing out my commitment to him, almost like I was already skipping. Perhaps this step, this quitting, was the prelude to my next decision, my greater shame. The thought was uncomfortable. It made me unwilling to listen to whatever the message said, though I wasn't in any real hurry to leave.

I looked around the empty apartment one more time. There was no sense of leaving anything behind me, no fondness for these rooms. I had the strange feeling that this world — not just Melanie, but the entire orb of the planet — did not want me, no matter how much I wanted *it.* I just couldn't seem to get my roots in. I smiled wryly at the thought of roots. This feeling was just superstitious nonsense.

I'd never had a host that was capable of superstition. It was an interesting sensation. Like knowing you were being watched without being able to find the watcher. It raised goose bumps on the nape of my neck.

I shut the door firmly behind me but did not touch the obsolete locks. No one would disturb this place until I returned or it was given to someone new.

Without looking at the Seeker, I climbed into the car. I hadn't done much driving, and neither had Melanie, so this made me a bit nervous. But I was sure I would get used to it soon enough.

"I'll be waiting for you in Tucson," the Seeker said, leaning in the open passenger-side window as I started the engine.

"I have no doubt of that," I muttered.

I found the controls on the door panel. Trying to hide a smile, I hit the button to raise the glass and watched her jump back.

"Maybe . . . ," she said, raising her voice to almost a shout so that I could hear her over the engine noise and through the closed window, "maybe I'll try it your way. Maybe I'll see you on the road."

She smiled and shrugged.

She was just saying it to upset me. I tried not to let her see that she had. I focused my eyes on the road ahead and pulled carefully away from the curb.

It was easy enough to find the freeway and then follow the signs out of San Diego. Soon there were no signs to follow, no wrong turns to take. In eight hours I would be in Tucson. It wasn't long enough. Perhaps I would stay a night in some small town along the way. If I could be sure that the Seeker would be ahead, waiting impatiently, rather than following behind, a stop would be a nice delay.

I found myself looking in the rearview mirror often, searching for a sign of pursuit. I was driving slower than anyone else, unwilling to reach my destination, and the other cars passed me without pause. There were no faces I recognized as they moved ahead. I shouldn't have let the Seeker's taunt bother me; she clearly didn't have the temperament to go anywhere slowly. Still . . . I continued to watch for her.

I'd been west to the ocean, north and south up and down the pretty California coastline, but I'd never been east for any distance at all. Civilization fell behind me quickly, and I was soon surrounded by the blank hills and rocks that were the precursors to the empty desert wastelands.

It was very relaxing to be away from civilization, and this bothered me. I should not have found the loneliness so welcoming. Souls were sociable. We lived and worked and grew together in harmony. We were all the same: peaceful, friendly, honest. Why should I feel better away from my kind? Was it Melanie who made me this way?

I searched for her but found her remote, dreaming in the back of my head.

This was the best it had been since she'd started talking again.

The miles passed quickly. The dark, rough rocks and the dusty plains covered in scrub flew by with monotonous uniformity. I realized I was driving faster than I'd meant to. There wasn't anything to keep my mind occupied here, so I found it hard to linger. Absently, I wondered why the desert was so much more colorful in Melanie's memories, so much more compelling. I let my mind coast with hers, trying to see what it was that was special about this vacant place.

But she wasn't seeing the sparse, dead land surrounding us. She was dreaming of another desert, canyoned and red, a magical place. She didn't try to keep me out. In fact, she seemed almost unaware of my presence. I questioned again what her detachment meant. I sensed no thought of attack. It felt more like a preparation for the end.

She was living in a happier place in her memory, as if she were saying goodbye. It was a place she had never allowed me to see before.

There was a cabin, an ingenious dwelling tucked into a nook in the red sandstone, perilously close to the flash flood line. An unlikely place, far from any trail or path, built in what seemed a senseless location. A rough place, without any of the conveniences of modern technology. She remembered laughing at the sink one had to pump to pull water up from the ground.

"It beats pipes," Jared says, the crease between his eyes deepening as his brows pull together. He seems worried by my laugh. Is he afraid I don't like it? "Nothing to trace, no evidence that we're here."

"I love it," I say quickly. "It's like an old movie. It's perfect."

The smile that never truly leaves his face — he smiles even in his sleep — grows wide. "They don't tell you the worst parts in the movies. C'mon, I'll show you where the latrine is."

I hear Jamie's laughter echo through the narrow canyon as he runs ahead of us. His black hair bounces with his body.

He bounces all the time now, this thin boy with the sun-darkened skin. I hadn't realized how much weight those narrow shoulders were carrying. With Jared, he is positively buoyant. The anxious expression has faded, replaced by grins. We are both more resilient than I gave us credit for.

"Who built this place?"

"My father and older brothers. I helped, or rather hindered, a little. My dad loved to get away from everything. And he didn't care much about convention. He never bothered to find out who the land actually *belonged* to or file permits or any of that pesky stuff." Jared laughs, throwing his head back. The sun dances off the blond bits in his hair. "Officially, this place doesn't exist. Convenient, isn't it?" Without seeming to think about it, he reaches out and takes my hand.

My skin burns where it meets his. It feels better than good, but it sets off a strange aching in my chest.

He is forever touching me this way, always seeming to need to reassure himself that I am here. Does he realize what it does to me, the simple pressure of his warm palm next to mine? Does his pulse jump in his veins, too? Or is he just happy to not be alone anymore?

He swings our arms as we walk beneath a little stand of cottonwood trees, their green so vivid against the red that it plays tricks on my eyes, confusing my focus. He is happy here, happier than in other places. I feel happy, too. The feeling is still unfamiliar.

He hasn't kissed me since that first night, when I screamed, finding the scar on his neck. Does he not want to kiss me again? Should I kiss him? What if he doesn't like that?

He looks down at me and smiles, the lines around his eyes crinkling into little webs. I wonder if he is as handsome as I think he is, or if it's just that he's the only person left in the whole world besides Jamie and me.

No, I don't think that's it. He really is beautiful.

"What are you thinking, Mel?" he asks. "You seem to be concentrating on something very important." He laughs.

I shrug, and my stomach flutters. "It's beautiful here."

He looks around us. "Yes. But then, isn't home always beautiful?"

"Home." I repeat the word quietly. "Home."

"Your home, too, if you want it."

"I want it." It seems like every mile I've walked in the past three years has been toward this place. I never want to leave, though I know we'll have to. Food doesn't grow on trees. Not in the desert, at least.

He squeezes my hand, and my heart punches against my ribs. It's just like pain, this pleasure.

There was a blurring sensation as Melanie skipped ahead, her thoughts dancing through the hot day until hours after the sun had fallen behind the red canyon walls. I went along, almost hypnotized by the endless road stretching ahead of me, the skeletal bushes flying by with mind-numbing sameness.

I peek into the one narrow little bedroom. The full-size mattress is only inches away from the rough stone walls on either side.

It gives me a deep, rich sense of joy to see Jamie asleep on a real bed, his head on a soft pillow. His lanky arms and legs sprawl out, leaving little room for me where I am meant to sleep. He is so much bigger in reality than the way I see him in my head. Almost ten — soon he won't be a child at all. Except that he will always be a child to me.

Jamie breathes evenly, sleeping sound. There is no fear in his dream, for this moment at least.

I shut the door quietly and go back to the small couch where Jared waits.

"Thank you," I whisper, though I know shouting the words wouldn't wake Jamie now. "I feel bad. This couch is much too short for you. Maybe you should take the bed with Jamie."

Jared chuckles. "Mel, you're only a few inches shorter than I am. Sleep comfortably, for once. Next time I'm out, I'll steal myself a cot or something."

I don't like this, for lots of reasons. Will he be leaving soon? Will he take us with him when he goes? Does he see this room assignment as a permanent thing?

He drops his arm around my shoulders and tucks me against his side. I scoot closer, though the heat of touching him has my heart aching again.

"Why the frown?" he asks.

"When will you . . . when will we have to leave again?"

He shrugs. "We scavenged enough on our way up that we're set for a few months. I can do a few short raids if you want to stay in one place for a while. I'm sure you're tired of running."

"Yes, I am," I agree. I take a deep breath to make me brave. "But if you go, I go."

He hugs me tighter. "I'll admit, I prefer it that way. The thought of being separated from you . . ." He laughs quietly. "Does it sound crazy to say that I'd rather die? Too melodramatic?"

"No, I know what you mean."

He *must* feel the same way I do. Would he say these

things if he thought of me as just another human, and not as a woman?

I realize that this is the first time we've ever been really alone since the night we met — the first time there's been a door to close between a sleeping Jamie and the two of us. So many nights we've stayed awake, talking in whispers, telling all of our stories, the happy stories and the horror stories, always with Jamie's head cradled on my lap. It makes my breath come faster, that simple closed door.

"I don't think you need to find a cot, not yet."

I feel his eyes on me, questioning, but I can't meet them. I'm embarrassed now, too late. The words are out.

"We'll stay here until the food is gone, don't worry. I've slept on worse things than this couch."

"That's not what I mean," I say, still looking down.

"You get the bed, Mel. I'm not budging on that."

"That's not what I mean, either." It's barely a whisper. "I meant the couch is plenty big for Jamie. He won't outgrow it for a long time. I could share the bed with . . . you."

There is a pause. I want to look up, to read the expression on his face, but I'm too mortified. What if he is disgusted? How will I stand it? Will he make me go away?

His warm, callused fingers tug my chin up. My heart throbs when our eyes meet.

"Mel, I . . ." His face, for once, has no smile.

I try to look away, but he holds my chin so that my gaze can't escape his. Does he not feel the fire between his body and mine? Is that all me? How can it all be me? It feels like a flat sun trapped between us — pressed like a flower between the pages of a thick book, burning the paper. Does it feel like something else to him? Something bad?

After a moment, his head turns; he's the one looking

away now, still keeping his grip on my chin. His voice is quiet. "You don't owe me that, Melanie. You don't owe me anything at all."

It's hard for me to swallow. "I'm not saying . . . I didn't mean that I felt *obligated*. And . . . you shouldn't, either. Forget I said anything."

"Not likely, Mel."

He sighs, and I want to disappear. Give up — lose my mind to the invaders if that's what it takes to erase this huge blunder. Trade the future to blot out the last two minutes of the past. Anything.

Jared takes a deep breath. He squints at the floor, his eyes and jaw tight. "Mel, it doesn't have to be like that. Just because we're together, just because we're the last man and woman on Earth . . ." He struggles for words, something I don't think I've ever seen him do before. "That doesn't mean you have to do anything you don't want to. I'm not the kind of man who would expect . . . You don't have to . . ."

He looks so upset, still frowning away, that I find myself speaking, though I know it's a mistake before I start. "That's not what I mean," I mutter. "'Have to' is not what I'm talking about, and I don't think you're 'that kind of man.' No. Of course not. It's just that —"

Just that I love him. I grit my teeth together before I can humiliate myself more. I should bite my tongue off right now before it ruins anything else.

"Just that . . . ?" he asks.

I try to shake my head, but he's still holding my chin tight between his fingers.

"Mel?"

I yank free and shake my head fiercely.

He leans closer to me, and his face is different suddenly.

There's a new conflict I don't recognize in his expression, and even though I don't understand it completely, it erases the feeling of rejection that's making my eyes sting.

"Will you talk to me? Please?" he murmurs. I can feel his breath on my cheek, and it's a few seconds before I can think at all.

His eyes make me forget that I am mortified, that I wanted to never speak again.

"If I got to pick anyone, anyone at all, to be stranded on a deserted planet with, it would be you," I whisper. The sun between us burns hotter. "I always want to be with you. And not just . . . not just to talk to. When you touch me . . ." I dare to let my fingers brush lightly along the warm skin of his arm, and it feels like the flames are flowing from their tips now. His arm tightens around me. Does he feel the fire? "I don't want you to stop." I want to be more exact, but I can't find the words. That's fine. It's bad enough having admitted this much. "If you don't feel the same way, I understand. Maybe it isn't the same for you. That's okay." Lies.

"Oh, Mel," he sighs in my ear, and pulls my face around to meet his.

More flames in his lips, fiercer than the others, blistering. I don't know what I'm doing, but it doesn't seem to matter. His hands are in my hair, and my heart is about to combust. I can't breathe. I don't *want* to breathe.

But his lips move to my ear, and he holds my face when I try to find them again.

"It was a miracle — more than a miracle — when I found you, Melanie. Right now, if I was given the choice between having the world back and having you, I wouldn't be able to give you up. Not to save five billion lives."

"That's wrong."

"Very wrong but very true."

"Jared," I breathe. I try to reach for his lips again. He pulls away, looking like he has something to say. What more can there be?

"But . . ."

"But?" How can there be a *but*? What could possibly follow all this fire that starts with a *but*?

"But you're seventeen, Melanie. And I'm twenty-six."

"What's that got to do with anything?"

He doesn't answer. His hands stroke my arms slowly, painting them with fire.

"You've got to be kidding me." I lean back to search his face. "You're going to worry about *conventions* when we're past the end of the world?"

He swallows loudly before he speaks. "Most conventions exist for a reason, Mel. I would feel like a bad person, like I was taking advantage. You're very young."

"No one's young anymore. Anyone who's survived this long is ancient."

There's a smile pulling up one corner of his mouth. "Maybe you're right. But this isn't something we need to rush."

"What is there to wait for?" I demand.

He hesitates for a long moment, thinking.

"Well, for one thing, there are some . . . practical matters to consider."

I wonder if he is just searching for a distraction, trying to stall. That's what it feels like. I raise one eyebrow. I can't believe the turn this conversation has taken. If he really does want me, this is senseless.

"See," he explains, hesitating. Under the deep golden tan of his skin, it looks like he might be blushing. "When I was stocking this place, I wasn't much planning for . . . guests. What I mean is . . ." The rest comes out in a rush. "Birth control was pretty much the last thing on my mind."

I feel my forehead crease. "Oh."

The smile is gone from his face, and for one short second there is a flash of anger I've never seen there before. It makes him look dangerous in a way I hadn't imagined he could. "This isn't the kind of world I'd want to bring a child into."

The words sink in, and I cringe at the thought of a tiny, innocent baby opening his eyes to this place. It's bad enough to watch Jamie's eyes, to know what this life will bring him, even in the best possible circumstances.

Jared is suddenly Jared again. The skin around his eyes crinkles. "Besides, we've got plenty of time to . . . think about this." Stalling again, I suspect. "Do you realize how very, very little time we've been together so far? It's been just four weeks since we found each other."

This floors me. "That can't be."

"Twenty-nine days. I'm counting."

I think back. It's not possible that it has been only twenty-nine days since Jared changed our lives. It seems like Jamie and I have been with Jared every bit as long as we were alone. Two or three years, maybe.

"We've got time," Jared says again.

An abrupt panic, like a warning premonition, makes it impossible for me to speak for a long moment. He watches the change on my face with worried eyes.

"You don't know that." The despair that softened when he found me strikes like the lash of a whip. "You can't know how much time we'll have. You don't know if we should be counting in months or days or hours."

He laughs a warm laugh, touching his lips to the tense

place where my eyebrows pull together. "Don't worry, Mel. Miracles don't work that way. I'll never lose you. I'll never let you get away from me."

She brought me back to the present — to the thin ribbon of the highway winding through the Arizona wasteland, baking under the fierce noon sun — without my choosing to return. I stared at the empty place ahead and felt the empty place inside.

Her thought sighed faintly in my head: *You never know how much time you'll have.*

The tears I was crying belonged to both of us.

# CHAPTER 9

# Discovered

I drove quickly through the I-10 junction as the sun fell behind me. I didn't see much besides the white and yellow lines on the pavement, and the occasional big green sign pointing me farther east. I was in a hurry now.

I wasn't sure exactly what I was in a hurry *for*, though. To be out of this, I supposed. Out of pain, out of sadness, out of aching for lost and hopeless loves. Did that mean out of this body? I couldn't think of any other answer. I would still ask my questions of the Healer, but it felt as though the decision was made. *Skipper. Quitter.* I tested the words in my head, trying to come to terms with them.

If I could find a way, I would keep Melanie out of the Seeker's hands. It would be very hard. No, it would be impossible.

I would try.

I promised her this, but she wasn't listening. She was still dreaming. Giving up, I thought, now that it was too late for giving up to help.

I tried to stay clear of the red canyon in her head, but I was there, too. No matter how hard I tried to see the cars zooming beside me, the shuttles gliding in toward the port, the few, fine clouds drifting overhead, I couldn't pull completely free of her dreams. I memorized Jared's face from a thousand different angles. I watched Jamie shoot up in a sudden growth spurt, always skin and bones. My arms ached for them both — no, the feeling was sharper than an ache, blade-edged and violent. It was intolerable. I had to get out.

I drove almost blindly along the narrow two-lane freeway. The desert was, if anything, more monotonous and dead than before. Flatter, more colorless. I would make it to Tucson long before dinnertime. Dinner. I hadn't eaten yet today, and my stomach rumbled as I realized that.

The Seeker would be waiting for me there. My stomach rolled then, hunger momentarily replaced with nausea. Automatically, my foot eased off the gas.

I checked the map on the passenger seat. Soon I would reach a little pit stop at a place called Picacho Peak. Maybe I would stop to eat something there. Put off seeing the Seeker a few precious moments.

As I thought of this unfamiliar name — Picacho Peak — there was a strange, stifled reaction from Melanie. I couldn't make it out. Had she been here before? I searched for a memory, a sight or a smell that corresponded, but found nothing. Picacho Peak. Again, there was that spike of interest that Melanie repressed. What did the words mean to her? She retreated into faraway memories, avoiding me.

This made me curious. I drove a little faster, wondering if the sight of the place would trigger something.

A solitary mountain peak — not massive by normal standards, but towering above the low, rough hills closer to me — was beginning to take shape on the horizon. It had an unusual, distinctive shape. Melanie watched it grow as we traveled, pretending indifference to it.

Why did she pretend not to care when she so obviously did? I was disturbed by her strength when I tried to find out. I couldn't see any way around the old blank wall. It felt thicker than usual, though I'd thought it was almost gone.

I tried to ignore her, not wanting to think about that — that she was growing stronger. I watched the peak instead, tracing its shape against the pale, hot sky. There was something familiar about it. Something I was sure I recognized, even as I was positive that neither of us had been here before.

Almost as if she was trying to distract me, Melanie plunged into a vivid memory of Jared, catching me by surprise.

I shiver in my jacket, straining my eyes to see the muted glare of the sun dying behind the thick, bristly trees. I tell myself that it is not as cold as I think it is. My body just isn't used to this.

The hands that are suddenly there on my shoulders do not startle me, though I am afraid of this unfamiliar place and I did not hear his silent approach. Their weight is too familiar.

"You're easy to sneak up on."

Even now, there is a smile in his voice.

"I saw you coming before you took the first step," I say without turning. "I have eyes in the back of my head."

Warm fingers stroke my face from my temple to my chin, dragging fire along my skin.

"You look like a dryad hidden here in the trees," he whispers in my ear. "One of them. So beautiful that you must be fictional."

"We should plant more trees around the cabin."

He chuckles, and the sound makes my eyes close and my lips stretch into a grin.

"Not necessary," he says. "You always look that way."

"Says the last man on Earth to the last woman on Earth, on the eve of their separation."

My smile fades as I speak. Smiles cannot last today.

He sighs. His breath on my cheek is warm compared to the chill forest air.

"Jamie might resent that implication."

"Jamie's still a boy. Please, please keep him safe."

"I'll make you a deal," Jared offers. "You keep *yourself* safe, and I'll do my best. Otherwise, no deal."

Just a joke, but I can't take it lightly. Once we are apart, there are no guarantees. "No matter what happens," I insist.

"Nothing's going to happen. Don't worry." The words are nearly meaningless. A waste of effort. But his voice is worth hearing, no matter the message.

"Okay."

He pulls me around to face him, and I lean my head against his chest. I don't know what to compare his scent to. It is his own, as unique as the smell of juniper or the desert rain.

"You and I won't lose each other," he promises. "I will always find you again." Being Jared, he cannot be completely serious for more than a heartbeat or two. "No matter how well you hide. I'm unstoppable at hide-and-seek."

"Will you give me to the count of ten?"

"Without peeking."

"You're on," I mumble, trying to disguise the fact that my throat is thick with tears.

"Don't be afraid. You'll be fine. You're strong, you're fast, and you're smart." He's trying to convince himself, too.

Why am I leaving him? It's such a long shot that Sharon is still human.

But when I saw her face on the news, I was so sure.

It was just a normal raid, one of a thousand. As usual when we felt isolated enough, safe enough, we had the TV on as we cleaned out the pantry and fridge. Just to get the weather forecast; there isn't much entertainment in the dead-boring everything-is-perfect reports that pass for news among the parasites. It was the hair that caught my eye — the flash of deep, almost pink red that I'd only ever seen on one person.

I can still see the look on her face as she peeked at the camera from the corner of one eye. The look that said, *I'm trying to be invisible; don't see me.* She walked not quite slowly enough, working too hard at keeping a casual pace. Trying desperately to blend in.

No body snatcher would feel that need.

What is Sharon doing walking around human in a huge city like Chicago? Are there others? Trying to find her doesn't even seem like a choice, really. If there is a chance there are more humans out there, we have to locate them.

And I have to go alone. Sharon will run from anyone but

me — well, she will run from me, too, but maybe she will pause long enough for me to explain. I am sure I know her secret place.

"And you?" I ask him in a thick voice. I'm not sure I can physically bear this looming goodbye. "Will you be safe?"

"Neither heaven nor hell can keep me apart from you, Melanie."

Without giving me a chance to catch my breath or wipe away the fresh tears, she threw another at me.

Jamie curls up under my arm — he doesn't fit the way he used to. He has to fold in on himself, his long, gangly limbs poking out in sharp angles. His arms are starting to turn hard and sinewy, but in this moment he's a child, shaking, cowering almost. Jared is loading the car. Jamie would not show this fear if he were here. Jamie wants to be brave, to be like Jared.

"I'm scared," he whispers.

I kiss his night-dark hair. Even here among the sharp, resinous trees, it smells like dust and sun. It feels like he is part of me, that to separate us will tear the skin where we are joined.

"You'll be fine with Jared." I have to sound brave, whether I feel that way or not.

"I know that. I'm scared for *you*. I'm scared you won't come back. Like Dad."

I flinch. When Dad didn't come back — though his body did eventually, trying to lead the Seekers to us — it was the most horror and the most fear and the most pain I'd ever felt. What if I do that to Jamie again?

"I'll come back. I always come back."

"I'm scared," he says again.

I have to be brave.

"I promise everything will be fine. I'm coming back. I promise. You know I won't break a promise, Jamie. Not to you."

The shaking slows. He believes me. He trusts me.

And another:

I can hear them on the floor below. They will find me in minutes, or seconds. I scrawl the words on a dirty shred of newsprint. They are nearly illegible, but if he finds them, he will understand:

*Not fast enough. Love you love Jamie. Don't go home.*

Not only do I break their hearts, I steal their refuge, too. I picture our little canyon home abandoned, as it must be forever now. Or if not abandoned, a tomb. I see my body leading the Seekers to it. My face smiling as we catch them there ...

"Enough," I said out loud, cringing away from the whiplash of pain. "Enough! You've made your point! I can't live without them either now. Does that make you happy? Because it doesn't leave me many choices, does it? Just one — to get rid of you. Do you *want* the Seeker inside you? Ugh!" I recoiled from the thought as if I would be the one to house her.

*There* is *another choice*, Melanie thought softly.

"Really?" I demanded with heavy sarcasm. "Show me one."

*Look and see.*

I was still staring at the mountain peak. It dominated

the landscape, a sudden upthrust of rock surrounded by flat scrubland. Her interest pulled my eyes over the outline, tracing the uneven two-pronged crest.

A slow, rough curve, then a sharp turn north, another sudden turn back the other way, twisting back to the north for a longer stretch, and then the abrupt southern decline that flattened out into another shallow curve.

Not north and south, the way I'd always seen the lines in her piecemeal memories; it was up and down.

The profile of a mountain peak.

The lines that led to Jared and Jamie. This was the first line, the starting point.

I could find them.

We *could find them*, she corrected me. *You don't know all the directions. Just like with the cabin, I never gave you everything.*

"I don't understand. Where does it lead? *How* does a mountain lead us?" My pulse beat faster as I thought of it: Jared was close. Jamie, within my reach.

She showed me the answer.

"They're just lines. And Uncle Jeb is just an old lunatic. A nut job, like the rest of my dad's family." I try to tug the book out of Jared's hands, but he barely seems to notice my effort.

"A nut job, like Sharon's mom?" he counters, still studying the dark pencil marks that deface the back cover of the old photo album. It's the one thing I haven't lost in all the running. Even the graffiti loony Uncle Jeb left on it during his last visit has sentimental value now.

"Point taken." If Sharon is still alive, it will be because her mother, loony Aunt Maggie, could give loony Uncle Jeb a run for the title of Craziest of the Crazy Stryder Siblings. My father had been only slightly touched by the Stryder madness — he didn't have a secret bunker in the backyard or anything. The rest of them, his sister and brothers, Aunt Maggie, Uncle Jeb, and Uncle Guy, were the most devoted of conspiracy theorists. Uncle Guy had died before the others disappeared during the invasion, in a car accident so commonplace that even Maggie and Jeb had struggled to make an intrigue out of it.

My father always affectionately referred to them as *the Crazies.* "I think it's time we visited the Crazies," Dad would announce, and then Mom would groan — which is why such announcements had happened so seldom.

On one of those rare visits to Chicago, Sharon had snuck me into her mother's hidey-hole. We got caught — the woman had booby traps everywhere. Sharon was scolded soundly, and though I was sworn to secrecy, I'd had a sense Aunt Maggie might build a new sanctuary.

But I remember where the first is. I picture Sharon there now, living the life of Anne Frank in the middle of an enemy city. We have to find her and bring her home.

Jared interrupts my reminiscing. "Nut jobs are exactly the kind of people who will have survived. People who saw Big Brother when he wasn't there. People who suspected the rest of humanity before the rest of humanity turned dangerous. People with hiding places ready." Jared grins, still studying the lines. And then his voice is heavier. "People like *my* father. If he and my brothers had hidden rather than fought. . . . Well, they'd still be here."

My tone is softer, hearing the pain in his. "Okay, I agree with the theory. But these lines don't *mean* anything."

"Tell me again what he said when he drew them."

I sigh. "They were arguing — Uncle Jeb and my dad. Uncle Jeb was trying to convince him that something was wrong, telling him not to trust anyone. Dad laughed it off. Jeb grabbed the photo album from the end table and started . . . almost *carving* the lines into the back cover with a pencil. Dad got mad, said my mom would be angry. Jeb said, 'Linda's mom asked you all to come up for a visit, right? Kind of strange, out of the blue? Got a little upset when only Linda would come? Tell you the truth, Trev, I don't think Linda will be minding anything much when she gets back. Oh, she might act like it, but you'll be able to tell the difference.' It didn't make sense at the time, but what he said really upset my dad. He ordered Uncle Jeb out of the house. Jeb wouldn't leave at first. Kept warning us not to wait until it was too late. He grabbed my shoulder and pulled me into his side. 'Don't let 'em get you, honey,' he whispered. 'Follow the lines. Start at the beginning and follow the lines. Uncle Jeb'll keep a safe place for you.' That's when Dad shoved him out the door."

Jared nods absently, still studying. "The beginning . . . the beginning . . . It has to mean something."

"Does it? They're just squiggles, Jared. It's not like a map — they don't even connect."

"There's something about the first one, though. Something familiar. I could swear I've seen it somewhere before."

I sigh. "Maybe he told Aunt Maggie. Maybe she got better directions."

"Maybe," he says, and continues to stare at Uncle Jeb's squiggles.

She dragged me back in time, to a much, much older memory — a memory that had escaped her for a long while. I was surprised to realize that she had only put these memories, the old and the fresh, together recently. After I was here. That was why the lines had slipped through her careful control despite the fact that they were one of the most precious of her secrets — because of the urgency of her discovery.

In this blurry early memory, Melanie sat in her father's lap with the same album — not so tattered then — open in her hands. Her hands were tiny, her fingers stubby. It was very strange to remember being a child in this body.

They were on the first page.

"Do you remember where this is?" Dad asks, pointing to the old gray picture at the top of the page. The paper looks thinner than the other photographs, as if it has worn down — flatter and flatter and flatter — since some great-great-grandpa took it.

"It's where we Stryders come from," I answer, repeating what I've been taught.

"Right. That's the old Stryder ranch. You went there once, but I bet you don't remember it. I think you were eighteen months old." Dad laughs. "It's been Stryder land since the very beginning. . . ."

And then the memory of the picture itself. A picture she'd looked at a thousand times without ever *seeing* it. It was black and white, faded to grays. A small rustic wooden house, far away on the other side of a desert field; in the foreground, a split-rail fence; a few equine shapes between the fence and the house. And then, behind it all, the sharp, familiar profile . . .

There were words, a label, scrawled in pencil across the top white border:

*Stryder Ranch, 1904, in the morning shadow of . . .*

"Picacho Peak," I said quietly.

*He'll have figured it out, too, even if they never found Sharon. I know Jared will have put it together. He's smarter than me, and he has the picture; he probably saw the answer before I did. He could be so close. . . .*

The thought had her so filled with yearning and excitement that the blank wall in my head slipped entirely.

I saw the whole journey now, saw her and Jared's and Jamie's careful trek across the country, always by night in their inconspicuous stolen vehicle. It took weeks. I saw where she'd left them in a wooded preserve outside the city, so different from the empty desert they were used to. The cold forest where Jared and Jamie would hide and wait had felt safer in some ways — because the branches were thick and concealing, unlike the spindly desert foliage that hid little — but also more dangerous in its unfamiliar smells and sounds.

Then the separation, a memory so painful we skipped through it, flinching. Next came the abandoned building she'd hidden in, watching the house across the street for her chance. There, concealed within the walls or in the secret basement, she hoped to find Sharon.

*I shouldn't have let you see that,* Melanie thought. The faintness of her silent voice gave away her fatigue. The assault of memories, the persuasion and coercion, had tired her. *You'll tell them where to find her. You'll kill her, too.*

"Yes," I mused aloud. "I have to do my duty."

*Why?* she murmured, almost sleepily. *What happiness will it bring you?*

I didn't want to argue with her, so I said nothing.

The mountain loomed larger ahead of us. In moments, we would be beneath it. I could see a little rest stop with a convenience store and a fast food restaurant bordered on one side by a flat, concrete space — a place for mobile homes. There were only a few in residence now, with the heat of the coming summer making things uncomfortable.

What now? I wondered. Stop for a late lunch or an early dinner? Fill my gas tank and then continue on to Tucson in order to reveal my fresh discoveries to the Seeker?

The thought was so repellent that my jaw locked against the sudden heave of my empty stomach. I slammed on the brake reflexively, screeching to a stop in the middle of the lane. I was lucky; there were no cars to hit me from behind. There were also no drivers to stop and offer their help and concern. For this moment, the highway was empty. The sun beat down on the pavement, making it shimmer, disappear in places.

This shouldn't have felt like a betrayal, the idea of continuing on my right and proper course. My first language, the true language of the soul that was spoken only on our planet of origin, had no word for *betrayal* or *traitor*. Or even *loyalty* — because without the existence of an opposite, the concept had no meaning.

And yet I felt a deep well of guilt at the very idea of the Seeker. It would be wrong to tell her what I knew. *Wrong, how?* I countered my own thought viciously. If I stopped here and listened to the seductive suggestions of my host, I would truly be a traitor. That was impossible. I was a soul.

And yet I knew what I wanted, more powerfully and

vividly than anything I had ever wanted in all the eight lives I'd lived. The image of Jared's face danced behind my eyelids when I blinked against the sun — not Melanie's memory this time, but my memory of hers. She forced nothing on me now. I could barely feel her in my head as she waited — I imagined her holding her breath, as if that were possible — for me to make my decision.

I could not separate myself from this body's wants. It was me, more than I'd ever intended it to be. Did I want or did it want? Did that distinction even matter now?

In my rearview mirror, the glint of the sun off a distant car caught my eye.

I moved my foot to the accelerator, starting slowly toward the little store in the shadow of the peak. There was really only one thing to do.

# CHAPTER 10

# Turned

The electric bell rang, announcing another visitor to the convenience store. I started guiltily and ducked my head behind the shelf of goods we were examining.

*Stop acting like a criminal,* Melanie advised.

*I'm not acting,* I replied tersely.

The palms of my hands felt cold under a thin sheen of sweat, though the small room was quite hot. The wide windows let in too much sun for the loud and laboring air-conditioning unit to keep up.

*Which one?* I demanded.

*The bigger one,* she told me.

I grabbed the larger pack of the two available, a canvas sling that looked well able to hold more than I could carry. Then I walked around the corner to where the bottled water was shelved.

*We can carry three gallons,* she decided. *That gives us three days to find them.*

I took a deep breath, trying to tell myself that I wasn't going along with this. I was simply trying to get more coordinates from her, that was all. When I had the whole story, I would find someone — a different Seeker, maybe, one less repulsive than the one assigned to me — and pass the information along. I was just being thorough, I promised myself.

My awkward attempt to lie to myself was so pathetic that Melanie didn't pay any attention to it, felt no worry at all. It must be too late for me, as the Seeker had warned. Maybe I should have taken the shuttle.

*Too late? I wish!* Melanie grumbled. *I can't make you do anything you don't want to do. I can't even raise my hand!* Her thought was a moan of frustration.

I looked down at my hand, resting against my thigh rather than reaching for the water as she wanted to do so badly. I could feel her impatience, her almost desperate desire to be on the move. On the run again, just as if my existence were no more than a short interruption, a wasted season now behind her.

She gave the mental equivalent of a snort at that, and then she was back to business. *C'mon,* she urged me. *Let's get going! It will be dark soon.*

With a sigh, I pulled the largest shrink-wrapped flat of water bottles from the shelf. It nearly hit the floor before I caught it against a lower shelf edge. My arms felt as though they'd popped halfway out of their sockets.

"You're kidding me!" I exclaimed aloud.

*Shut up!*

"Excuse me?" a short, stooped man, the other customer, asked from the end of the aisle.

"Uh — nothing," I mumbled, not meeting his gaze. "This is heavier than I expected."

"Would you like some help?" he offered.

"No, no," I answered hastily. "I'll just take a smaller one."

He turned back to the selection of potato chips.

*No, you will not,* Melanie assured me. *I've carried heavier loads than this. You've let us get all soft, Wanderer,* she added in irritation.

*Sorry,* I responded absently, bemused by the fact that she had used my name for the first time.

*Lift with your legs.*

I struggled with the flat of water, wondering how far I could possibly be expected to carry it. I managed to get it to the front register, at least. With great relief, I edged its weight onto the counter. I put the bag on top of the water, and then added a box of granola bars, a roll of doughnuts, and a bag of chips from the closest display.

*Water is way more important than food in the desert, and we can only carry so much —*

*I'm hungry,* I interrupted. *And these are light.*

*It's your back, I guess,* she said grudgingly, and then she ordered, *Get a map.*

I placed the one she wanted, a topographical map of the county, on the counter with the rest. It was no more than a prop in her charade.

The cashier, a white-haired man with a ready smile, scanned the bar codes.

"Doing some hiking?" he asked pleasantly.

"The mountain is very beautiful."

"The trailhead is just up that —" he said, starting to gesture.

"I'll find it," I promised quickly, pulling the heavy, badly balanced load back off the counter.

"Head down before it gets dark, sweetie. You don't want to get lost."

"I will."

Melanie was thinking sulfurous thoughts about the kind old man.

*He was being nice. He's sincerely concerned about my welfare,* I reminded her.

*You're all very creepy,* she told me acidly. *Didn't anyone ever tell you not to talk to strangers?*

I felt a deep tug of guilt as I answered. *There* are *no strangers among my kind.*

*I can't get used to not paying for things,* she said, changing the subject. *What's the point of scanning them?*

*Inventory, of course. Is he supposed to remember everything we took when he needs to order more? Besides, what's the point of money when everyone is perfectly honest?* I paused, feeling the guilt again so strongly that it was an actual pain. *Everyone but me, of course.*

Melanie shied away from my feelings, worried by the depth of them, worried that I might change my mind. Instead she focused on her raging desire to be away from here, to be moving toward her objective. Her anxiety leaked through to me, and I walked faster.

I carried the stack to the car and set it on the ground beside the passenger door.

"Let me help you with that."

I jerked up to see the other man from the store, a plastic bag in his hand, standing beside me.

"Ah . . . thank you," I finally managed, my pulse thudding behind my ears.

We waited, Melanie tensed as if to run, while he lifted our acquisitions into the car.

*There's nothing to fear. He's being kind, too.*

She continued to watch him distrustfully.

"Thank you," I said again as he shut the door.

"My pleasure."

He walked off to his own vehicle without a backward glance at us. I climbed into my seat and grabbed the bag of potato chips.

*Look at the map,* she said. *Wait till he's out of sight.*

*No one is watching us,* I promised her. But, with a sigh, I unfolded the map and ate with one hand. It was probably a good idea to have some sense of where we were headed.

*Where* are *we headed?* I asked her. *We've found the starting point, so what now?*

*Look around,* she commanded. *If we can't see it here, we'll try the south side of the peak.*

*See what?*

She placed the memorized image before me: a ragged zigzagging line, four tight switchbacks, the fifth point strangely blunt, like it was broken. Now I saw it as I should, a jagged range of four pointed mountain peaks with the broken-looking fifth . . .

I scanned the skyline, east to west across the northern horizon. It was so easy it felt false, as though I'd made the image up only *after* seeing the mountain silhouette that created the northeast line of the horizon.

*That's it,* Melanie almost sang in her excitement. *Let's go!* She wanted me to be out of the car, on my feet, moving.

I shook my head, bending over the map again. The mountain ridge was so far in the distance I couldn't guess at the miles between us and it. There was no way I was walking out of this parking lot and into the empty desert unless I had no other option.

*Let's be rational,* I suggested, tracing my finger along a thin ribbon on the map, an unnamed road that connected to the freeway a few miles east and then continued in the general direction of the range.

*Sure,* she agreed complacently. *The faster the better.*

We found the unpaved road easily. It was just a pale scar of flat dirt through the sparse shrubbery, barely wide enough for one vehicle. I had a feeling that the road would be overgrown with lack of use in a different region — some place with more vital vegetation, unlike the desert plants that needed decades to recover from such a violation. There was a rusted chain stretched across the entrance, screwed into a wooden post on one end, looped loosely around another post at the other. I moved quickly, pulling the chain free and piling it at the base of the first post, hurrying back to my running car, hoping no one would pass and stop to offer me help. The highway stayed clear as I drove onto the dirt and then rushed back to refasten the chain.

We both relaxed when the pavement disappeared behind us. I was glad that there was apparently no one left I would have to lie to, whether with words or silence. Alone, I felt less of a renegade.

Melanie was perfectly at home here in the middle of

nothing. She knew the names of all the spiny plants around us. She hummed their names to herself, greeting them like old friends.

*Creosote, ocotillo, cholla, prickly pear, mesquite . . .*

Away from the highway, the trappings of civilization, the desert seemed to take on a new life for Melanie. Though she appreciated the speed of the jolting car — our vehicle didn't have the ground clearance necessary for this off-road trip, as the shocks reminded me with every pit in the dirt — she itched to be on her feet, loping through the safety of the baking desert.

We would probably have to walk, and all too soon for my taste, but when that time came, I doubted it would satisfy her. I could feel the real desire beneath the surface. Freedom. To move her body to the familiar rhythm of her long stride with only her will for guidance. For a moment, I allowed myself to see the prison that was life without a body. To be carried inside but unable to influence the shape around you. To be trapped. To have no choices.

I shuddered and refocused on the rough road, trying to stave off the mingled pity and horror. No other host had made me feel such guilt for what I was. Of course, none of the others had stuck around to complain about the situation.

The sun was close to the tips of the western hills when we had our first disagreement. The long shadows created strange patterns across the road, making it hard to avoid the rocks and craters.

*There it is!* Melanie crowed as we caught sight of another formation farther east: a smooth wave of rock, interrupted by a sudden spur that swung a thin, long finger out against the sky.

She was all for turning immediately into the brush, no matter what that did to the car.

*Maybe we're supposed to go all the way to the first landmark,* I pointed out. The little dirt road continued to wind in more or less the right direction, and I was terrified to leave it. How else would I find my way back to civilization? Wasn't I going back?

I imagined the Seeker right at this moment, as the sun touched the dark, zigzagging line of the western horizon. What would she think when I didn't arrive in Tucson? A spasm of glee made me laugh out loud. Melanie also enjoyed the picture of the Seeker's furious irritation. How long would it take her to go back to San Diego to see if this had all been a ploy to get rid of her? And then what steps would she take when I wasn't there? When I wasn't anywhere?

I just couldn't picture very clearly where *I* would be at that point.

*Look, a dry wash. It's wide enough for the car — let's follow it,* Melanie insisted.

*I'm not sure we're supposed to go that way yet.*

*It will be dark soon and we'll have to stop. You're wasting time!* She was silently shouting in her frustration.

*Or saving time, if I'm right. Besides, it's* my *time, isn't it?*

She didn't answer in words. She seemed to stretch inside my mind, reaching back toward the convenient wash.

*I'm the one doing this, so I'm doing it my way.*

Melanie fumed wordlessly in response.

*Why don't you show me the rest of the lines?* I suggested. *We could see if anything is visible before night falls.*

*No,* she snapped. *I'll do that part* my *way.*

*You're being childish.*

Again she refused to answer. I continued toward the four sharp peaks, and she sulked.

When the sun disappeared behind the hills, night washed across the landscape abruptly; one minute the desert was sunset orange, and then it was black. I slowed, my hand fumbling around the dashboard, searching for the switch for the headlights.

*Have you lost your mind?* Melanie hissed. *Do you have any idea how visible headlights would be out here? Someone is sure to see us.*

*So what do we do now?*

*Hope the seat reclines.*

I let the engine idle as I tried to think of options besides sleeping in the car, surrounded by the black emptiness of the desert night. Melanie waited patiently, knowing I would find none.

*This is crazy, you know,* I told her, throwing the car into park and twisting the keys out of the ignition. *The whole thing. There can't really be anyone out here. We won't find anything. And we're going to get hopelessly lost trying.* I had an abstract sense of the physical danger in what we were planning — wandering out into the heat with no backup plan, no way to return. I knew Melanie understood the danger far more clearly, but she held the specifics back.

She didn't respond to my accusations. None of these problems bothered her. I could see that she'd rather wander alone in the desert for the rest of her life than go back to the life I'd had before. Even without the threat of the Seeker, this was preferable to her.

I leaned the seat back as far as it would go. It wasn't close to far enough for comfort. I doubted that I would be able to sleep, but there were so many things I wasn't allowing myself to think about that my mind was vacant and uninteresting. Melanie was silent, too.

I closed my eyes, finding little difference between my lids and the moonless night, and drifted into unconsciousness with unexpected ease.

# *Dehydrated*

O kay! You were right, you were right!" I said the words out loud. There was no one around to hear me.

Melanie wasn't *saying* "I told you so." Not in so many words. But I could feel the accusation in her silence.

I was still unwilling to leave the car, though it was useless to me now. When the gas ran out, I had let it roll forward with the remaining momentum until it took a nosedive into a shallow gorge — a thick rivulet cut by the last big rain. Now I stared out the windshield at the vast, vacant plain and felt my stomach twist with panic.

*We have to move, Wanderer. It's only going to get hotter.*

If I hadn't wasted more than a quarter of a tank of gas stubbornly pushing on to the very base of the second landmark — only to find that the third milestone was no longer visible from that vantage and to have to turn around and backtrack — we would have been so much farther down this sandy wash, so much closer to our next goal. Thanks to me, we were going to have to travel on foot now.

I loaded the water, one bottle at a time, into the pack, my motions unnecessarily deliberate; I added the remaining granola bars just as slowly. All the while, Melanie ached for me to hurry. Her impatience made it hard to think, hard to concentrate on anything. Like what was going to happen to us.

*C'mon, c'mon, c'mon,* she chanted until I lurched, stiff and awkward, out of the car. My back throbbed as I straightened up. It hurt from sleeping so contorted last night, not from the weight of the pack; the pack wasn't that heavy when I used my shoulders to lift it.

*Now cover the car,* she instructed, picturing me ripping thorny branches from the nearby creosotes and palo verdes and draping them over the silver top of the car.

"Why?"

Her tone implied that I was quite stupid for not understanding. *So no one finds us.*

*But what if I want to be found? What if there's nothing out here but heat and dirt? We have no way to get home!*

*Home?* she questioned, throwing cheerless images at me: the vacant apartment in San Diego, the Seeker's most obnoxious expression, the dot that marked Tucson on the map . . . a brief, happier flash of the red canyon that slipped in by accident. *Where would that be?*

I turned my back on the car, ignoring her advice. I was in too far already. I wasn't going to give up all hope of return. Maybe someone would find the car and then find me. I could easily and honestly explain what I was doing here to any rescuer: I was lost. I'd lost my way . . . lost my control . . . lost my mind.

I followed the wash at first, letting my body fall into its natural long-strided rhythm. It wasn't the way I walked on the sidewalks to and from the university — it wasn't *my* walk at all. But it fit the rugged terrain here and moved me smoothly forward with a speed that surprised me until I got used to it.

"What if I hadn't come this way?" I wondered as I walked farther into the desert waste. "What if Healer Fords were still in Chicago? What if my path hadn't taken us so close to them?"

It was that urgency, that lure — the thought that Jared and Jamie might be *right here,* somewhere in this empty place — that had made it impossible to resist this senseless plan.

*I'm not sure,* Melanie admitted. *I think I might still have tried, but I was afraid while the other souls were near. I'm still afraid. Trusting you could kill them both.*

We flinched together at the thought.

*But being here, so close . . . It seemed like I had to try. Please* — and suddenly she was pleading with me, begging me, no trace of resentment in her thoughts — *please don't use this to hurt them. Please.*

"I don't want to. . . . I don't know if I *can* hurt them. I'd rather . . ."

What? Die myself? Than give a few stray humans up to the Seekers?

Again we flinched at the thought, but my revulsion at the idea comforted her. And it frightened me more than it soothed her.

When the wash started angling too far toward the

north, Melanie suggested that we forget the flat, ashen path and take the direct line to the third landmark, the eastern spur of rock that seemed to point, fingerlike, toward the cloudless sky.

I didn't like leaving the wash, just as I'd resisted leaving the car. I could follow this wash all the way back to the road, and the road back to the highway. It was miles and miles, and it would take me days to traverse, but once I stepped off this wash I was officially adrift.

*Have faith, Wanderer. We'll find Uncle Jeb, or he'll find us.*

*If he's still alive,* I added, sighing and loping off my simple path into the brush that was identical in every direction. *Faith isn't a familiar concept for me. I don't know that I buy into it.*

*Trust, then?*

*In who? You?* I laughed. The hot air baked my throat when I inhaled.

*Just think,* she said, changing the subject, *maybe we'll see them by tonight.*

The yearning belonged to us both; the image of their faces, one man, one child, came from both memories. When I walked faster, I wasn't sure that I was completely in command of the motion.

It did get hotter — and then hotter, and then hotter still. Sweat plastered my hair to my scalp and made my pale yellow T-shirt cling unpleasantly wherever it touched. In the afternoon, scorching gusts of wind kicked up, blowing sand in my face. The dry air sucked the sweat away, crusted my hair with grit, and fanned my shirt out from my body; it moved as stiffly as cardboard with the dried salt. I kept walking.

I drank water more often than Melanie wanted me to. She begrudged me every mouthful, threatening me that we would want it much more tomorrow. But I'd already given her so much today that I was in no mood to listen. I drank when I was thirsty, which was most of the time.

My legs moved me forward without any thought on my part. The crunching rhythm of my steps was background music, low and tedious.

There was nothing to see; one twisted, brittle shrub looked exactly the same as the next. The empty homogeny lulled me into a sort of daze — I was only really aware of the shape of the mountains' silhouettes against the pale, bleached sky. I read their outlines every few steps, till I knew them so well I could have drawn them blindfolded.

The view seemed frozen in place. I constantly whipped my head around, searching for the fourth marker — a big dome-shaped peak with a missing piece, a curved absence scooped from its side that Melanie had only shown me this morning — as if the perspective would have changed from my last step. I hoped this last clue was it, because we'd be lucky to get that far. But I had a sense that Melanie was keeping more from me, and our journey's end was impossibly distant.

I snacked on my granola bars through the afternoon, not realizing until it was too late that I'd finished the last one.

When the sun set, the night descended with the same speed as it had yesterday. Melanie was prepared, already scouting out a place to stop.

*Here,* she told me. *We'll want to stay as far from the cholla as possible. You toss in your sleep.*

I eyed the fluffy-looking cactus in the failing light, so

thick with bone-colored needles that it resembled fur, and
shuddered. *You want me to just sleep on the ground?
Right here?*

*You see another option?* She felt my panic, and her
tone softened, as if with pity. *Look — it's better than the
car. At least it's flat. It's too hot for any critters to be attracted to your body heat and —*

"Critters?" I demanded aloud. *"Critters?"*

There were brief, very unpleasant flashes of deadly-
looking insects and coiled serpents in her memories.

*Don't worry.* She tried to soothe me as I arched up on
my tiptoes, away from anything that might be hiding in
the sand below, my eyes searching the blackness for some
escape. *Nothing's going to bother you unless you bother
it first. After all, you're bigger than anything else out
here.* Another flash of memory, this time a medium-size
canine scavenger, a coyote, flitted through our thoughts.

"Perfect," I moaned, sinking down into a crouch,
though I was still afraid of the black ground beneath me.
"Killed by wild dogs. Who would have thought it would
end so . . . so trivially? How anticlimactic. The claw beast
on the Mists Planet, sure. At least there'd be some dignity
in being taken down by *that*."

Melanie's answering tone made me picture her rolling
her eyes. *Stop being a baby. Nothing is going to eat you.
Now lie down and get some rest. Tomorrow will be harder
than today.*

"Thanks for the good news," I grumbled. She was
turning into a tyrant. It made me think of the human ax-
iom *Give him an inch and he'll take a mile.* But I was
more exhausted than I realized, and as I settled unwill-

ingly to the ground, I found it impossible not to slump down on the rough, gravelly dirt and let my eyes close.

It seemed like just minutes later when the morning dawned, blindingly bright and already hot enough to have me sweating. I was crusted in dirt and rocks when I woke; my right arm was pinned under me and had lost feeling. I shook out the tingles and then reached into my pack for some water.

Melanie did not approve, but I ignored her. I looked for the half-empty bottle I'd last drunk from, rummaging through the fulls and empties until I began to see a pattern.

With a slowly growing sense of alarm, I started counting. I counted twice. There were two more empties than there were fulls. I'd already used up more than half my water supply.

*I told you that you were drinking too much.*

I didn't answer her, but I pulled the pack on without taking a drink. My mouth felt horrible, dry and sandy and tasting of bile. I tried to ignore that, tried to stop running my sandpaper tongue over my gritty teeth, and started walking.

My stomach was harder to ignore than my mouth as the sun rose higher and hotter above me. It twisted and contracted at regular intervals, anticipating meals that didn't appear. By afternoon, the hunger had gone from uncomfortable to painful.

*This is nothing,* Melanie reminded me wryly. *We've been hungrier.*

*You* have, I retorted. I didn't feel like being an audience to her endurance memories right now.

I was beginning to despair when the good news came. As I swung my head across the horizon with a routine, halfhearted movement, the bulbous shape of the dome jumped out at me from the middle of a northern line of small peaks. The missing part was only a faint indentation from this vantage point.

*Close enough,* Melanie decided, as thrilled as I was to be making some progress. I turned north eagerly, my steps lengthening. *Keep a lookout for the next.* She remembered another formation for me, and I started craning my head around at once, though I knew it was useless to search for it this early.

It would be to the east. North and then east and then north again. That was the pattern.

The lift of finding another milestone kept me moving despite the growing weariness in my legs. Melanie urged me on, chanting encouragements when I slowed, thinking of Jared and Jamie when I turned apathetic. My progress was steady, and I waited till Melanie okayed each drink, even though the inside of my throat felt as though it was blistering.

I had to admit that I was proud of myself for being so tough. When the dirt road appeared, it seemed like a reward. It snaked toward the north, the direction I was already headed, but Melanie was skittish.

*I don't like the look of it,* she insisted.

The road was just a sallow line through the scrub, defined only by its smoother texture and lack of vegetation. Ancient tire tracks made a double depression, centered in the single lane.

*When it goes the wrong way, we'll leave it.* I was already walking down the middle of the tracks. *It's easier than weaving through the creosote and watching out for cholla.*

She didn't answer, but her unease made me feel a little paranoid. I kept up my search for the next formation — a perfect *M*, two matching volcanic points — but I also watched the desert around me more carefully than before.

Because I was paying extra attention, I noticed the gray smudge in the distance long before I could make out what it was. I wondered if my eyes were playing tricks on me and blinked against the dust that clouded them. The color seemed wrong for a rock, and the shape too solid for a tree. I squinted into the brightness, making guesses.

Then I blinked again, and the smudge suddenly jumped into a structured shape, closer than I'd been thinking. It was some kind of house or building, small and weathered to a dull gray.

Melanie's spike of panic had me dancing off the narrow lane and into the dubious cover of the barren brush.

*Hold on,* I told her. *I'm sure it's abandoned.*

*How do you know?* She was holding back so hard that I had to concentrate on my feet before I could move them forward.

*Who would live out here? We souls live for society.* I heard the bitter edge to my explanation and knew it was because of where I now stood — physically and metaphorically in the middle of nowhere. Why did I no longer belong to the society of souls? Why did I feel like I didn't . . . like I didn't *want* to belong? Had I ever really been a part of the community that was meant to be my own, or was that the reason behind my long line of lives lived in transience? Had I always been an aberration, or was this something Melanie was making me into? Had this planet changed me, or revealed me for what I already was?

Melanie had no patience for my personal crisis — she

wanted me to get far away from that building as fast as possible. Her thoughts yanked and twisted at mine, pulling me out of my introspection.

*Calm down,* I ordered, trying to focus my thoughts, to separate them from hers. *If there is anything that actually lives here, it would be human. Trust me on this; there is no such thing as a hermit among souls. Maybe your Uncle Jeb —*

She rejected that thought harshly. *No one could survive out in the open like this. Your kind would have searched any habitation thoroughly. Whoever lived here ran or became one of you. Uncle Jeb would have a better hiding place.*

*And if whoever lived here became one of us,* I assured her, *then they left this place. Only a human would live this way. . . .* I trailed off, suddenly afraid, too.

*What?* She reacted strongly to my fright, freezing us in place. She scanned my thoughts, looking for something I'd seen to upset me.

But I'd seen nothing new. *Melanie, what if there are humans out here — not Uncle Jeb and Jared and Jamie? What if someone else found us?*

She absorbed the idea slowly, thinking it through. *You're right. They'd kill us immediately. Of course.*

I tried to swallow, to wash the taste of terror from my dry mouth.

*There won't be anyone else. How could there be?* she reasoned. *Your kind are far too thorough. Only someone already in hiding would have had a chance. So let's go check it out — you're sure there are none of you, and I'm sure there are none of me. Maybe we can find something helpful, something we can use as a weapon.*

I shuddered at her thoughts of sharp knives and long metal tools that could be turned into clubs. *No weapons.*

*Ugh. How did such spineless creatures beat us?*

*Stealth and superior numbers. Any one of you, even your young, is a hundred times as dangerous as one of us. But you're like one termite in an anthill. There are millions of us, all working together in perfect harmony toward our goal.*

Again, as I described the unity, I felt the dragging sense of panic and disorientation. Who was I?

We kept to the creosote as we approached the little structure. It looked to be a house, just a small shack beside the road, with no hint at all of any other purpose. The reason for its location here was a mystery — this spot had nothing to offer but emptiness and heat.

There was no sign of recent habitation. The door frame gaped, doorless, and only a few shards of glass clung to the empty window frames. Dust gathered on the threshold and spilled inside. The gray weathered walls seemed to lean away from the wind, as if it always blew from the same direction here.

I was able to contain my anxiety as I walked hesitantly to the vacant door frame; we must be just as alone here as we had been all day and all yesterday.

The shade the dark entry promised drew me forward, trumping my fears with its appeal. I still listened intently, but my feet moved ahead with swift, sure steps. I darted through the doorway, moving quickly to one side so as to have a wall at my back. This was instinctual, a product of Melanie's scavenging days. I stood frozen there, unnerved by my blindness, waiting for my eyes to adjust.

The little shack was empty, as we'd known it would

be. There were no more signs of occupation inside than out. A broken table slanted down from its two good legs in the middle of the room, with one rusted metal chair beside it. Patches of concrete showed through big holes in the worn, grimy carpet. A kitchenette lined the wall with a rusted sink, a row of cabinets — some doorless — and a waist-high refrigerator that hung open, revealing its moldy black insides. A couch frame sat against the far wall, all the cushions gone. Still mounted above the couch, only a little crooked, was a framed print of dogs playing poker.

*Homey,* Melanie thought, relieved enough to be sarcastic. *It's got more decor than your apartment.*

I was already moving for the sink.

*Dream on,* Melanie added helpfully.

Of course it would be wasteful to have water running to this secluded place; the souls managed details like that better than to leave such an anomaly behind. I still had to twist the ancient knobs. One broke off in my hand, rusted through.

I turned to the cupboards next, kneeling on the nasty carpet to peek carefully inside. I leaned away as I opened the door, afraid I might be disturbing one of the venomous desert animals in its lair.

The first was empty, backless, so that I could see the wooden slats of the outside wall. The next had no door, but there was a stack of antique newspapers inside, covered with dust. I pulled one out, curious, shaking the dirt to the dirtier floor, and read the date.

*From human times,* I noted. Not that I needed a date to tell me that.

"Man Burns Three-Year-Old Daughter to Death," the

headline screamed at me, accompanied by a picture of an angelic blond child. This wasn't the front page. The horror detailed here was not so hideous as to rate priority coverage. Beneath this was the face of a man wanted for the murders of his wife and two children two years before the print date; the story was about a possible sighting of the man in Mexico. Two people killed and three injured in a drunk-driving accident. A fraud and murder investigation into the alleged suicide of a prominent local banker. A suppressed confession setting an admitted child molester free. House pets found slaughtered in a trash bin.

I cringed, shoving the paper away from me, back into the dark cupboard.

*Those were the exceptions, not the norm,* Melanie thought quietly, trying to keep the fresh horror of my reaction from seeping into her memories of those years and recoloring them.

*Can you see how we thought we might be able to do better, though? How we could have supposed that maybe you didn't deserve all the excellent things of this world?*

Her answer was acidic. *If you wanted to cleanse the planet, you could have blown it up.*

*Despite what your science fiction writers dream, we simply don't have the technology.*

She didn't think my joke was funny.

*Besides,* I added, *that would have been such a waste. It's a lovely planet. This unspeakable desert excepted, of course.*

*That's how we realized you were here, you know,* she said, thinking of the sickening news headlines again. *When the evening news was nothing but inspiring human-interest stories, when pedophiles and junkies were lining up at the hospitals to turn themselves in, when everything morphed into Mayberry, that's when you tipped your hand.*

"What an awful alteration!" I said dryly, turning to the next cupboard.

I pulled the stiff door back and found the mother lode.

"Crackers!" I shouted, seizing the discolored, half-smashed box of Saltines. There was another box behind it, one that looked like someone had stepped on it. "Twinkies!" I crowed.

*Look!* Melanie urged, pointing a mental finger at three dusty bottles of bleach at the very back of the cupboard.

*What do you want bleach for?* I asked, already ripping into the cracker box. *To throw in someone's eyes? Or to brain them with the bottle?*

To my delight, the crackers, though reduced to crumbs, were still inside their plastic sleeves. I tore one open and started shaking the crumbs into my mouth, swallowing them half chewed. I couldn't get them into my stomach fast enough.

*Open a bottle and smell it,* she instructed, ignoring my commentary. *That's how my dad used to store water in the garage. The bleach residue kept the water from growing anything.*

*In a minute.* I finished one sleeve of crumbs and started on the next. They were very stale, but compared to the taste in my mouth, they were ambrosia. When I finished the third, I became aware that the salt was burning the cracks in my lips and at the corners of my mouth.

I heaved out one of the bleach bottles, hoping Melanie was right. My arms felt weak and noodley, barely able to lift it. This concerned us both. How much had our condition deteriorated already? How much farther would we be able to go?

The bottle's cap was so tight, I wondered if it had melted into place. Finally, though, I was able to twist it off with my teeth. I sniffed at the opening carefully, not especially wanting to pass out from bleach fumes. The chemical scent was very faint. I sniffed deeper. It was water, definitely. Stagnant, musty water, but water all the same. I took a small mouthful. Not a fresh mountain stream, but wet. I started guzzling.

*Easy there,* Melanie warned me, and I had to agree. We'd lucked into this cache, but it made no sense to squander it. Besides, I wanted something solid now that the salt burn had eased. I turned to the box of Twinkies and licked three of the smooshed-up cakes from the inside of the wrappers.

The last cupboard was empty.

As soon as the hunger pangs had eased slightly, Melanie's impatience began to leak into my thoughts. Feeling no resistance this time, I quickly loaded my spoils into my pack, pitching the empty water bottles into the sink to make room. The bleach jugs were heavy, but theirs was a comforting weight. It meant I wouldn't stretch out to sleep on the desert floor thirsty and hungry again tonight. With the sugar energy beginning to buzz through my veins, I loped back out into the bright afternoon.

# CHAPTER 12

# *Failed*

I t's impossible! You've got it wrong! Out of order! That can't be it!"

I stared into the distance, sick with disbelief that was turning quickly to horror.

Yesterday morning I'd eaten the last mangled Twinkie for breakfast. Yesterday afternoon I'd found the double peak and turned east again. Melanie had given me what she promised was the last formation to find. The news had made me nearly hysterical with joy. Last night, I'd drunk the last of the water. That was day four.

This morning was a hazy memory of blinding sun and desperate hope. Time was running out, and I'd searched the skyline for the last milestone with a growing sense of panic. I couldn't see any place where it could fit; the long, flat line of a mesa flanked by blunt peaks on either end, like sentinels. Such a thing would take space, and the mountains to the east and north were thick with toothy points. I couldn't see where the flat mesa could be hiding between them.

Midmorning — the sun was still in the east, in my eyes — I'd stopped to rest. I'd felt so weak that it frightened me. Every muscle in my body had begun to ache, but it was not from all the walking. I could feel the ache of exertion and also the ache from sleeping on the ground, and these were different from the new ache. My body was drying out, and this ache was my muscles protesting the torture of it. I knew that I couldn't keep going much longer.

I'd turned my back on the east to get the sun off my face for a moment.

That's when I'd seen it. The long, flat line of the mesa, unmistakable with the bordering peaks. There it was, so far away in the distant west that it seemed to shimmer above a mirage, floating, hovering over the desert like a dark cloud. Every step we'd walked had been in the wrong direction. The last marker was farther to the west than we'd come in all our journeying.

"Impossible," I whispered again.

Melanie was frozen in my head, unthinking, blank, trying desperately to reject this new comprehension. I waited for her, my eyes tracing the undeniably familiar shapes, until the sudden weight of her acceptance and grief knocked me to my knees. Her silent keen of defeat echoed in my head and added one more layer to the pain. My breathing turned ragged — a soundless, tearless sobbing. The sun crept up my back; its heat soaked deep into the darkness of my hair.

My shadow was a small circle beneath me when I

regained control. Painstakingly, I got back on my feet. Tiny sharp rocks were embedded in the skin on my legs. I didn't bother to brush these off. I stared at the floating mesa mocking me from the west for a long, hot time.

And finally, not really sure why I did it, I started walking forward. I knew only this: that it was me who moved and no one else. Melanie was so small in my brain — a tiny capsule of pain wrapped tightly in on her herself. There was no help from her.

My footsteps were a slow *crunch, crunch* across the brittle ground.

"He was just a deluded old lunatic, after all," I murmured to myself. A strange shudder rocked my chest, and a hoarse coughing ripped its way up my throat. The stream of gravelly coughs rattled on, but it wasn't until I felt my eyes pricking for tears that couldn't come that I realized I was laughing.

"There was . . . never . . . ever . . . anything out here!" I gasped between spasms of hysteria. I staggered forward as though I were drunk, my footprints trailing unevenly behind me.

*No.* Melanie uncurled from her misery to defend the faith she still clung to. *I got it wrong or something. My fault.*

I laughed at her now. The sound was sucked away by the scorching wind.

*Wait, wait,* she thought, trying to pull my attention from the joke of it all. *You don't think . . . I mean, do you think that maybe* they *tried this?*

Her unexpected fear caught me midlaugh. I choked on the hot air, my chest throbbing from my fit of morbid hysteria. By the time I could breathe again, all trace of my black humor was gone. Instinctively, my eyes swept the desert void, looking for some evidence that I was not the first to waste my life this way. The plain was impossibly vast, but I couldn't halt my frantic search for . . . remains.

*No, of course not.* Melanie was already comforting herself. *Jared's too smart. He would never come out here unprepared like we did. He'd never put Jamie in danger.*

*I'm sure you're right,* I told her, wanting to believe it as much as she did. *I'm sure no one else in the whole universe could be this stupid. Besides, he probably never came to look. He probably never figured it out. Wish you hadn't.*

My feet kept moving. I was barely aware of the action. It meant so little in the face of the distance ahead. And even if we were magically transported to the very base of the mesa, what then? I was absolutely positive there was nothing there. No one waited at the mesa to save us.

"We're going to die," I said. I was surprised that there was no fear in my rasping voice. This was just a fact like any other. The sun is hot. The desert is dry. We are going to die.

*Yes.* She was calm, too. This, death, was easier to accept than that our efforts had been guided by insanity.

"That doesn't bother you?"

She thought for a moment before answering.

*At least I died trying. And I won. I never gave them away. I never hurt them. I did my best to find them. I tried to keep my promise. . . . I die for them.*

I counted nineteen steps before I could respond. Nineteen sluggish, futile crunches across the sand.

"Then what am I dying for?" I wondered, the pricking

feeling returning in my desiccated tear ducts. "I guess it's because I lost, then, right? Is that why?"

I counted thirty-four crunches before she had an answer to my question.

*No*, she thought slowly. *It doesn't feel that way to me. I think . . . Well, I think that maybe . . . you're dying to be human.* There was almost a smile in her thought as she heard the silly double meaning to the phrase. *After all the planets and all the hosts you've left behind, you've finally found the place and the body you'd die for. I think you've found your home, Wanderer.*

Ten crunches.

I didn't have the energy to open my lips anymore. *Too bad I didn't get to stay here longer, then.*

I wasn't sure about her answer. Maybe she was trying to make me feel better. A sop for dragging her out here to die. She had won; she had never disappeared.

My steps began to falter. My muscles screamed out to me for mercy, as if I had any means to soothe them. I think I would have stopped right there, but Melanie was, as always, tougher than I.

I could feel her now, not just in my head but in my limbs. My stride lengthened; the path I made was straighter. By sheer force of will, she dragged my half-dead carcass toward the impossible goal.

There was an unexpected joy to the pointless struggle. Just as I could feel her, she could feel my body. Our body, now; my weakness ceded control to her. She gloried in the freedom of moving our arms and legs forward, no matter how useless such a motion was. It was bliss simply because she *could* again. Even the pain of the slow death we had begun dimmed in comparison.

*What do you think is out there?* she asked me as we marched on toward the end. *What will you see, after we're dead?*

*Nothing.* The word was empty and hard and sure. *There's a reason we call it the* final *death.*

*The souls have no belief in an afterlife?*

*We have so many lives. Anything more would be . . . too much to expect. We die a little death every time we leave a host. We live again in another. When I die here, that will be the end.*

There was a long pause while our feet moved more and more slowly.

*What about you?* I finally asked. *Do you still believe in something more, even after all of this?* My thoughts raked over her memories of the end of the human world.

*It seems like there are some things that* can't *die.*

In our mind, their faces were close and clear. The love we felt for Jared and Jamie *did* feel very permanent. In that moment, I wondered if death was strong enough to dissolve something so vital and *sharp*. Perhaps this love would live on with her, in some fairytale place with pearly gates. Not with me.

*Would it be a relief to be free of it?* I wasn't sure. It felt like it was part of who I was now.

We only lasted a few hours. Even Melanie's tremendous strength of mind could ask no more than that of our failing body. We could barely see. We couldn't seem to find the oxygen in the dry air we sucked in and spit back out. The pain brought rough whimpers breaking through our lips.

*You've never had it* this *bad,* I teased her feebly as we staggered toward a dried stick of a tree standing a few feet taller than the low brush. We wanted to get to the thin streaks of shade before we fell.

*No,* she agreed. *Never this bad.*

We attained our purpose. The dead tree threw its cobwebby shadow over us, and our legs fell out from under us. We sprawled forward, never wanting the sun on our face again. Our head turned to the side on its own, searching for the burning air. We stared at the dust inches from our nose and listened to the gasping of our breath.

After a time, long or short we didn't know, we closed our eyes. Our lids were red and bright inside. We couldn't feel the faint web of shade; maybe it no longer touched us.

*How long?* I asked her.

*I don't know, I've never died before.*

*An hour? More?*

*Your guess is as good as mine.*

*Where's a coyote when you really need one?*

*Maybe we'll get lucky... escaped claw beast or something . . .* Her thought trailed off incoherently.

That was our last conversation. It was too hard to concentrate enough to form words. There was more pain than we thought there should be. All the muscles in our body rioted, cramping and spasming as they fought death.

We didn't fight. We drifted and waited, our thoughts dipping in and out of memories without a pattern. While we were still lucid, we hummed ourselves a lullaby in our head. It was the one we'd used to comfort Jamie when the ground was too hard, or the air was too cold, or the fear was too great to sleep. We felt his head press into the hollow just below our shoulder and the shape of his back under our arm. And then it seemed that it was *our* head cradled against a broader shoulder, and a new lullaby comforted *us*.

Our lids turned black, but not with death. Night had fallen, and this made us sad. Without the heat of day, we would probably last longer.

It was dark and silent for a timeless space. Then there was a sound.

It barely roused us. We weren't sure if we imagined it. Maybe it was a coyote, after all. Did we want that? We didn't know. We lost our train of thought and forgot the sound.

Something shook us, pulled our numb arms, dragged at them. We couldn't form the words to wish that it would be quick now, but that was our hope. We waited for the cut of teeth. Instead, the dragging turned to pushing, and we felt our face roll toward the sky.

It poured over our face — wet, cool, and impossible. It dribbled over our eyes, washing the grit from them. Our eyes fluttered, blinking against the dripping.

We did not care about the grit in our eyes. Our chin arched up, desperately searching, our mouth opening and closing with blind, pathetic weakness, like a newly hatched bird.

We thought we heard a sigh.

And then the water flowed into our mouth, and we gulped at it and choked on it. The water vanished while we choked, and our weak hands grasped out for it. A flat, heavy thumping pounded our back until we could breathe. Our hands kept clutching the air, looking for the water.

We definitely heard a sigh this time.

Something pressed to our cracked lips, and the water flowed again. We guzzled, careful not to inhale it this time. Not that we cared if we choked, but we did not want the water taken away again.

We drank until our belly stretched and ached. The water trickled to a stop, and we cried out hoarsely in protest. Another rim was pressed to our lips, and we gulped frantically until it was empty, too.

Our stomach would explode with another mouthful, yet we blinked and tried to focus, to see if we could find more. It was too dark; we could not see a single star. And then we blinked again and realized that the darkness was much closer than the sky. A figure hovered over us, blacker than the night.

There was a low sound of fabric rubbing against itself and sand shifting under a heel. The figure leaned away, and we heard a sharp rip — the sound of a zipper, deafening in the absolute stillness of the night.

Like a blade, light cut into our eyes. We moaned at the pain of it, and our hand flew up to cover our closed eyes. Even behind our lids, the light was too bright. The light disappeared, and we felt the breath of the next sigh hit our face.

We opened our eyes carefully, more blind than before. Whoever faced us sat very still and said nothing. We began to feel the tension of the moment, but it felt far away, outside ourself. It was hard to care about anything but the water in our belly and where we could find more. We tried to concentrate, to see what had rescued us.

The first thing we could make out, after minutes of blinking and squinting, was the thick whiteness that fell from the dark face, a million splinters of pale in the night. When we grasped that this was a beard — like Santa Claus, we thought chaotically — the other pieces of the face were supplied by our memory. Everything fit into place: the big cleft-tipped nose, the wide cheekbones, the thick white brows, the eyes set deep into the wrinkled fabric of skin. Though we could see only hints of each feature, we knew how light would expose them.

"Uncle Jeb," we croaked in surprise. "You found us."

Uncle Jeb, squatting next to us, rocked back on his heels when we said his name.

"Well, now," he said, and his gruff voice brought back a hundred memories. "Well, now, here's a pickle."

# CHAPTER 13

# *Sentenced*

A re they here?" We choked out the words — they
burst from us like the water in our lungs had,
expelled. After water, this question was all that mattered.
"Did they make it?"

Uncle Jeb's face was impossible to read in the darkness. "Who?" he asked.

"Jamie, Jared!" Our whisper burned like a shout.
"Jared was with Jamie. Our brother! Are they here? Did
they come? Did you find them, too?"

There was barely a pause.

"No." His answer was forceful, and there was no pity
in it, no feeling at all.

"No," we whispered. We were not echoing him, we
were protesting against getting our life back. What was
the point? We closed our eyes again and listened to the

pain in our body. We let that drown out the pain in our mind.

"Look," Uncle Jeb said after a moment. "I, uh, have something to take care of. You rest for a bit, and I'll be back for you."

We didn't hear the meaning in his words, just the sounds. Our eyes stayed closed. His footsteps crunched quietly away from us. We couldn't tell which direction he went. We didn't care anyway.

They were gone. There was no way to find them, no hope. Jared and Jamie had disappeared, something they knew well how to do, and we would never see them again.

The water and the cooler night air were making us lucid, something we did not want. We rolled over, to bury our face against the sand again. We were so tired, past the point of exhaustion and into some deeper, more painful state. Surely we could sleep. All we had to do was not think. We could do that.

We did.

When we woke, it was still night, but dawn was threatening on the eastern horizon — the mountains were lined with dull red. Our mouth tasted of dust, and at first we were sure that we had dreamed Uncle Jeb's appearance. Of course we had.

Our head was clearer this morning, and we noticed quickly the strange shape near our right cheek — something that was not a rock or a cactus. We touched it, and it was hard and smooth. We nudged it, and the delicious sound of sloshing water came from inside.

Uncle Jeb was real, and he'd left us a canteen.

We sat up carefully, surprised when we didn't break in

two like a withered stick. Actually, we felt better. The water must have had time to work its way through some of our body. The pain was dull, and for the first time in a long while, we felt hungry again.

Our fingers were stiff and clumsy as we twisted the cap from the top of the canteen. It wasn't all the way full, but there was enough water to stretch the walls of our belly again — it must have shrunk. We drank it all; we were done with rationing.

We dropped the metal canteen to the sand, where it made a dull thud in the predawn silence. We felt wide awake now. We sighed, preferring unconsciousness, and let our head fall into our hands. What now?

"Why did you give it water, Jeb?" an angry voice demanded, close behind our back.

We whirled, twisting onto our knees. What we saw made our heart falter and our awareness splinter apart.

There were eight humans half-circled around where I knelt under the tree. There was no question they were humans, all of them. I'd never seen faces contorted into such expressions — not on my kind. These lips twisted with hatred, pulled back over clenched teeth like wild animals. These brows pulled low over eyes that burned with fury.

Six men and two women, some of them very big, most of them bigger than me. I felt the blood drain from my face as I realized why they held their hands so oddly — gripped tightly in front of them, each balancing an object. They held weapons. Some held blades — a few short ones like those I had kept in my kitchen, and some longer, one huge and menacing. This knife had no purpose in a kitchen. Melanie supplied the name: a *machete*.

Others held long bars, some metal, some wooden. Clubs.

I recognized Uncle Jeb in their midst. Held loosely in his hands was an object I'd never seen in person, only in Melanie's memories, like the big knife. It was a rifle.

I saw horror, but Melanie saw all this with wonder, her mind boggling at their numbers. Eight human survivors. She'd thought Jeb was alone or, in the best case scenario, with only two others. To see so many of her kind alive filled her with joy.

*You're an idiot,* I told her. *Look at them. See them.*

I forced her to see it from my perspective: to see the threatening shapes inside the dirty jeans and light cotton shirts, brown with dust. They might have been human — as she thought of the word — once, but at this moment they were something else. They were barbarians, monsters. They hung over us, slavering for blood.

There was a death sentence in every pair of eyes.

Melanie saw all this and, though grudgingly, she had to admit that I was right. At this moment, her beloved humans were at their worst — like the newspaper stories we'd seen in the abandoned shack. We were looking at killers.

We should have been wiser; we should have died yesterday.

Why would Uncle Jeb keep us alive for this?

A shiver passed through me at the thought. I'd skimmed through the histories of human atrocities. I'd had no stomach for them. Perhaps I should have concentrated better. I knew there were reasons why humans let their enemies live, for a little while. Things they wanted from their minds or their bodies . . .

Of course it sprang into my head immediately — the one secret they would want from me. The one I could never, never tell them. No matter what they did to me. I would have to kill myself first.

I did not let Melanie see the secret I protected. I used her own defenses against her and threw up a wall in my head to hide behind while I thought of the information for the first time since implantation. There had been no reason to think of it before.

Melanie was hardly even curious on the other side of the wall; she made no effort to break through it. There were much more immediate concerns than the fact that she had not been the only one keeping information in reserve.

Did it matter that I protected my secret from her? I wasn't as strong as Melanie; I had no doubt she could endure torture. How much pain could I stand before I gave them anything they wanted?

My stomach heaved. Suicide was a repugnant option — worse because it would be murder, too. Melanie would be part of either torture or death. I would wait for that until I had absolutely no other choice.

*No, they can't. Uncle Jeb would never let them hurt me.*

*Uncle Jeb doesn't know you're here,* I reminded her.

*Tell him!*

I focused on the old man's face. The thick white beard kept me from seeing the set of his mouth, but his eyes did not seem to burn like the others'. From the corner of my eye, I could see a few of the men shift their gaze from me to him. They were waiting for him to answer the question that had alerted me to their presence. Uncle Jeb stared at me, ignoring them.

*I can't tell him, Melanie. He won't believe me. And if they think I'm lying to them, they'll think I'm a Seeker. They must have experience enough to know that only a Seeker would come out here with a lie, a story designed for infiltration.*

Melanie recognized the truth of my thought at once. The very word *Seeker* made her recoil with hatred, and she knew these strangers would have the same reaction.

*It doesn't matter anyway. I'm a soul — that's enough for them.*

The one with the machete — the biggest man there, black-haired with oddly fair skin and vivid blue eyes — made a sound of disgust and spit on the ground. He took a step forward, slowly raising the long blade.

Better fast than slow. Better that it was this brutal hand and not mine that killed us. Better that I didn't die a creature of violence, accountable for Melanie's blood as well as my own.

"Hold it, Kyle." Jeb's words were unhurried, almost casual, but the big man stopped. He grimaced and turned to face Melanie's uncle.

"Why? You said you made sure. It's one of them."

I recognized the voice — he was the same one who'd asked Jeb why he'd given me water.

"Well, yes, she surely is. But it's a little complicated."

"How?" A different man asked the question. He stood next to the big, dark-haired Kyle, and they looked so much alike that they had to be brothers.

"See, this here is my niece, too."

"Not anymore she's not," Kyle said flatly. He spit again

and took another deliberate step in my direction, knife ready. I could see from the way his shoulders leaned into the action that words would not stop him again. I closed my eyes.

There were two sharp metallic clicks, and someone gasped. My eyes flew open again.

"I said hold it, Kyle." Uncle Jeb's voice was still relaxed, but the long rifle was gripped tightly in his hands now, and the barrels were pointed at Kyle's back. Kyle was frozen just steps from me; his machete hung motionless in the air above his shoulder.

"Jeb," the brother said, horrified, "what are you doing?"

"Step away from the girl, Kyle."

Kyle turned his back to us, whirling on Jeb in fury. "It's not a *girl,* Jeb!"

Jeb shrugged; the gun stayed steady in his hands, pointed at Kyle. "There are things to be discussed."

"The doctor might be able to learn something from it," a female voice offered gruffly.

I cringed at the words, hearing in them my worst fears. When Jeb had called me his niece just now, I'd foolishly let a spark of hope flame to life — perhaps there would be pity. I'd been stupid to think that, even for a second. Death would be the only pity I could hope for from these creatures.

I looked at the woman who'd spoken, surprised to see that she was as old as Jeb, maybe older. Her hair was dark gray rather than white, which is why I hadn't noticed her age before. Her face was a mass of wrinkles, all of them turning down into angry lines. But there was something familiar about the features behind the lines.

Melanie made the connection between this ancient face and another, smoother face in her memory.

"Aunt Maggie? You're here? How? Is Sharon —" The words were all Melanie, but they gushed from my mouth, and I was unable to stop them. Sharing for so long in the desert had made her stronger, or me weaker. Or maybe it was just that I was concentrating on which direction the deathblow was going to fall from. I was bracing for our murder, and she was having a family reunion.

Melanie got only halfway through her surprised exclamation. The much-aged woman named Maggie lunged forward with a speed that belied her brittle exterior. She didn't raise the hand that held the black crowbar. That was the hand I was watching, so I didn't see her free hand swing out to slap me hard across the face.

My head snapped back and then forward. She slapped me again.

"You won't *fool* us, you parasite. We know how you work. We know how well you can mimic us."

I tasted blood inside my cheek.

*Don't do that again,* I scolded Melanie. *I told you what they'd think.*

Melanie was too shocked to answer.

"Now, Maggie," Jeb began in a soothing tone.

"Don't you 'Now, Maggie' me, you old fool! She's probably led a legion of them down on us." She backed away from me, her eyes measuring my stillness as if I were a coiled snake. She stopped beside her brother.

"I don't see anyone," Jeb retorted. *"Hey!"* he yelled, and I flinched in surprise. I wasn't the only one. Jeb waved his left hand over his head, the gun still clenched in the right. *"Over here!"*

"Shut up," Maggie growled, shoving his chest. Though I had good reason to know she was strong, Jeb didn't wobble.

"She's alone, Mag. She was pretty much dead when I found her — she's not in such great shape now. The centipedes don't sacrifice their own that way. They would have come for her much sooner than I did. Whatever else she is, she's alone."

I saw the image of the long, many-legged insect in my head, but I didn't make the connection.

*He's talking about* you, Melanie translated. She placed the picture of the ugly bug next to my memory of a bright silver soul. I didn't see a resemblance.

*I wonder how he knows what you look like,* Melanie wondered absently. My memories of a soul's true appearance had been new to her in the beginning.

I didn't have time to wonder with her. Jeb was walking toward me, and the others were close behind. Kyle's hand hovered at Jeb's shoulder, ready to restrain him or throw him out of the way, I couldn't tell.

Jeb put his gun in his left hand and extended the right to me. I eyed it warily, waiting for it to hit me.

"C'mon," he urged gently. "If I could carry you that far, I woulda brought you home last night. You're gonna have to walk some more."

"No!" Kyle grunted.

"I'm takin' her back," Jeb said, and for the first time there was a harsher tone to his voice. Under his beard, his jaw flexed into a stubborn line.

"Jeb!" Maggie protested.

"'S my place, Mag. I'll do what I want."

"Old fool!" she snapped again.

Jeb reached down and grabbed my hand from where it lay curled into a fist against my thigh. He yanked me to my feet. It was not cruelty; it was merely as if he was in a hurry. Yet was it not the very worst form of cruelty to prolong my life for the reasons he had?

I rocked unsteadily. I couldn't feel my legs very well — just prickles like needle points as the blood flowed down.

There was a hiss of disapproval behind him. It came from more than one mouth.

"Okay, whoever you are," he said to me, his voice still kind. "Let's get out of here before it heats up."

The one who must have been Kyle's brother put his hand on Jeb's arm.

"You can't just show it where we live, Jeb."

"I suppose it doesn't matter," Maggie said harshly. "It won't get a chance to tell tales."

Jeb sighed and pulled a bandanna — all but hidden by his beard — from around his neck.

"This is silly," he muttered, but he rolled the dirty fabric, stiff with dry sweat, into a blindfold.

I kept perfectly still as he tied it over my eyes, fighting the panic that increased when I couldn't see my enemies.

I couldn't see, but I knew it was Jeb who put one hand on my back and guided me; none of the others would have been so gentle.

We started forward, toward the north, I thought. No one spoke at first — there was just the sound of sand grinding under many feet. The ground was even, but I stumbled on my numb legs again and again. Jeb was patient; his guiding hand was almost chivalrous.

I felt the sun rise as we walked. Some of the footsteps

were faster than others. They moved ahead of us until they were hard to hear. It sounded like it was the minority that stayed with Jeb and me. I must not have looked like I needed many guards — I was faint with hunger, and I swayed with every step; my head felt dizzy and hollow.

"You aren't planning to tell him, are you?"

It was Maggie's voice; it came from a few feet behind me, and it sounded like an accusation.

"He's got a right to know," Jeb replied. The stubborn note was back in his voice.

"It's an unkind thing you are doing, Jebediah."

"Life is unkind, Magnolia."

It was hard to decide who was the more terrifying of the two. Was it Jeb, who seemed so intent on keeping me alive? Or Maggie, who had first suggested *the doctor* — an appellation that filled me with instinctive, nauseated dread — but who seemed more worried about cruelty than her brother?

We walked in silence again for a few hours. When my legs buckled, Jeb lowered me to the ground and held a canteen to my lips as he had in the night.

"Let me know when you're ready," Jeb told me. His voice sounded kind, though I knew that was a false interpretation.

Someone sighed impatiently.

"Why are you doing this, Jeb?" a man asked. I'd heard the voice before; it was one of the brothers. "For Doc? You could have just told Kyle that. You didn't have to pull a gun on him."

"Kyle needs a gun pulled on him more often," Jeb muttered.

"Please tell me this wasn't about sympathy," the man continued. "After all you've seen . . ."

"After all I've seen, if I hadn't learned compassion, I wouldn't be worth much. But no, it was not about sympathy. If I had enough sympathy for this poor creature, I would have let her die."

I shivered in the oven-hot air.

"What, then?" Kyle's brother demanded.

There was a long silence, and then Jeb's hand touched mine. I grasped it, needing the help to get back on my feet. His other hand pressed against my back, and I started forward again.

"Curiosity," Jeb said in a low voice.

No one replied.

As we walked, I considered a few sure facts. One, I was not the first soul they'd captured. There was already a set routine here. This "Doc" had tried to get his answer from others before me.

Two, he had tried unsuccessfully. If any soul had forgone suicide only to crack under the humans' torture, they would not need me now. My death would have been mercifully swift.

Oddly, I couldn't bring myself to hope for a quick end, though, or to try to effect that outcome. It would be easy to do, even without doing the deed myself. I would only have to tell them a lie — pretend to be a Seeker, tell them my colleagues were tracking me right now, bluster and threaten. Or tell them the truth — that Melanie lived on inside me, and that she had brought me here.

They would see another lie, and one so richly irresistible — the idea that the human could live on after implantation — so tempting to believe from their perspective, so insidious, that they would believe I was a Seeker more surely than if I claimed it. They would assume a trap, get rid of me quickly, and find a new place to hide, far away from here.

*You're probably right,* Melanie agreed. *It's what I would do.*

But I wasn't in pain yet, and so either form of suicide was hard to embrace; my instinct for survival sealed my lips. The memory of my last session with my Comforter — a time so civilized it seemed to belong to a different planet — flashed through my head. Melanie challenging me to have her removed, a seemingly suicidal impulse, but only a bluff. I remembered thinking how hard it was to contemplate death from a comfortable chair.

Last night Melanie and I had wished for death, but death had been only inches away at the time. It was different now that I was on my feet again.

*I don't want to die, either,* Melanie whispered. *But maybe you're wrong. Maybe that's not why they're keeping us alive. I don't understand why they would. . . .* She didn't want to imagine the things they might do to us — I was sure she could come up with worse than I. *What answer would they want from you that bad?*

*I'll never tell. Not you, not any human.*

A bold declaration. But then, I wasn't in pain yet. . . .

Another hour had passed — the sun was directly overhead, the heat of it like a crown of fire on my hair — when the sound changed. The grinding steps that I barely heard anymore turned to echoes ahead of me. Jeb's feet still crunched against the sand like mine, but someone in front of us had reached a new terrain.

"Careful, now," Jeb warned me. "Watch your head."

I hesitated, not sure what I was watching for, or how to watch with no eyes. His hand left my back and pressed down on my head, telling me to duck. I bent forward. My neck was stiff.

He guided me forward again, and I heard our footsteps make the same echoing sound. The ground didn't give like sand, didn't feel loose like rock. It was flat and solid beneath my feet.

The sun was gone — I could no longer feel it burn my skin or scorch my hair.

I took another step, and a new air touched my face. It was not a breeze. This was stagnant — *I* moved into *it*. The dry desert wind was gone. This air was still and cooler. There was the faintest hint of moisture to it, a mustiness that I could both smell and taste.

There were so many questions in my mind, and in Melanie's. She wanted to ask hers, but I kept silent. There was nothing either of us could say that would help us now.

"Okay, you can straighten up," Jeb told me.

I raised my head slowly.

Even with the blindfold, I could tell that there was no light. It was utterly black around the edges of the bandanna. I could hear the others behind me, shuffling their feet impatiently, waiting for us to move forward.

"This way," Jeb said, and he was guiding me again. Our footsteps echoed back from close by — the space we were in must have been quite small. I found myself ducking my head instinctively.

We went a few steps farther, and then we rounded a sharp curve that seemed to turn us back the way we'd

come. The ground started to slant downward. The angle
got steeper with every step, and Jeb gave me his rough
hand to keep me from falling. I don't know how long I
slipped and skidded my way through the darkness. The
hike probably felt longer than it was with each minute
slowed by my terror.

We took another turn, and then the floor started to
climb upward. My legs were so numb and wooden that as
the path got steeper, Jeb had to half drag me up the in-
cline. The air got mustier and moister the farther we went,
but the blackness didn't change. The only sounds were
our footsteps and their nearby echoes.

The pathway flattened out and began to turn and twist
like a serpent.

Finally, finally, there was a brightness around the top
and bottom of my blindfold. I wished that it would slip, as
I was too frightened to pull it off myself. It seemed to me
that I wouldn't be so terrified if I could just *see* where I
was and who was with me.

With the light came noise. Strange noise, a low murmuring babble. It sounded almost like a waterfall.

The babble got louder as we moved forward, and the
closer it got, the less it sounded like water. It was too varied, low and high pitches mingling and echoing. If it had
not been so discordant, it might have sounded like an ug-
lier version of the constant music I'd heard and sung on
the Singing World. The darkness of the blindfold suited
that memory, the memory of blindness.

Melanie understood the cacophony before I did. I'd
never heard the sound because I'd never been with humans before.

*It's an argument,* she realized. *It sounds like so many people arguing.*

She was drawn by the sound. Were there more people here, then? That there were even eight had surprised us both. What was this place?

Hands touched the back of my neck, and I shied away from them.

"Easy now," Jeb said. He pulled the blindfold off my eyes.

I blinked slowly, and the shadows around me settled into shapes I could understand: rough, uneven walls; a pocked ceiling; a worn, dusty floor. We were underground somewhere in a natural cave formation. We couldn't be that deep. I thought we'd hiked upward longer than we'd slid downward.

The rock walls and ceiling were a dark purpley brown, and they were riddled with shallow holes like Swiss cheese. The edges of the lower holes were worn down, but over my head the circles were more defined, and their rims looked sharp.

The light came from a round hole ahead of us, its shape not unlike the holes that peppered the cavern, but larger. This was an entrance, a doorway to a brighter place. Melanie was eager, fascinated by the concept of more humans. I held back, suddenly worried that blindness might be better than sight.

Jeb sighed. "Sorry," he muttered, so low that I was certainly the only one to hear.

I tried to swallow and could not. My head started to spin, but that might have been from hunger. My hands were trembling like leaves in a stiff breeze as Jeb prodded me through the big hole.

The tunnel opened into a chamber so vast that at first I couldn't accept what my eyes told me. The ceiling was too bright and too high — it was like an artificial sky. I tried to see what brightened it, but it sent down sharp lances of light that hurt my eyes.

I was expecting the babble to get louder, but it was abruptly dead quiet in the huge cavern.

The floor was dim compared to the brilliant ceiling so far above. It took a moment for my eyes to make sense of all the shapes.

A crowd. There was no other word for it — there was a crowd of humans standing stock-still and silent, all staring at me with the same burning, hate-filled expressions I'd seen at dawn.

Melanie was too stunned to do anything more than count. Ten, fifteen, twenty . . . twenty-five, twenty-six, twenty-seven . . .

I didn't care how many there were. I tried to tell her how little it mattered. It wouldn't take twenty of them to kill me. To kill us. I tried to make her see how precarious our position was, but she was beyond my warnings at the moment, lost in this human world she'd never dreamed was here.

One man stepped forward from the crowd, and my eyes darted first to his hands, looking for the weapon they would carry. His hands were clenched in fists but empty of any other threat. My eyes, adjusting to the dazzling light, made out the sun-gilded tint of his skin and then recognized it.

Choking on the sudden hope that dizzied me, I lifted my eyes to the man's face.

# CHAPTER 14

# *Disputed*

It was too much for both of us, seeing him here, now, after already accepting that we'd never see him again, after believing that we'd lost him forever. It froze me solid, made me unable to react. I wanted to look at Uncle Jeb, to understand his heartbreaking answer in the desert, but I couldn't move my eyes. I stared at Jared's face, uncomprehending.

Melanie reacted differently.

"Jared," she cried; through my damaged throat the sound was just a croak.

She jerked me forward, much the same way as she had in the desert, assuming control of my frozen body. The only difference was that this time, it was by force.

I wasn't able to stop her fast enough.

She lurched forward, raising my arms to reach out for him. I screamed a warning at her in my head, but she wasn't listening to me. She was barely aware that I was even there.

No one tried to stop her as she staggered toward him. No one but me. She was within inches of touching him, and still she didn't see what I saw. She didn't see how his face had changed in the long months of separation, how it had hardened, how the lines pulled in different directions now. She didn't see that the unconscious smile she remembered would not physically fit on this new face. Only once had she seen his face turn dark and dangerous, and that expression was nothing to the one he wore now. She didn't see, or maybe she didn't care.

His reach was longer than mine.

Before Melanie could make my fingers touch him, his arm shot out and the back of his hand smashed into the side of my face. The blow was so hard that my feet left the ground before my head slammed into the rock floor. I heard the rest of my body hit the floor with dull thumps, but I didn't feel it. My eyes rolled back in my head, and a ringing sound shimmered in my ears. I fought the dizziness that threatened to spin me unconscious.

*Stupid, stupid,* I whimpered at her. *I* told *you not to do that!*

*Jared's here, Jared's alive, Jared's here.* She was incoherent, chanting the words like they were lyrics to a song.

I tried to focus my eyes, but the strange ceiling was blinding. I twisted my head away from the light and then swallowed a sob as the motion sent daggers of agony through the side of my face.

I could barely handle the pain of this one spontaneous blow. What hope did I have of enduring an intensive, calculated onslaught?

There was a shuffle of feet beside me; my eyes moved instinctively to find the threat, and I saw Uncle Jeb standing over me. He had one hand half stretched out toward me, but he hesitated, looking away. I raised my head an inch, stifling another moan, to see what he saw.

Jared was walking toward us, and his face was the same as those of the barbarians in the desert — only it was beautiful rather than frightening in its fury. My heart faltered and then beat unevenly, and I wanted to laugh at myself. Did it matter that he was beautiful, that I loved him, when he was going to kill me?

I stared at the murder in his expression and tried to hope that rage would win out over expediency, but a true death wish evaded me.

Jeb and Jared locked eyes for a long moment. Jared's jaw clenched and unclenched, but Jeb's face was calm. The silent confrontation ended when Jared suddenly exhaled in an angry gust and took a step back.

Jeb reached down for my hand and put his other arm around my back to pull me up. My head whirled and ached; my stomach heaved. If it hadn't been empty for days, I might have thrown up. It was like my feet weren't touching the ground. I wobbled and pitched forward. Jeb steadied me and then gripped my elbow to keep me standing.

Jared watched all this with a teeth-baring grimace. Like an idiot, Melanie struggled to move toward him again. But I was over the shock of seeing him here and less stupid than she was now. She wouldn't break through again. I locked her away behind every bar I could create in my head.

*Just be quiet. Can't you see how he loathes me? Anything you say will make it worse. We're dead.*

*But Jared's alive, Jared's here,* she crooned.

The quiet in the cavern dissolved; whispers came from every side, all at the same time, as if I'd missed some cue. I couldn't make out any meanings in the hissing murmurs.

My eyes darted around the mob of humans — every one of them an adult, no smaller, younger figure among them. My heart ached at the absence, and Melanie fought to voice the question. I hushed her firmly. There wasn't anything to see here, nothing but anger and hatred on strangers' faces, or the anger and hatred on Jared's face.

Until another man pushed his way through the whispering throng. He was built slim and tall, his skeletal structure more obvious under his skin than most. His hair was washed out, either pale brown or a dark, nondescript blond. Like his bland hair and his long body, his features were mild and thin. There was no anger in his face, which was why it held my eye.

The others made way for this apparently unassuming man as if he had some status among them. Only Jared didn't defer to him; he held his ground, staring only at me. The tall man stepped around him, not seeming to notice the obstacle in his path any more than he would a pile of rock.

"Okay, okay," he said in an oddly cheery voice as he circled Jared and came to face me. "I'm here. What have we got?"

It was Aunt Maggie who answered him, appearing at his elbow.

"Jeb found it in the desert. Used to be our niece Melanie. It seemed to be following the directions he gave her." She flashed a dirty look at Jeb.

"Mm-hm," the tall, bony man murmured, his eyes appraising me curiously. It was strange, that appraisal. He looked as if he liked what he saw. I couldn't fathom why he would.

My gaze shied away from his, to another woman — a young woman who peered around his side, her hand resting on his arm — my eyes drawn by her vivid hair.

*Sharon!* Melanie cried.

Melanie's cousin saw the recognition in my eyes, and her face hardened.

I pushed Melanie roughly to the back of my head. *Shhh!*

"Mm-hm," the tall man said again, nodding. He reached one hand out to my face and seemed surprised when I recoiled from it, flinching into Jeb's side.

"It's okay," the tall man said, smiling a little in encouragement. "I won't hurt you."

He reached toward my face again. I shrunk into Jeb's side like before, but Jeb flexed his arm and nudged me forward. The tall man touched my jaw below my ear, his fingers gentler than I expected, and turned my face away. I felt his finger trace a line on the back of my neck, and I realized that he was examining the scar from my insertion.

I watched Jared's face from the corner of my eye. What this man was doing clearly upset him, and I thought I knew why — how he must have hated that slender pink line on my neck.

Jared frowned, but I was surprised that some of the anger had drained from his expression. His eyebrows pulled together. It made him look confused.

The tall man dropped his hands and stepped away from me. His lips were pursed, his eyes alight with some challenge.

"She looks healthy enough, aside from some recent exhaustion, dehydration, and malnourishment. I think you've put enough water back into her so that the dehydration won't interfere. Okay, then." He made an odd, unconscious motion with his hands, as if he were washing them. "Let's get started."

Then his words and his brief examination fit together and I understood — this gentle-seeming man who had just promised not to hurt me was the doctor.

Uncle Jeb sighed heavily and closed his eyes.

The doctor held a hand out to me, inviting me to put mine in his. I clenched my hands into fists behind my back. He looked at me carefully again, appraising the terror in my eyes. His mouth turned down, but it was not a frown. He was considering how to proceed.

"Kyle, Ian?" he called, craning his neck to search the assembly for the ones he summoned. My knees wobbled when the two big black-haired brothers pressed their way forward.

"I think I need some help. Maybe if you were to carry —" the doctor, who did not look quite so tall standing beside Kyle, began to say.

"No."

Everyone turned to see where the dissent had come from. I didn't need to look, because I recognized the voice. I looked at him anyway.

Jared's eyebrows pressed down hard over his eyes; his mouth was twisted into a strange grimace. So many emotions ran across his face, it was hard to pin one down. Anger, defiance, confusion, hatred, fear . . . pain.

The doctor blinked, his face going slack with surprise. "Jared? Is there a problem?"

"Yes."

Everyone waited. Beside me, Jeb was holding the corners of his lips down as if they were trying to lift into a grin. If that was the case, then the old man had an odd sense of humor.

"And it is?" the doctor asked.

Jared answered through his teeth. "I'll tell you the problem, Doc. What's the difference between letting you have it or Jeb putting a bullet in its head?"

I trembled. Jeb patted my arm.

The doctor blinked again. "Well" was all he said.

Jared answered his own question. "The difference is, if Jeb kills it, at least it dies cleanly."

"Jared." The doctor's voice was soothing, the same tone he'd used on me. "We learn so much each time. Maybe this will be the time —"

"Hah!" Jared snorted. "I don't see much progress being made, Doc."

*Jared will protect us,* Melanie thought faintly.

It was hard to concentrate enough to form words. *Not us, just your body.*

*Close enough . . .* Her voice seemed to come from some distance, from outside my pounding head.

Sharon took a step forward so that she stood half in front of the doctor. It was a strangely protective stance.

"There's no point in wasting an opportunity," she said fiercely. "We all realize that this is hard for you, Jared, but in the end it's not your decision to make. We have to consider what's best for the majority."

Jared glowered at her. "No." The word was a snarl.

I could tell he had not whispered the word, yet it was very quiet in my ears. In fact, everything was suddenly

quiet. Sharon's lips moved, her finger jabbed at Jared viciously, but all I heard was a soft hissing. Neither one of
them took a step, but they seemed to be drifting away
from me.

I saw the dark-haired brothers step toward Jared with
angry faces. I felt my hand try to rise in protest, but it only
twitched limply. Jared's face turned red when his lips
parted, and the tendons in his neck strained like he was
shouting, but I heard nothing. Jeb let go of my arm, and I
saw the dull gray of the rifle's barrel swing up beside me.
I cringed away from the weapon, though it was not pointed
in my direction. This upset my balance, and I watched the
room tip very slowly to one side.

"Jamie," I sighed as the light swirled away from my
eyes.

Jared's face was suddenly very close, leaning over me
with a fierce expression.

"Jamie?" I breathed again, this time a question.
"Jamie?"

Jeb's gruff voice answered from somewhere far away.

"The kid is fine. Jared brought him here."

I looked at Jared's tormented face, fast disappearing
into the dark mist that covered my eyes.

"Thank you," I whispered.

And then I was lost in the darkness.

# CHAPTER 15

# *Guarded*

When I came to, there was no disorientation. I knew exactly where I was, roughly speaking, and I kept my eyes closed and my breathing even. I tried to learn as much as I could about my exact situation without giving away the fact that I was conscious again.

I was hungry. My stomach knotted and clenched and made angry noises. I doubted these noises would betray me — I was sure it had gurgled and complained as I slept.

My head ached fiercely. It was impossible to know how much of this was from fatigue and how much was from the knocks I'd taken.

I was lying on a hard surface. It was rough and . . . pocked. It was not flat, but oddly curved, as though I was lying in a shallow bowl. It was not comfortable. My back and hips throbbed from being curled into this position.

That pain was probably what had woken me; I felt far from rested.

It was dark — I could tell that without opening my eyes. Not pitch-black, but very dark.

The air was even mustier than before — humid and corroded, with a peculiar acrid bite that seemed to cling to the back of my throat. The temperature was cooler than it had been in the desert, but the incongruous moisture made it almost as uncomfortable. I was sweating again, the water Jeb had given me finding its way out through my pores.

I could hear my breathing echo back to me from a few feet away. It could be that I was only close to one wall, but I guessed that I was in a very small space. I listened as hard as I could, and it sounded like my breathing echoed back from the other side as well.

Knowing that I was probably still somewhere in the cavern system Jeb had brought me to, I was fairly sure what I would see when I opened my eyes. I must be in some small hole in the rock, dark purple brown and riddled with holes like cheese.

It was silent except for the sounds my body made. Afraid to open my eyes, I relied on my ears, straining harder and harder against the silence. I couldn't hear anyone else, and this made no sense. They wouldn't have left me without a warden, would they? Uncle Jeb and his omnipresent rifle, or someone less sympathetic. To leave me alone . . . that wouldn't be in character with their brutality, their natural fear and hatred of what I was.

Unless . . .

I tried to swallow, but terror closed my throat. They

wouldn't leave me alone. Not unless they thought I was dead, or had made sure that I *would* be. Not unless there were places in these caves that no one came back from.

The picture I'd been forming of my surroundings shifted dizzyingly in my head. I saw myself now at the bottom of a deep shaft or walled into a cramped tomb. My breathing sped up, tasting the air for staleness, for some sign that my oxygen was running low. The muscles around my lungs pulled outward, filling with air for the scream that was on the way. I clenched my teeth to keep it from escaping.

Sharp and close, something grated across the ground beside my head.

I shrieked, and the sound of it was piercing in the small space. My eyes flew open. I jerked away from the sinister noise, throwing myself against a jagged rock wall. My hands swung up to protect my face as my head *thunk*ed painfully against the low ceiling.

A dim light illuminated the perfectly round exit to the tiny bubble of a cave I was curled in. Jared's face was half lit as he leaned into the opening, one arm reaching toward me. His lips were tight with anger. A vein in his forehead pulsed as he watched my panicked reaction.

He didn't move; he just stared furiously while my heart restarted and my breathing evened out. I met his glare, remembering how quiet he had always been — like a wraith when he wanted. No wonder I hadn't heard him sitting guard outside my cell.

But I had heard *something*. As I remembered that, Jared shoved his extended arm closer, and the grating noise repeated. I looked down. At my feet was a broken sheet of plastic serving as a tray. And on it . . .

I lunged for the open bottle of water. I was barely aware that Jared's mouth twisted with disgust as I jerked the bottle to my lips. I was sure that would bother me later, but all I cared about now was the water. I wondered if ever in my life I would take the liquid for granted again. Given that my life was not likely to be prolonged here, the answer was probably no.

Jared had disappeared, back through the circular entry. I could see a piece of his sleeve and nothing more. The dull light came from somewhere beside him. It was an artificial bluish color.

I'd gulped half the water down when a new scent caught my attention, informing me that water was not the only gift. I looked down at the tray again.

Food. They were feeding me?

It was the bread — a dark, unevenly shaped roll — that I smelled first, but there was also a bowl of some clear liquid with the tang of onions. As I leaned closer, I could see darker chunks on the bottom. Beside this were three stubby white tubes. I guessed they were vegetables, but I didn't recognize the variety.

It took only seconds for me to make these discoveries, but even in that short time, my stomach nearly jumped through my mouth trying to reach the food.

I ripped into the bread. It was very dense, studded with whole-grain kernels that caught in my teeth. The texture was gritty, but the flavor was wonderfully rich. I couldn't remember anything tasting more delicious to me, not even my mushed-up Twinkies. My jaw worked as fast as it could, but I swallowed most of the mouthfuls of tough bread half-chewed. I could hear each mouthful hit my stomach with a gurgle. It didn't feel as good as I thought it would. Too long empty, my stomach reacted to the food with discomfort.

I ignored that and moved on to the liquid — it was soup. This went down easier. Aside from the onions I'd smelled, the taste was mild. The green chunks were soft and spongy. I drank it straight from the bowl and wished the bowl were deeper. I tipped it back to make sure I'd gotten every drop.

The white vegetables were crunchy in texture, woody in taste. Some kind of root. They weren't as satisfying as the soup or as tasty as the bread, but I was grateful for their bulk. I wasn't full — not close — and I probably would have started on the tray next if I thought I'd be able to chew through it.

It didn't occur to me until I was finished that they shouldn't be feeding me. Not unless Jared had lost the confrontation with the doctor. Though why would Jared be my guard if that were the case?

I slid the tray away when it was empty, cringing at the noise it made. I stayed pressed against the back wall of my bubble as Jared reached in to retrieve it. This time he didn't look at me.

"Thank you," I whispered as he disappeared again. He said nothing; there was no change in his face. Even the bit of his sleeve did not show this time, but I was sure he was there.

*I can't believe he hit me,* Melanie mused, her thought incredulous rather than resentful. She was not over the surprise of it yet. I hadn't been surprised in the first place. Of course he had hit me.

*I wondered where you were,* I answered. *It would*

*be poor manners to get me into this mess and then abandon me.*

She ignored my sour tone. *I wouldn't have thought he'd be able to do it, no matter what. I don't think I could hit him.*

*Sure you could. If he'd come at you with reflective eyes, you'd have done the same. You're naturally violent.* I remembered her daydreams of strangling the Seeker. That seemed like months ago, though I knew it was only days. It would make sense if it had been longer. It ought to take time to get oneself stuck in such a disastrous mire as the one I was in now.

Melanie tried to consider it impartially. *I don't think so. Not Jared . . . and Jamie, there's no way I could hurt Jamie, even if he was . . .* She trailed off, hating that line of thought.

I considered this and found it true. Even if the child had become something or someone else, neither she nor I could ever raise a hand to him.

*That's different. You're like . . . a mother. Mothers are irrational here. Too many emotions involved.*

*Motherhood is always emotional — even for you souls.*

I didn't answer that.

*What do you think is going to happen now?*

*You're the expert on humans,* I reminded her. *It's probably not a good thing that they're giving me food. I can think of only one reason they'd want me strong.*

The few specifics I remembered of historical human brutalities tangled in my head with the stories in the old newspaper we'd read the other day. Fire — that was a bad one. Melanie had burned all the fingerprints off her right hand once in a stupid accident, grabbing a pan she hadn't realized was hot. I remembered how the pain had shocked her — it was so unexpectedly sharp and demanding.

It was just an accident, though. Quickly treated with ice, salves, medicine. No one had done it on purpose, continued on from the first sickening pain, drawing it out longer and longer . . .

I'd never lived on a planet where such atrocities could happen, even before the souls came. This place was truly the highest and the lowest of all worlds — the most beautiful senses, the most exquisite emotions . . . the most malevolent desires, the darkest deeds. Perhaps it was meant to be so. Perhaps without the lows, the highs could not be reached. Were the souls the exception to that rule? Could they have the light without the darkness of this world?

*I . . . felt something when he hit you,* Melanie interrupted. The words came slowly, one by one, as if she didn't want to think them.

*I felt something, too.* It was amazing how natural it was to use sarcasm now, after spending so much time with Melanie. *He's got quite a backhand, doesn't he?*

*That's not what I meant. I mean . . .* She hesitated for a long moment, and then the rest of the words came in a rush. *I thought it was all me — the way we feel about him. I thought I was . . . in control of that.*

The thoughts behind her words were clearer than the words themselves.

*You thought you were able to bring me here because* you *wanted it so much. That you were controlling me instead of the other way around.* I tried not to be annoyed. *You thought you were manipulating me.*

*Yes.* The chagrin in her tone was not because I was upset, but because she did not like being wrong. *But . . .*

I waited.

It came in a rush once more. *You're in love with him, too, separately from me. It feels different from the way I feel. Other. I didn't see that until he was there with us, until you saw him for the first time. How did that happen? How does a three-inch-long worm fall in love with a human being?*

*Worm?*

*Sorry. I guess you sort of have . . . limbs.*

*Not really. They're more like antennae. And I'm quite a bit longer than three inches when they're extended.*

*My point is, he's not your species.*

*My body is human,* I told her. *While I'm attached to it, I'm human, too. And the way you see Jared in your memories . . . Well, it's all your fault.*

She considered that for a moment. She didn't like it much.

*So if you had gone to Tucson and gotten a new body, you wouldn't love him anymore now?*

*I really, really hope that's true.*

Neither of us was happy with my answer. I leaned my head against the top of my knees. Melanie changed the subject.

*At least Jamie is safe. I knew Jared would take care of him. If I had to leave him, I couldn't have left him in better hands. . . . I wish I could see him.*

*I'm not asking that!* I cringed at the thought of the response *that* request would receive.

At the same time, I yearned to see the boy's face for myself. I wanted to be sure that he was really here, really safe — that they were feeding him and caring for him the way Melanie never could again. The way I, mother to no one, wanted to care for him. Did he have someone to sing to him at night? To tell him stories? Would this new, angry Jared think of little things like that? Did he have someone to curl up against when he was frightened?

*Do you think they will tell him that I'm here?* Melanie asked.

*Would that help or hurt him?* I asked back.

Her thought was a whisper. *I don't know. . . . I wish I could tell him that I kept my promise.*

*You certainly did.* I shook my head, amazed. *No one can say that you didn't come back, just like always.*

*Thanks for that.* Her voice was faint. I couldn't tell if she meant for my words now, or if she meant the bigger picture, bringing her here.

I was suddenly exhausted, and I could feel that she was, too. Now that my stomach had settled a bit and felt almost halfway full, the rest of my pains were not sharp enough to keep me awake. I hesitated before moving, afraid to make any noise, but my body wanted to uncurl and stretch out. I did so as silently as I could, trying to find a piece of the bubble long enough for me. Finally, I had to stick my feet almost out the round opening. I didn't like doing it, worried that Jared would hear the movement close to him and think I was trying to escape, but he didn't react in any way. I pillowed the good side of my face against my arm, tried to ignore the way the curve of the floor cramped my spine, and closed my eyes.

I think I slept, but if I did, it wasn't deeply. The sound of footsteps was still very far away when I came fully awake.

This time I opened my eyes at once. Nothing had changed — I still could see the dull blue light through the round hole; I still could not see if Jared was outside it. Someone was coming this way — it was easy to hear that the footsteps were coming closer. I pulled my legs away from the opening, moving as quietly as I could, and curled up against the back wall again. I would have liked to be able to stand; it would have made me feel less vulnerable, more prepared to face whatever was coming. The low ceiling of the cave bubble would barely have allowed me to kneel.

There was a flash of movement outside my prison. I saw part of Jared's foot as he rose silently to his feet.

"Ah. Here you are," a man said. The words were so loud after all the empty silence that I jumped. I recognized the voice. One of the brothers I'd seen in the desert — the one with the machete, Kyle.

Jared didn't speak.

"We're not going to allow this, Jared." It was a different speaker, a more reasonable voice. Probably the younger brother, Ian. The brothers' voices were very similar — or they would have been, if Kyle weren't always half shouting, his tone always twisted with anger. "We've all lost somebody — hell, we've all lost everybody. But this is ridiculous."

"If you won't let Doc have it, then it's got to die," Kyle added, his voice a growl.

"You can't keep it prisoner here," Ian continued. "Eventually, it will escape and we'll all be exposed."

Jared didn't speak, but he took one side step that put him directly in front of the opening to my cell.

My heart pumped hard and fast as I understood what

the brothers were saying. Jared had won. I was not to be tortured. I was not to be killed — not immediately, anyway. Jared was keeping me prisoner.

It seemed a beautiful word under the circumstances.

*I told you he would protect us.*

"Don't make this difficult, Jared," said a new male voice I didn't recognize. "It has to be done."

Jared said nothing.

"We don't want to hurt you, Jared. We're all brothers here. But we will if you make us." There was no bluff in Kyle's tone. "Move aside."

Jared stood rock still.

My heart started thumping faster than before, jerking against my ribs so hard that the hammering disrupted the rhythm of my lungs, made it difficult to breathe. Melanie was incapacitated with fear, unable to think in coherent words.

They were going to hurt him. Those lunatic humans were going to attack one of their own.

"Jared . . . please," Ian said.

Jared didn't answer.

A heavy footfall — a lunge — and the sound of something heavy hitting something solid. A gasp, a choking gurgle —

"No!" I cried, and launched myself through the round hole.

# CHAPTER 16

# *Assigned*

The ledge of the rock exit was worn down, but it scraped my palms and shins as I scrambled through it. It hurt, stiff as I was, to wrench myself erect, and my breath caught. My head swam as the blood flowed downward.

I looked for only one thing — where Jared was, so that I could put myself between him and his attackers.

They all stood frozen in place, staring at me. Jared had his back to the wall, his hands balled into fists and held low. In front of him, Kyle was hunched over, clutching his stomach. Ian and a stranger flanked him a few feet back, their mouths open with shock. I took advantage of their surprise. In two long, shaky strides, I moved between Kyle and Jared.

Kyle was the first to react. I was less than a foot from him, and his primary instinct was to shove me away. His hand struck my shoulder and heaved me toward the floor. Before I could fall, something caught my wrist and yanked me back to my feet.

As soon as he realized what he'd done, Jared dropped my wrist like my skin was oozing acid.

"Get back in there," he roared at me. He shoved my shoulder, too, but it wasn't as hard as Kyle's push. It sent me staggering two feet back toward the hole in the wall.

The hole was a black circle in the narrow hallway. Outside the small prison, the bigger cave looked just the same, only longer and taller, a tube rather than a bubble. A small lamp — powered by what, I couldn't guess — lit the hallway dimly from the ground. It cast strange shadows on the features of the men, turning them into scowling monster faces.

I took a step toward them again, turning my back to Jared.

"I'm what you want," I said directly to Kyle. "Leave him alone."

No one said anything for a long second.

"Tricky bugger," Ian finally muttered, eyes wide with horror.

"I said get back in there," Jared hissed behind me.

I turned halfway, not wanting Kyle out of my sight. "It's not your duty to protect me at your own expense."

Jared grimaced, one hand rising to push me back toward the cell again.

I skipped out of the way; the motion moved me toward the ones who wanted to kill me.

Ian grabbed my arms and pinned them behind me. I struggled instinctively, but he was very strong. He bent my joints too far back and I gasped.

"Get your hands off her!" Jared shouted, charging.

Kyle caught him and spun him around into a wrestling hold, forcing his neck forward. The other man grabbed one of Jared's thrashing arms.

"Don't hurt him!" I screeched. I strained against the hands that imprisoned me.

Jared's free elbow rammed into Kyle's stomach. Kyle gasped and lost his grip. Jared twisted away from his attackers and then lunged back, his fist connecting with Kyle's nose. Dark red blood spattered the wall and the lamp.

"Finish it, Ian!" Kyle yelled. He put his head down and hurtled into Jared, throwing him into the other man.

"No!" Jared and I cried at the same moment.

Ian dropped my arms, and his hands wrapped around my throat, choking off my air. I clawed at his hands with my useless, stubby nails. He gripped me tighter, dragging my feet off the floor.

It hurt — the strangling hands, the sudden panic of my lungs. It was agony. I writhed, more trying to escape the pain than the murdering hands.

*Click, click.*

I'd only heard the sound once before, but I recognized it. So did everyone else. They all froze, Ian with his hands locked hard on my neck.

"Kyle, Ian, Brandt — back off!" Jeb barked.

No one moved — just my hands, still clawing, and my feet, twitching in the air.

Jared suddenly darted under Kyle's motionless arm and sprang at me. I saw his fist flying toward my face, and closed my eyes.

A loud *thwack* sounded inches behind my head. Ian

howled, and I dropped to the floor. I crumpled there at his feet, gasping. Jared retreated after an angry glance in my direction and went to stand at Jeb's elbow.

"You're guests here, boys, and don't forget it," Jeb growled. "I told you not to go looking for the girl. She's my guest, too, for the moment, and I don't take kindly to any of my guests killing any of the others."

"Jeb," Ian moaned above me, his voice muffled by the hand held to his mouth. "Jeb. This is insane."

"What's your plan?" Kyle demanded. His face was smeared with blood, a violent, macabre sight. But there was no evidence of pain in his voice, only controlled and simmering anger. "We have a right to know. We have to decide whether this place is safe or if it's time to move on. So . . . how long will you keep this thing as your pet? What will you do with it when you're finished playing God? All of us deserve to know the answers to these questions."

Kyle's extraordinary words echoed behind the pulse thudding in my head. Keep me as a pet? Jeb had called me his *guest*. . . . Was that another word for prisoner? Was it possible that *two* humans existed that did not demand either my death or my torture-wrung confession? If so, it was nothing less than a miracle.

"Don't have your answers, Kyle," Jeb said. "It's not up to me."

I doubted any other response Jeb could have given would have confused them more. All four men, Kyle, Ian, the one I didn't know, and even Jared, stared at him with shock. I still crouched gasping at Ian's feet, wishing there was some way I could climb back into my hole unnoticed.

"Not up to you?" Kyle finally echoed, still disbelieving. "Who, then? If you're thinking of putting it to a vote, that's already been done. Ian, Brandt, and I are the duly designated appointees of the result."

Jeb shook his head — a tight movement that never took his eyes off the man in front of him. "It's not up for a vote. This is still my house."

*"Who, then?"* Kyle shouted.

Jeb's eyes finally flickered — to another face and then back to Kyle. "It's Jared's decision."

Everyone, me included, shifted their eyes to stare at Jared.

He gaped at Jeb, just as astonished as the rest, and then his teeth ground together with an audible sound. He threw a glare of pure hate in my direction.

"Jared?" Kyle asked, facing Jeb again. "That makes no sense!" He was not in control of himself now, almost spluttering in rage. "He's more biased than anyone else! Why? How can he be rational about this?"

"Jeb, I don't . . ." Jared muttered.

"She's your responsibility, Jared," Jeb said in a firm voice. "I'll help you out, of course, if there's any more trouble like this, and with keeping track of her and all that. But when it comes to making decisions, that's all yours." He raised one hand when Kyle tried to protest again. "Look at it this way, Kyle. If somebody found your Jodi on a raid and brought her back here, would you want me or Doc or a vote deciding what we did with her?"

"Jodi is dead," Kyle hissed, blood spraying off his lips. He glared at me with much the same expression Jared had just used.

"Well, if her body wandered in here, it would still be up to you. Would you want it any other way?"

"The majority —"

"My house, my rules," Jeb interrupted harshly. "No more discussion on this. No more votes. No more execution attempts. You three spread the word — this is how it works from now on. New rule."

"*Another* one?" Ian muttered under his breath.

Jeb ignored him. "If, unlikely as it may be, somehow this ever happens again, whoever the body belongs to makes the call." Jeb poked the barrel of the gun toward Kyle, then jerked it a few inches toward the hall behind him. "Get out of here. I don't want to see you anywhere around this place again. You let everyone know that this corridor is off-limits. No one's got any reason for being here except Jared, and if I catch someone skulking around, I'm asking questions second. You got that? Move. Now." He jabbed the gun at Kyle again.

I was amazed that the three assassins immediately stalked back up the hallway, not even pausing to give me or Jeb a parting grimace.

I deeply wanted to believe that the gun in Jeb's hands was a bluff.

From the first time I'd seen him, Jeb had shown every outward appearance of kindness. He had not touched me once in violence; he had not even looked at me with recognizable hostility. Now it seemed that he was one of only two people here who meant me no harm. Jared might have fought to keep me alive, but it was plain that he was intensely conflicted about that decision. I sensed that he could change his mind at any time. From his expression, it was clear that part of him wanted this over with —

especially now that Jeb had put the decision on his shoulders. While I made this analysis, Jared glowered at me with disgust in every line of his expression.

However, as much as I wanted to believe that Jeb was bluffing, while I watched the three men disappear into the darkness away from me, it was obvious there was no way he could be. Under the front he presented, Jeb must have been just as deadly and cruel as the rest of them. If he hadn't used that gun in the past — used it to kill, not just to threaten — no one would have obeyed him this way.

*Desperate times,* Melanie whispered. *We can't afford to be kind in the world you've created. We're fugitives, an endangered species. Every choice is life-or-death.*

*Shh. I don't have time for a debate. I need to focus.*

Jared was facing Jeb now, one hand held out in front of him, palm up, fingers curled limply. Now that the others were gone, their bodies slumped into a looser stance. Jeb was even grinning under his thick beard, as though he'd enjoyed the standoff at gunpoint. Strange human.

"Please don't put this on me, Jeb," Jared said. "Kyle is right about one thing — I *can't* make a rational decision."

"No one said you had to decide this second. She's not going anywhere." Jeb glanced down at me, still grinning. The eye closest to me — the one Jared couldn't see — closed quickly and opened again. A wink. "Not after all the trouble she took to get here. You've got plenty of time to think it through."

"There's nothing to think through. Melanie *is* dead. But I can't — I can't — Jeb, I can't just . . ." Jared couldn't seem to finish the sentence.

*Tell him.*

*I'm not ready to die right this second.*

"Don't think about it, then," Jeb told him. "Maybe you'll figure something out later. Give it some time."

"What are we going to *do* with it? We can't keep watch on it round the clock."

Jeb shook his head. "That's *exactly* what we're going to have to do for a while. Things will calm down. Even Kyle can't preserve a murderous rage for more than a few weeks."

"A few *weeks?* We can't afford to play guard down here for a few *weeks.* We have other things —"

"I know, I know." Jeb sighed. "I'll figure something out."

"And that's only half the problem." Jared looked at me again; a vein in his forehead pulsed. "Where do we keep it? It's not like we have a cell block."

Jeb smiled down at me. "You're not going to give us any trouble, now, are you?"

I stared at him mutely.

"Jeb," Jared muttered, upset.

"Oh, don't worry about her. First of all, we'll keep an eye on her. Secondly, she'd never be able to find her way out of here — she'd wander around lost until she ran into somebody. Which leads us to number three: she's not that stupid." He raised one thick white eyebrow at me. "You're not going to go looking for Kyle or the rest of them, are you? I don't think any of them are very fond of you."

I just stared, wary of his easy, chatty tone.

"I wish you wouldn't talk to it like that," Jared muttered.

"I was raised in a politer time, kid. I can't help myself." Jeb put one hand on Jared's arm, patting lightly.

"Look, you've had a full night. Let me take the next watch here. Get some sleep."

Jared seemed about to object, but then he looked at me again and his expression hardened.

"Whatever you want, Jeb. And . . . I don't — I won't accept responsibility for this thing. Kill it if you think that's best."

I flinched.

Jared scowled at my reaction, then turned his back abruptly and walked the same way the others had gone. Jeb watched him go. While he was distracted, I crept back into my hole.

I heard Jeb settle slowly to the ground beside the opening. He sighed and stretched, popping a few joints. After a few minutes, he started whistling quietly. It was a cheery tune.

I curled myself around my bent knees, pressing my back into the farthest recess of the little cell. Tremors started at the small of my back and ran up and down my spine. My hands shook, and my teeth chattered softly together, despite the soggy heat.

"Might as well lie down and get some sleep," Jeb said, whether to me or to himself, I wasn't sure. "Tomorrow's bound to be a tough one."

The shivers passed after a time — maybe half an hour. When they were gone, I felt exhausted. I decided to take Jeb's advice. Though the floor felt even more uncomfortable than before, I was unconscious in seconds.

◆

The smell of food woke me. This time I *was* groggy and disoriented when I opened my eyes. An instinctive sense of panic had my hands trembling again before I was fully conscious.

The same tray sat on the ground beside me, identical offerings on it. I could both see and hear Jeb. He sat in front of the cave in profile, looking straight ahead down the long round corridor and whistling softly.

Driven by my fierce thirst, I sat up and grabbed the open bottle of water.

"Morning," Jeb said, nodding in my direction.

I froze, my hand on the bottle, until he turned his head and started whistling again.

Only now, not quite so desperately thirsty as before, did I notice the odd, unpleasant aftertaste to the water. It matched the acrid taste of the air, but it was slightly stronger. The tang lingered in my mouth, inescapable.

I ate quickly, this time saving the soup for last. My stomach reacted more happily today, accepting the food with better grace. It barely gurgled.

My body had other needs, though, now that the loudest ones had been sated. I looked around my dark, cramped hole. There weren't a lot of options visible. But I could barely contain my fear at the thought of speaking up and making a request, even of the bizarre but friendly Jeb.

I rocked back and forth, debating. My hips ached from curving to the bowled shape of the cave.

"Ahem," Jeb said.

He was looking at me again, his face a deeper color under the white hair than usual.

"You've been stuck in here for a while," he said. "You need to . . . get out?"

I nodded.

"Don't mind a walk myself." His voice was cheerful. He sprang to his feet with surprising agility.

I crawled to the edge of my hole, staring out at him cautiously.

"I'll show you our little washroom," he continued. "Now, you should know that we're going to have to go through . . . kind of the main plaza, so to speak. Don't worry. I think everyone will have gotten the message by now." Unconsciously, he stroked the length of his gun.

I tried to swallow. My bladder was so full it was a constant pain, impossible to ignore. But to parade right through the middle of the hive of angry killers? Couldn't he just bring me a bucket?

He measured the panic in my eyes — watched the way I automatically shrank back farther into the hole — and his lips pursed in speculation. Then he turned and started walking down the dark hall. "Follow me," he called back, not looking to see if I obeyed.

I had one vivid flash of Kyle finding me here alone, and was after Jeb before a second passed, scrambling awkwardly through the opening and then hobbling along on my stiff legs as fast as I could to catch up. It felt both horrible and wonderful to stand straight again — the pain was sharp, but the relief was greater.

I was close behind him when we reached the end of the hall; darkness loomed through the tall broken oval of the exit. I hesitated, looking back at the small lamp he'd left on the floor. It was the only light in the dark cave. Was I supposed to bring it?

He heard me stop and turned to peer at me over his shoulder. I nodded toward the light, then looked back at him.

"Leave it. I know my way." He held out his free hand to me. "I'll guide you."

I stared at the hand for a long moment, and then, feeling the urgency in my bladder, I slowly put my hand on his palm, barely touching it — the way I would have touched a snake if for some reason I was ever forced to.

Jeb led me through the blackness with sure, quick steps. The long tunnel was followed by a series of bewildering twists in opposing directions. As we rounded yet another sharp V in the path, I knew I was hopelessly turned around. I was sure this was on purpose, and the reason Jeb had left the lamp behind. He wouldn't want me knowing too much about how to find my way out of this labyrinth.

I was curious as to how this place had come to be, how Jeb had found it, and how the others had wound up here. But I forced my lips tightly together. It seemed to me that keeping silent was my best bet now. What I was hoping for, I wasn't sure. A few more days of life? Just a cessation of pain? Was there anything else left? All I knew was that I wasn't ready to die, as I'd told Melanie before; my survival instinct was every bit as developed as the average human's.

We turned another corner, and the first light reached us. Ahead, a tall, narrow crevice glowed with light from another room. This light was not artificial like the little lamp by my cave. It was too white, too pure.

We couldn't move through the narrow fracture in the rock side by side. Jeb went first, towing me close behind. Once through — and able to see again — I pulled my hand out of Jeb's light grip. He didn't react in any way except to put his newly freed hand back on the gun.

We were in a short tunnel, and a brighter light shone through a rough arched doorway. The walls were the same holey purple rock.

I could hear voices now. They were low, less urgent than the last time I'd heard the babble of a human crowd. No one was expecting us today. I could only imagine what the response would be to my appearance with Jeb. My palms were cold and wet; my breath came in shallow gasps. I leaned as close as I could to Jeb without actually touching him.

"Easy," he murmured, not turning. "They're more afraid of you than you are of them."

I doubted that. And even if there were any way that it could be true, fear turned into hatred and violence in the human heart.

"I won't let anybody hurt you," Jeb mumbled as he reached the archway. "Anyway, might as well get used to this."

I wanted to ask what that meant, but he stepped through into the next room. I crept in after him, half a step behind, keeping myself hidden by his body as much as possible. The only thing harder than moving myself forward into that room was the thought of falling behind Jeb and being caught alone here.

Sudden silence greeted our entrance.

We were in the gigantic, bright cavern again, the one they'd first brought me to. How long ago was that? I had no idea. The ceiling was still too bright for me to make out exactly how it was lit. I hadn't noticed before, but the walls were not unbroken — dozens of irregular gaps opened to adjoining tunnels. Some of the openings were huge, others barely large enough for a man to fit through stooped over; some were natural crevices, others were, if not man-made, at least enhanced by someone's hands.

Several people stared at us from the recesses of those crevices, frozen in the act of coming or going. More people were out in the open, their bodies caught in the middle of whatever movement our entrance had interrupted. One woman was bent in half, reaching for her shoelaces. A man's motionless arms hung in the air, raised to illustrate some point he'd been making to his companions. Another man wobbled, caught off balance in a sudden stop. His foot came down hard as he struggled to keep steady; the thud of its fall was the only sound in the vast space. It echoed through the room.

It was fundamentally wrong for me to feel grateful to that hideous weapon in Jeb's hands . . . but I did. I knew that without it we would probably have been attacked. These humans would not stop themselves from hurting Jeb if it meant they could get to me. Though we might be attacked despite the gun. Jeb could only shoot one of them at a time.

The picture in my head had turned so grisly that I couldn't bear it. I tried to focus on my immediate surroundings, which were bad enough.

Jeb paused for a moment, the gun held at his waist, pointing outward. He stared all around the room, seeming to lock his gaze one by one with each person in it. There were fewer than twenty here; it did not take long. When he was satisfied with his study, he headed for the left wall of the cavern. Blood thudding in my ears, I followed in his shadow.

He did not walk directly across the cavern, instead keeping close to the curve of the wall. I wondered at his path until I noticed a large square of darker ground that took up the center of the floor — a very large space. No one stood on this darker ground. I was too frightened to do more than notice the anomaly; I didn't even guess at a reason.

There were small movements as we circled the silent room. The bending woman straightened, twisting at the waist to watch us go. The gesturing man folded his arms across his chest. All eyes narrowed, and all faces tightened into expressions of rage. However, no one moved toward us, and no one spoke. Whatever Kyle and the others had told these people about their confrontation with Jeb, it seemed to have had the effect Jeb was hoping for.

As we passed through the grove of human statues, I recognized Sharon and Maggie eyeing us from the wide mouth of one opening. Their expressions were blank, their eyes cold. They did not look at me, only Jeb. He ignored them.

It felt like years later when we finally reached the far side of the cavern. Jeb headed for a medium-sized exit, black against the brightness of this room. The eyes on my back made my scalp tingle, but I didn't dare to look behind me. The humans were still silent, but I worried that they might follow. It was a relief to slip into the darkness of the new passageway. Jeb's hand touched my elbow to guide me, and I did not shrink away from it. The babble of voices didn't pick up again behind us.

"That went better than I expected," Jeb muttered as he steered me through the cave. His words surprised me, and I was glad I didn't know what he'd thought would happen.

The ground sloped downward under my feet. Ahead, a dim light kept me from total blindness.

"Bet you've never seen anything like my place here." Jeb's voice was louder now, back to the chatty tone he'd used before. "It's really something, isn't it?"

He paused briefly in case I might respond, and then went on.

"Found this place back in the seventies. Well, it found me. I fell through the roof of the big room — probably shoulda died from the fall, but I'm too tough for my own good. Took me a while to find a way out. I was hungry enough to eat rock by the time I managed it.

"I was the only one left on the ranch by then, so I didn't have anyone to show it to. I explored every nook and cranny, and I could see the possibilities. I decided this might be a good card to keep up my sleeve, just in case. That's how we Stryders are — we like to be prepared."

We passed the dim light — it came from a fist-sized hole in the ceiling, making a small circle of brightness on the floor. When it was behind us, I could see another spot of illumination far ahead.

"You're probably curious as to how this all got here." Another pause, shorter than the last. "I know I was. I did a little research. These are lava tubes — can you beat that? This used to be a volcano. Well, still is a volcano, I expect. Not quite dead, as you'll see in a bit. All these caves and holes are bubbles of air that got caught in the cooling lava. I've put quite a bit of work into it over the last few decades. Some of it was easy — connecting the tubes just took a little elbow grease. Other parts took more imagination. Did you see the ceiling in the big room? That took me *years* to get right."

I wanted to ask him how, but I couldn't bring myself to speak. Silence was safest.

The floor began to slant downward at a steeper angle. The terrain was broken into rough steps, but they seemed secure enough. Jeb led me down them confidently. As we dropped lower and lower into the ground, the heat and humidity increased.

I stiffened when I heard a babble of voices again, this time from ahead. Jeb patted my hand kindly.

"You'll like this part — it's always everyone's favorite," he promised.

A wide, open arch shimmered with moving light. It was the same color as the light in the big room, pure and white, but it flickered at a strange dancing pace. Like everything else that I couldn't understand in this cavern, the light frightened me.

"Here we are," Jeb said enthusiastically, pulling me through the archway. "What do you think?"

# CHAPTER 17

# *Visited*

The heat hit me first — like a wall of steam, the moist, thick air rolled over me and dewed on my skin. My mouth opened automatically as I tried to pull a breath from the abruptly denser air. The smell was stronger than before — that same metallic tang that clung in my throat and flavored the water here.

The murmuring babble of bass and soprano voices seemed to issue from every side, echoing off the walls. I squinted anxiously through the swirling cloud of moisture, trying to make out where the voices came from. It was bright here — the ceiling was dazzling, like in the big room but much closer. The light danced off the vapor, creating a shimmering curtain that almost blinded me. My eyes struggled to adjust, and I clutched at Jeb's hand in panic.

I was surprised that the strangely fluid babble did not

respond in any way to our entrance. Perhaps they couldn't see us yet, either.

"It's a bit close in here," Jeb said apologetically, fanning at the steam in front of his face. His voice was relaxed, conversational in tone, and loud enough to make me jump. He spoke as if we were not surrounded. And the babble continued, oblivious to his voice.

"Not that I'm complaining," he continued. "I'd be dead several times over if this place didn't exist. The very first time I got stuck in the caves, of course. And now, we'd never be able to hide out here without it. With no hiding place, we're all dead, right?"

He nudged me with his elbow, a conspiratorial gesture.

"Mighty convenient, how it's laid out. Couldn't have planned it much better if I'd sculpted it myself out of play dough."

His laugh cleared a section of mist, and I saw the room for the first time.

Two rivers flowed through the dank, high-domed space. This was the chatter that filled my ears — the water gushing over and under the purple volcanic rock. Jeb spoke as if we were alone because we were.

It was really only one river and one small stream. The stream was closest; a shallow braided ribbon of silver in the light from above, coursing between low stone banks that it seemed constantly in danger of overrunning. A feminine, high-pitched murmur purred from its gentle ripples.

The male, bass gurgle came from the river, as did the thick clouds of vapor that rose from the gaping holes in the ground by the far wall. The river was black, submerged under the floor of the cavern, exposed by wide, round erosions along the length of the room. The holes looked dark and dangerous, the river barely visible as it rushed powerfully toward an invisible and unfathomable destination. The water seemed to simmer, such was the heat and steam it produced. The sound of it, too, was like that of boiling water.

From the ceiling hung a few long, narrow stalactites, dripping toward the stalagmites beneath each one. Three of them had met, forming thin black pillars between the two bodies of flowing water.

"Got to be careful in here," Jeb said. "Quite a current in the hot spring. If you fall in, you're gone. Happened once before." He bowed his head at the memory, his face sober.

The swift black eddies of the subterranean river were suddenly horrible to me. I imagined being caught in their scalding current and shuddered.

Jeb put his hand lightly on my shoulder. "Don't worry. Just watch your step and you'll be fine. Now," he said, pointing to the far end of the cavern, where the shallow stream ran into a dark cave, "the first cave back there is the bathing room. We've dug the floor out to make a nice, deep tub. There's a schedule for taking baths, but privacy's not usually an issue — it's black as pitch. The room's nice and warm so close to the steam, but the water won't burn you like the hot spring here. There's another cave just past that one, through a crevice. We've widened the entrance up to a comfortable size. That room is the farthest we can follow the stream — it drops underground there. So we've got that room fixed up as the latrine. Convenient and sanitary." His voice had assumed a complacent tone, as if he felt credit was due to him for nature's creations. Well, he had discovered and improved the place — I supposed some pride was justified.

"We don't like to waste batteries, and most of us know the floor here by heart, but since it's your first time, you can find your way with this."

Jeb pulled a flashlight from his pocket and held it out. The sight of it reminded me of the moment he'd found me dying in the desert, when he'd checked my eyes and known what I was. I didn't know why the memory made me sad.

"Don't get any crazy ideas about maybe the river taking you out of here or something. Once that water goes underground, it doesn't come back up," he cautioned me.

Since he seemed to be waiting for some acknowledgment of his warning, I nodded once. I took the flashlight from his hand slowly, being careful not to make any quick movements that might startle him.

He smiled in encouragement.

I followed his directions quickly — the sound of the rushing water was not making my discomfort any easier to bear. It felt very strange to be out of his sight. What if someone had hidden in these caves, guessing I would have to come here eventually? Would Jeb hear the struggle over the cacophony of the rivers?

I shone the flashlight all around the bathing room, looking for any sign of an ambush. The odd flickering shadows it made were not comforting, but I found no substance to my fears. Jeb's tub was more the size of a small swimming pool and black as ink. Under the surface, a person would be invisible as long as they could hold their breath. . . . I hurried through the slender crack at the back of the room to escape my imaginings. Away from Jeb, I was nearly overwhelmed with panic — I couldn't breathe normally; I could barely hear over the sound of my pulse racing behind my ears. I was more running than walking when I made my way back to the room with the rivers.

To find Jeb standing there, still in the same pose, still alone, was like a balm to my splintered nerves. My breathing and my heartbeat slowed. Why this crazy human should be such a comfort to me, I couldn't understand. I supposed it was like Melanie had said, *desperate times.*

"Not too shabby, eh?" he asked, a grin of pride on his face.

I nodded once again and returned the flashlight.

"These caves are a great gift," he said as we started back toward the dark passageway. "We wouldn't be able to survive in a group like this without them. Magnolia and Sharon were getting along real well — shockingly well — up there in Chicago, but they were pushing their luck hiding two. It's mighty nice to have a community again. Makes me feel downright human."

He took my elbow once more as we climbed the rough staircase out.

"I'm sorry about the, um, accommodations we've got you in. It was the safest place I could think of. I'm surprised those boys found you as quick as they did." Jeb sighed. "Well, Kyle gets real . . . motivated. But I suppose it's all for the best. Might as well get used to how things are going to be. Maybe we can find something more hospitable for you. I'll think on it. . . . While I'm with you, at least, you don't really have to cram yourself into that little hole. You can sit in the hall with me if you prefer. Though with Jared . . ." He trailed off.

I listened to his apologetic words in wonder; this was so much more kindness than I'd hoped for, more compassion than I'd thought this species was capable of giving their enemies. I patted the hand on my elbow lightly, hesitantly, trying to convey that I understood and wouldn't cause a problem. I was sure Jared much preferred to have me out of sight.

Jeb had no trouble translating my wordless communication. "That's a good girl," he said. "We'll figure this all out somehow. Doc can just concentrate on healin' human folks. You're much more interesting alive, *I* think."

Our bodies were close enough that he was able to feel me tremble.

"Don't worry. Doc's not going to bother you now."

I couldn't stop shivering. Jeb could only promise me *now*. There was no guarantee that Jared would not decide my secret was more important than protecting Melanie's body. I knew that such a fate would make me wish Ian had succeeded last night. I swallowed, feeling the bruising that seemed to go all the way through my neck to the inside walls of my throat.

*You never know how much time you'll have,* Melanie had said so many days ago, when my world was still under control.

Her words echoed in my head as we reentered the big room, the main plaza of Jeb's human community. It was full, like the first night, everyone there to glare at us with eyes that blazed anger and betrayal when they looked at him and murder when they looked at me. I kept my gaze down on the rock under my feet. From the corner of my eye, I could see that Jeb held his gun ready again.

It was only a matter of time, indeed. I could feel it in

the atmosphere of hate and fear. Jeb could not protect me long.

It was a relief to scrape back through the narrow crevice, to look forward to the winding black labyrinth and my cramped hiding place; I could hope to be alone there.

Behind me, a furious hissing, like a nest of goaded snakes, echoed in the big cavern. The sound made me wish Jeb would lead me through the labyrinth at a quicker pace.

Jeb chuckled under his breath. He seemed to get stranger the longer I was around him. His sense of humor mystified me as much as his motivations did.

"It gets a bit tedious down here sometimes, you know," he murmured to me, or to himself. With Jeb, it was hard to tell. "Maybe when they get over being cheesed off at me, they'll realize they appreciate all the excitement I'm providing."

Our path through the dark twisted in a serpentine fashion. It didn't feel at all familiar. Perhaps he took a different route to keep me lost. It seemed to take more time than before, but finally I could see the dim blue light of the lamp shining from around the next curve.

I braced myself, wondering if Jared would be there again. If he was, I knew he would be angry. I was sure he wouldn't approve of Jeb taking me for a field trip, no matter how necessary it might have been.

As soon as we rounded the corner, I could see that there *was* a figure slumped against the wall beside the lamp, casting a long shadow toward us, but it was obviously not Jared. My hand clutched at Jeb's arm, an automatic spasm of fear.

And then I really looked at the waiting figure. It was

smaller than me — that was how I'd known it was not Jared — and thin. Small, but also too tall and too wiry. Even in the dim light of the blue lamp, I could see that his skin was dyed to a deep brown by the sun, and that his silky black hair now fell unkempt past his chin.

My knees buckled.

My hand, grasping Jeb's arm in panic, held on for support.

"Well, for Pete's sake!" Jeb exclaimed, obviously irritated. "Can't nobody keep a secret around this place for more'n twenty-four hours? Gol' durn, this burns me up! Bunch of gossipmongers . . ." He trailed off into a grumble.

I didn't even try to understand the words Jeb was saying; I was locked in the fiercest battle of my life — of every life I'd ever lived.

I could feel Melanie in each cell of my body. My nerve endings tingled in recognition of her familiar presence. My muscles twitched in anticipation of her direction. My lips trembled, trying to open. I leaned forward toward the boy in the hall, my body reaching because my arms would not.

Melanie had learned many things the few times I'd ceded or lost my command to her, and I truly had to struggle against her — so hard that fresh sweat beaded on my brow. But I was not dying in the desert now. Nor was I weak and dizzy and taken off guard by the appearance of someone I'd given up for lost; I'd known this moment might come. My body was resilient, quick to heal — I was strong again. The strength of my body gave strength to my control, to my determination.

I drove her from my limbs, chased her from every

hold she'd found, thrust her back into the recesses of my mind, and chained her there.

Her surrender was sudden and total. *Aaah,* she sighed, and it was almost a moan of pain.

I felt strangely guilty as soon as I'd won.

I'd already known that she was more to me than a resistant host who made life unnecessarily difficult. We'd become companions, even confidantes during our past weeks together — ever since the Seeker had united us against a common enemy. In the desert, with Kyle's knife over my head, I'd been glad that if I *had* to die I would not be the one to kill Melanie; even then, she was more than a body to me. But now it seemed like something beyond that. I regretted causing her pain.

It was necessary, though, and she didn't seem to grasp that. Any word we said wrong, any poorly considered action would mean a quick execution. Her reactions were too wild and emotional. She would get us into trouble.

*You have to trust me now,* I told her. *I'm just trying to keep us alive. I know you don't want to believe your humans could hurt us . . .*

*But it's Jamie,* she whispered. She yearned for the boy with an emotion so strong that it weakened my knees again.

I tried to look at him impartially — this sullen-faced teenager slumped against the tunnel wall with his arms folded tightly across his chest. I tried to see him as a stranger and plan my response, or lack of response, accordingly. I tried, but I failed. He was Jamie, he was beautiful, and my arms — mine, not Melanie's — longed to hold him. Tears filled my eyes and trickled down my face. I could only hope they were invisible in the dim light.

"Jeb," Jamie said — a gruff greeting. His eyes passed swiftly over me and away.

His voice was so deep! Could he really be so old? I realized with a double pang of guilt that I'd just missed his fourteenth birthday. Melanie showed me the day, and I saw that it was the same day as the first dream with Jamie. She'd struggled so hard all through the waking hours to keep her pain to herself, to cloud her memories in order to protect the boy, that he'd come out in her dream. And I'd e-mailed the Seeker.

I shuddered now in disbelief that I'd ever been so callous.

"Whatcha doing here, kid?" Jeb demanded.

"Why didn't you tell me?" Jamie demanded back.

Jeb went silent.

"Was that Jared's idea?" Jamie pressed.

Jeb sighed. "Okay, so you know. What good does that do you, eh? We only wanted to —"

"To protect me?" he interrupted, surly.

When did he get so bitter? Was it my fault? Of course it was.

Melanie began sobbing in my head. It was distracting, loud — it made Jeb and Jamie's voices sound farther away.

"Fine, Jamie. So you don't need protecting. What do you want?"

This quick capitulation seemed to throw Jamie off. His eyes darted between Jeb's face and mine while he struggled to come up with a request.

"I — I want to talk with her . . . with it," he finally said. His voice was higher when he was unsure.

"She doesn't say much," Jeb told him, "but you're welcome to try, kid."

Jeb pried my fingers off his arm. When he was free, he turned his back to the nearest wall, leaning into it as he eased himself to the floor. He settled in there, fidgeting until he found a comfortable position. The gun stayed balanced in the cradle of his lap. Jeb's head lolled back against the wall, and his eyes closed. In seconds, he looked like he was asleep.

I stood where he'd left me, trying to keep my eyes off Jamie's face and failing.

Jamie was surprised again by Jeb's easy acquiescence. He watched the old man recline on the floor with wide eyes that made him look younger. After a few minutes of perfect stillness from Jeb, Jamie looked back up at me, and his eyes tightened.

The way he stared at me — angry, trying hard to be brave and grown-up, but also showing the fear and pain so clearly in his dark eyes — had Melanie sobbing louder and my knees shaking. Rather than take a chance with another collapse, I moved slowly to the tunnel wall across from Jeb and slid down to the floor. I curled up around my bent legs, trying to be as small as possible.

Jamie watched me with cautious eyes and then took four slow steps forward until he stood over me. His glance flitted to Jeb, who hadn't moved or opened his eyes, and then Jamie knelt down at my side. His face was suddenly intense, and it made him look more adult than any expression yet. My heart throbbed for the sad man in the little boy's face.

"You're not Melanie," he said in a low voice.

It was harder not to speak to him because *I* was the

one who wanted to speak. Instead, after a brief hesitation, I shook my head.

"You're inside her body, though."

Another pause, and I nodded.

"What happened to your . . . to her face?"

I shrugged. I didn't know what my face looked like, but I could imagine.

"Who did this to you?" he pressed. With a hesitant finger, he almost touched the side of my neck. I held still, feeling no urge to cringe away from *this* hand.

"Aunt Maggie, Jared, and Ian," Jeb listed off in a bored voice. We both jumped at the sound. Jeb hadn't moved, and his eyes were still closed. He looked so peaceful, as if he had answered Jamie's question in his sleep.

Jamie waited for a moment, then turned back to me with the same intense expression.

"You're not Melanie, but you know all her memories and stuff, right?"

I nodded again.

"Do you know who I am?"

I tried to swallow the words, but they slipped through my lips. "You're Jamie." I couldn't help how my voice wrapped around the name like a caress.

He blinked, startled that I had broken my silence. Then he nodded. "Right," he whispered back.

We both looked at Jeb, who remained still, and back at each other.

"Then you remember what happened to her?" he asked.

I winced, and then nodded slowly.

"I want to know," he whispered.

I shook my head.

"I want to know," Jamie repeated. His lips trembled. "I'm not a kid. Tell me."

"It's not . . . pleasant," I breathed, unable to stop myself. It was very hard to deny this boy what he wanted.

His straight black eyebrows pulled together and up in the middle over his wide eyes. "Please," he whispered.

I glanced at Jeb. I thought that maybe he was peeking from between his lashes now, but I couldn't be sure.

My voice was soft as breathing. "Someone saw her go into a place that was off-limits. They knew something was wrong. They called the Seekers."

He flinched at the title.

"The Seekers tried to get her to surrender. She ran from them. When they had her cornered, she jumped into an open elevator shaft."

I recoiled from the memory of pain, and Jamie's face went white under his tan.

"She didn't die?" he whispered.

"No. We have very skilled Healers. They mended her quickly. Then they put me in her. They hoped I would be able to tell them how she had survived so long." I had not meant to say so much; my mouth snapped shut. Jamie didn't seem to notice my slip, but Jeb's eyes opened slowly and fixed on my face. No other part of him moved, and Jamie didn't see the change.

"Why didn't you let her die?" he asked. He had to swallow hard; a sob was threatening in his voice. This was all the more painful to hear because it was not the sound a child makes, frightened of the unknown, but the fully comprehending agony of an adult. It was so hard not to reach out and put my hand on his cheek. I wanted to hug him to me and beg him not to be sad. I curled my hands into fists and tried to concentrate on his question. Jeb's eyes flickered to my hands and back to my face.

"I wasn't in on the decision," I murmured. "I was still in a hibernation tank in deep space when that happened."

Jamie blinked again in surprise. My answer was nothing he'd expected, and I could see him struggling with some new emotion. I glanced at Jeb; his eyes were bright with curiosity.

The same curiosity, though more wary, won out with Jamie. "Where were you coming from?" he asked.

In spite of myself, I smiled at his unwilling interest. "Far away. Another planet."

"What was —" he started to ask, but he was interrupted by another question.

"What the hell?" Jared shouted at us, frozen with fury in the act of rounding the corner at the end of the tunnel. "Damn it, Jeb! We agreed not to —"

Jamie wrenched himself upright. "Jeb didn't bring me here. But *you* should have."

Jeb sighed and got slowly to his feet. As he did so, the gun rolled from his lap onto the floor. It stopped only a few inches from me. I scooted away, uncomfortable.

Jared had a different reaction. He lunged toward me, closing the length of the hallway in a few running strides. I cowered into the wall and covered my face with my arms. Peeking around my elbow, I watched him jerk the gun up from the floor.

"Are you trying to get us killed?" he almost screamed at Jeb, shoving the gun into the old man's chest.

"Calm down, Jared," Jeb said in a tired voice. He took the gun in one hand. "She wouldn't touch this thing if I left it down here alone with her all night. Can't you see that?" He stabbed the barrel of the gun toward me, and I cringed away. "She's no Seeker, this one."

"Shut up, Jeb, just shut up!"

"Leave him alone," Jamie shouted. "He didn't do anything wrong."

"You!" Jared shouted back, turning on the slim, angry figure. "You get out of here *now,* or so *help* me!"

Jamie balled his fists and stood his ground.

Jared's fists came up, too.

I was rooted in place with shock. How could they scream at each other this way? They were family, the bonds between them stronger than any blood tie. Jared wouldn't hit Jamie — he couldn't! I wanted to do something, but I didn't know what to do. Anything that brought me to their attention would only make them angrier.

For once, Melanie was calmer than I was. *He can't hurt Jamie,* she thought confidently. *It's not possible.*

I looked at them, facing off like enemies, and panicked.

*We should never have come here. See how unhappy we've made them,* I moaned.

"You shouldn't have tried to keep this a secret from me," Jamie said between his teeth. "And you shouldn't have hurt her." One of his hands unclenched and flew out to point at my face.

Jared spit on the floor. "That's not Melanie. She's never coming back, Jamie."

"That's her face," Jamie insisted. "And her neck. Don't the bruises there *bother* you?"

Jared dropped his hands. He closed his eyes and took a deep breath. "You will either leave right now, Jamie, and give me some space, or I will *make* you leave. I am not bluffing. I can't deal with any more right now, okay? I'm at my limit. So can we please have this conversation later?" He opened his eyes again; they were full of pain.

Jamie looked at him, and the anger drained slowly from his face. "Sorry," he muttered after a moment. "I'll go . . . but I'm not promising that I won't come back."

"I can't think about that now. Go. Please."

Jamie shrugged. He threw one more searching look at me, and then he left, his quick, long stride making me ache again for the time I'd missed.

Jared looked at Jeb. "You, too," he said in a flat voice.

Jeb rolled his eyes. "I don't think you've had a long enough break, to be honest. I'll keep an eye on —"

"Go."

Jeb frowned thoughtfully. "Okay. Sure." He started down the hall.

"Jeb?" Jared called after him.

"Yeah?"

"If I asked you to shoot it right now, would you do it?"

Jeb kept walking slowly, not looking at us, but his words were clear. "I'd have to. I follow my own rules. So don't ask me unless you really mean it."

He disappeared into the dark.

Jared watched him go. Before he could turn his glower on me, I ducked into my uncomfortable sanctuary and curled up in the back corner.

# CHAPTER 18

# *Bored*

I spent the rest of the day, with one brief exception, in total silence.

That exception occurred when Jeb brought food for both Jared and me several hours later. As he set the tray inside the entrance to my tiny cave, he smiled at me apologetically.

"Thank you," I whispered.

"You're welcome," he told me.

I heard Jared grunt, irritated by our small exchange.

That was the only sound Jared made all day. I was sure he was out there, but there was never so much as an audible breath to confirm that conviction.

It was a very long day — very cramped and very dull. I tried every position I could imagine, but I could never quite manage to get all of me stretched out comfortably at once. The small of my back began a steady throbbing.

Melanie and I thought a lot about Jamie. Mostly we worried that we had damaged him by coming here, that we were injuring him now. What was a kept promise in comparison with that?

Time lost meaning. It could have been sunset, it could have been dawn — I had no references here, buried in the earth. Melanie and I ran out of topics for discussion. We flipped through our joint memories apathetically, like switching TV channels without stopping to watch anything in particular. I napped once but could not fall soundly asleep because I was so uncomfortable.

When Jeb finally came back, I could have kissed his leathery face. He leaned into my cell with a grin stretching his cheeks.

"'Bout time for another walk?" he asked me.

I nodded eagerly.

"I'll do it," Jared growled. "Give me the gun."

I hesitated, crouched awkwardly in the mouth of my cave, until Jeb nodded at me.

"Go ahead," he told me.

I climbed out, stiff and unsteady, and took Jeb's offered hand to balance myself. Jared made a sound of revulsion and turned his face away. He was holding the gun tightly, his knuckles white over the barrel. I didn't like to see it in his hands. It bothered me more than it did with Jeb.

Jared didn't make allowances for me the way Jeb had. He stalked off into the black tunnel without pausing for me to catch up.

It was hard — he didn't make much noise and he didn't guide me, so I had to walk with one hand in front of my face and one hand on the wall, trying not to run into the rock. I fell twice on the uneven floor. Though he did not help me, he did wait till he could hear that I was on my feet again to continue. Once, hurrying through a straighter section of the tube, I got too close and my searching hand touched his back, traced across the shape of his shoulders, before I realized that I hadn't reached another wall. He jumped ahead, jerking out from under my fingers with an angry hiss.

"Sorry," I whispered, feeling my cheeks turn warm in the darkness.

He didn't respond, but sped his pace so that following was even more difficult.

I was confused when, finally, some light appeared ahead of me. Had we taken a different route? This was not the white brilliance of the biggest cavern. It was muted, pale and silvery. But the narrow crevice we'd had to pass through seemed the same. . . . It wasn't until I was inside the giant, echoing space that I realized what caused the difference.

It was nighttime; the light that shone dimly from above mimicked the light of the moon rather than the sun. I used the less-blinding illumination to examine the ceiling, trying to ferret out its secret. High, so very high above me, a hundred tiny moons shone their diluted light toward the dim, distant floor. The little moons were scattered in patternless clusters, some farther away than others. I shook my head. Even though I could look directly at the light now, I still didn't understand it.

"C'mon," Jared ordered angrily from several paces ahead.

I flinched and hurried to follow. I was sorry I'd let my

attention wander. I could see how much it irritated him to have to speak to me.

I didn't expect the help of a flashlight when we reached the room with the rivers, and I didn't receive it. It was dimly lit now, too, like the big cave, but with only twenty-odd miniature moons here. Jared clenched his jaw and stared at the ceiling while I walked hesitantly into the room with the inky pool. I guessed that if I stumbled into the fierce underground hot spring and disappeared, Jared would probably see it as a kind intervention of fate.

*I think he would be sad,* Melanie disagreed as I edged my way around the black bathing room, hugging the wall. *If we fell.*

*I doubt it. He might be reminded of the pain of losing you the first time, but he would be happy if I disappeared.*

*Because he doesn't know you,* Melanie whispered, and then faded away as if she were suddenly exhausted.

I stood frozen where I was, surprised. I wasn't sure, but it felt as though Melanie had just given me a compliment.

"Move it," Jared barked from the other room.

I hurried as fast as the darkness and my fear would allow.

When we returned, Jeb was waiting by the blue lamp; at his feet were two lumpy cylinders and two uneven rectangles. I hadn't noticed them before. Perhaps he'd gone to get them while we were away.

"Are you sleeping here tonight or am I?" Jeb asked Jared in a casual tone.

Jared looked at the shapes by Jeb's feet.

"I am," he answered curtly. "And I only need one bedroll."

Jeb raised a thick eyebrow.

"It's not one of us, Jeb. You left this on me — so butt out."

"She's not an animal, either, kid. And you wouldn't treat a dog this way."

Jared didn't answer. His teeth ground together.

"Never figured you for a cruel man," Jeb said softly. But he picked up one of the cylinders, put his arm through a strap, and slung it over his shoulder, then stuffed one rectangle — a pillow — under his arm.

"Sorry, honey," he said as he passed me, patting my shoulder.

"Cut that out!" Jared growled.

Jeb shrugged and ambled away. Before he was out of sight, I hurried to disappear into my cell; I hid in its darkest reaches, coiling myself into a tight ball that I hoped was too small to see.

Instead of lurking silently and invisibly in the outside tunnel, Jared spread his bedroll directly in front of the mouth of my prison. He plumped his pillow a few times, possibly trying to rub it in that he had one. He lay down on the mat and crossed his arms over his chest. That was the piece of him that I could see through the hole — just his crossed arms and half of his stomach.

His skin was that same dark gold tan that had haunted my dreams for the last half year. It was very strange to have that piece of my dream in solid reality not five feet from me. Surreal.

"You won't be able to sneak past me," he warned. His

voice was softer than before — sleepy. "If you try . . ." He yawned. "I *will* kill you."

I didn't respond. The warning struck me as a bit of an insult. Why would I try to sneak past him? Where would I go? Into the hands of the barbarians out there waiting for me, all of them wishing that I would make exactly that kind of stupid attempt? Or, supposing I *could* somehow sneak past them, back out into the desert that had nearly baked me to death the last time I'd tried to cross it? I wondered what he thought me capable of. What plan did he think I was hatching to overthrow their little world? Did I really seem so powerful? Wasn't it clear how pathetically defenseless I was?

I could tell when he was deeply asleep because he started twitching the way Melanie remembered he occasionally did. He only slept so restlessly when he was upset. I watched his fingers clench and unclench, and I wondered if he was dreaming that they were wrapped around my neck.

◆

The days that followed — perhaps a week of them, it was impossible to keep track — were very quiet. Jared was like a silent wall between me and everything else in the world, good or bad. There was no sound but that of my own breathing, my own movements; there were no sights but the black cave around me, the circle of dull light, the familiar tray with the same rations, the brief, stolen glimpses of Jared; there were no touches but the pitted rocks against my skin; there were no tastes but the bitter water, the hard bread, the bland soup, the woody roots, over and over again.

It was a very strange combination: constant terror, persistent aching physical discomfort, and excruciating monotony. Of the three, the killer boredom was the hardest to take. My prison was a sensory-deprivation chamber.

Together, Melanie and I worried that we were going to go mad.

*We both hear a voice in our head,* she pointed out. *That's never a good sign.*

*We're going to forget how to speak,* I worried. *How long has it been since anyone talked to us?*

*Four days ago you thanked Jeb for bringing us food, and he said you were welcome. Well, I think it was four days ago. Four long sleeps ago, at least.* She seemed to sigh. *Stop chewing your nails — it took me years to break that habit.*

But the long, scratchy nails bothered me. *I don't really think we need to worry about bad habits in the long term.*

Jared didn't let Jeb bring food again. Instead, someone brought it to the end of the hall and Jared retrieved it. I got the same thing — bread, soup, and vegetables — twice every day. Sometimes there were extra things for Jared, packaged foods with brand names I recognized — Red Vines, Snickers, Pop-Tarts. I tried to imagine how the humans had gotten their hands on these delicacies.

I didn't expect him to share — of course not — but I wondered sometimes if he thought I was hoping he would. One of my few entertainments was hearing him eat his treats, because he always did so ostentatiously, perhaps rubbing it in the way he had with the pillow that first night.

Once, Jared slowly ripped open a bag of Cheetos —
showy about it as usual — and the rich smell of fake pow-
dered cheese rolled through my cave . . . delicious, irresistible. He ate one slowly, letting me hear each distinct
crunch.

My stomach growled loudly, and I laughed at myself.
I hadn't laughed in so long; I tried to remember the last
time and couldn't — just that strange bout of macabre
hysteria in the desert, which really didn't count as *laughter*. Even before I'd come here, there hadn't been much I'd
found funny.

But this seemed hilarious to me for some reason —
my stomach yearning after that one small Cheeto — and
I laughed again. A sign of madness, surely.

I didn't know how my reaction offended him, but he
got up and disappeared. After a long moment, I could
hear him eating the Cheetos again, but from farther away.
I peeked out of the hole to see that he was sitting in the
shadows at the end of the corridor, his back to me. I pulled
my head inside, afraid he might turn and catch me watching. From then on, he stayed down at that end of the hall
as much as possible. Only at night did he stretch out in
front of my prison.

Twice a day — or rather twice a night, as he never
took me when the others were about — I got to walk to
the room with the rivers; it was a highlight, despite the
terror, as it was the only time I was not hunched into the
unnatural shapes my small cave forced on me. Each time
I had to crawl back inside was harder than the last.

Three times that week, always during the sleeping
hours, someone came to check on us.

The first time it was Kyle.

Jared's sudden lunge to his feet woke me. "Get out of here," he warned, holding the gun ready.

"Just checking," Kyle said. His voice was far away but loud and rough enough that I was sure it was not his brother. "Someday you might not be here. Someday you might sleep too soundly."

Jared's only answer was to cock the gun.

I heard Kyle's laughter trailing behind him as he left.

The other two times I didn't know who it was. Kyle again, or maybe Ian, or maybe someone whose name I hadn't learned. All I knew was that twice more I was woken by Jared jumping to his feet with the gun pointed at the intruder. No more words were spoken. Whoever was *just checking* didn't bother to make conversation. When they were gone, Jared went back to sleep quickly. It took me longer to quiet my heart.

The fourth time was something new.

I was not quite asleep when Jared started awake, rolling to his knees in a swift movement. He came up with the gun in his hands and a curse on his lips.

"Easy," a voice murmured from the distance. "I come in peace."

"Whatever you're selling, I'm not buying," Jared growled.

"I just want to talk." The voice came closer. "You're buried down here, missing the important discussions. . . . We miss your take on things."

"I'm sure," Jared said sarcastically.

"Oh, put the gun down. If I was planning to fight you, I would have come with four guys this time."

There was a short silence, and when Jared spoke again, his voice carried a hint of dark humor. "How's your brother these days?" he asked. Jared seemed to enjoy the question. It relaxed him to tease his visitor. He sat down and slouched against the wall halfway in front of my prison, at ease, but with the gun still ready.

My neck ached, seeming to comprehend that the hands that had crushed and bruised it were very close by.

"He's still fuming about his nose," Ian said. "Oh, well — it's not the first time it's been broken. I'll tell him you said you were sorry."

"I'm not."

"I know. No one is ever sorry for hitting Kyle."

They laughed quietly together; there was a sense of camaraderie in their amusement that seemed wildly out of place while Jared held a gun loosely pointed in Ian's direction. But then, the bonds that were forged in this desperate place must have been very strong. Thicker than blood.

Ian sat down on the mat next to Jared. I could see his profile in silhouette, a black shape against the blue light. I noticed that his nose was perfect — straight, aquiline, the kind of nose that I'd seen in pictures of famous sculptures. Did that mean that others found him more bearable than the brother whose nose was often broken? Or that he was better at ducking?

"So what do you want, Ian? Not just an apology for Kyle, I imagine."

"Did Jeb tell you?"

"I don't know what you're talking about."

"They've given up the search. Even the Seekers."

Jared didn't comment, but I could feel the sudden tension in the air around him.

"We've been keeping a close watch for some change,

but they never seemed overly anxious. The search never strayed from the area where we abandoned the car, and for the past few days they were clearly looking for a body rather than a survivor. Then two nights ago we caught a lucky break — the search party left some trash in the open, and a pack of coyotes raided their base camp. One of *them* was coming back late and surprised the animals. The coyotes attacked and dragged the Seeker a good hundred yards into the desert before the rest of them heard its screams and came to the rescue. The other Seekers were armed, of course. They scared the coyotes off easily, and the victim wasn't seriously hurt, but the event seems to have answered any questions they might have had about what happened to our guest here."

I wondered how they were able to spy on the Seekers who searched for me — to see so much. I felt strangely exposed by the idea. I didn't like the picture in my head: the humans invisible, watching the souls they hated. The thought made the skin on the back of my neck prickle.

"So they packed up and left. The Seekers gave up the search. All the volunteers went home. No one is looking for it." His profile turned toward me, and I hunched down, hoping it was too dark to see me in here — that, like his face, I would appear as only a black shape. "I imagine it's been declared officially dead, if they keep track of those things the way we used to. Jeb's been saying 'I told you so' to anyone who'll stand still long enough to hear it."

Jared grumbled something incoherent; I could only pick out Jeb's name. Then he inhaled a sharp breath, blew it out, and said, "All right, then. I guess that's the end of it."

"That's what it looks like." Ian hesitated for a moment

and then added, "Except . . . Well, it's probably nothing at all."

Jared tensed again; he didn't like having his intelligence edited. "Go on."

"No one but Kyle thinks much of it, and you know how Kyle is."

Jared grunted his assent to that.

"You've got the best instincts for this kind of thing; I wanted your opinion. That's why I'm here, taking my life into my hands to infiltrate the restricted area," Ian said dryly, and then his voice was utterly serious again. "You see, there's this one . . . a Seeker, no doubt about that — it packs a Glock."

It took me a second to understand the word he used. It wasn't a familiar part of Melanie's vocabulary. When I understood that he was talking about a kind of gun, the wistful, envious tone in his voice made me feel slightly ill.

"Kyle was the first to notice how this one stood out. It didn't seem important to the rest — certainly not part of the decision-making process. Oh, it had suggestions enough, from what we could see, but no one seemed to listen to it. Wish we could've heard what it was saying. . . ."

My skin prickled anxiously again.

"Anyway," Ian continued, "when they called off the search, this one wasn't happy with the decision. You know how the parasites are always so . . . very *pleasant?* This was weird — it's the closest I've ever seen them come to an argument. Not a real argument, because none of the others argued back, but the unhappy one sure looked like it was arguing with *them*. The core group of Seekers disregarded it — they're all gone."

"But the unhappy one?" Jared asked.

"It got in a car and drove halfway to Phoenix. Then it drove back to Tucson. Then it drove west again."

"Still searching."

"Or very confused. It stopped at that convenience store by the peak. Talked to the parasite that worked there, though that one had already been questioned."

"Huh," Jared grunted. He was interested now, concentrating on the puzzle.

"Then it went for a hike up the peak — stupid little thing. Had to be burning alive, wearing black from head to toe."

A spasm rocked through my body; I found myself off the floor, cringing against the back wall of my cell. My hands flew up instinctively to protect my face. I heard a hiss echo through the small space, and only after it faded did I realize it was mine.

"What was *that?*" Ian asked, his voice shocked.

I peeked through my fingers to see both of their faces leaning through the hole toward me. Ian's was black, but part of Jared's was lit, his features hard as stone.

I wanted to be still, invisible, but tremors I couldn't control were shaking violently down my spine.

Jared leaned away and came back with the lamp in his hands.

"Look at its eyes," Ian muttered. "It's frightened."

I could see both their expressions now, but I looked only at Jared. His gaze was tightly focused on me, calculating. I guessed he was thinking through what Ian had said, looking for the trigger to my behavior.

My body wouldn't stop shaking.

*She'll never give up,* Melanie moaned.

*I know, I know,* I moaned back.

When had our distaste turned to fear? My stomach knotted and heaved. Why couldn't she just let me be dead like the rest of them had? When I *was* dead, would she hunt me still?

"Who is the Seeker in black?" Jared suddenly barked at me.

My lips trembled, but I didn't answer. Silence was safest.

"I know you can talk," Jared growled. "You talk to Jeb and Jamie. And now you're going to talk to me."

He climbed into the mouth of the cave, huffing with surprise at how tightly he had to fold himself to manage it. The low ceiling forced him to kneel, and that didn't make him happy. I could see he'd rather stand over me.

I had nowhere to run. I was already wedged into the deepest corner. The cave barely had room for the two of us. I could feel his breath on my skin.

"Tell me what you know," he ordered.

# CHAPTER 19

## *Abandoned*

Who is the Seeker in black? Why is it still searching?"
Jared's shout was deafening, echoing at me from
all sides.

I hid behind my hands, waiting for the first blow.

"Ah — Jared?" Ian murmured. "Maybe you should let
me . . ."

"Stay out of it!"

Ian's voice got closer, and the rocks grated as he tried
to follow Jared into the small space that was already too
full. "Can't you see it's too scared to talk? Leave it alone
for a sec —"

I heard something scrape the floor as Jared moved,
and then a thud. Ian cursed. I peered through my fingers
to see that Ian was no longer visible and Jared had his
back to me.

Ian spit and groaned. "That's twice," he growled, and

I understood that the punch meant for me had been diverted by Ian's interference.

"I'm ready to go for three," Jared muttered, but he turned back around to face me, bringing light with him; he'd grabbed the lamp with the hand that had struck Ian. The cave seemed almost brilliant after so much darkness.

Jared spoke to me again, scrutinizing my face in the new illuminations, making each word a sentence. "Who. Is. The. Seeker."

I dropped my hands and stared into his pitiless eyes. It bothered me that someone else had suffered for my silence — even someone who had once tried to kill me. This was not how torture was supposed to work.

Jared's expression wavered as he read the change in mine. "I don't have to hurt you," he said quietly, not as sure of himself. "But I do have to know the answer to my question."

This wasn't even the right question — not a secret I was in any way bound to protect.

"Tell me," he insisted, his eyes tight with frustration and deep unhappiness.

Was I truly a coward? I would rather have believed that I was — that my fear of pain was stronger than anything else. The real reason I opened my mouth and spoke was so much more pathetic.

I wanted to *please* him, this human who hated me so fiercely.

"The Seeker," I began, my voice rough and hoarse; I hadn't spoken in a long time.

He interrupted, impatient. "We already know it's a Seeker."

"No, not just any Seeker," I whispered. "*My* Seeker."

"What do you mean, *your* Seeker?"

"Assigned to me, following me. She's the reason —" I caught myself just before I spoke the word that would have meant our death. Just before I could say *we*. The ultimate truth that he would see as the ultimate lie — playing on his deepest wishes, his deepest pain. He would never see that it was possible for his wish to be true. He would only see a dangerous liar looking out through the eyes he'd loved.

"The reason?" he prompted.

"The reason I ran away," I breathed. "The reason I came here."

Not entirely true, but not entirely a lie, either.

Jared stared at me, his mouth half-open, as he tried to process this. From the corner of my eye, I could see that Ian was peering through the hole again, his vivid blue eyes wide with surprise. There was blood, dark on his pale lips.

"You ran away from a Seeker? But you're one of them!" Jared struggled to compose himself, to get back to his interrogation. "Why would it follow you? What did it want?"

I swallowed; the sound seemed unnaturally loud. "She wanted you. You and Jamie."

His expression hardened. "And you were trying to lead it here?"

I shook my head. "I didn't . . . I . . ." How could I explain it? He'd never accept the truth.

"What?"

"I . . . didn't want to tell her. I don't like her."

He blinked, confused again. "Don't you all have to like everyone?"

"We're supposed to," I admitted, coloring with shame.

"Who did you tell about this place?" Ian asked over Jared's shoulder. Jared scowled but kept his eyes on my face.

"I couldn't tell — I didn't know. . . . I just saw the lines. The lines on the album. I drew them for the Seeker . . . but we didn't know what they were. She still thinks they're a road map." I couldn't seem to stop talking. I tried to make the words come slower, to protect myself from a slip.

"What do you mean you didn't know what they were? You're here." Jared's hand flexed toward me but dropped before it closed the small distance.

"I . . . I was having trouble with my . . . with the . . . with her memory. I didn't understand . . . I couldn't access everything. There were walls. That's why the Seeker was assigned to me, waiting for me to unlock the rest." Too much, too much. I bit my tongue.

Ian and Jared exchanged a look. They'd never heard anything like this before. They didn't trust me, but they wanted so desperately to believe it was possible. They wanted it too much. That made them fear.

Jared's voice whipped out with a sudden harshness. "Were you able to *access* my cabin?"

"Not for a long time."

"And then you told the Seeker."

"No."

"No? Why not?"

"Because . . . by the time I could remember it . . . I didn't *want* to tell her."

Ian's eyes were frozen wide.

Jared's voice changed, became low, almost tender. So much more dangerous than the shouting. "Why didn't you want to tell her?"

My jaw locked hard. It was not *the* secret, but still, it was a secret he would have to beat out of me. In this moment, my determination to hold my tongue had less to do with self-preservation than it did with a stupid, grudging kind of pride. I would *not* tell this man who despised me that I loved him.

He watched the defiance flash in my eyes, and he seemed to understand what it would take to get this answer. He decided to skip it — or maybe to come back to it later, save it for last, in case I wouldn't be able to answer any more questions when he was done with me.

"Why weren't you able to access everything? Is that . . . normal?"

This question was very dangerous, too. For the first time so far, I told an outright lie.

"She fell a long way. The body was damaged."

Lying did not come easily to me; this lie fell flat. Jared and Ian both reacted to the false note. Jared's head cocked to the side; one of Ian's ink black eyebrows rose.

"Why isn't this Seeker giving up like the rest?" Ian asked.

I was abruptly exhausted. I knew they could keep this up all night, *would* keep this up all night if I continued to answer, and eventually I would make a mistake. I slumped against the wall and closed my eyes.

"I don't know," I whispered. "She's not like other souls. She's . . . *annoying.*"

Ian laughed once — a startled sound.

"And you — are you like other . . . *souls?*" Jared asked.

I opened my eyes and stared at him wearily for a long moment. *What a stupid question,* I thought. Then I shut my eyes tight, buried my face against my knees, and wrapped my arms around my head.

Either Jared understood that I was done speaking or his body was complaining too loudly to be ignored. He grunted a few times as he squeezed himself out of the opening of my cave, taking the lamp with him, and then groaned quietly as he stretched.

"That was unexpected," Ian whispered.

"Lies, of course," Jared whispered back. I could just barely make out their words. They probably didn't realize how the sound echoed back to me in here. "Only . . . I can't quite figure out what it wants us to believe — where it's trying to lead us."

"I don't think it's lying. Well, except the one time. Did you notice?"

"Part of the act."

"Jared, when have you ever met a parasite who could lie about anything? Except a Seeker, of course."

"Which it must be."

"Are you serious?"

"It's the best explanation."

"She — *it* is the furthest thing from a Seeker I've ever seen. If a Seeker had any idea how to find us, it would have brought an army."

"And they wouldn't have found anything. But she — it got in, didn't it?"

"It's almost been killed half a dozen —"

"Yet it's still breathing, isn't it?"

They were quiet for a long time. So long that I started to think about moving out of the cramped ball I was curled in, but I didn't want to make any noise by lying down. I wished Ian would leave so I could sleep. The adrenaline left me so worn out when it drained from my system.

"I think I'm going to go talk to Jeb," Ian eventually whispered.

"Oh, *that's* a great idea." Jared's voice was thick with sarcasm.

"Do you remember that first night? When it jumped between you and Kyle? That was bizarre."

"It was just trying to find a way to stay alive, to escape. . . ."

"By giving Kyle the go-ahead to kill her — it? Good plan."

"It worked."

"Jeb's gun worked. Did she know he was on his way?"

"You're overthinking this, Ian. That's what it wants."

"I don't think you're right. I don't know why . . . but I don't think she wants us to think about her at all." I heard Ian get to his feet. "You know what's really twisted?" he muttered, his voice no longer a whisper.

"What's that?"

"I felt *guilty* — guilty as hell — watching her flinch away from us. Seeing the black marks on her neck."

"You can't let it get to you like that." Jared was suddenly disturbed. "It's not human. Don't forget that."

"Just because she isn't human, do you think that means she doesn't feel pain?" Ian asked as his voice faded into the distance. "That she doesn't feel just like a girl who's been beaten — beaten by us?"

"Get a hold of yourself," Jared hissed after him.

"See you around, Jared."

Jared didn't relax for a long time after Ian left; he paced for a while, back and forth in front of the cave, and then sat on the mat, blocking my light, and muttered incomprehensibly to himself. I gave up waiting for him to fall asleep, and stretched out as well as I could on the bowl-like floor. He jumped when my movement made noise, and then started muttering to himself again.

*"Guilty,"* he grumbled in scathing tones. "Letting it get to him. Just like Jeb, like Jamie. Can't let this go on. Stupid to let it live."

Goose bumps rose on my arms, but I tried to ignore them. If I panicked every time he thought about killing me, I'd never have a moment's peace. I turned onto my stomach to bend my spine in the other direction, and he jerked again and then lapsed into silence. I was sure he was still brooding when I finally drifted to sleep.

◆

When I woke up, Jared was sitting on the mat where I could see him, elbows on knees, his head leaning against one fist.

I didn't feel as if I'd slept more than an hour or two, but I was too sore to try to go back to sleep right away. Instead, I fretted about Ian's visit, worrying that Jared would work even harder to keep me secluded after Ian's strange reaction. Why couldn't Ian have kept his mouth shut about feeling guilty? If he knew he was capable of guilt, why did he go around strangling people in the first place? Melanie was irritated with Ian, too, and nervous about the outcome of his qualms.

Our worries were interrupted after just a few minutes.

"'S just me," I heard Jeb call. "Don't get worked up."

Jared cocked the gun.

"Go ahead and shoot me, kid. Go ahead." The sound of Jeb's voice got closer with every word.

Jared sighed and put the gun down. "Please leave."

"Need to talk to you," Jeb said, huffing as he sat down across from Jared. "Hey, there," he said in my direction, nodding.

"You know how much I hate that," Jared muttered.

"Yep."

"Ian already told me about the Seekers —"

"I know. I was just talkin' with him about it."

"Great. Then what do you want?"

"Not so much what *I* want. It's what everybody needs. We're running low on just about everything. We need a real comprehensive supply run."

"Oh," Jared muttered; this topic was not what he'd been tensed for. After a short pause he said, "Send Kyle."

"Okay," Jeb said easily, bracing himself against the wall to rise again.

Jared sighed. It seemed his suggestion had been a bluff. He folded as soon as Jeb took him up on it. "No. Not Kyle. He's too . . ."

Jeb chuckled. "Almost got us in some real hot water the last time he was out alone, didn't he? Not one to think things through. Ian, then?"

"He thinks things through *too* much."

"Brandt?"

"He's no good for the long trips. Starts getting panicked a few weeks in. Makes mistakes."

"Okay, you tell me who, then."

The seconds passed and I heard Jared suck in a breath now and then, each time as if he was about to give Jeb an answer, but then he just exhaled and said nothing.

"Ian and Kyle together?" Jeb asked. "Maybe they could balance each other out."

Jared groaned. "Like the last time? Okay, okay, I know it has to be me."

"You're the best," Jeb agreed. "You changed our lives when you showed up here."

Melanie and I nodded to ourselves; this didn't surprise either of us.

*Jared is magic. Jamie and I were perfectly safe while Jared's instincts guided us; we never came close to getting caught. If it had been Jared in Chicago, I'm sure he would have made it out fine.*

Jared jerked his shoulder toward me. "What about . . . ?"

"I'll keep an eye on her when I can. And I'll expect you to take Kyle with you. That oughta help."

"That won't be enough — Kyle gone and you keeping an eye on her when you can. She . . . it won't last long."

Jeb shrugged. "I'll do my best. That's all I can do."

Jared started to shake his head slowly back and forth.

"How long can you stay down here?" Jeb asked him.

"I don't know," Jared whispered.

There was a long silence. After a few minutes, Jeb began whistling tunelessly.

Finally, Jared let out a huge breath that I hadn't realized he'd been holding.

"I'll leave tonight." The words were slow, full of resignation but also relief. His voice changed slightly, got a little less defensive. It was as though he was making the transition back to who he'd been here before I showed up. Letting one responsibility slide from his shoulders and putting another, more welcome one in its place.

He was giving up on keeping me alive, letting nature — or rather mob justice — take its course. When he returned, and I was dead, he wouldn't hold anyone responsible. He would not mourn. All this I could hear in those three words.

I knew the human exaggeration for sorrow — a *broken heart*. Melanie remembered speaking the phrase herself. But I'd always thought of it as a hyperbole, a traditional description for something that had no real physiological link, like a green thumb. So I wasn't expecting the pain in my chest. The nausea, yes, the swelling in my throat, yes, and, yes, the tears burning in my eyes. But what was the ripping sensation just under my rib cage? It made no logical sense.

And it wasn't just ripping, but twisting and pulling in different directions. Because Melanie's heart broke, too, and it was a separate sensation, as if we'd grown another organ to compensate for our twin awarenesses. A double heart for a double mind. Twice the pain.

*He's leaving,* she sobbed. *We'll never see him again.* She didn't question the fact that we were going to die.

I wanted to weep with her, but someone had to keep her head. I bit my hand to hold the moan back.

"That's probably best," Jeb said.

"I'll need to get some things organized. . . ." Already Jared's mind was far, far away from this claustrophobic corridor.

"I'll take over here, then. Have a safe trip."

"Thanks. Guess I'll see you when I see you, Jeb."

"Guess so."

Jared handed the gun back to Jeb, stood up, and brushed absently at the dust on his clothes. Then he was off, hurrying down the hall with his familiar quick step, his mind on other things. Not one glance in my direction, not one more thought for my fate.

I listened to the fading sound of his footsteps until they were gone. Then, forgetting Jeb's existence, I pressed my face into my hands and sobbed.

# CHAPTER 20

# Freed

Jeb let me cry myself out without interrupting. He didn't comment all through the following sniffles. It was only when I'd been completely silent for a good half hour that he spoke.

"Still awake in there?"

I didn't answer. I was too much in the habit of silence.

"You want to come out here and stretch?" he offered. "My back is aching just thinking about that stupid hole."

Ironically, considering my week of maddening silence, I wasn't in the mood for company. But his offer wasn't one I could refuse. Before I could think about it, my hands were pulling me through the exit.

Jeb was sitting with crossed legs on the mat. I watched him for some reaction as I shook out my arms and legs and rolled my shoulders, but he had his eyes closed. Like the time of Jamie's visit, he looked asleep.

How long had it been since I'd seen Jamie? And how was he now? My already sore heart gave a painful little lurch.

"Feel better?" Jeb asked, his eyes opening.

I shrugged.

"It's going to be okay, you know." He grinned a wide, face-stretching grin. "That stuff I said to Jared . . . Well, I won't say I *lied,* exactly, because it's all true if you look at it from a certain angle, but from another angle, it wasn't so much the truth as it was what he needed to hear."

I just stared; I didn't understand a word of what he was saying.

"Anyway, Jared needs a break from this. Not from you, kid," he added quickly, "but from the situation. He'll gain some perspective while he's away."

I wondered how he seemed to know exactly which words and phrases would cut at me. And, more than that, why should Jeb care if his words hurt me, or even if my back was aching and throbbing? His kindness toward me was frightening in its own way because it was incomprehensible. At least Jared's actions made sense. Kyle's and Ian's murder attempts, the doctor's cheerful eagerness to hurt me — these behaviors also were logical. Not kindness. What did Jeb want from me?

"Don't look so glum," Jeb urged. "There's a bright side to this. Jared was being real pigheaded about you, and now that he's temporarily out of the picture, it's bound to make things more comfortable."

My eyebrows furrowed as I tried to decide what he meant.

"For example," he went on. "This space here we usually use for storage. Now, when Jared and the guys get back, we're going to need someplace to put all the stuff they bring home with them. So we might as well find a new place for you now. Something a little bigger, maybe? Something with a bed?" He smiled again as he dangled the carrot in front of me.

I waited for him to snatch it away, to tell me he was joking.

Instead, his eyes — the color of faded blue jeans — became very, very gentle. Something about the expression in them brought the lump back to my throat.

"You don't have to go back in that hole, honey. The worst part's over."

I found that I couldn't doubt the earnest look on his face. For the second time in an hour, I put my face in my hands and cried.

He got to his feet and patted me awkwardly on the shoulder. He didn't seem comfortable with tears. "There, there," he mumbled.

I got control of myself more quickly this time. When I wiped the wet from my eyes and smiled tentatively at him, he nodded in approval.

"That's a girl," he said, patting me again. "Now, we'll have to hang out here until we're sure Jared's really gone and can't catch us." He grinned conspiratorially. "Then we'll have some fun!"

I remembered that his idea of fun was usually along the lines of an armed standoff.

He chuckled at my expression. "Don't worry about it. While we're waiting, you might as well try to get some rest. I'll bet even that skinny mattress would feel pretty good to you right now."

I looked from his face to the mat on the floor and back.

"Go on," he said. "You look like you could use a good sleep. I'll keep watch over you."

Touched, new moisture in my eyes, I sank down on the mat and laid my head on the pillow. It was heavenly, despite Jeb's calling it thin. I stretched out to my full height, pointing my toes and reaching out with my fingers. I heard my joints popping. Then I let myself wilt into the mattress. It felt as if it were hugging me, erasing all the sore spots. I sighed.

"Does me good to see that," Jeb muttered. "It's like an itch you can't scratch, knowing someone is suffering under your own roof."

He eased himself to the floor a few yards away and started humming quietly. I was asleep before he'd finished the first bar.

When I woke up, I knew that I'd been solidly asleep for a long time — a longer stretch than I'd slept since coming here. No pains, no frightening interruptions. I would have felt pretty good, except that waking on the pillow reminded me that Jared was gone. It still smelled like him. And in a good way, not the way I smelled.

*Back to just dreams.* Melanie sighed forlornly.

I remembered my dream only vaguely, but I knew it had featured Jared, as was usual when I was able to sleep deeply enough to dream.

"Morning, kid," Jeb said, sounding chipper.

I peeled back my lids to look at him. Had he sat against

the wall all night? He didn't look tired, but I suddenly felt guilty for monopolizing the better accommodations.

"So the guys are long gone," he said enthusiastically. "How 'bout a tour?" He stroked the gun slung through a strap at his waist with an unconscious gesture.

My eyes opened wider, stared at him in disbelief. A tour?

"Now, don't turn sissy on me. Nobody's going to bother you. And you'll need to be able to find your way around eventually."

He held out a hand to help me up.

I took it automatically, my head spinning as I tried to process what he was saying. I would need to find my way around? Why? And what did he mean "eventually"? How long did he expect me to last?

He pulled me to my feet and led me forward.

I'd forgotten what it was like to move through the dark tunnels with a hand guiding me. It was so easy — walking barely took any concentration at all.

"Let's see," Jeb murmured. "Maybe the right wing first. Set up a decent place for you. Then the kitchens . . ." He went on planning his tour, continuing as we stepped through the narrow crevice into the bright tunnel that led to the even brighter big room. When the sound of voices reached us, I felt my mouth go dry. Jeb kept right on chatting at me, either missing or ignoring my terror.

"I'll bet the carrots are sprouted today," he was saying as he led me into the main plaza. The light blinded me, and I couldn't see who was there, but I could feel their eyes on me. The sudden silence was as ominous as ever.

"Yep," Jeb answered himself. "Now, I always think

that looks real pretty. A nice spring green like that is a treat to see."

He stopped and held his hand out, inviting me to look. I squinted in the direction he gestured, but my eyes kept darting around the room as I waited for them to adjust. It took a moment, but then I saw what he was talking about. I also saw that there were maybe fifteen people here today, all of them regarding me with hostile eyes. But they were busy with something else, too.

The wide, dark square that took up the center of the big cavern was no longer dark. Half of it was fuzzy with spring green, just as Jeb had said. It *was* pretty. And amazing.

No wonder no one stood on this space. It was a garden.

"Carrots?" I whispered.

He answered at normal volume. "This half that's greening up. The other half is spinach. Should be up in a few days."

The people in the room had gone back to work, still peeking at me now and then but mostly concentrating on what they were doing. It was easy enough to understand their actions — and the big barrel on wheels, and the hoses — now that I recognized the garden.

"Irrigating?" I whispered again.

"That's right. Dries out pretty quick in this heat."

I nodded in agreement. It was still early, I guessed, but I was already sweaty. The heat from the intense radiance overhead was stifling in the caves. I tried to examine the ceiling again, but it was too bright to stare at.

I tugged Jeb's sleeve and squinted up at the dazzling light. "How?"

Jeb smiled, seeming thrilled with my curiosity. "Same way the magicians do it — with mirrors, kid. Hundreds of 'em. Took me long enough to get them all up there. It's nice to have extra hands around here when they need cleaning. See, there's only four small vents in the ceiling here, and that wasn't enough light for what I had in mind. What do you think of it?"

He pulled his shoulders back, proud again.

"Brilliant," I whispered. "Astonishing."

Jeb grinned and nodded, enjoying my reaction.

"Let's keep on," he suggested. "Got a lot to do today."

He led me to a new tunnel, a wide, naturally shaped tube that ran off from the big cave. This was new territory. My muscles all locked up; I moved forward with stiff legs, unbending knees.

Jeb patted my hand but otherwise ignored my nerves. "This is mostly sleeping quarters and some storage. The tubes are closer to the surface here, so it was easier to get some light."

He pointed up at a bright, slender crack in the tunnel ceiling overhead. It threw a hand-sized spot of white onto the floor.

We reached a broad fork — not really a fork, because there were too many tines. It was an octopus-like branching of passageways.

"Third from the left," he said, and looked at me expectantly.

"Third from the left?" I repeated.

"That's right. Don't forget. It's easy to get lost around here, and that wouldn't be safe for you. Folks'd just as soon stab you as send you in the right direction."

I shuddered. "Thanks," I muttered with quiet sarcasm.

He laughed as if my answer had delighted him. "No point in ignoring the truth. Doesn't make it worse to have it said out loud."

It didn't make it better, either, but I didn't say that. I was beginning to enjoy myself just a little. It was so nice to have someone talk to me again. Jeb was, if nothing else, interesting company.

"One, two, three," he counted off, then he led me down the third hallway from the left. We started passing round entrances covered by a variety of makeshift doors. Some were curtained off with patterned sheets of fabric; others had big pieces of cardboard duct-taped together. One hole had two real doors — one red-painted wood, one gray metal — leaning over the opening.

"Seven," Jeb counted, and stopped in front of a small-ish circle, the tallest point just a few inches higher than my head. This one protected its privacy with a pretty jade green screen — the kind that might divide the space in an elegant living room. There was a pattern of cherry blossoms embroidered across the silk.

"This is the only space I can think of for now. The only one that's fitted up decent for human habitation. It will be empty for a few weeks, and we'll figure something better out for you by the time it's needed again."

He folded the screen aside, and a light that was brighter than that in the hallway greeted us.

The room he revealed gave me a strange feeling of vertigo — probably because it was so much taller than it was wide. Standing inside it was like standing in a tower or a silo, not that I had ever been in such places, but those were the comparisons Melanie made. The ceiling, twice as high as the room was wide, was a maze of cracks. Like vines of light, the cracks circled around and almost met. This seemed dangerous to me — unstable. But Jeb showed no fear of cave-ins as he led me farther in.

There was a double-sized mattress on the floor, with about a yard of space on three sides of it. The two pillows and two blankets twisted into two separate configurations on either half of the mattress made it look as if this room housed a couple. A thick wooden pole — something like a rake handle — was braced horizontally against the far wall at shoulder height with the ends lodged in two of the Swiss cheese holes in the rock. Over it were draped a handful of T-shirts and two pairs of jeans. A wooden stool was flush with the wall beside the makeshift clothes rack, and on the floor beneath it was a stack of worn paperback books.

"Who?" I said to Jeb, whispering again. This space so obviously belonged to someone that I no longer felt like we were alone.

"Just one of the guys out on the raid. Won't be back for a while. We'll find you something by then."

I didn't like it — not the room, but the idea of staying in it. The presence of the owner was strong despite the simple belongings. No matter who he was, he would not be happy to have me here. He would hate it.

Jeb seemed to read my mind — or maybe the expression on my face was clear enough that he didn't have to.

"Now, now," he said. "Don't worry about that. This is *my* house, and this is just one of my many guest rooms. I say who is and isn't my guest. Right now, you are my guest, and I am offering you this room."

I still didn't like it, but I wasn't going to upset Jeb,

either. I vowed that I would disturb nothing, if it meant sleeping on the floor.

"Well, let's keep moving. Don't forget: third from the left, seventh in."

"Green screen," I added.

"Exactly."

Jeb took me back through the big garden room, around the perimeter to the opposite side, and through the biggest tunnel exit. When we passed the irrigators, they stiffened and turned, afraid to have me behind their backs.

This tunnel was well lit, the bright crevices coming at intervals too regular to be natural.

"We go even closer to the surface now. It gets drier, but it gets hotter, too."

I noticed that almost immediately. Instead of being steamed, we were now being baked. The air was less stuffy and stale. I could taste the desert dust.

There were more voices ahead. I tried to steel myself against the inevitable reaction. If Jeb insisted on treating me like . . . like a human, like a welcome guest, I was going to have to get used to this. No reason to let it make me nauseous over and over again. My stomach began an unhappy rolling anyway.

"This way's the kitchen," Jeb told me.

At first I thought we were in another tunnel, one crowded with people. I pressed myself against the wall, trying to keep my distance.

The kitchen was a long corridor with a high ceiling, higher than it was wide, like my new quarters. The light was bright and hot. Instead of thin crevices through deep rock, this place had huge open holes.

"Can't cook in the daytime, of course. Smoke, you

know. So we mainly use this as the mess hall until night-fall."

All conversation had come to an abrupt halt, so Jeb's words were clear for everyone to hear. I tried to hide behind him, but he kept walking farther in.

We'd interrupted breakfast, or maybe it was lunch.

The humans — almost twenty at a quick estimate — were very close here. It wasn't like the big cavern. I wanted to keep my eyes on the floor, but I couldn't stop them from flashing around the room. Just in case. I could feel my body tensing to run for it, though where I would run, I didn't know.

Against both sides of the hallway, there were long piles of rock. Mostly rough, purple volcanic stone, with some lighter-colored substance — cement? — running between them, creating seams, holding them together. On top of these piles were different stones, browner in color, and flat. They were glued together with the light gray grout as well. The final product was a relatively even surface, like a counter or a table. It was clear that they were used for both.

The humans sat on some, leaned on others. I recognized the bread rolls they held suspended between the table and their mouths, frozen with disbelief as they took in Jeb and his one-person tour.

Some of them were familiar. Sharon, Maggie, and the doctor were the closest group to me. Melanie's cousin and aunt glared at Jeb furiously — I had an odd conviction that I could have stood on my head and bellowed songs out of Melanie's memory at the top of my lungs and they still would not have looked at me — but the doctor eyed me with a frank and almost friendly curiosity that made me feel cold deep inside my bones.

At the back end of the hall-shaped room, I recognized the tall man with ink black hair and my heart stuttered. I'd thought Jared was supposed to take the hostile brothers with him to make Jeb's job of keeping me alive slightly easier. At least it was the younger one, Ian, who had belatedly developed a conscience — not quite as bad as leaving Kyle behind. That consolation did not slow my racing pulse, however.

"Everybody full so quick?" Jeb asked loudly and sarcastically.

"Lost our appetites," Maggie muttered.

"How 'bout you," he said, turning to me. "You hungry?"

A quiet groan went through our audience.

I shook my head — a small but frantic motion. I didn't even know whether I was hungry, but I knew I couldn't eat in front of this crowd that would gladly have eaten me.

"Well, I am," Jeb grumbled. He walked down the aisle between the counters, but I did not follow. I couldn't stand the thought of being within easy reach of the rest. I stayed pressed against the wall where I stood. Only Sharon and Maggie watched him go to a big plastic bin on one counter and grab a roll. Everyone else watched me. I was certain that if I moved an inch, they would pounce. I tried not to breathe.

"Well, let's just keep on movin'," Jeb suggested around a mouthful of bread as he ambled back to me. "Nobody seems able to concentrate on their lunch. Easily distracted, this set."

I was watching the humans for sudden movements, not really seeing their faces after that first moment when I recognized the few I could put names to. So it wasn't until Jamie stood up that I noticed him there.

He was a head shorter than the adults beside him, but taller than the two smaller children who perched on the counter on his other side. He hopped lightly off his seat and followed behind Jeb. His expression was tight, compressed, like he was trying to solve a difficult equation in his head. He examined me through narrow eyes as he approached on Jeb's heels. Now I wasn't the only one in the room holding my breath. The others' gazes shifted back and forth between Melanie's brother and me.

*Oh, Jamie,* Melanie thought. She hated the sad, adult expression on his face, and I probably hated it even more. She didn't feel as guilty as I did for putting it there.

*If only we could take it away.* She sighed.

*It's too late. What could we do to make it better now?*

I didn't mean the question more than rhetorically, but I found myself searching for an answer, and Melanie searched, too. We found nothing in the brief second we had to consider the matter; there was nothing to be found, I was sure. But we both knew we would be searching again when we were done with this asinine tour and had a chance to think. If we lived that long.

"Whatcha need, kid?" Jeb asked without looking at him.

"Just wondering what you're doing," Jamie answered, his voice striving for nonchalance and only just failing.

Jeb stopped when he got to me and turned to look at

Jamie. "Takin' her for a tour of the place. Just like I do for any newcomer."

There was another low grumble.

"Can I come?" Jamie asked.

I saw Sharon shake her head feverishly, her expression outraged. Jeb ignored her.

"Doesn't bother me . . . if you can mind your manners."

Jamie shrugged. "No problem."

I had to move then — to knot my fingers together in front of me. I wanted so badly to push Jamie's untidy hair out of his eyes and then leave my arm around his neck. Something that would not go over well, I was sure.

"Let's go," Jeb said to us both. He took us back out the way we had come. Jeb walked on one side of me, Jamie on the other. Jamie seemed to be trying to stare at the floor, but he kept glancing up at my face — just like I couldn't help glancing down at his. Whenever our eyes met, we looked away again quickly.

We were about halfway down the big hall when I heard the quiet footsteps behind us. My reaction was instantaneous and unthinking. I skittered to one side of the tunnel, sweeping Jamie along with one arm so that I was between him and whatever was coming for me.

"Hey!" he protested, but he did not knock my arm away.

Jeb was just as quick. The gun twirled out of its strap with blinding speed.

Ian and the doctor both raised their hands above their heads.

"We can mind our manners, too," the doctor said. It was hard to believe that this soft-spoken man with the friendly expression was the resident torturer; he was all the more terrifying to me because his exterior was so benign. A person would be on her guard on a dark and ominous night, a person would be ready. But on a clear, sunny day? How would she know to flee when she couldn't see any place for danger to hide?

Jeb squinted at Ian, the barrel of the gun shifting to follow his gaze.

"I don't mean any trouble, Jeb. I'll be just as mannerly as Doc."

"Fine," Jeb said curtly, stowing his gun. "Just don't test me. I haven't shot anybody in a real long time, and I sort of miss the thrill of it."

I gasped. Everyone heard that and turned to see my horrified expression. The doctor was the first one to laugh, but even Jamie joined in briefly.

"It's a joke," Jamie whispered to me. His hand strayed from his side, almost as if he was reaching for mine, but he quickly shoved it into the pocket of his shorts. I let my arm — still stretched protectively in front of his body — drop, too.

"Well, the day's wasting," Jeb said, still a little surly. "You'll all have to keep up, 'cause I'm not waiting on you." He stalked forward before he was done speaking.

# CHAPTER 21

# Named

I kept tight to Jeb's side, a little in front of him. I wanted to be as far as possible from the two men following us. Jamie walked somewhere in the middle, not sure of where he wanted to be.

I wasn't able to concentrate much on the rest of Jeb's tour. My attention was not focused on the second set of gardens he led me through — one with corn growing waist-high in the blistering heat of the brilliant mirrors — or the wide but low-ceilinged cavern he called the "rec room." That one was pitch-black and deep underground, but he told me they brought in lights when they wanted to play. The word *play* didn't make sense to me, not here in this group of tense, angry survivors, but I didn't ask him to explain. There was more water here, a tiny, noxiously sulfurous spring that Jeb said they sometimes used as a second latrine because it was no good for drinking.

My attention was divided between the men walking behind us and the boy at my side.

Ian and the doctor did mind their manners surprisingly well. No one attacked me from behind — though I thought my eyes might get lodged in the back of my head from trying to see if they were about to. They just followed quietly, sometimes talking to each other in low voices. Their comments revolved around names I didn't know and nicknames for places and things that might or might not have been inside these caves. I couldn't understand any of it.

Jamie said nothing, but he looked at me a lot. When I wasn't trying to keep an eye on the others, I was often peeking at him, too. This left little time to admire the things Jeb showed me, but he didn't seem to notice my preoccupations.

Some of the tunnels were very long — the distances hidden beneath the ground here were mind-boggling. Often they were pitch-black, but Jeb and the others never so much as paused, clearly familiar with their whereabouts and long since accustomed to traveling in darkness. It was harder for me than it was when Jeb and I were alone. In the dark, every noise sounded like an attack. Even the doctor's and Ian's casual chatter seemed like a cover for some nefarious move.

*Paranoid,* Melanie commented.

*If that's what it takes to keep us alive, so be it.*

*I wish you would pay more attention to Uncle Jeb. This is fascinating.*

*Do what you want with your time.*

*I can only hear and see what you hear and see,*

*Wanderer,* she told me. Then she changed the subject. *Jamie looks okay, don't you think? Not too unhappy.*

*He looks . . . wary.*

We were just coming into some light after the longest trek so far in the humid blackness.

"This here is the southernmost spur of the tube system," Jeb explained as we walked. "Not super convenient, but it gets good light all day long. That's why we made it the hospital wing. This is where Doc does his thing."

The moment Jeb announced where we were, my body froze and my joints locked; I skidded to a halt, my feet planted against the rock floor. My eyes, wide with terror, flickered between Jeb's face and the face of the doctor.

Had this all been a ruse, then? Wait for stubborn Jared to be out of the picture and then lure me back here? I couldn't believe I'd walked to this place under my own power. How stupid I was!

Melanie was just as aghast. *We might as well have gift-wrapped ourselves for them!*

They stared back at me, Jeb expressionless, the doctor looking as surprised as I felt — though not as horrified.

I would have flinched, ripped myself away from the touch of a hand on my arm, if the hand had not been so familiar.

"No," Jamie said, his hand hesitantly resting just below my elbow. "No, it's okay. Really. Right, Uncle Jeb?" Jamie looked trustingly at the old man. "It's okay, right?"

"Sure it is." Jeb's faded blue eyes were calm and clear. "Just showing you my place, kid, that's all."

"What are you talking about?" Ian grumbled from behind us, sounding annoyed that he didn't understand.

"Did you think we brought you here on purpose, for Doc?" Jamie said to me instead of answering Ian. "Because we wouldn't do that. We promised Jared."

I stared at his earnest face, trying to believe.

"Oh!" Ian said as he understood, and then he laughed. "That wasn't a bad plan. I'm surprised I didn't think of it."

Jamie scowled at the big man and patted my arm before removing his hand. "Don't be scared," he said.

Jeb took up where he'd left off. "So this big room here is fitted up with a few cots in case anyone gets sick or hurt. We've been pretty lucky on that count. Doc doesn't have much to work with in an emergency." Jeb grinned at me. "Your folks threw out all *our* medicines when they took over things. Hard to get our hands on what we need."

I nodded slightly; the movement was absentminded. I was still reeling, trying to get my bearings. This room looked innocent enough, as if it were only used for healing, but it made my stomach twist and contract.

"What do you know about alien medicine?" the doctor asked suddenly, his head cocked to the side. He watched my face with expectant curiosity.

I stared at him wordlessly.

"Oh, you can talk to Doc," Jeb encouraged me. "He's a pretty decent guy, all things considered."

I shook my head once. I meant to answer the doctor's question, to tell them that I knew nothing, but they misunderstood.

"She's not giving away any trade secrets," Ian said sourly. "Are you, sweetheart?"

"Manners, Ian," Jeb barked.

"Is it a secret?" Jamie asked, guarded but clearly curious.

I shook my head again. They all stared at me in confusion. Doc shook his head, too, slowly, baffled.

I took a deep breath, then whispered, "I'm not a Healer. I don't know how they — the medications — work. Only that they *do* work — they heal, rather than merely treating symptoms. No trial and error. Of course the human medicines were discarded."

All four of them stared with blank expressions. First they were surprised when I didn't answer, and now they were surprised when I did. Humans were impossible to please.

"Your kind didn't change too much of what we left behind," Jeb said thoughtfully after a moment. "Just the medical stuff, and the spaceships instead of planes. Other than that, life seems to go on just the same as ever . . . on the surface."

"We come to experience, not to change," I whispered. "Health takes priority over that philosophy, though."

I shut my mouth with an audible snap. I had to be more careful. The humans hardly wanted a lecture on soul philosophy. Who knew what would anger them? Or what would snap their fragile patience?

Jeb nodded, still thoughtful, and then ushered us onward. He wasn't as enthusiastic as he continued my tour through the few connecting caves here in the medical wing, not as involved in the presentation. When we turned around and headed back into the black corridor, he lapsed into silence. It was a long, quiet walk. I thought through what I'd said, looking for something that might have offended. Jeb was too strange for me to guess if that was the case. The other humans, hostile and suspicious as they were, at least made sense. How could I hope to make sense of Jeb?

The tour ended abruptly when we reentered the huge garden cavern where the carrot sprouts made a bright green carpet across the dark floor.

"Show's over," Jeb said gruffly, looking at Ian and the doctor. "Go do something useful."

Ian rolled his eyes at the doctor, but they both turned good-naturedly enough and made their way toward the biggest exit — the one that led to the kitchen, I remembered. Jamie hesitated, looking after them but not moving.

"You come with me," Jeb told him, slightly less gruff this time. "I've got a job for you."

"Okay," Jamie said. I could see that he was pleased to have been chosen.

Jamie walked beside me again as we headed back toward the sleeping-quarters section of the caves. I was surprised, as we chose the third passageway from the left, that Jamie seemed to know exactly where we were going. Jeb was slightly behind us, but Jamie stopped at once when we reached the green screen that covered the seventh apartment. He moved the screen aside for me but stayed in the hall.

"You okay to sit tight for a while?" Jeb asked me.

I nodded, grateful at the thought of hiding again. I ducked through the opening and then stood a few feet in, not sure what to do with myself. Melanie remembered that there were books here, but I reminded her of my vow to not touch anything.

"I got things to do, kid," Jeb said to Jamie. "Food ain't gonna fix itself, you know. You up to guard duty?"

"Sure," Jamie said with a bright smile. His thin chest swelled with a deep breath.

My eyes widened in disbelief as I watched Jeb place the rifle in Jamie's eager hands.

"Are you *crazy?*" I shouted. My voice was so loud that I didn't recognize it at first. It felt like I'd been whispering forever.

Jeb and Jamie looked up at me, shocked. I was out in the hallway with them in a second.

I almost reached for the hard metal of the barrel, almost ripped it from the boy's hands. What stopped me wasn't the knowledge that a move like that would surely get me killed. What stopped me was the fact that I was weaker than the humans in this way; even to save the boy, I could not make myself touch the weapon.

I turned on Jeb instead.

"What are you thinking? Giving the weapon to a child? He could kill himself!"

"Jamie's been through enough to be called a man, I think. He knows how to handle himself around a gun."

Jamie's shoulders straightened at Jeb's praise, and he gripped the gun tighter to his chest.

I gaped at Jeb's stupidity. "What if they come for me with him here? Did you think of what could happen? This isn't a joke! They'll hurt him to get to me!"

Jeb remained calm, his face placid. "Don't think there'll be any trouble today. I'd bet on it."

"Well, I wouldn't!" I was yelling again. My voice echoed off the tunnel walls — someone was sure to hear, but I didn't care. Better they come while Jeb was still here.

"If you're so sure, then leave me here alone. Let what happens happen. But don't put Jamie in danger!"

"Is it the kid you're worried about, or are you just afraid that he'll turn the gun on you?" Jeb asked, his voice almost languid.

I blinked, my anger derailed. That thought had not even occurred to me. I glanced blankly at Jamie, met his surprised gaze, and saw that the idea was shocking to him, too.

It took me a minute to recover my side of the argument, and by the time I did, Jeb's expression had changed. His eyes were intent, his mouth pursed — as if he were about to fit the last piece into a frustrating puzzle.

"Give the gun to Ian or any of the others. I don't care," I said, my voice slow and even. "Just leave the boy out of this."

Jeb's sudden face-wide grin reminded me, strangely, of a pouncing cat.

"It's my house, kid, and I'll do what I want. I always do."

Jeb turned his back and ambled away down the hall, whistling as he went. I watched him go, my mouth hanging open. When he disappeared, I turned to Jamie, who was watching me with a sullen expression.

"I'm not a child," he muttered in a deeper tone than usual, his chin jutting out belligerently. "Now, you should . . . you should go in your room."

The order was less than severe, but there was nothing else I could do. I'd lost this disagreement by a large margin.

I sat down with my back against the rock that formed one side of the cave opening — the side where I could hide behind the half-opened screen but still watch Jamie. I wrapped my arms around my legs and began doing what I knew I would be doing as long as this insane situation continued: I worried.

I also strained my eyes and ears for some sound of approach, to be ready. No matter what Jeb said, I would prevent anyone from challenging Jamie's guard. I would give myself up before they asked.

*Yes,* Melanie agreed succinctly.

Jamie stood in the hallway for a few minutes, the gun tight in his hands, unsure as to how to do his job. He started pacing after that, back and forth in front of the screen, but he seemed to feel silly after a couple of passes. Then he sat down on the floor beside the open end of the screen. The gun eventually settled on his folded legs, and his chin into his cupped hands. After a long time, he sighed. Guard duty was not as exciting as he'd been expecting.

I did not get bored watching him.

After maybe an hour or two, he started looking at me again, flickering glances. His lips opened a few times, and then he thought better of whatever he was going to say.

I laid my chin on my knees and waited as he struggled. My patience was rewarded.

"That planet you were coming from before you were in Melanie," he finally said. "What was it like there? Was it like here?"

The direction of his thoughts caught me off guard. "No," I said. With only Jamie here, it felt right to speak normally instead of whispering. "No, it was very different."

"Will you tell me what it was like?" he asked, cocking his head to one side the way he used to when he was really interested in one of Melanie's bedtime stories.

So I told him.

I told him all about the See Weeds' waterlogged planet. I told him about the two suns, the elliptical orbit, the gray waters, the unmoving permanence of roots, the stunning vistas of a thousand eyes, the endless conversations of a million soundless voices that all could hear.

He listened with wide eyes and a fascinated smile.

"Is that the only other place?" he asked when I fell silent, trying to think of anything I'd missed. "Are the *See Weeds*" — he laughed once at the pun — "the only other aliens?"

I laughed, too. "Hardly. No more than I'm the only alien on this world."

"Tell me."

So I told him about the Bats on the Singing World — how it was to live in musical blindness, how it was to fly. I told him about the Mists Planet — how it felt to have thick white fur and four hearts to keep warm, how to give claw beasts a wide berth.

I started to tell him about the Planet of the Flowers, about the color and the light, but he interrupted me with a new question.

"What about the little green guys with the triangle heads and the big black eyes? The ones who crashed in Roswell and all that. Was that you guys?"

"Nope, not us."

"Was it all fake?"

"I don't know — maybe, maybe not. It's a big universe, and there's a lot of company out there."

"How did you come here, then — if you weren't the little green guys, who were you? You had to have bodies to move and stuff, right?"

"Right," I agreed, surprised at his grasp of the facts at hand. I shouldn't have been surprised — I knew how bright he was, his mind like a thirsty sponge. "We used our Spider selves in the very beginning, to get things started."

"Spiders?"

I told him about the Spiders — a fascinating species. Brilliant, the most incredible minds we'd ever come across, and each Spider had three of them. Three brains, one in each section of their segmented bodies. We'd yet to find a problem they couldn't solve for us. And yet they were so coldly analytical that they rarely came up with a problem they were curious enough to solve for themselves. Of all our hosts, the Spiders welcomed our occupation the most. They barely noticed the difference, and when they did, they seemed to appreciate the direction we provided. The few souls who had walked on the surface of the Spiders' planet before implantation told us that it was cold and gray — no wonder the Spiders only saw in black and white and had a limited sense of temperature. The Spiders lived short lives, but the young were born knowing everything their parent had, so no knowledge was lost.

I'd lived out one of the short life terms of the species and then left with no desire to return. The amazing clarity of my thoughts, the easy answers that came to any question almost without effort, the march and dance of numbers were no substitute for emotion and color, which I could only vaguely understand when inside that body. I wondered how any soul could be content there, but the planet had been self-sufficient for thousands of Earth years. It was still open for settling only because the Spiders reproduced so quickly — great sacs of eggs.

I started to tell Jamie how the offensive had been launched here. The Spiders were our best engineers — the ships they made for us danced nimbly and undetectably through the stars. The Spiders' bodies were almost as useful as their minds: four long legs to each segment — from which they'd earned their nickname on this planet — and twelve-fingered hands on each leg. These six-jointed fingers were as slender and strong as steel threads, capable of the most delicate procedures. About the mass of a cow, but short and lean, the Spiders had no trouble with the first insertions. They were stronger than humans, smarter than humans, and prepared, which the humans were not. . . .

I stopped short, midsentence, when I saw the crystalline sparkle on Jamie's cheek.

He was staring straight ahead at nothing, his lips pressed in a tight line. A large drop of salt water rolled slowly down the cheek closest to me.

*Idiot,* Melanie chastised me. *Didn't you think what your story would mean to him?*

*Didn't* you *think of warning me sooner?*

She didn't answer. No doubt she'd been as caught up in the storytelling as I was.

"Jamie," I murmured. My voice was thick. The sight of his tear had done strange things to my throat. "Jamie, I'm so sorry. I wasn't thinking."

Jamie shook his head. "'S okay. I asked. I wanted to know how it happened." His voice was gruff, trying to hide the pain.

It was instinctive, the desire to lean forward and wipe that tear away. I tried at first to ignore it; I was not Melanie. But the tear hung there, motionless, as if it would never fall. Jamie's eyes stayed fixed on the blank wall, and his lips trembled.

He wasn't far from me. I stretched my arm out to brush my fingers against his cheek; the tear spread thin across his skin and disappeared. Acting on instinct again, I left my hand against his warm cheek, cradling his face.

For a short second, he pretended to ignore me.

Then he rolled toward me, his eyes closed, his hands reaching. He curled into my side, his cheek against the hollow of my shoulder, where it had once fit better, and sobbed.

These were not the tears of a child, and that made them more profound — made it more sacred and painful that he would cry them in front of me. This was the grief of a man at the funeral for his entire family.

My arms wound around him, not fitting as easily as they used to, and I cried, too.

"I'm sorry," I said again and again. I apologized for everything in those two words. That we'd ever found this place. That we'd chosen it. That I'd been the one to take his sister. That I'd brought her back here and hurt him again. That I'd made him cry today with my insensitive stories.

I didn't drop my arms when his anguish quieted; I was in no hurry to let him go. It seemed as though my body had been starving for this from the beginning, but I'd never understood before now what would feed the hunger. The mysterious bond of mother and child — so strong on this planet — was not a mystery to me any longer. There was no bond greater than one that required your life for another's. I'd understood this truth before; what I had not understood was *why*. Now I knew why a mother would give her life for her child, and this knowledge would forever shape the way I saw the universe.

"I know I've taught you better than that, kid."

We jumped apart. Jamie lurched to his feet, but I curled closer to the ground, cringing into the wall.

Jeb leaned down and picked up the gun we'd both forgotten from the floor. "You've got to mind a gun better than this, Jamie." His tone was very gentle — it softened the criticism. He reached out to tousle Jamie's shaggy hair.

Jamie ducked under Jeb's hand, his face scarlet with mortification.

"Sorry," he muttered, and turned as if to flee. He stopped after just a step, though, and swiveled back to look at me. "I don't know your name," he said.

"They called me Wanderer," I whispered.

"Wanderer?"

I nodded.

He nodded, too, then hurried away. The back of his neck was still red.

When he was gone, Jeb leaned against the rock and slid down till he was seated where Jamie had been. Like Jamie, he kept the gun cradled in his lap.

"That's a real interesting name you've got there," he told me. He seemed to be back to his chatty mood. "Maybe sometime you'll tell me how you got it. Bet that's a good story. But it's kind of a mouthful, don't you think? Wanderer?"

I stared at him.

"Mind if I call you Wanda, for short? It flows easier."

He waited this time for a response. Finally, I shrugged. It didn't matter to me whether he called me "kid" or some strange human nickname. I believed it was meant kindly.

"Okay, then, Wanda." He smiled, pleased at his invention. "It's nice to have a handle on you. Makes me feel like we're old friends."

He grinned that huge, cheek-stretching grin, and I couldn't help grinning back, though my smile was more rueful than delighted. He was supposed to be my enemy. He was probably insane. And he *was* my friend. Not that he wouldn't kill me if things turned out that way, but he wouldn't like doing it. With humans, what more could you ask of a friend?

# CHAPTER 22

# Cracked

Jeb put his hands behind his head and looked up at the dark ceiling, his face thoughtful. His chatty mood had not passed.

"I've wondered a lot what it's like — getting caught, you know. Saw it happen more than once, come close a few times myself. What would it be like, I wondered. Would it hurt, having something put in your head? I've seen it done, you know."

My eyes widened in surprise, but he wasn't looking at me.

"Seems like you all use some kind of anesthetic, but that's just a guess. Nobody was screaming in agony or anything, though, so it couldn't be too torturous."

I wrinkled my nose. Torture. No, that was the humans' specialty.

"Those stories you were telling the kid were real interesting."

I stiffened and he laughed lightly. "Yeah, I was listening. Eavesdropping, I'll admit it. I'm not sorry — it was great stuff, and you won't talk to me the way you do with Jamie. I really got a kick out of those bats and the plants and spiders. Gives a man lots to think about. Always liked to read crazy, out-there stuff, science fiction and whatnot. Ate that stuff up. And the kid's like me — he's read all the books I've got, two, three times apiece. Must be a treat for him to get some new stories. Sure is for me. You're a good storyteller."

I kept my eyes down, but I felt myself softening, losing my guard a bit. Like anyone inside these emotional bodies, I was a sucker for flattery.

"Everyone here thinks you hunted us out to turn us over to the Seekers."

The word sent a shock jolting through me. My jaw stiffened and my teeth cut my tongue. I tasted blood.

"What other reason could there be?" he went on, oblivious to my reaction or ignoring it. "But they're just trapped in fixed notions, I think. I'm the only one with questions. . . . I mean, what kind of a plan was that, to wander off into the desert without any way to get back?" He chuckled. "Wandering — guess that's your specialty, eh, Wanda?"

He leaned toward me and nudged me with one elbow. Wide with uncertainty, my eyes flickered to the floor, to his face, and back to the floor. He laughed again.

"That trek was just a few steps shy of a successful suicide, in my opinion. Definitely not a Seeker's MO, if you know what I mean. I've tried to reason it out. Use logic, right? So, if you didn't have backup, which I've seen no sign of, and you had no way to get back, then you must've had a different goal. You haven't been real talkative since you got here, 'cept with the kid just now, but I've listened to what you *have* said. Kind of seems to me like the reason you almost died out there was 'cause you were hell-bent on finding that kid and Jared."

I closed my eyes.

"Only why would *you* care?" Jeb asked, expecting no answer, just musing. "So, this is how I see it: either you're a really good actress — like a super-Seeker, some new breed, sneakier than the first — with some kind of a plan I can't figure out, or you're not acting. The first seems like a pretty complicated explanation for your behavior, then and now, and I don't buy it.

"But if you're not acting . . ."

He paused for a moment.

"Spent a lot of time watching your kind. I was always waiting for them to change, you know, when they didn't have to act like us anymore, because there was no one to act *for*. I kept on watching and waiting, but they just kept on actin' like humans. Staying with their bodies' families, going out for picnics in good weather, plantin' flowers and paintin' pictures and all the rest of it. I've been wondering if you all aren't turning sort of human. If we don't have some real influence, in the end."

He waited, giving me a chance to respond. I didn't.

"Saw something a few years ago that stuck with me. Old man and woman, well, the bodies of an old man and an old woman. Been together so long that the skin on their fingers grew in ridges around their wedding rings. They were holding hands, and he kissed her on her cheek, and she blushed under all those wrinkles. Occurred to me that you have all the same feelings we have, because you're really us, not just hands in a puppet."

"Yes," I whispered. "We have all the same feelings. Human feelings. Hope, and pain, and love."

"So, if you aren't acting . . . well, then I'd swear to it that you loved them both. *You* do. Wanda, not just Mel's body."

I put my head down on my arms. The gesture was tantamount to an admission, but I didn't care. I couldn't hold it up anymore.

"So that's you. But I wonder about my niece, too. What it was like for her, what it would be like for me. When they put somebody inside your head, are you just . . . gone? Erased? Like being dead? Or is it like being asleep? Are you aware of the outside control? Is it aware of you? Are you trapped there, screaming inside?"

I sat very still, trying to keep my face smooth.

"Plainly, your memories and behaviors, all that is left behind. But your consciousness . . . Seems like some people wouldn't go down without a fight. Hell, I know I would try to stay — never been one to take no for an answer, anyone will tell you that. I'm a fighter. All of us who are left are fighters. And, you know, I woulda pegged Mel for a fighter, too."

He didn't move his eyes from the ceiling, but I looked at the floor — stared at it, memorizing the patterns in the purple gray dust.

"Yeah, I've wondered about that a lot."

I could feel his eyes on me now, though my head was still down. I didn't move, except to breathe slowly in and out. It took a great deal of effort to keep that slow rhythm smooth. I had to swallow; the blood was still flowing in my mouth.

*Why did we ever think he was crazy?* Mel wondered. *He sees everything. He's a genius.*

*He's both.*

*Well, maybe this means we don't have to keep quiet anymore. He knows.* She was hopeful. She'd been very quiet lately, absent almost half the time. It wasn't as easy for her to concentrate when she was relatively happy. She'd won her big fight. She'd gotten us here. Her secrets were no longer in jeopardy; Jared and Jamie could never be betrayed by her memories.

With the fight taken out of her, it was harder for her to find the will to speak, even to me. I could see how the idea of discovery — of having the other humans recognize her existence — invigorated her.

*Jeb knows, yes. Does that really change anything?*

She thought about the way the other humans looked at Jeb. *Right.* She sighed. *But I think Jamie . . . well, he doesn't know or guess, but I think he feels the truth.*

*You might be right. I guess we'll see if that does him or us any good, in the end.*

Jeb could only manage to keep quiet for a few seconds, and then he was off again, interrupting us. "Pretty interesting stuff. Not as much *bang! bang!* as the movies I used to like. But still pretty interesting. I'd like to hear more about those spider thingies. I'm real curious . . . real curious, for sure."

I took a deep breath and raised my head. "What do you want to know?"

He smiled at me warmly, his eyes crinkling into half moons. "Three brains, right?"

I nodded.

"How many eyes?"

"Twelve — one at each juncture of the leg and the body. We didn't have lids, just a lot of fibers — like steel wool eyelashes — to protect them."

He nodded, his eyes bright. "Were they furry, like tarantulas?"

"No. Sort of . . . armored — scaled, like a reptile or a fish."

I slouched against the wall, settling myself in for a long conversation.

Jeb didn't disappoint on that count. I lost track of how many questions he asked me. He wanted details — the Spiders' looks, their behaviors, and how they'd handled Earth. He didn't flinch away from the invasion details; on the contrary, he almost seemed to enjoy that part more than the rest. His questions came fast on the heels of my answers, and his grins were frequent. When he was satisfied about the Spiders, hours later, he wanted to know more about the Flowers.

"You didn't half explain that one," he reminded me.

So I told him about that most beautiful and placid of planets. Almost every time I stopped to breathe, he interrupted me with a new question. He liked to guess the answers before I could speak and didn't seem to mind getting them wrong in the least.

"So did ya eat flies, like a Venus flytrap? I'll bet you did — or maybe something bigger, like a bird — like a pterodactyl!"

"No, we used sunlight for food, like most plants here."

"Well, that's not as much fun as my idea."

Sometimes I found myself laughing with him.

We were just moving on to the Dragons when Jamie showed up with dinner for three.

"Hi, Wanderer," he said, a little embarrassed.

"Hi, Jamie," I answered, a little shy, not sure if he would regret the closeness we'd shared. I was, after all, the bad guy.

But he sat down right next to me, between me and Jeb, crossing his legs and setting the food tray in the middle of our little conclave. I was starving, and parched from all the talking. I took a bowl of soup and downed it in a few gulps.

"Shoulda known you were just being polite in the mess hall today. Gotta speak up when you're hungry, Wanda. I'm no mind reader."

I didn't agree with that last part, but I was too busy chewing a mouthful of bread to answer.

"Wanda?" Jamie asked.

I nodded, letting him know that I didn't mind.

"Kinda suits her, doncha think?" Jeb was so proud of himself, I was surprised he didn't pat himself on the back, just for effect.

"Kinda, I guess," Jamie said. "Were you guys talking about dragons?"

"Yeah," Jeb told him enthusiastically, "but not the lizardy kind. They're all made up of jelly. They can fly, though . . . sort of. The air's thicker, sort of jelly, too. So it's almost like swimming. And they can breathe acid — that's about as good as fire, wouldn't you say?"

I let Jeb fill Jamie in on the details while I ate more than my share of food and drained a water bottle. When my mouth was free, Jeb started in with the questions again.

"Now, this acid . . ."

Jamie didn't ask questions the way Jeb did, and I was more careful about what I said with him there. However, this time Jeb never asked anything that might lead to a touchy subject, whether by coincidence or design, so my caution wasn't necessary.

The light slowly faded until the hallway was black. Then it was silver, a tiny, dim reflection from the moon that was just enough, as my eyes adjusted, to see the man and the boy beside me.

Jamie edged closer to me as the night wore on. I didn't realize that I was combing my fingers through his hair as I talked until I noticed Jeb staring at my hand.

I folded my arms across my body.

Finally, Jeb yawned a huge yawn that had me and Jamie doing the same.

"You tell a good story, Wanda," Jeb said when we were all done stretching.

"It's what I did . . . before. I was a teacher, at the university in San Diego. I taught history."

"A teacher!" Jeb repeated, excited. "Well, ain't that amazin'? There's something we could use around here. Mag's girl Sharon does the teaching for the three kids, but there's a lot she can't help with. She's most comfortable with math and the like. History, now —"

"I only taught *our* history," I interrupted. Waiting for him to take a breath wasn't going to work, it seemed. "I wouldn't be much help as a teacher here. I don't have any training."

"Your history is better than nothing. Things we human folks ought to know, seeing as we live in a more populated universe than we were aware of."

"But I wasn't a real teacher," I told him, desperate. Did he honestly think anyone wanted to hear my voice, let alone listen to my stories? "I was sort of an honorary professor, almost a guest lecturer. They only wanted me because . . . well, because of the story that goes along with my name."

"That's the next one I was going to ask for," Jeb said complacently. "We can talk about your teaching experience later. Now — why did they call you Wanderer? I've heard a bunch of odd ones, Dry Water, Fingers in the Sky, Falling Upward — all mixed in, of course, with the Pams and the Jims. I tell you, it's the kind of thing that can drive a man crazy with curiosity."

I waited till I was sure he was done to begin. "Well, the way it usually works is that a soul will try out a planet or two — two's the average — and then they'll settle in their favorite place. They just move to new hosts in the same species on the same planet when their body gets close to death. It's very disorienting moving from one kind of body to the next. Most souls really hate that. Some never move from the planet they are born on. Occasionally, someone has a hard time finding a good fit. They may try three planets. I met a soul once who'd been to five before he'd settled with the Bats. I liked it there — I suppose that's the closest I've ever come to choosing a planet. If it hadn't been for the blindness . . ."

"How many planets have you lived on?" Jamie asked in a hushed voice. Somehow, while I'd been talking, his hand had found its way into mine.

"This is my ninth," I told him, squeezing his fingers gently.

"Wow, nine!" he breathed.

"That's why they wanted me to teach. Anybody can tell them our statistics, but I have personal experience from most of the planets we've . . . taken." I hesitated at that word, but it didn't seem to bother Jamie. "There are only three I've never been to — well, now four. They just opened a new world."

I expected Jeb to jump in with questions about the new world, or the ones I'd skipped, but he just played absently with the ends of his beard.

"Why did you never stay anywhere?" Jamie asked.

"I never found a place I liked enough to stay."

"What about Earth? Do you think you'll stay here?"

I wanted to smile at his child's confidence — as if I were going to get the chance to ever move on to another host. As if I were going to get the chance to live out even another month in the one I had.

"Earth is . . . very interesting," I murmured. "It's harder than any place I've been before."

"Harder than the place with the frozen air and the claw beasts?" he asked.

"In its own way, yes." How could I explain that the Mists Planet only came at you from the outside — it was much more difficult to be attacked from within.

*Attacked,* Melanie scoffed.

I yawned. *I wasn't actually thinking of you,* I told her. *I was thinking of these unstable emotions, always betraying me. But you did attack me. Pushing your memories on me that way.*

*I learned my lesson,* she assured me dryly. I could feel

how intensely aware she was of the hand in mine. There was an emotion slowly building in her that I didn't recognize. Something on the edge of anger, with a hint of desire and a portion of despair.

*Jealousy,* she enlightened me.

Jeb yawned again. "I'm being downright rude, I guess. You must be bushed — walking all over today and then me keepin' you up half the night talking. Ought to be a better host. C'mon, Jamie, let's go and let Wanda get some sleep."

I was exhausted. It felt as if it had been a very long day, and, from Jeb's words, perhaps that wasn't in my imagination.

"Okay, Uncle Jeb." Jamie jumped lightly to his feet and then offered his hand to the old man.

"Thanks, kid." Jeb groaned as he got up. "And thanks to you, too," he added in my direction. "Most interesting conversation I've had in . . . well, probably forever. Rest your voice up, Wanda, because my curiosity is a powerful thing. Ah, there he is! 'Bout time."

Only then did I hear the sound of approaching footsteps. Automatically, I shrank against the wall and scooted farther back into the cave-room, and then felt more exposed because the moonlight was brighter inside.

I was surprised that this was the first person to turn in for the night; the corridor appeared to house many.

"Sorry, Jeb. I got to talking with Sharon, and then I sort of dozed off."

It was impossible not to recognize this easy, gentle voice. My stomach rolled, unstable, and I wished it were empty.

"We didn't even notice, Doc," Jeb said. "We were

having the time of our lives here. Someday you'll have to get her to tell you some of her stories — great stuff. Not tonight, though. She's got to be pretty worn out, I'd bet. We'll see you in the morning."

The doctor was spreading a mat out in front of the cave entrance, just as Jared had.

"Keep an eye on this," Jeb said, laying the gun beside the mat.

"Are you okay, Wanda?" Jamie asked. "You're shaking."

I hadn't realized it, but my whole body was quivering. I didn't answer him — my throat felt swollen shut.

"Now, now," Jeb said in a soothing voice. "I asked Doc if he minded taking a shift. You don't need to worry about anything. Doc's an honorable man."

The doctor smiled a sleepy smile. "I'm not going to hurt you . . . Wanda, is it? I promise. I'll just keep watch while you sleep."

I bit my lip, and the quivering didn't stop.

Jeb seemed to think everything was settled, though. "Night, Wanda. Night, Doc," he said as he started back down the hall.

Jamie hesitated, looking at me with a worried expression. "Doc's okay," he promised in a whisper.

"C'mon, boy, it's late!"

Jamie hurried off after Jeb.

I watched the doctor when they were gone, waiting for some change. Doc's relaxed expression didn't waver, though, and he didn't touch the gun. He stretched his long frame out on the mat, his calves and feet hanging off the end. Lying down, he looked much smaller, he was so rail thin.

"Good night," he murmured drowsily.

Of course I didn't answer. I watched him in the dull moonlight, timing the rise and fall of his chest by the sound of the pulse thudding in my ears. His breathing slowed and got deeper, and then he began to quietly snore.

It could have been an act, but even if it was, there wasn't much I could do about it. Silently, I crept deeper into the room, till I felt the edge of the mattress against my back. I'd promised myself that I would not disturb this place, but it probably wouldn't hurt anything if I just curled up on the foot of the bed. The floor was rough and so hard.

The sound of the doctor's soft snoring was comforting; even if it was put on to calm me, at least I knew exactly where he was in the darkness.

Live or die, I figured I might as well go ahead and sleep. I was dog tired, as Melanie would say. I let my eyes close. The mattress was softer than anything I'd touched since coming here. I relaxed, sinking in . . .

There was a low shuffling sound — it was inside the room with me. My eyes popped open, and I could see a shadow between the moonlit ceiling and me. Outside, the doctor's snores continued uninterrupted.

# CHAPTER 23

# *Confessed*

The shadow was huge and misshapen. It loomed over me, top-heavy, swinging closer to my face.

I think I meant to scream, but the sound got trapped in my throat, and all that came out was a breathless squeak.

"Shh, it's just me," Jamie whispered. Something bulky and roundish rolled from his shoulders and plopped softly to the floor. When it was gone I could see his true, lithe shadow against the moonlight.

I caught a few gasps of air, my hand clutching at my throat.

"Sorry," he whispered, sitting down on the edge of the mattress. "I guess that was pretty stupid. I was trying not to wake Doc — I didn't even think how I would scare you. You okay?" He patted my ankle, which was the part of me closest to him.

"Sure," I huffed, still breathless.

"Sorry," he muttered again.

"What are you doing here, Jamie? Shouldn't you be asleep?"

"That's why I'm here. Uncle Jeb was snoring like you wouldn't believe. I couldn't stand it anymore."

His answer didn't make sense to me. "Don't you usually sleep with Jeb?"

Jamie yawned and bent to untie the bulky bedroll he'd dropped to the floor. "No, I usually sleep with Jared. He doesn't snore. But you know that."

I did.

"Why don't you sleep in Jared's room, then? Are you afraid to sleep alone?" I wouldn't have blamed him for that. It seemed like I was constantly terrified here.

"Afraid," he grumbled, offended. "No. This *is* Jared's room. And mine."

"What?" I gasped. "Jeb put me in Jared's room?"

I couldn't believe it. Jared would kill me. No, he would kill Jeb first, and *then* he would kill me.

"It's my room, too. And I told Jeb you could have it."

"Jared will be furious," I whispered.

"I can do what I want with my room," Jamie muttered rebelliously, but then he bit his lip. "We won't tell him. He doesn't have to know."

I nodded. "Good idea."

"You don't mind if I sleep in here, do you? Uncle Jeb's really loud."

"No, *I* don't mind. But Jamie, I don't think you should."

He frowned, trying to be tough instead of hurt. "Why not?"

"Because it's not safe. Sometimes people come looking for me at night."

His eyes went wide. "They do?"

"Jared always had the gun — they went away."

"Who?"

"I don't know — Kyle sometimes. But there are surely others who are still here."

He nodded. "All the more reason why I should stay. Doc might need help."

"Jamie —"

"I'm not a kid, Wanda. I can take care of myself."

Obviously, arguing was only going to make him more stubborn. "At least take the bed," I said, surrendering. "I'll sleep on the floor. It's your room."

"That's not right. You're the guest."

I snorted quietly. "Ha. No, the bed is yours."

"No way." He lay down on the mat, folding his arms tightly across his chest.

Again, I saw that arguing was the wrong approach to take with Jamie. Well, this one I could rectify as soon as he was asleep. Jamie slept so deeply it was almost a coma. Melanie could carry him anywhere once he was out.

"You can use my pillow," he told me, patting the one next to the side where he lay. "You don't need to scrunch up at the bottom there."

I sighed but crawled to the top of the bed.

"That's right," he said approvingly. "Now, could you throw me Jared's?"

I hesitated, about to reach for the pillow under my head; he jumped up, leaned over me, and snatched the other pillow. I sighed again.

We lay in silence for a while, listening to the low whistle of the doctor's breathing.

"Doc has a nice snore, doesn't he?" Jamie whispered.

"It won't keep you up," I agreed.

"You tired?"

"Yeah."

"Oh."

I waited for him to say something more, but he was quiet.

"Was there something you wanted?" I asked.

He didn't answer right away, but I could feel him struggling, so I waited.

"If I asked you something, would you tell me the truth?"

It was my turn to hesitate. "I don't know everything," I hedged.

"You would know this. When we were walking . . . me and Jeb . . . he was telling me some things. Things he thought, but I don't know if he's right."

Melanie was suddenly very *there* in my head.

Jamie's whisper was hard to hear, quieter than my breathing. "Uncle Jeb thinks that Melanie might still be alive. Inside there with you, I mean."

*My Jamie.* Melanie sighed.

I said nothing to either of them.

"I didn't know that could happen. Does that happen?" His voice broke, and I could hear that he was fighting tears. He was not a boy to cry, and here I'd grieved him this deeply twice in one day. A pain pierced through the general region of my chest.

"Does it, Wanda?"

*Tell him. Please tell him that I love him.*

"Why won't you answer me?" Jamie was really crying now but trying to muffle the sound.

I crawled off the bed, squeezing into the hard space between the mattress and the mat, and threw my arm over his shaking chest. I leaned my head against his hair and felt his tears, warm on my neck.

"Is Melanie still alive, Wanda? Please?"

He was probably a tool. The old man could have sent him just for this; Jeb was smart enough to see how easily Jamie broke through my defenses. It was possible that Jeb was seeking confirmation for his theory, and he wasn't against using the boy to get it. What would Jeb do when he was certain of the dangerous truth? How would he use the information? I didn't think he meant me harm, but could I trust my own judgment? Humans were deceitful, treacherous creatures. I couldn't anticipate their darker agendas when such things were unthinkable to my species.

Jamie's body shook beside me.

*He's suffering,* Melanie cried. She battered ineffectually at my control.

But I couldn't blame this on Melanie if it turned out to be a huge mistake. I knew who was speaking now.

"She promised she would come back, didn't she?" I murmured. "Would Melanie break a promise to you?"

Jamie slid his arms around my waist and clung to me for a long time. After a few minutes, he whispered, "Love you, Mel."

"She loves you, too. She's so happy that you're here and safe."

He was silent long enough for the tears on my skin to dry, leaving a fine, salty dust behind.

"Is everybody like that?" Jamie whispered long after I thought he'd fallen asleep. "Does everybody stay?"

"No," I told him sadly. "No. Melanie is special."

"She's strong and brave."

"Very."

"Do you think . . ." He paused to sniff. "Do you think that maybe Dad is still there, too?"

I swallowed, trying to move the lump farther down my throat. It didn't work. "No, Jamie. No, I don't think so. Not like Melanie is."

"Why?"

"Because he brought the Seekers looking for you. Well, the soul inside him did. Your father wouldn't have let that happen if he were still there. Your sister never let me see where the cabin was — she didn't even let me know that you existed for the longest time. She didn't bring me here until she was sure that I wouldn't hurt you."

It was too much information. Only as I finished speaking did I realize that the doctor wasn't snoring anymore. I could hear no noise from his breathing. Stupid. I cursed myself internally.

"Wow," Jamie said.

I whispered into his ear, so close that there was no way the doctor could possibly overhear. "Yes, she's very strong."

Jamie strained to hear me, frowning, and then glanced at the opening to the dark hall. He must have realized the same thing I had, because he turned his face to my ear and whispered back softer than before. "Why would you do that? Not hurt us? Isn't that what you want?"

"No. I don't want to hurt you."

"Why?"

"Your sister and I have . . . spent a lot of time together. She shared you with me. And . . . I started to . . . to love you, too."

"And Jared, too?"

I gritted my teeth for a second, chagrined that he had made the connection so easily. "Of course I don't want anything to hurt Jared, either."

"He hates you," Jamie told me, plainly grieved by the fact.

"Yes. Everyone does." I sighed. "I can't blame them."

"Jeb doesn't. And I don't."

"You might, after you think about it more."

"But you weren't even here when they took over. You didn't pick my dad or my mom or Melanie. You were in outer space then, right?"

"Yes, but I am what I am, Jamie. I did what souls do. I've had many hosts before Melanie, and nothing's stopped me from . . . taking lives. Again and again. It's how I live."

"Does Melanie hate you?"

I thought for a minute. "Not as much as she used to."

*No. I don't hate you at all. Not anymore.*

"She says she doesn't hate me at all anymore," I murmured almost silently.

"How . . . how is she?"

"She's happy to be here. She's so happy to see you. She doesn't even care that they're going to kill us."

Jamie stiffened under my arm. "They can't! Not if Mel's still alive!"

*You've upset him,* Melanie complained. *You didn't have to say that.*

*It won't be any easier for him if he's unprepared.*

"They won't believe that, Jamie," I whispered. "They'll think I'm lying to trick you. They'll just want to kill me more if you tell them that. Only Seekers lie."

The word made him shudder.

"But you're not lying. I know it," he said after a moment.

I shrugged.

"I won't let them kill her."

His voice, though quiet as a breath, was fierce with determination. I was paralyzed at the thought of him becoming more involved with this situation, with me. I thought of the barbarians he lived with. Would his age protect him from them if he tried to protect me? I doubted it. My thoughts scrambled, searching for some way to dissuade him without triggering his stubbornness.

Jamie spoke before I could say anything; he was suddenly calm, as if the answer was plain in front of him. "Jared will think of something. He always does."

"Jared won't believe you, either. He'll be the angriest of them all."

"Even if he doesn't believe it, he'll protect her. Just in case."

"We'll see," I muttered. I'd find the perfect words later — the argument that would not sound like an argument.

Jamie was quiet, thinking. Eventually, his breathing got slower, and his mouth fell open. I waited until I was sure he was deeply under, and then I crawled over him and very carefully shifted him from the floor to the bed. He was heavier than before, but I managed. He didn't wake.

I put Jared's pillow back where it belonged, and then stretched out on the mat.

*Well,* I thought, *I just hurled myself out of the frying pan.* But I was too tired to care what this would mean tomorrow. Within seconds, I was unconscious.

When I woke, the crevices in the ceiling were bright with echoed sunlight, and someone was whistling.

The whistling stopped.

"Finally," Jeb muttered when my eyes fluttered.

I rolled onto my side so that I could look at him; as I moved, Jamie's hand slid from my arm. Sometime in the night he must have reached out to me — well, not to me, to his sister.

Jeb was leaning against the natural rock door frame, his arms folded across his chest. "Morning," he said. "Get enough sleep?"

I stretched, decided that I felt acceptably rested, and then nodded.

"Oh, don't give me the silent treatment again," he complained, scowling.

"Sorry," I murmured. "I slept well, thank you."

Jamie stirred at the sound of my voice.

"Wanda?" he asked.

I was ridiculously touched that it was my silly nick-name that he spoke on the edge of sleep.

"Yes?"

Jamie blinked and pulled his tangled hair out of his eyes. "Oh, hey, Uncle Jeb."

"My room not good enough for you, kid?"

"You snore real loud," Jamie said, and then yawned.

"Haven't I taught you anything?" Jeb asked him.

"Since when do you let a guest and a lady sleep on the floor?"

Jamie sat up suddenly, staring around, disoriented. He frowned.

"Don't upset him," I told Jeb. "He insisted on taking the mat. I moved him when he was asleep."

Jamie snorted. "Mel always used to do that, too."

I widened my eyes slightly at him, trying to convey a warning.

Jeb chuckled. I looked up at him, and he had that same pouncing-cat expression he'd had yesterday. The solved-puzzle expression. He walked over and kicked the edge of the mattress.

"You've already missed your morning class. Sharon's bound to be testy about that, so get a move on."

"Sharon is *always* testy," Jamie complained, but he got to his feet quickly.

"On your way, boy."

Jamie looked at me again, then he turned and disappeared into the hall.

"Now," Jeb said as soon as we were alone. "I think all this babysitting nonsense has gone on long enough. I'm a busy man. Everyone is busy here — too busy to sit around playin' guard. So today you're going to have to come along with me while I get my chores done."

I felt my mouth pop open.

He stared at me, no smile.

"Don't look so terrified," he grumbled. "You'll be fine." He patted his gun. "My house is no place for babies."

I couldn't argue with *that*. I took three quick, deep breaths, trying to steady my nerves. Blood pulsed so loudly in my ears that his voice seemed quiet in comparison when he spoke again.

"C'mon, Wanda. Day's wasting."

He turned and stomped out of the room.

I was frozen for a moment, and then I lurched out after him. He wasn't bluffing — he was already invisible around the first corner. I raced after him, horrified by the thought that I might run into someone else in this obviously inhabited wing. I caught up to him before he reached the big intersection of the tunnels. He didn't even look at me as I slowed beside him to match his pace.

"'Bout time that northeast field was planted. We'll have to work the soil first. Hope you don't mind getting your hands dirty. After we're done, I'll see that you get a chance to clean yourself up. You need it." He sniffed pointedly, then laughed.

I felt the back of my neck get hot, but I ignored the last part. "I don't mind getting my hands dirty," I murmured. As I recalled, the empty northeastern field was out of the way. Perhaps we would be able to work alone.

Once we got to the big plaza cave, we started passing humans. They all stared, infuriated, as usual. I was beginning to recognize most of them: the middle-aged woman with the long salt-and-pepper braid I had seen with the irrigation team yesterday. The short man with the round belly, thinning sandy hair, and ruddy cheeks had been with her. The athletic-looking woman with the caramel brown skin had been the one bent to tie her shoe the first time I'd come out here during the day. Another dark-skinned woman with thick lips and sleepy eyes had been in the kitchen, near the two black-haired children — perhaps she was their mother? Now we passed Maggie;

she glowered at Jeb and turned her face away from me. We passed a pale, sick-looking man with white hair whom I was sure I'd never seen before. Then we passed Ian.

"Hey, Jeb," he said cheerfully. "Whatcha up to?"

"Turning the soil in the east field," Jeb grunted.

"Want some help?"

"*Ought* to make yourself useful," Jeb muttered.

Ian took this as an assent and fell into step behind me. It gave me goose bumps, feeling his eyes on my back.

We passed a young man who couldn't have been many years older than Jamie — his dark hair stood up from his olive-toned forehead like steel wool.

"Hey, Wes," Ian greeted him.

Wes watched in silence as we passed. Ian laughed at his expression.

We passed Doc.

"Hey, Doc," Ian said.

"Ian." Doc nodded. In his hands was a big wad of dough. His shirt was covered with dark, coarse flour. "Morning, Jeb. Morning, Wanda."

"Morning," Jeb answered.

I nodded uneasily.

"See you 'round," Doc said, hurrying off with his burden.

"Wanda, huh?" Ian asked.

"My idea," Jeb told him. "Suits her, I think."

"Interesting" was all Ian said.

We finally made it to the northeastern field, where my hopes were dashed.

There were more people here than there had been in the passageways — five women and nine men. They all stopped what they were doing and scowled, naturally.

"Pay 'em no mind," Jeb murmured to me.

Jeb proceeded to follow his own advice; he went to a jumbled pile of tools against the closest wall, shoved his gun through the strap at his waist, and grabbed a pick and two shovels.

I felt exposed, having him so far away. Ian was just a step behind me — I could hear him breathing. The others in the room continued to glower, their tools still in their hands. I didn't miss the fact that the picks and hoes that were breaking the earth could easily be used to break a body. It seemed to me, in reading a few of their expressions, that I wasn't the only one with that idea.

Jeb came back and handed me a shovel. I gripped the smooth, worn wooden handle, feeling its weight. After seeing the bloodlust in the humans' eyes, it was hard not to think of it as a weapon. I didn't like the idea. I doubted I could raise it as one, even to block a blow.

Jeb gave Ian the pick. The sharp, blackened metal looked deadly in his hands. It took all my willpower not to skip out of range.

"Let's take the back corner."

At least Jeb took me to the least crowded spot in the long, sunny cave. He had Ian pulverize the hard-baked dirt ahead of us, while I flipped the clods over and he followed behind, crushing the chunks into usable soil with the edge of his shovel.

Watching the sweat run down Ian's fair skin — he'd removed his shirt after a few seconds in the dry scorch of the mirror light — and hearing Jeb's grunted breaths behind me, I could see that I had the easiest job. I wished I had something more difficult to do, something that would keep me from being distracted by the movements of the other humans. Their every motion had me cringing and flinching.

I couldn't do Ian's job — I didn't have the thick arm and back muscles needed to really chew into the hard soil. But I decided to do what I could of Jeb's, prechopping the clods into smaller bits before I moved on. It helped a little bit — kept my eyes busy and tired me out so that I had to concentrate on making myself work.

Ian brought us water now and then. There was a woman — short and fair, I'd seen her in the kitchen yesterday — who seemed to have the job of bringing water to the others, but she ignored us. Ian brought enough for three every time. I found his about-face in regard to me unsettling. Was he really no longer intent on my death? Or just looking for an opportunity? The water always tasted funny here — sulfurous and stale — but now that taste seemed suspicious. I tried to ignore the paranoia as much as possible.

I was working hard enough to keep my eyes busy and my mind numb; I didn't notice when we hit the end of the last row. I stopped only when Ian did. He stretched, pulling the pick overhead with two hands and popping his joints. I shied away from the raised pick, but he didn't see. I realized that everyone else had stopped, too. I looked at the fresh-turned dirt, even across the entire floor, and realized that the field was complete.

"Good work," Jeb announced in a loud voice to the group. "We'll seed and water tomorrow."

The room was filled with soft chatter and clanks as the tools were piled against the wall once more. Some of the talk was casual; some was still tense because of me. Ian held his hand out for my shovel, and I handed it to him, feeling my already low mood sink right to the floor. I had no doubt that I would be included in Jeb's "we." Tomorrow would be just as hard as today.

I looked at Jeb mournfully, and he was smiling in my direction. There was a smugness to his grin that made me believe he knew what I was thinking — not only did he guess my discomfort, but he was enjoying it.

He winked at me, my crazy friend. I realized again that this was the best to be expected from human friendship.

"See you tomorrow, Wanda," Ian called from across the room, and laughed to himself.

Everyone stared.

# CHAPTER 24

# *Tolerated*

It was true that I did not smell good.

I'd lost count of how many days I'd spent here — was it more than a week now? more than two? — and all of them sweating into the same clothes I'd worn on my disastrous desert trek. So much salt had dried into my cotton shirt that it was creased into rigid accordion wrinkles. It used to be pale yellow; now it was a splotchy, diseased-looking print in the same dark purple color as the cave floor. My short hair was crunchy and gritty; I could feel it standing out in wild tangles around my head, with a stiff crest on top, like a cockatoo's. I hadn't seen my face recently, but I imagined it in two shades of purple: cave-dirt purple and healing-bruise purple.

So I could understand Jeb's point — yes, I needed a bath. And a change of clothes as well, to make the bath worth the effort. Jeb offered me some of Jamie's clothes to wear while mine dried, but I didn't want to ruin Jamie's few things by stretching them. Thankfully, he didn't try to offer me anything of Jared's. I ended up with an old but clean flannel shirt of Jeb's that had the sleeves ripped off, and a pair of faded, holey cutoff sweatpants that had gone unclaimed for months. These were draped over my arm — and a bumpy mound of vile-smelling, loosely molded chunks that Jeb claimed was homemade cactus soap was in my hand — as I followed Jeb to the room with the two rivers.

Again we were not alone, and again I was miserably disappointed that this was the case. Three men and one woman — the salt-and-pepper braid — were filling buckets with water from the smaller stream. A loud splashing and laughing echoed from the bathing room.

"We'll just wait our turn," Jeb told me.

He leaned against the wall. I stood stiffly beside him, uncomfortably conscious of the four pairs of eyes on me, though I kept my own on the dark hot spring rushing by underneath the porous floor.

After a short wait, three women exited the bathing room, their wet hair dripping down the backs of their shirts — the athletic caramel-skinned woman, a young blonde I didn't remember seeing before, and Melanie's cousin Sharon. Their laughter stopped abruptly as soon as they caught sight of us.

"Afternoon, ladies," Jeb said, touching his forehead as if it were the brim of a hat.

"Jeb," the caramel woman acknowledged dryly.

Sharon and the other girl ignored us.

"Okay, Wanda," he said when they'd passed. "It's all yours."

I gave him a glum look, then made my way carefully into the black room.

I tried to remember how the floor went — I was sure I had a few feet before the edge of the water. I took off my shoes first, so that I could feel for the water with my toes.

It was just so dark. I remembered the inky appearance of the pool — ripe with suggestions of what might lurk beneath its opaque surface — and shuddered. But the longer I waited, the longer I would have to be here, so I put the clean clothes next to my shoes, kept the smelly soap, and shuffled forward carefully until I found the lip of the pool.

The water was cool compared to the steamy air of the outer cavern. It felt nice. That didn't keep me from being terrified, but I could still appreciate the sensation. It had been a long time since anything had been *cool*. Still fully dressed in my dirty clothes, I waded in waist deep. I could feel the stream's current swirl around my ankles, hugging the rock. I was glad the water was not stagnant — it would be upsetting to sully it, filthy as I was, if that were the case.

I crouched down into the ink until I was immersed to my shoulders. I ran the coarse soap over my clothes, thinking this would be the easiest way to make sure they were clean. Where the soap touched my skin, it burned mildly.

I took off the soapy clothes and scrubbed them under the water. Then I rinsed them again and again until there was no way any of my sweat or tears could have survived, wrung them out, and laid them on the floor beside where I thought my shoes were.

The soap burned more strongly against my bare skin, but the sting was bearable because it meant I could be clean again. When I was done lathering, my skin prickled everywhere and my scalp felt scalded. It seemed as if the places where the bruises had formed were more sensitive than the rest of me — they must still have been there. I was happy to put the acidic soap on the rock floor and rinse my body again and again, the way I had my clothes.

It was with a strange mingling of relief and regret that I sloshed my way out of the pool. The water was very pleasant, as was the feeling of clean, if prickling, skin. But I'd had quite enough of the blindness and the things I could imagine into the darkness. I felt around until I found the dry clothes, then I pulled them quickly on and shoved my water-wrinkled feet into my shoes. I carried my wet clothes in one hand and the soap gingerly between two fingers of the other.

Jeb laughed when I emerged; his eyes were on the soap in my cautious grasp.

"Smarts a bit, don't it? We're trying to fix that." He held out his hand, protected by the tail of his shirt, and I placed the soap in it.

I didn't answer his question because we weren't alone; there was a line waiting silently behind him — five people, all of them from the field turning.

Ian was first in line.

"You look better," he told me, but I couldn't tell from his tone if he was surprised or annoyed that I did.

He raised one arm, extending his long, pale fingers toward my neck. I flinched away, and he dropped his hand quickly.

"Sorry about that," he muttered.

Did he mean for scaring me now or for marking up my neck in the first place? I couldn't imagine that he was apologizing for trying to kill me. Surely he still wanted me dead. But I wasn't going to ask. I started walking, and Jeb fell into step behind me.

"So, today wasn't that bad," Jeb said as we walked through the dark corridor.

"Not that bad," I murmured. After all, I hadn't been murdered. That was always a plus.

"Tomorrow will be even better," he promised. "I always enjoy planting — seeing the miracle of the little dead-looking seeds having so much life in them. Makes me feel like a withered old guy might have some potential left in him. Even if it's only to be fertilizer." Jeb laughed at his joke.

When we got to the big garden cavern, Jeb took my elbow and steered me east rather than west.

"Don't try to tell me you're not hungry after all that digging," he said. "It's not my job to provide room service. You're just going to have to eat where everyone else eats."

I grimaced at the floor but let him lead me to the kitchen.

It was a good thing the food was exactly the same thing as always, because if, miraculously, a filet mignon or a bag of Cheetos had materialized, I wouldn't have been able to taste a thing. It took all my concentration just to make myself swallow — I hated to make even that small sound in the dead silence that followed my appearance. The kitchen wasn't crowded, just ten people lounging against the counters, eating their tough rolls and drinking their watery soup. But I killed all conversation again. I wondered how long things could last like this.

The answer was exactly four days.

It also took me that long to understand what Jeb was up to, what the motivation was behind his switch from the courteous host to the curmudgeonly taskmaster.

The day after turning the soil I spent seeding and irrigating the same field. It was a different group of people than the day before; I imagined there was some kind of rotation of the chores here. Maggie was in this group, and the caramel-skinned woman, but I didn't learn her name. Mostly everyone worked in silence. The silence felt unnatural — a protest against my presence.

Ian worked with us, when it was clearly not his turn, and this bothered me.

I had to eat in the kitchen again. Jamie was there, and he kept the room from total silence. I knew he was too sensitive not to notice the awkward hush, but he deliberately ignored it, seeming to pretend that he and Jeb and I were the only people in the room. He chattered about his day in Sharon's class, bragging a little about some trouble he'd gotten into for speaking out of turn, and complaining about the chores she'd given him as punishment. Jeb chastised him halfheartedly. They both did a very good job of acting normal. I had no acting ability. When Jamie asked me about my day, the best I could do was stare intently at my food and mumble one-word answers. This seemed to make him sad, but he didn't push me.

At night it was a different story — he wouldn't let me stop talking until I begged to be allowed to sleep. Jamie had reclaimed his room, taking Jared's side of the bed and insisting that I take his. This was very much as

Melanie remembered things, and she approved of the arrangement.

Jeb did, too. "Saves me the trouble of finding someone to play guard. Keep the gun close and don't forget it's there," he told Jamie.

I protested again, but both the man and the boy refused to listen to me. So Jamie slept with the gun on the other side of his body from me, and I fretted and had nightmares about it.

The third day of chores, I worked in the kitchen. Jeb taught me how to knead the coarse bread dough, how to lay it out in round lumps and let it rise, and, later on, how to feed the fire in the bottom of the big stone oven when it was dark enough to let the smoke out.

In the middle of the afternoon, Jeb left.

"I'm gonna get some more flour," he muttered, playing with the strap that held the gun to his waist.

The three silent women who kneaded alongside us didn't look up. I was up to my elbows in the sticky dough, but I started to scrape it off so I could follow him.

Jeb grinned, flashed a look at the unobserving women, and shook his head at me. Then he spun around and dashed out of the room before I could free myself.

I froze there, no longer breathing. I stared at the three women — the young blonde from the bathing room, the salt-and-pepper braid, and the heavy-lidded mother — waiting for them to realize that they could kill me now. No Jeb, no gun, my hands trapped in the gluey dough — nothing to stop them.

But the women kept on kneading and shaping, not seeming to realize this glaring truth. After a long, breathless moment, I started kneading again, too. My stillness would probably alert them to the situation sooner than if I kept working.

Jeb was gone for an eternity. Perhaps he had meant that he needed to *grind* more flour. That seemed like the only explanation for his endless absence.

"Took you long enough," the salt-and-pepper-braid woman said when he got back, so I knew it wasn't just my imagination.

Jeb dropped a heavy burlap sack to the floor with a deep thud. "That's a lot of flour there. You try carryin' it, Trudy."

Trudy snorted. "I imagine it took a lot of rest stops to get it this far."

Jeb grinned at her. "It sure did."

My heart, which had been thrumming like a bird's for the entire episode, settled into a less frantic rhythm.

The next day we were cleaning mirrors in the room that housed the cornfield. Jeb told me this was something they had to do routinely, as the combination of humidity and dust caked the mirrors until the light was too dim to feed the plants. It was Ian, working with us again, who scaled the rickety wooden ladder while Jeb and I tried to keep the base steady. It was a difficult task, given Ian's weight and the homemade ladder's poor balance. By the end of the day, my arms were limp and aching.

I didn't even notice until we were done and heading for the kitchen that the improvised holster Jeb always wore was empty.

I gasped out loud, my knees locking like a startled colt's. My body tottered to a halt.

"What's wrong, Wanda?" Jeb asked, too innocent.

I would have answered if Ian hadn't been right beside

him, watching my strange behavior with fascination in his vivid blue eyes.

So I just gave Jeb a wide-eyed look of mingled disbelief and reproach, and then slowly began walking beside him again, shaking my head. Jeb chuckled.

"What's that about?" Ian muttered to Jeb, as if I were deaf.

"Beats me," Jeb said; he lied as only a human could, smooth and guileless.

He was a good liar, and I began to wonder if leaving the gun behind today, and leaving me alone yesterday, and all this effort forcing me into human company was his way of getting me killed without doing the job himself. Was the friendship all in my head? Another lie?

This was my fourth day eating in the kitchen.

Jeb, Ian, and I walked into the long, hot room — into a crowd of humans chatting in low voices about the day's events — and nothing happened.

Nothing happened.

There was no sudden silence. No one paused to stare daggers at me. No one seemed to notice us at all.

Jeb steered me to an empty counter and then went to get enough bread for three. Ian lounged next to me, casually turning to the girl on his other side. It was the young blonde — he called her Paige.

"How are things going? How are you holding up with Andy gone?" he asked her.

"I'd be fine if I weren't so worried," she told him, biting her lip.

"He'll be home soon," Ian assured her. "Jared always brings everyone home. He's got a real talent. We've had no accidents, no problems since he showed up. Andy will be fine."

My interest sparked when he mentioned Jared — and Melanie, so somnolent these days, stirred — but Ian didn't say anything else. He just patted Paige's shoulder and turned to take his food from Jeb.

Jeb sat next to me and surveyed the room with a deep sense of satisfaction plain on his face. I looked around the room, too, trying to see what he saw. This must have been what it was usually like here, when I wasn't around. Only today I didn't seem to bother them. They must have been tired of letting me interrupt their lives.

"Things are settling down," Ian commented to Jeb.

"Knew they would. We're all reasonable folks here."

I frowned to myself.

"That's true, at the moment," Ian said, laughing. "My brother's not around."

"Exactly," Jeb agreed.

It was interesting to me that Ian counted himself among the reasonable folks. Had he noticed that Jeb was unarmed? I was burning with curiosity, but I couldn't risk pointing it out in case he hadn't.

The meal continued as it had begun. My novelty had apparently worn off.

When the meal was over, Jeb said I deserved a rest. He walked me all the way to my door, playing the gentleman again.

"Afternoon, Wanda," he said, tipping his imaginary hat.

I took a deep breath for bravery. "Jeb, wait."

"Yes?"

"Jeb . . ." I hesitated, trying to find a polite way to put

it. "I . . . well, maybe it's stupid of me, but I sort of thought we were friends."

I scrutinized his face, looking for any change that might indicate that he was about to lie to me. He only looked kind, but what did I know of a liar's tells?

"Of course we are, Wanda."

"Then why are you trying to get me killed?"

His furry brows pulled together in surprise. "Now, why would you think that, honey?"

I listed my evidence. "You didn't take the gun today. And yesterday you left me alone."

Jeb grinned. "I thought you hated that gun."

I waited for an answer.

"Wanda, if I wanted you dead, you wouldn't have lasted that first day."

"I know," I muttered, starting to feel embarrassed without understanding why. "That's why it's all so *confusing*."

Jeb laughed cheerfully. "No, I don't want you dead! That's the whole point, kid. I've been getting them all used to seeing you around, getting them to accept the situation without realizing it. It's like boiling a frog."

My forehead creased at the eccentric comparison.

Jeb explained. "If you throw a frog in a pot of boiling water, it will hop right out. But if you put that frog in a pot of tepid water and slowly warm it, the frog doesn't figure out what's going on until it's too late. Boiled frog. It's just a matter of working by slow degrees."

I thought about that for a second — remembered how the humans had ignored me at lunch today. Jeb had gotten them used to me. The realization made me feel strangely hopeful. Hope was a silly thing in my situation, but it seeped into me anyway, coloring my perceptions more brightly than before.

"Jeb?"

"Yeah?"

"Am I the frog or the water?"

He laughed. "I'll leave that one for you to puzzle over. Self-examination is good for the soul." He laughed again, louder this time, as he turned to leave. "No pun intended."

"Wait — can I ask one more?"

"Sure. I'd say it's your turn anyway, after all I've asked you."

"*Why* are you my friend, Jeb?"

He pursed his lips for a second, considering his answer.

"You know I'm a curious man," he began, and I nodded. "Well, I get to watch your souls a lot, but I never get to talk with 'em. I've had so many questions just piling up higher and higher. . . . Plus, I've always thought that if a person wants to, he can get along with just about anybody. I like putting my theories to the test. And see, here you are, one of the nicest gals I ever met. It's real interesting to have a soul as a friend, and it makes me feel super special that I've managed it."

He winked at me, bowed from the waist, and walked away.

◆

Just because I now understood Jeb's plan, it didn't make things easier when he escalated it.

He never took the gun anywhere anymore. I didn't know where it was, but.I was grateful that Jamie wasn't sleeping with it, at least. It made me a little nervous to have Jamie with me unprotected, but I decided he was actually in less danger without the gun. No one would feel the need to hurt him when he wasn't a threat. Besides, no one came looking for me anymore.

Jeb started sending me on little errands. Run back to the kitchen for another roll, he was still hungry. Go fetch a bucket of water, this corner of the field was dry. Pull Jamie out of his class, Jeb needed to speak with him. Were the spinach sprouts up yet? Go and check. Did I remember my way through the south caves? Jeb had a message for Doc.

Every time I had to carry out one of these simple directives, I was in a sweaty haze of fear. I concentrated on being invisible and walked as quickly as I could without running through the big rooms and the dark corridors. I tended to hug the walls and keep my eyes down. Occasionally, I would stop conversation the way I used to, but mostly I was ignored. The only time I felt in immediate danger of death was when I interrupted Sharon's class to get Jamie. The look Sharon gave me seemed designed to be followed by hostile action. But she let Jamie go with a nod after I choked out my whispered request, and when we were alone, he held my shaking hand and told me Sharon looked the same way at anyone who interrupted her class.

The very worst was the time I had to find Doc, because Ian insisted on showing me the way. I could have refused, I suppose, but Jeb didn't have a problem with the arrangement, and that meant Jeb trusted Ian not to kill me. I was far from comfortable with testing *that* theory, but it seemed the test was inevitable. If Jeb was wrong to trust Ian, then Ian would find his opportunity soon enough.

So I went with Ian through the long black southern tunnel as if it were a trial by fire.

I lived through the first half. Doc got his message. He seemed unsurprised to see Ian tagging along beside me. Perhaps it was my imagination, but I thought they exchanged a significant glance. I half expected them to strap me to one of Doc's gurneys at that point. These rooms continued to make me feel nauseated.

But Doc just thanked me and sent me on my way as if he were busy. I couldn't really tell what he was doing — he had several books open and stacks and stacks of papers that seemed to contain nothing but sketches.

On the way back, curiosity overcame my fear.

"Ian?" I asked, having a bit of difficulty saying the name for the first time.

"Yes?" He sounded surprised that I'd addressed him.

"Why haven't you killed me yet?"

He snorted. "That's direct."

"You could, you know. Jeb might be annoyed, but I don't think he'd shoot you." What was I saying? It sounded like I was trying to convince him. I bit my tongue.

"I know," he said, his tone complacent.

It was quiet for a moment, just the sounds of our footsteps echoing, low and muffled, from the tunnel walls.

"It doesn't seem fair," Ian finally said. "I've been thinking about it a lot, and I can't see how killing you would make anything right. It would be like executing a private for a general's war crimes. Now, I don't buy all of Jeb's crazy theories — it would be nice to believe, sure, but just because you want something to be true doesn't make it that way. Whether he's right or wrong, though, you don't appear to mean us any harm. I have to admit, you seem honestly fond of that boy. It's very strange to watch. Anyway, as long as you don't put us in danger, it seems . . . *cruel* to kill you. What's one more misfit in this place?"

I thought about the word *misfit* for a moment. It might have been the truest description of me I'd ever heard. Where had I ever fit in?

How strange that Ian, of all the humans, should have such a surprisingly gentle interior. I didn't realize that *cruelty* would seem a negative to him.

He waited in silence while I considered all this.

"If you don't want to kill me, then why did you come with me today?" I asked.

He paused again before answering.

"I'm not sure that . . ." He hesitated. "Jeb thinks things have calmed down, but I'm not completely sure about that. There're still a few people . . . Anyway, Doc and I have been trying to keep an eye on you when we can. Just in case. Sending you down the south tunnel seemed like pushing your luck, to me. But that's what Jeb does best — he pushes luck as far as it will go."

"You . . . you and Doc are trying to *protect* me?"

"Strange world, isn't it?"

It was a few seconds before I could answer.

"The strangest," I finally agreed.

# CHAPTER 25

# *Compelled*

Another week passed, maybe two — there seemed little point in keeping track of time here, where it was so irrelevant — and things only got stranger for me.

I worked with the humans every day, but not always with Jeb. Some days Ian was with me, some days Doc, and some days only Jamie. I weeded fields, kneaded bread, and scrubbed counters. I carried water, boiled onion soup, washed clothes in the far end of the black pool, and burned my hands making that acidic soap. Everyone did their part, and since I had no right to be here, I tried to work twice as hard as the others. I could not earn a place, I knew that, but I tried to make my presence as light a burden as possible.

I got to know a little about the humans around me, mostly just by listening to them. I learned their names, at least. The caramel-skinned woman was named Lily, and she was from Philadelphia. She had a dry sense of humor and got along well with everyone because she never got ruffled. The young man with the bristly black hair, Wes, stared at her a lot, but she never seemed to notice that. He was only nineteen, and he'd escaped from Eureka, Montana. The sleepy-eyed mother was named Lucina, and her two boys were Isaiah and Freedom — Freedom had been born right here in the caves, delivered by Doc. I didn't see much of these three; it seemed that the mother kept her children as separate from me as was possible in this limited space. The balding, red-cheeked man was Trudy's husband; his name was Geoffrey. They were often with another older man, Heath, who had been Geoffrey's best friend since early childhood; the three had escaped the invasion together. The pallid man with the white hair was Walter. He was sick, but Doc didn't know what was wrong with him — there was no way to find out, not without labs and tests, and even if Doc could diagnose the problem, he had no medicine to treat it. As the symptoms progressed, Doc was starting to think it was a form of cancer. This pained me — to watch someone actually *dying* from something so easily fixed. Walter tired easily but was always cheerful. The white-blond woman — her eyes contrastingly dark — who'd brought water to the others that first day in the field was Heidi. Travis, John, Stanley, Reid, Carol, Violetta, Ruth Ann . . . I knew all the names, at least. There were thirty-five humans in the colony, with six of them gone on the raid, Jared included. Twenty-nine humans in the caves now, and one mostly unwelcome alien.

I also learned more about my neighbors.

Ian and Kyle shared the cave on my hallway with the

two real doors propped over the entrance. Ian had begun bunking with Wes in another corridor in protest of my presence here, but he'd moved back after just two nights. The other nearby caves had also gone vacant for a while. Jeb told me the occupants were afraid of me, which made me laugh. Were twenty-nine rattlesnakes afraid of a lone field mouse?

Now Paige was back, next door, in the cave she shared with her partner, Andy, whose absence she mourned. Lily was with Heidi in the first cave, with the flowered sheets; Heath was in the second, with the duct-taped cardboard; and Trudy and Geoffrey were in the third, with a striped quilt. Reid and Violetta were one cave farther down the hall than mine, their privacy protected by a stained and threadbare oriental carpet.

The fourth cave in this corridor belonged to Doc and Sharon, and the fifth to Maggie, but none of these three had returned.

Doc and Sharon were partnered, and Maggie, in her rare moments of sarcastic humor, teased Sharon that it had taken the end of humanity for Sharon to find the perfect man: every mother wanted a doctor for her daughter.

Sharon was not the girl I'd seen in Melanie's memories. Was it the years of living alone with the dour Maggie that had changed her into a more brightly colored version of her mother? Though her relationship with Doc was newer to this world than I was, she showed none of the softening effects of new love.

I knew the duration of that relationship from Jamie — Sharon and Maggie rarely forgot when I was in a room with them, and their conversation was guarded. They were still the strongest opposition, the only people here whose ignoring me continued to feel aggressively hostile.

I'd asked Jamie how Sharon and Maggie had gotten here. Had they found Jeb on their own, beaten Jared and Jamie here? He seemed to understand the real question: had Melanie's last effort to find them been entirely a waste?

Jamie told me no. When Jared had showed him Melanie's last note, explained that she was gone — it took him a moment to be able to speak again after that word, and I could see in his face what this moment had done to them both — they'd gone to look for Sharon themselves. Maggie had held Jared at the point of an antique sword while he tried to explain; it had been a close thing.

It had not taken long with Maggie and Jared working together for them to decipher Jeb's riddle. The four of them had gotten to the caves before I'd moved from Chicago to San Diego.

When Jamie and I spoke of Melanie, it was not as difficult as it should have been. She was always a part of these conversations — soothing his pain, smoothing my awkwardness — though she had little to say. She rarely spoke to me anymore, and when she did it was muted; now and then I wasn't sure if I really heard her or just my own idea of what she might think. But she made an effort for Jamie. When I heard her, it was always with him. When she didn't speak, we both felt her there.

"Why is Melanie so quiet now?" Jamie asked me late one night. For once, he wasn't grilling me about Spiders and Fire-Tasters. We were both tired — it had been a long day pulling carrots. The small of my back was in knots.

"It's hard for her to talk. It takes so much more effort

than it takes you and me. She doesn't have anything she wants to say that badly."

"What does she *do* all the time?"

"She listens, I think. I guess I don't know."

"Can you hear her now?"

"No."

I yawned, and he was quiet. I thought he was asleep. I drifted in that direction, too.

"Do you think she'll go away? Really gone?" Jamie suddenly whispered. His voice caught on the last word.

I was not a liar, and I don't think I could have lied to Jamie if I were. I tried not to think about the implications of my feelings for him. Because what did it mean if the greatest love I'd ever felt in my nine lives, the first true sense of family, of maternal instinct, was for an alien life-form? I shoved the thought away.

"I don't know," I told him. And then, because it was true, I added, "I hope not."

"Do you like her like you like me? Did you used to hate her, like she hated you?"

"It's different than how I like you. And I never really hated her, not even in the beginning. I was very afraid of her, and I was angry that because of her I couldn't be like everyone else. But I've always, always admired strength, and Melanie is the strongest person I've ever known."

Jamie laughed. "*You* were afraid of *her?*"

"You don't think your sister can be scary? Remember the time you went too far up the canyon, and when you came home late she 'threw a raging hissy fit,' according to Jared?"

He chuckled at the memory. I was pleased, having distracted him from his painful question.

I was eager to keep the peace with all my new companions in any way I could. I thought I was willing to do anything, no matter how backbreaking or smelly, but it turned out I was wrong.

"So I was thinking," Jeb said to me one day, maybe two weeks after everyone had "calmed down."

I was beginning to hate those words from Jeb.

"Do you remember what I was saying about you maybe teaching a little here?"

My answer was curt. "Yes."

"Well, how 'bout it?"

I didn't have to think it through. "No."

My refusal sent an unexpected pang of guilt through me. I'd never refused a Calling before. It felt like a selfish thing to do. Obviously, though, this was not the same. The souls would have never asked me to do something so suicidal.

He frowned at me, scrunching his caterpillar eyebrows together. "Why not?"

"How do you think Sharon would like that?" I asked him in an even voice. It was just one example, but perhaps the most forceful.

He nodded, still frowning, acknowledging my point.

"It's for the greater good," he grumbled.

I snorted. "The greater good? Wouldn't that be shooting me?"

"Wanda, that's shortsighted," he said, arguing with me as if my answer had been a serious attempt at persuasion. "What we have here is a very unusual opportunity for learning. It would be wasteful to squander that."

"I really don't think anyone wants to learn from me. I don't mind talking to you or Jamie —"

"Doesn't matter what they want," Jeb insisted. "It's what's good for them. Like chocolate versus broccoli. Ought to know more about the universe — not to mention the new tenants of our planet."

"How does it help them, Jeb? Do you think I know something that could destroy the souls? Turn the tide? Jeb, it's over."

"It's not over while we're still here," he told me, grinning so I knew he was teasing me again. "I don't expect you to turn traitor and give us some super-weapon. I just think we should know more about the world we live in."

I flinched at the word *traitor*. "I couldn't give you a weapon if I wanted to, Jeb. We don't have some great weakness, an Achilles' heel. No archenemies out there in space who could come to your aid, no viruses that will wipe us out and leave you standing. Sorry."

"Don't sweat it." He made a fist and tapped it playfully against my arm. "You might be surprised, though. I told you it gets boring in here. People might want your stories more than you think."

I knew Jeb would not leave it alone. Was Jeb capable of conceding defeat? I doubted it.

At mealtimes I usually sat with Jeb and Jamie, if he was not in school or busy elsewhere. Ian always sat near, though not really with us. I could not fully accept the idea of his self-appointed role as my bodyguard. It seemed too good to be true and thus, by human philosophy, clearly false.

A few days after I'd refused Jeb's request to teach the humans "for their own good," Doc came to sit by me during the evening meal.

Sharon remained where she was, in the corner farthest

from my usual place. She was alone today, without her mother. She didn't turn to watch Doc walking toward me. Her vivid hair was wound into a high bun, so I could see that her neck was stiff, and her shoulders were hunched, tense and unhappy. It made me want to leave at once, before Doc could say whatever he meant to say to me, so that I could not be considered in collusion with him.

But Jamie was with me, and he took my hand when he saw the familiar panicked look come into my eyes. He was developing an uncanny ability to sense when I was turning skittish. I sighed and stayed where I was. It should probably have bothered me more that I was such a slave to this child's wishes.

"How are things?" Doc asked in a casual voice, sliding onto the counter next to me.

Ian, a few feet down from us, turned his body so it looked like he was part of the group.

I shrugged.

"We boiled soup today," Jamie announced. "My eyes are still stinging."

Doc held up a pair of bright red hands. "Soap."

Jamie laughed. "You win."

Doc gave a mocking bow from the waist, then turned to me. "Wanda, I had a question for you. . . ." He let the words trail off.

I raised my eyebrows.

"Well, I was wondering. . . . Of all the different planets you're familiar with, which species is physically the closest to humankind?"

I blinked. "Why?"

"Just good old-fashioned biological curiosity. I guess I've been thinking about your Healers. . . . Where do they get the knowledge to cure, rather than just treat symptoms, as you said?" Doc was speaking louder than necessary, his mild voice carrying farther than usual. Several people looked up — Trudy and Geoffrey, Lily, Walter . . .

I wrapped my arms tightly around myself, trying to take up less space. "Those are two different questions," I murmured.

Doc smiled and gestured with one hand for me to proceed.

Jamie squeezed my hand.

I sighed. "The Bears on the Mists Planet, probably."

"With the claw beasts?" Jamie whispered.

I nodded.

"How are they similar?" Doc prodded.

I rolled my eyes, feeling Jeb's direction in this, but continued. "They're close to mammals in many ways. Fur, warm-blooded. Their blood isn't exactly the same as yours, but it does essentially the same job. They have similar emotions, the same need for societal interaction and creative outlets —"

"Creative?" Doc leaned forward, fascinated — or feigning fascination. "How so?"

I looked at Jamie. "You know. Why don't you tell Doc?"

"I might get it wrong."

"You won't."

He looked at Doc, who nodded.

"Well, see, they have these awesome hands." Jamie was enthusiastic almost immediately. "Sort of double-jointed — they can curl both ways." He flexed his own fingers, as if trying to bend them backward. "One side is soft, like my palm, but the other side is like razors! They cut the ice — ice sculpting. They make cities that are all crystal castles that never melt! It's beautiful, isn't it, Wanda?" He turned to me for backup.

I nodded. "They see a different range of colors — the ice is full of rainbows. Their cities are a point of pride for them. They're always trying to make them more beautiful. I knew of one Bear who we called . . . well, something like Glitter Weaver, but it sounds better in that language, because of the way the ice seemed to know what he wanted and shaped itself into his dreams. I met him once and saw his creations. That's one of my most beautiful memories."

"They dream?" Ian asked quietly.

I smiled wryly. "Not as vividly as humans."

"How do your Healers get their knowledge about the physiology of a new species? They came to this planet prepared. I watched it start — watched the terminal patients walk out of the hospital whole. . . ." A frown etched a V-shaped crease into Doc's narrow forehead. He hated the invaders, like everyone, but unlike the others, he also envied them.

I didn't want to answer. Everyone was listening to us by this point, and this was no pretty fairytale about ice-sculpting Bears. This was the story of their defeat.

Doc waited, frowning.

"They . . . they take samples," I muttered.

Ian grinned in understanding. "Alien abductions."

I ignored him.

Doc pursed his lips. "Makes sense."

The silence in the room reminded me of my first time here.

"Where did your kind begin?" Doc asked. "Do you remember? I mean, as a species, do you know how you evolved?"

"The Origin," I answered, nodding. "We still live there. It's where I was . . . born."

"That's kind of special," Jamie added. "It's rare to meet someone from the Origin, isn't it? Most souls try to stay there, right, Wanda?" He didn't wait for my response. I was beginning to regret answering his questions so thoroughly each night. "So when someone moves on, it makes them almost . . . like a celebrity? Or like a member of a royal family."

I could feel my cheeks getting warm.

"It's a cool place," Jamie went on. "Lots of clouds, with a bunch of different-colored layers. It's the only planet where the souls can live outside of a host for very long. The hosts on the Origin planet are really pretty, too, with sort of wings and lots of tentacles and big silver eyes."

Doc was leaning forward with his face in his hands. "Do they remember how the host-parasite relationship was formed? How did the colonization begin?"

Jamie looked at me, shrugging.

"We were always that way," I answered slowly, still unwilling. "As far back as we were intelligent enough to know ourselves, at least. We were discovered by another species — the Vultures, we call them here, though more for their personalities than for their looks. They were . . . not kind. Then we discovered that we could bond with them just as we had with our original hosts. Once we controlled them, we made use of their technology. We took their planet first, and then followed them to the Dragon

Planet and the Summer World — lovely places where the Vultures had also not been kind. We started colonizing; our hosts reproduced so much slower than we did, and their life spans were short. We began exploring farther into the universe. . . ."

I trailed off, conscious of the many eyes on my face. Only Sharon continued to look away.

"You speak of it almost as if you were there," Ian noted quietly. "How long ago did this happen?"

"After dinosaurs lived here but before you did. I was not there, but I remember some of what my mother's mother's mother remembered of it."

"How old are *you?*" Ian asked, leaning toward me, his brilliant blue eyes penetrating.

"I don't know in Earth years."

"An estimate?" he pressed.

"Thousands of years, maybe." I shrugged. "I lose track of the years spent in hibernation."

Ian leaned back, stunned.

"Wow, that's old," Jamie breathed.

"But in a very real sense, I'm younger than you," I murmured to him. "Not even a year old. I feel like a child all the time."

Jamie's lips pulled up slightly at the corners. He liked the idea of being more mature than I was.

"What's the aging process for your kind?" Doc asked. "The natural life span?"

"We don't have one," I told him. "As long as we have a healthy host, we can live forever."

A low murmur — angry? frightened? disgusted? I couldn't tell — swirled around the edges of the cave. I saw that my answer had been unwise; I understood what these words would mean to them.

"Beautiful." The low, furious word came from Sharon's direction, but she hadn't turned.

Jamie squeezed my hand, seeing again in my eyes the desire to bolt. This time I gently pulled my hand free.

"I'm not hungry anymore," I whispered, though my bread sat barely touched on the counter beside me. I hopped down and, hugging the wall, made my escape.

Jamie followed right behind me. He caught up to me in the big garden plaza and handed me the remains of my bread.

"It was real interesting, honest," he told me. "I don't think anyone's too upset."

"Jeb put Doc up to this, didn't he?"

"You tell good stories. Once everyone knows that, they'll want to hear them. Just like me and Jeb."

"What if I don't *want* to tell them?"

Jamie frowned. "Well, I guess then . . . you shouldn't. But it seems like you don't mind telling me stories."

"That's different. You like me." I could have said, *You don't want to kill me,* but the implications would have upset him.

"Once people get to know you, they'll all like you. Ian and Doc do."

"Ian and Doc do not like me, Jamie. They're just morbidly curious."

"Do so."

"Ugh," I groaned. We were to our room by now. I shoved the screen aside and threw myself onto the mattress. Jamie sat down less forcefully beside me and looped his arms around his knees.

"Don't be mad," he pleaded. "Jeb means well."

I groaned again.

"It won't be so bad."

"Doc's going to do this every time I go in the kitchen, isn't he?"

Jamie nodded sheepishly. "Or Ian. Or Jeb."

"Or you."

"We all want to know."

I sighed and rolled onto my stomach. "Does Jeb have to get his way every single time?"

Jamie thought for a moment, then nodded. "Pretty much, yeah."

I took a big bite of bread. When I was done chewing, I said, "I think I'll eat in here from now on."

"Ian's going to ask you questions tomorrow when you're weeding the spinach. Jeb's not making him — he wants to."

"Well, that's wonderful."

"You're pretty good with sarcasm. I thought the parasites — I mean the souls — didn't like negative humor. Just the happy stuff."

"They'd learn pretty quick in here, kid."

Jamie laughed and then took my hand. "You don't hate it here, do you? You're not miserable, are you?"

His big chocolate-colored eyes were troubled.

I pressed his hand to my face. "I'm fine," I told him, and at that moment, it was entirely the truth.

# CHAPTER 26

*Returned*

Without ever actually agreeing to do it, I became the teacher Jeb wanted.

My "class" was informal. I answered questions every night after dinner. I found that as long as I was willing to do this, Ian and Doc and Jeb would leave me alone during the day so that I could concentrate on my chores. We always convened in the kitchen; I liked to help with the baking while I spoke. It gave me an excuse to pause before answering a difficult question, and somewhere to look when I didn't want to meet anyone's eyes. In my head, it seemed fitting; my words were sometimes upsetting, but my actions were always for their good.

I didn't want to admit that Jamie was right. Obviously, people didn't *like* me. They couldn't; I wasn't one of them. Jamie liked me, but that was just some strange chemical reaction that was far from rational. Jeb liked me, but Jeb was crazy. The rest of them didn't have either excuse.

No, they didn't like me. But things changed when I started talking.

The first time I noticed it was the morning after I answered Doc's questions at dinner; I was in the black bathing room, washing clothes with Trudy, Lily, and Jamie.

"Could you hand me the soap, please, Wanda?" Trudy asked from my left.

An electric current ran through my body at the sound of my name spoken by a female voice. Numbly, I passed her the soap and then rinsed the sting off my hand.

"Thank you," she added.

"You're welcome," I murmured. My voice cracked on the last syllable.

I passed Lily in the hall a day later on my way to find Jamie before dinner.

"Wanda," she said, nodding.

"Lily," I answered, my throat dry.

Soon it wasn't just Doc and Ian who asked questions at night. It surprised me who the most vocal were: exhausted Walter, his face a worrisome shade of gray, was endlessly interested in the Bats of the Singing World. Heath, usually silent, letting Trudy and Geoffrey talk for him, was outspoken during these evenings. He had some fascination with Fire World, and though it was one of my least favorite stories to tell, he peppered me with questions until he'd heard every detail I knew. Lily was concerned with the mechanics of things — she wanted to know about the ships that carried us from planet to planet, their pilots, their fuel. It was to Lily that I explained the cryotanks — something they had all seen but few understood the purpose of. Shy Wes, usually sitting close to Lily, asked not about other planets but about this one. How did it work? No money, no recompense for work — why did our souls' society not fall apart? I tried to explain that it was not so different from life in the caves. Did we not all work without money and share in the products of our labor equally?

"Yes," he interrupted me, shaking his head. "But it's different here — Jeb has a gun for the slackers."

Everyone looked at Jeb, who winked, and then they all laughed.

Jeb was in attendance about every other night. He didn't participate; he just sat thoughtfully in the back of the room, occasionally grinning.

He was right about the entertainment factor; oddly, for we all had legs, the situation reminded me of the See Weeds. There had been a special title for entertainers there, like *Comforter* or *Healer* or *Seeker*. I was one of the *Storytellers,* so the transition to a teacher here on Earth had not been such a change, profession-wise, at least. It was much the same in the kitchen after dark, with the smell of smoke and baking bread filling the room. Everyone was stuck here, as good as planted. My stories were something new, something to think about besides the usual — the same endlessly repeated sweaty chores, the same thirty-five faces, the same memories of other faces that brought the same grief with them, the same fear and the same despair that had long been familiar companions. And so the kitchen was always full for my casual lessons. Only Sharon and Maggie were conspicuously and consistently absent.

I was in about my fourth week as an informal teacher when life in the caves changed again.

The kitchen was crowded, as was usual. Jeb and Doc

were the only ones missing besides the normal two. On the counter next to me was a metal tray of dark, doughy rolls, swollen to twice the size they'd started at. They were ready for the oven, as soon as the current tray was done. Trudy checked every few minutes to make sure nothing was burning.

Often, I tried to get Jamie to talk for me when he knew the story well. I liked to watch the enthusiasm light up his face, and the way he used his hands to draw pictures in the air. Tonight, Heidi wanted to know more about the Dolphins, so I asked Jamie to answer her questions as well as he could.

The humans always spoke with sadness when they asked about our newest acquisition. They saw the Dolphins as mirrors of themselves in the first years of the occupation. Heidi's dark eyes, disconcerting underneath her fringe of white-blond hair, were tight with sympathy as she asked her questions.

"They look more like huge dragonflies than fish, right, Wanda?" Jamie almost always asked for corroboration, though he never waited for my answer. "They're all leathery, though, with three, four, or five sets of wings, depending on how old they are, right? So they kind of fly through the water — it's lighter than water here, less dense. They have five, seven, or nine legs, depending on which gender they are, right, Wanda? They have three different genders. They have really long hands with tough, strong fingers that can build all kinds of things. They make cities under the water out of hard plants that grow there, kind of like trees but not really. They aren't as far along as we are, right, Wanda? Because they've never made a spaceship or, like, telephones for communication. Humans were more advanced."

Trudy pulled out the tray of baked rolls, and I bent to shove the next tray of risen dough into the hot, smoking hole. It took a little jostling and balancing to get it in just right.

As I sweated in front of the fire, I heard some kind of commotion outside the kitchen, echoing down the hall from somewhere else in the caves. It was hard, with all the random sound reverberations and strange acoustics, to judge distances here.

"Hey!" Jamie shouted behind me, and I turned just in time to see the back of his head as he sprinted out the door.

I straightened out of my crouch and took a step after him, my instinct to follow.

"Wait," Ian said. "He'll be back. Tell us more about the Dolphins."

Ian was sitting on the counter beside the oven — a hot seat that I wouldn't have chosen — which made him close enough to reach out and touch my wrist. My arm flinched away from the unexpected contact, but I stayed where I was.

"What's going on out there?" I asked. I could still hear some kind of jabbering — I thought I could hear Jamie's excited voice in the mix.

Ian shrugged. "Who knows? Maybe Jeb . . ." He shrugged again, as if he wasn't interested enough to bother with figuring it out. Nonchalant, but there was a tension in his eyes I didn't understand.

I was sure I would find out soon enough, so I shrugged, too, and started explaining the incredibly complex famil-

ial relationships of the Dolphins while I helped Trudy
stack the warm bread in plastic containers.

"Six of the nine . . . grandparents, so to speak, traditionally stay with the larvae through their first stage of
development while the three parents work with *their* six
grandparents on a new wing of the family dwelling for the
young to inhabit when they are mobile," I was explaining,
my eyes on the rolls in my hands rather than my audience,
as usual, when I heard the gasp from the back of the room.
I continued with my next sentence automatically as I
scanned the crowd to see who I'd upset. "The remaining
three grandparents are customarily involved . . ."

No one was upset with me. Every head was turned in
the same direction I was looking. My eyes skipped across
the backs of their heads to the dark exit.

The first thing I saw was Jamie's slight figure, clinging to someone's arm. Someone so dirty, head to toe, that
he almost blended right in with the cave wall. Someone
too tall to be Jeb, and anyway, there was Jeb just behind
Jamie's shoulder. Even from this distance, I could see that
Jeb's eyes were narrowed and his nose wrinkled, as if he
were anxious — a rare emotion for Jeb. Just as I could see
that Jamie's face was bright with sheer joy.

"Here we go," Ian muttered beside me, his voice barely
audible above the crackle of the flames.

The dirty man Jamie was still clinging to took a step
forward. One of his hands rose slowly, like an involuntary
reflex, and curled into a fist.

From the dirty figure came Jared's voice — flat, perfectly devoid of any inflection. "What is the meaning of
this, Jeb?"

My throat closed. I tried to swallow and found the way

blocked. I tried to breathe and was not successful. My heart drummed unevenly.

*Jared!* Melanie's exultant voice was loud, a silent shriek of elation. She burst into radiant life inside my head. *Jared is home!*

"Wanda is teaching us all about the universe," Jamie babbled eagerly, somehow not catching on to Jared's fury — he was too excited to pay attention, maybe.

*"Wanda?"* Jared repeated in a low voice that was almost a snarl.

There were more dirty figures in the hall behind him. I only noticed them when they echoed his snarl with an outraged muttering.

A blond head rose from the frozen audience. Paige lurched to her feet. "Andy!" she cried, and stumbled through the figures seated around her. One of the dirty men stepped around Jared and caught her as she nearly fell over Wes. "Oh, Andy!" she sobbed, the tone of her voice reminding me of Melanie's.

Paige's outburst changed the atmosphere momentarily. The silent crowd began to murmur, most of them rising to their feet. The sound was one of welcome now, as the majority went to greet the returned travelers. I tried to read the strange expressions on their faces as they forced grins onto their lips and peeked furtively back at me. I realized after a long, slow second — time seemed to be congealing around me, freezing me into place — that the expression I wondered at was *guilt*.

"It's going to be okay, Wanda," Ian murmured under his breath.

I glanced at him wildly, searching for that same guilt

on his face. I didn't find it, only a defensive tightening around his vivid eyes as he stared at the newcomers.

"What the hell, people?" a new voice boomed.

Kyle — easily identifiable by his size despite the grime — was shoving his way around Jared and heading toward . . . me.

"You're letting it tell you its lies? Have you all gone crazy? Or did it lead the Seekers here? Are you *all* parasites now?"

Many heads fell forward, ashamed. Only a few kept their chins stiffly in the air, their shoulders squared: Lily, Trudy, Heath, Wes . . . and frail Walter, of all people.

"Easy, Kyle," Walter said in his feeble voice.

Kyle ignored him. He walked with deliberate steps toward me, his eyes, the same vibrant cobalt as his brother's, glowing with rage. I couldn't keep my eyes on him, though — they kept returning to Jared's dark shape, trying to read his camouflaged face.

Melanie's love flowed through me like a lake bursting through a dam, distracting me even more from the enraged barbarian closing the distance quickly.

Ian slid into my view, moving to place himself in front of me. I strained my neck to the side to keep my view of Jared clear.

"Things changed while you were gone, brother."

Kyle halted, face slack with disbelief. "Did the Seekers come, then, Ian?"

"She's not a danger to us."

Kyle ground his teeth together, and from the corner of my eye, I saw him reach for something in his pocket.

This captured my attention at last. I cringed, expecting

a weapon. The words stumbled off my tongue in a choked whisper. "Don't get in his way, Ian."

Ian didn't respond to my plea. I was surprised at the amount of anxiety this caused me, at how much I didn't want him hurt. It wasn't the instinctive protection, the bone-deep *need* to protect, that I felt for Jamie or even Jared. I just knew that Ian should not be harmed trying to protect me.

Kyle's hand came back up, and a light shone out of it. He pointed it at Ian's face, held it there for a moment. Ian didn't flinch from the light.

"So, what, then?" Kyle demanded, putting the flash-light back in his pocket. "You're not a parasite. How did it get to you?"

"Calm down, and we'll tell you all about it."

"No."

The contradiction did not come from Kyle but from behind him. I watched Jared walk slowly toward us through the silent spectators. As he got closer, Jamie still clinging to his hand with a bewildered expression, I could read his face better under the mask of dirt. Even Melanie, all but delirious with happiness at his safe return, could not misunderstand the expression of loathing there.

Jeb had wasted his efforts on the wrong people. It didn't matter that Trudy or Lily was speaking to me, that Ian would put himself between his brother and me, that Sharon and Maggie made no hostile move toward me. The only one who had to be convinced had now, finally, decided.

"I don't think anyone needs to calm down," Jared said through his teeth. "Jeb," he continued, not looking to see if the old man had followed him forward, "give me the gun."

The silence that followed his words was so tense I could feel the pressure inside my ears.

From the instant I could clearly see his face, I'd known it was over. I knew what I had to do now; Melanie was in agreement. As quietly as I could, I took a step to the side and slightly back, so that I would be clear of Ian. Then I closed my eyes.

"Don't happen to have it on me," Jeb drawled.

I peeked through narrowed eyes as Jared whirled to assess the truth of Jeb's claim.

Jared's breath whistled angrily through his nostrils. "Fine," he muttered. He took another step toward me. "It will be slower this way, though. It would be more humane if you were to find that gun fast."

"Please, Jared, let's talk," Ian said, planting his feet firmly as he spoke, already knowing the answer.

"I think there's been too much talk," Jared growled. "Jeb left this up to me, and I've made my decision."

Jeb cleared his throat noisily. Jared spun halfway around to look at him again.

"What?" he demanded. "You made the rule, Jeb."

"Well, now, that's true."

Jared turned back toward me. "Ian, get out of my way."

"Well, well, hold on a sec," Jeb went on. "If you recall, the rule was that whoever the body belonged to got to make the decision."

A vein in Jared's forehead pulsed visibly. "And?"

"Seems to me like there's someone here with a claim just as strong as yours. Mebbe stronger."

Jared stared straight ahead, processing this. After a slow moment, understanding furrowed his brow. He looked down at the boy still hanging on his arm.

All the joy had drained from Jamie's face, leaving it pale and horrorstruck.

"You can't, Jared," he choked. "You wouldn't. Wanda's good. She's my friend! And Mel! What about Mel? You can't kill Mel! Please! You have to —" He broke off, his expression agonized.

I closed my eyes again, trying to block the picture of the suffering boy from my mind. It was already almost impossible not to go to him. I locked my muscles in place, promising myself that it wouldn't help him if I moved now.

"So," Jeb said, his tone far too conversational for the moment, "you can see that Jamie's not in agreement. I figure he's got as much say as you do."

There was no answer for so long that I had to open my eyes again.

Jared was staring at Jamie's anguished, fearful face with his own kind of horror.

"How could you let this happen, Jeb?" he whispered.

"There *is* a need for some talk," Jeb answered. "Why don't you take a breather first, though? Maybe you'll feel more up to conversation after a bath."

Jared glared balefully at the old man, his eyes full of the shock and pain of the betrayed. I had only human comparisons for such a look. Caesar and Brutus, Jesus and Judas.

The unbearable tension lasted through another long minute, and then Jared shook Jamie's fingers off his arm.

"Kyle," Jared barked, turning and stalking out of the room.

Kyle gave his brother a parting grimace and followed.

The other dirty members of the expedition went after them silently, Paige tucked securely under Andy's arm.

Most of the other humans, all those who had hung their

heads in shame for admitting me into their society, shuffled out behind them. Only Jamie, Jeb, and Ian beside me, and Trudy, Geoffrey, Heath, Lily, Wes, and Walter stayed.

No one spoke until the echoes of their footsteps faded away into silence.

"Whew!" Ian breathed. "That was close. Nice thinking, Jeb."

"Inspiration in desperation. But we're not out of the woods yet," Jeb answered.

"Don't I know it! You didn't leave the gun anywhere obvious, did you?"

"Nope. I figured this might be comin' on soon."

"That's something, at least."

Jamie was trembling, alone in the space left by the exodus. Surrounded by those I had to count as friends, I felt able to walk to his side. He threw his arms around my waist, and I patted his back with shaky hands.

"It's okay," I lied in a whisper. "It's okay." I knew even a fool would hear the false note in my voice, and Jamie was not a fool.

"He won't hurt you," Jamie said thickly, struggling against the tears I could see in his eyes. "I won't let him."

"Shh," I murmured.

I was appalled — I could feel that my face was fixed in lines of horror. Jared was right — how *could* Jeb have let this happen? If they'd killed me the first day here, before Jamie had ever seen me . . . Or that first week, while Jared kept me isolated from everyone, before Jamie and I had become friends . . . Or if I had just kept my mouth shut about Melanie . . . It was too late for all that. My arms tightened around the child.

Melanie was just as aghast. *My poor baby.*

*I told you it was a bad idea to tell him everything,* I reminded her.

*What will it do to him now, when we die?*

*It's going to be terrible. He'll be traumatized and scarred and devastated —*

Melanie interrupted me. *Enough. I know, I know. But what can we do?*

*Not die, I suppose.*

Melanie and I thought about the likelihood of our survival and felt despair.

Ian thumped Jamie on the back — I could feel the motion reverberate through both our bodies.

"Don't agonize over it, kid," he said. "You're not in this alone."

"They're just shocked, that's all." I recognized Trudy's alto voice behind me. "Once we get a chance to explain, they'll see reason."

"See reason? Kyle?" someone hissed almost unintelligibly.

"We knew this was coming," Jeb muttered. "Just got to weather it. Storms pass."

"Maybe you ought to find that gun," Lily suggested calmly. "Tonight might be a long one. Wanda can stay with Heidi and me —"

"I think it might be better to keep her somewhere else," Ian disagreed. "Maybe in the southern tunnels? I'll keep an eye on her. Jeb, wanna lend me a hand?"

"They wouldn't look for her with me." Walter's offer was just a whisper.

Wes spoke over the last of Walter's words. "I'll tag along with you, Ian. There're six of them."

"No," I finally managed to choke out. "No. That's not

right. You shouldn't fight with each other. You all belong here. You belong together. Not fighting, not because of me."

I pulled Jamie's arms from around my waist, holding his wrists when he tried to stop me.

"I just need a minute to myself," I told him, ignoring all the stares I could feel on my face. "I need to be alone." I turned my head to find Jeb. "And you should have a chance to discuss this without me listening. It's not fair — having to discuss strategy in front of the enemy."

"Now, don't be like that," Jeb said.

"Let me have some time to think, Jeb."

I stepped away from Jamie, dropping his hands. A hand fell on my shoulder, and I cringed.

It was just Ian. "It's not a good idea for you to be wandering around by yourself."

I leaned toward him and tried to pitch my voice so low that Jamie wouldn't hear me clearly. "Why prolong the inevitable? Will it get easier or harder for him?"

I thought I knew the answer to my last question. I ducked under Ian's hand and broke into a run, sprinting for the exit.

"Wanda!" Jamie called after me.

Someone quickly shushed him. There were no footsteps behind me. They must have seen the wisdom of letting me go.

The hall was dark and deserted. If I was lucky, I'd be able to cut around the edge of the big garden plaza in the dark with no one the wiser.

In all my time here, the one thing I'd never found was the way out. It seemed as if I'd been down every tunnel time and again, and I'd never seen an opening I hadn't

eventually explored in search of one thing or another. I
thought about it now as I crept through the deepest shadowed corners of the big cave. Where could the exit be?
And I thought about this: if I could figure that puzzle out,
would I be able to leave?

I couldn't think of anything worth leaving for — certainly not the desert waiting outside, but also not the
Seeker, not the Healer, not my Comforter, not my life before, which had left such a shallow impression on me. Everything that really mattered was with me here. Jamie.
Though he would kill me, Jared. I couldn't imagine walking away from either of them.

And Jeb. Ian. I had friends now. Doc, Trudy, Lily,
Wes, Walter, Heath. Strange humans who could overlook
what I was and see something they didn't have to kill.
Maybe it was just curiosity, but regardless of that, they
were willing to side with me against the rest of their tight-
knit family of survivors. I shook my head in wonder as I
traced the rough rock with my hands.

I could hear others in the cavern, on the far side from
me. I didn't pause; they could not see me here, and I'd just
found the crevice I was looking for.

After all, there was really only one place for me to go.
Even if I could somehow have guessed the way to escape,
I would still have gone this way. I crept into the blackest
darkness imaginable and hurried along my way.

# CHAPTER 27

# Undecided

I felt my way back to my prison hole.

It had been weeks and weeks since I'd been down this particular corridor; I hadn't been back since the morning after Jared had left and Jeb had set me free. It seemed to me that while I lived and Jared was in the caves, this must be where I belonged.

There was no dim light to greet me now. I was fairly sure I was in the last leg — the turns and twists were still vaguely familiar. I let my left hand drag against the wall as low as I could reach, feeling for the opening as I crept forward. I wasn't decided on crawling back *inside* the cramped hole, but at least it would give me a reference point, letting me know that I was where I meant to be.

As it happened, I didn't have the option of inhabiting my cell again.

In the same moment that my fingers brushed the rough

edge at the top of the hole, my foot hit an obstacle and I stumbled, falling to my knees. I threw my hands out to catch myself, and they landed with a crunch and a crackle, breaking through something that wasn't rock and didn't belong here.

The sound startled me; the unexpected object frightened me. Perhaps I'd made a wrong turn and wasn't anywhere near my hole. Perhaps I was in someone's living space. I ran through the memory of my recent journey in my head, wondering how I could have gotten so turned about. Meanwhile, I listened for some reaction to my crashing fall, holding absolutely still in the darkness.

There was nothing — no reaction, no sound. It was only dark and stuffy and humid, as it always was, and so silent that I knew I must be alone.

Carefully, trying to make as little noise as possible, I took stock of my surroundings.

My hands were stuck in something. I pulled them free, tracing the contours of what felt like a cardboard box — a cardboard box with a sheet of thin, crackly plastic on top that my hands had fallen through. I felt around inside the box and found a layer of more crackly plastic — small rectangles that made a lot of noise when I handled them. I retreated quickly, afraid of drawing attention to myself.

I remembered that I'd thought I'd found the top of the hole. I searched to my left and found more stacks of cardboard squares on that side. I tried to find the top of the stack and had to stand in order to do so — it was as high as my head. I searched until I found the wall, and then the hole, exactly where I'd thought it was. I tried to climb in to ascertain if it really was the same place — one second on that bowed floor and I would know it for certain — but

I could not get any farther than the opening. It, too, was crammed full of boxes.

Stymied, I explored with my hands, moving back out into the hall. I found I could go no deeper down the passageway; it was entirely filled with the mysterious cardboard squares.

As I hunted along the floor, trying to understand, I found something different from the crowd of boxes. It was rough fabric, like burlap, a sack full of something heavy that shifted with a quiet hissing sound when I nudged it. I kneaded the sack with my hands, less alarmed by the low hiss than by the plastic crackle — it seemed unlikely that this sound would alert anyone to my presence.

Suddenly, it all came clear. It was the smell that did it. As I played with the sand-like material inside the bag, I got an unexpected whiff of a familiar scent. It took me back to my bare kitchen in San Diego, to the low cupboard on the left side of the sink. In my head I could see so clearly the bag of uncooked rice, the plastic measuring cup I used to dole it out, the rows of canned food behind it . . .

Once I realized that I was touching a bag of rice, I understood. I *was* in the right place after all. Hadn't Jeb said they used this place for storage? And hadn't Jared just returned from a long raid? Now everything the raiders had stolen in the weeks they'd been gone was dumped in this out-of-the-way place until it could be used.

Many thoughts ran through my head at once.

First, I realized that I was surrounded by food. Not just rough bread and weak onion soup, but *food*. Somewhere in this stack, there could be peanut butter. Chocolate chip cookies. Potato chips. *Cheetos.*

Even as I imagined finding these things, tasting them again, being full for the first time since I'd left civilization, I felt guilty for thinking of it. Jared hadn't risked his life and spent weeks hiding and stealing to feed *me.* This food was for others.

I also worried that perhaps this wasn't the entire haul. What if they had more boxes to stow? Would Jared and Kyle be the ones to bring them? It didn't take any imagination at all to picture the scene that would result if they found me here.

But wasn't that why I was here? Wasn't that exactly what I'd needed to be alone to think about?

I slouched against the wall. The rice bag made a decent pillow. I closed my eyes — unnecessary in the inky darkness — and settled in for a consultation.

*Okay, Mel. What now?*

I was glad to find that she was still awake and alert. Opposition brought out her strength. It was only when things were going well that she drifted away.

*Priorities,* she decided. *What's most important to us? Staying alive? Or Jamie?*

She knew the answer. *Jamie,* I affirmed, sighing out loud. The sound of my breath whispered back from the black walls.

*Agreed. We could probably last awhile if we let Jeb and Ian protect us. Will that help him?*

*Maybe. Would he be more hurt if we just gave up? Or if we let this drag on, only to have it end badly, which seems inevitable?*

She didn't like that. I could feel her scrambling around, searching for alternatives.

*Try to escape?* I suggested.

*Unlikely,* she decided. *Besides, what would we do out there? What would we tell* them?

We imagined it together — how would I explain my months of absence? I could lie, make up some alternative story, or say I didn't remember. But I thought of the Seeker's skeptical face, her bulging eyes bright with suspicion, and knew my inept attempts at subterfuge would fail.

*They'd think I took over,* Melanie agreed. *Then they'd take you out and put* her *in.*

I squirmed, as if a new position on the rock floor would take me further away from the idea, and shuddered. Then I followed the thought to its conclusion. *She'd tell them about this place, and the Seekers would come.*

The horror washed through us.

*Right,* I continued. *So escape is out.*

*Right,* she whispered, emotion making her thought unstable.

*So the decision is . . . quick or slow. Which hurts him less?*

It seemed that as long as I focused on practicalities I could keep at least my side of the discussion numbly businesslike. Melanie tried to mimic my effort.

*I'm not sure. On the one hand, logically, the longer the three of us are together, the harder our . . . separation would be for him. Then again, if we didn't fight, if we just gave up . . . he wouldn't like that. He'd feel betrayed by us.*

I looked at both sides she'd presented, trying to be rational about it.

*So . . . quick, but we have to do our best not to die?*

*Go down fighting,* she affirmed grimly.

*Fighting. Fabulous.* I tried to imagine that — meeting violence with violence. Raising my hand to strike someone. I could form the words but not the mental picture.

*You can do it,* she encouraged. *I'll help you.*

*Thanks, but no thanks. There has to be some other way.*

*I don't get you, Wanda. You've given up on your species entirely, you're ready to die for my brother, you're in love with the man I love who is going to kill us, and yet you won't let go of customs that are entirely impractical here.*

*I am who I am, Mel. I can't change that, though everything else may change. You hold on to yourself; allow me to do the same.*

*But if we're going to —*

She would have continued to argue with me, but we were interrupted. A scuffing sound, shoe against rock, echoed from somewhere back down the corridor.

I froze — every function of my body arrested but my heart, and even that faltered jaggedly — and listened. I didn't have long to hope that I'd just imagined the sound. Within seconds, I could hear more quiet footsteps coming this way.

Melanie kept her cool, whereas I was lost to panic.

*Get on your feet,* she ordered.

*Why?*

*You won't fight, but you can run. You have to try something — for Jamie.*

I started breathing again, keeping it quiet and shallow. Slowly, I rolled forward till I was on the balls of my feet.

Adrenaline coursed through my muscles, making them tingle and flex. I would be faster than most who would try to catch me, but where would I run to?

"Wanda?" someone whispered quietly. "Wanda? Are you here? It's me."

His voice broke, and I knew him.

"Jamie!" I rasped. "What are you doing? I told you I needed to be alone."

Relief was plain in his voice, which he now raised from the whisper. "Everybody is looking for you. Well, you know, Trudy and Lily and Wes — *that* everybody. Only we're not supposed to let anyone know that's what we're doing. No one is supposed to guess that you're missing. Jeb's got his gun again. Ian's with Doc. When Doc's free, he'll talk to Jared and Kyle. Everybody listens to Doc. So you don't have to hide. Everybody's busy, and you're probably tired. . . ."

As Jamie explained, he continued forward until his fingers found my arm, and then my hand.

"I'm not really *hiding,* Jamie. I told you I had to think."

"You could think with Jeb there, right?"

"Where do you want me to go? Back to Jared's room? This is where I'm supposed to be."

"Not anymore." The familiar stubborn edge entered his voice.

"Why is everyone so busy?" I asked to distract him. "What's Doc doing?"

My attempt was unsuccessful; he didn't answer.

After a minute of silence, I touched his cheek. "Look, you should be with Jeb. Tell the others to stop looking for me. I'll just hang out here for a while."

"You can't sleep here."

"I have before."

I felt his head shake in my hand.

"I'll go get mats and pillows, at least."

"I don't need more than one."

"I'm not staying with Jared while he's being such a jerk."

I groaned internally. "Then you stay with Jeb and his snores. You belong with them, not with me."

"I belong wherever I want to be."

The threat of Kyle finding me here was heavy on my mind. But that argument would only make Jamie feel responsible for protecting me.

"Fine, but you have to get Jeb's permission."

"Later. I'm not going to bug Jeb tonight."

"What is Jeb doing?"

Jamie didn't answer. It was only at that point I realized he had deliberately not answered my question the first time. There was something he didn't want to tell me. Maybe the others were busy trying to find me, too. Maybe Jared's homecoming had returned them to their original opinion about me. It had seemed that way in the kitchen, when they'd hung their heads and eyed me with furtive guilt.

"What's going on, Jamie?" I pressed.

"I'm not supposed to tell you," he muttered. "And I'm not going to." His arms wrapped tightly around my waist, and his face pressed against my shoulder. "Everything is going to be all right," he promised me, his voice thick.

I patted his back and ran my fingers through his tangled mane. "Okay," I said, agreeing to accept his silence. After all, I had my secrets, too, didn't I? "Don't be upset,

Jamie. Whatever it is, it will all work out for the best. You're going to be fine." As I said the words, I willed them to be true.

"I don't know what to hope for," he whispered.

As I stared into the dark at nothing in particular, trying to understand what he wouldn't say, a faint glow caught my eye at the far end of the hallway — dim but conspicuous in the black cave.

"Shhh," I breathed. "Someone is coming. Quick, hide behind the boxes."

Jamie's head snapped up, toward the yellow light that was getting brighter by the second. I listened for the accompanying footsteps but heard nothing.

"I'm not going to hide," he breathed. "Get behind me, Wanda."

"No!"

"Jamie!" Jared shouted. "I know you're back here!"

My legs felt hollow, numb. Did it have to be Jared? It would be so much easier for Jamie if Kyle were the one to kill me.

"Go away!" Jamie shouted back.

The yellow light sped up and turned into a circle on the far wall.

Jared stalked around the corner, the flashlight in his hand sweeping back and forth across the rock floor. He was clean again, wearing a faded red shirt I recognized — it had hung in the room where I'd lived for weeks and so was a familiar sight. His face was also familiar — it wore exactly the same expression it had since the first moment I'd shown up here.

The beam of the flashlight hit my face and blinded me; I knew the light reflected brilliantly off the silver behind my eyes, because I felt Jamie jump — just a little start, and then he set himself more firmly than before.

"Get away from it!" Jared roared.

"Shut up!" Jamie yelled back. "You don't know her! Leave her alone!"

He clung to me while I tried to unlock his hands.

Jared came on like a charging bull. He grabbed the back of Jamie's shirt with one hand and yanked him away from me. He held on to his handful of fabric, shaking the boy while he yelled.

"You're being an idiot! Can't you see how it's using you?"

Instinctively, I shoved myself into the tight space between them. As I'd intended, my advance made him drop Jamie. I didn't want or need what else happened — the way his familiar smell assaulted my senses, the way the contours of his chest felt under my hands.

"Leave Jamie alone," I said, wishing for once that I could be more like Melanie wanted me to be — that my hands could be hard now, that my voice could be strong.

He snatched my wrists in one hand and used this leverage to hurl me away from him, into the wall. The impact caught me by surprise, knocked the breath out of me. I rebounded off the stone wall to the floor, landing in the boxes again, making another crinkly crash as I shredded through more cellophane.

The pulse thudded in my head as I lay awkwardly bent over the boxes, and for a moment, I saw strange lights pass in front of my eyes.

"Coward!" Jamie screamed at Jared. "She wouldn't hurt you to save her own life! Why can't you leave her alone?"

I heard the boxes shifting and felt Jamie's hands on my arm. "Wanda? Are you okay, Wanda?"

"Fine," I huffed, ignoring the throbbing in my head. I could see his anxious face hovering over me in the glow of the flashlight, which Jared must have dropped. "You should go now, Jamie," I whispered. "Run."

Jamie shook his head fiercely.

"Stay *away* from it!" Jared bellowed.

I watched as Jared grabbed Jamie's shoulders and yanked the boy up from his crouch. The boxes this displaced fell me like a small avalanche. I rolled away, covering my head with my arms. A heavy one caught me right between the shoulder blades, and I cried out in pain.

"Stop hurting her!" Jamie howled.

There was a sharp crack, and someone gasped.

I struggled to pull myself out from under the heavy carton, rising up on my elbows dizzily.

Jared had one hand over his nose, and something dark was oozing down over his lips. His eyes were wide with surprise. Jamie stood in front of him with both hands clenched into fists, a furious scowl on his face.

Jamie's scowl melted slowly while Jared stared at him in shock. Hurt took its place — hurt and a betrayal so deep that it rivaled Jared's expression in the kitchen.

"You aren't the man I thought you were," Jamie whispered. He looked at Jared as though Jared were very far away, as if there were a wall between them and Jamie was utterly isolated on his side.

Jamie's eyes started to swim, and he turned his head, ashamed of showing weakness in front of Jared. He walked away with quick, jerky movements.

*We tried,* Melanie thought sadly. Her heart ached after the child, even as she longed for me to return my eyes to the man. I gave her what she wanted.

Jared wasn't looking at me. He was staring at the blackness into which Jamie had disappeared, his hand still covering his nose.

"Aw, *damn it!*" he suddenly shouted. "Jamie! Get back here!"

There was no answer.

Jared threw one bleak glance in my direction — I cringed away, though his fury seemed to have faded — then scooped up the flashlight and stomped after Jamie, kicking a box out of his way.

"I'm sorry, okay? Don't cry, kid!" He called out more angry apologies as he turned the corner and left me lying in the darkness.

For a long moment, it was all I could do to breathe. I concentrated on the air flowing in, then out, then in. After I felt I had that part mastered, I worked on getting up off the floor. It took a few seconds to remember how to move my legs, and even then they were shaky and threatened to collapse under me, so I sat against the wall again, sliding over till I found my rice-filled pillow. I slumped there and took stock of my condition.

Nothing was broken — except maybe Jared's nose. I shook my head slowly. Jamie and Jared should not be fighting. I was causing them so much turmoil and unhappiness. I sighed and went back to my assessment. There was a vast sore spot in the center of my back, and the side of my face felt raw and moist where it had hit the wall. It stung when I touched it and left warm fluid on my fingers.

That was the worst of it, though. The other bruises and scrapes were mild.

As I realized that, I was unexpectedly overwhelmed by relief.

I was alive. Jared had had his chance to kill me and he had not used it. He'd gone after Jamie instead, to make things right between them. So whatever damage I was doing to their relationship, it was probably not irreparable.

It had been a long day — the day had already been long even before Jared and the others had shown up, and that seemed like eons ago. I closed my eyes where I was and fell asleep on the rice.

# CHAPTER 28

# *Unenlightened*

It was disorienting to wake in the absolute dark. In the past months, I'd gotten used to having the sun tell me it was morning. At first I thought it must still be night, but then, feeling the sting of my face and the ache of my back, I remembered where I was.

Beside me, I could hear the sound of quiet, even breathing; it did not frighten me, because it was the most familiar of sounds here. I was not surprised that Jamie had crept back and slept beside me last night.

Maybe it was the change in my breathing that woke him; maybe it was just that our schedules had become synchronized. But seconds after I was conscious, he gave a little gasp.

"Wanda?" he whispered.

"I'm right here."

He sighed in relief.

"It's really dark here," he said.

"Yes."

"You think it's breakfast time yet?"

"I don't know."

"I'm hungry. Let's go see."

I didn't answer him.

He interpreted my silence correctly, as the balk it was. "You don't have to hide out here, Wanda," he said earnestly, after waiting a moment for me to speak. "I talked to Jared last night. He's going to stop picking on you — he promised."

I almost smiled. Picking on me.

"Will you come with me?" Jamie pressed. His hand found mine.

"Is that what you really want me to do?" I asked in a low voice.

"Yes. Everything will be the same as it was before."

*Mel? Is this best?*

*I don't know.* She was torn. She knew she couldn't be objective; she wanted to see Jared.

*That's crazy, you know.*

*Not as crazy as the fact that you want to see him, too.*

"Fine, Jamie," I agreed. "But don't get upset when it's not the same as before, okay? If things get ugly . . . Well, just don't be surprised."

"It'll be okay. You'll see."

I let him lead the way out of the dark, towing me by the hand he still held. I braced myself as we entered the big garden cavern; I couldn't be sure of anyone's reaction to me today. Who knew what had been said as I slept?

But the garden was empty, though the sun was bright

in the morning sky. It reflected off the hundreds of mirrors, momentarily blinding me.

Jamie was not interested in the vacant cave. His eyes were on my face, and he sucked in a sharp breath through his teeth as the light touched my cheek.

"Oh," he gasped. "Are you okay? Does that hurt bad?"

I touched my face lightly. The skin felt rough — grit crusted in the blood. It throbbed where my fingers brushed.

"It's fine," I whispered; the empty cavern made me wary — I didn't want to speak too loudly. "Where is everybody?"

Jamie shrugged, his eyes still tight as they surveyed my face. "Busy, I guess." He didn't lower his voice.

This reminded me of last night, of the secret he wouldn't tell me. My eyebrows pulled together.

*What do you think he's not telling us?*

*You know what I know, Wanda.*

*You're human. Aren't you supposed to have intuition or something?*

*Intuition? My intuition tells me that we don't know this place as well as we thought we did,* Melanie said.

We pondered the ominous sound of that.

It was almost a relief to hear the normal noises of mealtime coming from the kitchen corridor. I didn't particularly want to see anyone — besides the sick yearning to see Jared, of course — but the unpopulated tunnels, combined with the knowledge that something was being kept from me, made me edgy.

The kitchen was not even half full — an oddity for this time of the morning. But I barely noticed that, because the smell coming from the banked stone oven over-ruled every other thought.

"Oooh," Jamie moaned. "Eggs!"

Jamie pulled me faster now, and I had no reluctance to keep pace with him. We hurried, stomachs growling, to the counter by the oven where Lucina, the mother, stood with a plastic ladle in her hand. Breakfast was usually serve-yourself, but then breakfast was also usually tough bread rolls.

She looked only at the boy as she spoke. "They tasted better an hour ago."

"They'll taste just fine now," Jamie countered enthusi-astically. "Has everyone eaten?"

"Pretty much. I think they took a tray down to Doc and the rest. . . ." Lucina trailed off, and her eyes flick-ered to me for the first time; Jamie's eyes did the same. I didn't understand the expression that crossed Lucina's features — it disappeared too quickly, replaced by something else as she appraised the new marks on my face.

"How much is left?" Jamie asked. His eagerness sounded a trifle forced now.

Lucina turned and bent, tugging a metal pan off the hot stones in the bottom of the oven with the bowl of the ladle. "How much do you want, Jamie? There's plenty," she told him without turning.

"Pretend I'm Kyle," he said with a laugh.

"A Kyle-sized portion it is," Lucina said, but when she smiled, her eyes were unhappy.

She filled one of the soup bowls to overflowing with slightly rubbery scrambled eggs, stood up, and handed it to Jamie.

She eyed me again, and I understood what *this* look was for.

"Let's sit over there, Jamie," I said, nudging him away from the counter.

He stared in amazement. "Don't you want any?"

"No, I'm —" I was about to say "fine" again, when my stomach gurgled disobediently.

"Wanda?" He looked at me, then back at Lucina, who had her arms folded across her chest.

"I'll just have bread," I muttered, trying to shove him away.

"No. Lucina, what's the problem?" He looked at her expectantly. She didn't move. "If you're done here, I'll take over," he suggested, his eyes narrowing and his mouth setting in a stubborn line.

Lucina shrugged and set the ladle on the stone counter. She walked away slowly, not looking at me again.

"Jamie," I muttered urgently under my breath. "This food isn't meant for me. Jared and the others weren't risking their lives so that I could have eggs for breakfast. Bread is fine."

"Don't be stupid, Wanda," Jamie said. "You live here now, just like the rest of us. Nobody minds it when you wash their clothes or bake their bread. Besides, these eggs aren't going to last much longer. If you don't eat them, they'll get thrown out."

I felt all the eyes in the room boring into my back.

"That might be preferable to some," I said even more quietly. No one but Jamie could possibly hear.

"Forget that," Jamie growled. He hopped over the counter and filled another bowl with eggs, which he then shoved at me. "You're going to eat every bite," he told me resolutely.

I looked at the bowl. My mouth watered. I pushed the eggs a few inches away from me and then folded my arms.

Jamie frowned. "Fine," he said, and shoved his own bowl across the counter. "You don't eat, I don't eat." His stomach grumbled audibly. He folded his arms across his chest.

We stared at each other for two long minutes, both our stomachs rumbling as we inhaled the smell of the eggs. Every now and then, he would peek down at the food out of the corner of his eye. That's what beat me — the longing look in his eyes.

"Fine," I huffed. I slid his bowl back to him and then retrieved my own. He waited until I took the first bite to touch his. I stifled a moan as the taste registered on my tongue. I knew the cooled, rubbery eggs weren't the best thing I'd ever tasted, but that's how it felt. This body lived for the present.

Jamie had a similar reaction. And then he started shoveling the food into his mouth so fast it seemed he didn't have time to breathe. I watched him to make sure he didn't choke.

I ate more slowly, hoping that I'd be able to convince him to eat some of mine when he was done.

That was when, with our minor standoff over and my stomach satisfied, I finally noticed the atmosphere in the kitchen.

I would have expected, with the excitement of eggs for breakfast after months of monotony, more of a feeling of celebration. But the air was somber, the conversations all whispered. Was this a reaction to the scene last night? I scanned the room, trying to understand.

People *were* looking at me, a few here and there, but they weren't the only ones talking in serious whispers, and the others paid me no mind at all. Besides, none of them seemed angry or guilty or tense or any of the other emotions I was expecting.

No, they were *sad*. Despair was etched on every face in the room.

Sharon was the last person I noticed, eating in a distant corner, keeping to herself as usual. She was so composed as she mechanically ate her breakfast that at first I didn't notice the tears dripping in streaks down her face. They fell into her food, but she ate as if she were beyond noticing.

"Is something wrong with Doc?" I whispered to Jamie, suddenly afraid. I wondered if I was being paranoid — maybe this had nothing to do with me. The sadness in the room seemed to be part of some other human drama from which I'd been excluded. Was this what was keeping everyone busy? Had there been an accident?

Jamie looked at Sharon and sighed before he answered me. "No, Doc's fine."

"Aunt Maggie? Is she hurt?"

He shook his head.

"Where's Walter?" I demanded, still whispering. I felt a gnawing anxiety as I thought of harm befalling one of my companions here, even those who hated me.

"I don't know. He's fine, I'm sure."

I realized now that Jamie was just as sad as everyone else here.

"What's wrong, Jamie? Why are you upset?"

Jamie looked down at his eggs, eating them slowly and deliberately now, and did not answer me.

He finished in silence. I tried to pass him what was left in my bowl, but he glowered so fiercely that I took it back and ate the rest without any more resistance.

We added our bowls to the big plastic bin of dirty dishes. It was full, so I took it from the counter. I wasn't sure what was going on in the caves today, but dishes ought to be a safe occupation.

Jamie came along beside me, his eyes alert. I didn't like that. I wouldn't allow him to act as my bodyguard, if the necessity arose. But then, as we made our way around the edge of the big field, my regular bodyguard found me, so it became a moot point.

Ian was filthy; light brown dust covered him from head to toe, darker where it was wet with his sweat. The brown streaks smeared across his face did not disguise the exhaustion there. I was not surprised to see that he was just as down as everyone else. But the dust did make me curious. It was not the purple black dust inside the caves. Ian had been outside this morning.

"There you are," he murmured when he saw us. He was walking swiftly, his long legs cutting the distance with anxious strides. When he reached us, he did not slow, but rather caught me under the elbow and hurried me forward. "Let's duck in here for a minute."

He pulled me into the narrow tunnel mouth that led toward the eastern field, where the corn was almost ripe. He did not lead me far, just into the darkness where we were invisible from the big room. I felt Jamie's hand rest lightly on my other arm.

After half a minute, deep voices echoed through the

big cavern. They were not boisterous — they were somber, as depressed as any of the faces I'd read this morning. The voices passed us, close by the crack where we hid, and Ian's hand tensed on my elbow, his fingers pressing into the soft spots above the bone. I recognized Jared's voice, and Kyle's. Melanie strained against my control, and my control was tenuous anyway. We both wanted to see Jared's face. It was a good thing Ian held us back.

". . . don't know why we let him keep trying. When it's over, it's over," Jared was saying.

"He really thought he had it this time. He was so sure. . . . Oh, well. It will be worth all this if he figures it out someday," Kyle disagreed.

"*If.*" Jared snorted. "I guess it's a good thing we found that brandy. Doc's going to blow through the whole crate by nightfall at the rate he's going."

"He'll pass out soon enough," Kyle said, his voice beginning to fade in the distance. "I wish Sharon would . . ." And then I couldn't make out any more.

Ian waited until the voices faded completely, and then a few minutes more, before he finally released my arm.

"Jared promised," Jamie muttered to him.

"Yeah, but Kyle didn't," Ian answered.

They walked back out into the light. I followed slowly behind them, not sure what I was feeling.

Ian noticed for the first time what I carried. "No dishes now," he told me. "Let's give them a chance to clean up and move on."

I thought about asking him why he was dirty, but probably, like Jamie, he would refuse to answer. I turned to stare at the tunnel that led toward the rivers, speculating.

Ian made an angry sound.

I looked back at him, frightened, and then realized what had upset him — he'd only just seen my face.

He raised his hand as if to lift my chin, but I flinched and he dropped it.

"That makes me so sick," he said, and his voice truly did sound as if he were nauseated. "And worse, knowing that if I hadn't stayed behind, I might have been the one to do it. . . ."

I shook my head at him. "It's nothing, Ian."

"I don't agree with *that*," he muttered, and then he spoke to Jamie. "You probably ought to get to school. It's better that we get everything back to normal as soon as possible."

Jamie groaned. "Sharon will be a *nightmare* today."

Ian grinned. "Time to take one for the team, kid. I don't envy you."

Jamie sighed and kicked the dirt. "Keep an eye on Wanda."

"Will do."

Jamie shuffled away, casting glances back at us every few minutes until he disappeared into another tunnel.

"Here, give me those," Ian said, pulling the bin of dishes from me before I could respond.

"They weren't too heavy for me," I told him.

He grinned again. "I feel silly standing here with my arms empty while you lug these around. Chalk it up to gallantry. C'mon — let's go relax somewhere out of the way until the coast is clear."

His words troubled me, and I followed him in silence. Why should gallantry apply to me?

He walked all the way to the cornfield, and then into

the cornfield, stepping in the low part of the furrow, between the stalks. I trailed behind him until he stopped, somewhere in the middle of the field, set the dishes aside, and sprawled out on the dirt.

"Well, this is out of the way," I said as I settled to the ground beside him, crossing my legs. "But shouldn't we be working?"

"You work too hard, Wanda. You're the only one who never takes a day off."

"It gives me something to do," I mumbled.

"Everyone is taking a break today, so you might as well."

I looked at him curiously. The light from the mirrors threw double shadows through the cornstalks that crisscrossed over him like zebra stripes. Under the lines and the dirt, his pale face was weary.

"You look like you've been working."

His eyes tightened. "But I'm resting now."

"Jamie won't tell me what's going on," I murmured.

"No. And neither will I." He sighed. "It's nothing you want to know anyway."

I stared at the ground, at the dark purple and brown dirt, as my stomach twisted and rolled. I could think of nothing worse than not knowing, but maybe I was just lacking in imagination.

"It's not really fair," Ian said after a silent moment, "seeing as I won't answer your question, but do you mind if I ask you one?"

I welcomed the distraction. "Go ahead."

He didn't speak at once, so I looked up to find the reason for his hesitation. He was staring down now, looking at the dirt streaked across the backs of his hands.

"I know you're not a liar. I know that now," he said quietly. "I'll believe you, whatever your answer is."

I waited again while he continued to stare at the dirt on his skin.

"I didn't buy Jeb's story before, but he and Doc are pretty convinced. . . . Wanda?" he asked, looking up at me. "Is she still in there with you? The girl whose body you wear?"

This was not just my secret anymore — both Jamie and Jeb knew the truth. Neither was it the secret that really mattered. At any rate, I trusted Ian not to go blabbing to anyone who would kill me over it. "Yes," I told him. "Melanie is still here."

He nodded slowly. "What is it like? For you? For her?"

"It's . . . frustrating, for us both. At first I would have given anything to have her disappear the way she should have. But now I . . . I've gotten used to her." I smiled wryly. "Sometimes it's nice to have the company. It's harder for her. She's like a prisoner in many ways. Locked away in my head. She prefers that captivity to disappearing, though."

"I didn't know there was a choice."

"There wasn't in the beginning. It wasn't until your kind discovered what was happening that any resistance started. That seems to be the key — knowing what's going to happen. The humans who were taken by surprise didn't fight back."

"So if I were caught?"

I appraised his fierce expression — the fire in his brilliant eyes.

"I doubt you would disappear. Things have changed,

though. When they catch full-grown humans now, they don't offer them as hosts. Too many problems." I half smiled again. "Problems like *me*. Going soft, getting sympathetic to my host, losing my way . . ."

He thought about that for a long time, sometimes looking at my face, sometimes at the cornstalks, sometimes at nothing at all.

"What would they do with me, then, if they caught me now?" he finally asked.

"They'd still do an insertion, I think. Trying to get information. Probably they'd put a Seeker in you."

He shuddered.

"But they wouldn't keep you as a host. Whether they found the information or not, you would be . . . discarded." The word was hard to say. The idea sickened me. Odd — it was usually the human things that made me sick. But I'd never looked at the situation from the body's perspective before; no other planet had forced me to. A body that didn't function right was quickly and painlessly disposed of because it was as useless as a car that could not run. What was the point of keeping it around? There were conditions of the mind, too, that made a body unusable: dangerous mental addictions, malevolent yearnings, things that could not be healed and made the body unsafe to others. Or, of course, a mind with a will too strong to be erased. An anomaly localized on this planet.

I had never seen the ugliness of treating an unconquerable spirit as a defect as clearly as I did now, looking into Ian's eyes.

"And if they caught *you?*" he asked.

"If they realized who I was . . . if anyone is still looking for me . . ." I thought of my Seeker and shuddered as he had. "They would take me out and put me in another host. Someone young, tractable. They would hope that I would be able to be myself again. Maybe they would ship me off-planet — get me away from the bad influences."

"Would you be yourself again?"

I met his gaze. "I *am* myself. I haven't lost myself to Melanie. I would feel the same as I do now, even as a Bear or a Flower."

"They wouldn't *discard* you?"

"Not a soul. We have no capital punishment for our kind. Or any punishment, really. Whatever they did, it would be to save me. I used to think there was no need for any other way, but now I have myself as proof against that theory. It would probably be right to discard me. I'm a traitor, aren't I?"

Ian pursed his lips. "More of an expatriate, I'd say. You haven't turned on them; you've just left their society."

We were quiet again. I wanted to believe what he said was true. I considered the word *expatriate,* trying to convince myself that I was nothing worse.

Ian exhaled loudly enough to make me jump. "When Doc sobers up, we'll get him to take a look at your face." He reached over and put his hand under my chin; this time I didn't flinch. He turned my head to the side so he could examine the wound.

"It's not important. I'm sure it looks worse than it is."

"I hope so — it looks awful." He sighed and then stretched. "I suppose we've hidden long enough that Kyle's clean and unconscious. Want some help with the dishes?"

Ian wouldn't let me wash the dishes in the stream the

way I usually did. He insisted that we go into the black bathing room, where I would be invisible. I scrubbed dishes in the shallow end of the dark pool, while he cleaned off the filth left behind by his mystery labors. Then he helped me with the last of the dirty bowls.

When we were done, he escorted me back to the kitchen, which was starting to fill up with the lunch crowd. More perishables were on the menu: soft white bread slices, slabs of sharp cheddar cheese, circles of lush pink bologna. People were scarfing down the delicacies with abandon, though the despair was still perceptible in the slump of their shoulders, in the absence of smiles or laughter.

Jamie was waiting for me at our usual counter. Two double stacks of sandwiches sat in front of him, but he wasn't eating. His arms were folded as he waited for me. Ian eyed his expression curiously but left to get his own food without asking.

I rolled my eyes at Jamie's stubbornness and took a bite. Jamie dug in as soon as I was chewing. Ian was back quickly, and we all ate in silence. The food tasted so good it was hard to imagine a reason for conversation — or anything else that would empty our mouths.

I stopped at two, but Jamie and Ian ate until they were groaning in pain. Ian looked as though he was about to collapse. His eyes struggled to stay open.

"Get back to school, kid," he said to Jamie.

Jamie appraised him. "Maybe I should take over. . . ."

"Go to school," I told him quickly. I wanted Jamie a safe distance from me today.

"I'll see you later, okay? Don't worry about . . . about anything."

"Sure." A one-word lie wasn't quite so obvious. Or maybe I was just being sarcastic again.

Once Jamie was gone, I turned on the somnolent Ian. "Go get some rest. I'll be fine — I'll stay someplace inconspicuous. Middle of a cornfield or something."

"Where did you sleep last night?" he asked, his eyes surprisingly sharp under his half-closed lids.

"Why?"

"I can sleep there now, and you can be inconspicuous beside me."

We were just murmuring, barely over a whisper now. No one paid us any attention.

"You can't watch me every second."

"Wanna bet?"

I shrugged, giving up. "I was back at the . . . the hole. Where I was kept in the beginning."

Ian frowned; he didn't like that. But he got up and led the way back to the storage corridor. The main plaza was busy again now, full of people moving around the garden, all of them grave, their eyes on their feet.

When we were alone in the black tunnel, I tried to reason with him again.

"Ian, what's the point of this? Won't it hurt Jamie more, the longer I'm alive? In the end, wouldn't it be better for him if —"

"Don't think like that, Wanda. We're not animals. Your death is not an inevitability."

"I don't think you're an animal," I said quietly.

"Thanks. I didn't say that as an accusation, though. I wouldn't blame you if you did."

That was the end of our conversation; that was the

moment we both saw the pale blue light reflecting dimly from around the next turn in the tunnel.

"Shh," Ian breathed. "Wait here."

He pressed my shoulder down gently, trying to stick me where I stood. Then he strode forward, making no attempt to hide the sound of his footsteps. He disappeared around the corner.

"Jared?" I heard him say, feigning surprise.

My heart felt heavy in my chest; the sensation was more pain than fear.

"I know it's with you," Jared answered. He raised his voice, so that anyone between here and the main plaza would hear. "Come out, come out, wherever you are," he called, his voice hard and mocking.

# CHAPTER 29

# *Betrayed*

M aybe I should have run the other way. But no one was holding me back now, and though his voice was cold and angry, Jared was calling to me. Melanie was even more eager than I was as I stepped carefully around the corner and into the blue light; I hesitated there.

Ian stood just a few feet ahead of me, poised on the balls of his feet, ready for whatever hostile movement Jared might make toward me.

Jared sat on the ground, on one of the mats Jamie and I had left here. He looked as weary as Ian, though his eyes, too, were more alert than the rest of his exhausted posture.

"At ease," Jared said to Ian. "I just want to talk to it. I promised the kid, and I'll stand by that promise."

"Where's Kyle?" Ian demanded.

"Snoring. Your cave might shake apart from the vibrations."

Ian didn't move.

"I'm not lying, Ian. And I'm not going to kill it. Jeb is right. No matter how messed up this stupid situation is, Jamie has as much say as I do, and he's been totally suckered, so I doubt he'll be giving me the go-ahead anytime soon."

"No one's been suckered," Ian growled.

Jared waved his hand, dismissing the disagreement over terminology. "It's not in any danger from me, is my point." For the first time he looked at me, evaluating the way I hugged the far wall, watching my hands tremble. "I won't hurt you again," he said to me.

I took a small step forward.

"You don't have to talk to him if you don't want to, Wanda," Ian said quickly. "This isn't a duty or a chore to be done. It's not mandatory. You have a choice."

Jared's eyebrows pulled low over his eyes — Ian's words confused him.

"No," I whispered. "I'll talk to him." I took another short step. Jared turned his hand palm up and curled his fingers twice, encouraging me forward.

I walked slowly, each step an individual movement followed by a pause, not part of a steady advance. I stopped a yard away from him. Ian shadowed each step, keeping close to my side.

"I'd like to talk to it alone, if you don't mind," Jared said to him.

Ian planted himself. "I do mind."

"No, Ian, it's okay. Go get some sleep. I'll be fine." I nudged his arm lightly.

Ian scrutinized my face, his expression dubious. "This isn't some death wish? Sparing the kid?" he demanded.

"No. Jared wouldn't lie to Jamie about this."

Jared scowled when I said his name, the sound of it full of confidence.

"Please, Ian," I pleaded. "I want to talk to him."

Ian looked at me for a long minute, then turned to scowl at Jared. He barked out each sentence like an order.

"Her name is *Wanda,* not *it.* You will not touch her. Any mark you leave on her, I will double on your worthless hide."

I winced at the threat.

Ian turned abruptly and stalked into the darkness.

It was silent for a moment as we both watched the empty space where he had disappeared. I looked at Jared's face first, while he still stared after Ian. When he turned to meet my gaze, I dropped my eyes.

"Wow. He's not kidding, is he?" Jared said.

I treated that as a rhetorical question.

"Why don't you have a seat?" he asked me, patting the mat beside him.

I deliberated for a moment, then went to sit against the same wall but close to the hole, putting the length of the mat between us. Melanie didn't like this; she wanted to be near him, for me to smell his scent and feel the warmth of his body beside me.

I did not want that — and it wasn't because I was afraid he would hurt me; he didn't look angry at the moment, only tired and wary. I just didn't want to be any closer to him. Something in my chest was hurting to have him so near — to have him hating me in such close proximity.

He watched me, his head tilted to the side; I could only meet his gaze fleetingly before I had to look away.

"I'm sorry about last night — about your face. I shouldn't have done that."

I stared at my hands, knotted together in a double fist on my lap.

"You don't have to be afraid of me."

I nodded, not looking at him.

He grunted. "Thought you said you would talk to me?"

I shrugged. I couldn't find my voice with the weight of his antagonism in the air between us.

I heard him move. He scooted down the mat until he sat right beside me — the way Melanie had hoped for. Too close — it was hard to think straight, hard to breathe right — but I couldn't bring myself to scoot away. Oddly, for this was what she'd wanted in the first place, Melanie was suddenly irritated.

*What?* I asked, startled by the intensity of her emotion.

*I don't like him next to you. It doesn't feel right. I don't like the way you want him there.* For the first time since we'd abandoned civilization together, I felt waves of hostility emanating from her. I was shocked. That was hardly fair.

"I just have one question," Jared said, interrupting us.

I met his gaze and then shied away — recoiling both from his hard eyes and from Melanie's resentment.

"You can probably guess what it is. Jeb and Jamie spent all night jabbering at me. . . ."

I waited for the question, staring across the dark hall

at the rice bag — last night's pillow. In my peripheral vision, I saw his hand come up, and I cringed into the wall.

"I'm not going to hurt you," he said again, impatient, and cupped my chin in his rough hand, pulling my face around so I had to look at him.

My heart stuttered when he touched me, and there was suddenly too much moisture in my eyes. I blinked, trying to clear them.

"Wanda." He said my name slowly — unwillingly, I could tell, though his voice was even and toneless. "Is Melanie still alive — still part of you? Tell me the truth."

Melanie attacked with the brute strength of a wrecking ball. It was physically painful, like the sudden stab of a migraine headache, where she tried to force her way out.

*Stop it! Can't you see?*

It was so obvious in the set of his lips, the tight lines under his eyes. It didn't matter what I said or what she said.

*I'm already a liar to him,* I told her. *He doesn't want the truth — he's just looking for evidence, some way to prove me a liar, a Seeker, to Jeb and Jamie so that he'll be allowed to kill me.*

Melanie refused to answer or believe me; it was a struggle to keep her silent.

Jared watched the sweat bead on my forehead, the strange shiver that shook down my spine, and his eyes narrowed. He held on to my chin, refusing to let me hide my face.

*Jared, I love you,* she tried to scream. *I'm right here.*

My lips didn't quiver, but I was surprised that he couldn't read the words spelled out plainly in my eyes.

Time passed slowly while he waited for my answer. It was agonizing, having to stare into his eyes, having to see the revulsion there. As if that weren't enough, Melanie's anger continued to slice at me from the inside. Her jealousy swelled into a bitter flood that washed through my body and left it polluted.

More time passed, and the tears welled up until they couldn't be contained in my eyes anymore. They spilled over onto my cheeks and rolled silently into Jared's palm. His expression didn't change.

Finally, I'd had enough. I closed my eyes and jerked my head down. Rather than hurt me, he dropped his hand.

He sighed, frustrated.

I expected he would leave. I stared at my hands again, waiting for that. My heartbeat marked the passing minutes. He didn't move. I didn't move. He seemed carved out of stone beside me. It fit him, this stonelike stillness. It fit his new, hard expression, the flint in his eyes.

Melanie pondered this Jared, comparing him with the man he used to be. She remembered an unremarkable day on the run . . .

"Argh!" Jared and Jamie groan together.

Jared lounges on the leather sofa and Jamie sprawls on the carpet in front of him. They're watching a basketball game on the big-screen TV. The parasites who live in this house are at work, and we've already filled the jeep with all it can hold. We have hours to rest before we need to disappear again.

On the TV, two players are disagreeing politely on the sideline. The cameraman is close; we can hear what they're saying.

"I believe I was the last one to touch it — it's your ball."

"I'm not sure about that. I wouldn't want to take any unfair advantage. We'd better have the refs review the tape."

The players shake hands, pat each other's shoulders.

"This is ridiculous," Jared grumbles.

"I can't stand it," Jamie agrees, mirroring Jared's tone perfectly; he sounds more like Jared every day — one of the many forms his hero worship has taken. "Is there anything else on?"

Jared flips through a few channels until he finds a track and field meet. The parasites are holding the Olympics in Haiti right now. From what we can see, the aliens are all hugely excited about it. Lots of them have Olympic flags outside their houses. It's not the same, though. Everyone who participates gets a medal now. Pathetic.

But they can't really screw up the hundred-meter dash. Individual parasite sports are much more entertaining than when they try to compete against each other directly. They perform better in separate lanes.

"Mel, come relax," Jared calls.

I stand by the back door out of habit, not because I'm tensed to run. Not because I'm frightened. Empty habit, nothing more.

I go to Jared. He pulls me onto his lap and tucks my head under his chin.

"Comfortable?" he asks.

"Yes," I say, because I really, truly am entirely comfortable. Here, in an alien's house.

Dad used to say lots of funny things — like he was speaking his own language sometimes. Twenty-three skidoo, salad days, nosy parker, bandbox fresh, the catbird seat, chocolate teapot, and something about Grandma sucking eggs. One of his favorites was *safe as houses*.

Teaching me to ride a bike, my mother worrying in the doorway: *"Calm down, Linda, this street is safe as houses."* Convincing Jamie to sleep without his nightlight: *"It's safe as houses in here, son, not a monster for miles."*

Then overnight the world turned into a hideous nightmare, and the phrase became a black joke to Jamie and me. Houses were the most dangerous places we knew.

Hiding in a patch of scrubby pines, watching a car pull out from the garage of a secluded home, deciding whether to make a food run, whether it was too dicey. *"Do you think the parasites'll be gone for long?"* *"No way — that place is safe as houses. Let's get out of here."*

And now I can sit here and watch TV like it is five years ago and Mom and Dad are in the other room and I've never spent a night hiding in a drainpipe with Jamie and a bunch of rats while body snatchers with spotlights search for the thieves who made off with a bag of dried beans and a bowl of cold spaghetti.

I know that if Jamie and I survived alone for twenty years we would never find this feeling on our own. The feeling of safety. More than safety, even — happiness. Safe and happy, two things I thought I'd never feel again.

Jared makes us feel that way without trying, just by being Jared.

I breathe in the scent of his skin and feel the warmth of his body under mine.

Jared makes everything safe, everything happy. Even houses.

*He still makes me feel safe*, Melanie realized, feeling

the warmth where his arm was just half an inch from mine. *Though he doesn't even know I'm here.*

*I* didn't feel safe. Loving Jared made me feel less safe than anything else I could think of.

I wondered if Melanie and I would have loved Jared if he'd always been who he was now, rather than the smiling Jared in our memories, the one who had come to Melanie with his hands full of hope and miracles. Would she have followed him if he'd always been so hard and cynical? If the loss of his laughing father and wild big brothers had iced him over the way nothing but Melanie's loss had?

*Of course.* Mel was certain. *I would love Jared in any form. Even like this, he belongs with me.*

I wondered if the same held true for me. Would I love him now if he were like this in her memory?

Then I was interrupted. Without any cue that I perceived, suddenly Jared was talking, speaking as if we were in the middle of a conversation.

"And so, because of you, Jeb and Jamie are convinced that it's possible to continue some kind of awareness after . . . being caught. They're both sure Mel's still kicking in there."

He rapped his fist lightly against my head. I flinched away from him, and he folded his arms.

"Jamie thinks she's talking to him." He rolled his eyes. "Not really fair to play the kid like that — but that's assuming a sense of ethics that clearly does not apply."

I wrapped my arms around myself.

"Jeb does have a point, though — that's what's killing me! What *are* you after? The Seekers' search wasn't well directed or even . . . suspicious. They only seemed to be looking for you — not for us. So maybe they didn't know what you were up to. Maybe you're freelancing? Some kind of undercover thing. Or . . ."

It was easier to ignore him when he was speculating so foolishly. I focused on my knees. They were dirty, as usual, purple and black.

"Maybe they're right — about the killing-you part, anyway."

Unexpectedly, his fingers brushed lightly once across the goose bumps his words had raised on my arm. His voice was softer when he spoke again. "Nobody's going to hurt you now. As long as you aren't causing any trouble . . ." He shrugged. "I can sort of see their point, and maybe, in a sick way, it *would* be wrong, like they say. Maybe there is no justifiable reason to . . . Except that Jamie . . ."

My head flipped up — his eyes were sharp, scrutinizing my reaction. I regretted showing interest and watched my knees again.

"It scares me how attached he's getting," Jared muttered. "Shouldn't have left him behind. I never imagined . . . And I don't know what to do about it now. He thinks Mel's alive in there. What will it do to him when . . . ?"

I noticed how he said *when*, not *if*. No matter what promises he'd made, he didn't see me lasting in the long term.

"I'm surprised you got to Jeb," he reflected, changing the subject. "He's a canny old guy. He sees through deceptions so easily. Till now."

He thought about that for a minute.

"Not much for conversation, are you?"

There was another long silence.

His words came in a sudden gush. "The part that keeps bugging me is what if they're right? How the hell would I know? I hate the way their logic makes sense to me. There's got to be another explanation."

Melanie struggled again to speak, not as viciously as before, this time without hope of breaking through. I kept my arms and lips locked.

Jared moved, shifting away from the wall so that his body was turned toward me. I watched the movement from the corner of my eye.

"Why are you here?" he whispered.

I peeked up at his face. It was gentle, kind, almost the way Melanie remembered it. I felt my control slipping; my lips trembled. Keeping my arms locked took all my strength. I wanted to touch his face. *I* wanted it. Melanie did not like this.

*If you won't let me talk, then at least keep your hands to yourself,* she hissed.

*I'm trying. I'm sorry.* I was sorry. This was hurting her. We were both hurting, different hurts. It was hard to know who had it worse at the moment.

Jared watched me curiously while my eyes filled again.

"Why?" he asked softly. "You know, Jeb has this crazy idea that you're here for me and Jamie. Isn't that nuts?"

My mouth half-opened; I quickly bit down on my lip.

Jared leaned forward slowly and took my face between both his hands. My eyes closed.

"Won't you tell me?"

My head shook once, fast. I wasn't sure who did it. Was it me saying won't or Melanie saying can't?

His hands tightened under my jaw. I opened my eyes, and his face was inches away from mine. My heart fluttered, my stomach dropped — I tried to breathe, but my lungs did not obey.

I recognized the intention in his eyes; I knew how he would move, exactly how his lips would feel. And yet it was so new to me, a first more shocking than any other, as his mouth pressed against mine.

I think he meant just to touch his lips to mine, to be soft, but things changed when our skin met. His mouth was abruptly hard and rough, his hands trapped my face to his while his lips moved mine in urgent, unfamiliar patterns. It was so different from remembering, so much stronger. My head swam incoherently.

The body revolted. I was no longer in control of it — it was in control of me. It was not Melanie — the body was stronger than either of us now. Our breathing echoed loudly: mine wild and gasping, his fierce, almost a snarl.

My arms broke free from my control. My left hand reached for his face, his hair, to wind my fingers in it.

My right hand was faster. Was not mine.

Melanie's fist punched his jaw, knocked his face away from mine with a blunt, low sound. Flesh against flesh, hard and angry.

The force of it was not enough to move him far, but he scrambled away from me the instant our lips were no longer connected, gaping with horrorstruck eyes at my horrorstruck expression.

I stared down at the still-clenched fist, as repulsed as if I'd found a scorpion growing on the end of my arm. A gasp of revulsion choked its way out of my throat. I grabbed the right wrist with my left hand, desperate to keep Melanie from using my body for violence again.

I glanced up at Jared. He was staring at the fist I restrained, too, the horror fading, surprise taking its place. In that second, his expression was entirely defenseless. I could easily read his thoughts as they moved across his unlocked face.

This was not what he had expected. And he'd had expectations; that was plain to see. This had been a test. A test he'd thought he was prepared to evaluate. A test with results he'd anticipated with confidence. But he'd been surprised.

Did that mean pass or fail?

The pain in my chest was not a surprise. I already knew that a breaking heart was more than an exaggeration.

In a fight-or-flight situation, I never had a choice; it would always be flight for me. Because Jared was between me and the darkness of the tunnel exit, I wheeled and threw myself into the box-packed hole.

The boxes crunched, crackled, and cracked as my weight shoved them into the wall, into the floor. I wriggled my way into the impossible space, twisting around the heavier squares and crushing the others. I felt his fingers scrape across my foot as he made a grab for my ankle, and I kicked one of the more solid boxes between us. He grunted, and despair wrapped choking hands around my throat. I hadn't meant to hurt him again; I hadn't meant to strike. I was only trying to escape.

I didn't hear my own sobbing, loud as it was, until I could go no farther into the crowded hole and the sound of my thrashing stopped. When I did hear myself, heard the ragged, tearing gasps of agony, I was mortified.

So mortified, so humiliated. I was horrified at myself, at the violence I'd allowed to flow through my body, whether consciously or not, but that was not why I was sobbing. I was sobbing because it had been a test, and, stupid, stupid, stupid, emotional creature that I was, I wanted it to be real.

Melanie was writhing in agony inside me, and it was hard to make sense of the double pain. I felt as though I was dying because it was not real; she felt as though she was dying because, to her, it had felt real enough. In all that she'd lost since the end of her world, so long ago, she'd never before felt betrayed. When her father had brought the Seekers after his children, she'd known it was not *him*. There was no betrayal, only grief. Her father was dead. But Jared was alive and himself.

*No one's betrayed you, stupid,* I railed at her. I wanted her pain to stop. It was too much, the extra burden of her agony. Mine was enough.

*How could he? How?* she ranted, ignoring me.

We sobbed, beyond control.

One word snapped us back from the edge of hysteria.

From the mouth of the hole, Jared's low, rough voice — broken and strangely childlike — asked, "Mel?"

# CHAPTER 30

# *Abbreviated*

M el?" he asked again, the hope he didn't want to feel coloring his tone.

My breath caught in another sob, an aftershock.

"You know that was for you, Mel. You *know* that. Not for h — it. You know I wasn't kissing it."

My next sob was louder, a moan. Why couldn't I shut up? I tried holding my breath.

"If you're in there, Mel . . ." He paused.

Melanie hated the "if." A sob burst up through my lungs, and I gasped for air.

"I love you," Jared said. "Even if you're not there, if you can't hear me. I love you."

I held my breath again, biting my lip until it bled. The physical pain didn't distract me as much as I wished it would.

It was silent outside the hole, and then silent inside, too, as I turned blue. I listened intently, concentrating only on what I could hear. I wouldn't think. There was no sound.

I was twisted into the most impossible position. My head was the lowest point, the right side of my face pressed against the rough rock floor. My shoulders were slanted around a crumpled box edge, the right higher than the left. My hips angled the opposite way, with my left calf pressed to the ceiling. Fighting with the boxes had left bruises — I could feel them forming. I knew I would have to find some way to explain to Ian and Jamie that I had done this to myself, but how? What should I say? How could I tell them that Jared had kissed me as a test, like giving a lab rat a jolt of electricity to observe its reaction?

And how long was I supposed to hold this position? I didn't want to make any noise, but it felt like my spine was going to snap in a minute. The pain got more difficult to bear every second. I wouldn't be able to bear it in silence for long. Already, a whimper was rising in my throat.

Melanie had nothing to say to me. She was quietly working through her own relief and fury. Jared had spoken to her, finally recognized her existence. He had told her he loved her. But he had kissed me. She was trying to convince herself that there was no reason to be wounded by this, trying to believe all the solid reasons why this wasn't what it felt like. Trying, but not yet succeeding. I could hear all this, but it was directed internally. She wasn't speaking to me — in the juvenile, petty sense of the phrase. I was getting the cold shoulder.

I felt an unfamiliar anger toward her. Not like the beginning, when I feared her and wished for her eradication from my mind. No, I felt my own sense of betrayal now. How could she be angry with *me* for what had happened?

How did that make sense? How was it my fault that I'd fallen in love because of the memories *she* forced on me and then been overthrown by this unruly body? I cared that she was suffering, yet my pain meant nothing to her. She enjoyed it. Vicious human.

Tears, much weaker than the others, flowed down my cheeks in silence. Her hostility toward me simmered in my mind.

Abruptly, the pain in my bruised, twisted back was too much. The straw on the camel.

"Ung," I grunted, pushing against stone and cardboard as I shoved myself backward.

I didn't care about the noise anymore, I just wanted out. I swore to myself that I would never cross the threshold of this wretched pit again — death first. Literally.

It was harder to worm out than it had been to dive in. I wiggled and squirmed around until I felt like I was making things worse, bending myself into the shape of a lopsided pretzel. I started to cry again, like a child, afraid that I would never get free.

Melanie sighed. *Hook your foot around the edge of the mouth and pull yourself out,* she suggested.

I ignored her, struggling to work my torso around a particularly pointy corner. It jabbed me just under the ribs.

*Don't be petty,* she grumbled.

*That's rich, coming from you.*

*I know.* She hesitated, then caved. *Okay, sorry. I am. Look, I'm human. It's hard to be fair sometimes. We don't always feel the right thing, do the right thing.* The resentment was still there, but she was trying to forgive and forget that I'd just made out with her true love — that's the way she thought of it, at least.

I hooked my foot around the edge and yanked. My knee hit the floor, and I used that leverage to lift my ribs off the point. It was easier then to get my other foot out and yank again. Finally, my hands found the floor and I shoved my way through, a breech birth, falling onto the dark green mat. I lay there for a moment, facedown, breathing. I was sure at this point that Jared was long gone, but I didn't make certain of that right away. I just breathed in and out until I felt prepared to lift my head.

I was alone. I tried to hold on to the relief and forget the sorrow this fact engendered. It was better to be alone. Less humiliating.

I curled up on the mat, pressing my face against the musty fabric. I wasn't sleepy, but I was tired. The crushing weight of Jared's rejection was so heavy it exhausted me. I closed my eyes and tried to think about things that wouldn't make my stinging eyes tear again. Anything but the appalled look on Jared's face when he'd broken away from me . . .

What was Jamie doing now? Did he know I was here, or was he looking for me? Ian would be asleep for a long time, he'd looked so exhausted. Would Kyle wake soon? Would he come in search? Where was Jeb? I hadn't seen him all day. Was Doc really drinking himself unconscious? That seemed so unlike him . . .

I woke slowly, roused by my growling stomach. I lay quietly for a few minutes, trying to orient myself. Was it day or night? How long had I slept here alone?

My stomach wouldn't be ignored for long, though, and I rolled up onto my knees. I must have slept for a while to be this hungry — missed a meal or two.

I considered eating something from the supply pile in

the hole — after all, I'd already damaged pretty much everything, maybe destroyed some. But that only made me feel guiltier about the idea of taking more. I'd go scavenge some rolls from the kitchen.

I was feeling a little hurt, on top of all the big hurt, that I'd been down here so long without anyone coming to look for me — what a vain attitude; why should anyone care what happened to me? — so I was relieved and appeased to find Jamie sitting in the doorway to the big garden, his back turned on the human world behind him, unmistakably waiting for me.

My eyes brightened, and so did his. He scrambled to his feet, relief washing over his features.

"You're okay," he said; I wished he were right. He began to ramble. "I mean, I didn't think Jared was lying, but he said he thought you wanted to be alone, and Jeb said I couldn't go check on you and that I had to stay right here where he could see that I wasn't sneaking back there, but even though I didn't *think* you were hurt or anything, it was hard to not know for sure, you know?"

"I'm fine," I told him. But I held my arms out, seeking comfort. He threw his arms around my waist, and I was shocked to find that his head could rest on my shoulder while we stood.

"Your eyes are red," he whispered. "Was he mean to you?"

"No." After all, people weren't intentionally cruel to lab rats — they were just trying to get information.

"Whatever you said to him, I think he believes us now. About Mel, I mean. How does she feel?"

"She's glad about that."

He nodded, pleased. "How about you?"

I hesitated, looking for a factual response. "Telling the truth is easier for me than trying to hide it."

My evasion seemed to answer the question enough to satisfy him.

Behind him, the light in the garden was red and fading. The sun had already set on the desert.

"I'm hungry," I told him, and I pulled away from our hug.

"I knew you would be. I saved you something good."

I sighed. "Bread's fine."

"Let it go, Wanda. Ian says you're too self-sacrificing for your own good."

I made a face.

"I think he's got a point," Jamie muttered. "Even if we all want you here, you don't belong until you decide you do."

"I can't ever belong. And nobody really wants me here, Jamie."

"I do."

I didn't fight with him, but he was wrong. Not lying, because he believed what he was saying. But what he really wanted was Melanie. He didn't separate us the way he should.

Trudy and Heidi were baking rolls in the kitchen and sharing a bright green, juicy apple. They took turns taking bites.

"It's good to see you, Wanda," Trudy said sincerely, covering her mouth while she spoke because she was still chewing her last bite. Heidi nodded in greeting, her teeth sunk in the apple. Jamie nudged me, trying to be inconspicuous about it — pointing out that people wanted me. He wasn't making allowances for common courtesy.

"Did you save her dinner?" he asked eagerly.

"Yep," Trudy said. She bent down beside the oven and came back with a metal tray in her hand. "Kept it warm. It's probably nasty and tough now, but it's better than the usual."

On the tray was a rather large piece of red meat. My mouth started to water, even as I rejected the portion I'd been allotted.

"It's too much."

"We have to eat all the perishables the first day," Jamie encouraged me. "Everyone eats themselves sick — it's a tradition."

"You need the protein," Trudy added. "We were on cave rations too long. I'm surprised no one's in worse shape."

I ate my protein while Jamie watched with hawk-like attention as each bite traveled from the tray to my mouth. I ate it all to please him, though it made my stomach ache to eat so much.

The kitchen started to fill up again as I was finishing. A few had apples in their hands — all sharing with someone else. Curious eyes examined the sore side of my face.

"Why's everyone coming here now?" I muttered to Jamie. It was black outside, the dinner hour long over.

Jamie looked at me blankly for a second. "To hear you teach." His tone added the words *of course.*

"Are you kidding me?"

"I told you nothing's changed."

I stared around the narrow room. It wasn't a full house. No Doc tonight, and none of the returned raiders, which meant no Paige, either. No Jeb, no Ian, no Walter. A few others missing: Travis, Carol, Ruth Ann. But more than I would have thought, if I'd thought anyone would consider following the normal routine after such an abnormal day.

"Can we go back to the Dolphins, where we left off?" Wes asked, interrupting my evaluation of the room. I could see that he'd taken it upon himself to start the ball rolling, rather than that he was vitally interested in the kinship circles of an alien planet.

Everyone looked at me expectantly. Apparently, life was not changing as much as I'd thought.

I took a tray of rolls from Heidi's hands and turned to shove it into the stone oven. I started talking with my back still turned.

"So . . . um . . . hmm . . . the, uh, third set of grand-parents . . . They traditionally serve the community, as they see it. On Earth, they would be the breadwinners, the ones who leave the home and bring back sustenance. They are farmers, for the most part. They cultivate a plant-like growth that they milk for its sap. . . ."

And life went on.

Jamie tried to talk me out of sleeping in the supply corridor, but his attempt was halfhearted. There just wasn't another place for me. Stubborn as usual, he insisted on sharing my quarters. I imagined Jared didn't like that, but as I didn't see him that night or the next day, I couldn't verify my theory.

It was awkward again, going about my usual chores, with the six raiders home — just like when Jeb had first forced me to join the community. Hostile stares, angry silences. It was harder for them than it was for me, though — *I* was used to it. They, on the other hand, were entirely unaccustomed to the way everyone else treated me. When I was helping with the corn harvest, for example, and Lily thanked me for a fresh basket with a smile, Andy's eyes bulged in their sockets at the exchange. Or when I was waiting for the bathing pool with Trudy and Heidi, and Heidi began playing with my hair. It was growing, always swinging in my eyes these days, and I was planning to shear it off again. Heidi was trying to find a style for me, flipping the strands this way and that. Brandt and Aaron — Aaron was the oldest man who'd gone on the long raid, someone I couldn't remember having seen before at all — came out and found us there, Trudy laughing at some silly atrocity Heidi was attempting to create atop my head, and both men turned a little green and stalked silently past us.

Of course, little things like that were nothing. Kyle roamed the caves now, and though he was obviously under orders to leave me in peace, his expression made it clear that this restriction was repugnant to him. I was always with others when I crossed his path, and I wondered if that was the only reason he did nothing more than glower at me and unconsciously curl his thick fingers into claws. This brought back all the panic from my first weeks here, and I might have succumbed to it — begun hiding again, avoiding the common areas — but something more important than Kyle's murderous glares came to my attention that second night.

The kitchen filled up again — I'm not sure how much was interest in my stories and how much was interest in the chocolate bars Jeb handed out. I declined mine, explaining to a disgruntled Jamie that I couldn't talk and chew at the same time; I suspected that he would save one for me, obstinate as ever. Ian was back in his usual hot seat by the fire, and Andy was there — eyes wary —

beside Paige. None of the other raiders, including Jared, of course, was in attendance. Doc was not there, and I wondered if he was still drunk or perhaps hungover. And again, Walter was absent.

Geoffrey, Trudy's husband, questioned me for the first time tonight. I was pleased, though I tried not to show it, that he seemed to have joined the ranks of the humans who tolerated me. But I couldn't answer his questions well, which was too bad. His questions were like Doc's.

"I don't really know anything about Healing," I admitted. "I never went to a Healer after . . . after I first got here. I haven't been sick. All I know is that we wouldn't choose a planet unless we were able to maintain the host bodies perfectly. There's nothing that can't be healed, from a simple cut, a broken bone, to a disease. Old age is the only cause of death now. Even healthy human bodies were only designed to last for so long. And there are accidents, too, I guess, though those don't happen as often with the souls. We're cautious."

"Armed humans aren't just an accident," someone muttered. I was moving hot rolls; I didn't see who spoke, and I didn't recognize the voice.

"Yes, that's true," I agreed evenly.

"So you don't know what they use to cure diseases, then?" Geoffrey pressed. "What's in their medications?"

I shook my head. "I'm sorry, I don't. It wasn't something I was interested in, back when I had access to the information. I'm afraid I took it for granted. Good health is simply a given on every planet I've lived on."

Geoffrey's red cheeks flushed brighter than usual. He looked down, an angry set to his mouth. What had I said to offend him?

Heath, sitting beside Geoffrey, patted his arm. There was a pregnant silence in the room.

"Uh — about the Vultures . . ." Ian said — the words were forced, a deliberate subject change. "I don't know if I missed this part sometime, but I don't remember you ever explaining about them being 'unkind' . . . ?"

It wasn't something I *had* explained, but I was pretty sure he wasn't really that interested — this was just the first question he'd been able to think of.

My informal class ended earlier than usual. The questions were slow, and most of them supplied by Jamie and Ian. Geoffrey's questions had left everyone else preoccupied.

"Well, we've got an early one tomorrow, tearing down the stalks . . ." Jeb mused after yet another awkward silence, making the words a dismissal. People rose to their feet and stretched, talking in low voices that weren't casual enough.

"What did I say?" I whispered to Ian.

"Nothing. They've got mortality on their minds." He sighed.

My human brain made one of those leaps in understanding that they called intuition.

"Where's Walter?" I demanded, still whispering.

Ian sighed again. "He's in the south wing. He's . . . not doing well."

"Why didn't anyone tell me?"

"Things have been . . . difficult for you lately, so . . ."

I shook my head impatiently at that consideration. "What's wrong with him?"

Jamie was there beside me now; he took my hand.

"Some of Walter's bones snapped, they're so brittle,"

he said in a hushed voice. "Doc's sure it's cancer — final stages, he says."

"Walt must have been keeping quiet about the pain for a long while now," Ian added somberly.

I winced. "And there's nothing to be done? Nothing at all?"

Ian shook his head, keeping his brilliant eyes on mine. "Not for us. Even if we weren't stuck here, there would be no help for him now. We never cured that one."

I bit my lip against the suggestion I wanted to make. Of course there was nothing to do for Walter. Any of these humans would rather die slowly and in pain than trade their mind for their body's cure. I could understand that . . . now.

"He's been asking for you," Ian continued. "Well, he says your name sometimes; it's hard to tell what he means — Doc's keeping him drunk to help with the pain."

"Doc feels real bad about using so much of the alcohol himself," Jamie added. "Bad timing, all around."

"Can I see him?" I asked. "Or will that make the others unhappy?"

Ian frowned and snorted. "Wouldn't that be just like some people, to get worked up over this?" He shook his head. "Who cares, though, right? If it's Walt's final wish . . ."

"Right," I agreed. The word *final* had my eyes burning. "If seeing me is what Walter wants, then I guess it doesn't matter what anyone else thinks, or if they get mad."

"Don't worry about that — I'm not going to let anybody harass you." Ian's white lips pressed into a thin line.

I felt anxious, like I wanted to look at a clock. Time had ceased to mean much to me, but suddenly I felt the weight of a deadline. "Is it too late to go tonight? Will we disturb him?"

"He's not sleeping regular hours. We can go see."

I started walking at once, dragging Jamie because he still gripped my hand. The sense of passing time, of endings and finality, propelled me forward. Ian caught up quickly, though, with his long stride.

In the moonlit garden cavern, we passed others who for the most part paid us no mind. I was too often in the company of Jamie and Ian to cause any curiosity, though we weren't headed for the usual tunnels.

The one exception was Kyle. He froze midstride when he saw his brother beside me. His eyes flashed down to see Jamie's hand in mine, and then his lips twisted into a snarl.

Ian squared his shoulders as he absorbed his brother's reaction — his mouth curled into a mirror of Kyle's — and he deliberately reached for my other hand. Kyle made a noise like he was about to be sick and turned his back on us.

When we were in the blackness of the long tunnel south, I tried to free that hand. Ian gripped it tighter.

"I wish you wouldn't make him angrier," I muttered.

"Kyle is wrong. Being wrong is sort of a habit with him. He'll take longer than anyone else to get over it, but that doesn't mean we should make allowances for him."

"He frightens me," I admitted in a whisper. "I don't want him to have more reasons to hate me."

Ian and Jamie squeezed my hands at the same time. They spoke simultaneously.

"Don't be afraid," Jamie said.

"Jeb's made his opinion very clear," Ian said.

"What do you mean?" I asked Ian.

"If Kyle can't accept Jeb's rules, then he's no longer welcome here."

"But that's wrong. Kyle belongs here."

Ian grunted. "He's staying . . . so he'll just have to learn to deal."

We didn't talk again through the long walk. I was feeling guilty — it seemed to be a permanent emotional state here. Guilt and fear and heartbreak. Why had I come?

*Because you do belong here, oddly enough,* Melanie whispered. She was very aware of the warmth of Ian's and Jamie's hands, wrapped around and twined with mine. *Where else have you ever had this?*

*Nowhere,* I confessed, feeling only more depressed. *But it doesn't make me belong. Not the way you do.*

*We're a package deal, Wanda.*

*As if I needed reminding. . . .*

I was a little surprised to hear her so clearly. She'd been quiet the last two days, waiting, anxious, hoping to see Jared again. Of course, I'd been similarly occupied.

*Maybe he's with Walter. Maybe that's where he's been,* Melanie thought hopefully.

*That's not why we're going to see Walter.*

*No. Of course not.* Her tone was repentant, but I realized that Walter did not mean as much to her as he did to me. Naturally, she was sad that he was dying, but she had accepted that outcome from the beginning. I, on the other hand, could not bring myself to accept it, even now. Walter was my friend, not hers. I was the one he'd defended.

One of those dim blue lights greeted us as we approached the hospital wing. (I knew now that the lanterns were solar powered, left in sunny corners during the day to charge.) We all moved more quietly, slowing at the same time without having to discuss it.

I hated this room. In the darkness, with the odd shadows thrown by the weak glow, it seemed only more forbidding. There was a new smell — the room reeked of slow decay and stinging alcohol and bile.

Two of the cots were occupied. Doc's feet hung over the edge of one; I recognized his light snore. On the other, looking hideously withered and misshapen, Walter watched us approach.

"Are you up for visitors, Walt?" Ian whispered when Walter's eyes drifted in his direction.

"Ungh," Walter moaned. His lips drooped from his slack face, and his skin gleamed wetly in the low light.

"Is there anything you need?" I murmured. I pulled my hands free — they fluttered helplessly in the air between me and Walter.

His loosely rolling eyes searched the darkness. I took a step closer.

"Is there anything we can do for you? Anything at all?"

His eyes roamed till they found my face. Abruptly, they focused through the drunken stupor and the pain.

"Finally," he gasped. His breath wheezed and whistled. "I knew you would come if I waited long enough. Oh, Gladys, I have so much to tell you."

# CHAPTER 31

# *Needed*

I froze and then looked quickly over my shoulder to see if someone was behind me.

"Gladys was his wife," Jamie whispered almost silently. "She didn't escape."

"Gladys," Walter said to me, oblivious to my reaction. "Would you believe I went and got cancer? What are the odds, eh? Never took a sick day in my life . . ." His voice faded out until I couldn't hear it, but his lips continued to move. He was too weak to lift his hand; his fingers dragged themselves toward the edge of the cot, toward me.

Ian nudged me forward.

"What should I do?" I breathed. The sweat beading on my forehead had nothing to do with the humid heat.

". . . grandfather lived to be a hundred and one," Walter wheezed, audible again. "Nobody ever had cancer in my family, not even the cousins. Didn't your aunt Regan have skin cancer, though?"

He looked at me trustingly, waiting for an answer. Ian poked me in the back.

"Um . . ." I mumbled.

"Maybe that was Bill's aunt," Walter allowed.

I shot a panicked glance at Ian, who shrugged. "Help," I mouthed at him.

He motioned for me to take Walter's searching fingers.

Walter's skin was chalk white and translucent. I could see the faint pulse of blood in the blue veins on the back of his hand. I lifted his hand gingerly, worried about the slender bones that Jamie had said were so brittle. It felt too light, as if it were hollow.

"Ah, Gladdie, it's been hard without you. It's a nice place here; you'll like it, even when I'm gone. Plenty of people to talk to — I know how you need to have your conversation. . . ." The volume of his voice sank until I couldn't make out the words anymore, but his lips still shaped the words he wanted to share with his wife. His mouth kept moving, even when his eyes closed and his head lolled to the side.

Ian found a wet cloth and began wiping Walter's shining face.

"I'm not good at . . . at deception," I whispered, watching Walter's mumbling lips to make sure he wasn't listening to me. "I don't want to upset him."

"You don't have to say anything," Ian reassured me. "He's not lucid enough to care."

"Do I look like her?"

"Not a bit — I've seen her picture. Stocky redhead."

"Here, let me do that."

Ian gave me the rag, and I cleaned the sweat off Walter's neck. Busy hands always made me feel more comfortable. Walter continued to mumble. I thought I heard him say, "Thanks, Gladdie, that's nice."

I didn't notice that Doc's snores had stopped. His familiar voice was suddenly there behind me, too gentle to startle.

"How is he?"

"Delusional," Ian whispered. "Is that the brandy or the pain?"

"More the pain, I would think. I'd trade my right arm for some morphine."

"Maybe Jared will produce another miracle," Ian suggested.

"Maybe," Doc sighed.

I wiped absently at Walter's pallid face, listening more intently now, but they didn't speak of Jared again.

*Not here,* Melanie whispered.

*Looking for help for Walter,* I agreed.

*Alone,* she added.

I thought about the last time I'd seen him — the kiss, the belief . . . *He probably wanted some time to himself.*

*I hope he isn't out there convincing himself that you're a very talented actress-slash-Seeker again. . . .*

*That's possible, of course.*

Melanie groaned silently.

Ian and Doc murmured in quiet voices about inconsequential things, mostly Ian catching Doc up on what was going on in the caves.

"What happened to Wanda's face?" Doc whispered, but I could still hear him easily.

"More of the same," Ian said in a tight voice.

Doc made an unhappy noise under his breath and then clicked his tongue.

Ian told him a bit about tonight's awkward class, about Geoffrey's questions.

"It would have been convenient if Melanie had been possessed by a Healer," Doc mused.

I flinched, but they were behind me and probably didn't notice.

"We're lucky it was Wanda," Ian murmured in my defense. "No one else —"

"I know," Doc interrupted, good-natured as always. "I guess I should say, it's too bad Wanda didn't have more of an interest in medicine."

"I'm sorry," I murmured. I *was* careless to reap the benefits of perfect health without ever being curious about the cause.

A hand touched my shoulder. "You have nothing to apologize for," Ian said.

Jamie was being very quiet. I looked around and saw that he was curled up on the cot where Doc had been napping.

"It's late," Doc noted. "Walter's not going anywhere tonight. You should get some sleep."

"We'll be back," Ian promised. "Let us know what we can bring, for either of you."

I laid Walter's hand down, patting it cautiously. His eyes snapped open, focusing with more awareness than before.

"Are you leaving?" he wheezed. "Do you have to go so soon?"

I took his hand again quickly. "No, I don't have to leave."

He smiled and closed his eyes again. His fingers locked around mine with brittle strength.

Ian sighed.

"You can go," I told him. "I don't mind. Take Jamie back to his bed."

Ian glanced around the room. "Hold on a sec," he said, and then he grabbed the cot closest to him. It wasn't heavy — he lifted it easily and slid it into place next to Walter's. I stretched my arm to the limit, trying not to jostle Walter, so that Ian could arrange the cot under it. Then he grabbed me up just as easily and set me on the cot beside Walter. Walter's eyes never fluttered. I gasped quietly, caught off guard by the casual way Ian was able to put his hands on me — as though I were human.

Ian jerked his chin toward Walter's hand clasped around mine. "Do you think you can sleep like that?"

"Yes, I'm sure I can."

"Sleep well, then." He smiled at me, then turned and lifted Jamie from the other cot. "Let's go, kid," he muttered, carrying the boy with no more effort than if he were an infant. Ian's quiet footsteps faded into the distance until I couldn't hear them anymore.

Doc yawned and went to sit behind the desk he'd constructed out of wooden crates and an aluminum door, taking the dim lamp with him. Walter's face was too dark to see, and that made me nervous. It was like he was already gone. I took comfort in his fingers, still curled stiffly around mine.

Doc began to shuffle through some papers, humming

almost inaudibly to himself. I drifted off to the sound of the gentle rustling.

Walter recognized me in the morning.

He didn't wake until Ian showed up to escort me back; the cornfield was due to be cleared of the old stalks. I promised Doc I would bring him breakfast before I got to work. The very last thing I did was to carefully loosen my numb fingers, freeing them from Walter's grasp.

His eyes opened. "Wanda," he whispered.

"Walter?" I wasn't sure how long he would know me, or if he would remember last night. His hand clutched at the empty air, so I gave him my left, the one that wasn't dead.

"You came to see me. That was nice. I know . . . with the others back . . . must be hard . . . for you . . . Your face . . ."

He seemed to be having a difficult time making his lips form the words, and his eyes went in and out of focus. How like him, that his first words to me would be full of concern.

"Everything's fine, Walter. How are you feeling?"

"Ah —" He groaned quietly. "Not so . . . Doc?"

"Right here," Doc murmured, close behind me.

"Got any more liquor?" he gasped.

"Of course."

Doc was already prepared. He held the mouth of a thick glass bottle to Walter's slack lips and carefully poured the dark brown liquid in slow drips into his mouth. Walter winced as each sip burned down his throat. Some of it trickled out the side of his mouth and onto his pillow. The smell stung my nose.

"Better?" Doc asked after a long moment of slow pouring.

Walter grunted. It didn't sound like assent. His eyes closed.

"More?" Doc asked.

Walter grimaced and then moaned.

Doc cursed under his breath. "Where's Jared?" he muttered.

I stiffened at the name. Melanie stirred and then drifted again.

Walter's face sagged. His head rolled back on his neck.

"Walter?" I whispered.

"The pain's too much for him to stay conscious. Let him be," Doc said.

My throat felt swollen. "What can I do?"

Doc's voice was desolate. "About as much as I can. Which is nothing. I'm useless."

"Don't be like that, Doc," I heard Ian murmur. "This isn't your fault. The world doesn't work the way it used to. No one expects more of you."

My shoulders hunched inward. No, their world didn't work the same way anymore.

A finger tapped my arm. "Let's go," Ian whispered.

I nodded and started to pull my hand free again.

Walter's eyes rolled open, unseeing. "Gladdie? Are you here?" he implored.

"Um . . . I'm here," I said uncertainly, letting his fingers lock around mine.

Ian shrugged. "I'll get you both some food," he whispered, and then he left.

I waited anxiously for him to return, unnerved by Walter's misconception. Walter murmured Gladys's name over and over, but he didn't seem to need anything from me, for which I was grateful. After a while, half an hour maybe, I began listening for Ian's footsteps in the tunnel, wondering what could be taking him so long.

Doc stood by his desk the whole time, staring into nothing with his shoulders slumped. It was easy to see how useless he felt.

And then I did hear something, but it wasn't footsteps.

"What is that?" I asked Doc in a whisper; Walter was quiet again, maybe unconscious. I didn't want to disturb him.

Doc turned to look at me, cocking his head to the side at the same time to listen.

The noise was a funny thrumming, a fast, soft beat. I thought I heard it get just a little louder, but then it seemed quieter again.

"That's weird," Doc said. "It almost sounds like . . ." He paused, his forehead furrowing in concentration as the unfamiliar sound faded.

We were listening intently, so we heard the footsteps when they were still far away. They did not match the expected, even pace of Ian's return. He was running — no, sprinting.

Doc reacted immediately to the sound of trouble. He jogged quickly out to meet Ian. I wished I could see what was wrong, too, but I didn't want to upset Walter by trying to free my hand again. I listened hard instead.

"Brandt?" I heard Doc say in surprise.

"Where is it? *Where is it?*" the other man demanded breathlessly. The running footsteps only paused for a second, then started up again, not quite as fast.

"What are you talking about?" Doc asked, calling back this way.

"The parasite!" Brandt hissed impatiently, anxiously, as he burst through the arched entry.

Brandt was not a big man like Kyle or Ian; he was probably only a few inches taller than me, but he was thick and solid as a rhinoceros. His eyes swept the room; his piercing gaze focused on my face for half a second, then took in Walter's oblivious form, and then raced around the room only to end up on me again.

Doc caught up with Brandt then, his long fingers gripping Brandt's shoulder just as the broader man took the first step in my direction.

"What are you doing?" Doc asked, his voice the closest to a growl I'd ever heard it.

Before Brandt answered, the odd sound returned, going from soft to screaming loud to soft again with a suddenness that had us all frozen. The beats thudded right on top of one another, shaking the air when they were at their loudest.

"Is that — is that a helicopter?" Doc asked, whispering.

"Yes," Brandt whispered back. "It's the Seeker — the one from before, the one who was looking for *it*." He jerked his chin at me.

My throat was suddenly too small — the breaths moving through it were thin and shallow, not enough. I felt dizzy.

*No. Not now. Please.*

*What is her problem?* Mel snarled in my head. *Why can't she leave us alone?*

*We can't let her hurt them!*

*But how do we stop her?*

*I don't know. This is all my fault!*

*Mine, too, Wanda. Ours.*

"Are you sure?" Doc asked.

"Kyle got a clear view through the binoculars while it was hovering. Same one he saw before."

"Is it looking *here?*" Doc's voice was suddenly horrified. He half spun, eyes flashing toward the exit. "Where's Sharon?"

Brandt shook his head. "It's just running sweeps. Starts at Picacho, then fans out in spokes. Doesn't look like it's focusing on anything close. Circled around a few times where we dumped the car."

"Sharon?" Doc asked again.

"She's with the kids and Lucina. They're fine. The boys are getting things packed in case we have to roll tonight, but Jeb says it's not likely."

Doc exhaled, then paced over to his desk. He slouched against it, looking as if he'd just run a long race. "So it's nothing new, really," he murmured.

"Naw. Just have to lay low for a few days," Brandt reassured him. His eyes were flickering around the room again, settling on me every other second. "Do you have any rope handy?" he asked. He pulled up the edge of the sheet on an empty cot, examining it.

"Rope?" Doc echoed blankly.

"For the parasite. Kyle sent me out here to secure it."

My muscles contracted involuntarily; my hand gripped Walter's fingers too tightly, and he whimpered. I tried to force it to relax while I kept my eyes on Brandt's hard face. He was waiting for Doc, expectant.

"You're here to *secure* Wanda?" Doc said, his voice

hard again. "And what makes you think that's necessary?"

"Come on, Doc. Don't be stupid. You've got some big vents in here, and a lot of reflective metal." Brandt gestured to a file cabinet against the far wall. "You let your attention wander for half a minute, and it'll be flashing signals to that Seeker."

I sucked in a shocked breath; it was loud in the still room.

"See?" Brandt said. "Guessed its plan in one."

I wanted to bury myself under a boulder to hide from the bulging, relentless eyes of my Seeker, yet he imagined I wanted to guide her in. Bring her here to kill Jamie, Jared, Jeb, Ian . . . I felt like gagging.

"You can go, Brandt," Doc said in an icy tone. "I will keep an eye on Wanda."

Brandt raised one eyebrow. "What happened to you guys? To you and Ian and Trudy and the rest? It's like you're all hypnotized. If your eyes weren't right, I'd have to wonder . . ."

"Go ahead and wonder all you want, Brandt. But get out while you're doing it."

Brandt shook his head. "I've got a job to do."

Doc walked toward Brandt, stopping when he was between Brandt and me. He folded his arms across his chest.

"You're not going to touch her."

The throbbing helicopter blades sounded in the distance. We were all very still, not breathing, until they faded.

Brandt shook his head when it was quiet again. He didn't speak; he just went to the desk and picked up Doc's chair. He carried it to the wall by the file cabinet, slammed it to the ground, and then sat down hard, making the metal legs squeal against the stone. He leaned forward, his hands on his knees, and stared at me. A vulture waiting for a dying hare to stop moving.

Doc's jaw tightened, making a little popping noise.

"Gladys," Walter muttered, surfacing from his dazed sleep. "You're here."

Too nervous to speak with Brandt watching, I just patted his hand. His clouded eyes searched my face, seeing features that weren't there.

"It hurts, Gladdie. It hurts a lot."

"I know," I whispered. "Doc?"

He was already there, the brandy in hand. "Open up, Walter."

The sound of the helicopter thumped quietly, far away but still much too close. Doc flinched, and a few drops of brandy splattered on my arm.

◆

It was a horrible day. The worst of my life on this planet, even including my first day in the caves and the last hot, dry day in the desert, hours from death.

The helicopter circled and circled. Sometimes more than an hour would pass, and I would think it was finally over. Then the sound would come back, and I would see the Seeker's obstinate face in my head, her protruding eyes scouring the blank desert for some sign of humans. I tried to will her away, concentrating hard on my memories of the desert's featureless, colorless plain, as if I could somehow make sure she saw nothing else, as if I could bore her into leaving.

Brandt never took his suspicious stare off of me. I could always feel it, though I rarely looked at him. It got a little better when Ian came back with both breakfast and lunch. He was all dirty from packing in case of an evacuation — whatever that meant. Did they have anywhere to go? Ian scowled so hard he looked like Kyle when Brandt explained in clipped phrases why he was there. Then Ian dragged another empty cot beside mine, so that he could sit in Brandt's line of sight and block his view.

The helicopter, Brandt's distrustful watch, these were not really so bad. On an ordinary day — if there was really such a thing anymore — either one of these might have seemed agonizing. Today, they were nothing.

By noon, Doc had given Walter the last of the brandy. It seemed like only minutes later that Walter was writhing, moaning, and gasping for breath. His fingers bruised and chafed mine, but if I ever pulled away, his moans turned to shrill screams. I ducked out once to use the latrine; Brandt followed me, which made Ian feel like he had to come, too. By the time we got back — after nearly running the whole way — Walter's screams no longer sounded human. Doc's face was hollow with echoed agony. Walter quieted after I spoke to him for a moment, letting him think his wife was near. It was an easy lie, a kind one. Brandt made little noises of irritation, but I knew that he was wrong to be upset. Nothing mattered beside Walter's pain.

The whimpers and the writhing continued, though, and Brandt paced back and forth at the other end of the room, trying to be as far from the sound as possible.

Jamie came looking for me, bringing food enough for four, when the light was growing orangey overhead. I wouldn't let him stay; I made Ian take him back to the kitchen to eat, made Ian promise to watch him all night so he wouldn't sneak back here. Walter couldn't help shrieking when his twisting moved his broken leg, and the sound of it was nearly unbearable. Jamie shouldn't have this night burned into his memory the way it would surely be burned into Doc's and mine. Perhaps Brandt's as well, though he did what he could to ignore Walter, plugging his ears and humming a dissonant tune.

Doc did not try to distance himself from Walter's hideous suffering; instead, he suffered with him. Walter's cries carved deep lines in Doc's face, like claws raking his skin.

It was strange to see such depths of compassion in a human, particularly Doc. I couldn't look at him the same way after watching him live Walter's pain. So great was his compassion, he seemed to bleed internally with it. As I watched, it became impossible to believe that Doc was a cruel person; the man simply could not be a torturer. I tried to remember what had been said to found my conjectures — had anyone made the accusation outright? I didn't think so. I must have jumped to false conclusions in my terror.

I doubted I could ever mistrust Doc again after this nightmarish day. However, I would always find his hospital a horrible place.

When the last of the daylight disappeared, so did the helicopter. We sat in the darkness, not daring to turn on even the dim blue light. It took a few hours before any of us would believe the hunt was over. Brandt was the first to accept it; he'd had enough of the hospital, too.

"Makes sense for it to give up," he muttered, edging

out the exit. "Nothing to see at night. I'll just take your light with me, Doc, so that Jeb's pet parasite can't get up to anything, and be on my way."

Doc didn't respond, didn't even look at the sullen man as he left.

"Make it stop, Gladdie, make it stop!" Walter begged me. I wiped the sweat from his face while he crushed my hand.

Time seemed to slow down and stop; the black night felt unending. Walter's screams got more and more frequent, more and more excruciating.

Melanie was far away, knowing she could do nothing useful. I would have hidden, too, if Walter hadn't needed me. I was all alone in my head — exactly what I had once wanted. It made me feel lost.

Eventually, a dim gray light started to creep in through the high vents overhead. I was hovering on the edge of sleep, Walter's moans and screams keeping me from sinking under. I could hear Doc snoring behind me. I was glad that he'd been able to escape for a little while.

I didn't hear Jared come in. I was mumbling weak assurances, barely coherent, trying to calm Walter.

"I'm here, I'm here," I murmured as he cried out his wife's name. "Shh, it's okay." The words were meaningless. It was something to say, though, and it did seem that my voice calmed the worst of his cries.

I don't know how long Jared watched me with Walter before I realized he was there. It must have been a while. I was sure his first reaction would be anger, but when I heard him speak, his voice was cool.

"Doc," he said, and I heard the cot behind me shake. "Doc, wake up."

I jerked my hand free, whirling, disoriented, to see the face that went with the unmistakable voice.

His eyes were on me as he shook the sleeping man's shoulder. They were impossible to read in the dim light. His face had no expression at all.

Melanie jolted into awareness. She pored over his features, trying to read the thoughts behind the mask.

"Gladdie! Don't leave! Don't!" Walter's screech had Doc bolting upright, nearly capsizing his cot.

I spun back to Walter, shoving my sore hand into his searching fingers.

"Shhh, shhh! Walter, I'm here. I won't leave. I won't, I promise."

He quieted down, whimpering like a small child. I wiped the damp cloth over his forehead; his sob hitched and turned into a sigh.

"What's that about?" Jared murmured behind me.

"She's the best painkiller I've been able to find," Doc said wearily.

"Well, I've found you something better than a tame Seeker."

My stomach knotted, and Melanie hissed in my head. *So stupidly, blindly stubborn!* she growled. *He wouldn't believe you if you told him the sun sets in the west.*

But Doc was beyond caring about the slight to me. "You found something!"

"Morphine — there's not much. I would have gotten here sooner if the Seeker hadn't pinned me down out there."

Doc was instantly in action. I heard him rustling through something papery, and he crowed in delight. "Jared, you're the miracle man!"

"Doc, just a sec . . ."

But Doc was at my side already, his haggard face alight with anticipation. His hands were busy with a small syringe. He stuck the tiny needle into the crease at Walter's elbow, on the arm that was attached to me. I turned my face away. It seemed so horribly invasive to stab something through his skin.

I couldn't argue with the results, though. Within half a minute, Walter's entire body relaxed, melting into a pile of loose flesh against the thin mattress. His breathing went from harsh and urgent to whispery and even. His hand relaxed, freeing mine.

I massaged my left hand with my right, trying to bring the blood back to my fingertips. Little prickles followed the flow of blood under my skin.

"Uh, Doc, there really isn't enough for that," Jared murmured.

I looked up from Walter's face, peaceful at last. Jared had his back to me, but I could see the surprise in Doc's expression.

"Enough for what? I'm not going to save this for a rainy day, Jared. I'm sure we'll wish we had it again, and too soon, but I'm not going to let Walter scream in agony while I have a way to help him!"

"That's not what I meant," Jared said. He spoke the way he did when he'd already thought about something long and hard. Slow and even, like Walter's breath.

Doc frowned, confused.

"There's enough to stop the pain for maybe three or four days, that's all," Jared said. "If you give it to him in doses."

I didn't understand what Jared was saying, but Doc did.

"Ah," he sighed. He turned to look at Walter again, and I saw a rim of fresh tears start to pool above his lower lids. He opened his mouth to speak, but nothing came out.

I wanted to know what they were talking about, but Jared's presence made me silent, brought back the reserve I rarely felt the need for anymore.

"You can't save him. You can only save him pain, Doc."

"I know," Doc said. His voice broke, like he was holding back a sob. "You're right."

*What's going on?* I asked. As long as Melanie was going to be around, I might as well make use of her.

*They're going to kill Walter,* she told me matter-of-factly. *There's enough morphine to give him an overdose.*

My gasp sounded loud in the quiet room, but it was really just a breath. I didn't look up to see how the two healthy men would react. My own tears pooled as I leaned over Walter's pillow.

*No,* I thought, *no. Not yet. No.*

*You'd rather he died screaming?*

*I just . . . I can't stand the . . . finality. It's so absolute. I'll never see my friend again.*

*How many of your other friends have you gone back to visit, Wanderer?*

*I've never had friends like this before.*

My friends on other planets were all blurred together in my head; the souls were so similar, almost interchangeable in some ways. Walter was distinctly himself. When he was gone, there would be no one who could fill his place.

I cradled Walter's head in my arms and let my tears fall onto his skin. I tried to stifle my crying, but it made its way out regardless, a keening rather than sobs.

*I know. Another first,* Melanie whispered, and there was compassion in her tone. Compassion for me — that was a first, too.

"Wanda?" Doc asked.

I just shook my head, not able to answer.

"I think you've been here too long," he said. I felt his hand, light and warm, on my shoulder. "You should take a break."

I shook my head again, still keening softly.

"You're worn out," he said. "Go clean up, stretch your legs. Eat something."

I glared up at him. "Will Walter be here when I get back?" I mumbled through my tears.

His eyes tightened anxiously. "Do you want that?"

"I'd like a chance to say goodbye. He's my friend."

He patted my arm. "I know, Wanda, I know. Me, too. I'm in no hurry. You get some air and then come back. Walter will be sleeping for a while."

I read his worn face, and I believed the sincerity there.

I nodded and carefully put Walter's head back on the pillow. Maybe if I got away from this place for a little bit, I'd find a way to handle this. I wasn't sure how — I had no experience with real goodbyes.

Because I was in love with him, no matter that it was unwilling, I had to look at Jared before I left. Mel wanted this, too, but wished that she could somehow exclude me from the process.

He was staring at me. I had a feeling his eyes had been on me for a long time. His face was carefully composed, but there was surprise and suspicion in there again. It made me tired. What would be the point of acting out a charade now, even if I were that talented a liar? Walter would never stand up for me again. I couldn't *sucker* him anymore.

I met Jared's gaze for one long second, then turned to hurry down the pitch-black corridor that was brighter than his expression.

# CHAPTER 32

# *Ambushed*

The caves were quiet; the sun had not yet risen. In the big plaza, the mirrors were a pale gray with the coming dawn.

My few clothes were still in Jamie and Jared's room. I snuck in, glad that I knew where Jared was.

Jamie was sound asleep, curled into a tight ball in the top corner of the mattress. He didn't usually sleep so compactly, but he had good reason to at the moment. Ian was sprawled across the rest of the space, his feet and hands hanging off the edges, one appendage to each of the four sides.

For some reason, this was hysterical to me. I had to put my fist in my mouth to choke back the laughter as I quickly snatched up my old dirt-dyed T-shirt and shorts. I hurried into the hall, still stifling the giggles.

*You're slaphappy,* Melanie told me. *You need some sleep.*

*I'll sleep later. When . . .* I couldn't finish the thought. It sobered me instantaneously, and everything was quiet again.

I was still rushing as I headed for the bathing room. I trusted Doc, but . . . Maybe he would change his mind. Maybe Jared would argue against what I wanted. I couldn't be all day.

I thought I heard something behind me when I reached the octopus-like juncture where all the sleeping halls met. I looked back, but I couldn't see anyone in the dim cave. People were beginning to stir. Soon it would be time for breakfast and another day of work. If they'd finished with the stalks, the ground in the east fields would need to be turned. Maybe I would have time to help . . . later . . .

I followed the familiar path to the underground rivers, my mind in a million other places. I couldn't seem to concentrate on anything in particular. Every time I tried to focus on a subject — Walter, Jared, breakfast, chores, baths — some other thought would pull my head away in seconds. Melanie was right; I needed to sleep. She was just as muddled. Her thoughts all spun around Jared, but she could make nothing coherent of them, either.

I'd gotten used to the bathing room. The utter blackness of it didn't bother me anymore. So many places were black here. Half my daylight hours were lived in darkness. And I'd been here too many times. There was never anything lurking under the water's surface, waiting to pull me under.

I knew I didn't have time to soak, though. Others would be up soon, and some people liked to start their day clean. I got to work, washing myself first, then moving on to my clothes. I scrubbed at my shirt fiercely, wishing I could scrub out my memory of the past two nights.

My hands were stinging when I was done, the dry cracks on my knuckles burning worst of all. I rinsed them in the water, but it made no noticeable difference. I sighed and climbed out to get dressed.

I'd left my dry clothes on the loose rocks in the back corner. I kicked a stone by accident, hard enough to hurt my bare foot, and it clattered loudly across the room, bouncing off the wall and landing with a plunk and a gurgle in the pool. The sound made me jump, though it wasn't all that loud next to the roar of the hot river in the outer room.

I was just shoving my feet into my scruffy tennis shoes when my turn was up.

"Knock, knock," a familiar voice called from the dark entry.

"Good morning, Ian," I said. "I'm just done. Did you sleep well?"

"Ian's still sleeping," Ian's voice answered. "I'm sure that won't last forever, though, so we'd best get on with this."

Splinters of ice pinned my joints in place. I couldn't move. I couldn't breathe.

I'd noticed it before, and then forgotten it in the long weeks of Kyle's absence: not only did Ian and his brother look very much alike, but — when Kyle spoke at a normal volume, which so rarely happened — they also had exactly the same voice.

There was no air. I was trapped in this black hole with Kyle at the door. There was no way out.

*Keep quiet!* Melanie shrieked in my head.

I could do that. There was no air to scream with.

*Listen!*

I did as I was told, trying to focus in spite of the fear that stabbed through my head like a million slender spears of ice.

I couldn't hear anything. Was Kyle waiting for a response? Was he sneaking around the room in silence? I listened harder, but the rush of the river covered any sounds.

*Quick, grab a rock!* Melanie ordered.

*Why?*

I saw myself crashing a rough stone against Kyle's head.

*I can't do it!*

*Then we're going to die!* she screamed back at me. *I can do it! Let me!*

*There has to be another way,* I moaned, but I forced my ice-locked knees to bend. My hands searched the darkness and came up with a large, jagged rock and a handful of pebbles.

Fight or flight.

In desperation, I tried to unlock Melanie, to let her out. I couldn't find the door — my hands were still my own, clutched uselessly around the objects I could never make into weapons.

A noise. A tiny splash as something entered the stream that drained the pool into the latrine room. Only a few yards away.

*Give me my hands!*

*I don't know how! Take them!*

I started to creep away, close to the wall, toward the

exit. Melanie struggled to find her way out of my head, but she couldn't find the door from her side, either.

Another sound. Not by the far stream. A breath, by the exit. I froze where I was.

*Where is he?*

*I don't know!*

Again, I could hear nothing but the river. Was Kyle alone? Was someone waiting by the door to catch me when he herded me around the pool? How close was Kyle now?

I felt the hairs on my arms and legs standing on end. There was some kind of pressure in the air, as though I could feel his silent movements. The door. I half turned, easing back in the direction I'd come, away from where I'd heard the breath.

He couldn't wait forever. The little he'd said told me he was in a hurry. Someone could come at any time. Odds were on his side, though. There were fewer who would be inclined to stop him than there were who might think this was for the best. And of those inclined to stop him, even fewer who'd have much of a chance of doing that. Only Jeb and his gun would make a difference. Jared was at least as strong as Kyle, but Kyle was more motivated. Jared would probably not fight him now.

Another noise. Was that a footstep by the door? Or just my imagination? How long had this silent standoff lasted? I couldn't guess how many seconds or minutes had passed.

*Get ready.* Melanie knew that the stalling would soon be at an end. She wanted me to clench the rock tighter.

But I would give flight a chance first. I would not be an effective fighter, even if I could bring myself to try. Kyle was probably twice my weight, and he had a much longer reach.

I raised the hand with the pebbles and aimed them toward the back passage to the latrine. Maybe I could make him think that I was going to hide and hope for rescue. I threw the handful of small stones and shied away from the noise when they clattered against the rock wall.

The breath at the door again, the sound of a light footfall headed toward my decoy. I edged as quietly along the wall as I could.

*What if there are two?*

*I don't know.*

I was almost to the exit. If I could just make the tunnel, I thought I could outrun him. I was lighter and fast. . . .

I heard a footstep, very clearly this time, disrupting the stream in the back of the room. I crept faster.

A gigantic splash shattered the tense standoff. Water pelted my skin, making me gasp. It spattered against the wall in a wave of wet sound.

*He's coming through the pool! Run!*

I hesitated just a second too long. Big fingers clutched at my calf, my ankle. I yanked against the pull, lurching forward. I stumbled, and the momentum that threw me down to the floor made his fingers slip. He caught my sneaker. I kicked it off, leaving it in his hand.

I was down, but he was down, too. It gave me enough time to scramble forward, ripping my knees against the rough stone.

Kyle grunted, and his hand clutched at my naked heel. There was nothing to catch hold of; I slid free again. I wrenched myself forward, pulling to my feet with my head still down, every second in danger of falling again because my body was moving almost parallel to the floor. I kept my balance through sheer force of will.

There was no one else. No one to catch me at the exit to the outer room. I sprinted forward, hope and adrenaline surging in my veins. I burst into the river room at full speed, my only thought to reach the tunnel. I could hear Kyle's heavy breath close behind but not close enough. With each step, I pushed harder against the ground, throwing myself ahead of him.

Pain lanced through my leg, crumpling it.

Over the babble of the river, I heard two heavy stones hit the ground and roll — the one I'd been clutching and the one he'd thrown to cripple me. My leg twisted under me, spinning me backward to the ground, and in the same second he was on top of me.

His weight knocked my head against the rock in a ringing blow and pinned me flat against the floor. No leverage.

*Scream!*

The air blew out of me in a siren of sound that surprised us all. My wordless shriek was more than I'd hoped for — surely someone would hear it. Please let that someone be Jeb. Please let him have the gun.

"Uhng!" Kyle protested. His hand was big enough to cover most of my face. His palm mashed against my mouth, cutting off my scream.

He rolled then, and the motion so took me by surprise that I had no time to try to find an advantage in it. He pulled me swiftly over and under and over his body. I was dizzy and confused, my head still spinning, but I understood as soon as my face hit the water.

His hand locked on the back of my neck, forcing my face into the shallow stream of cooler water that wound its way into the bathing pool. It was too late to hold my breath. I'd already inhaled a mouthful of water.

My body panicked when the water hit my lungs. Its flailing was stronger than he'd expected. My limbs all jerked and thrashed in different directions, and his grip on my neck slipped. He tried to get a better hold, and some instinct made me pull myself into him rather than away, as he was expecting. I only pulled half a foot closer to him, but that got my chin out of the stream, and enough of my mouth to choke some of the water back out and drag in a breath.

He fought to push me back into the stream, but I wriggled and wedged myself under him so that his own weight was working against his goal. I was still reacting to the water in my lungs, coughing and spasming out of control.

"Enough!" Kyle growled.

He pulled himself off me, and I tried to drag myself away.

"Oh, no, you *don't!*" he spit through his teeth.

It was over, and I knew it.

There was something wrong with my injured leg. It felt numb, and I couldn't make it do what I wanted. I could only push myself along the floor with my arms and my good leg. I was coughing too hard to do even that well. Too hard to scream again.

Kyle grabbed my wrist and yanked me up from the floor. The weight of my body made my leg buckle, and I slumped into him.

He got both my wrists in one hand and wrapped the

other arm around my waist. He pulled me off the floor and into his side, like an awkward bag of flour. I twisted, and my good leg kicked against the empty air.

"Let's get this over with."

He jumped over the smaller stream with a bound and carried me toward the closest sinkhole. The steam from the hot spring washed my face.

He was going to throw me into the dark, hot hole and let the boiling water pull me into the ground as it burned me.

"No, no!" I shouted, my voice too hoarse and low to carry.

I writhed frantically. My knee knocked against one of the ropy rock columns, and I hooked my foot around it, trying to yank myself out of his grip. He jerked me free with an impatient grunt.

At least that loosened his hold enough that I could make one more move. It had worked before, so I tried it again. Instead of trying to free myself, I twisted in and wrapped my legs around his waist, locking the good ankle around the bad, trying to ignore the pain so that I could get a good hold there.

"Get *off* me, you —" He fought to knock me loose, and I jerked one of my wrists free. I wrapped that arm around his neck and grabbed his thick hair. If I was going into the black river, so was he.

Kyle hissed and stopped prying at my leg long enough to punch my side.

I gasped in pain but got my other hand into his hair.

He wrapped both arms around me, as if we were embracing rather than locked in a killing struggle. Then he grabbed my waist from both sides and heaved with all his strength against my hold.

His hair started to come out in my hands, but he just grunted and pulled harder.

I could hear the steaming water rushing close by, right below me, it seemed. The steam billowed up in a thick cloud, and for a minute I couldn't see anything but Kyle's face, twisted with rage into something beastlike and merciless.

I felt my bad leg giving. I tried to pull myself closer to him, but his brute strength was winning against my desperation. He would have me free in a moment, and I would fall into the hissing steam and disappear.

*Jared! Jamie!* The thought, the agony, belonged to both Melanie and me. They would never know what had happened to me. Ian. Jeb. Doc. Walter. No goodbyes.

Kyle abruptly jumped into the air and came down with a thud. The jarring impact had the effect he wanted: my legs came loose.

But before he could take advantage, there was another result.

The cracking sound was deafening. I thought the whole cave was coming down. The floor shuddered beneath us.

Kyle gasped and jumped back, taking me — hands still locked in his hair — with him. The rock under his feet, with more cracking and groaning, began to crumble away.

Our combined weight had broken the brittle lip of the hole. As Kyle stumbled away, the crumbling followed his heavy steps. It was faster than he was.

A piece of the floor disappeared from under his heel,

and he went down with a thud. My weight pushed him back hard, and his head smacked sharply against a stone pillar. His arms fell away from me, limp.

The cracking of the floor settled into a sustained groan. I could feel it shiver beneath Kyle's body.

I was on his chest. Our legs dangled above empty space, the steam condensing into a million drops on our skin.

"Kyle?"

There was no answer.

I was afraid to move.

*You've got to get off him. You're too heavy together. Carefully — use the pillar. Pull away from the hole.*

Whimpering in fear, too terrified to think for myself, I did as Melanie ordered. I freed my fingers from Kyle's hair and climbed gingerly over his unconscious form, using the pillar as an anchor to pull myself forward. It felt steady enough, but the floor still moaned under us.

I pulled myself past the pillar and onto the ground beyond it. This ground stayed firm under my hands and knees, but I scrambled farther away, toward the safety of the exit tunnel.

There was another crack, and I glanced back. One of Kyle's legs drooped farther down as a rock fell from beneath it. I heard the splash this time as the chunk of stone met the river below. The ground shuddered under his weight.

*He's going to fall,* I realized.

*Good,* Melanie snarled.

*But . . . !*

*If he falls, he can't kill us, Wanda. If he doesn't fall, he will.*

*I can't just . . .*

*Yes, you can. Walk away. Don't you want to live?*

I did. I wanted to live.

Kyle could disappear. And if he did, there was a chance that no one would ever hurt me again. At least not among the people here. There was still the Seeker to consider, but maybe she would give up someday, and then I could stay here indefinitely with the humans I loved. . . .

My leg throbbed, pain replacing some of the numbness. Warm fluid trickled down my lips. I tasted the moisture without thinking and realized it was my blood.

*Walk away, Wanderer. I want to live. I want a choice, too.*

I could feel the tremors from where I stood. Another piece of floor splashed into the river. Kyle's weight shifted, and he slid an inch toward the hole.

*Let him go.*

Melanie knew better than I what she was talking about. This was her world. Her rules.

I stared at the face of the man who was about to die — the man who wanted me dead. With him unconscious, Kyle's face was no longer that of an angry animal. It was relaxed, almost peaceful.

The resemblance to his brother was very apparent.

*No!* Melanie protested.

I crawled back to him on my hands and knees — slowly, feeling the ground with care before each inch I moved. I was too afraid to go beyond the pillar, so I hooked my good leg around it, an anchor again, and leaned around to wedge my hands under Kyle's arms and over his chest.

I heaved so hard I nearly pulled my arms from their

sockets, but he didn't move. I heard a sound like the trickle of sand through an hourglass as the floor continued to dissolve into tiny pieces.

I yanked again, but the only result was that the trickle sped up. Shifting his weight was breaking the floor faster.

Just as I thought that, a large chunk of rock plummeted into the river, and Kyle's precarious balance was overthrown. He began to fall.

*"No!"* I screamed, the siren bursting from my throat again. I flattened myself against the column and managed to pin him to the other side, locking my hands around his wide chest. My arms ached.

"Help me!" I shrieked. "Somebody! Help!"

# CHAPTER 33

# Doubted

Another splash. Kyle's weight tortured my arms.

"Wanda? Wanda!"

"Help me! Kyle! The floor! Help!"

I had my face pressed against the stone, my eyes toward the cave entrance. The light was bright overhead as the day dawned. I held my breath. My arms screamed.

"Wanda! Where are you?"

Ian leaped through the door, the rifle in his hands, held low and ready. His face was the angry mask his brother had worn.

"Watch out!" I screamed at him. "The floor is breaking up! I can't hold him much longer!"

It took him two long seconds to process the scene that was so different from the one he'd been expecting — Kyle, trying to kill me. The scene that had been, just seconds ago.

Then he threw the gun to the cave floor and started toward me with a long stride.

"Get down — disperse your weight!"

He dropped to all fours and scuttled to me, his eyes burning in the light of dawn.

"Don't let go," he cautioned.

I groaned in pain.

He assessed for another second, and then slid his body behind mine, pushing me closer to the rock. His arms were longer than mine. Even with me in the way, he was able to get his hands around his brother.

"One, two, three," he grunted.

He pulled Kyle up against the rock, much more securely than I'd had him. The movement smashed my face into the pillar. The bad side, though — it couldn't get much more scarred at this point.

"I'm going to pull him to this side. Can you squeeze out?"

"I'll try."

I loosened my hold on Kyle, feeling my shoulders ache in relief, making sure Ian had him. Then I wriggled out from between Ian and the rock, careful not to put myself on a dangerous section of the floor. I crawled backward a few feet toward the door, ready to make a grab for Ian if he started slipping.

Ian hauled his inert brother around one side of the pillar, dragging him in jerks, a foot at a time. More of the floor crumbled, but the foundation of the pillar remained intact. A new shelf formed about two feet out from the column of rock.

Ian crawled backward the way I had, dragging his brother along in short surges of muscle and will. Within a minute, we were all three in the mouth of the corridor, Ian and I breathing in gasps.

"What . . . the hell . . . happened?"

"Our weight . . . was too . . . much. Floor caved in."

"What were you doing . . . by the edge? With Kyle?"

I put my head down and concentrated on breathing.

*Well, tell him.*

*What will happen then?*

*You know what will happen. Kyle broke the rules. Jeb will shoot him, or they'll kick him out. Maybe Ian will beat the snot out of him first. That would be fun to watch.*

Melanie didn't really mean it — I didn't think so, anyway. She was just still mad at me for risking our lives to save our would-be murderer.

*Exactly,* I told her. *And if they kick Kyle out for me . . . or kill him . . .* I shuddered. *Well, can't you see how little sense that would make? He's one of you.*

*We've got a life here, Wanda. You're jeopardizing that.*

*It's my life, too. And I'm . . . well, I'm me.*

Melanie groaned in disgust.

"Wanda?" Ian demanded.

"Nothing," I muttered.

"You're a rotten liar. You know that, right?"

I kept my head down and breathed.

"What did he do?"

"Nothing," I lied. Poorly.

Ian put his hand under my chin, pulled my face up. "Your nose is bleeding." He twisted my head to the side. "And there's more blood in your hair."

"I — hit my head when the floor fell."

"On both sides?"

I shrugged.

Ian glared at me for a long moment. The darkness of the tunnel muted the brilliance of his eyes.

"We should get Kyle to Doc — he really cracked his head when he went down."

"Why are you protecting him? He tried to kill you." It was a statement of fact, not a question. His expression slowly melted from anger to horror. He was imagining what we had been doing on that unstable shelf — I could see that in his eyes. When I did not answer, he spoke again in a whisper. "He was going to throw you in the river. . . .." A strange tremor shook his body.

Ian had one arm around Kyle — he'd collapsed that way and seemed too tired to move. Now he shoved his unconscious brother away roughly, sliding farther from him in disgust. He slid into me and wrapped his arms around my shoulders. He pulled me close against his chest — I could feel his breath go in and out, still more ragged than normal.

It felt very strange.

"I should roll him right back in there and kick him over the edge myself."

I shook my head frantically, making it throb in pain. "No."

"Saves time. Jeb made the rules clear. You try to hurt someone here, there are penalties. There'll be a tribunal."

I tried to pull away from him, but he tightened his grip. It wasn't frightening, not like the way Kyle had grabbed me. But it was upsetting — it threw me off balance. "No. You can't do that, because no one broke the rules. The floor collapsed, that's all."

"Wanda —"

"He's your brother."

"He knew what he was doing. He's my brother, yes, but he did what he did, and you are . . . you are . . . my friend."

"He did nothing. He is human," I whispered. "This is his place, not mine."

"We're not having this discussion again. Your definition of human is not the same as mine. To you, it means something . . . negative. To me, it's a compliment — and by my definition, you are and he isn't. Not after this."

"Human isn't a negative to me. I know you now. But Ian, he's your *brother*."

"A fact that shames me."

I pushed away from him again. This time, he let me go. It might have had something to do with the moan of pain that escaped my lips when I moved my leg.

"Are you okay?"

"I think so. We need to find Doc, but I don't know if I can walk. I — I hit my leg, when I fell."

A growl strangled in his throat. "Which leg? Let me see."

I tried to straighten out my hurt leg — it was the right one — and groaned again. His hands started at my ankle, testing the bones, the joints. He rotated my ankle carefully.

"Higher. Here." I pulled his hand to the back of my thigh, just above the knee. I moaned again when he pressed the sore place. "It's not broken or anything, I don't think. Just really sore."

"Deep muscle bruise, at least," he muttered. "And how did this happen?"

"Must have . . . landed on a rock when I fell."

He sighed. "Okay, let's get you to Doc."

"Kyle needs him more than I do."

"I have to go find Doc anyway — or some help. I can't carry Kyle that far, but I can certainly carry you. Oops — hold on."

He turned abruptly and ducked back into the river room. I decided I wouldn't argue with him. I wanted to see Walter before . . . Doc had promised to wait for me. Would that first dose of painkiller wear off soon? My head swam. There was so much to worry about, and I was so tired. The adrenaline had drained, leaving me empty.

Ian came back with the gun. I frowned because this reminded me that I'd wished for it before. I didn't like that.

"Let's go."

Without thinking, he handed the gun to me. I let it fall into my open palms, but I couldn't curl my hands around it. I decided it was a suitable punishment, to have to carry the thing.

Ian chuckled. "How anyone could be afraid of you . . ." he mumbled to himself.

He picked me up easily and was moving before I was settled. I tried to keep the tenderest parts — the back of my head, the back of my leg — from resting on him too hard.

"How'd your clothes get so wet?" he asked. We were passing under one of the fist-sized skylights, and I could see the hint of a grim smile on his pale lips.

"I don't know," I muttered. "Steam?"

We passed into darkness again.

"You're missing a shoe."

"Oh."

We passed through another beam of light, and his eyes flashed sapphire. They were serious now, locked on my face.

"I'm . . . *very* glad that you weren't hurt, Wanda. Hurt worse, I should say."

I didn't answer. I was afraid of giving him something to use against Kyle.

Jeb found us just before we hit the big cave. There was enough light for me to see the sharp glint of curiosity in his eyes when he saw me in Ian's arms, face bleeding, the gun resting gingerly on my open hands.

"You were right, then," Jeb guessed. The curiosity was strong, but the steel in his tone was stronger. His jaw was tight beneath the fan of his beard. "I didn't hear a shot. Kyle?"

"He's unconscious," I said in a rush. "You need to warn everyone — part of the floor collapsed in the river room. I don't know how stable it is now. Kyle hit his head really hard trying to get out of the way. He needs Doc."

Jeb raised one eyebrow so high it almost touched the faded bandanna at his hairline.

"That's the story," Ian said, making no effort to conceal his doubt. "And she's apparently sticking to it."

Jeb laughed. "Let me take that off your hands," he said to me.

I let him have the gun willingly. He laughed again at my expression.

"I'll get Andy and Brandt to help me with Kyle. We'll follow behind you."

"Keep a close eye on him when he wakes up," Ian said in a hard tone.

"Can do."

Jeb slouched off, looking for more hands. Ian hurried me toward the hospital cave.

"Kyle could be really hurt. . . . Jeb should hurry."

"Kyle's head is harder than any rock in this place."

The long tunnel felt longer than usual. Was Kyle dying, despite my efforts? Was he conscious again and looking for me? What about Walter? Was he sleeping . . . or gone? Had the Seeker given up her hunt, or would she be back now that it was light again?

*Will Jared still be with Doc?* Mel added her questions to mine. *Will he be angry when he sees you? Will he know me?*

When we reached the sunlit southern cave, Jared and Doc didn't look like they'd moved much. They leaned, side by side, against Doc's makeshift desk. It was quiet as we approached. They weren't talking, just watching Walter sleep.

They started up with wide eyes as Ian carried me into the light and laid me on the cot next to Walter's. He straightened my right leg carefully.

Walter was snoring. That sound eased some of my tension.

"What now?" Doc demanded angrily. He was bending over me as soon as the words were out, wiping at the blood on my cheek.

Jared's face was frozen in surprise. He was being careful, not letting the expression give way to anything else.

"Kyle," Ian answered at the same time that I said, "The floor —"

Doc looked back and forth between us, confused.

Ian sighed and rolled his eyes. Absently, he laid one

hand lightly on my forehead. "The floor crumbled by the first river hole. Kyle fell back and cracked his head on a rock. Wanda saved his worthless life. She says she fell, too, when the floor gave." Ian gave Doc a meaningful look. *"Something,"* he said the word sarcastically, "bashed the back of her head pretty good." He started listing. "Her nose is bleeding but not broken, I don't think. She's got some damage to the muscle here." He touched my sore thigh. "Knees sliced up pretty good, got her face again, but I think maybe I did that, trying to pull Kyle out of the hole. Shouldn't have bothered." Ian muttered the last part.

"Anything else?" Doc asked. At that moment, his fingers, probing along my side, reached the place where Kyle had punched me. I gasped.

Doc tugged my shirt up, and I heard both Ian and Jared hiss at what they saw.

"Let me guess," Ian said in a voice like ice. "You fell on a rock."

"Good guess," I agreed, breathless. Doc was still touching my side, and I was trying to hold back whimpers.

"Might have broken a rib, not sure," Doc murmured. "I wish I could give you something for the pain —"

"Don't worry about that, Doc," I panted. "I'm okay. How's Walter? Did he wake up at all?"

"No, it will take some time to sleep that dose off," Doc said. He took my hand and started bending my wrist, my elbow.

"I'm okay."

His kind eyes were soft as he met my gaze. "You will be. You'll just have to rest for a while. I'll keep an eye on you. Here, turn your head."

I did as he asked, and then winced while he examined my wound.

"Not here," Ian muttered.

I couldn't see Doc, but Jared threw Ian a sharp look.

"They're bringing Kyle. I'm not having them in the same room."

Doc nodded. "Probably wise."

"I'll get a place ready for her. I'll need you to keep Kyle here until . . . until we decide what to do with him."

I started to speak, but Ian put his fingers on my lips.

"All right," Doc agreed. "I'll tie him down, if you want."

"If we have to. Is it okay to move her?" Ian glanced toward the tunnel, his face anxious.

Doc hesitated.

"No," I whispered, Ian's fingers still touching my mouth. "Walter. I want to be here for Walter."

"You've saved all the lives you can save today, Wanda," Ian said, his voice gentle and sad.

"I want to say . . . to say good — goodbye."

Ian nodded. Then he looked at Jared. "Can I trust you?"

Jared's face flushed with anger. Ian held up his hand.

"I don't want to leave her here unprotected while I find her a safe place," Ian said. "I don't know if Kyle will be conscious when he arrives. If Jeb shoots him, it will upset her. But you and Doc should be able to handle him. I don't want Doc to be on his own, and force Jeb's hand."

Jared spoke through clenched teeth. "Doc won't be on his own."

Ian hesitated. "She's been through hell in the past couple of days. Remember that."

Jared nodded once, teeth still clamped together.

"I'll be here," Doc reminded Ian.

Ian met his gaze. "Okay." He leaned over me, and his luminous eyes held mine. "I'll be back soon. Don't be afraid."

"I'm not."

He ducked in and touched his lips to my forehead.

No one was more surprised than I, though I heard Jared gasp quietly. My mouth hung open as Ian wheeled and nearly sprinted from the room.

I heard Doc pull a breath in through his teeth, like a backward whistle. "Well," he said.

They both stared at me for a long moment. I was so tired and sore, I barely cared what they were thinking.

"Doc —" Jared started to say something in an urgent tone, but a clamor from the tunnel interrupted him.

Five men struggled through the opening. Jeb, in front, had Kyle's left leg in his arms. Wes had the right leg, and behind them, Andy and Aaron worked to support his torso. Kyle's head lolled back over Andy's shoulder.

"Stars, but he's heavy," Jeb grunted.

Jared and Doc sprang forward to help. After a few minutes of cursing and groaning, Kyle was lying on a cot a few feet away from mine.

"How long has he been out, Wanda?" Doc asked me. He pulled Kyle's eyelids back, letting the sunlight shine into his pupils.

"Um . . ." I thought quickly. "As long as I've been here, the ten minutes or so it took Ian to carry me here, and then maybe five more minutes before that?"

"At least twenty minutes, would you say?"

"Yes. Close to that."

While we were consulting, Jeb had made his own diagnosis. No one paid any attention as he came to stand at the head of Kyle's cot. No one paid any attention — until he turned an open bottle of water over Kyle's face.

"Jeb," Doc complained, knocking his hand away.

But Kyle sputtered and blinked, and then moaned. "What happened? Where did it go?" He started to shift his weight, trying to look around. "The floor . . . is moving. . . ."

Kyle's voice had my fingers clenching the sides of my cot and panic washing through me. My leg ached. Could I limp away? Slowly, perhaps . . .

"'S okay," someone murmured. Not someone. I would always know that voice.

Jared moved to stand between my cot and Kyle's, his back to me, his eyes on the big man. Kyle rolled his head back and forth, groaning.

"You're safe," Jared said in a low voice. He didn't look at me. "Don't be afraid."

I took a deep breath.

Melanie wanted to touch him. His hand was close to mine, resting on the edge of my cot.

*Please, no,* I told her. *My face hurts quite enough as it is!*

*He won't hit you.*

*You* think. *I'm not willing to risk it.*

Melanie sighed; she yearned to move toward him. It wouldn't have been so hard to bear if I weren't yearning also.

*Give him time,* I pleaded. *Let him get used to us. Wait till he really believes.*

She sighed again.

"Aw, hell!" Kyle grumbled. My gaze flickered toward him at the sound of his voice. I could just see his bright eyes around Jared's elbow, focused on me. "It didn't fall!" he complained.

# CHAPTER 34

# Buried

Jared lunged forward, away from me. With a loud smacking sound, his fist hit Kyle's face.

Kyle's eyes rolled back in his head, and his mouth fell slack.

The room was very quiet for a few seconds.

"Um," Doc said in a mild voice, "medically speaking, I'm not sure that was the most helpful thing for his condition."

"But *I* feel better," Jared answered, sullen.

Doc smiled the tiniest smile. "Well, maybe a few more minutes of unconsciousness won't kill him."

Doc began looking under Kyle's lids again, taking his pulse . . .

"What happened?" Wes was by my head, speaking in a murmur.

"Kyle tried to kill it," Jared answered before I could. "Are we really surprised?"

"Did not," I muttered.

Wes looked at Jared.

"Altruism seems to come more naturally to it than lies," Jared noted.

"Are you *trying* to be annoying?" I demanded. My patience was not waning, but entirely gone. How long had it been since I'd slept? The only thing that ached worse than my leg was my head. Every breath hurt my side. I realized, with some surprise, that I was in a truly bad mood. "Because if you are, then be assured, you have succeeded."

Jared and Wes looked at me with shocked eyes. I was sure that if I could see the others, their expressions would match. Maybe not Jeb's. He was the master of the poker face.

"I *am* female," I complained. "That 'it' business is really getting on my nerves."

Jared blinked in surprise. Then his face settled back into harder lines. "Because of the body you wear?"

Wes glared at him.

"Because of *me*," I hissed.

"By whose definition?"

"How about by yours? In my species, I am the one that bears young. Is that not female enough for you?"

That stopped him short. I felt almost smug.

*As you should,* Melanie approved. *He's wrong, and he's being a pig about it.*

*Thank you.*

*We girls have to stick together.*

"That's a story you've never told us," Wes murmured,

while Jared struggled for a rebuttal. "How does that work?"

Wes's olive-toned face darkened, as if he'd just realized he had spoken the words out loud. "I mean, I guess you don't have to answer that, if I'm being rude."

I laughed. My mood was swinging around wildly, out of control. Slaphappy, like Mel had said. "No, you're not asking anything . . . inappropriate. We don't have such a complicated . . . elaborate setup as your species." I laughed again, and then felt warmth in my face. I remembered only too clearly how elaborate it could be.

*Get your mind out of the gutter.*

*It's your mind,* I reminded her.

"Then . . . ?" Wes asked.

I sighed. "There are only a few of us who are . . . Mothers. Not Mothers. That's what they call us, but it's just the potential to be one . . ." I was sober again, thinking of it. There were no Mothers, no surviving Mothers, only the memories of them.

"You have that *potential?*" Jared asked stiffly.

I knew the others were listening. Even Doc had paused in the act of putting his ear to Kyle's chest.

I didn't answer his question. "We're . . . a little like your hives of bees, or your ants. Many, many sexless members of the family, and then the queen . . ."

"Queen?" Wes repeated, looking at me with a strange expression.

"Not like that. But there is only one Mother for every five, ten thousand of my kind. Sometimes less. There's no hard-and-fast rule."

"How many drones?" Wes wondered.

"Oh, no — there aren't drones. No, I told you, it's simpler than that."

They waited for me to explain. I swallowed. I shouldn't have brought this up. I didn't want to talk about it anymore. Was it really such a big thing to have Jared call me "it"?

They still waited. I frowned, but then I spoke. I'd started this. "The Mothers . . . divide. Every . . . cell, I guess you could call it, though our structure isn't the same as yours, becomes a new soul. Each new soul has a little of the Mother's memory, a piece of her that remains."

"How many cells?" Doc asked, curious. "How many young?"

I shrugged. "A million or so."

The eyes that I could see widened, looked a little wilder. I tried not to feel hurt when Wes cringed away from me.

Doc whistled under his breath. He was the only one who was still interested in continuing. Aaron and Andy had wary, disturbed expressions on their faces. They'd never heard me teach before. Never heard me speak so much.

"When does that happen? Is there a catalyst?" Doc asked.

"It's a choice. A voluntary choice," I told him. "It's the only way we ever willingly choose to die. A trade, for a new generation."

"You could choose now, to divide all your cells, just like that?"

"Not quite just like that, but yes."

"Is it complicated?"

"The decision is. The process is . . . painful."

"Painful?"

Why should that have surprised him so? Wasn't it the same for his kind?

*Men.* Mel snorted.

"Excruciating," I told him. "We all remember how it was for our Mothers."

Doc was stroking his chin, entranced. "I wonder what the evolutionary track would be . . . to produce a hive society with suiciding queens. . . ." He was lost on another plane of thought.

"Altruism," Wes murmured.

"Hmm," Doc said. "Yes, that."

I closed my eyes, wishing my mouth had stayed closed. I felt dizzy. Was I just tired or was it my head wound?

"Oh," Doc muttered. "You've slept even less than I have, haven't you, Wanda? We should let you get some rest."

" 'M fine," I mumbled, but I didn't open my eyes.

"That's just great," someone said under his breath. "We've got a bloody *queen mother alien* living with us. She could blow into a million new buggers at any moment."

"Shh."

"They couldn't hurt you," I told whoever it was, not opening my eyes. "Without host bodies, they would die quickly." I winced, imagining the unimaginable grief. A million tiny, helpless souls, tiny silver babies, withering . . .

No one answered me, but I could feel their relief in the air.

I was so tired. I didn't care that Kyle was three feet from me. I didn't care that two of the men in the room would side with Kyle if he came around. I didn't care about anything but sleep.

Of course, that was when Walter woke up.

"Uuuh," he groaned, just a whisper. "Gladdie?"

With a groan of my own, I rolled toward him. The pain in my leg made me wince, but I couldn't twist my torso. I reached out to him, found his hand.

"Here," I whispered.

"Ahh," Walter sighed in relief.

Doc hushed the men who began to protest. "Wanda's given up sleep and peace to help him through the pain. Her hands are bruised from holding his. What have you done for him?"

Walter groaned again. The sound began low and guttural but turned quickly to a high-pitched whimper.

Doc winced. "Aaron, Andy, Wes . . . would you, ah, go get Sharon for me, please?"

"All of us?"

"Get out," Jeb translated.

The only answer was a shuffling of feet as they left.

"Wanda," Doc whispered, close beside my ear. "He's in pain. I can't let him come all the way around."

I tried to breathe evenly. "It's better if he doesn't know me. It's better if he thinks Gladdie is here."

I pulled my eyes open. Jeb was beside Walter, whose face still looked as if he slept.

"Bye, Walt," Jeb said. "See you on the other side."

He stepped back.

"You're a good man. You'll be missed," Jared murmured.

Doc was fumbling in the package of morphine again. The paper crackled.

"Gladdie?" Walt sobbed. "It hurts."

"Shhh. It won't hurt much longer. Doc will make it stop."

"Gladdie?"

"Yes?"

"I love you, Gladdie. I've loved you my whole life long."

"I know, Walter. I — I love you, too. You know how I love you."

Walter sighed.

I closed my eyes when Doc leaned over Walter with the syringe.

"Sleep well, friend," Doc murmured.

Walter's fingers relaxed, loosened. I held on to them — I was the one clinging now.

The minutes passed, and all was quiet except my breathing. It was hitching and breaking, tending toward quiet sobs.

Someone patted my shoulder. "He's gone, Wanda," Doc said, his voice thick. "He's out of pain."

He pulled my hand free and rolled me carefully out of my awkward position into one that was less agonizing. But only slightly so. Now that I knew Walter wouldn't be disturbed, the sobs were not so quiet. I clutched at my side, where it throbbed.

"Oh, go ahead. You won't be happy otherwise," Jared muttered in a grudging tone. I tried to open my eyes, but I couldn't do it.

Something stung my arm. I didn't remember having hurt my arm. And in such a strange place, just inside my elbow . . .

*Morphine,* Melanie whispered.

We were already drifting now. I tried to be alarmed, but I couldn't be. I was too far gone.

*No one said goodbye,* I thought dully. I couldn't expect Jared . . . but Jeb . . . Doc . . . Ian wasn't here . . .

*No one's dying,* she promised me. *Just sleeping this time . . .*

◆

When I woke, the ceiling above me was dim, starlit. Nighttime. There were so many stars. I wondered where I was. There were no black obstructions, no pieces of ceiling in my view. Just stars and stars and stars . . .

Wind fanned my face. It smelled like . . . dust and . . . something I couldn't put my finger on. An absence. The musty smell was gone. No sulfur, and it was so dry.

"Wanda?" someone whispered, touching my good cheek.

My eyes found Ian's face, white in the starlight, leaning over me. His hand on my skin was cooler than the breeze, but the air was so dry it wasn't uncomfortable. Where was I?

"Wanda? Are you awake? They won't wait any longer."

I whispered because he did. "What?"

"They're starting already. I knew you would want to be here."

"She comin' around?" Jeb's voice asked.

"What's starting?" I asked.

"Walter's funeral."

I tried to sit up, but my body was all rubbery. Ian's hand moved to my forehead, holding me down.

I twisted my head under his hand, trying to see . . .

I was outside.

*Outside.*

On my left, a rough, tumbled pile of boulders formed a miniature mountain, complete with scrubby brush. On my right, the desert plain stretched away from me, disappearing in the darkness. I looked down past my feet, and I could see the huddle of humans, ill at ease in the open air. I knew just how they felt. Exposed.

I tried to get up again. I wanted to be closer, to see. Ian's hand restrained me.

"Easy there," he said. "Don't try to stand."

"Help me," I pleaded.

"Wanda?"

I heard Jamie's voice, and then I saw him, his hair bobbing as he ran to where I was lying.

My fingertips traced the edges of the mat beneath me. How did I get here, sleeping under the stars?

"They didn't wait," Jamie said to Ian. "It will be over soon."

"Help me up," I said.

Jamie reached for my hand, but Ian shook his head. "I got her."

Ian slid his arms under me, very careful to avoid the worst of the sore spots. He pulled me up off the ground, and my head spun like a ship about to capsize. I groaned.

"What did Doc do to me?"

"He gave you a little of the leftover morphine, so that he could check you out without hurting you. You needed sleep anyway."

I frowned, disapproving. "Won't someone else need the medicine more?"

"Shh," he said, and I could hear a low voice in the distance. I turned my head.

I could see the group of humans again. They stood at the mouth of a low, dark, open space carved out by the wind under the unstable-looking pile of boulders. They stood in a ragged line, facing the shadowed grotto.

I recognized Trudy's voice.

"Walter always saw the bright side of things. He could see the bright side of a black hole. I'll miss that."

I saw a figure step forward, saw the gray-and-black braid swing as she moved, and watched Trudy toss a handful of something into the darkness. Sand scattered from her fingers, falling to the ground with a faint hiss.

She went back to stand beside her husband. Geoffrey moved away from her, stepped forward toward the black space.

"He'll find his Gladys now. He's happier where he is." Geoffrey threw his handful of dirt.

Ian carried me to the right side of the line of people, close enough to see into the murky grotto. There was a darker space on the ground in front of us, a big oblong around which the entire human population stood in a loose half circle.

Everyone was there — everyone.

Kyle stepped forward.

I trembled, and Ian squeezed me gently.

Kyle did not look in our direction. I saw his face in profile; his right eye was nearly swollen shut.

"Walter died human," Kyle said. "None of us can ask for more than that." He threw a fistful of dirt into the dark shape on the ground.

Kyle rejoined the group.

Jared stood beside him. He took the short walk and stopped at the edge of Walter's grave.

"Walter was good through and through. Not one of us is his equal." He threw his sand.

Jamie walked forward, and Jared patted his shoulder once as they passed each other.

"Walter was brave," Jamie said. "He wasn't afraid to die, he wasn't afraid to live, and . . . he wasn't afraid to *believe*. He made his own decisions, and he made good ones." Jamie threw his handful. He turned and walked back, his eyes locked on mine the whole way.

"Your turn," he whispered when he was at my side.

Andy was already moving forward, a shovel in his hands.

"Wait," Jamie said in a low voice that carried in the silence. "Wanda and Ian haven't said anything."

There was an unhappy mutter around me. My brain felt like it was pitching and heaving inside my skull.

"Let's have some respect," Jeb said, louder than Jamie. It felt too loud to me.

My first instinct was to wave Andy ahead and make Ian carry me away. This was human mourning, not mine.

But I did mourn. And I did have something to say.

"Ian, help me get some sand."

Ian crouched down so I could scoop up a handful of the loose rocks at our feet. He rested my weight on his knee to get his own share of dirt. Then he straightened and carried me to the edge of the grave.

I couldn't see into the hole. It was dark under the overhang of rock, and the grave seemed to be very deep.

Ian began speaking before I could.

"Walter was the best and brightest of what is human," he said, and scattered his sand into the hole. It fell for a long time before I heard it hiss against the bottom.

Ian looked down at me.

It was absolutely silent in the starlit night. Even the wind was calm. I whispered, but I knew my voice carried to everyone.

"There was no hatred in your heart," I whispered. "That you existed is proof that we were wrong. We had no right to take your world from you, Walter. I hope your fairytales are true. I hope you find your Gladdie."

I let the rocks trickle through my fingers and waited until I heard them fall with a soft patter onto Walter's body, obscured in the deep, dark grave.

Andy started to work as soon as Ian took the first step back, shoveling from a mound of pale, dusty earth that was piled a few feet farther into the grotto. The shovel load hit with a thump rather than a whisper. The sound made me cringe.

Aaron stepped past us with another shovel. Ian turned slowly and carried me away to make room for them. The heavy thuds of falling dirt echoed behind us. Low voices began to murmur. I heard footsteps as people milled and huddled to discuss the funeral.

I really looked at Ian for the first time as he walked back to the dark mat where it lay on the open dirt — out of place, not belonging. Ian's face was streaked with pale dust, his expression weary. I'd seen his face like that before. I couldn't pinpoint the memory before Ian had laid me on the mat again, and I was distracted. What was I supposed to do out here in the open? Sleep? Doc was right behind us; he and Ian both knelt down in the dust beside me.

"How are you feeling?" Doc asked, already prodding at my side.

I wanted to sit up, but Ian pressed my shoulder down when I tried.

"I'm fine. I think maybe I could walk . . ."

"No need to push it. Let's give that leg a few days, okay?" Doc pulled my left eyelid up, absentminded, and shone a tiny beam of light into it. My right eye saw the bright reflection that danced across his face. He squinted away from the light, recoiling a few inches. Ian's hand on my shoulder didn't flinch. That surprised me.

"Hmm. That doesn't help a diagnosis, does it? How does your head feel?" Doc asked.

"A little dizzy. I think it's the drugs you gave me, though, not the wound. I don't like them — I'd rather feel the pain, I think."

Doc grimaced. So did Ian.

"What?" I demanded.

"I'm going to have to put you under again, Wanda. I'm sorry."

"But . . . why?" I whispered. "I'm really not that hurt. I don't want —"

"We have to take you back inside," Ian said, cutting me off, his voice low, as if he didn't want it to carry back to the others. I could hear the voices behind us, echoing quietly off the rocks. "We promised . . . that you wouldn't be conscious."

"Blindfold me again."

Doc pulled the little syringe from his pocket. It was already depressed, only a quarter left. I shied away from

it, toward Ian. His hand on my shoulder became a restraint.

"You know the caves too well," Doc murmured. "They
don't want you having the chance to guess . . ."

"But where would I go?" I whispered, my voice frantic. "If I knew the way out? Why would I leave now?"

"If it eases their minds . . ." Ian said.

Doc took my wrist, and I didn't fight him. I looked
away as the needle bit into my skin, looked at Ian. His
eyes were midnight in the dark. They tightened at the look
of betrayal in mine.

"Sorry," he muttered. It was the last thing I heard.

# CHAPTER 35

# *Tried*

I groaned. My head felt all swirly and disconnected. My stomach rolled nauseatingly.

"Finally," someone murmured in relief. Ian. Of course. "Hungry?"

I thought about that and then made an involuntary gagging sound.

"Oh. Never mind. Sorry. Again. We had to do it. People got all . . . paranoid when we took you outside."

"'S okay," I sighed.

"Want some water?"

"No."

I opened my eyes, trying to focus in the darkness. I could see two stars through the cracks overhead. Still night. Or night again, who knew?

"Where am I?" I asked. The shapes of the cracks were

unfamiliar. I would swear I'd never stared at this ceiling before.

"Your room," Ian said.

I searched for his face in the darkness but could only make out the black shape that was his head. With my fingers, I examined the surface I lay on; it was a real mattress. There was a pillow under my head. My searching hand touched his, and he caught my fingers before I could withdraw them.

"Whose room is it really?"

"Yours."

"Ian . . ."

"It used to be ours — Kyle's and mine. Kyle's being . . . held in the hospital wing until things can be decided. I can move in with Wes."

"I'm not taking your room. And what do you mean, until things can be decided?"

"I told you there would be a tribunal."

"When?"

"Why do you want to know?"

"Because if you're going through with that, then I have to be there. To explain."

"To lie."

"When?" I asked again.

"First light. I won't take you."

"Then I'll take myself. I know I'll be able to walk as soon as my head stops spinning."

"You would, wouldn't you?"

"Yes. It's not fair if you don't let me speak."

Ian sighed. He dropped my hand and straightened slowly to his feet. I could hear his joints pop as he stood. How long had he been sitting in the dark, waiting for me to wake? "I'll be back soon. You might not be hungry, but I'm starving."

"You had a long night."

"Yes."

"If it gets light, I won't sit here waiting for you."

He chuckled without humor. "I'm sure that's true. So I'll be back before that, and I will help you get where you're going."

He leaned one of the doors away from the entrance to his cave, stepped around it, and then let it fall back into place. I frowned. That might be hard to do on one leg. I hoped Ian truly was coming back.

While I waited for him, I stared up at the two stars I could see and let my head slowly become stationary. I really didn't like human drugs. Ugh. My body hurt, but the lurching in my head was worse.

Time passed slowly, but I didn't fall asleep. I'd been sleeping most of the last twenty-four hours. I probably *was* hungry, too. I would have to wait for my stomach to calm before I was sure.

Ian came back before the light, just as he'd promised.

"Feeling any better?" he asked as he stepped around the door.

"I think so. I haven't moved my head yet."

"Do you think it's *you* reacting to the morphine, or Melanie's body?"

"It's Mel. She reacts badly to most painkillers. She found that out when she broke her wrist ten years ago."

He thought about that for a moment. "It's . . . odd. Dealing with two people at once."

"Odd," I agreed.

"Are you hungry yet?"

I smiled. "I thought I smelled bread. Yes, I think my stomach is past the worst."

"I was hoping you'd say that."

His shadow sprawled out beside me. He felt for my hand, then pulled my fingers open and placed a familiar round shape in it.

"Help me up?" I asked.

He put his arm carefully around my shoulders and folded me up in one stiff piece, minimizing the ache in my side. I could feel something foreign on the skin there, tight and rigid.

"Thanks," I said, a little breathless. My head spun slowly. I touched my side with my free hand. Something adhered to my skin, under my shirt. "Are my ribs broken, then?"

"Doc's not sure. He's doing as much as he can."

"He tries so hard."

"He does."

"I feel bad . . . that I used to not like him," I admitted.

Ian laughed. "Of course you didn't. I'm amazed you can like any of us."

"You've got that turned around," I mumbled, and dug my teeth into the hard roll. I chewed mechanically and then swallowed, setting the bread down as I waited to see how it hit my stomach.

"Not very appetizing, I know," Ian said.

I shrugged. "Just testing — to see if the nausea's really passed."

"Maybe something more appealing . . ."

I looked at him, curious, but I couldn't see his face. I listened to a sharp crackle and a ripping sound . . . and then I could smell, and I understood.

"Cheetos!" I cried. "Really? For me?"

Something touched my lip, and I crunched into the delicacy he offered.

"I've been dreaming about this." I sighed as I chewed.

That made him laugh. He put the bag in my hands.

I downed the contents of the small bag quickly, and then finished my roll, seasoned by the cheese flavor still in my mouth. He handed me a bottle of water before I could ask.

"Thank you. For more than the Cheetos, you know. For so much."

"You're more than welcome, Wanda."

I stared into his dark blue eyes, trying to decipher everything he was saying with that sentence — there seemed to be something more than just courtesy in the words. And then I realized that I could see the color of Ian's eyes; I glanced quickly up at the cracks above. The stars were gone, and the sky was turning pale gray. Dawn was coming. First light.

"Are you sure you have to do this?" Ian asked, his hands already half-extended as if to pick me up.

I nodded. "You don't have to carry me. My leg feels better."

"We'll see."

He helped me to my feet, leaving his arm around my waist and pulling my arm around his neck.

"Careful, now. How's that?"

I hobbled forward a step. It hurt, but I could do it. "Great. Let's go."

*I think Ian likes you too much.*

*Too much?* I was surprised to hear from Melanie, and

so distinctly. Lately, she only spoke up like this when Jared was around.

*I'm here, too. Does he even care about that?*

*Of course he does. He believes us more than anyone besides Jamie and Jeb.*

*I don't mean that.*

*What do you mean?*

But she was gone.

It took us a long time. I was surprised by how far we had to go. I'd been thinking we were going to the big plaza or the kitchen — the usual places for congregating. But we went through the eastern field and kept going until we finally reached the big, deep black cave that Jeb had called the game room. I hadn't been here since my first tour. The biting scent of the sulfurous spring greeted me.

Unlike most of the caverns here, the game room was much wider than it was tall. I could see that now because the dim blue lights hung from the ceiling rather than resting on the floor. The ceiling was only a few feet over my head, the height of a normal ceiling in a house. But I couldn't even see the walls, they were so distant from the lights. I couldn't see the smelly spring, tucked away in some far corner, but I could hear it dribble and gush.

Kyle sat in the brightest spot of light. He had his long arms wrapped around his legs. His face was set in a stiff mask. He didn't look up when Ian helped me limp in.

On either side of him were Jared and Doc, on their feet, both with their arms hanging loose and ready at their sides. As though they were . . . guards.

Jeb stood beside Jared, his gun slung over one shoulder. He appeared relaxed, but I knew how quickly that could change. Jamie held his free hand . . . no, Jeb had his hand around Jamie's wrist, and Jamie didn't seem happy about it. When he saw me come in, though, he smiled and waved. He took a deep breath and looked pointedly at Jeb. Jeb dropped Jamie's wrist.

Sharon stood beside Doc, with Aunt Maggie at her other side.

Ian pulled me toward the edge of the darkness surrounding the tableau. We weren't alone there. I could see the shapes of many others, but not their faces.

It was strange; through the caves, Ian had supported most of my weight with ease. Now, though, he seemed to have tired. His arm around my waist was slack. I lurched and hopped forward as best I could until he picked the spot he wanted. He settled me to the floor, and then sat beside me.

"Ouch," I heard someone whisper.

I turned and could just make out Trudy. She scooted closer to us, Geoffrey and then Heath copying her.

"You look rotten," she told me. "How bad are you hurt?"

I shrugged. "I'm fine." I started to wonder if Ian had let me struggle just to make a show of my injuries — to make me testify against Kyle without words. I frowned at his innocent expression.

Wes and Lily arrived then and came to sit with my little group of allies. Brandt entered a few seconds later, and then Heidi, and then Andy and Paige. Aaron was last.

"That's everybody," he said. "Lucina's staying with her kids. She doesn't want them here — she said to go on without her."

Aaron sat beside Andy, and there was a short moment of silence.

"Okay, then," Jeb said in a loud voice meant to be heard by all. "Here's how it's gonna work. Straight-up majority vote. As usual, I'll make my own decision if I have a problem with the majority, 'cause this —"

"Is my house," several voices interjected in chorus. Someone chuckled but stopped quickly. This wasn't funny. A human was on trial for trying to kill an alien. This had to be a horrible day for all of them.

"Who's speaking against Kyle?" Jeb asked.

Ian started to stand beside me.

"No!" I whispered, tugging on his elbow.

He shrugged me off and rose to his feet.

"This is simple enough," Ian said. I wanted to jump up and clap my hand over his mouth, but I didn't think I could get to my feet without help. "My brother was warned. He was not in any doubt about Jeb's ruling on this. Wanda is one of our community — the same rules and protections apply to her as to any of us. Jeb told Kyle point-blank that if he couldn't live with her here, he should move on. Kyle decided to stay. He knew then and he knows now the penalty for murder in this place."

"It's still alive," Kyle grunted.

"Which is why I'm not asking for your death," Ian snapped back. "But you can't live here anymore. Not if you're a murderer at heart."

Ian stared at his brother for a moment, then sat on the ground beside me again.

"But he could get caught, and we'd have no idea," Brandt protested, rising to his feet. "He'll lead them back here, and we'd have no warning."

There was a murmur through the room.

Kyle glared at Brandt. "They'll never get me alive."

"Then it's a death sentence after all," someone muttered at the same time that Andy said, "You can't guarantee that."

"One at a time," Jeb warned.

"I've survived on the outside before," Kyle said angrily.

Another voice came from the darkness. "It's a risk." I couldn't make out the owners of the voices — they were just hissing whispers.

And another. "What did Kyle do wrong? Nothing."

Jeb took a step toward the voice, glowering. "My rules."

"She's not one of us," someone else protested.

Ian started to rise again.

"Hey!" Jared exploded. His voice was so loud that everyone jumped. "Wanda's not on trial here! Does someone have a concrete complaint against her — against Wanda herself? Then ask for another tribunal. But we all know she hasn't harmed anyone here. In fact, she saved his life." He stabbed one finger toward Kyle's back. Kyle's shoulders hunched, like he'd felt the jab. "Just seconds after he tried to throw her into the river, she risked her life to keep him from the same painful death. She had to know that if she let him fall she would be safer here. She saved him anyway. Would any of you have done the same — rescue your enemy? He tried to kill her, and yet will she even speak against him?"

I felt all the eyes in the dark room on my face as Jared now held his hand out, palm up, toward me.

"*Will* you speak against him, Wanda?"

I stared at him wide-eyed, stunned that he was speaking for me, that he was speaking *to* me, that he was using my name. Melanie was in shock, too, torn in half. She was overjoyed at the kindness in his face as he looked at us, the softness in his eyes that had been absent so long. But it was *my* name he'd said . . .

It was a few seconds before I could find my voice.

"This is all a misunderstanding," I whispered. "We both fell when the floor caved in. Nothing else happened." I hoped the whisper would make it harder to hear the lie in my voice, but as soon as I was done, Ian chuckled. I nudged him with my elbow, but that didn't stop him.

Jared actually smiled at me. "You see. She even tries to lie in his defense."

"*Tries* being the operative word," Ian added.

"Who says it's lying? Who can prove that?" Maggie asked harshly, stepping forward into the empty space beside Kyle. "Who can prove that it's not the truth that sounds so false on its lips?"

"Mag —" Jeb started.

"Shut up, Jebediah — I'm speaking. There is no reason for us to be here. No human was attacked. The insidious trespasser offers no complaint. This is a waste of all our time."

"I second that," Sharon added in a clear, loud voice.

Doc shot her a pained look.

Trudy jumped to her feet. "We can't house a murderer — and just wait around for him to be successful!"

"*Murder* is a subjective term," Maggie hissed. "I only consider it murder when something human is killed."

I felt Ian's arm wrap around my shoulder. I didn't realize that I was trembling until his motionless body was against mine.

"*Human* is a subjective term as well, Magnolia," Jared said, glowering at her. "I thought the definition embraced *some* compassion, some little bit of mercy."

"Let's vote," Sharon said before her mother could answer him. "Raise your hand if you think Kyle should be allowed to stay here, with no penalty for the . . . misunderstanding." She shot a glance not at me, but at Ian beside me when she used the word I'd used.

Hands began to rise. I watched Jared's face as his features settled into a scowl.

I struggled to raise my hand, but Ian tightened his hold around my arms and made an irritated noise through his nose. I held my palm as high as I could get it. In the end, though, my vote wasn't necessary.

Jeb counted out loud. "Ten . . . fifteen . . . twenty . . . twenty-three. Okay, that's a clear majority."

I didn't look around to see who had voted how. It was enough that in my little corner all arms were crossed tightly over chests and all eyes stared at Jeb with expectant expressions.

Jamie walked away from Jeb to come squeeze in between Trudy and me. He put his arm around me, under Ian's.

"Maybe your souls were right about us," he said, loud enough for most to hear his high, hard voice. "The majority are no better than —"

"Hush!" I hissed at him.

"Okay," Jeb said. Everyone went silent. Jeb looked down at Kyle, then at me, and then at Jared. "Okay, I'm inclined to go with the majority on this."

"Jeb —" Jared and Ian said simultaneously.

"My house, my rules," Jeb reminded them. "Never forget that. So you listen to me, Kyle. And you'd better listen, too, I think, Magnolia. Anyone who tries to hurt Wanda again will not get a tribunal, they will get a burial." He slapped the butt of his gun for emphasis.

I flinched.

Magnolia glared hatefully at her brother.

Kyle nodded, as if accepting the terms.

Jeb looked around the unevenly spaced audience, locking eyes with each member except the little group beside me.

"Tribunal's over," Jeb announced. "Who's up for a game?"

# CHAPTER 36

# Believed

The congregation relaxed, and a more enthusiastic murmur ran around the half circle.

I looked at Jamie. He pursed his lips and shrugged. "Jeb's just trying to get things back to normal. It's been a bad couple of days. Burying Walter . . .".

I winced.

I saw that Jeb was grinning at Jared. After a moment of resistance, Jared sighed and rolled his eyes at the strange old man. He turned and strode quickly from the cave.

"Jared got a new ball?" someone asked.

"Cool," Wes said beside me.

"Playing games," Trudy muttered, and shook her head.

"If it eases the tension," Lily responded quietly, shrugging.

Their voices were low, close beside me, but I could also hear other, louder voices.

"Easy on the ball this time," Aaron said to Kyle. He stood over him, offering his hand.

Kyle took the offered hand and got slowly to his feet. When he was standing, his head almost hit the hanging lanterns.

"The last ball was weak," Kyle said, grinning at the older man. "Structurally deficient."

"I nominate Andy for captain," someone shouted.

"I nominate Lily," Wes called out, getting to his feet and stretching.

"Andy and Lily."

"Yeah, Andy and Lily."

"I want Kyle," Andy said quickly.

"Then I get Ian," Lily countered.

"Jared."

"Brandt."

Jamie got to his feet and stood on his toes, trying to look tall.

"Paige."

"Heidi."

"Aaron."

"Wes."

The roll call continued. Jamie glowed when Lily chose him before half the adults were taken. Even Maggie and Jeb were picked for teams. The numbers were even until Lucina came back with Jared, her two small boys bouncing in excitement. Jared had a shiny new soccer ball in his hand; he held it out, and Isaiah, the older child, jumped up and down trying to knock it from his hand.

"Wanda?" Lily asked.

I shook my head and pointed to my leg.

"Right. Sorry."

*I'm good at soccer,* Mel grumbled. *Well, I used to be. I can hardly walk,* I reminded her.

"I think I'll sit this one out," Ian said.

"No," Wes complained. "They've got Kyle and Jared. We're dead without you."

"Play," I told him. "I'll . . . I'll keep score."

He looked at me, his lips pressed into a thin, rigid line. "I'm not really in the mood for playing a game."

"They need you."

He snorted.

"C'mon, Ian," Jamie urged.

"I want to watch," I said. "But it will be . . . boring if one team has too much advantage."

"Wanda." Ian sighed. "You really are the worst liar I've ever met."

But he got up and started stretching with Wes.

Paige set up goalposts, four lanterns.

I tried to get to my feet — I was right in the middle of the field. Nobody noticed me in the dim light. All around, the atmosphere was upbeat now, charged with anticipation. Jeb had been right. This was something they needed, odd as it seemed to me.

I was able to get onto all fours, and then I pulled my good leg forward so I was kneeling on the bad. It hurt. I tried to hop up onto my good leg from there. My balance was all off, thanks to the awkward weight of my sore leg.

Strong hands caught me before I could fall on my face. I looked up, a little rueful, to thank Ian.

The words caught in my throat when I saw that it was Jared whose arms held me up.

"You could have just asked for help," he said conversationally.

"I —" I cleared my throat. "I should have. I didn't want to . . ."

"Call attention to yourself?" He said the words as if he were truly curious. There was no accusation in them. He helped me hobble toward the cave entrance.

I shook my head once. "I didn't want to . . . make anyone do anything, out of courtesy, that they didn't want to do." That didn't explain it exactly right, but he seemed to understand my meaning.

"I don't think Jamie or Ian would begrudge you a helping hand."

I glanced back at them over my shoulder. In the low light, neither had noticed I was gone yet. They were bouncing the ball off their heads, and laughing when Wes caught it in the face.

"But they're having fun. I wouldn't want to interrupt that."

Jared examined my face. I realized I was smiling in affection.

"You care about the kid quite a bit," he said.

"Yes."

He nodded. "And the man?"

"Ian is . . . Ian believes me. He watches over me. He can be so very kind . . . for a human." Almost like a soul, I'd wanted to say. But that wouldn't have sounded like the compliment it was to this audience.

Jared snorted. "For a human. A more important distinction than I'd realized."

He lowered me to the lip of the entrance. It made a shallow bench that was more comfortable than the flat floor.

"Thank you," I told him. "Jeb did the right thing, you know."

"I don't agree with that." Jared's tone was milder than his words.

"Thank you also — for before. You didn't have to defend me."

"Every word was the truth."

I looked at the floor. "It's true that I would never do anything to hurt anyone here. Not on purpose. I'm sorry that I hurt you when I came here. And Jamie. So sorry."

He sat down right beside me, his face thoughtful. "Honestly . . ." He hesitated. "The kid is better since you came. I'd sort of forgotten what his laugh sounded like."

We both listened to it now, echoing above the lower pitch of adult laughter.

"Thank you for telling me that. It's been my . . . biggest worry. I hoped I hadn't damaged anything permanently."

"Why?"

I looked up at him, confused.

"Why do you love him?" he asked, his voice still curious but not intense.

I bit my lip.

"You can tell me. I'm . . . I've . . ." He couldn't find the words to explain. "You can tell me," he repeated.

I looked at my feet as I answered. "In part because Melanie does." I didn't peek to see if the name made him flinch. "Remembering him the way she does . . . that's a powerful thing. And then, when I met him in person . . ." I shrugged. "I can't *not* love him. It's part of my . . . the very makeup of these cells to love him. I hadn't realized before how much influence a host had on me. Maybe it's just human bodies. Maybe it's just Melanie."

"She talks to you?" He kept his voice even, but I could hear the strain now.

"Yes."

"How often?"

"When she wants to. When she's interested."

"How about today?"

"Not much. She's . . . kind of mad at me."

He barked out a surprised laugh. "She's mad? Why?"

"Because of . . ." Was there such a thing as double jeopardy here? "Nothing."

He heard the lie again and made the connection.

"Oh. Kyle. She wanted him to fry." He laughed again. "She would."

"She can be . . . violent," I agreed. I smiled, to soften the insult.

It was no insult to him. "Really? How?"

"She wants me to fight back. But I . . . I can't do that. I'm not a fighter."

"I can see that." He touched my battered face with one fingertip. "Sorry."

"No. Anyone would do the same. I know what you must have felt."

"You wouldn't —"

"If I were human, I would. Besides, I wasn't thinking of that. . . . I was remembering the Seeker."

He stiffened.

I smiled again, and he relaxed a little. "Mel wanted me to throttle her. She really hates that Seeker. And I can't . . . find it in myself to blame her."

"She's still searching for you. Looks like she had to return the helicopter, at least."

I closed my eyes, clenched my fists, and concentrated on breathing for several seconds.

"I didn't used to be afraid of her," I whispered. "I don't know why she scares me so much now. Where is she?"

"Don't worry. She was just up and down the highway yesterday. She won't find you."

I nodded, willing myself to believe.

"Can you . . . can you hear Mel now?" he murmured.

I kept my eyes closed. "I'm . . . aware of her. She's listening very hard."

"What's she thinking?" His voice was just a whisper.

*Here's your chance,* I told her. *What do you want to tell him?*

She was cautious, for once. The invitation unsettled her. *Why? Why does he believe you now?*

I opened my eyes and found him staring at my face, holding his breath.

"She wants to know what happened to make you . . . different now. Why do you believe us?"

He thought for a moment. "An . . . accumulation of things. You were so . . . kind to Walter. I've never seen anyone but Doc be that compassionate. And you saved Kyle's life, where most of us would have let him fall just to protect ourselves, intended murder aside. And then you're such an appalling liar." He laughed once. "I kept trying to see these things as evidence of some grand plot. Maybe I'll wake up tomorrow and feel that way again."

Mel and I flinched.

"But when they started attacking you today . . . well, I snapped. I could see in them everything that shouldn't have been in me. I realized I already did believe, and that I was just being obstinate. Cruel. I think I've believed since . . . well, a little bit since that first night when you put yourself in front of me to *save* me from Kyle." He laughed as if he didn't think Kyle was dangerous. "But I'm better at lying than you are. I can even lie to myself."

"She hopes you won't change your mind. She's afraid you will."

He closed his eyes. "Mel."

My heart thudded faster in my chest. It was her joy that sped it, not mine. He must have guessed how I loved him. After his questions about Jamie, he must have seen that.

"Tell her . . . that won't happen."

"She hears you."

"How . . . straightforward is the connection?"

"She hears what I hear, sees what I see."

"Feels what you feel?"

"Yes."

His nose wrinkled. He touched my face again, softly, a caress. "You don't know how sorry I am."

My skin felt hotter where he had touched it; it was a good heat, but his words burned hotter than his touch. Of course he was sorrier for hurting her. Of course. That shouldn't bother me.

"C'mon, Jared! Let's go!"

We looked up. Kyle was calling to Jared. He seemed utterly at ease, as if he had not been on trial for his life today. Maybe he'd known it would go his way. Maybe he was quick to get over anything. He didn't seem to notice me there beside Jared.

I realized, for the first time, that others had.

Jamie was watching us with a satisfied smile. This probably looked like a good thing to him. Was it?

*What do you mean?*

*What does he see when he looks at us? His family, put back together?*

*Isn't it? Sort of?*

*With the one unwelcome addition.*

*But better than it was yesterday.*

*I guess . . .*

*I know,* she admitted. *I'm glad Jared knows I'm here . . . but I still don't like him touching you.*

*And I like it too much.* My face tingled where Jared's fingers had brushed it. *Sorry about that.*

*I don't blame you. Or, at least, I know I* shouldn't.

*Thanks.*

Jamie wasn't the only one watching.

Jeb was curious, that little smile gathering up the corners of his beard.

Sharon and Maggie watched with fire in their eyes. Their expressions were so much the same that the youthful skin and bright hair did nothing to make Sharon look younger than her grizzled mother.

Ian was worried. His eyes were tight, and he seemed on the verge of coming to protect me again. To make sure Jared wasn't upsetting me. I smiled, to reassure him. He didn't smile back, but he took a deep breath.

*I don't think that's why he's worried,* Mel said.

"Are you listening to her now?" Jared was on his feet but still watching my face.

His question distracted me before I could ask her what she meant. "Yes."

"What's she saying?"

"We're noticing what the others think of your . . . change of heart." I nodded toward Melanie's aunt and cousin. They turned their backs on me in synchronization.

"Tough nuts," he acknowledged.

"Fine, then," Kyle boomed, turning his body toward

the ball that sat under the brightest spot of light. "We'll win it without you."

"I'm coming!" Jared threw one wistful glance at me — at us — and ran to get in on the game.

I wasn't the best scorekeeper. It was too dark to see the ball from where I sat. It was too dark even to see the players well when they weren't right under the lights. I began counting from Jamie's reactions. His shout of victory when his team scored, his groan when the other team did. The groans outnumbered the shouts.

Everyone played. Maggie was the goalie for Andy's team, and Jeb was the goalie for Lily's. They were both surprisingly good. I could see their silhouettes in the light from the goalpost lamps, moving as lithely as if they were decades younger. Jeb was not afraid to hit the floor to stop a goal, but Maggie was more effective without resorting to such extremes. She was like a magnet for the invisible ball. Every time Ian or Wes got off a shot . . . *thunk!* It landed in her hands.

Trudy and Paige quit after a half hour or so and passed me on their way out, chattering with excitement. It seemed impossible that we'd started the morning with a trial, but I was relieved that things had changed so drastically.

The women weren't gone long. They came back with arms full of boxes. Granola bars — the kind with fruit filling. The game came to a halt. Jeb called halftime, and everyone hurried over to eat breakfast.

The goods were divvied up at the center line. It was a mob scene at first.

"Here you go, Wanda," Jamie said, ducking out of the group. He had his hands full of the bars, and water bottles tucked under his arms.

"Thanks. Having fun?"

"Yeah! Wish you could play."

"Next time," I said.

"Here you go . . ." Ian was there, his hands full of granola bars.

"Beat ya," Jamie told him.

"Oh," Jared said, appearing on Jamie's other side. He also had too many bars for one.

Ian and Jared exchanged a long glance.

"Where's all the food?" Kyle demanded. He stood over an empty box, his head swiveling around the room, looking for the culprit.

"Catch," Jared said, tossing granola bars one by one, hard, like knives.

Kyle plucked them out of the air with ease, then jogged over to see if Jared was holding out on him.

"Here," Ian said, shoving half of his haul toward his brother without looking at him. "Now go."

Kyle ignored him. For the first time today, he looked at me, staring down at me where I sat. His irises were black with the light behind him. I couldn't read his expression.

I recoiled, and caught my breath when my ribs protested.

Jared and Ian closed ranks in front of me like stage curtains.

"You heard him," Jared said.

"Can I say something first?" Kyle asked. He peered down through the space between them.

They didn't respond.

"I'm not sorry," Kyle told me. "I still think it was the right thing to do."

Ian shoved his brother. Kyle reeled back but then stepped forward again.

"Hold on, I'm not done."

"Yeah, you are," Jared said. His hands were clenched, the skin over his knuckles white.

Everyone had noticed now. The room was hushed, all the fun of the game lost.

"No, I'm not." Kyle held his hands up, a gesture of surrender, and spoke to me again. "I don't think I was wrong, but you did save my life. I don't know why, but you did. So I figure, a life for a life. I won't kill you. I'll pay the debt that way."

"You stupid jackass," Ian said.

"Who's got the crush on a worm, bro? You gonna call *me* stupid?"

Ian lifted his fists, leaning forward.

"I'll tell you why," I said, making my voice louder than I wanted to. But it had the effect I was after. Ian and Jared and Kyle turned to stare at me, fight forgotten for the moment.

It made me nervous. I cleared my throat. "I didn't let you fall because . . . because I'm not *like* you. I'm not saying that I'm not . . . like humans. Because there are others here who would do the same. There are kind and good people here. People like your brother, and Jeb, and Doc . . . I'm saying that I'm not like you *personally.*"

Kyle stared at me for a minute and then chuckled. "Ouch," he said, still laughing. He turned away from us then, his message given, and walked back to get some water. "Life for a life," he called over his shoulder.

I wasn't sure I believed him. Not sure at all. Humans were good liars.

# CHAPTER 37

# Wanted

There was a pattern to the wins. If Jared and Kyle played together, they won. If Jared played with Ian, then that team would win. It seemed to me that Jared could not be defeated, until I saw the brothers play together.

At first it seemed to be a strained thing, for Ian at least, playing as teammates with Kyle. But after a few minutes of running in the dark, they fell into a familiar pattern — a pattern that had existed since long before I'd come to this planet.

Kyle knew what Ian would do before Ian did it, and vice versa. Without having to speak, they told each other everything. Even when Jared pulled all the best players to his side — Brandt, Andy, Wes, Aaron, Lily, and Maggie as goalie — Kyle and Ian were victorious.

"Okay, okay," Jeb said, catching Aaron's goal attempt with one hand and tucking the ball under his arm. "I think we all know the winners. Now, I hate to be a party pooper, but there's work waiting . . . and, to be honest, I'm bushed."

There were a few halfhearted protests and a few moans, but more laughter. No one seemed too upset to have the fun end. From the way a few people sat down right where they were and put their heads between their knees to breathe, it was clear Jeb wasn't the only one who was tired out.

People began to drift out in twos and threes. I scooted to one side of the corridor's mouth, making room for them to pass, probably on their way to the kitchen. It had to be past time for lunch, though it was hard to mark the hour in this black hole. Through the gaps in the line of exiting humans, I watched Kyle and Ian.

When the game was called, Kyle had raised his hand for a high five, but Ian had stalked past him without acknowledging the gesture. Then Kyle caught his brother's shoulder and spun him around. Ian knocked Kyle's hand away. I tensed for a fight — and it seemed like one at first. Kyle threw a punch toward Ian's stomach. Ian dodged it easily, though, and I saw that there was no force behind it. Kyle laughed and used his superior reach to rub his fist into Ian's scalp. Ian smacked that hand away, but this time he halfway smiled.

"Good game, bro," I heard Kyle say. "You've still got it."

"You're such an idiot, Kyle," Ian answered.

"You got the brains; I got the looks. Seems fair."

Kyle threw another half-strength punch. This time, Ian caught it and twisted his brother into a headlock. Now he was really smiling, and Kyle was cussing and laughing at the same time.

It all looked very violent to me; my eyes narrowed, tight with the stress of watching. But at the same time, it brought to mind one of Melanie's memories: three puppies rolling on the grass, yapping furiously and baring their teeth as if their only desire was to rip out their brothers' throats.

*Yes, they're playing,* Melanie confirmed. *The bonds of brotherhood go deep.*

*As they should. This is right. If Kyle really doesn't kill us, this will be a good thing.*

*If,* Melanie repeated morosely.

"Hungry?"

I looked up, and my heart stopped beating for a slightly painful moment. It seemed that Jared was still a believer.

I shook my head. This gave me the moment I needed to be able to speak to him. "I'm not sure why, since I've done nothing besides sit here, but I'm just tired."

He held out his hand.

*Get a hold of yourself,* Melanie warned me. *He's just being courteous.*

*You think I don't know that?*

I tried to keep my hand from shaking as I reached for his.

He pulled me carefully to my feet — to my foot, really. I balanced there on my good leg, not sure how to proceed. He was confused, too. He still held my hand, but there was a wide space between us. I thought of how ridiculous I would look hopping through the caves, and felt my neck get warm. My fingers curled around his, though I wasn't really using him for support.

"Where to?"

"Ah . . ." I frowned. "I don't really know. I suppose there's still a mat by the ho — in the storage area."

He frowned back, liking that idea no better than I did.

And then a strong arm was under my arms, supporting my weight.

"I'll get her where she needs to go," Ian said.

Jared's face was careful, the way he looked at me when he didn't want me to know what he was thinking. But he was looking at Ian now.

"We were just discussing where exactly that would be. She's tired. Maybe the hospital . . . ?"

I shook my head at the same time Ian did. After the past horrible days spent there, I didn't think I could bear the room I'd once misguidedly feared. Especially Walter's empty bed . . .

"I've got a better place for her," Ian said. "Those cots aren't much softer than rock, and she's got a lot of sore spots."

Jared still held my hand. Did he realize how tightly he was gripping it? The pressure was starting to get uncomfortable, but he didn't seem aware. And I certainly wasn't going to complain.

"Why don't you get lunch?" Jared suggested to Ian. "You look hungry. I'll take her wherever you had planned . . . ?"

Ian chuckled, a low, dark sound. "I'm fine. And honestly, Jared, Wanda needs a bit more help than a hand. I don't know if you're . . . comfortable enough with the situation to give her that. You see —"

Ian paused to lean down and pull me quickly up

into his arms. I gasped as the movement tugged at my side. Jared didn't free my hand. My fingertips were turning red. .

"— she's actually had enough exercise for one day, I think. You go on ahead to the kitchen."

They stared at each other while my fingertips turned purple.

"I can carry her," Jared finally said in a low voice.

"Can you?" Ian challenged. He held me out, away from his body.

An offer.

Jared stared at my face for a long minute. Then he sighed and dropped my hand.

*Ow, that hurts!* Melanie complained. She was referring to the sudden lance of pain that shot through my chest, not the return of blood to my fingers.

*Sorry. What do you want me to do about it?*

*He's not yours.*

*Yes. I know that.*

*Ow.*

*Sorry.*

"I think I'll tag along," Jared said as Ian, with a tiny, triumphant smile hovering around the edges of his mouth, turned and headed toward the exit. "There's something I want to discuss with you."

"Suit yourself."

Jared didn't discuss anything at all as we walked through the dark tunnel. He was so quiet, I wasn't sure he was still there. But when we broke out into the light of the cornfield again, he was right beside us.

He didn't speak until we were through the big plaza — until there was no one around but the three of us.

"What's your take on Kyle?" he asked Ian.

Ian snorted. "He prides himself on being a man of his word. Usually, I would trust a promise from him. In this situation . . . I'm not letting her out of my sight."

"Good."

"It will be fine, Ian," I said. "I'm not afraid."

"You don't have to be. I promise — no one is ever going to do something like this to you again. You *will* be safe here."

It was hard to look away from his eyes when they blazed like that. Hard to doubt anything he said.

"Yes," Jared agreed. "You will."

He was walking just behind Ian's shoulder. I couldn't see his expression.

"Thanks," I whispered.

No one spoke again until Ian paused at the red and gray doors that leaned over the entrance to his cave.

"Would you mind getting that?" Ian said to Jared, nodding toward the doors.

Jared didn't move. Ian turned around so we could both see him; his face was careful again.

"*Your* room? This is your better place?" Jared's voice was full of skepticism.

"It's her room now."

I bit my lip. I wanted to tell Ian that of course this wasn't my room, but I didn't get a chance before Jared began questioning him.

"Where's Kyle staying?"

"With Wes, for now."

"And you?"

"I'm not exactly sure."

They stared at each other with appraising eyes.

"Ian, this is —" I started to say.

"Oh," he interrupted, as if just remembering me . . . as if my weight was so insignificant that he'd forgotten I was here. "You're exhausted, aren't you? Jared, could you get the door, please?"

Wordlessly, Jared wrenched the red door back with a bit too much force and shoved it on top of the gray one.

I now really saw Ian's room for the first time, with the noon sun filtering down through the narrow cracks in the ceiling. It wasn't as bright as Jamie and Jared's room, or as tall. It was smaller, more proportionate. Roundish — sort of like my hole, only ten times the size. There were two twin mattresses on the floor, shoved against opposite walls to make a narrow aisle between them. Against the back wall, there was a long, low wooden cupboard; the left side had a pile of clothes on top, two books, and a stack of playing cards. The right side was completely empty, though there were shapes in the dust that indicated this was a recent occurrence.

Ian set me carefully down on the right mattress, arranging my leg and straightening the pillow under my head. Jared stood in the doorway, facing the passageway.

"That okay?" Ian asked me.

"Yes."

"You look tired."

"I shouldn't be — I've done nothing but sleep lately."

"Your body needs sleep to heal."

I nodded. I couldn't deny that it was hard to hold up my eyelids.

"I'll bring you food later — don't worry about anything."

"Thank you. Ian?"

"Yeah?"

"This is your room," I mumbled. "You'll sleep here, of course."

"You don't mind?"

"Why would I?"

"It's probably a good idea — best way to keep an eye on you. Get some sleep."

"Okay."

My eyes were already closed. He patted my hand, and then I heard him get to his feet. A few seconds later, the wooden door clunked softly against stone.

*What do you think you're doing?* Melanie demanded.

*What? What did I do now?*

*Wanda, you're . . . mostly human. You must realize what Ian will think of your invitation.*

*Invitation?* I could see the direction of her thoughts now. *It's not like that. This is his room. There are two beds here. There aren't enough sleeping areas for me to have my own space. Of course we should share. Ian knows that.*

*Does he? Wanda, open your eyes. He's starting to . . . How do I explain it so that you'll understand right? To feel about you . . . the way you feel about Jared. Can't you see that?*

I couldn't answer for two heartbeats.

*That's impossible,* I finally said.

"Do you think what happened this morning will influence Aaron or Brandt?" Ian asked in a low voice from the other side of the doors.

"You mean Kyle getting a bye?"

"Yeah. They didn't have to . . . *do* anything before.

Not when it looked so likely that Kyle would do it for them."

"I see your point. I'll speak to them."

"You think that will be enough?" Ian asked.

"I've saved both their lives. They owe me. If I ask them for something, they'll do it."

"You'd bet her life on that?"

There was a pause.

"We'll keep an eye on her," Jared finally said.

Another long silence.

"Aren't you going to go eat?" Jared asked.

"I think I'll hang out here for a bit. . . . How about you?"

Jared didn't answer.

"What?" Ian asked. "Is there something you want to say to me, Jared?"

"The girl in there . . ." Jared said slowly.

"Yes?"

"That body doesn't belong to her."

"Your point?"

Jared's voice was hard when he answered. "Keep your hands off it."

A low chuckle from Ian. "Jealous, Howe?"

"That's not really the issue."

"Really." Ian was sarcastic now.

"Wanda seems to be, more or less, cooperating with Melanie. It sounds like they're almost . . . on friendly terms. But obviously Wanda's making the decisions. What if it were you? How would you feel if you were Melanie? What if you were the one . . . invaded that way? What if you were trapped, and someone else was telling your body what to do? If you couldn't speak for yourself? Wouldn't you want your wishes — as much as they could be known — respected? At the very least by other humans?"

"Okay, okay. Point taken. I'll keep that in mind."

"What do you mean, you'll *keep that in mind?*" Jared demanded.

"I mean that I'll think about it."

"There's nothing to think about," Jared retorted. I knew how he would look from the sound of his voice — teeth clenched, jaw strained. "The body and the person locked inside it belong to *me*."

"You're sure that Melanie still feels the —"

"Melanie will always be mine. And I will always be hers."

*Always.*

Melanie and I were suddenly at opposite ends of the spectrum. She was flying, elated. I was . . . not.

We waited anxiously through the next silence.

"But what if it were you?" Ian asked in little more than a whisper. "What if you were stuffed in a human body and let loose on this planet, only to find yourself lost among your own kind? What if you were such a good . . . person that you tried to save the life you'd taken, that you almost died trying to get her back to her family? What if you then found yourself surrounded by violent aliens who hated you and hurt you and tried to murder you, over and *over* again?" His voice faltered momentarily. "What if you just kept doing whatever you could to save and heal these people despite that? Wouldn't you deserve a life, too? Wouldn't you have earned that much?"

Jared didn't answer. I felt my eyes getting moist. Did

Ian really think so highly of me? Did he really think I'd earned the right to a life here?

"Point taken?" Ian pressed.

"I — I'll have to think about that one."

"Do that."

"But still —"

Ian interrupted him with a sigh. "Don't get worked up. Wanda isn't exactly human, despite the body. She doesn't seem to respond to . . . physical contact the same way a human would."

Now Jared laughed. "Is that your theory?"

"What's funny?"

"She is quite capable of responding to physical contact," Jared informed him, his tone suddenly sober again. "She's human enough for that. Or her body is, anyway."

My face went hot.

Ian was silent.

"Jealous, O'Shea?"

"Actually . . . I am. Surprisingly so." Ian's voice was strained. "How would you know that?"

Now Jared hesitated. "It was . . . sort of an experiment."

"An *experiment?*"

"It didn't go the way I thought it would. Mel punched me." I could hear that he was grinning at the memory, and I could see, in my head, the little lines fanning out around his eyes.

"Melanie . . . punched . . . you?"

"It sure wasn't Wanda. You should have seen her face. . . . What? Hey, Ian, easy, man!"

"Did you think for one moment what that must have done to her?" Ian hissed.

"Mel?"

"No, you fool, Wanda!"

"Done to *Wanda?*" Jared asked, sounding bewildered by the idea.

"Oh, get out of here. Go eat something. Stay away from me for a few hours."

Ian didn't give him a chance to answer. He yanked the door out of his way — roughly but very quietly — and then slid into his room and put the door back in its place.

He turned and met my gaze. From his expression, he was surprised to find me awake. Surprised and chagrined. The fire in his eyes blazed and then slowly dimmed. He pursed his lips.

He cocked his head to one side, listening. I listened, too, but Jared's retreat made no sound. Ian waited for another moment, then sighed and plunked down on the edge of his mattress, across from me.

"I guess we weren't as quiet as I thought," he said.

"Sound carries in these caves," I whispered.

He nodded. "So . . ." he finally said. "What do you think?"

# CHAPTER 38

## *Touched*

W hat do I think about what?"

"About our . . . discussion out there," Ian clarified.

What did I think about it? I didn't know.

Somehow, Ian was able to look at things from my perspective, my *alien* perspective. He thought I had earned a right to my life.

But he was . . . jealous? Of Jared?

He knew what I was. He knew I was just a tiny creature fused into the back of Melanie's brain. A worm, as Kyle had said. Yet even Kyle thought Ian had a "crush" on me. On *me?* That wasn't possible.

Or did he want to know what I thought about Jared? My feelings on the experiment? More details about my responses to physical contact? I shuddered.

Or my thoughts on Melanie? Melanie's thoughts on

their conversation? Whether I agreed with Jared about *her* rights?

I didn't know what I thought. About any of it.

"I really don't know," I said.

He nodded. "That's understandable."

"Only because you are very understanding."

He smiled at me. It was odd how his eyes could both scorch and warm. Especially with a color that was closer to ice than fire. They were quite warm at the moment.

"I like you very much, Wanda."

"I'm only just beginning to see that. I guess I'm a little slow."

"It's a surprise to me, too."

We both thought that over.

He pursed his lips. "And . . . I suppose . . . *that* is one of the things you don't know how you feel about?"

"No. I mean yes, I . . . *don't* know. I . . . I —"

"That's okay. You haven't had long to think about it. And it must seem . . . strange."

I nodded. "Yes. More than strange. Impossible."

"Tell me something," Ian said after a moment.

"If I know the answer."

"It's not a hard question."

He didn't ask it right away. Instead, he reached across the narrow space and picked up my hand. He held it in both of his for a moment, and then he trailed the fingers of his left hand slowly up my arm, from my wrist to my shoulder. Just as slowly, he pulled them back again. He looked at the skin of my arm rather than my face, watching the goose bumps that formed along the path of his fingers.

"Does that feel good or bad to you?" he asked.

*Bad,* Melanie insisted.

*But it doesn't hurt,* I protested.

*That's not what he's asking. When he says good . . . Oh, it's like talking to a child!*

*I'm not even a year old, you know. Or am I now?* I was sidetracked, trying to figure out the date.

Melanie was not distracted. *Good, to him, means the way it feels when Jared touches us.* The memory she provided was not one from the caves. It was in the magic canyon, at sunset. Jared stood behind her and let his hands follow the shape of her arms, from her shoulders to her wrists. I shivered at the pleasure of the simple touch. *Like that.*

*Oh.*

"Wanda?"

"Melanie says bad," I whispered.

"What do *you* say?"

"I say . . . I don't know."

When I could meet his eyes, they were warmer than I expected. "I can't even imagine how confusing this all must be to you."

It was comforting that he understood. "Yes. I'm confused."

His hand traced up and down my arm again. "Would you like me to stop?"

I hesitated. "Yes," I decided. "That . . . what you're doing . . . makes it hard for me to think. And Melanie is . . . angry at me. That also makes it hard to think."

*I'm not angry at you. Tell him to leave.*

*Ian is my friend. I don't want him to leave.*

He leaned away, folding his arms across his chest.

"I don't suppose she'd give us a minute alone?"

I laughed. "I doubt it."

Ian tilted his head to one side, his expression speculative.

"Melanie Stryder?" he asked, addressing her.

We both started at the name.

Ian went on. "I'd like the chance to speak with Wanda privately, if you don't mind. Is there any way that could be arranged?"

*Of all the nerve! You tell him I said no chance in hell! I do not like this man.*

My nose wrinkled up.

"What did she say?"

"She said no." I tried to say the words as gently as they could be said. "And that she doesn't . . . like you."

Ian laughed. "I can respect that. I can respect *her*. Well, it was worth a try." He sighed. "Kind of puts a damper on things, having an audience."

*What things?* Mel growled.

I grimaced. I didn't like feeling her anger. It was so much more vicious than mine.

*Get used to it.*

Ian put his hand on my face. "I'll let you think about things, okay? So you can decide how you feel."

I tried to be objective about that hand. It was soft against my face. It felt . . . nice. Not like when Jared touched me. But also different from the way it felt when Jamie hugged me. Other.

"It might take a while. None of this makes any sense, you know," I told him.

He grinned. "I know."

I realized, when he smiled then, that I wanted him to like me. The rest — the hand on my face, the fingers on my arm — I still wasn't sure at all about those. But I wanted him to like me, and to think kind things about me. Which is why it was hard to tell him the truth.

"You don't really feel that way about *me,* you know," I whispered. "It's this body. . . . She's pretty, isn't she?"

He nodded. "She is. Melanie is a very pretty girl. Even beautiful." His hand moved to touch my bad cheek, to stroke the rough, scarring skin with gentle fingers. "In spite of what I've done to her face."

Normally, I would have denied that automatically. Reminded him that the wounds on my face weren't his fault. But I was so confused that my head was spinning and I couldn't form a coherent sentence.

Why should it bother me that he thought Melanie was beautiful?

*You've got me there.* My feelings were no clearer to her than they were to me.

He brushed my hair back from my forehead.

"But, pretty as she is, she's a stranger to me. She's not the one I . . . care about."

That made me feel better. Which was even more confusing.

"Ian, you don't . . . Nobody here *separates* us the way they should. Not you, not Jamie, not Jeb." The truth came out in a rush, more heated than I'd meant it to be. "You *couldn't* care about me. If you could hold me in your hand, *me,* you would be disgusted. You would throw me to the ground and grind me under your foot."

His pale forehead creased as his black brows pulled together. "I . . . not if I knew it was you."

I laughed without humor. "How would you know? You couldn't tell us apart."

His mouth turned down.

"It's just the body," I repeated.

"That's not true at all," he disagreed. "It's not the face, but the expressions on it. It's not the voice, but what you say. It's not how you look in that body, but the things you do with it. *You* are beautiful."

He moved forward as he spoke, kneeling beside the bed where I lay and taking my hand again in both of his.

"I've never known anyone like you."

I sighed. "Ian, what if I'd come here in Magnolia's body?"

He grimaced and then laughed. "Okay. That's a good question. I don't know."

"Or Wes's?"

"But you're female — you yourself are."

"And I always request whatever a planet's equivalent is. It seems more . . . right. But I could be put into a man and I would function just fine."

"But you're not in a man's body."

"See? That's my point. Body and soul. Two different things, in my case."

"I wouldn't want it without you."

"You wouldn't want *me* without *it*."

He touched my cheek again and left his hand there, his thumb under my jaw. "But this body is part of you, too. It's part of who you are. And, unless you change your mind and turn us all in, it's who you will always be."

Ah, the finality of it. Yes, I would die in this body. The final death.

*And I will never live in it again,* Melanie whispered.

*It's not how either of us planned our future, is it?*

*No. Neither of us planned to have no future.*

"Another internal conversation?" Ian guessed.

"We're thinking of our mortality."

"You could live forever if you left us."

"Yes, I could." I sighed. "You know, humans have the shortest life span of any species I've ever been, except the Spiders. You have so little time."

"Don't you think, then . . ." Ian paused and leaned closer to me so that I couldn't seem to see anything around his face, just snow and sapphire and ink. "That maybe you should make the most of what time you have? That you should *live* while you're alive?"

I didn't see it coming the way I had with Jared. Ian was not as familiar to me. Melanie realized what he was going to do before I did, just a second before his lips touched mine.

*No!*

It wasn't like kissing Jared. With Jared, there was no thought, only desire. No control. A spark to gasoline — inevitable. With Ian, I didn't even know what I felt. Everything was muddled and confused.

His lips were soft and warm. He pressed them only lightly to mine, and then brushed them back and forth across my mouth.

"Good or bad?" he whispered against my lips.

*Bad! Bad, bad!*

"I — I can't think." When I moved my mouth to speak, he moved his with it.

"That sounds . . . good."

His mouth pressed down with more force now. He caught my lower lip between his and pulled on it gently.

Melanie wanted to hit him — so much more than she'd wanted to punch Jared. She wanted to shove him

away and then kick his face. The image was horrible. It
conflicted jarringly with the sensation of Ian's kiss.

"Please," I whispered.

"Yes?"

"Please stop. I can't think. Please."

He sat back at once, clasping his hands in front of him.
"Okay," he said, his tone cautious.

I pressed my hands against my face, wishing I could
push out Melanie's anger.

"Well, at least nobody punched me." Ian grinned.

"She wanted to do more than that. Ugh. I don't like it
when she's mad. It hurts my head. Anger is so . . . ugly."

"Why didn't she?"

"Because I didn't lose control. She only breaks free
when I'm . . . overwhelmed."

He watched as I kneaded my forehead.

*Calm down,* I begged her. *He's not touching me.*

*Has he forgotten that I'm* here? *Doesn't he care? This
is me, it's me!*

*I tried to explain that.*

*What about you? Have you forgotten Jared?*

She threw the memories at me the way she'd done in
the beginning, only this time they were like blows. A
thousand punches of his smile, his eyes, his lips on mine,
his hands on my skin . . .

*Of course not. Have you forgotten that you don't want
me to love him?*

"She's talking to you."

"Yelling at me," I corrected.

"I can tell now. I can see you concentrate on the conversation. I never noticed before today."

"She's not always this vocal."

"I *am* sorry, Melanie," he said. "I know this must be impossible for you."

Again, she visualized smashing her foot into his sculpted nose, leaving it crooked like Kyle's. *Tell him I don't want his apologies.*

I winced.

Ian half smiled, half grimaced. "She doesn't accept."

I shook my head.

"So she can break free? If you're overwhelmed?"

I shrugged. "Sometimes, if she takes me by surprise and I'm too . . . emotional. Emotion makes it hard to concentrate. But it's been more difficult for her lately. It's like the door between us is locked. I don't know why. I *tried* to let her out when Kyle —" I stopped talking abruptly, grinding my teeth together.

"When Kyle tried to kill you," he finished matter-of-factly. "You wanted her free? Why?"

I just stared at him.

"To fight him?" he guessed.

I didn't answer.

He sighed. "Okay. Don't tell me. Why do you think the . . . door is locked?"

I frowned. "I don't know. Maybe the time passing . . . It worries us."

"But she broke through before, to punch Jared."

"Yes." I shuddered at the memory of my fist striking his jaw.

"Because you were overwhelmed and emotional?"

"Yes."

"What did he do? Just kiss you?"

I nodded.

Ian flinched. His eyes tightened.

"What?" I asked. "What's wrong?"

"When Jared kisses you, you are . . . overwhelmed by emotion."

I stared at him, worried by the expression on his face. Melanie enjoyed it. *That's right!*

He sighed. "And when I kiss you . . . you aren't sure if you like it. You are not . . . overwhelmed."

"Oh." Ian was jealous. How very strange this world was. "I'm sorry."

"Don't be. I told you I'd give you time, and I don't mind waiting for you to think things through. I don't mind that at all."

"What do you mind?" Because he minded something very much.

He took a deep breath and blew it out slowly. "I saw how you loved Jamie. That was always really obvious. I guess I should have seen that you loved Jared, too. Maybe I didn't want to. It makes sense. You came here for the two of them. You love them both, the same way Melanie did. Jamie like a brother. And Jared . . ."

He was looking away, staring at the wall over me. I had to look away, too. I stared at the sunlight where it touched the red door.

"How much of that is Melanie?" he wanted to know.

"I don't know. Does it matter?"

I could barely hear his answer. "Yes. It does to me." Without looking at me or seeming to notice what he was doing, Ian took my hand again.

It was very quiet for a minute. Even Melanie was still. That was nice.

Then, as though a switch had been flipped, Ian was his normal self again. He laughed.

"Time is on my side," he said, grinning. "We've got the rest of our lives in here. One day you'll wonder what you ever saw in Jared."

*In your dreams.*

I laughed with him, happy he was joking again.

"Wanda? Wanda, can I come in?"

Jamie's voice started from down the hall and, accompanied by the sound of his jogging steps, ended right outside the door.

"Of course, Jamie."

I already had my hand held out to him before he shrugged the door aside. I hadn't seen him nearly enough lately. Unconscious or crippled, I hadn't been free to seek him out.

"Hey, Wanda! Hey, Ian!" Jamie was all grins, his messy hair bouncing when he moved. He headed for my reaching hand, but Ian was in his way. So he settled for sitting on the edge of my mattress and resting his hand on my foot. "How are you feeling?"

"Better."

"Hungry yet? There's beef jerky and corn on the cob! I could get you some."

"I'm okay for now. How are you? I haven't seen you much lately."

Jamie made a face. "Sharon gave me detention."

I smiled. "What did you do?"

"Nothing. I was totally framed." His innocent expression was a bit overdone, and he quickly changed the subject. "Guess what? Jared was saying at lunch that he didn't think it was fair for you to have to move out of the room you were used to. He said we weren't being good hosts. He said you should move back in with me! Isn't that great?

I asked him if I could tell you right away, and he said that was a good idea. He said you would be in here."

"I'll bet he did," Ian murmured.

"So what do you think, Wanda? We get to be roomies again!"

"But Jamie, where will Jared stay?"

"Wait — let me guess," Ian interrupted. "I bet he said the room was big enough for three. Am I right?"

"Yeah. How did you know?"

"Lucky guess."

"So that's good, isn't it, Wanda? It will be just like before we came here!"

It felt sort of like a razor sliding between my ribs when he said that — too clean and precise a pain to be compared to a blow or a break.

Jamie analyzed my tortured expression with alarm. "Oh. No, I mean but with you, too. It will be nice. The four of us, right?"

I tried to laugh through the pain; it didn't hurt any worse than not laughing.

Ian squeezed my hand.

"The four of us," I mumbled. "Nice."

Jamie crawled up the mattress, worming his way around Ian, to put his arms around my neck.

"Sorry. Don't be sad."

"Don't worry about it."

"You know I love you, too."

So sharp, so piercing, the emotions of this planet. Jamie had never said those words to me before. My whole body suddenly felt a few degrees warmer.

*So sharp,* Melanie agreed, wincing at her own pain.

"Will you come back?" Jamie begged against my shoulder.

I couldn't answer right away.

"What does Mel want?" he asked.

"She wants to live with you," I whispered. I didn't have to check to know that.

"And what do you want?"

"Do you want me to live with you?"

"You know I do, Wanda. Please."

I hesitated.

"Please?"

"If that's what you want, Jamie. Okay."

"Woo hoo!" Jamie crowed in my ear. "Cool! I'm gonna go tell Jared! I'll get you some food, too, okay?" He was already on his feet, bouncing the mattress so that I felt it in my ribs.

"Okay."

"You want something, Ian?"

"Sure, kid. I want you to tell Jared he's shameless."

"Huh?"

"Never mind. Go get Wanda some lunch."

"Sure. And I'll ask Wes for his extra bed. Kyle can come back in here, and everything will be like it should be!"

"Perfect," Ian said, and though I didn't look at his face, I knew he was rolling his eyes.

"Perfect," I whispered, and felt the razor's edge again.

# CHAPTER 39

# Worried

*Perfect*, I grumbled to myself. *Just perfect.*

Ian was coming to join me for lunch, a big smile glued into place on his face. Trying to cheer me up . . . again.

*I think you're overdoing the sarcasm lately,* Melanie told me.

*I'll keep that in mind.*

I hadn't heard from her much in the past week. Neither of us was good company right now. It was better if we avoided social interaction, even with each other.

"Hey, Wanda," Ian greeted me, hopping up onto the counter beside me. He had a bowl of tomato soup in one hand, still steaming. Mine was beside me, cooled and half full. I was toying with a piece of roll, ripping it into tiny pieces.

I didn't answer him.

"Oh, come on." He put his hand on my knee. Mel's angry reaction was lethargic. She was too used to this kind of thing to really work up a good fit anymore. "They'll be back today. Before sunset, without a doubt."

"You said that three days ago, and two days ago, and again yesterday," I reminded him.

"I have a good feeling about today. Don't sulk — it's so human," he teased.

"I'm not sulking." I *wasn't*. I was so worried I could barely think straight. It didn't leave me energy to do anything else.

"This isn't the first raid Jamie's gone on."

"That makes me feel so much better." Again with the sarcasm. Melanie was right — I really was overusing it.

"He's got Jared and Geoffrey and Trudy with him. And Kyle's *here*." Ian laughed. "So there's no way they'll get into any trouble."

"I don't want to talk about it."

"Okay."

He turned his attention to his food and let me stew. Ian was nice that way — always trying to give me what I wanted, even when what I wanted was unclear to either of us. His insistent attempts to distract me from the present anxiety excepted, of course. I knew I didn't want *that*. I wanted to worry; it was the only thing I could do.

It had been a month since I'd moved back into Jamie and Jared's room. For three weeks of that time, the four of us had lived together. Jared slept on a mattress wedged above the head of the bed where Jamie and I slept.

I'd gotten used to it — the sleeping part, at least; I was having a hard time sleeping now in the empty room. I missed the sound of two other bodies breathing.

I hadn't gotten used to waking up every morning with Jared there. It still took me a second too long to return his morning greeting. He was not at ease, either, but he was always polite. We were both very polite.

It was almost scripted at this point.

*"Good morning, Wanda, how did you sleep?"*

*"Fine, thank you, and you?"*

*"Fine, thanks. And . . . Mel?"*

*"She's good, too, thanks."*

Jamie's constant state of euphoria and his happy chattering kept things from becoming too strained. He talked about — and to — Melanie often, until her name was no longer the source of stress it had once been when Jared was present. Every day, it got a little bit more comfortable, the pattern of my life here a little bit more pleasant.

We were . . . sort of happy. Both Melanie and I.

And then, a week ago, Jared had left for another short raid — mostly to replace broken tools — and taken Jamie with him.

"You tired?" Ian asked.

I realized I was rubbing at my eyes. "Not really."

"Still not sleeping well?"

"It's too quiet."

"I could sleep with you — Oh, calm down, Melanie. You know what I meant."

Ian always noticed when Melanie's antagonism made me cringe.

"I thought they were going to be back today," I challenged.

"You're right. I guess there's no need for rearranging."

I sighed.

"Maybe you should take the afternoon off."

"Don't be silly," I told him. "I've got plenty of energy for work."

He grinned as though I'd said something that pleased him. Something he'd been hoping I would say.

"Good. I could use some help with a project."

"What's the project?"

"I'll show you — you finished there?"

I nodded.

He took my hand as he led me out of the kitchen. Again, this was so common that Melanie barely protested.

"Why are we going this way?" The eastern field did not need attention. We'd been part of the group that had irrigated it this morning.

Ian didn't answer. He was still grinning.

He led me down the eastern tunnel, past the field and into the corridor that led to only one place. As soon as we were in the tunnel, I could hear voices echoing and a sporadic *thud, thud* that it took me a moment to place. The stale, bitter sulfur odor helped link the sound to the memory.

"Ian, I'm not in the mood."

"You said you had plenty of energy."

"To work. Not to play soccer."

"But Lily and Wes will be really disappointed. I promised them a game of two-on-two. They worked so hard this morning to free up the afternoon . . ."

"Don't try to make me feel guilty," I said as we rounded the last curve. I could see the blue light of several lamps, shadows flitting in front of them.

"Isn't it working?" he teased. "C'mon, Wanda. It will be good for you."

He pulled me into the low-ceilinged game room, where Lily and Wes were passing the ball back and forth across the length of the field.

"Hey, Wanda. Hey, Ian," Lily called to us.

"This one's mine, O'Shea," Wes warned him.

"You're not going to let me lose to Wes, are you?" Ian murmured.

"You could beat them alone."

"It would still be a forfeit. I'd never live it down."

I sighed. "Fine. *Fine.* Be that way."

Ian hugged me with what Melanie thought was unnecessary enthusiasm. "You're my very favorite person in the known universe."

"Thanks," I muttered dryly.

"Ready to be humiliated, Wanda?" Wes taunted. "You may have taken the planet, but you're losing this game."

Ian laughed, but I didn't respond. The joke made me uneasy. How could Wes make a joke about that? Humans were always surprising me.

Melanie included. She'd been in just as miserable a mood as I was, but now she was suddenly excited.

*We didn't get to play last time,* she explained. I could feel her yearning to run — to run for pleasure rather than in fear. Running was something she used to love. *Doing nothing won't get them home any faster. A distraction might be nice.* She was already thinking strategy, sizing up our opponents.

"Do you know the rules?" Lily asked me.

I nodded. "I remember them."

Absently, I bent my leg at the knee and grabbed my ankle behind me, pulling it to stretch out the muscles. It was a familiar position to my body. I stretched the other leg and was pleased that it felt whole. The bruise on the back of my thigh was faded yellow, almost gone. My side felt fine, which made me think that my rib had never really been broken.

I'd seen my face while I was cleaning mirrors two weeks ago. The scar forming on my cheek was dark red and as big as the palm of my hand, with a dozen jagged points around the edges. It bothered Melanie more than it did me.

"I'll take the goal," Ian told me, while Lily fell back and Wes paced beside the ball. A mismatch. Melanie liked this. Competition appealed to her.

From the moment the game started — Wes kicking the ball back to Lily and then sprinting ahead to get around me for her pass — there was very little time to think. Only to react and to feel. See Lily shift her body, measure the direction this would send the ball. Cut Wes off — ah, but he was surprised by how fast I was — launch the ball to Ian and move up the field. Lily was playing too far forward. I raced her to the lantern goalpost and won. Ian aimed the pass perfectly, and I scored the first goal.

It felt good: the stretch and pull of muscle, the sweat of exertion rather than plain heat, the teamwork with Ian. We were well matched. I was quick, and his aim was deadly. Wes's goading dried up before Ian scored the third goal.

Lily called the game when we hit twenty-one. She was breathing hard. Not me; I felt good, muscles warm and limber.

Wes wanted another round, but Lily was done.

"Face it, they're better."

"We got hustled."

"No one ever said she couldn't play."

"No one ever said she was a pro, either."

I liked that — it made me smile.

"Don't be a sore loser," Lily said, reaching out to tickle Wes's stomach playfully. He caught her fingers and pulled her closer to him. She laughed, tugging away, but Wes reeled her in and planted a solid kiss on her laughing mouth.

Ian and I exchanged a quick, startled glance.

"For you, I will lose with grace," Wes told her, and then set her free.

Lily's smooth caramel skin had taken on a bit of pink on her cheeks and neck. She peeked at Ian and me to see our reaction.

"And now," Wes continued, "I'm off to get reinforcements. We'll see how your little ringer does against Kyle, Ian." He lobbed the ball into the far dark corner of the cave, where I heard it splash into the spring.

Ian trotted off to retrieve it, while I continued to look at Lily curiously.

She laughed at my expression, sounding self-conscious, which was unusual for her. "I know, I know."

"How long has . . . that been going on?" I wondered.

She grimaced.

"Not my business. Sorry."

"It's okay. It's not a secret — how could anything be a secret here, anyway? It's just really . . . new to me. It's sort of your fault," she added, smiling to show that she was teasing me.

I felt a little guilty anyway. And confused. "What did I do?"

"Nothing," she assured me. "It was Wes's . . . reaction to you that surprised me. I didn't know he had so much depth to him. I was never really aware of him before that. Oh, well. He's too young for me, but what does that matter here?" She laughed again. "It's strange how life and love go on. I didn't expect that."

"Yeah. Kind of funny how that happens," Ian agreed. I hadn't heard him return. He slung his arm around my shoulders. "It's nice, though. You do know Wes has been infatuated with you since he first got here, right?"

"So he says. I hadn't noticed."

Ian laughed. "Then you're the only one. So, Wanda, how about some one-on-one while we're waiting?"

I could feel Melanie's wordless enthusiasm. "Okay."

He let me have the ball first, holding back, hugging the goal area. My first shot cut between him and the post, scoring. I rushed him when he kicked off, and got the ball back. I scored again.

*He's letting us win,* Mel grumbled.

"Come on, Ian. Play."

"I am."

*Tell him he's playing like a girl.*

"Playing like a girl."

He laughed, and I slipped the ball away from him again. The taunt wasn't enough. I had an inspiration then, and I shot the ball through his goal, guessing it would probably be the last time I got to do it.

Mel objected. *I don't like this idea.*

*I'll bet it works, though.*

I put the ball back at center field. "You win, and you can sleep in my room while they're gone." I needed a good night's rest.

"First to ten." With a grunt, he launched the ball past me so hard that it rebounded off the distant, invisible wall behind my goal and came back to us.

I looked at Lily. "Was that wide?"

"No, it looked dead center to me."

"One–three," Ian announced.

It took him fifteen minutes to win, but at least I got to really work. I even squeezed in one more goal, of which I was proud. I was gasping for air when he stole the ball from me and sailed it through my goalposts for the last time.

He wasn't winded. "Ten–four, I win."

"Good game," I huffed.

"Tired?" he asked, the innocence in his tone a bit overdone. Being funny. He stretched. "I think I'm ready for bed myself." He leered in a melodramatic way.

I winced.

"Aw, Mel, you know I'm joking. Be nice."

Lily eyed us, mystified.

"Jared's Melanie objects to me," Ian told her, winking.

Her eyebrows rose. "That's . . . interesting."

"I wonder what's taking Wes so long?" Ian muttered, not taking much notice of her reaction. "Should we go find out? I could use some water."

"Me, too," I agreed.

"Bring some back." Lily didn't move from where she was half sprawled on the floor.

As we entered the narrow tunnel, Ian threw one arm lightly around my waist.

"You know," he said, "it's really unfair for Melanie to make *you* suffer when she's angry at me."

"Since when are humans fair?"

"Good point."

"Besides, she'd be glad to make you suffer, if I'd let her."

He laughed.

"That's nice about Wes and Lily, don't you think?" he said.

"Yes. They both seem very happy. I like that."

"I like it, too. Wes finally got the girl. Gives me hope." He winked at me. "Do you think Melanie would make you very uncomfortable if I were to kiss you right now?"

I stiffened for a second, then took a deep breath. "Probably."

*Oh, yes.*

"Definitely."

Ian sighed.

We heard Wes shouting at the same time. His voice came from the end of the tunnel, getting closer with each word.

"They're back! Wanda, they're back!"

It took me less than a second to process, and then I was sprinting. Behind me, Ian mumbled something about wasted effort.

I nearly knocked Wes down. "Where?" I gasped.

"In the plaza."

And I was off again. I flew into the big garden room with my eyes already searching. It wasn't hard to find them. Jamie was standing at the front of a group of people near the entrance to the southern tunnel.

"Hey, Wanda!" he yelled, waving.

Trudy held his arm as I ran around the edges of the field, as if she were holding him back from running to meet me.

I grabbed his shoulders with both hands and pulled him to me. "Oh, Jamie!"

"Did ya miss me?"

"Just a tiny bit. Where is everyone? Is everyone home? Is everyone okay?" Besides Jamie, Trudy was the only person here who was back from the raid. Everyone else in the little crowd — Lucina, Ruth Ann, Kyle, Travis, Violetta, Reid — was welcoming them home.

"Everyone's back and well," Trudy assured me.

My eyes swept the big cave. "Where are they?"

"Uh . . . getting cleaned up, unloading . . ."

I wanted to offer my help — anything that would get me to where Jared was so I could see with my own eyes that he was safe — but I knew I wouldn't be allowed to see where the goods were coming in.

"You look like you need a bath," I told Jamie, rumpling his dirty, knotted hair without letting go of him.

"He's supposed to go lie down," Trudy said.

"*Trudy,*" Jamie muttered, giving her a dark look.

Trudy glanced at me quickly, then looked away.

"Lie down . . . ?" I stared at Jamie, pulling back to get a good look at him. He didn't seem tired — his eyes were bright, and his cheeks flushed under his tan. My eyes raked over him once and then froze on his right leg.

There was a ragged hole in his jeans a few inches above his knee. The fabric around the hole was a dark reddish brown, and the ominous color spread in a long stain all the way to the cuff.

*Blood,* Melanie realized with horror.

"Jamie! What happened?"

"Thanks, Trudy."

"She was going to notice soon enough. C'mon, we'll talk while you limp."

Trudy put her arm under his and helped him hop forward one slow step at a time, keeping his weight on his left leg.

"Jamie, tell me what happened!" I put my arm around him from the other side, trying to carry as much of his weight as I could.

"It's really stupid. And totally my fault. *And* it could have happened here."

"Tell me."

He sighed. "I tripped with a knife in my hand."

I shuddered. "Shouldn't we be taking you the other way? You need to see Doc."

"That's where I'm coming from. That's where we went first."

"What did Doc say?"

"It's fine. He cleaned it and bandaged it and said to go lie down."

"And have you walk all this way? Why didn't you stay in the hospital?"

Jamie made a face and glanced up at Trudy, like he was looking for an answer.

"Jamie will be more comfortable on his bed," she suggested.

"Yeah," he agreed quickly. "Who wants to lie around on one of those awful cots?"

I looked at them and then behind me. The crowd was gone. I could hear their voices echoing back down the southern corridor.

*What was that about?* Mel wondered warily.

It occurred to me that Trudy wasn't a much better liar

than I was. When she'd said the others from the raid were unloading and cleaning up, there was a false note to her voice. I thought I remembered her eyes flickering to the right, back toward that tunnel.

"Hey, kid! Hey, Trudy!" Ian had caught up to us.

"Hi, Ian," they greeted him at the same time.

"What happened here?"

"Fell on a knife," Jamie grunted, ducking his head.

Ian laughed.

"I don't think it's funny," I told him, my voice tight. Melanie, frantic with worry in my head, imagined slapping him. I ignored her.

"Could happen to anybody," Ian said, planting a light punch on Jamie's arm.

"Right," Jamie muttered.

"Where's everybody?"

I watched Trudy from the corner of my eye as she answered him.

"They, uh, had some unloading to finish up." This time her eyes moved toward the southern tunnel very deliberately, and Ian's expression hardened, turned enraged for half a second. Then Trudy glanced back at me and caught me watching.

*Distract them,* Melanie whispered.

I looked down at Jamie quickly.

"Are you hungry?" I asked him.

"Yeah."

"When *aren't* you hungry?" Ian teased. His face was relaxed again. He was better at deception than Trudy.

When we reached our room, Jamie sank gratefully onto the big mattress.

"You sure you're okay?" I checked.

"It's nothing. Really. Doc says I'll be fine in a few days."

I nodded, though I was not convinced.

"I'm going to go clean up," Trudy murmured as she left.

Ian propped himself against the wall, going nowhere.

*Keep your face down when you lie,* Melanie suggested.

"Ian?" I stared intently at Jamie's bloody leg. "Do you mind getting us some food? I'm hungry, too."

"Yeah. Get us something good."

I could feel Ian's eyes on me, but I didn't look up.

"Okay," he agreed. "I'll be back in just a second." He emphasized the short time.

I kept my gaze down, as if I were examining the wound, until I heard his footsteps fade.

"You aren't mad at me?" Jamie asked.

"Of course not."

"I know you didn't want me to go."

"You're safe now; that's all that matters." I patted his arm absentmindedly. Then I got to my feet and let my hair, now chin length, fall forward to hide my face.

"I'll be right back — I forgot something I wanted to tell Ian."

"What?" he asked, confused by my tone.

"You'll be okay here by yourself?"

"Course I will," he retorted, sidetracked.

I ducked out around the screen before he could ask anything else.

The hall was clear, Ian out of sight. I had to hurry. I knew he was already suspicious. He'd noticed that *I'd* noticed Trudy's awkward and artificial explanation. He wouldn't be gone long.

I walked quickly, but didn't run, as I moved through the big plaza. Purposeful, as if I were on an errand. There were only a few people there — Reid, headed for the passageway that led to the bathing pool; Ruth Ann and Heidi, paused by the eastern corridor, chatting; Lily and Wes, their backs to me, holding hands. No one paid me any attention. I stared ahead as if I were not focused on the southern tunnel, only turning in at the very last second.

As soon as I was in the pitch-black of the corridor, I sped up, jogging along the familiar path.

Some instinct told me this was the same thing — that this was a repeat of the last time Jared and the others had come home from a raid, and everyone was sad, and Doc had gotten drunk, and no one would answer my questions. It was happening again, whatever I wasn't supposed to know about. What I didn't want to know about, according to Ian. I felt prickles on the back of my neck. Maybe I *didn't* want to know.

*Yes, you do. We both do.*

*I'm frightened.*

*Me, too.*

I ran as quietly as I could down the dark tunnel.

# CHAPTER 40

# Horrified

I slowed when I heard the sound of voices. I was not close enough to the hospital for it to be Doc. Others were on their way back. I pressed myself against the rock wall and crept forward as quietly as I could. My breathing was ragged from running. I covered my mouth with my hand to stifle the sound.

". . . why we keep doing this," someone complained.

I wasn't sure whose voice it was. Someone I didn't know well. Maybe Violetta? It held that same depressed tone that I recognized from before. It erased any notion that I'd been imagining things.

"Doc didn't want to. It was Jared's idea this time."

I was sure that it was Geoffrey who spoke now, though his voice was a little changed by the subdued revulsion in it. Geoffrey had been with Trudy on the raid, of course. They did everything together.

"I thought he was the biggest opponent to this business."

That was Travis, I guessed.

"He's more . . . motivated now," Geoffrey answered. His voice was quiet, but I could tell he was angry about something.

They passed just half a foot from where I cringed into the rocks. I froze, holding my breath.

"I think it's sick," Violetta muttered. "Disgusting. It's never going to work."

They walked slowly, their steps weighted with despair.

No one answered her. No one spoke again in my hearing. I stayed motionless until their footsteps had faded a little, but I couldn't wait until the sound disappeared completely. Ian might be following me already.

I crept forward as quickly as I could and then started jogging again when I decided it was safe.

I saw the first faint hints of daylight streaming around the curving tunnel ahead, and I shifted into a quieter lope that still kept me moving swiftly. I knew that once I was around the gradual arc, I would be able to see the doorway into Doc's realm. I followed the bend, and the light grew brighter.

I moved cautiously now, putting each foot down with silent care. It was very quiet. For a moment, I wondered if I was wrong and there was no one here at all. Then, as the uneven entrance came into view, throwing a block of white sunlight against the opposite wall, I could hear the sound of quiet sobbing.

I tiptoed right to the edge of the gap and paused, listening.

The sobbing continued. Another sound, a soft, rhythmic thudding, kept time with it.

"There, there." It was Jeb's voice, thick with some emotion. "'S okay. 'S okay, Doc. Don't take it so hard."

Hushed footsteps, more than one set, were moving around the room. Fabric rustling. A brushing sound. It reminded me of the sounds of cleaning.

There was a smell that didn't belong here. Strange . . . not quite metallic, but not quite anything else, either. The smell was not familiar — I was sure I had never smelled it before — and yet I had an odd feeling that it *should* be familiar to me.

I was afraid to move around the corner.

*What's the worst they will do to us?* Mel pointed out. *Make us leave?*

*You're right.*

Things had definitely changed if that was the worst I could fear from the humans now.

I took a deep breath — noticing again that strange, *wrong* smell — and eased around the rocky edge into the hospital.

No one noticed me.

Doc was kneeling on the floor, his face buried in his hands, his shoulders heaving. Jeb leaned over him, patting his back.

Jared and Kyle were laying a crude stretcher beside one of the cots in the middle of the room. Jared's face was hard — the mask had come back while he was away.

The cots were not empty, as they usually were. Something, hidden under dark green blankets, filled the length of both of them. Long and irregular, with familiar curves and angles . . .

Doc's homemade table was arranged at the head of these cots, in the brightest spot of sunlight. The table glittered with silver — shiny scalpels and an assortment of antiquated medical tools that I couldn't put a name to.

Brighter than these were other silver things. Shimmering segments of silver stretched in twisted, tortured pieces across the table . . . tiny silver strands plucked and naked and scattered . . . splatters of silver liquid smeared on the table, the blankets, the walls . . .

The quiet in the room was shattered by my scream. The whole *room* was shattered. It spun and shook to the sound, whirled around me so that I couldn't find the way out. The walls, the silver-stained walls, rose up to block my escape no matter which way I turned.

Someone shouted my name, but I couldn't hear whose voice it was. The screaming was too loud. It hurt my head. The stone wall, oozing silver, slammed into me, and I fell to the floor. Heavy hands held me there.

"Doc, help!"

"What's wrong with her?"

"Is it having a fit?"

"What did she see?"

"Nothing — nothing. The bodies were covered!"

That was a lie! The bodies were hideously uncovered, strewn in obscene contortions across the glittering table. Mutilated, dismembered, tortured bodies, ripped into grotesque shreds . . .

I had clearly seen the vestigial feelers still attached to the truncated anterior section of a child. Just a child! A baby! A baby thrown haphazardly in maimed pieces across the table smeared with its own blood . . .

My stomach rolled like the walls were rolling, and acid clawed its way up my throat.

"Wanda? Can you hear me?"

"Is she conscious?"

"I think she's going to throw up."

The last voice was right. Hard hands held my head while the acid in my stomach violently overflowed.

"What do we do, Doc?"

"Hold on to her — don't let her hurt herself."

I coughed and squirmed, trying to escape. My throat cleared.

"Let me go!" I was finally able to choke out. The words were garbled. "Get away from me! Get away; you're monsters! Torturers!"

I shrieked wordlessly again, twisting against the restraining arms.

"Calm down, Wanda! Shh! It's okay!" That was Jared's voice. For once, it didn't matter that it was Jared.

"Monster!" I screamed at him.

"She's hysterical," Doc told him. "Hold on."

A sharp, stinging blow whipped across my face.

There was a gasp, far away from the immediate chaos.

"What are you *doing?*" Ian roared.

"It's having a seizure or something, Ian. Doc's trying to bring it around."

My ears were ringing, but not from the slap. It was the smell — the smell of the silver blood dripping down the walls — the smell of the blood of souls. The room writhed around me as though it were alive. The light twisted into strange patterns, curved into the shapes of monsters from my past. A Vulture unfurled its wings . . .

a claw beast swung its heavy pincers toward my face . . . Doc smiled and reached for me with silver trickling from his fingertips . . .

The room spun once more, slowly, and then went black.

◆

Unconsciousness didn't claim me for long. It must have been only seconds later when my head cleared. I was all too lucid; I wished I could stay oblivious longer.

I was moving, rocking back and forth, and it was too black to see. Mercifully, the horrible smell had faded. The musty, humid air of the caves was like perfume.

The feeling of being carried, being cradled, was familiar. That first week after Kyle had injured me, I'd traveled many places in Ian's arms.

". . . thought she'd have guessed what we were up to. Looks like I was wrong," Jared was murmuring.

"You think that's what happened?" Ian's voice cut hard in the quiet tunnel. "That she was scared because Doc was trying to take the other souls out? That she was afraid for herself?"

Jared didn't answer for a minute. "You don't?"

Ian made a sound in the back of his throat. "No. I don't. As disgusted as *I* am that you would bring back more . . . victims for Doc, bring them back *now!* — as much as that turns my stomach, that's not what upset her. How can you be so blind? Can't you imagine what that must have looked like to her in there?"

"I know we had the bodies covered before —"

"The *wrong bodies,* Jared. Oh, I'm sure Wanda would be upset by a human corpse — she's so gentle; violence and death aren't a part of her normal world. But think what the things on that table must have meant to her."

It took him another moment. "Oh."

"Yes. If you or I had walked in on a human vivisection, with torn body parts, with blood splattered on everything, it wouldn't have been as bad for us as it was for her. We'd have seen it all before — even before the invasion, in horror movies, at least. I'd bet she's never been exposed to anything like that in all her lives."

I was getting sick again. His words were bringing it back. The sight. The smell.

"Let me go," I whispered. "Put me down."

"I didn't mean to wake you. I'm sorry." The last words were fervent, apologizing for more than waking me.

"Let me go."

"You're not well. I'll take you to your room."

"No. Put me down now."

"Wanda —"

"Now!" I shouted. I shoved against Ian's chest, kicking my legs free at the same time. The ferocity of my struggle surprised him. He lost his hold on me, and I half fell into a crouch on the floor.

I sprang up from the crouch running.

"Wanda!"

"Let her go."

"Don't touch me! Wanda, come back!"

It sounded like they were wrestling behind me, but I didn't slow. Of course they were fighting. They were humans. Violence was pleasure to them.

I didn't pause when I was back in the light. I sprinted through the big cavern without looking at any of the monsters there. I could feel their eyes on me, and I didn't care.

I didn't care where I was going, either. Just somewhere I could be alone. I avoided the tunnels that had people near them, running down the first empty one I could find.

It was the eastern tunnel. This was the second time I'd sprinted through this corridor today. Last time in joy, this time in horror. It was hard to remember how I'd felt this afternoon, knowing the raiders were home. Everything was dark and gruesome now, including their return. The very stones seemed evil.

This way was the right choice for me, though. No one had any reason to come here, and it was empty.

I ran to the farthest end of the tunnel, into the deep night of the empty game room. Could I really have played games with them such a short time ago? Believed the smiles on their faces, not seeing the beasts underneath . . .

I moved forward until I stumbled ankle deep into the oily waters of the dark spring. I backed away, my hand outstretched, searching for a wall. When I found a rough ridge of stone — sharp-edged beneath my fingers — I turned into the depression behind the protrusion and curled myself into a tight ball on the ground there.

*It wasn't what we thought. Doc wasn't hurting anyone on purpose; he was just trying to save —*

*GET OUT OF MY HEAD!* I shrieked.

As I thrust her away from me — gagged her so that I wouldn't have to bear her justifications — I realized how weak she'd grown in all these months of friendliness. How much I'd been allowing. Encouraging.

It was almost too easy to silence her. As easy as it should have been from the beginning.

It was only me now. Just me, and the pain and the horror that I would never escape. I would never *not* have that image in my head again. I would never be free of it. It was forever a part of me.

I didn't know how to mourn here. I could not mourn in human ways for these lost souls whose names I would never know. For the broken child on the table.

I had never had to mourn on the Origin. I didn't know how it was done there, in the truest home of my kind. So I settled for the way of the Bats. It seemed appropriate, here where it was as black as being blind. The Bats mourned with silence — not singing for weeks on end until the pain of the nothingness left behind by the lack of music was worse than the pain of losing a soul. I'd known loss there. A friend, killed in a freak accident, a falling tree in the night, found too late to save him from the crushed body of his host. Spiraling . . . Upward . . . Harmony; those were the words that would have held his name in this language. Not exact, but close enough. There had been no horror in his death, only grief. An accident.

The bubbling stream was too discordant to remind me of our songs. I could grieve beside its harmony-free clatter.

I wrapped my arms tightly around my shoulders and mourned for the child and the other soul who had died with it. My siblings. My family. If I had found a way free of this place, if I had warned the Seekers, their remains would not be so casually mangled and mixed together in that blood-steeped room.

I wanted to cry, to keen in misery. But that was the

human way. So I locked my lips and hunched in the darkness, holding the pain inside.

My silence, my mourning, was stolen from me.

It took them a few hours. I heard them looking, heard their voices echo and warp in the long tubes of air. They were calling for me, expecting an answer. When they received no answer, they brought lights. Not the dim blue lanterns that might never have revealed my hiding place here, buried under all this blackness, but the sharp yellow lances of flashlights. They swept back and forth, pendulums of light. Even with the flashlights, they didn't find me until the third search of the room. Why couldn't they leave me alone?

When the flashlight's beam finally disinterred me, there was a gasp of relief.

"I found her! Tell the others to get back inside! She's in here after all!"

I knew the voice, but I didn't put a name to it. Just another monster.

"Wanda? Wanda? Are you all right?"

I didn't raise my head or open my eyes. I was in mourning.

"Where's Ian?"

"Should we get Jamie, do you think?"

"He shouldn't be on that leg."

Jamie. I shuddered at his name. My Jamie. He was a monster, too. He was just like the rest of them. My Jamie. It was a physical pain to think of him.

"Where is she?"

"Over here, Jared. She's not . . . responding."

"We didn't touch her."

"Here, give me the light," Jared said. "Now, the rest of

you, get out of here. Emergency over. Give her some air, okay?"

There was a shuffling noise that didn't travel far.

"Seriously, people. You're not helping. Leave. All the way out."

The shuffling was slow at first, but then became more productive. I could hear many footsteps fading away in the room and then disappearing out of it.

Jared waited until it was silent again.

"Okay, Wanda, it's just you and me."

He waited for some kind of answer.

"Look, I guess that must have been pretty . . . bad. We never wanted you to see that. I'm sorry."

Sorry? Geoffrey'd said it was Jared's idea. He wanted to cut me out, slice me into little pieces, fling my blood on the wall. He'd slowly mangle a million of me if he could find a way to keep his favorite monster alive with him. Slash us all to slivers.

He was quiet for a long time, still waiting for me to react.

"You look like you want to be alone. That's okay. I can keep them away, if that's what you want."

I didn't move.

Something touched my shoulder. I cringed away from it, into the sharp stones.

"Sorry," he muttered.

I heard him stand, and the light — red behind my closed eyes — began to fade as he walked away.

He met someone in the mouth of the cave.

"Where is she?"

"She wants to be alone. Let her be."

"Don't get in my way again, Howe."

"Do you think she wants comfort from you? From a human?"

"I wasn't party to this —"

Jared answered in a lower voice, but I could still hear the echoes. "Not *this* time. You're one of us, Ian. Her enemy. Did you hear what she said in there? She was screaming *monsters*. That's how she sees us now. She doesn't want your comfort."

"Give me the light."

They didn't speak again. A minute passed, and I heard one set of slow footsteps moving around the edge of the room. Eventually, the light swept across me, turning my lids red again.

I huddled myself more tightly together, expecting him to touch me.

There was a quiet sigh, and then the sound of him sitting on the stone, not as close beside me as I would have expected.

With a click, the light disappeared.

I waited in the silence for a long time for him to speak, but he was just as silent as I was.

Finally, I stopped waiting and returned to my mourning. Ian did not interrupt. I sat in the blackness of the big hole in the ground and grieved for lost souls with a human at my side.

# CHAPTER 41

# Vanished

Ian sat with me for three days in the darkness.

He left for only a few short minutes at a time, to get us food and water. At first, Ian ate, though I did not. Then, as he realized that it wasn't a loss of appetite that left my tray full, he stopped eating, too.

I used his brief absences to deal with the physical needs that I could not ignore, thankful for the proximity of the odorous stream. As my fast lengthened, those needs vanished.

I couldn't keep from sleeping, but I did not make myself comfortable. The first day, I woke to find my head and shoulders cradled on his lap. I recoiled from him, shuddering so violently that he did not repeat the gesture. After that, I slumped against the stones where I was, and when I woke, I would curl back up into my silent ball at once.

"Please," Ian whispered on the third day — at least I thought it was the third day; there was no way to be sure of the passing time in this dark, silent place. It was the first time he'd spoken.

I knew a tray of food was in front of me. He pushed it closer, till it touched my leg. I cringed away.

"Please, Wanda. Please eat something."

He put his hand on my arm but moved away quickly when I flinched out from under it.

"Please don't hate me. I'm so sorry. If I'd known . . . I would have stopped them. I won't let it happen again."

He would never stop them. He was just one among many. And, as Jared had said, he'd had no objections before. I was the enemy. Even in the most compassionate, humankind's limited scope of mercy was reserved for their own.

I knew Doc could never intentionally inflict pain on another person. I doubted he would even be capable of watching such a thing, tender as his feelings were. But a worm, a centipede? Why would he care about the agony of a strange alien creature? Why would it bother him to murder a baby — slowly, slicing it apart piece by piece — if it had no human mouth to scream with?

"I should have told you," Ian whispered.

Would it have mattered if I'd simply been told rather than having seen the tortured remains for myself? Would the pain be less strong?

"Please eat."

The silence returned. We sat in it for a while, maybe another hour.

Ian got up and walked quietly away.

I could make no sense of my emotions. In that

moment, I hated the body I was bound to. How did it make sense that his going depressed me? Why should it pain me to have the solitude I craved? I wanted the monster back, and that was plainly wrong.

I wasn't alone for long. I didn't know if Ian had gone to get him or if he'd been waiting for Ian to leave, but I recognized Jeb's contemplative whistle as it approached in the darkness.

The whistling stopped a few feet from me, and there was a loud click. A beam of yellow light burned my eyes. I blinked against it.

Jeb set the flashlight down, bulb up. It threw a circle of light on the low ceiling and made a wider, more diffuse sphere of light around us.

Jeb settled himself against the wall beside me.

"Gonna starve yourself, then? Is that the plan?"

I glared at the stone floor.

If I was being honest with myself, I knew that my mourning was over. I had grieved. I hadn't known the child or the other soul in the cave of horrors. I could not grieve for strangers forever. No, now I was angry.

"You wanna die, there are easier and faster ways."

As if I wasn't aware of *that*.

"So give me to Doc, then," I croaked.

Jeb wasn't surprised to hear me speak. He nodded to himself, as if this was exactly what he'd known would come out of my mouth.

"Did you expect us to just give up, Wanderer?" Jeb's voice was stern and more serious than I had ever heard it before. "We have a stronger survival instinct than that. Of course we want to find a way to get our minds back. It could be any one of us someday. So many people we love are already lost.

"It isn't easy. It nearly kills Doc each time he fails — you've seen that. But this is our reality, Wanda. This is our world. We've lost a war. We are about to be extinct. We're trying to find ways to save ourselves."

For the first time, Jeb spoke to me as if I were a soul and not a human. I had a sense that the distinction had always been clear to him, though. He was just a courteous monster.

I couldn't deny the truth of what he was saying, or the sense of it. The shock had worn off, and I was myself again. It was in my nature to be fair.

Some few of these humans could see my side of things; Ian, at least. Then I, too, could consider their perspective. They were monsters, but maybe monsters who were justified in what they were doing.

Of course they would think violence was the answer. They wouldn't be able to imagine any other solution. Could I blame them that their genetic programming restricted their problem-solving abilities in this way?

I cleared my throat, but my voice was still hoarse with disuse. "Hacking up babies won't save anyone, Jeb. Now they're *all* dead."

He was quiet for a moment. "We can't tell your young from your old."

"No, I know that."

"Your kind don't spare our babies."

"We don't torture them, though. We never intentionally cause anyone pain."

"You do worse than that. You erase them."

"You do both."

"We do, yes — because we have to try. We have to keep fighting. It's the only way we know. It's keep trying or turn our faces to the wall and die." He raised one eyebrow at me.

That must have been what it looked like I was doing.

I sighed and took the water bottle Ian had left close to my foot. I drained it in one long pull, and then cleared my throat again.

"It will never work, Jeb. You can keep cutting us out in pieces, but you'll just murder more and more sentient creatures of both species. We do not willingly kill, but our bodies are not weak, either. Our attachments may look like soft silver hair, but they're stronger than your organs. That's what's happening, isn't it? Doc slices up *my* family, and their limbs shred through the brains of *yours*."

"Like cottage cheese," he agreed.

I gagged and then shuddered at the image.

"It makes me sick, too," he admitted. "Doc gets real bent out of shape. Every time he thinks he's got it cracked, it goes south again. He's tried everything he can think of, but he can't save them from getting turned into oatmeal. Your souls don't respond to injected sedation . . . or poison."

My voice came out rough with new horror. "Of course not. Our chemical makeup is completely different."

"Once, one of yours seemed to guess what was going to happen. Before Doc could knock the human out, the silver thingy tore up his brain from the inside. Course, we didn't know that until Doc opened him up. The guy just collapsed."

I was surprised, strangely impressed. That soul must

have been very brave. I had not had the courage to take that step, even in the beginning when I was sure they were going to try to torture this very information from me. I didn't imagine they would try to slash the answer out for themselves; that course was so obviously doomed to failure, it had never occurred to me.

"Jeb, we are relatively tiny creatures, utterly dependent on unwilling hosts. We wouldn't have lasted very long if we didn't have some defenses."

"I'm not denying that your kind have a right to those defenses. I'm just telling you that we're gonna keep fighting back, however we can. We don't mean to cause anyone pain. We're makin' this up as we go. But we *will* keep fighting."

We looked at each other.

"Then maybe you *should* have Doc slice me up. What else am I good for?"

"Now, now. Don't be silly, Wanda. We humans aren't so logical as all that. We have a greater range of good and bad in us than you do. Well, maybe mostly the bad."

I nodded at that, but he kept going, ignoring me.

"We value the individual. We probably put *too* much emphasis on the individual, if it comes right down to it. How many people, in the abstract, would . . . let's say Paige . . . how many people would she sacrifice to keep Andy alive? The answer wouldn't make any sense if you were looking at the whole of humanity as equals.

"The way you are valued here . . . Well, that don't make much sense when you look at it from humanity's perspective, either. But there's some who would value you above a human stranger. Have to admit, I put myself in that group. I count you as a friend, Wanda. Course, that's not gonna work well if you hate me."

"I don't hate you, Jeb. But . . ."

"Yeah?"

"I just don't see how I can live here anymore. Not if you're going to be slaughtering my family in the other room. And I can't leave, obviously. So you see what I mean? What else is there for me but Doc's pointless cutting?" I shuddered.

He nodded seriously. "Now, that's a real valid point. It's not fair to ask you to live with that."

My stomach dropped. "If I get a choice, I'd rather you shot me, actually," I whispered.

Jeb laughed. "Slow down there, honey. Nobody's shooting my friends, or hackin' 'em up. I know you're not lying, Wanda. If you say doing it our way isn't going to work, then we're going to have to rethink things. I'll tell the boys they're not to bring any more souls back for now. Besides, I think Doc's nerves are toast. He can't take much more of this."

"You could be lying to me," I reminded him. "I probably couldn't tell."

"You'll have to trust me, then. Because I'm not going to shoot you. And I'm not going to let you starve yourself, either. Eat something, kid. That's an order."

I took a deep breath, trying to think. I wasn't sure if we'd come to an accommodation or not. Nothing made sense in this body. I liked the people here too much. They were friends. Monstrous friends that I couldn't see in the proper light while sunk in emotion.

Jeb picked up a thick square of cornbread soaked through with stolen honey and shoved it into my hand.

It made a mess there, crumbling into gluey morsels that stuck to my fingers. I sighed again and started cleaning them off with my tongue.

"That's a girl! We'll get over this rough spot. Things are gonna work out here, you'll see. Try to think positive."

"Think positive," I mumbled around a mouthful of food, shaking my head with disbelief. Only Jeb . . .

Ian came back then. When he walked into our circle of light and saw the food in my hand, the look that spread across his face filled me with guilt. It was a look of joyous relief.

No, I had never intentionally caused anyone physical pain, but I had hurt Ian deeply enough just by hurting myself. Human lives were so impossibly tangled. What a mess.

"Here you are, Jeb," he said in a subdued voice as he sat down across from us, just slightly closer to Jeb. "Jared guessed you might be here."

I dragged myself half a foot toward him, my arms aching from being motionless so long, and put my hand on his.

"Sorry," I whispered.

He turned his hand up to hold mine. "Don't apologize to me."

"I should have known. Jeb's right. Of course you fight back. How can I blame you for that?"

"It's different with you here. It should have stopped."

But my being here had only made it that much more important to solve the problem. How to rip me out and keep Melanie here. How to erase me to bring her back.

"All's fair in war," I murmured, trying to smile.

He grinned weakly back. "And love. You forgot that part."

"Okay, break it up," Jeb mumbled. "I'm not done here."

I looked at him curiously. What more was there?

"Now." He took a deep breath. "Try not to freak out again, okay?" he asked, looking at me.

I froze, gripping Ian's hand tighter.

Ian threw an anxious glance at Jeb.

"You're going to tell her?" Ian asked.

"What now?" I gasped. "What is it *now*?"

Jeb had his poker face on. "It's Jamie."

Those two words turned the world upside down again.

For three long days, I'd been Wanderer, a soul among humans. I was suddenly Wanda again, a very confused soul with human emotions that were too powerful to control.

I jumped to my feet — yanking Ian up with me, my hand locked on his like a vise — and then swayed, my head spinning.

"Sheesh. I said don't freak out, Wanda. Jamie's okay. He's just really anxious about you. He heard what happened, and he's been asking for you — worried out of his mind, that kid is — and I don't think it's good for him. I came down here to ask you to go see him. But you can't go like this. You look horrible. It will just upset him for no good reason. Sit down and eat some more food."

"His leg?" I demanded.

"There's a little infection," Ian murmured. "Doc wants him to stay down or he'd have come to get you a long time ago. If Jared wasn't practically pinning him to the bed, he would have come anyway."

Jeb nodded. "Jared almost came here and carried you out by force, but I told him to let me speak to you first. It wouldn't do the kid any good to see you catatonic."

My blood felt as though it had changed into ice water. Surely just my imagination.

"What's being done?"

Jeb shrugged. "Nothin' *to* do. Kid's strong; he'll fight it off."

"Nothing to do? What do you mean?"

"It's a bacterial infection," Ian said. "We don't have antibiotics anymore."

"Because they don't work — the bacteria are smarter than your medicines. There has to be something better, something else."

"Well, we don't have anything else," Jeb said. "He's a healthy kid. It just has to run its course."

"Run . . . its . . . course." I murmured the words in a daze.

"Eat something," Ian urged. "You'll worry him if he sees you like this."

I rubbed my eyes, trying to think straight.

Jamie was sick. There was nothing to treat him with here. No options but waiting to see if his body could heal itself. And if it couldn't . . .

"No," I gasped.

I felt as if I were standing on the edge of Walter's grave again, listening to the sound of sand falling into the darkness.

"No," I moaned, fighting against the memory.

I turned mechanically and started walking with stiff strides toward the exit.

"Wait," Ian said, but he didn't pull against the hand he still held. He kept pace with me.

Jeb caught up to me on the other side and shoved more food into my free hand.

"Eat for the kid's sake," he said.

I bit into it without tasting, chewed without thinking, swallowed without feeling the food go down.

"Knew she was gonna overreact," Jeb grumbled.

"So why did you tell her?" Ian asked, frustrated.

Jeb didn't answer. I wondered why he didn't. Was this worse even than I imagined?

"Is he in the hospital?" I asked in an emotionless, inflectionless voice.

"No, no," Ian assured me quickly. "He's in your room."

I didn't even feel relief. Too numb for that.

I would have gone into that room again for Jamie, even if it was still reeking of blood.

I didn't see the familiar caves I walked through. I barely noticed that it was day. I couldn't meet the eyes of any of the humans who stopped to stare at me. I could only put one foot in front of the other until I finally reached the hallway.

There were a few people clustered in front of the seventh cave. The silk screen was pushed far aside, and they craned their necks to see into Jared's room. They were all familiar, people I'd considered friends. Jamie's friends, too. Why were they here? Was his condition so unstable that they needed to check on him often?

"Wanda," someone said. Heidi. "Wanda's here."

"Let her through," Wes said. He slapped Jeb on the back. "Good job."

I walked through the little group without looking at them. They parted for me; I might have walked right into them if they hadn't. I couldn't concentrate on anything but moving myself forward.

It was bright in the high-ceilinged room. The room itself was not crowded. Doc or Jared had kept everyone out. I was vaguely aware of Jared, leaning against the far wall with his hands clasped behind him — a posture he assumed only when he was really worried. Doc knelt beside the big bed where Jamie lay, just where I had left him.

Why had I left him?

Jamie's face was red and sweaty. The right leg of his jeans had been cut away, and the bandage was peeled back from his wound. It wasn't as big as I'd expected. Not as horrible as I would have imagined. Just a two-inch gash with smooth edges. But the edges were a frightening shade of red, and the skin around the cut was swollen and shiny.

"Wanda," Jamie exhaled when he saw me. "Oh, you're okay. Oh." He took a deep breath.

I stumbled and fell to my knees beside him, dragging Ian down with me. I touched Jamie's face and felt the skin burn under my hand. My elbow brushed Doc's, but I barely noticed. He scooted away, but I didn't look to see what emotion was on his face, whether it was aversion or guilt.

"Jamie, baby, how are you?"

"Stupid," he said, grinning. "Just plain stupid. Can

you believe this?" He gestured to his leg. "Of all the luck."

I found a wet rag on his pillow and wiped it across his forehead.

"You're going to be fine," I promised. I was surprised at how fierce my voice sounded.

"Of course. It's nothing. But Jared wouldn't let me come talk to you." His face was suddenly anxious. "I heard about . . . and Wanda, you know I —"

"Shh. Don't even think of it. If I'd had any idea you were sick I would have been here sooner."

"I'm not really sick. Just a stupid infection. I'm glad you're here, though. I hated not knowing how you were."

I couldn't swallow down the lump in my throat. Monster? My Jamie? Never.

"So I heard you schooled Wes the day we got back," Jamie said, changing the subject with a wide grin. "Man, I wish I could seen that! I bet Melanie loved it."

"Yes, she did."

"She okay? Not too worried?"

"Of course she's worried," I murmured, watching the cloth travel across his forehead as if it were someone else's hand moving it.

Melanie.

Where was she?

I searched through my head for her familiar voice. There was nothing but silence. Why wasn't she here? Jamie's skin was burning where my fingers brushed it. The feel of it — that unwholesome heat — should have had her in the same panic I was feeling.

"You okay?" Jamie asked. "Wanda?"

"I'm . . . tired. Jamie, I'm sorry. I'm just . . . out of it."

He eyed me carefully. "You don't look so good."

What had I done?

"I haven't cleaned up in a while."

"I'm fine, you know. You should go eat or something. You're pale."

"Don't worry about me."

"I'll get you some food," Ian said. "You hungry, kid?"

"Ah . . . no, not really."

My eyes flashed back to Jamie. Jamie was always hungry.

"Send someone else," I told Ian, gripping his hand tighter.

"Sure." His face was smooth, but I could sense both surprise and worry. "Wes, could you get some food? Something for Jamie, too. I'm sure he'll find that appetite by the time you get back."

I measured Jamie's face. He was flushed, but his eyes were bright. He would be okay for a few minutes if I left him here.

"Jamie, do you mind if I go wash my face? I feel sort of . . . grimy."

He frowned at the false note in my voice. "Course not."

I pulled Ian up with me again as I rose. "I'll be right back. I mean it this time."

He smiled at my weak joke.

I felt someone's eyes on me as I left the room. Jared's or Doc's, I didn't know. I didn't care.

Only Jeb still stood in the hallway now; the others had gone, reassured, perhaps, that Jamie was doing okay. Jeb's head tilted to the side, curious, as he tried to figure out what I was doing. He was surprised to see me leave Jamie's side so soon and so abruptly. He, too, had heard the sham in my excuse.

I hurried past his inquisitive gaze, towing Ian with me.

I dragged Ian back through the room where the tunnels to all the living quarters met in a big tangle of openings. Instead of keeping on toward the main plaza, I pulled him into one of the dark corridors, picking at random. It was deserted.

"Wanda, what —"

"I need you to help me, Ian." My voice was strained, frantic.

"Whatever you need. You know that."

I put my hands on either side of his face, staring into his eyes. I could barely see a glint of their blue in the darkness.

"I need you to kiss me, Ian. Now. Please."

# CHAPTER 42

# Forced

Ian's jaw fell slack. "You . . . what?"

"I'll explain in a minute. This isn't fair to you, but . . . please. Just kiss me."

"It won't upset you? Melanie won't bother you?"

"Ian!" I complained. "Please!"

Still confused, he put his hands on my waist and pulled my body against his. His face was so worried, I wondered if this would even work. I hardly needed the romance, but maybe he did.

He closed his eyes as he leaned toward me, an automatic thing. His lips pressed lightly against mine once, and then he pulled back to look at me with the same worried expression.

Nothing.

"No, Ian. Really *kiss* me. Like . . . like you're *trying* to get slapped. Do you understand?"

"No. What's wrong? Tell me first."

I put my arms around his neck. It felt strange; I wasn't at all sure how to do this right. I pushed up on my toes and pulled his head down at the same time until I could reach his lips with mine.

This wouldn't have worked with another species. Another mind wouldn't have been so easily overwhelmed by its body. Other species had their priorities in better order. But Ian was human, and his body responded.

I shoved my mouth against his, gripping his neck tighter with my arms when his first reaction was to hold me away. Remembering how his mouth had moved with mine before, I tried to mimic that movement now. His lips opened with mine, and I felt an odd thrill of triumph at my success. I caught his lower lip between my teeth and heard a low, wild sound break from his throat in surprise.

And then I didn't have to try anymore. One of Ian's hands trapped my face, while the other clamped around the small of my back, holding me so close that it was hard to pull a breath into my constricted chest. I was gasping, but so was he. His breath mingled with mine. I felt the stone wall touch my back, press against it. He used it to bind me even closer. There was no part of me that wasn't fused to part of him.

It was just the two of us, so close that we hardly counted as two.

Just us.

No one else.

Alone.

Ian felt it when I gave up. He must have been waiting for this — not as entirely ruled by his body as I'd imagined. He eased back as soon as my arms went limp, but kept his face next to mine, the tip of his nose touching the tip of mine.

I dropped my arms, and he took a deep breath. Slowly, he loosened both his hands and then placed them lightly on my shoulders.

"Explain," he said.

"She's not here," I whispered, still breathing in gasps. "I can't find her. Not even now."

"Melanie?"

"I can't hear her! Ian, how can I go back in to Jamie? He'll know that I'm lying! How can I tell him that I've lost his sister *now?* Ian, he's sick! I can't tell him that! I'll upset him, make it harder for him to get well. I —"

Ian's fingers pressed against my lips. "Shh, shh. Okay. Let's think about this. When was the last time you heard her?"

"Oh, Ian! It was right after I saw . . . in the hospital. And she tried to defend them . . . and I screamed at her . . . and I — I made her go away! And I haven't heard her since. I can't find her!"

"Shh," he said again. "Calmly. Okay. Now, what do you really want? I know you don't want to upset Jamie, but he's going to be fine regardless. So, consider — would it be better, just for you, if —"

"No! I can't erase Melanie! I can't. That would be wrong! That would make me a monster, too!"

"Okay, okay! Okay. Shh. So we have to find her?"

I nodded urgently.

He took another deep breath. "Then you need to . . . really be overwhelmed, don't you?"

"I don't know what you mean."

I was afraid I did, though.

Kissing Ian was one thing — even a pleasant thing, maybe, if I wasn't so racked with worry — but anything more . . . elaborate . . . Could I? Mel would be furious if I used her body that way. Was that what I had to do to find her? But what about Ian? It was so grossly unfair to him.

"I'll be right back," Ian promised. "Stay *here*."

He pressed me against the wall for emphasis and then ducked back out into the hallway.

It was hard to obey. I wanted to follow him, to see what he was doing and where he was going. We had to talk about this; I had to think it through. But I had no time. Jamie was waiting for me, with questions that I couldn't answer with lies. No, he wasn't waiting for me; he was waiting for Melanie. How could I have done this? What if she was really gone?

*Mel, Mel, Mel, come back! Melanie, Jamie needs you. Not me — he needs you. He's sick, Mel. Mel, can you hear that? Jamie is sick!*

I was talking to myself. No one heard.

My hands were trembling with fear and stress. I wouldn't be able to wait here much longer. I felt like the anxiety was going to make me swell until I popped.

Finally, I heard footsteps. And voices. Ian wasn't alone. Confusion swept through me.

"Just think of it as . . . an experiment," Ian was saying.

"Are you crazy?" Jared answered. "Is this some sick joke?"

My stomach dropped through the floor.

Overwhelmed. *That's* what he'd meant.

Blood burned in my face, hot as Jamie's fever. What

was Ian doing to me? I wanted to run, to hide somewhere better than my last hiding place, somewhere I could never, ever be found, no matter how many flashlights they used. But my legs were shaking, and I couldn't move.

Ian and Jared came into view in the room where the tunnels met. Ian's face was expressionless; he had one hand on Jared's shoulder and was guiding him, almost pushing him forward. Jared was staring at Ian with anger and doubt.

"Through here," Ian encouraged, forcing Jared toward me. I flattened my back against the rock.

Jared saw me, saw my mortified expression, and stopped.

"Wanda, what's this about?"

I threw Ian one blazing glance of reproach and then tried to meet Jared's eyes.

I couldn't do it. I looked at his feet instead.

"I lost Melanie," I whispered.

"You *lost* her!"

I nodded miserably.

His voice was hard and angry. "How?"

"I'm not sure. I made her be quiet . . . but she always comes back . . . always before . . . I can't hear her now . . . and Jamie . . ."

"She's gone?" Muted agony in his voice.

"I don't know. I can't find her."

Deep breath. "Why does Ian think I have to kiss you?"

"Not kiss *me*," I said, my voice so faint I could barely hear it myself. "Kiss her. Nothing upset her more than when you kissed us . . . before. Nothing pulled her to the surface like that. Maybe . . . No. You don't have to. I'll try to find her myself."

I still had my eyes on his feet, so I saw him step toward me.

"You think, if I kiss her . . . ?"

I couldn't even nod. I tried to swallow.

Familiar hands brushed my neck, tracing down either side to my shoulders. My heart thudded loud enough that I wondered if he could hear it.

I was so embarrassed, forcing him to touch me this way. What if he thought it was a trick — my idea, not Ian's?

I wondered if Ian was still there, watching. How much would this hurt him?

One hand continued, as I knew it would, down my arm to my wrist, leaving a trail of fire behind it. The other cupped beneath my jaw, as I knew it must, and pulled my face up.

His cheek pressed against mine, the skin burning where we were connected, and he whispered in my ear.

"Melanie. I know you're there. Come back to me."

His cheek slowly slid back, and his chin tilted to the side so that his mouth covered mine.

He *tried* to kiss me softly. I could tell that he tried. But his intentions went up in smoke, just like before.

There was fire *everywhere,* because *he* was everywhere. His hands traced my skin, burning it. His lips tasted every inch of my face. The rock wall slammed into my back, but there was no pain. I couldn't feel anything besides the burning.

My hands knotted in his hair, pulling him to me as if there were any possible way for us to be closer. My legs wrapped around his waist, the wall giving me the leverage I needed. His tongue twisted with mine, and there was no part of my mind that was not invaded by the insane desire that possessed me.

He pulled his mouth free and pressed his lips to my ear again.

"Melanie Stryder!" It was so loud in my ear, a growl that was almost a shout. "You will *not* leave me. Don't you love me? Prove it! *Prove it!* Damn it, Mel! Get back here!"

His lips attacked mine again.

*Ahhh,* she groaned weakly in my head.

I couldn't think to greet her. I was on fire.

The fire burned its way to her, back to the tiny corner where she drooped, nearly lifeless.

My hands fisted around the fabric of Jared's T-shirt, yanking it up. This was their idea; I didn't tell them what to do. His hands burned on the skin of my back.

*Jared?* she whispered. She tried to orient herself, but the mind we shared was so disoriented.

I felt the muscles of his stomach under my palms, my hands crushed between us.

*What? Where . . .* Melanie struggled.

I broke away from his mouth to breathe, and his lips scorched their way down my throat. I buried my face in his hair, inhaling the scent.

*Jared! Jared! NO!*

I let her flow through my arms, knowing this was what I wanted, though I could barely pay attention now. The hands on his stomach turned hard, angry. The fingers clawed at his skin and then shoved him as hard as they could.

"NO!" she shouted through my lips.

Jared caught her hands, then caught me against the wall before I could fall. I sagged, my body confused by the conflicting directions it was receiving.

"Mel? Mel!"

"What are you *doing?*"

He groaned in relief. "I knew you could do it! Ah, Mel!"

He kissed her again, kissed the lips that she now controlled, and we could both taste the tears that ran down his face.

She bit him.

Jared jumped back from us, and I slid to the floor, landing in a wilted heap.

He started laughing. "That's my girl. You still got her, Wanda?"

"Yes," I gasped.

*What the hell, Wanda?* she screeched at me.

*Where have you* been? *Do you have any idea what I've been going through trying to find you?*

*Yeah, I can see that you were really suffering.*

*Oh, I'll suffer,* I promised her. I could already feel it coming on. Just like before . . .

She was flipping through my thoughts as fast as she could. *Jamie?*

*That's what I've been trying to tell you. He needs you.*

*Then why aren't we with him?*

*Because he's probably a bit young to watch this kind of thing.*

She searched through some more. *Wow, Ian, too. I'm glad I missed that part.*

*I was so worried. I didn't know what to do. . . .*

*Well, c'mon. Let's go.*

"Mel?" Jared asked.

"She's here. She's furious. She wants to see Jamie."

Jared put his arm around me and helped me up. "You can be as mad as you want, Mel. Just stick around."

*How long was I gone?*

*Three days is all.*

Her voice was suddenly smaller. *Where was I?*

*You don't know?*

*I can't remember . . . anything.*

We shuddered.

"You okay?" Jared asked.

"Sort of."

"Was that her before, talking to me — talking out loud?"

"Yes."

"Can she . . . can you let her do that now?"

I sighed. I was already exhausted. "I can try." I closed my eyes.

*Can you get past me?* I asked her. *Can you talk to him?*

*I . . . How? Where?*

I tried to flatten myself against the inside of my head. "C'mon," I murmured. "Here."

Melanie struggled, but there was no way out.

Jared's lips came down on mine, hard. My eyes flew open in shock. His gold-flecked eyes were open, too, half an inch away.

She jerked our head back. "Cut that *out!* Don't touch her!"

He smiled, the little creases feathering out around his eyes. "Hey, baby."

*That's not funny.*

I tried to breathe again. "She's not laughing."

He left his arm around me. Around us. We walked out into the tunnel junction, and there was no one there. No Ian.

"I'm warning you, Mel," Jared said, still smiling widely. Teasing. "You better stay right here. I'm not making any guarantees about what I will or won't do to get you back."

My stomach fluttered.

*Tell him I'll throttle him if he touches you like that again.* But her threat was a joke, too.

"She's threatening your life right now," I told him. "But I think she's being facetious."

He laughed, giddy with relief. "You're so serious all the time, Wanda."

"Your jokes aren't funny," I muttered. Not to me.

Jared laughed again.

*Ah,* Melanie said. *You are suffering.*

*I'll try not to let Jamie see.*

*Thank you for bringing me back.*

*I won't erase you, Melanie. I'm sorry I can't give you more than that.*

*Thank you.*

"What's she saying?"

"We're just . . . making up."

"Why couldn't she talk before, when you were trying to let her?"

"I don't know, Jared. There really isn't enough room for both of us. I can't seem to get myself out of the way completely. It's like . . . not like holding your breath. Like trying to pause your heartbeats. I can't make myself not exist. I don't know how."

He didn't answer, and my chest throbbed with pain. How joyful he would be if I *could* figure out how to erase myself!

Melanie wanted to . . . not to contradict me, but to make me feel better; she struggled to find words to soften my agony. She couldn't come up with the right ones.

*But Ian would be devastated. And Jamie. Jeb would miss you. You have so many friends here.*

*Thanks.*

I was glad that we were back to our room now. I needed to think about something else before I started crying. Now wasn't the time for self-pity. There were more important issues at hand than my heart, breaking yet again.

# CHAPTER 43

# Frenzied

I imagined that from the outside, I looked as still as a statue. My hands were folded in front of me, my face was without expression, my breathing was too shallow to move my chest.

Inside, I was spinning apart, as if the pieces of my atoms were reversing polarity and blowing away from one another.

Bringing Melanie back had not saved him. All that I could do was not enough.

The hall outside our room was crowded. Jared, Kyle, and Ian were back from their desperate raid, empty-handed. A cooler of ice — that was all they had to show for three days of risking their lives. Trudy was making compresses and laying them across Jamie's forehead, the back of his neck, his chest.

Even if the ice cooled the fever, raging out of control,

how long until it was all melted? An hour? More? Less? How long until he was dying again?

I would have been the one to put the ice on him, but I couldn't move. If I moved, I would fall into microscopic pieces.

"Nothing?" Doc murmured. "Did you check —"

"Every spot we could think of," Kyle interrupted. "It's not like painkillers, drugs — lots of people had reason to keep those hidden. The antibiotics were always kept in the open. They're gone, Doc."

Jared just stared down at the red-faced child on the bed, not speaking.

Ian stood beside me. "Don't look like that," he whispered. "He'll pull through. He's tough."

I couldn't respond. Couldn't even hear the words, really.

Doc knelt beside Trudy and pulled Jamie's chin down. With a bowl he scooped up some of the ice water from the cooler and let it trickle into Jamie's mouth. We all heard the thick, painful sound of Jamie's swallowing. But his eyes didn't open.

I felt as though I would never be able to move again. That I would turn into part of the stone wall. I wanted to be stone.

If they dug a hole for Jamie in the empty desert, they would have to put me in it, too.

*Not good enough,* Melanie growled.

I was despairing, but she was filled with fury.

*They tried.*

*Trying solves nothing. Jamie will not die. They have to go back out.*

*For what purpose? Even if they did find your old*

*antibiotics, what are the chances they would still be any good? They only worked half the time anyway. Inferior. He doesn't need your medicine. He needs more than that. Something that really works . . .*

My breathing sped up, deepened as I saw it.

*He needs* mine, I realized.

Mel and I were both awestruck by the obviousness of this idea. The simplicity of it.

My stone lips cracked apart. "Jamie needs real medicines. The ones the souls have. We need to get him those."

Doc frowned at me. "We don't even know what those things do, how they work."

"Does it matter?" Some of Melanie's anger was seeping into my voice. "They do work. They can save him."

Jared stared at me. I could feel Ian's eyes on me, too, and Kyle's, and all the rest in the room. But I saw only Jared.

"We can't get 'em, Wanda," Jeb said, his tone already one of defeat. Giving up. "We can only get into deserted places. There's always a bunch of your kind in a hospital. Twenty-four hours a day. Too many eyes. We won't do Jamie any good if we get caught."

"Sure," Kyle said in a hard voice. "The centipedes will be only too happy to heal his body when they find us here. And make him one of them. Is that what you're after?"

I turned to glare at the big, sneering man. My body tensed and leaned forward. Ian put his hand on my shoulder as if he were holding me back. I didn't think I would have made any aggressive move toward Kyle, but maybe I was wrong. I was so far from my normal self.

When I spoke, my voice was dead even, no inflection. "There has to be a way."

Jared was nodding. "Maybe someplace small. The gun would make too much noise, but if there were enough of us to overwhelm them, we could use knives."

"No." My arms came unfolded, my hands falling open in shock. "No. That's not what I meant. Not killing —"

No one even listened to me. Jeb was arguing with Jared.

"There's no way, kid. Somebody'd get a call off to the Seekers. Even if we were in and out, something like that would bring 'em down on us in force. We'd be hard-pressed to make it out at all. And they'd follow."

"Wait. Can't you —"

They still weren't listening to me.

"I don't want the boy to die, either, but we can't risk everyone's lives for one person," Kyle said. "People die here; it happens. We can't get crazy to save one boy."

I wanted to choke him, to cut off his air in order to stop his calm words. Me, not Melanie. *I* was the one who wanted to turn his face purple. Melanie felt the same way, but I could tell how much of the violence came directly from me.

"We have to save him," I said, louder now.

Jeb looked at me. "Hon, we can't just walk in there and ask."

Right then, another very simple and obvious truth occurred to me.

"You can't. But I can."

The room fell dead silent.

I was caught up in the beauty of the plan forming in my head. The perfection of it. I spoke mostly to myself, and to Melanie. She was impressed. This would work. We could save Jamie.

"They aren't *suspicious*. Not at all. Even if I'm a horrible liar, they would never suspect me of anything. They wouldn't be listening for lies. Of course not. I'm one of them. They would do anything to help me. I'd say I got hurt hiking or something . . . and then I'd find a way to be alone and I'd take as much as I could hide. Think of it! I could get enough to heal everyone here. To last for years. And Jamie would be fine! Why didn't I think of this before? Maybe it wouldn't have been too late even for Walter."

I looked up then, with shining eyes. It was just so perfect!

So perfect, so absolutely right, so obvious to me, that it took me forever to understand the expressions on their faces. If Kyle's had not been so explicit, it might have taken me longer.

Hatred. Suspicion. Fear.

Even Jeb's poker face was not enough. His eyes were tight with mistrust.

Every face said *no*.

*Are they insane? Can't they see how this would help us all?*

*They don't believe me. They think I'll hurt them, hurt Jamie!*

"Please," I whispered. "It's the only way to save him."

"Patient, isn't it?" Kyle spit. "Bided its time well, don't you think?"

I fought the desire to choke him again.

"Doc?" I begged.

He didn't meet my eyes. "Even if there was any way we could let you outside, Wanda . . . I just couldn't trust drugs I don't understand. Jamie's a tough kid. His system will fight this off."

"We'll go out again, Wanda," Ian murmured. "We'll find something. We won't come back until we do."

"That's not good enough." The tears were pooling in my eyes. I looked to the one person who might possibly be in as much pain as I was. "Jared. You know. You *know* I would never let anything hurt Jamie. You know I can do this. Please."

He met my gaze for one long moment. Then he looked around the room, at every other face. Jeb, Doc, Kyle, Ian, Trudy. Out the door at the silent audience whose expressions mirrored Kyle's: Sharon, Violetta, Lucina, Reid, Geoffrey, Heath, Heidi, Andy, Aaron, Wes, Lily, Carol. My friends mixed in with my enemies, all of them wearing Kyle's face. He stared at the next row, which I couldn't see. Then he looked down at Jamie. There was no sound of breathing in the whole room.

"No, Wanda," he said quietly. "No."

A sigh of relief from the rest.

My knees buckled. I fell forward and yanked free of Ian's hands when he tried to pull me back up. I crawled to Jamie and pushed Trudy aside with my elbow. The silent room watched. I took the compress from his head and refilled the melted ice. I didn't meet the stares I could feel on my skin. I couldn't see anyway. The tears swam in front of my eyes.

"Jamie, Jamie, Jamie," I crooned. "Jamie, Jamie, Jamie."

I couldn't seem to do anything but sob out his name

and touch the packets of ice over and over, waiting for the moment they would need changing.

I heard them leave, a few at a time. I heard their voices, mostly angry, fade away down the halls. I couldn't make sense of the words, though.

*Jamie, Jamie, Jamie . . .*

"Jamie, Jamie, Jamie . . ."

Ian knelt beside me when the room was almost empty.

"I know you wouldn't . . . but Wanda, they'll kill you if you try," he whispered. "After what happened . . . in the hospital. They're afraid you have good reason to destroy us. . . . Anyway, he'll be all right. You have to trust that."

I turned my face from him, and he went away.

"Sorry, kid," Jeb mumbled when he left.

Jared left. I didn't hear him go, but I knew when he was gone. That seemed right to me. He didn't love Jamie the way we did. He had proved that. He *should* go.

Doc stayed, watching helplessly. I didn't look at him.

The daylight faded slowly, turned orange and then gray. The ice melted and was gone. Jamie started to burn alive under my hands.

"Jamie, Jamie, Jamie . . ." My voice was cracked and hoarse now, but I couldn't stop. "Jamie, Jamie, Jamie . . ."

The room turned black. I couldn't see Jamie's face. Would he leave in the night? Had I already seen his face, his living face, for the last time?

His name was just a whisper on my lips now, low enough that I could hear Doc's quiet snoring.

I wiped the tepid cloth across his body without ceasing. As the water dried, it cooled him a little. The burn lessened. I began to believe that he wouldn't die tonight.

But I wouldn't be able to hold him here forever. He would slip away from me. Tomorrow. The next day. And then I would die, too. I would not live without Jamie.

*Jamie, Jamie, Jamie . . .* Melanie groaned.

*Jared didn't believe us.* The lament was both of ours. We thought it at the same time.

It was still silent. I didn't hear anything. Nothing alerted me.

Then, suddenly, Doc cried out. The sound was oddly muffled, like he was shouting into a pillow.

My eyes couldn't make sense of the shapes in the darkness at first. Doc was jerking strangely. And he seemed too big — like he had too many arms. It was terrifying. I leaned over Jamie's inert form, to protect him from whatever was happening. I could not flee while he lay helpless. My heart pounded against my ribs.

Then the flailing arms were still. Doc's snore started up again, louder and thicker than before. He slumped to the ground, and the shape separated. A second figure pulled itself away from his and stood in the darkness.

"Let's go," Jared whispered. "We don't have time to waste."

My heart nearly exploded.

*He believes.*

I jumped to my feet, forcing my stiff knees to unbend. "What did you do to Doc?"

"Chloroform. It won't last long."

I turned quickly and poured the warm water over Jamie, soaking his clothes and the mattress. He didn't stir. Perhaps that would keep him cool until Doc woke up.

"Follow me."

I was on his heels. We moved silently, almost

touching, almost running but not quite. Jared hugged the walls, and I did the same.

He stopped when we reached the light of the moon-bright garden room. It was deserted and still.

I could see Jared clearly for the first time. He had the gun slung behind his back and a knife sheathed at his waist. He held out his hands, and there was a length of dark fabric in them. I understood at once.

The whispered words raced out of my mouth. "Yes, blindfold me."

He nodded, and I closed my eyes while he tied the cloth over them. I would keep them closed anyway.

The knot was quick and tight. When he was done, I spun myself in a fast circle — once, twice . . .

His hands stopped me. "That's okay," he said. And then he gripped me harder and lifted me off the ground. I gasped in surprise as he threw me against his shoulder. I folded there, my head and chest hanging over his back, beside the gun. His arms held my legs against his chest, and he was already moving. I bounced as he jogged, my face brushing against his shirt with each stride.

I had no sense of which way we were going; I didn't try to guess or think or feel. I concentrated only on the bouncing of his gait, counting steps. Twenty, twenty-one, twenty-two, twenty-three . . .

I could feel him lean as the path took him down and then up. I tried not to think about it.

Four hundred twelve, four hundred thirteen, four hundred fourteen . . .

I knew when we were out. I smelled the dry, clean breeze of the desert. The air was hot, though it had to be close to midnight.

He pulled me down and set me on my feet.

"The ground is flat. Do you think you can run blind-folded?"

"Yes."

He grabbed my elbow tightly in his hand and took off, setting a rigorous pace. It wasn't easy. He caught me time and time again before I could fall. I started to get used to it after a while, and I kept my balance better over the tiny pits and rises. We ran until we were both gasping.

"If . . . we can get . . . to the jeep . . . we'll be in . . . the clear."

The jeep? I felt a strange wave of nostalgia. Mel hadn't seen the jeep since the first leg of that disastrous trip to Chicago, hadn't known it had survived.

"If we . . . can't?" I asked.

"They catch us . . . they'll kill you. Ian's . . . right about . . . that part."

I tried to run faster. Not to save my life, but because I was the only one who could save Jamie's. I stumbled again.

"Going to . . . take off the blindfold. You'll be . . . faster."

"You sure?"

"Don't . . . look around. 'Kay?"

"Promise."

He yanked at the knots behind my head. As the fabric fell away from my eyes, I focused them only on the ground at my feet.

It made a world of difference. The moonlight was bright, and the sand was very smooth and pale. Jared dropped his arm and broke into a faster stride. I kept up easily now. Distance running was familiar to my body. I settled into my preferred stride. Just over a six-minute mile, I'd guess. I couldn't keep up that pace forever, but I'd run myself into the ground trying.

"You hear . . . anything?" he asked.

I listened. Just two sets of running feet on the sand.

"No."

He grunted in approval.

I guessed this was the reason he'd stolen the gun. They couldn't stop us from a distance without it.

It took about an hour more. I was slowing then, and so was he. My mouth burned for water.

I'd never looked up from the ground, so it startled me when he put his hand over my eyes. I faltered, and he pulled us to a walk.

"We're okay now. Just ahead . . ."

He left his hand over my eyes and tugged me forward. I heard our footsteps echo off something. The desert wasn't as flat here.

"Get in."

His hand disappeared.

It was nearly as dark as it was with him covering my eyes. Another cave. Not a deep one. If I turned around, I would be able to see out of it. I didn't turn.

The jeep faced into the darkness. It looked just the same as I remembered it, this vehicle I had never seen. I swung myself over the door into the seat.

Jared was in his seat already. He leaned over and tied the blindfold over my eyes again. I held still to make it easier.

The noise of the engine scared me. It seemed too dangerous. There were so many people who shouldn't find us now.

We moved in reverse briefly, and then the wind was blasting my face. There was a funny sound behind the jeep, something that didn't fit Melanie's memories.

"We're going to Tucson," he told me. "We never raid there — it's too close. But we don't have time for anything else. I know where a small hospital is, not too deep into town."

"Not Saint Mary's?"

He heard the alarm in my voice. "No, why?"

"I know someone there."

He was quiet for a minute. "Will you be recognized?"

"No. No one will know my face. We don't have . . . wanted people. Not like you did."

"Okay."

But he had me thinking now, thinking about my appearance. Before I could voice my concerns, he took my hand and folded it around something very small.

"Keep that close to you."

"What is it?"

"If they guess that you're . . . with us, if they're going to . . . put someone else in Mel's body, you put that in your mouth and bite down on it hard."

"Poison?"

"Yes."

I thought about that for a moment. And then I laughed; I couldn't help it. My nerves were frayed with worry.

"It's not a joke, Wanda," he said angrily. "If you can't do it, then I have to take you back."

"No, no, I can." I tried to get a hold of myself. "I know I can. That's why I'm laughing."

His voice was harsh. "I don't get the joke."

"Don't you see? For millions of my own kind, I've never been able to do that. Not for my own . . . children. I was always too afraid to die that final time. But I can do it for one alien child." I laughed again. "It doesn't make any sense. Don't worry, though. I can die to protect Jamie."

"I'm trusting you to do just that."

It was silent for a moment, and then I remembered what I looked like.

"Jared, I don't look right. For walking into a hospital."

"We've got better clothes stashed with the . . . less-conspicuous vehicles. That's where we're headed now. About five more minutes."

That wasn't what I meant, but he was right. These clothes would never do. I waited to talk to him about the rest. I needed to look at myself first.

The jeep stopped, and he pulled off the blindfold.

"You don't have to keep your eyes down," he told me when my head ducked automatically. "There's nothing here to give us away. Just in case this place was ever discovered."

It wasn't a cave. It was a rock slide. A few of the bigger boulders had been carefully excavated, leaving clever dark spaces under them that no one would suspect of housing anything but dirt and smaller rocks.

The jeep was already lodged in a tight space. I was so close to the rock, I had to climb over the back of the jeep to get out. There was something odd attached to the bumper — chains and two very dirty tarps, all ragged and torn.

"Here," Jared said, and led the way to a shadowy crevice just a little shorter than he was. He brushed aside a dusty, dirt-colored tarp and rifled through a pile hiding behind it. He pulled out a T-shirt, soft and clean, with tags still attached. He ripped those off and threw the shirt to me. Then he dug until he found a pair of khaki pants. He checked the size, then flipped them to me, too.

"Put them on."

I hesitated for a moment while he waited, wondering what my problem was. I flushed and then turned my back to him. I yanked my ragged shirt over my head and replaced it as quickly as my fumbling fingers could manage.

I heard him clear his throat. "Oh. I'll, uh, get the car." His footsteps moved away.

I stripped off my tattered cutoff sweats and pulled the crisp new pants into place. My shoes were in bad shape, but they weren't that noticeable. Besides, comfortable shoes weren't always easy to come by. I could pretend I had an attachment to this pair.

Another engine came to life, quieter than the jeep's. I turned to see a modest, unremarkable sedan pull out of a deep shadow under a boulder. Jared got out and chained the tattered tarps from the jeep to this car's rear bumper. Then he drove it to where I stood, and as I saw the heavy tarps wipe the tire tracks from the dirt, I comprehended their purpose.

Jared leaned across the seat to open the passenger door. There was a backpack on the seat. It lay flat, empty. I nodded to myself. Yes, this I needed.

"Let's go."

"Hold on," I said.

I crouched to look at myself in the side mirror.

Not good. I flipped my chin-length hair over my cheek, but it wasn't enough. I touched my cheek and bit my lip.

"Jared. I can't go in with my face like this." I pointed to the long, jagged scar across my skin.

"What?" he demanded.

"No soul would have a scar like this. They would have had it treated. They'll wonder where I've been. They'll ask questions."

His eyes widened and then narrowed. "Maybe you should have thought of this before I snuck you out. If we go back now, they'll think it was a ploy for you to learn the way out."

"We're not going back without medicine for Jamie." My voice was harder than his.

His got harder to match it. "What do you propose we do, then, Wanda?"

"I'll need a rock." I sighed. "You're going to have to hit me."

# CHAPTER 44

# Healed

"Wanda . . ."

"We don't have time. I'd do it myself, but I can't get the angle right. There's no other way."

"I don't think I can . . . do it."

"For Jamie, even?" I pushed the good side of my face as hard as I could against the headrest of the passenger seat and closed my eyes.

Jared was holding the rough fist-sized stone I'd found. He'd been weighing it in his hand for five minutes.

"You just have to get the first few layers of skin off. Just hide the scar, that's all. C'mon, Jared, we have to hurry. Jamie . . ."

*Tell him I said to do it now. And make it a good one.*

"Mel says do it now. And make sure you do it hard enough. Get it all the first time."

Silence.

"Do it, Jared!"

He took a deep breath, a gasp. I felt the air move and squeezed my eyes tighter.

It made a squishing sound and a thud — that was the first thing I noticed — and then the shock of the blow wore off, and I felt it, too.

"Ungh," I groaned. I hadn't meant to make any sound. I knew that would make it worse for him. But so much was involuntary with this body. Tears sprang up in my eyes, and I coughed to hide a sob. My head rang, vibrated in aftershock.

"Wanda? Mel? I'm sorry!"

His arms wrapped around us, pulled us into his chest.

"'S okay," I whimpered. "We're okay. Did you get it all?"

His hand touched my chin, turned my head.

"Ahh," he gasped, sickened. "I took half your face off. I'm so sorry."

"No, that's good. That's good. Let's go."

"Right." His voice was still weak, but he leaned me back into my seat, settling me carefully, and then the car rumbled beneath us.

Ice-cold air blew in my face, shocking me, stinging my raw cheek. I'd forgotten what air-conditioning felt like.

I opened my eyes. We were driving down a smooth wash — smoother than it should have been, carefully altered to be this way. It snaked away from us, coiling around the brush. I couldn't see very far ahead.

I pulled the visor down and flipped open the mirror. In the shadowy moonlight, my face was black and white. Black all across the right side, oozing down my chin, dripping across my neck, and seeping into the collar of my new, clean shirt.

My stomach heaved.

"Good job," I whispered.

"How much pain are you in?"

"Not much," I lied. "Anyway, it won't hurt much longer. How far are we from Tucson?"

Just then, we reached pavement. Funny how the sight of it made my heart race in panic. Jared stopped, keeping the car hidden in the brush. He got out and removed the tarps and chains from the bumper, putting them in the trunk. He got back in and eased the car forward, checking carefully to make sure the highway was empty. He reached for the headlights.

"Wait," I whispered. I couldn't speak louder. I felt so exposed here. "Let me drive."

He looked at me.

"It can't look like I *walked* to the hospital like this. Too many questions. I have to drive. You hide in the back and tell me where to go. Is there something you can hide under?"

"Okay," he said slowly. He put the car into reverse and pulled it back into the deeper brush. "Okay. I'll hide. But if you take us somewhere I don't tell you to go . . ."

*Oh!* Melanie was stung by his doubt, as was I.

My voice was flat. "Shoot me."

He didn't answer. He got out, leaving the engine running. I slid across the cup holders into his seat. I heard the trunk slam.

Jared climbed into the backseat, a thick plaid blanket under his arm.

"Turn right at the road," he said.

The car was an automatic, but it had been a long time and I was unsure behind the wheel. I moved ahead carefully, pleased to find that I remembered how to drive. The highway was still empty. I pulled out onto the road, my heart reacting to the open space again.

"Lights," Jared said. His voice came from low on the bench.

I searched till I found the switch, then flicked them on. They seemed horribly bright.

We weren't far from Tucson — I could see a yellowish glow of color against the sky. The lights of the city ahead.

"You could drive a little faster."

"I'm right at the limit," I protested.

He paused for a second. "Souls don't speed?"

I laughed. The sound was only a tad hysterical. "We obey all laws, traffic laws included."

The lights became more than a glow — they turned into individual points of brightness. Green signs informed me of my exit options.

"Take Ina Road."

I followed his instructions. He kept his voice low, though, enclosed as we were, we could both have shouted.

It was hard to be in this unfamiliar city. To see houses and apartments and stores with signs lit up. To know I was surrounded, outnumbered. I imagined what it must feel like for Jared. His voice was remarkably calm. But he'd done this before, many times.

Other cars were on the road now. When their lights washed my windshield, I cringed in terror.

*Don't fall apart now, Wanda. You have to be strong for Jamie. This won't work if you can't do that.*

*I can. I can do it.*

I concentrated on Jamie, and my hands were steadier on the wheel.

Jared directed me through the mostly sleeping city. The Healing facility was just a small place. It must have been a medical building once — doctors' offices, rather than an actual hospital. The lights were bright through most of the windows, through the glass front. I could see a woman behind a greeting desk. She didn't look up at my headlights. I drove to the darkest corner of the parking lot.

I slid my arms through the straps of the backpack. It wasn't new, but it was in good shape. Perfect. There was just one more thing to do.

"Quick, give me the knife."

"Wanda . . . I know you love Jamie, but I really don't think you could use it. You're not a fighter."

"Not for them, Jared. I need a wound."

He gasped. "You *have* a wound. That's enough!"

"I need one like Jamie's. I don't know enough about Healing. I have to see exactly what to do. I would have done it before, but I wasn't sure I'd be able to drive."

"No. Not again."

"Give it to me now. Someone will notice if I don't go inside soon."

Jared thought it through quickly. He was the best, as Jeb had said, because he could see what had to be done and do it fast. I heard the steely sound of the knife coming out of the sheath.

"Be very careful. Not too deep."

"You want to do it?"

He inhaled sharply. "No."

"Okay."

I took the ugly knife. It had a heavy handle and was very sharp; it came to a tapered point at the tip.

I didn't let myself think about it. I didn't want to give myself a chance to be a coward. The arm, not the leg — that's all I paused to decide. My knees were scarred. I didn't want to have to hide that, too.

I held my left arm out; my hand was shaking. I braced it against the door and then twisted my head so that I could bite down on the headrest. I held the knife's handle awkwardly but tightly in my right hand. I pressed the point against the skin of my forearm so I wouldn't miss. Then I closed my eyes.

Jared was breathing too hard. I had to be fast or he would stop me.

*Just pretend it's a shovel opening the ground,* I told myself.

I jammed the knife into my arm.

The headrest muffled my scream, but it was still too loud. The knife fell from my hand — jerking sickeningly out from the muscle — and then clunked against the floor.

"Wanda!" Jared rasped.

I couldn't answer yet. I tried to choke back the other screams I felt coming. I'd been right not to do this before driving.

"Let me see!"

"Stay there," I gasped. "Don't move."

I heard the blanket rustling behind me despite my warning. I pulled my left arm against my body and yanked the door open with my right hand. Jared's hand brushed my back as I half fell out the door. It wasn't a restraint. It was comfort.

"I'll be right back," I coughed out, and then I kicked the door shut behind me.

I stumbled across the lot, fighting nausea and panic. They seemed to balance each other out — one keeping the other from taking control of my body. The pain wasn't too bad — or rather, I couldn't feel it as much anymore. I was going into shock. Too many kinds of pain, too close together. Hot liquid rolled down my fingers and dripped to the pavement. I wondered if I could move those fingers. I was afraid to try.

The woman behind the reception desk — middle-aged, with dark chocolate skin and a few silver threads in her black hair — jumped to her feet when I lurched through the automatic doors.

"Oh, no! Oh, dear!" She grabbed a microphone, and her next words echoed from the ceiling, magnified. "Healer Knits! I need you in reception! This is an emergency!"

"No." I tried to speak calmly, but I swayed in place. "I'm okay. Just an accident."

She put the microphone down and hurried around to where I stood swaying. Her arm went around my waist.

"Oh, honey, what happened to you?"

"So careless," I muttered. "I was hiking. . . . I fell down the rocks. I was . . . cleaning up after dinner. A knife was in my hand. . . ."

My hesitations seemed like part of the shock to her. She didn't look at me with suspicion — or humor, the way Ian sometimes did when I lied. Only concern.

"You poor dear! What's your name?"

"Glass Spires," I told her, using the rather generic name of a herd member from my time with the Bears.

"Okay, Glass Spires. Here comes the Healer. You'll be fine in just a moment."

I didn't feel panicked at all anymore. The kindly woman patted my back. So gentle, so caring. She would never harm me.

The Healer was a young woman. Her hair, skin, and eyes were all a similar shade of light brown. It made her unusual looking — monochromatic. She wore tan scrubs that only added to that impression.

"Wow," she said. "I'm Healer Knits Fire. I'll get you fixed up directly. What happened?"

I told my story again as the two women led me down a hallway and then through the very first door. They had me lie down on the paper-covered bed.

The room was familiar. I'd been in only one place like this, but Melanie's childhood was full of such memories. The short row of double cabinets, the sink where the Healer was washing her hands, the bright, clean white walls . . .

"First things first," Knits Fire said cheerfully. She pulled a cabinet open. I tried to focus my eyes, knowing this was important. The cabinet was full of rows and rows of stacked white cylinders. She took one down, reaching for it without searching; she knew what she wanted. The small container had a label, but I couldn't read it. "A little no pain should help, don't you think?"

I saw the label again as she twisted the lid off. Two short words. *No Pain?* Was that what it said?

"Open your mouth, Glass Spires."

I obeyed. She took a small, thin square — it looked like tissue paper — and laid it on my tongue. It dissolved at once. There was no flavor. I swallowed automatically.

"Better?" the Healer asked.

And it was. Already. My my head was clear — I could concentrate without difficulty. The pain had melted away with the tiny square. Disappeared. I blinked, shocked.

"Yes."

"I know you feel fine now, but please don't move. Your injuries are not treated yet."

"Of course."

"Cerulean, could you get us some water? Her mouth seems dry."

"At once, Healer Knits."

The older woman left the room.

The Healer turned back to her cabinets, opening a different one this time. This, too, was filled with white containers. "Here we are." She pulled one from the top of a stack, then took another from the other side.

Almost as if she were trying to help me fulfill my mission, she listed the names as she reached for them.

"Clean — inside and out . . . Heal . . . Seal . . . And where is . . . ah, Smooth. Don't want a scar on that pretty face, do we?"

"Ah . . . no."

"Don't worry. You'll be perfect again."

"Thank you."

"You're very welcome."

She leaned over me with another white cylinder. The top of this one came off with a pop, and there was an aerosol spray nozzle underneath. She sprayed my forearm first, coating the wound with clear, odorless mist.

"Healing must be a fulfilling profession." My voice sounded just right. Interested, but not unduly so. "I haven't been in a Healing facility since insertion. This is very interesting."

"Yes, I like it." She started spraying my face.

"What are you doing now?"

She smiled. I guessed that I was not the first curious soul. "This is Clean. It will make sure nothing foreign stays in the wound. It kills off any of the microbes that might infect the wound."

"Clean," I repeated to myself.

"And the Inside Clean, just in case anything has snuck into your system. Inhale this, please."

She had a different white cylinder in her hand, a thinner bottle with a pump rather than an aerosol top. She puffed a cloud of mist into the air above my face. I sucked in a breath. The mist tasted like mint.

"And this is Heal," Knits Fire continued, twisting the cap off the next canister, revealing a small pouring spout. "It encourages your tissues to rejoin, to grow the way they should."

She dribbled a tiny bit of the clear liquid into the wide cut on my arm, then she pushed the edges of the wound together. I could feel her touch, but there was no pain.

"I'll seal this up before I move on." She opened another container, this one a pliable tube, and then squeezed out a line of thick, clear jelly onto her finger. "Like glue," she told me. "It holds everything together and lets the Heal do its job." She wiped it over my arm in one swift pass. "Okay, you can move that now. Your arm is fine."

I held it up to look. A faint pink line was visible under the shiny gel. The blood was still wet on my arm, but there was no source anymore. As I watched, the Healer cleaned my skin with one quick pass of a damp towel.

"Turn your face this way, please. Hmm, you must have hit those rocks just exactly wrong. What a mess."

"Yes. It was a bad fall."

"Well, thank goodness you were able to drive yourself here."

She was lightly dripping Heal onto my cheek, smearing it with the tips of her fingers. "Ah, I love to watch it work. Looks much better already. Okay . . . around the edges." She smiled to herself. "Maybe one more coat. I want this to be erased." She worked for a minute longer. "Very nice."

"Here's some water," the older woman said as she came through the door.

"Thank you, Cerulean."

"Let me know if you need anything more. I'll be up front."

"Thanks."

Cerulean left. I wondered if she was from the Flower Planet. Blue flowers were rare — one might take a name from that.

"You can sit now. How do you feel?"

I pulled myself up. "Perfect." It was true. I hadn't felt so healthy in a long time. The sharp shift from pain to ease made the sensation more powerful.

"That's just how it should be. Okay, let's dust on a little Smooth."

She twisted the last cylinder's top and shook an iridescent powder into her hand. She patted it into my cheek, then patted another handful onto my arm.

"You'll always have a small line on your arm," she said apologetically. "Like your neck. A deep wound . . ." She shrugged. Absentmindedly, she brushed the hair back from my neck and examined the scar. "This was nicely done. Who was your Healer?"

"Um . . . Faces Sunward," I said, pulling the name from one of my old students. "I was in . . . Eureka, Montana. I didn't like the cold. I moved south."

So many lies. I felt a twist of anxiety in my stomach.

"I started out in Maine," she said, not noticing anything amiss in my voice. As she spoke, she cleaned the blood from my neck. "It was too cold for me, too. What's your Calling?"

"Um . . . I serve food. In a Mexican restaurant in . . . Phoenix. I like spicy food."

"Me, too." She wasn't looking at me funny. She was wiping my cheek now.

"Very nice. No worries, Glass Spires. Your face looks great."

"Thank you, Healer."

"Of course. Would you like some water?"

"Yes, please." I kept a grip on myself. It wouldn't do to bolt the glass down the way I wanted to. I wasn't able to stop myself from finishing it all, though. It tasted too good.

"Would you like more?"

"I . . . yes, that would be nice. Thank you."

"I'll be right back."

The second she was out the door, I slid off the mattress. The paper crackled, freezing me in place. She didn't dart back in. I had only seconds. It had taken Cerulean a few minutes to get the water. Maybe it would take the Healer just as long. Maybe the cool, pure water was far away from this room. Maybe.

I ripped the pack off my shoulders and wrenched the drawstrings open. I started with the second cabinet. There was the stacked column of Heal. I grabbed the whole column and let it clatter quietly into the bottom of my pack.

What would I say if she caught me? What lie could I tell?

I took the two kinds of Clean next, from the first cabinet. There was a second stack behind the first of each, and I took half of those, too. Then the No Pain, both stacks of that. I was about to turn back for the Seal, when the label of the next row of cylinders caught my attention.

Cool. For fevers? There were no instructions, just the label. I took the stack. Nothing here would hurt a human body. I was sure of that.

I grabbed all the Seal and two cans of Smooth. I couldn't press my luck any further. I closed the cabinets quietly and threw my arms through the straps of the pack. I leaned against the mattress, making another crackle. I tried to look relaxed.

She didn't come back.

I checked the clock. It had been one minute. How far away was the water?

Two minutes.

Three minutes.

Had my lies been as obvious to her as they were to me?

Sweat started to dew up on my forehead. I wiped it away quickly.

What if she brought back a Seeker?

I thought of the small pill in my pocket, and my hands shook. I could do it, though. For Jamie.

I heard quiet footsteps then, two sets, coming down the hall.

# CHAPTER 45

# *Succeeded*

Healer Knits Fire and Cerulean walked through the door together. The Healer handed me a tall glass of water. It didn't feel as cold as the first — my fingers were cold with fear now. The dark-skinned woman had something for me, too. She handed me a flat rectangle with a handle.

"I thought you would want to see," Knits Fire said with a warm smile.

The tension flooded out of me. There was no suspicion or fear. Just more kindness from the souls who had dedicated their lives to Healing.

Cerulean had given me a mirror.

I held it up and then tried to stifle my gasp.

My face looked the way I remembered it from San Diego. The face I'd taken for granted there. The skin was smooth and peachy across my right cheekbone. If I looked carefully, it was just a little lighter and pinker in color than the tan on the other cheek.

It was a face that belonged to Wanderer, the soul. It belonged here, in this civilized place where there was no violence and no horror.

I realized why it was so easy to lie to these gentle creatures. Because it felt right to talk with them, because I understood their communication and their rules. The lies could be . . . maybe *should* be true. I should be filling a Calling somewhere, whether teaching at a university or serving food in a restaurant. A peaceful, easy life contributing to a greater good.

"What do you think?" the Healer asked.

"I look perfect. Thank you."

"It was my pleasure to heal you."

I looked at myself again, seeing details beyond the perfection. My hair was ragged — dirty, with uneven ends. There was no gloss to it — homemade soap and poor nutrition were to blame for that. Though the Healer had cleaned the blood from my neck, it was still smudged with purple dust.

"I think it's time I called the camping trip quits. I need to clean up," I murmured.

"Do you camp often?"

"In all my free time, lately. I . . . can't seem to keep away from the desert."

"You must be brave. I find the city much more comfortable."

"Not brave — just different."

In the mirror, my eyes were familiar rings of hazel. Dark gray on the outside, a circle of moss green, and then another circle of caramel brown around the pupil.

Underlying it all, a faint shimmer of silver that would reflect the light, magnify it.

*Jamie?* Mel asked urgently, beginning to feel nervous. I was too comfortable here. She could see the logic of the other path laid out before me, and that frightened her.

*I know who I am,* I told her.

I blinked, then looked back at the friendly faces beside me.

"Thank you," I said again to the Healer. "I suppose I'd better be on my way."

"It's very late. You could sleep here if you'd like."

"I'm not tired. I feel . . . perfect."

The Healer grinned. "No Pain does that."

Cerulean walked me to the reception area. She put her hand on my shoulder as I stepped through the door.

My heart beat faster. Had she noticed that my pack, once flat, was now bulging?

"Be more careful, dear," she said, and patted my arm.

"I will. No more hikes in the dark."

She smiled and went back to her desk.

I kept my pace even as I walked through the parking lot. I wanted to run. What if the Healer looked in her cabinets? How soon would she realize why they were half empty?

The car was still there, in the pocket of darkness created by a gap between streetlights. It looked empty. My breath came fast and uneven. Of course it should look empty. That was the whole point. But my lungs didn't calm until I could glimpse the vague shape under the blanket on the backseat.

I opened the door and put the backpack on the passenger seat — it settled there with a reassuring clatter —

then I climbed in and shut the door. There was no reason to slam the locks down; I ignored the urge.

"Are you okay?" Jared whispered as soon as the door was closed. His voice was a strained, anxious rasp.

"Shh," I said, keeping my lips as still as I could. "Wait."

I drove past the bright entrance and answered Cerulean's wave with one of my own.

"Making friends?"

We were on the dark road. No one was watching me anymore. I slumped in the seat. My hands started to shake. I could allow that, now that it was over. Now that I'd succeeded.

"All souls are friends," I told him, using my normal volume.

"Are you all right?" he demanded again.

"I'm healed."

"Let me see."

I stretched my left arm across my body, so he could see the tiny pink line.

He sucked in a surprised breath.

The blanket rustled; he sat up and then climbed through the space between the seats. He pushed the backpack out of the way, then pulled it onto his lap, testing its weight.

He looked up at me as we passed under a streetlamp, and he gasped.

"Your face!"

"It's healed, too. Naturally."

He raised one hand, holding it in the air near my cheek, unsure. "Does it hurt?"

"Of course not. It feels like nothing happened to it in the first place."

His fingers brushed the new skin. It tingled, but that was from his touch. Then he was back to business.

"Did they suspect anything? Do you think they'll call the Seekers?"

"No. I told you they wouldn't be suspicious. They didn't even check my eyes. I was hurt, so they healed me." I shrugged.

"What did you get?" he asked, opening the drawstrings on the backpack.

"The right things for Jamie . . . if we get back in time . . ." I glanced at the clock on the dashboard automatically, though the hours it marked were meaningless. "And more for the future. I only took what I understood."

"We'll be back in time," he promised. He examined the white containers. "Smooth?"

"Not a necessity. But I know what it does, so . . ."

He nodded, digging through the bag. He muttered the names to himself. "No Pain? Does it work?"

I laughed. "It's amazing. If you stab yourself, I could show you. . . . That's a joke."

"I know."

He was staring at me with an expression I didn't understand. His eyes were wide, like something had deeply surprised him.

"What?" My joke hadn't been *that* bad.

"You did it." His tone was full of wonder.

"Wasn't that the idea?"

"Yes, but . . . I guess I didn't really think we were going to make it out."

"You didn't? Then why . . . ? Why did you let me try?"

He answered in a soft almost-whisper. "I figured it was better to die trying than to live without the kid."

For a moment, my throat was choked with emotion. Mel was too overcome to speak as well. We were a family in that one instant. All of us.

I cleared my throat. No need to feel things that would only come to nothing.

"It was very easy. Probably any of you could get away with it, if you acted naturally. She did look at my neck." I touched it reflexively. "Your scar is too obviously home-made, but with the medicines I took, Doc could fix that."

"I doubt any of us could act so natural."

I nodded. "Yes. It's easy for me. I know what they expect." I laughed briefly to myself. "I'm one of them. If you trusted me, I could probably get you anything in the world you wanted." I laughed again. It was just the stress fading, making me giddy. But it was funny to me. Did he realize that I would do exactly that for him? Anything in the world he wanted.

"I do trust you," he whispered. "With all our lives, I trust you."

And he *had* trusted me with every single human life. His, and Jamie's, and everyone else's.

"Thank you," I whispered back.

"You did it," he repeated in wonder.

"We're going to save him."

*Jamie is going to live,* Mel rejoiced. *Thank you, Wanda.*

*Anything for them,* I told her, and then I sighed, because it was so true.

After reattaching the tarps when we reached the wash, Jared took over the driving. The way was familiar to him, and he drove faster than I would have. He had me get out before he pulled the car into its impossibly small hiding place under the rock slide. I waited for the sound of rock against metal, but Jared found a way in.

And then we were back in the jeep and flying through the night. Jared laughed, triumphant, as we jolted across the open desert, and the wind carried his voice away.

"Where's the blindfold?" I asked.

"Why?"

I looked at him.

"Wanda, if you wanted to turn us in, you had your chance. No one can deny that you're one of us now."

I thought about that. "I think some still could. It would make them feel better."

"Your *some* need to get over themselves."

I was shaking my head now, picturing our reception. "It's not going to be easy, getting back in. Imagine what they're thinking right now. What they're waiting for . . ."

He didn't answer. His eyes narrowed.

"Jared . . . if they . . . if they don't listen . . . if they don't wait . . ." I started talking faster, feeling a sudden pressure, trying to get him all the information before it was too late. "Give Jamie the No Pain first — lay that on his tongue. Then the Inside Clean spray — he just has to inhale it. You'll need Doc to —"

"Hey, hey! You're going to be the one giving the directions."

"But let me tell you how —"

"No, Wanda. It's not going to go down that way. I'll shoot anyone who touches you."

"Jared —"

"Don't panic. I'll aim low, and then you can use that stuff to heal 'em back up again."

"If that's a joke, it's not funny."

"No joke, Wanda."

"Where's the blindfold?"

He pressed his lips together.

But I had my old shirt — Jeb's raggy hand-me-down. That would work almost as well.

"This will make it a little bit easier for them to let us in," I said as I folded it up into a thick band. "And that means getting to Jamie faster." I tied it over my eyes.

It was quiet for a time. The jeep bounced along the uneven terrain. I remembered nights like this when Melanie had been the passenger. . . .

"I'm taking us right to the caves. There's a place the jeep will be fairly well hidden for a day or two. It will save us time."

I nodded. Time was the key now.

"Almost there," he said after a minute. He exhaled. "They're waiting."

I heard him fumbling beside me, heard a metal clank as he pulled the gun from the backseat.

"Don't shoot anyone."

"No promises."

"Stop!" someone shouted. The sound carried in the empty desert air.

The jeep slowed and then idled.

"It's just us," Jared said. "Yes, yes, look. See? I'm still me."

There was hesitation from the other side.

"Look — I'm bringing the jeep in under cover, okay?

We've got meds for Jamie, and we're in a hurry. I don't care what you're thinking, you're not going to get in my way tonight."

The jeep pulled forward. The sound changed and echoed as he found his cover.

"Okay, Wanda, everything's fine. Let's go."

I already had the pack on my shoulders. I got out of the jeep carefully, not sure where the wall was. Jared caught my searching hands.

"Up you go," he said, and lifted me over his shoulder again.

I wasn't as secure as before. He used only one arm to hold me. The other must have had the gun. I didn't like that.

But I was worried enough to be grateful for it when I heard the running footsteps approaching.

"Jared, you *idiot!*" Kyle shouted. "What were you thinking?"

"Ease up, Kyle," Jeb said.

"Is she hurt?" Ian demanded.

"Get out of my way," Jared said, his voice calm. "I'm in a hurry. Wanda's in perfect shape, but she insisted on being blindfolded. How is Jamie?"

"Hot," Jeb said.

"Wanda's got what we need." He was moving fast now, sliding downhill.

"I can carry her." Ian, of course.

"She's fine where she is."

"I'm really okay," I told Ian, my voice bouncing with Jared's movement.

Uphill again, a steady jog despite my weight. I could hear the others running with us.

I knew when we were through to the main cavern — the angry hiss of voices swelled around us, turning into a clamor of sound.

"Out of my way," Jared roared over their voices. "Is Doc with Jamie?"

I couldn't make out the answer. Jared could have put me down, but he was in too much of a hurry to pause for that second.

The angry voices echoed behind us, the sound constricting as we entered the smaller tunnel. I could feel where we were now, follow the turns in my head as we raced through the junction to the third sleeping hall. I could almost count the doors as they passed me invisibly.

Jared jerked to a halt and let the sudden stop slide me down from his shoulder. My feet hit the floor. He ripped the blindfold from my eyes.

Our room was lit by several of the dim blue lanterns. Doc was standing rigidly, as if he'd just sprung to his feet. Kneeling beside him, her hand still holding a wet cloth to Jamie's forehead, was Sharon. Her face was almost unrecognizable, it was so contorted with fury. Maggie was struggling to her feet on Jamie's other side.

Jamie still lay limp and red, eyes closed, his chest barely moving to pull in air.

"You!" Sharon spit, and then she launched herself from her crouch. Like a cat, she sprang at Jared, nails reaching for his face.

Jared caught her hands and twisted her away from him, pulling her arms behind her back.

Maggie looked as if she was about to join her daughter, but Jeb stepped around the struggling Sharon and Jared to stand toe-to-toe with her.

"Let her go!" Doc cried.

Jared ignored him. "Wanda — heal him!"

Doc moved to put himself between Jamie and me.

"Doc," I choked. The violence in the room, swirling around Jamie's still form, scared me. "I need your help. Please. For Jamie."

Doc didn't move, his eyes on Sharon and Jared.

"C'mon, Doc," Ian said. The little room was too crowded, claustrophobic, as Ian came to stand with his hand on my shoulder. "You gonna let the kid die for your pride?"

"It's not pride. You don't know what these foreign substances will do to him!"

"He can't get much worse, can he?"

"Doc," I said. "Look at my face."

Doc wasn't the only one who responded to my words. Jeb, Ian, and even Maggie looked and then did a double take. Maggie glanced away quickly, angry that she'd betrayed any interest.

"How?" Doc demanded.

"I'll show you. Please. Jamie doesn't need to suffer."

Doc hesitated, staring at my face, and then let out a big sigh. "Ian's right — he can't get much worse. If this kills him . . ." He shrugged, and his shoulders slumped. He took a step back.

"No," Sharon cried.

No one paid any attention to her.

I knelt beside Jamie, yanking the backpack off my shoulders and tugging it open. I fumbled until I found the No Pain. A bright light switched on beside me, pointed at Jamie's face.

"Water, Ian?"

I twisted the lid open and pinched out one of the little tissue squares. When I pulled Jamie's chin down, his skin burned my hand. I laid the square on his tongue and then held out my hand without looking up. Ian placed the bowl of water in it.

Carefully, I dripped enough water into his mouth to wash the medicine down his throat. The sound of his swallow was dry and painful.

I searched frantically for the thinner spray bottle. When I found it, I had the lid off and the mist sprayed into the air above him in one fast movement. I waited, watching his chest until he inhaled.

I touched his face, and it was so hot! I scrambled for the Cool, praying it would be easy to use. The lid screwed off, and I found that the cylinder was full of more tissue squares, light blue this time. I breathed a sigh of relief and placed one on Jamie's tongue. I picked up the bowl again and dribbled another mouthful of water through his parched lips.

His swallow was quicker this time, less strained.

Another hand touched Jamie's face. I recognized Doc's long bony fingers.

"Doc, do you have a sharp knife?"

"I have a scalpel. You want me to open the wound?"

"Yes, so I can clean it."

"I thought about trying that . . . to drain it, but the pain . . ."

"He'll feel nothing now."

"Look at his face," Ian leaned in beside me to whisper.

Jamie's face was no longer red. It was a natural, healthy tan. The sweat still glistened on his brow, but I knew it was just left over from before. Doc and I touched his forehead at the same time.

*It's working. Yes!* Exultation swept through both Mel and me.

"Remarkable," Doc breathed.

"The fever has cooled, but the infection may remain in his leg. Help me with his wound, Doc."

"Sharon, could you hand me —" he began absent-mindedly. Then he looked up. "Oh. Ah, Kyle, do you mind handing me that bag right there by your foot?"

I scooted down so that I was over the red, swollen cut. Ian redirected the light so I could see it clearly. Doc and I both rustled through our bags at the same time. He came up with the silver scalpel, a sight that sent a quiver of un-ease down my spine. I ignored it and readied the bigger Clean spray.

"He won't feel it?" Doc checked, hesitating.

"Hey," Jamie croaked. His eyes were open wide, roaming the room until they found my face. "Hey, Wanda. What's going on? What's everyone doing here?"

# CHAPTER 46

# Encircled

Jamie started to sit up.

"Easy there, kid. How you feelin'?" Ian moved to press Jamie's shoulders against the mattress.

"I feel . . . really good. Why is everyone here? I don't remember . . ."

"You've been sick. Hold still so we can finish fixing you."

"Can I have some water?"

"Sure, kid. Here you go."

Doc was staring at Jamie with disbelieving eyes.

I could barely talk, my throat was so tight with joy. "It's the No Pain," I muttered. "It feels wonderful."

"Why does Jared have Sharon in a headlock?" Jamie whispered to Ian.

"She's in a bad mood," Ian stage-whispered back.

"Hold very still, Jamie," Doc cautioned. "We're going to . . . clean out your injury. Okay?"

"Okay," Jamie agreed in a small voice. He'd noticed the scalpel in Doc's hands. He eyed it warily.

"Tell me if you can feel this," Doc said.

"If it hurts," I amended.

With practiced skill, Doc slid the scalpel gently through the diseased skin in one swift movement. We both glanced at Jamie. He was staring straight up at the dark ceiling.

"That feels weird," Jamie said. "But it doesn't hurt."

Doc nodded to himself and brought the scalpel down again, making a cross cut. Red blood and dark yellow discharge oozed from the gash.

As soon as Doc's hand was clear, I was spraying Clean back and forth across the bloody X. When it hit the oozing secretion, the unhealthy yellow seemed to sizzle silently. It began to recede. Almost like suds hit by a spray of water. It melted. Doc was breathing fast beside me.

"Look at *that*."

I sprayed the area twice for good measure. Already the darker red was gone from Jamie's skin. All that was left was the normal red color of the human blood that flowed out.

"Okay, Heal," I muttered. I found the right canister and tipped the little spout over the gashes in his skin. The clear liquid trickled in, coating the raw flesh and glistening there. The bleeding stopped wherever the Heal spread. I poured half the container — surely twice as much as was needed — into the wound.

"Okay, hold the edges together for me, Doc."

Doc was speechless as this point, though his mouth

hung wide. He did as I asked, using two hands to get both cuts.

Jamie laughed. "That tickles."

Doc's eyes bulged.

I smeared Seal across the X, watching with deep satisfaction as the edges fused together and faded to pink.

"Can I see?" Jamie asked.

"Let him up, Ian. We're almost done."

Jamie pulled himself up on his elbows, his eyes bright and curious. His sweaty, dirty hair was matted to his head. It didn't make sense now, next to the healthy glow of his skin.

"See, I put this on," I said, brushing a handful of glitter across the cuts, "and it makes the scar very faint. Like this." I showed him the one on my arm.

Jamie laughed. "But don't scars impress girls? Where did you get this stuff, Wanda? It's like magic."

"Jared took me on a raid."

"Seriously? That's *awesome.*"

Doc touched the glistening powder residue on my hand, then held his fingers to his nose.

"You should have seen her," Jared said. "She was incredible."

I was surprised to hear his voice close behind me. I looked around for Sharon automatically and just caught sight of the flame of her hair leaving the room. Maggie was right behind her.

How sad. How frightening. To be filled with so much hate that you could not even rejoice in the healing of a child. . . . How did anyone ever come to that point?

"She walked right into a hospital, right up to the alien there, and asked them to treat her injuries, bold as anything. Then, when they turned their backs, she robbed them blind!" Jared made it sound exciting. Jamie was enjoying it, too; his smile was huge. "Walked right out of there with medicine enough to last us all for a long time. She even waved at the bugger behind the counter as she drove away." Jared laughed.

*I couldn't do this for them,* Melanie said, suddenly chagrined. *You're of more value to them than I would be.*

*Hush,* I said. It was not a time for sadness or jealousy. Only joy. *I wouldn't be here to help them without you. You saved him, too.*

Jamie was staring at me with big eyes.

"It wasn't that exciting, really," I told him. He took my hand, and I squeezed his, my heart swollen with gratitude and love. "It was very easy. I'm a bugger, too, after all."

"I didn't mean —" Jared started to apologize.

I waved his protest away, smiling.

"How did you explain the scar on your face?" Doc asked. "Didn't they wonder why you hadn't —"

"I had to have fresh injuries, of course. I was careful to leave them nothing to be suspicious about. I told them I'd fallen with a knife in my hand." I nudged Jamie with my elbow. "It could happen to anyone."

I was really flying high now. Everything seemed to glow from inside — the fabrics, the faces, the very walls. The crowd inside and outside the room had begun to murmur and question, but that noise was just a ringing in my ears — like the lingering sound after a bell is struck. A shimmer in the air. Nothing seemed real but the little circle of people I loved. Jamie and Jared and Ian and Jeb. Even Doc belonged in this perfect moment.

"Fresh injuries?" Ian asked in a flat voice.

I stared at him, surprised at the anger in his eyes.

"It was necessary. I had to hide my scar. And learn how to heal Jamie."

Jared picked up my left wrist and stroked his finger over the faint pink line a few inches above it. "It was horrible," he said, all the humor suddenly gone from his sober voice. "She about hacked her hand off. I thought she'd never use it again."

Jamie's eyes widened in horror. "You cut yourself?"

I squeezed his hand again. "Don't be anxious — it wasn't that bad. I knew it would be healed quickly."

"You should have seen her," Jared repeated in a low voice, still stroking my arm.

Ian's fingers brushed across my cheek. It felt nice, and I leaned into his hand when he left it there. I wondered if it was the No Pain or just the joy of saving Jamie that made everything warm and glowing.

"No more raids for you," Ian murmured.

"Of course she'll go out again," Jared said, his voice louder with surprise. "Ian, she was absolutely phenomenal. You'd have to see to really understand. I'm only just beginning to guess at all the possibilities —"

"Possibilities?" Ian's hand slid down my neck to my shoulder. He pulled me closer to his side, away from Jared. "At what cost to her? You *let* her almost *hack* her own *hand* off?" His fingers flexed around the top of my arm with his inflections.

The anger didn't belong with the glow. "No, Ian, it wasn't like that," I said. "It was my idea. I had to."

"Of course it was your idea," Ian growled. "You'd do anything. . . . You have no *limits* when it comes to these two. But Jared shouldn't have let you —"

"What other way was there, Ian?" Jared argued. "Did you have a better plan? Do you think she'd be happier if she was unhurt but Jamie was gone?"

I flinched at the hideous thought.

Ian's voice was less hostile when he answered. "No. But I don't understand how you could sit there and watch her do that to herself." Ian shook his head in disgust, and Jared's shoulders hunched in response. "What kind of a man —"

"A practical one," Jeb interrupted.

We all looked up. Jeb stood over us, a bulky cardboard box in his arms.

"It's why Jared's the best at getting what we need. Because he can do what has to be done. Or watch what has to be done. Even when watching's harder than doing.

"Now, I know it's closer to breakfast than supper, but I figured some of you haven't eaten in a while," Jeb went on, changing the subject without subtlety. "Hungry, kid?"

"Uh . . . I'm not sure," Jamie admitted. "I feel real hollow, but it doesn't feel . . . *bad*."

"That's the No Pain," I said. "You should eat."

"And drink," Doc said. "You need liquids."

Jeb let the unwieldy box fall onto the mattress. "Thought we might have a bit of a celebration. Dig in."

"Wow, yum!" Jamie said, pawing through the box of dehydrated meals of the sort that hikers used. "Spaghetti. Excellent."

"Dibs on the garlic chicken," Jeb said. "I've been missin' garlic quite a bit — though I imagine no one misses it on my breath." He chuckled.

Jeb was prepared, with bottles of water and several portable stoves. People began to gather around, squeezing together in the small space. I was wedged between Jared and Ian, and I'd pulled Jamie onto my lap. Though he was much too old for this, he didn't protest. He must have sensed how much both of us needed that — Mel and I *had* to feel him alive and healthy and in our arms.

The shimmering circle seemed to widen, enveloping the entire late-night supper party, making them family, too. Everyone waited contentedly for Jeb to prepare the unexpected treats, in no hurry. Fear had been replaced by relief and happy news. Even Kyle, compressed into the small space on the other side of his brother, was not unwelcome in the circle.

Melanie sighed in contentment. She was vibrantly aware of the warmth of the boy in my lap and the touch of the man who still stroked his hand against my arm. She wasn't even upset by Ian's arm around my shoulders.

*You're feeling the No Pain, too,* I teased her.

*I don't think it's the No Pain. Not for either of us.*

*No, you're right. This is more than I've ever had.*

*This is so much of what I lost.*

What was it that made this human love so much more desirable to me than the love of my own kind? Was it because it was exclusive and capricious? The souls offered love and acceptance to all. Did I crave a greater challenge? This love was tricky; it had no hard-and-fast rules — it might be given for free, as with Jamie, or earned through time and hard work, as with Ian, or completely and heartbreakingly unattainable, as with Jared.

Or was it simply better somehow? Because these humans could hate with so much fury, was the other end of the spectrum that they could love with more heart and zeal and fire?

I didn't know why I had yearned after it so desperately. All I knew was that, now that I had it, it was worth every ounce of risk and agony it had cost. It was better than I'd imagined.

It was everything.

By the time the food was prepared and consumed, the late — or rather early — hour had gotten to us all. People stumbled out of the crowded room toward their beds. As they left, there was more space.

Those remaining slouched down where we were as room became available. Gradually, we melted in place until we were horizontal. My head ended up pillowed on Jared's stomach; his hand stroked my hair now and then. Jamie's face was against my chest, and his arms were around my neck. One of my arms wrapped around his shoulders. Ian's head was cushioned on my stomach, and he held my other hand to his face. I could feel Doc's long leg stretched beside mine, his shoe by my hip. Doc was asleep — I could hear him snoring. I may have even been touching Kyle somewhere.

Jeb was sprawled on the bed. He belched, and Kyle chuckled.

"Nicer night than I was plannin' for. I like it when pessimism goes unrewarded," Jeb mused. "Thanks, Wanda."

"Mmm," I sighed, half asleep.

"Next time she raids . . ." Kyle said, somewhere on the other side of Jared's body. A big yawn interrupted his sentence. "Next time she raids, I'm coming, too."

"She's not going out again," Ian answered, his body tensing. I brushed my hand against his face, trying to soothe him.

"Of course not," I murmured to him. "I don't have to go anywhere unless I'm needed. I don't mind staying in here."

"I'm not talking about keeping you prisoner, Wanda," Ian explained, irritated. "You can go anywhere you want as far as I'm concerned. Jogging on the highway, if you'd like that. But not a raid. I'm talking about keeping you safe."

"We need her," Jared said, his voice harder than I wanted to hear it.

"We got by fine without her before."

"Fine? Jamie would have died without her. She can get things for us that no one else can."

"She's a person, Jared, not a tool."

"I know that. I didn't say that —"

"'S up to Wanda, I'd say." Jeb interrupted the argument just as I was about to. My hand was holding Ian down now, and I could feel Jared's body shifting under my head as he prepared to get up. Jeb's words froze them in place.

"You can't leave it up to her, Jeb," Ian protested.

"Why not? Seems like she's got her own mind. 'S it your job to make decisions for her?"

"I'll tell you why not," Ian grumbled. "Wanda?"

"Yes, Ian?"

"Do you *want* to go out on raids?"

"If I can help, of course I should go."

"That's not what I asked, Wanda."

I was quiet for a moment, trying to remember his question to see how I'd gotten it wrong.

"See, Jeb? She never takes into account her own wants — her own happiness, her own *health,* even. She'd do anything we asked her to, even if it got her killed. It's not fair to ask her things the way we'd ask each other. *We* stop to think about ourselves. She doesn't."

It was quiet. No one answered Ian. The silence dragged on until I felt compelled to speak for myself.

"That's not true," I said. "I think about myself all the time. And I . . . I *want* to help. Doesn't that count? It made me so happy to help Jamie tonight. Can't I find happiness the way *I* want to?"

Ian sighed. "See what I mean?"

"Well, I can't tell her she can't go if she wants to," Jeb said. "She's not a prisoner anymore."

"But we don't have to ask."

Jared was very quiet through all this. Jamie was quiet, too, but I was pretty sure he was asleep. I knew Jared wasn't; his hand was tracing random patterns on the side of my face. Glowing, burning patterns.

"You don't need to ask," I said. "I volunteer. It really wasn't . . . frightening. Not at all. The other souls are very kind. I'm not afraid of them. It was almost too easy."

"Easy? Cutting your —"

I interrupted Ian quickly. "That was an emergency. I won't have to do that again." I paused for a second. "Right?" I checked.

Ian groaned. "If she goes, I'm going, too," he said in a bleak tone. "*Someone* has to protect her from herself."

"And I'll be there to protect the rest of us from *her,*" Kyle said with a chuckle. Then he grunted and said, "Ow."

I was too tired to lift my head to see who had hit Kyle now.

"And I'll be there to bring you all back alive," Jared murmured.

# CHAPTER 47

# Employed

"This is too easy. It's not really even fun anymore," Kyle complained.

"You wanted to come," Ian reminded him.

He and Ian were in the windowless back of the van, sorting through the nonperishable groceries and toiletries I'd just collected from the store. It was the middle of the day, and the sun was shining on Wichita. It was not as hot as the Arizona desert, but it was more humid. The air swarmed with tiny flying bugs.

Jared drove toward the highway out of town, carefully keeping below the speed limit. This continued to irritate him.

"Getting tired of shopping yet, Wanda?" Ian asked me.

"No. I don't mind it."

"You always say that. Isn't there *anything* you mind?"

"I mind . . . being away from Jamie. And I mind being

outside, a little bit. During the day especially. It's like the opposite of claustrophobia. Everything is too open. Does that bother you, too?"

"Sometimes. We don't go out during the day much."

"At least she gets to stretch her legs," Kyle muttered. "I don't know why you want to hear *her* complain."

"Because it's so uncommon. Which makes it a nice change from listening to *you* complain."

I tuned them out. Once Ian and Kyle got started, they usually went on for a while. I consulted the map.

"Oklahoma City next?" I asked Jared.

"And a few small towns on the way, if you're up for it," he answered, eyes on the road.

"I am."

Jared rarely lost his focus when on a raid. He didn't relax into relieved banter the way Ian and Kyle did every time I completed another mission successfully. It made me smile when they used that word — *mission*. That sounded so formidable. In reality, it was just a trip to the store. Just like I'd done a hundred times in San Diego when I was only feeding myself.

Like Kyle said, it was too easy to provide any excitement. I pushed my cart up and down the aisles. I smiled at the souls who smiled at me, and I filled my cart with things that would last. I usually grabbed a few things that wouldn't, for the men hiding in the back of the van. Pre-made sandwiches from the deli — things like that for our meals. And maybe a treat or two. Ian had a fondness for mint chocolate chip ice cream. Kyle liked caramel sweets best. Jared ate anything he was offered; it seemed as if he'd given up favorites many years before, embracing a life where wants were unwelcome and even needs were carefully assessed before they were met. Another reason he was good at this life — he saw priorities uncontaminated by personal desire.

Occasionally, in the smaller towns, someone would notice me, would speak to me. I had my lines down so well that I could probably have fooled a human by this point.

*"Hi there. New in town?"*

*"Yes. Brand-new."*

*"What brings you to Byers?"*

I was always careful to check the map before I left the van, so the town's name would be familiar.

*"My partner travels a lot. He's a photographer."*

*"How wonderful! An Artist. Well, there's certainly a lot of beautiful land around here."*

Originally, I'd been the Artist. But I'd found that throwing in the information that I was already partnered saved me some time when I was speaking to males.

*"Thank you so much for your help."*

*"You're very welcome. Come back soon."*

I'd only had to speak to a pharmacist once, in Salt Lake City; after that, I'd known what to look for.

A sheepish smile. *"I'm not sure I'm getting the right nutrition. I can't seem to avoid the junk food. This body has such a sweet tooth."*

*"You need to be wise, Thousand Petals. I know it's easy to give in to your cravings, but try to think about what you're eating. In the meantime, you should take a supplement."*

Health. Such an obvious title on the bottle, it made me feel silly for asking.

*"Would you like the ones that taste like strawberries or the ones that taste like chocolate?"*

*"Could I try both?"*

And the pleasant soul named Earthborn gave me both of the large bottles.

Not very challenging. The only fear or sense of danger I ever felt came when I thought of the small cyanide pill that I always kept in an easily reachable pocket. Just in case.

"You should get new clothes in the next town," Jared said.

"Again?"

"Those are looking a little creased."

"Okay," I agreed. I didn't like the excess, but the steadily growing pile of dirty laundry wouldn't go to waste. Lily and Heidi and Paige were all close to my size, and they would be grateful for something new to wear. The men rarely bothered with things like clothes when they were raiding. Every foray was life-or-death — clothes were not a priority. Nor were the gentle soaps and shampoos that I'd been collecting at every store.

"You should probably clean up, too," Jared said with a sigh. "Guess that means a hotel tonight."

Keeping up appearances was not something they'd worried about before. Of course, I was the only one who had to look as if I were a part of civilization from close up. The men wore jeans and dark T-shirts now, things that didn't show dirt or attract attention in the brief moments they might be seen.

They all hated sleeping in the roadside inns — succumbing to unconsciousness inside the very mouth of the enemy. It scared them more than anything else we did. Ian said he'd rather charge an armed Seeker.

Kyle simply refused. He mostly slept in the van during the day and then sat up at night, acting as sentry.

For me, it was as easy as shopping in the stores. I checked us in, made conversation with the clerk. Told the story about my photographer partner and the friend who was traveling with us (just in case someone saw all three of us enter the room). I used generic names from unremarkable planets. Sometimes we were Bats: Word Keeper, Sings the Egg Song, and Sky Roost. Sometimes we were See Weeds: Twisting Eyes, Sees to the Surface, and Second Sunrise. I changed the names every time, not that anyone was trying to trace our path. It just made Melanie feel safer to do that. All this made her feel like a character in a human movie about espionage.

The hard part, the part I really minded — not that I would say this in front of Kyle, who was so quick to doubt my intentions — was all the taking without giving anything back. It had never bothered me to shop in San Diego. I took what I needed and nothing more. Then I spent my days at the university giving back to the community by sharing my knowledge. Not a taxing Calling, but one I took seriously. I took my turns at the less-appealing chores. I did my day collecting garbage and cleaning streets. We all did.

And now I took so much more and gave nothing in return. It made me feel selfish and wrong.

*It's not for yourself. It's for others,* Mel reminded me when I brooded.

*It still feels wrong. Even you can feel that, can't you?*

*Don't think about it* was her solution.

I was glad we were on the homestretch of our long raid. Tomorrow we would visit our growing cache — a moving truck we kept hidden within a day's reach of our path — and clean out the van for the last time. Just a few more cities, a few more days, down through Oklahoma, then New Mexico, and then a straight drive through Arizona with no stops.

Home again. At last.

When we slept in hotels rather than in the crowded van, we usually checked in after dark and left before dawn to keep the souls from getting a good look at us. Not really necessary.

Jared and Ian were beginning to realize that. This night, because we'd had such a successful day — the van was completely full; Kyle would have little space — and because Ian thought I looked tired, we stopped early. The sun had not set when I returned to the van with the plastic key card.

The little inn was not very busy. We parked close to our room, and Jared and Ian went straight from the van to the room in a matter of five or six steps, their eyes on the ground. On their necks, small, faint pink lines provided camouflage. Jared carried a half-empty suitcase. No one looked at them or me.

Inside, the room-darkening curtains were drawn, and the men relaxed a little bit.

Ian lounged on the bed he and Jared would use, and flipped on the TV. Jared put the suitcase on the table, took out our dinner — cooled greasy breaded chicken strips I'd ordered from the deli in the last store — and passed it around. I sat by the window, peeking through the corner at the falling sun as I ate.

"You have to admit, Wanda, we humans had better entertainment," Ian teased.

On the television screen, two souls were speaking their lines clearly, their bodies held with perfect posture. It wasn't hard to pick up what was happening in the story because there wasn't a lot of variety in the scripts souls wrote. In this one, two souls were reconnecting after a long separation. The male's stint with the See Weeds had come between them, but he'd chosen to be human because he guessed his partner from the Mists Planet would be drawn to these warm-blooded hosts. And, miracle of miracles, he'd found her here.

They all had happy endings.

"You have to consider the intended audience."

"True. I wish they'd run old human shows again." He flipped through the channels and frowned. "Used to be a few of them on."

"They were too disturbing. They had to be replaced with things that weren't so . . . violent."

"*The Brady Bunch*?"

I laughed. I'd seen that show in San Diego, and Melanie knew it from her childhood. "It condoned aggression. I remember one where a little male child punched a bully, and that was portrayed as being the right thing to do. There was blood."

Ian shook his head in disbelief but returned to the show with the former See Weed. He laughed at the wrong parts, the parts that were supposed to be touching.

I stared out the window, watching something much more interesting than the predictable story on television.

Across the two-lane road from the inn was a small park, bordered on one side by a school and on the other by a field where cows grazed. There were a few young trees, and an old-fashioned playground with a sandbox, a slide, a set of monkey bars, and one of those hand-pulled merry-go-rounds. Of course there was a swing set, too, and that was the only equipment being used currently.

A little family was taking advantage of the cooler evening air. The father had some silver in his dark hair at the temples; the mother looked many years his junior. Her red brown hair was pulled back in a long ponytail that bobbed when she moved. They had a little boy, no more than a year old. The father pushed the child in the swing from behind, while the mother stood in front, leaning in to kiss his forehead when he swung her way, making him giggle so hard that his chubby little face was bright red. This had her laughing, too — I could see her body shake with it, her hair dancing.

"What are you staring at, Wanda?"

Jared's question wasn't anxious, because I was smiling softly at the surprising scene.

"Something I've never seen in all my lives. I'm staring at . . . hope."

Jared came to stand behind me, peeking out over my shoulder. "What do you mean?" His eyes swept across the buildings and the road, not pausing on the playing family.

I caught his chin and pointed his face in the right direction. He didn't so much as flinch at my unexpected touch, and that gave me a strange jolt of warmth in the pit of my stomach. "Look," I said.

"What am I looking at?"

"The only hope for survival I've ever seen for a host species."

"Where?" he demanded, bewildered.

I was aware of Ian close behind us now, listening silently.

"See?" I pointed at the laughing mother. "See how she loves her human child?"

At that moment, the woman snatched her son from the swing and squeezed him in a tight embrace, covering his face with kisses. He cooed and flailed — just a baby. Not the miniature adult he would have been if he carried one of my kind.

Jared gasped. "The baby is *human?* How? Why? For how long?"

I shrugged. "I've never seen this before — I don't know. She has not given him up for a host. I can't imagine that she would be . . . forced. Motherhood is all but worshipped among my kind. If she is unwilling . . ." I shook my head. "I have no idea how that will be handled. This doesn't happen elsewhere. The emotions of these bodies are so much stronger than logic."

I glanced up at Jared and Ian. They were both staring openmouthed at the interspecies family in the park.

"No," I murmured to myself. "No one would force the parents if they wanted the child. And just *look* at them."

The father had his arms around both the mother and the child now. He looked down at his host body's biological son with staggering tenderness in his eyes.

"Aside from ourselves, this is the first planet we've discovered with live births. Yours certainly isn't the easiest or most prolific system. I wonder if that's the difference . . . or if it's the helplessness of your young. Everywhere else, reproduction is through some form of eggs or seeds. Many parents never even meet their young. I wonder . . ." I trailed off, my thoughts full of speculation.

The mother lifted her face to her partner, and he kissed her lips. The human child crowed with delight.

"Hmm. Perhaps, someday, some of my kind and some of yours will live in peace. Wouldn't that be . . . strange?"

Neither man could tear his eyes from the miracle in front of them.

The family was leaving. The mother dusted the sand off her jeans while the father took the boy. Then, holding hands that they swung between them, the souls strolled toward the apartments with their human child.

Ian swallowed loudly.

We didn't speak for the rest of the evening, all of us made thoughtful by what we'd seen. We went to sleep early, so we could rise early and get back to work.

I slept alone, in the bed farthest from the door. This made me uncomfortable. The two big men did not fit easily on the other bed; Ian tended to sprawl when he was deeply asleep, and Jared was not above throwing punches when that happened. Both of them would be more comfortable if I shared. I slept in a small ball now; maybe it was the too-open spaces I moved in all day that had me constricting in on myself at night, or maybe I was just so used to curling up to sleep in the tiny space behind the passenger seat on the van's floor that I'd forgotten how to sleep straight.

But I knew why no one asked me to share. The first night the men had unhappily realized the necessity of a hotel shower for me, I'd heard Ian and Jared talking about me over the whir of the bathroom fan.

". . . not fair to ask her to choose," Ian was saying. He kept his voice low, but the fan was not loud enough to drown it out. The hotel room was very small.

"Why not? It's fairer to *tell* her where she's going to sleep? Don't you think it's more polite —"

"For someone else. But Wanda will agonize over this. She'll be trying so hard to please us both, she'll make herself miserable."

"Jealous again?"

"Not this time. I just know how she thinks."

There was a silence. Ian was right. He *did* know how I thought. He'd probably already foreseen that given the slightest hint that Jared would prefer it, I would choose to sleep beside Jared, and then keep myself awake worrying that I'd made Jared unhappy by being there and that I'd hurt Ian's feelings in the bargain.

"Fine," Jared snapped. "But if you try cuddling up to me tonight . . . so help me, O'Shea."

Ian chuckled. "Not to sound overly arrogant, but to be perfectly honest, Jared, were I so inclined, I think I could do better."

Despite feeling a little guilty about wasting so much needed space, I probably did sleep better alone.

We didn't have to go to a hotel again. The days started to pass more quickly, as if even the seconds were trying to run home. I could feel a strange western pull on my body. We were all eager to get back to our dark, crowded haven.

Even Jared got careless.

It was late, no sunlight left lingering behind the western mountains. Behind us, Ian and Kyle were taking turns driving the big moving truck loaded with our spoils, just as Jared and I took turns with the van. They had to drive the heavy vehicle more carefully than Jared did the van. The headlights had faded slowly into the distance, until they disappeared around a wide curve in the road.

We were on the homestretch. Tucson was behind us. In a few short hours, I would see Jamie. We would unload the welcome provisions, surrounded by smiling faces. A real homecoming.

My first, I realized.

For once the return would bring nothing but joy. We carried no doomed hostages this time.

I wasn't paying attention to anything but anticipation. The road didn't seem to be flying by too fast; it couldn't fly past fast enough as far as I was concerned.

The truck's headlights reappeared behind us.

"Kyle must be driving," I murmured. "They're catching up."

And then the red and blue lights suddenly spun out in the dark night behind us. They reflected off all the mirrors, dancing spots of color across the roof, the seats, our frozen faces, and the dashboard, where the needle on the speed gauge showed that we were traveling twenty miles over the speed limit.

The sound of a siren pierced the desert calm.

# CHAPTER 48

# Detained

The red and blue lights swirled in time with the siren's cry.

Before the souls had come to this place, these lights and sounds had had only one meaning. The law, the keepers of the peace, the punishers of offenders.

Now, again, the flashing colors and angry noise had only one meaning. A very similar meaning. Still the keepers of the peace. Still the punishers.

Seekers.

It wasn't as common a sight or sound as it had been before. The police force was only needed to help in cases of accidents or other emergencies, not to enforce laws. Most civil servants didn't have vehicles with sirens, unless the vehicle was an ambulance or a fire truck.

This low, sleek car behind us was not for any accident. This was a vehicle made for pursuit. I'd never seen anything quite like it before, but I knew exactly what it meant.

Jared was frozen, his foot still pushing down on the gas pedal. I could see that he was trying to find a solution, a way to outrun them in this decrepit van or a way to evade them — to hide our wide white profile in the low, gaunt brush of the desert — without leading them back to the rest. Without giving everyone away. We were so close to the others now. They slumbered, unaware . . .

When he gave up after two seconds of frantic thought, he exhaled.

"I'm so sorry, Wanda," he whispered. "I blew it."

"Jared?"

He reached for my hand and eased up on the gas. The car started to slow.

"Got your pill?" he choked.

"Yes," I whispered.

"Can Mel hear me?"

*Yes.* The thought was a sob.

"Yes." My voice only barely escaped being a sob, too.

"I love you, Mel. Sorry."

"She loves you. More than anything."

A short, aching silence.

"Wanda, I . . . I care about you, too. You're a good person, Wanda. You deserve better than what I've given you. Better than this."

He had something small, much too small to be so deadly, between his fingers.

"Wait," I gasped.

He could not die.

"Wanda, we can't take the chance. We can't outrun

them, not in this. If we try to run, a thousand of them will swarm after us. Think of Jamie."

The van was slowing, drifting to the shoulder.

"Give me one try," I begged. I fumbled quickly for the pill in my pocket. I pinched it between my thumb and forefinger and held it up. "Let me try to lie us out of this. I'll swallow it right away if anything goes wrong."

"You'll never lie your way past a Seeker!"

"Let me try. Quick!" I pulled off my seat belt and crouched beside him, unfastening his. "Switch with me. Fast, before they're close enough to see."

"Wanda —"

"One try. Hurry!"

He was the best at split-second decisions. Smooth and fast, he was out of the driver's seat and over my crouched body. I rolled up into his seat while he took mine.

"Seat belt," I ordered tersely. "Close your eyes. Turn your head away."

He did as I said. It was too dark to see it, but his new soft pink scar would be visible from this angle.

I strapped my seat belt on and then leaned my head back.

Lying with my body, that was the key. It was simply a matter of the right movements. Imitation. Like the actors on the TV program, only better. Like a human.

"Help me, Mel," I murmured.

*I can't help you be a better soul, Wanda. But you* can *do this. Save him. I know you can.*

A better soul. I only had to be myself.

It was late. I was tired. I wouldn't have to act that part.

I let my eyelids droop, let my body sag against the seat.

Chagrin. I could do chagrin. I could feel it now.

My mouth turned down into a sheepish grimace.

The Seekers' car did not park behind us, the way I could feel Mel expected. It stopped across the road, on the shoulder, facing the wrong way for that lane's traffic flow. A dazzling light exploded through the window of the other car. I blinked into it, raising my hand to shade my face with deliberate slowness. Faintly, past the glare of the spotlight, I saw the gleam of my eyes bounce against the road as I looked down.

A car door slammed. One set of footsteps made a pattern of low thuds as someone crossed the pavement. There was no sound of dirt or rocks, so the Seeker had emerged from the passenger side. Two of them, at least, but only one coming to interrogate me. This was a good sign, a sign of comfort and confidence.

My glowing eyes were a talisman. A compass that could not fail — like the North Star, undoubtable.

Lying with my body was *not* the key. Telling the truth with it was enough. I had something in common with the human baby in the park: nothing like me had ever existed before.

The Seeker's body blocked the light, and I could see again.

It was a man. *Probably* middle-aged — his features conflicted with one another, making it hard to tell; his hair was all white, but his face was smooth and unwrinkled. He wore a T-shirt and shorts, a blocky gun clearly visible on his hip. One hand rested on the butt of the weapon. In his other hand was a dark flashlight. He didn't turn it on.

"Having a problem, miss?" he said when he was a few feet away. "You were going much too fast for safety."

His eyes were restless. They swiftly appraised my expression — which was, hopefully, sleepy — and then ran along the length of the van, darted into the darkness behind us, flashed forward to the stretch of highway ahead, lit by our headlights, and came back to my face. They repeated the course another time.

He was anxious. This knowledge made my palms sweaty, but I tried to keep the panic from my voice.

"I'm so sorry," I apologized in a loud whisper. I glanced at Jared, as if checking to see whether our words had woken him. "I think . . . well, I think I might have fallen asleep. I didn't realize I was so tired."

I tried to smile remorsefully. I could tell I sounded stiff, like the too-careful actors on the television.

The Seeker's eyes traced their route again, this time lingering on Jared. My heart jumped painfully against the inside of my ribs. I pinched the pill tighter.

"It was irresponsible for me to drive for so long without sleep," I said quickly, trying again to smile a little. "I thought we could make it to Phoenix before I would need rest. I'm very sorry."

"What's your name, miss?"

His voice was not harsh, but neither was it warm. He kept it low, though, following my cue.

"Leaves Above," I said, using the name from the last hotel. Would he want to check my story? I might need someplace to refer him to.

"Upside-down Flower?" he guessed. His eyes flickered around their course.

"Yes, I was."

"My partner, too. Were you on the island?"

"No," I said quickly. "The mainland. Between the great rivers."

He nodded, perhaps a little disappointed.

"Should I go back to Tucson?" I asked. "I think I'm quite awake now. Or maybe I should take a nap right here first —"

"No!" he interrupted me in a louder voice.

I jumped, startled, and the little pill slipped from my fingers. It dropped to the metal floor with a faintly audible *clink*. I felt the blood drain from my face as though a plug had been pulled.

"Didn't mean to startle you," he apologized quickly, his eyes repeating their restless circle. "But you shouldn't linger here."

"Why?" I managed to whisper. My fingers twitched anxiously at the empty air.

"There was a . . . disappearance recently."

"I don't understand. A disappearance?"

"It could have been an accident . . . but there might be . . ." He hesitated, unwilling to say the word. "Humans may be in this area."

"Humans?" I squeaked, too loud. He heard the fear in my voice and interpreted it the only way he could.

"There's no proof of that, Leaves Above. No sightings or anything. Don't be anxious. But you *should* proceed on to Phoenix without unnecessary delay."

"Of course. Or maybe Tucson? That would be closer."

"There's no danger. You can continue with your plans."

"If you're sure, Seeker . . ."

"I'm quite sure. Just don't go wandering off into the desert, Flower." He smiled. The expression warmed his face, making it kind. Just like all the other souls I'd dealt with. He wasn't anxious *about* me, but *for* me. He wasn't listening for lies. And he probably wouldn't recognize them if he was. Just another soul.

"I wasn't planning on it." I smiled back at him. "I'll be more careful. I know I couldn't fall asleep now." I glanced at the desert out Jared's window with a wary expression, so the Seeker would think that fear was making me alert. My expression tensed into a taut mask as I caught sight of a pair of lights reflected in the side mirror.

Jared's spine stiffened at the same time, but he held his pose. It looked too tight.

My eyes darted back to the Seeker's face.

"I can help with that," he said, still smiling but looking down now as he fumbled to remove something from his pocket.

He hadn't seen the change in my face. I tried to control the muscles in my cheeks, to make them relax, but I couldn't concentrate hard enough to make it happen.

In the rearview mirror, the headlights got closer.

"You should not use this often," the Seeker went on, searching the other pocket now. "It's not harmful, of course, or the Healers wouldn't have us give it out. But if you use it frequently, it *will* alter your sleep cycles. . . . Ah, here it is. Awake."

The lights slowed as they approached.

*Just drive by,* I begged in my head. *Don't stop, don't stop, don't stop.*

*Let it be Kyle at the wheel,* Melanie added, thinking the words like a prayer.

*Don't stop. Just drive. Don't stop. Just drive.*

"Miss?"

I blinked, trying to focus. "Um, Awake?"

"Just inhale this, Leaves Above."

He had a thin white aerosol can in his hand. He sprayed a puff of mist into the air in front of my face. I leaned forward obediently and took a sniff, my eyes darting to the mirror at the same time.

"It's grapefruit scented," the Seeker said. "Nice, don't you think?"

"Very nice." My brain was suddenly sharp, focused.

The big moving truck slowed and then idled on the road behind us.

*No!* Mel and I shouted together. I searched the dark floor for one half second, hoping against hope that the little pill would be visible. I couldn't even make out my feet.

The Seeker glanced absently at the truck and then waved it forward.

I looked back at the truck, too, a forced smile on my face. I couldn't see who was driving. My eyes reflected the headlights, shot out faint beams of their own.

The truck hesitated.

The Seeker waved again, more broadly this time. "Go ahead," he muttered to himself.

*Drive! Drive! Drive!*

Beside me, Jared's hand was clenched in a fist.

Slowly, the big truck shuddered into first gear and then

inched forward through the space between the Seeker's vehicle and ours. The Seeker's spotlight outlined two silhouettes, two black profiles, both facing straight forward. The one in the driver's seat had a crooked nose.

Mel and I both exhaled in relief.

"How do you feel?"

"Alert," I told the Seeker.

"It will wear off in about four hours."

"Thank you."

The Seeker chuckled. "Thank *you,* Leaves Above. When we saw you racing down the road, we thought we might have humans on our hands. I was sweating, but not from the heat!"

I shuddered.

"Don't worry. You'll be perfectly fine. If you'd like, we can follow you to Phoenix."

"I'm just fine. You don't need to trouble yourself."

"It was nice to meet you. I'll be pleased when my shift is over, so that I can go home and tell my partner I met another green-first Flower. She'll be so excited."

"Um . . . tell her, 'Brightest sun, longest day' for me," I said, giving him the Earthly translation of the common greeting and farewell on the Flower Planet.

"Certainly. Have a pleasant journey."

"And you have a pleasant night."

He stepped back, and the spotlight hit my eyes again. I blinked furiously.

"Cut it, Hank," the Seeker said, shading his eyes as he turned to walk toward the car. The night turned black again, and I forced another smile toward the invisible Seeker named Hank.

I started the engine with shaking hands.

The Seekers were faster. The little black car with the incongruous light bar atop it purred to life. It executed a sharp U-turn, and then the taillights were all I could see. They disappeared quickly into the night.

I pulled back onto the road. My heart pumped the blood through my veins in hard little bursts. I could feel the fierce pulse throbbing through to my fingertips.

"They're gone," I whispered through my suddenly chattering teeth.

I heard Jared swallow.

"That was . . . close," he said.

"I thought Kyle was going to stop."

"Me, too."

Neither of us could speak above a whisper.

"The Seeker bought it." His teeth were still clenched in anxiety.

"Yes."

"I wouldn't have. Your acting hasn't improved much."

I shrugged. My body was so rigid, it all moved together. "They can't *not* believe me. What I am . . . well, it's something impossible. Something that shouldn't exist."

"Something unbelievable," he agreed. "Something wonderful."

His praise thawed some of the ice in my stomach, in my veins.

"Seekers aren't all that different from the rest of them," I murmured to myself. "Nothing to be especially afraid of."

He shook his head back and forth slowly. "There really isn't anything you can't do, is there?"

I wasn't sure how to respond to that.

"Having you with us is going to change everything," he continued under his breath, talking to himself now.

I could feel how his words made Melanie sad, but she was not angry this time. She was resigned.

*You can help them. You can protect them better than I could.* She sighed.

The slow-moving taillights did not frighten me when they appeared on the road ahead. They were familiar, a relief. I sped up — just a little, still a few miles below the limit — to pass them.

Jared pulled a flashlight out of the glove compartment. I understood what he was doing: reassurance.

He held the light to his own eyes as we passed the cab of the truck. I looked past him, through the other window. Kyle nodded once at Jared and took a deep breath. Ian was leaning anxiously around him, his eyes focused on me. I waved once, and he grimaced.

We were getting close to our hidden exit.

"Should I go all the way to Phoenix?"

Jared thought about it. "No. They might see us on the way back and stop us again. I don't think they're following. They're focused on the road."

"No, they won't follow." I was sure of this.

"Let's go home, then."

"Home," I agreed wholeheartedly.

We killed the lights, and so did Kyle behind us.

We would take both vehicles right to the caves and unload quickly so they could be hidden before morning. The little overhang by the entrance would not hide them from view.

I rolled my eyes as I thought of the way into and out of

the caves. The *big mystery* I hadn't been able to solve for myself. Jeb was so tricky.

Tricky — just like the directions he'd given Mel, the lines he'd carved onto the back of her photo album. They didn't lead to his cave hideout at all. No, instead they made the person following them parade back and forth in front of his secret place, giving him ample opportunity to decide whether or not to extend an invitation inside.

"What do you think happened?" Jared asked, interrupting my thoughts.

"What do you mean?"

"The recent disappearance the Seeker mentioned."

I stared ahead blankly. "Wouldn't that be me?"

"I don't think you would count as *recent*, Wanda. Besides, they weren't watching the freeway before we left. That's new. They're looking for us. Here."

His eyes narrowed, while mine widened.

"What have they been doing?" Jared suddenly exploded, slapping his hand loudly against the dashboard. I jumped.

"You think Jeb and the others did something?"

He didn't answer me; he just stared out across the star-bright desert with furious eyes.

I didn't understand. Why would the Seekers be looking for humans just because someone had disappeared in the desert? Accidents did happen. Why would they jump to that particular conclusion?

And why was Jared angry? Our family in the caves wouldn't do anything to draw attention to themselves. They knew better than that. They wouldn't go outside unless there was an emergency of some kind.

Or something they *felt* was urgent. Necessary.

Had Doc and Jeb been taking advantage of my absence?

Jeb had only agreed to stop slaughtering people and souls while I was under the same roof. Was this their compromise?

"You okay?" Jared asked.

My throat was too thick to answer. I shook my head. Tears streamed down my cheeks and fell from my chin to my lap.

"Maybe I'd better drive."

I shook my head again. I could see well enough.

He didn't argue with me.

I was still crying silently when we got to the little mountain that hid our vast cave system. It was actually just a hill — an insignificant outcropping of volcanic rock, like so many others, sparsely decorated with spindly creosote and flat-bladed prickly pears. The thousands of tiny vents were invisible, lost in the jumble of loose purple rocks. Somewhere, smoke would be rising, black on black.

I got out of the van and leaned against the door, wiping my eyes. Jared came to stand beside me. He hesitated, then put a hand on my shoulder.

"Sorry. I didn't know they were planning this. I had no idea. They shouldn't have . . ."

But he only thought that because they'd somehow gotten caught.

The moving truck rumbled to a stop behind us. Two doors slammed shut, and then feet were running toward us.

"What happened?" Kyle demanded, there first.

Ian was right behind him. He took one look at my

expression, at the tears still running down my cheeks, at Jared's hand on my shoulder, and then rushed forward and threw his arms around me. He pulled me into his chest. I didn't know why this made me cry harder. I clung to him while my tears leaked onto his shirt.

"It's okay. You did great. It's over."

"Seeker's not the problem, Ian," Jared said, voice strained, his hand still touching me, though he had to lean forward to preserve that point of contact.

"Huh?"

"They were watching the road for a reason. Sounds like Doc's been . . . working in our absence."

I shuddered, and for a moment, it seemed like I could taste silver blood in the back of my throat.

"Why, those —!" Ian's fury robbed him of speech. He couldn't finish his sentence.

"Nice," Kyle said in a disgusted tone. "Idiots. We're gone for a few weeks, and they've got the Seekers on patrol. They could have just asked us to —"

"Shut up, Kyle," Jared said harshly. "That's neither here nor there at the moment. We've got to get this all unloaded fast. Who knows how many are watching for us? Let's grab a load and then get some more hands."

I shook Ian off so that I could help. The tears did not stop running. Ian stayed close to my side, taking the heavy flat of canned soup I picked up and replacing it with a big but light box of pasta.

We started down the steep pathway in, Jared leading. The utter blackness did not bother me. I still didn't know this path well, but it wasn't difficult. Straight down, then straight up.

We were halfway there when a familiar voice called

out from a distance. It echoed down the tunnel, fracturing.

"They're back . . . ack . . . back!" Jamie was shouting.

I tried to dry my tears on my shoulder, but I couldn't get them all.

A blue light approached, bouncing as the carrier ran. Then Jamie bounded into view.

His face threw me.

I was trying to compose myself to greet him, assuming he would be joyful and not wanting to upset him. But Jamie was already upset. His face was white and tense, his eyes rimmed in red. His dirty cheeks had rivulets through the dust there, tracks made by tears.

"Jamie?" Jared and I said together, dropping our boxes to the floor.

Jamie ran straight for me and threw his arms around my waist.

"Oh, Wanda! Oh, Jared!" he sobbed. "Wes is dead! He's *dead!* The Seeker killed him!"

# CHAPTER 49

# Interrogated

I killed Wes.

My hands, scratched and bruised and painted with purple dust in the course of the frantic unloading, might as well have been painted red with his blood.

Wes was dead, and it was as much my fault as if I'd pulled the trigger myself.

All of us but five were gathered in the kitchen now that the truck was unloaded, eating some of the perishables we'd picked up on the final shopping trip — cheese and fresh bread with milk — and listening to Jeb and Doc as they explained everything to Jared, Ian, and Kyle.

I sat a little space away from the others, my head in my hands, too numb with grief and guilt to ask questions the way they did. Jamie sat with me. He patted my back now and then.

Wes was already buried in the dark grotto beside

Walter. He had died four days ago, the night that Jared and Ian and I had sat watching the family in the park. I would never see my friend again, never hear his voice . . .

Tears splashed on the stone beneath me, and Jamie's pats increased in tempo.

Andy and Paige were not here.

They'd driven the truck and the van back to their hiding places. They would take the jeep from there to its usual rough garage, and then they'd have to walk the rest of the way home. They would be back before sunrise.

Lily was not here.

"She's not . . . doing so well," Jamie had murmured when he'd caught me scanning the room for her. I didn't want to know any more. I could imagine well enough.

Aaron and Brandt were not here.

Brandt now bore a smooth, pink, circular scar in the hollow space beneath his left collarbone. The bullet had missed his heart and lungs by a hair and then burrowed halfway through his shoulder blade trying to escape. Doc had used most of the Heal getting it out of him. Brandt was fine now.

Wes's bullet had been better aimed. It had pierced his high olive-skinned forehead and blown out the back of his head. There was nothing Doc could have done, even if he'd been right there with them, a gallon of Heal at his disposal.

Brandt, who now carried in a holster on his hip a boxy, heavy trophy from the encounter, was with Aaron. They were in the tunnel where we would have stored our spoils if it had not been occupied. If it was not being used as a prison again.

As if losing Wes was not enough.

It seemed hideously wrong to me that the numbers remained the same. Thirty-five living bodies, just like before I'd come to the caves. Wes and Walter were gone, but I was here.

And now so was the Seeker.

My Seeker.

If I'd just gone straight to Tucson. If I had just stayed in San Diego. If I had just skipped this planet and gone somewhere entirely different. If I'd given myself as a Mother like anyone else would have after five or six planets. If, if, if . . . If I had not come here, if I had not given the Seeker the clues she needed to follow, then Wes would be alive. It had taken her longer than me to figure them out, but when she did, she didn't have to pursue them with caution. She'd barreled through the desert in an all-terrain SUV, leaving bright new scars across the fragile desert landscape, each pass getting closer.

They had to do something. They had to stop her.

I had killed Wes.

*They still would have caught me in the first place, Wanda. I led them here, not you.*

I was too miserable to answer her.

*Besides, if we hadn't come here, Jamie would be dead. And maybe Jared, too. He would have died tonight, without you.*

Death on every side. Death everywhere I looked.

*Why did she have to follow me?* I moaned to myself. *I'm not* hurting *the other souls here, not really. I'm even saving some of their lives by being here, by keeping Doc from his doomed efforts. Why did she have to follow?*

*Why did they keep her?* Mel snarled. *Why didn't they*

*kill her right away? Or kill her slow — I don't care how! Why is she still alive?*

Fear fluttered in my stomach. The Seeker was alive; the Seeker was here.

I shouldn't have been afraid of her.

Of course, it made sense to be afraid that her disappearance would bring the other Seekers down on us. Everyone was afraid of that. Spying on the search for my body, the humans had seen how vocal she was about her convictions. She'd been trying to convince the other Seekers that there were humans hiding in this desert wasteland. None seemed to take her seriously. They had gone home; she was the only one who kept looking.

But now she'd vanished in the middle of her search. That changed everything.

Her vehicle had been moved far away, left in the desert on the other side of Tucson. It looked as though she'd disappeared in the same way it was believed I had: pieces of her bag left torn nearby, the snacks she'd carried with her chewed open and scattered. Would the other souls accept such a coincidence?

We already knew they would not. Not entirely. They were looking. Would the search become more intense?

But to be afraid of the Seeker herself . . . That didn't make much sense. She was physically insignificant, probably smaller than Jamie. I was stronger and faster than she was. I was surrounded by friends and allies, and she, inside these caves at least, was all alone. Two guns, the rifle and her own Glock — the very gun Ian had once envied, the gun that had killed my friend Wes — were trained on her at every moment. Only one thing had kept her alive until now, and it couldn't save her for long.

Jeb had thought I might want to talk to her. That was all.

Now that I was back, she was condemned to die within hours whether I spoke to her or not.

So why did I feel as though I was at the disadvantage? Why this strange premonition that *she* would be the one to walk away from our confrontation?

I hadn't decided if I wanted to talk to her. At least, that was what I'd told Jeb.

Without a doubt, I did *not* want to talk to her. I was terrified to ever see her face again — a face that, no matter how I tried, I could not imagine looking frightened.

But if I told them I had no desire for conversation, Aaron would shoot her. It would be like I'd given him the order to fire. Like I'd pulled the trigger.

Or worse, Doc would try to cut her out of the human body. I flinched away from the memory of the silver blood smeared all over the hands of my friend.

Melanie twisted uneasily, trying to escape the torment in my head.

*Wanda? They're just going to shoot her. Don't panic.*

Should this comfort me? I couldn't avoid the imagined tableau. Aaron, the Seeker's gun in his hand; the Seeker's body slowly crumpling to the stone floor, the red blood pooling around her . . .

*You don't have to watch.*

That wouldn't stop it from happening.

Melanie's thoughts became a little frantic. *But we want her to die. Right? She killed Wes! Besides, she can't stay alive. No matter what.*

She was right about everything, of course. It was true that there was no way the Seeker could stay alive. Imprisoned, she would work doggedly to escape. Freed, she would quickly be the death of all my family.

It was true she had killed Wes. He was so young and so loved. His death left a burning agony in its wake. I understood the claim of human justice that demanded her life in return.

It was also true that I wanted her to die.

"Wanda? Wanda?"

Jamie shook my arm. It took me a moment to realize that someone had called my name. Perhaps many times already.

"Wanda?" Jeb's voice asked again.

I looked up. He was standing over me. His face was expressionless, the blank facade that meant he was in the grip of some strong emotion. His poker face.

"The boys want to know if you have any questions for the Seeker."

I put one hand to my forehead, trying to block the images there. "If I don't?"

"They're ready to be done with guard duty. It's a hard time. They'd rather be with their friends right now."

I nodded. "Okay. I guess I'd better . . . go and see her at once, then." I shoved myself away from the wall and to my feet. My hands were shaking, so I clenched them into fists.

*You don't have any questions.*

*I'll think of some.*

*Why prolong the inevitable?*

*I have no idea.*

*You're trying to save her,* Melanie accused, full of outrage.

*There's no way to do that.*

*No. There isn't. And you want her dead anyway. So let them shoot her.*

I cringed.

"You okay?" Jamie asked.

I nodded, not trusting my voice enough to speak.

"You don't have to," Jeb told me, his eyes sharp on my face.

"It's okay," I whispered.

Jamie's hand wrapped around mine, but I shook it off. "Stay here, Jamie."

"I'll come with you."

My voice was stronger now. "Oh, no, you will *not*."

We stared at each other for a moment, and for once I won the argument. He stuck his chin out stubbornly but slouched back against the wall.

Ian, too, seemed inclined to follow me out of the kitchen, but I stopped him in his tracks with a single look. Jared watched me go with an unfathomable expression.

"She's a complainer," Jeb told me in a low voice as we walked back toward the hole. "Not quiet like you were. Always asking for more — food, water, pillows . . . She threatens a lot, too. 'The Seekers will get you all!' That kinda thing. It's been hard on Brandt especially. She's pushed his temper right to the edge."

I nodded. This did not surprise me one bit.

"She hasn't tried to escape, though. A lot of talk and no action. Once the guns come up, she backs right down."

I recoiled.

"My guess is, she wants to live pretty dang bad," Jeb murmured to himself.

"Are you sure this is the . . . safest place to keep her?" I asked as we started down the black, twisting tunnel.

Jeb chuckled. "You didn't find your way out," he reminded me. "Sometimes the best hiding place is the one that's in plain sight."

My answer was flat. "She's more motivated than I was."

"The boys're keepin' a sharp eye on her. Nothin' to worry about."

We were almost there. The tunnel turned back on itself in a sharp V.

How many times had I rounded this corner, my hand tracing along the inside of the pointed switchback, just like this? I'd never traced along the outside wall. It was uneven, with jutting rocks that would leave bruises and cause me to trip. Staying on the inside was a shorter walk anyway.

When they'd first showed me that the V was not a V but a Y — two branches forking off from another tunnel, *the* tunnel — I'd felt pretty stupid. Like Jeb said, hiding things in plain sight was sometimes the cleverest route. The times I'd been desperate enough to even consider escaping the caves, my mind had skipped right over this place in my speculations. This was the hole, the prison. In my head, it was the darkest, deepest well in the caves. This was where they'd buried me.

Even Mel, sneakier than I was, had never dreamed that they'd held me captive just a few paces from the exit.

It wasn't even the only exit. But the other was small and tight, a crawl space. I hadn't found that one because I'd walked into these caves standing upright. I hadn't been looking for *that* kind of tunnel. Besides, I'd never explored the edges of Doc's hospital; I'd avoided it from the beginning.

The voice, familiar even though it seemed part of another life, interrupted my thoughts.

"I wonder how you're still alive, eating like this. Ugh!"

Something plastic clattered against the rocks.

I could see the blue light as we rounded the last corner.

"I didn't know humans had the patience to starve someone to death. That seems like too complex a plan for you shortsighted creatures to grasp."

Jeb chuckled. "Gotta say, I'm impressed with those boys. Surprised they held up this long."

We turned into the lit dead-end tunnel. Brandt and Aaron, both sitting as far as possible from the end of the tunnel where the Seeker paced, both with guns in their hands, sighed with relief when they saw us approaching.

"Finally," Brandt muttered. His face was etched in hard lines of grief.

The Seeker halted in her pacing.

I was surprised to see the conditions she was kept in.

She was not stuffed into the tiny cramped hole, but comparatively free, stomping to and fro across the short width of the tunnel. On the floor, against the flat end of the tunnel, were a mat and a pillow. A plastic tray was tilted at an angle against the wall at about the midpoint of the cave; a few jicama roots lay scattered near it with a soup bowl. A little soup was splattered out from where that lay. This explained the clatter I'd just heard — she'd thrown her food. It looked as though she'd eaten most of it first, though.

I stared at this relatively humane setup and felt an odd pain in my stomach.

*Who did* we *kill?* Melanie muttered sullenly. This stung her, too.

"You want a minute with her?" Brandt asked me, and the pain stabbed again. Had Brandt ever referred to *me* using a feminine pronoun? I wasn't surprised that Jeb had done this for the Seeker, but everyone else?

"Yes," I whispered.

"Careful," Aaron cautioned. "She's an angry little thing."

I nodded.

The others stayed where they were. I walked down the tunnel alone.

It was hard to lift my eyes, to meet the gaze that I could feel like cold fingers pressing against my face.

The Seeker was glaring at me, a harsh sneer twisting her features. I'd never seen a soul use that expression before.

"Well, hello there, *Melanie*," she mocked me. "What took you so long to come visit?"

I didn't answer. I walked toward her slowly, trying hard to believe that the hate coursing through my body really did not belong to me.

"Did your little friends think I would talk to you? Spill all my secrets because you carry a gagged and lobotomized soul around in your head, reflecting through your eyes?" She laughed abrasively.

I stopped two long strides away from her, my body tensed to run. She made no aggressive move toward me, but I could not relax my muscles. This was not like meeting the Seeker on the highway — I didn't have the usual sensation of safety that I felt around the gentle others of my kind. Again, the strange conviction that she would live long after I was gone swept through me.

*Don't be ridiculous. Ask her your questions. Have you come up with any?*

"So, what do you want? Did you request permission to kill me personally, Melanie?" the Seeker hissed.

"They call me Wanda here," I said.

She flinched slightly when I opened my lips to speak, as if expecting me to shout. My low, even voice seemed to upset her more than the scream she anticipated.

I examined her face while she glared at me with her bulging eyes. It was dirty, stained with purple dust and dried sweat. Other than that, there wasn't a mark on it. Again, this gave me an odd ache.

"Wanda," she repeated in a flat voice. "Well, what are you waiting for? Didn't they give you the okay? Were you planning to use your bare hands or my gun?"

"I'm not here to kill you."

She smiled sourly. "To interrogate me, then? Where are your instruments of torture, human?"

I cringed. "I won't hurt you."

Insecurity flickered across her face and then vanished behind her sneer. "What are they keeping me for, then? Do they think I can be tamed, like your pet soul?"

"No. They just . . . they didn't want to kill you until they had . . . consulted me. In case I wanted to talk to you first."

Her lids lowered, narrowing her protruding eyes. "Do you have something to say?"

I swallowed. "I was wondering . . ." I only had the same question I'd been unable to answer for myself. "Why? Why couldn't you let me be dead, like the rest of them? Why were you so determined to hunt me down? I didn't want to hurt anyone. I just wanted . . . to go my own way."

She leaped up onto her toes, shoving her face toward mine. Someone moved behind me, but I couldn't hear more than that — she was shouting in my face.

"Because I was *right!*" she shrieked. "More than right! *Look* at them all! A vile nest of killers, lurking in wait! Just like I thought, only so much *worse!* I *knew* you were out here with them! *One* of them! I *told* them there was danger! I *told* them!"

She stopped, panting, and took a step back from me, staring over my shoulder. I didn't look away to see what had made her retreat. I assumed it had something to do with what Jeb had just told me — *once the guns come up, she backs right down.* I analyzed her expression for a moment as her heavy breathing slowed.

"But they didn't listen to you. So you came for us alone."

The Seeker didn't answer. She took another step back from me, doubt twisting her expression. She looked oddly vulnerable for a second, as if my words had stripped away the shield she'd been hiding behind.

"They'll look for you, but in the end, they never believed you at all, did they?" I said, watching as each word was confirmed in her desperate eyes. It made me very sure. "So they won't take the search further than that. When they don't find you, their interest will fade. We'll be careful, as usual. They won't find us."

Now I could see true fear in her eyes for the first time. The terrible — to her — knowledge that I was right. And I felt better for my nest of humans, my little family. I *was* right. They would be safe. Yet, incongruously, I didn't feel any better for myself.

I had no more questions for the Seeker. When I walked away, she would die. Would they wait until I was far enough not to hear the shot? Was there anywhere in the caves that was far enough for that?

I stared at her angry, fearful face, and I knew how deeply I hated her. How much I never wanted to see that face again for the rest of my lives.

The hate that made it impossible for me to allow her to die.

"I don't know how to save you," I whispered, too low for the humans to hear. Why did that sound like a lie in my ears? "I can't think of a way."

"Why would you want to? You're one of them!" But a spasm of hope sparked in her eyes. Jeb was right. All the bluster, all the threats . . . She wanted very much to stay alive.

I nodded at her accusation, a little absently because I was thinking hard and fast. "But still me," I murmured. "I don't want . . . I don't want . . ."

How to finish that sentence? I didn't want . . . the Seeker to die? No. That wasn't true.

I didn't want . . . to hate the Seeker? To hate her so much that I wanted her to die. To have her die while I hated her. Almost as if she died *because* of my hate.

If I truly did not want her death, would I be able to think of a way to save her? Was it my hate that was blocking an answer? Would I be responsible if she died?

*Are you insane?* Melanie protested.

She'd killed my friend, shot him dead in the desert, broken Lily's heart. She'd put my family in danger. As long as she lived, she was a danger to them. To Ian, to Jamie, to Jared. She would do everything in her power to see them all dead.

*That's more like it.* Melanie approved of this train of thought.

*But if she dies, and I could have saved her if I'd wanted to . . . who am I then?*

*You have to be practical, Wanda. This is a war. Whose side are you on?*

*You know the answer to that.*

*I do. And that's who you are, Wanda.*

*But . . . but what if I could do both? What if I could save her life and keep everyone here safe at the same time?*

A heavy wave of nausea rolled in my stomach as I saw the answer I'd been trying to believe didn't exist.

The only wall I'd ever built between Melanie and me crumbled to dust.

*No!* Mel gasped. And then screamed, *NO!*

The answer I must have known I would find. The answer that explained my strange premonition.

Because I could save the Seeker. Of course I could. But it would cost me. A trade. What had Kyle said? A life for a life.

The Seeker stared at me, her dark eyes full of venom.

# CHAPTER 50

# Sacrificed

The Seeker scrutinized my face while Mel and I fought.

*No, Wanda, no!*

*Don't be stupid, Mel. You of all people should see the potential of this choice. Isn't this what you want?*

But even as I tried to look at the happy ending, I couldn't escape the horror of this choice. This was the secret I should die to protect. The information I'd been desperate to keep safe no matter what hideous torture I was put through.

This was not the kind of torture I'd expected: a personal crisis of conscience, confused and complicated by love for my human family. Very painful, nevertheless.

I could not claim to be an expatriate if I did this. No, I would be purely a traitor.

*Not for her, Wanda! Not for her!* Mel howled.

*Should I wait? Wait until they catch another soul? An innocent soul whom I have no reason to hate? I'll have to make the decision sometime.*

*Not now! Wait! Think about this!*

My stomach rolled again, and I had to hunch my body forward and take a deep breath. I just managed not to gag.

"Wanda?" Jeb called in concern.

*I could do it, Mel. I could justify letting her die if she was one of those innocent souls. I could let them kill her then. I could trust myself to make an objective decision.*

*But she's horrible, Wanda! We hate her!*

*Exactly. And I can't trust myself. Look at how I almost didn't see the answer . . .*

"Wanda, you all right?"

The Seeker glared past me, toward Jeb's voice.

"Fine, Jeb," I gasped. My voice was breathy, strained. I was surprised at how bad it sounded.

The Seeker's dark eyes flickered between us, unsure. Then she recoiled from me, cringing into the wall. I recognized the pose — remembered exactly how it felt to hold it.

A gentle hand came down on my shoulder and spun me around.

"What's going on with you, hon?" Jeb asked.

"I need a minute," I told him breathlessly. I looked straight into his faded-denim eyes and told him something that was most definitely not a lie. "I have one more question. But I really need a minute to myself. Can you . . . wait for me?"

"Sure, we can wait a little while more. Take a breather."

I nodded and walked as quickly as I could from the prison. My legs were stiff with terror at first, but I found my stride as I moved. By the time I passed Aaron and Brandt, I was almost running.

"What happened?" I heard Aaron whisper to Brandt, his voice bewildered.

I wasn't sure where to hide while I thought. My feet, like a shuttle on automatic pilot, took me through the corridors toward my sleeping room. I could only hope that it would be empty.

It was dark, barely any light from the stars trickling down through the cracked ceiling. I didn't see Lily till I tripped over her in the darkness.

I almost didn't recognize her tear-swollen face. She was curled into a tight, tiny ball on the floor in the middle of the passageway. Her eyes were wide, not quite comprehending who I was.

"Why?" she asked me.

I stared at her wordlessly.

"I said that life and love go on. But *why* do they? They shouldn't. Not anymore. What's the point?"

"I don't know, Lily. I'm not sure what the point is."

"Why?" she asked again, not speaking to me anymore. Her glassy eyes looked right through me.

I stepped carefully past her and hurried to my room. I had my own question that had to be answered.

To my great relief, the room was empty. I threw myself facedown on the mattress where Jamie and I slept.

When I'd told Jeb I had one more question, that was the truth. But the question was not for the Seeker. The question was for me.

The question was would I — not *could* I — do it?

I *could* save the Seeker's life. I knew how. It would not endanger any of the lives here. Except my own. I would have to trade that.

*No.* Melanie tried to be firm through her panic.

*Please let me think.*

*No.*

*This is the thing, Mel. It's inevitable anyway. I can see that now. I should have seen it long ago. It's so obvious.*

*No, it isn't.*

I remembered our conversation when Jamie was ill. When we were making up. I'd told her that I wouldn't erase her and that I was sorry that I couldn't give her more than that.

It wasn't so much a lie as it was an unfinished sentence. I couldn't give her more than that — and stay alive myself.

The actual lie had been given to Jared. I'd told him, just seconds later, that I didn't know how to make myself not exist. In the context of our discussion, it was true. I didn't know how to fade away, here inside Melanie. But I was surprised I hadn't heard the obvious lie right then, hadn't seen in that moment what I was seeing now. Of course I knew how to make myself not exist.

It was just that I had never considered that option viable, ultimate betrayal that it was to every soul on this planet.

Once the humans knew that I had this answer, the one they had murdered for over and over again, it would cost me.

*No, Wanda!*

*Don't you want to be free?*

A long pause.

*I wouldn't ask you for this,* she finally said. *And I wouldn't do it for you. And I sure as hell wouldn't do it for the Seeker!*

*You don't have to ask. I think I might have volunteered . . . eventually.*

*Why do you think that?* she demanded, her tone close to a sob. It touched me. I expected her to be elated.

*In part because of them. Jared and Jamie. I can give them the whole world, everything they want. I can give them you. I probably would have realized that . . . someday. Who knows? Maybe Jared would have asked. You know I wouldn't have said no.*

*Ian's right. You're too self-sacrificing. You don't have any limits. You need limits, Wanda!*

*Ah, Ian,* I moaned. A new pain twisted through me, surprisingly close to my heart.

*You'll take the whole world away from him. Everything he wants.*

*It would never work with Ian. Not in this body, even though he loves it. It doesn't love him.*

*Wanda, I . . .* Melanie struggled for words. Still, the joy I expected from her did not come. Again, this touched me. *I don't think I can let you do this. You're more important than that. In the bigger picture, you are of much more value to them than I am. You can help them; you can save them. I can't do any of that. You have to stay.*

*I can't see any other way, Mel. I wonder how I didn't see it sooner. It seems so completely obvious.* Of course *I have to go.* Of course *I have to give you yourself back. I already knew we souls were wrong to come here. So I don't have any choice now but to do the right thing, and leave. You all survived without me before; you'll do it again. You've learned so much about the souls from me — you'll help them. Can't you see? This is the happy ending. It's the way they all need the story to finish. I can give them hope. I can give them . . . not a future. Maybe not that. But as much as I can. Everything I can.*

*No, Wanda, no.*

She was crying, becoming incoherent. Her sorrow brought tears to my eyes. I'd no idea that she cared so much for me. Almost as much as I cared for her. I hadn't realized that we loved each other.

Even if Jared had never asked me for this, even if Jared did not exist . . . Once this path had occurred to me, I would have had to proceed down it. I loved her that much.

No wonder the success rate for resistant hosts was so low here on Earth. Once we learned to love our human host, what hope did we souls have? We could not exist at the expense of one we loved. Not a soul. A soul could not live that way.

I rolled myself over and, in the starlight, I looked at my body.

My hands were dirty and scratched, but under the surface blemishes, they were beautiful. The skin was a pretty sun-browned color; even bleached in the pale light, it was pretty. The nails were chewed short but still healthy and smooth, with little half moons of white at the bases. I fluttered my fingers, watching the muscles pull the bones in graceful patterns. I let them dance above me, where they became black fluid shapes against the stars.

I ran them through my hair. It was almost to my shoulders now. Mel would like that. After a few weeks of shampoo in hotel showers and Health vitamins, it was glossy and soft again.

I stretched my arms out as far as they would go, tugging against the tendons until some of my joints cracked. My arms felt strong. They could pull me up a mountainside, they could carry a heavy load, they could plow a field. But they were also soft. They could hold a child, they could comfort a friend, they could love . . . but that was not for me.

I took a deep breath, and tears welled out of the corners of my eyes and rolled down my temples into my hair.

I tensed the muscles in my legs, felt their ready strength and speed. I wanted to run, to have an open field that I could race across just to see how fast I could go. I wanted to do this barefoot, so I could feel the earth beneath my feet. I wanted to feel the wind fly through my hair. I wanted it to rain, so that I could smell it in the air as I ran.

My feet flexed and pointed slowly, to the rhythm of my breathing. In and out. Flex and point. It felt nice.

I traced my face with my fingertips. They were warm on my skin, skin that was smooth and pretty. I was glad I was giving Melanie her face back the way it had been. I closed my eyes and stroked my eyelids.

I'd lived in so many bodies, but never one I loved like this. Never one that I craved in this way. Of course, this would be the one I'd have to give up.

The irony made me laugh, and I concentrated on the feel of the air that popped in little bubbles from my chest and up through my throat. Laughter was like a fresh breeze — it cleaned its way through the body, making everything feel good. Did other species have such a simple healer? I couldn't remember one.

I touched my lips and remembered how it felt to kiss Jared, and how it felt to kiss Ian. Not everyone got to kiss so many other beautiful bodies. I'd had more than some, even in this short time.

It was just so short! Maybe a year now, I wasn't completely sure. Just one quick revolution of a blue green planet around an unexceptional yellow star. The shortest life of any I'd ever lived.

The shortest, the most important, the most heartbreaking of lives. The life that would forever define me. The life that had finally tied me to one star, to one planet, to one small family of strangers.

A little more time . . . would that be so wrong?

*No,* Mel whispered. *Just take a little more time.*

*You never know how much time you'll have,* I whispered back.

But I did. I knew exactly how much time I had. I couldn't take any more time. My time was up.

I was going anyway. I had to do the right thing, be my true self, with what time I had left.

With a sigh that seemed to come all the way from the soles of my feet and the palms of my hands, I got up.

Aaron and Brandt wouldn't wait forever. And now I had a few more questions that I needed answered. This time, the questions were for Doc.

The caves were full of sad, cast-down eyes. It was easy enough to slip unobtrusively past them all. No one cared what I was doing right now, except maybe Jeb, Brandt, and Aaron, and they weren't here.

I didn't have an open, rainy field, but at least I had the

long south tunnel. It was too dark to run flat out the way I wanted, but I kept up a steady jog. It felt good as my muscles warmed.

I expected I would find Doc already there, but I'd wait if I had to. He would be alone. Poor Doc, that was usually the case now.

Doc had been sleeping alone in his hospital since the night we'd saved Jamie's life. Sharon had taken her things from their room and moved them to her mother's, and Doc wouldn't sleep in the empty room.

Such a great hatred. Sharon would rather kill her own happiness, and Doc's, too, than forgive him for helping me heal Jamie.

Sharon and Maggie were barely a presence in the caves anymore. They looked past everyone now, the way they used to look past only me. I wondered if that would change when I was gone, or if they were both so rigid in their grudge that it would be too late for them to change.

What an extraordinarily stupid way to waste time.

For the first time ever, the south tunnel felt short. Before I thought I'd gone halfway, I could see Doc's light glowing dimly from the rough arch ahead. He was home.

I slowed myself to a walk before I interrupted him. I didn't want to scare him, to make him think there was an emergency.

He was still startled when I appeared, a little breathless, in the stone doorway.

He jumped up from behind his desk. The book he was reading fell out of his hands.

"Wanda? Is something wrong?"

"No, Doc," I reassured him. "Everything's fine."

"Does someone need me?"

"Just me." I gave him a weak smile.

He walked around his desk to meet me, his eyes wide with curiosity. He paused half a step away and raised one eyebrow.

His long face was gentle, the opposite of alarming. It was hard to remember how he'd looked like a monster to me before.

"You are a man of your word," I began.

He nodded and opened his mouth to speak, but I held one hand up.

"No one will ever test that more than I will test it now," I warned him.

He waited, eyes confused and wary.

I took a deep breath, felt it expand my lungs.

"I know how to do what you've been ending so many lives to discover. I know how to take the souls from your bodies without harm to either. Of course I know that. We all have to, in case of an emergency. I even performed the emergency procedure once, when I was a Bear."

I stared at him, waiting for his response. It took him a long moment, and his eyes grew wilder every second.

"Why are you telling me this?" he finally gasped.

"Because I . . . I am going to give you the knowledge you need." I held up my hand again. "But only if you will give me what I want in return. I'm warning you right now, it won't be any easier for you to give me what I want than it will be for me to give you what you want."

His face was fiercer than I'd ever seen it. "Name your terms."

"You can't kill them — the souls you remove. You must give me your word — your promise, your oath, your vow — that you will give them safe conduct on to another life. This means some danger; you will have to have cryo-tanks, and you will have to get those souls onto shuttles off-planet. You have to send them to another world to live. But they won't be able to hurt you. By the time they reach their next planet, your grandchildren will be dead."

Would my conditions mitigate my guilt in this? Only if Doc could be trusted.

He was thinking very hard as I explained. I watched his face to see what he would make of my demand. He didn't look angry, but his eyes were still wild.

"You don't want us to kill the Seeker?" he guessed.

I didn't answer his question because he wouldn't understand the answer; I did want them to kill her. That was the whole problem. Instead, I explained further.

"She'll be the first, the test. I want to make sure, while I'm still here, that you're going to follow through. I will do the separation myself. When she is safe, I'll teach you how it's done."

"On who?"

"Kidnapped souls. The same as before. I can't guarantee you that the human minds will come back. I don't know if the erased can return. We'll see with the Seeker."

Doc blinked, processing something. "What do you mean, while you are still here? Are you leaving?"

I stared at him, waiting for the realization to hit. He stared back, uncomprehending.

"Don't you realize what I'm giving you?" I whispered.

Finally, comprehension slammed home in his expression.

I spoke quickly, before he could. "There's something

else I'm going to ask you for, Doc. I don't want to . . . I *won't* be shipped off to another planet. This is my planet, it truly is. And yet, there's really no place for me here. So . . . I know it might . . . offend some of the others. Don't tell them if you think they won't allow it. Lie if you have to. But I'd like to be buried by Walt and Wes. Can you do that for me? I won't take up much space." I smiled weakly again.

*No!* Melanie was howling. *No, no, no, no . . .*

"No, Wanda," Doc objected, too, with a shocked expression.

"Please, Doc," I whispered, wincing against the protest in my head, which was getting louder. "I don't think Wes or Walt will mind."

"That's not what I meant! I can't kill you, Wanda. Ugh! I'm so sick of death, so sick of killing my friends." Doc's voice caught in a sob.

I put my hand on his thin arm, rubbed it. "People die here. It happens." Kyle had said something to that effect. Funny that I should quote Kyle of all people twice in one night.

"What about Jared and Jamie?" Doc asked in a choked voice.

"They'll have Melanie. They'll be fine."

"Ian?"

Through my teeth. "Better off without me."

Doc shook his head, wiping at his eyes. "I need to think about this, Wanda."

"We don't have long. They won't wait forever before they kill the Seeker."

"I don't mean about that part. I agree to those terms. But I don't think I can kill you."

"It's all or none, Doc. You have to decide right now. And . . ." I realized I had one more demand. "And you can't tell anyone else about the last part of our agreement. No one. Those are my terms, take them or leave them. Do you want to know how to remove a soul from a human body?"

Doc shook his head again. "Let me think."

"You already know the answer, Doc. This is what you've been searching for."

He just kept shaking his head slowly back and forth.

I ignored that symbol of denial because we both knew his choice was made.

"I'll get Jared," I said. "We'll make a quick raid for cryotanks. Hold off the others. Tell them . . . tell them the truth. Tell them I'm going to help you get the Seeker out of that body."

# CHAPTER 51

# *Prepared*

I found Jared and Jamie in our room, waiting for me, worry on both their faces. Jared must have talked to Jeb.

"Are you all right?" Jared asked me, while Jamie jumped up and threw his arms around my waist.

I wasn't sure how to answer his question. I didn't know the answer. "Jared, I need your help."

Jared was on his feet as soon as I was done speaking. Jamie leaned back to look at my face. I didn't meet Jamie's gaze. I wasn't sure how much I could bear right now.

"What do you need me to do?" Jared asked.

"I'm making a raid. I could use some . . . extra muscle."

"What are we after?" He was intense, already shifting into his mission mode.

"I'll explain on the way. We don't have a lot of time."

"Can I come?" Jamie said.

"No!" Jared and I said together.

Jamie frowned and let me go, sinking down onto the mattress and crossing his legs. He put his face in his hands and sulked. I couldn't look directly at him before I ducked out of the room. I was already yearning to sit beside him, to hold him tight and forget this whole mess.

Jared followed as I retraced my path through the south tunnel.

"Why this way?" he asked.

"I . . ." He would know if I tried to lie or evade. "I don't want to run into anyone. Jeb, Aaron, or Brandt, particularly."

"Why?"

"I don't want to have to explain myself to them. Not yet."

He was quiet, trying to make sense of my answer.

I changed the subject. "Do you know where Lily is? I don't think she should be alone. She seems . . ."

"Ian's with her."

"That's good. He's the kindest."

Ian would help Lily — he was exactly what she needed now. Who would help Ian when . . . ? I shook my head, shaking the thought away.

"What are we in such a hurry to get?" Jared asked me.

I took a deep breath before I answered him. "Cryotanks."

The south tunnel was black. I could not see his face. His footsteps did not falter beside me, and he didn't say anything for several minutes. When he spoke again, I could hear that he was focusing on the raid — singleminded, setting aside whatever curiosity he felt until after the mission was planned to his satisfaction.

"Where do we get them?"

"Empty cryotanks are stored outside Healing facilities until they're needed. With more souls coming in than leaving, there will be a surplus. No one will guard them; no one will notice if some go missing."

"Are you sure? Where did you get this information?"

"I saw them in Chicago, piles and piles of them. Even the little facility we went to in Tucson had a small store of them, crated outside the delivery bay."

"If they were crated, then how can you be sure —"

"Haven't you noticed our fondness for labels?"

"I'm not doubting you," he said. "I just want to make sure that you've thought this through."

I heard the double meaning in his words.

"I have."

"Let's get it done, then."

Doc was already gone — already with Jeb, as we hadn't passed him on the way. He must have left right behind me. I wondered how his news was being taken. I hoped they weren't stupid enough to discuss it in front of the Seeker. Would she shred her human host's brain if she guessed what I was doing? Would she assume I'd turned traitor entirely? That I would give the humans what they needed with no restrictions?

Wasn't that what I was about to do, though? When I was gone, would Doc bother to keep his word?

Yes, he *would* try. I believed that. I had to believe that. But he couldn't do it alone. And who would help him?

We scrambled up the tight black vent that opened onto the southern face of the rocky hill, about halfway up the low peak. The eastern edge of the horizon was turning gray, with just a hint of pink bleeding into the line between sky and rock.

My eyes were locked on my feet as I climbed down. It was necessary; there was no path, and the loose rocks made for treacherous footing. But even if the way had been paved and smooth, I doubted I would have been able to lift my eyes. My shoulders, too, seemed trapped in a slump.

Traitor. Not a misfit, not a wanderer. Just a traitor. I was putting my gentle brothers' and sisters' lives into the angry and motivated hands of my adopted human family.

My humans had every right to hate the souls. This was a war, and I was giving them a weapon. A way to kill with impunity.

I considered this as we ran through the desert in the growing light of dawn — ran because, with the Seekers looking, we shouldn't be out in the daylight.

Focusing on this angle — viewing my choice not as a sacrifice but rather as arming the humans in exchange for the Seeker's life — I knew that it was wrong. And if I was trying to save only the Seeker, this would be the moment when I would change my mind and turn around. She wasn't worth selling out the others. Even she would agree with that.

Or would she? I suddenly wondered. The Seeker didn't seem to be as . . . what was the word Jared had used? *Altruistic.* As altruistic as the rest of us. Maybe she would count her own life dearer than the lives of many.

But it was too late to change my mind. I'd already thought far beyond just saving the Seeker. For one thing, this would happen again. The humans would kill any souls they came across unless I gave them another option. More than that, I was going to save Melanie, and that was worth the sacrifice. I was going to save Jared and Jamie, too. Might as well save the repugnant Seeker while I was at it.

The souls were wrong to be here. My humans deserved their world. I could not give it back to them, but I could give them this. If only I could be sure that they would not be cruel.

I would just have to trust Doc, and hope.

And maybe wring the promise from a few more of my friends, just in case.

I wondered how many human lives I would save. How many souls' lives I *might* save. The only one I couldn't save now was myself.

I sighed heavily. Even over the sound of our exerted breathing, Jared heard that. In my peripheral vision, I saw his face turn, felt his eyes boring into me, but I did not look over to meet his gaze. I stared at the ground.

We got to the jeep's hiding place before the sun had climbed over the eastern peaks, though the sky was already light blue. We ducked into the shallow cave just as the first rays painted the desert sand gold.

Jared grabbed two bottles of water out of the backseat, tossed one to me, and then lounged against the wall. He gulped down half a bottle and wiped his mouth with the back of his hand before he spoke.

"I could tell you were in a hurry to get out of there, but we need to wait until dark if you're planning a smash and grab."

I swallowed my mouthful of water. "That's fine. I'm sure they'll wait for us now."

His eyes searched my face.

"I saw your Seeker," he told me, watching my reaction. "She's . . . energetic."

I nodded. "And vocal."

He smiled and rolled his eyes. "She doesn't seem to enjoy the accommodations we provided."

My gaze dropped to the floor. "Could be worse," I mumbled. The strangely jealous hurt I'd been feeling leaked, uninvited, into my voice.

"That's true," he agreed, his voice subdued.

"Why are they so kind to her?" I whispered. "She killed Wes."

"Well, that's your fault."

I stared up at him, surprised to see the slight curve of his mouth; he was teasing me.

"Mine?"

His small smile wavered. "They didn't want to feel like monsters. Not again. They're trying to make up for before, only a little too late — and with the wrong soul. I didn't realize that would . . . hurt your feelings. I would have thought you'd like it better that way."

"I do." I didn't want them to hurt anyone. "It's always better to be kind. I just . . ." I took a deep breath. "I'm glad I know why."

Their kindess was for me, not for her. My shoulders felt lighter.

"It's not a good feeling — knowing that you profoundly deserve the title of *monster*. It's better to be kind than to feel guilty." He smiled again and then yawned. That made me yawn.

"Long night," he commented. "And we've got another one coming. We should sleep."

I was glad for his suggestion. I knew he had many

questions about exactly what this raid meant. I also knew he would have already put several things together. And I didn't want to discuss any of it.

I stretched out on the smooth patch of sand beside the jeep. To my shock, Jared came to lie beside me, *right* beside me. He curled around the curve of my back.

"Here," he said, and he reached around to slide his fingers under my face. He pulled my head up from the ground and then moved his arm under it, making a pillow for me. He let his other arm drape over my waist.

It took a few seconds before I was able to respond. "Thanks."

He yawned. I felt his breath warm the back of my neck. "Get some rest, Wanda."

Holding me in what could only be considered an embrace, Jared fell asleep quickly, as he had always been able to do. I tried to relax with his arm warm around me, but it took a long time.

This embrace made me wonder how much he had already guessed.

My weary thoughts tangled and twisted. Jared was right — it had been a very long night. Though not half long enough. The rest of my days and nights were going to fly by as if they were only minutes.

The next thing I knew, Jared was shaking me awake. The light in the little cavern was dim and orangey. Sunset.

Jared pulled me to my feet and handed me a hiker's meal bar — this was the kind of rations they kept with the jeep. We ate, and drank the rest of our water, in silence. Jared's face was serious and focused.

"Still in a hurry?" he asked as we climbed into the jeep.

No. I wanted the time to stretch out forever.

"Yes." What was the point in putting it off? The Seeker and her body would die if we waited too long, and I would still have to make the same choice.

"We'll hit Phoenix, then. It's logical that they wouldn't notice this kind of raid. It doesn't make sense for humans to take your cold-storage tanks. What possible use could we have for them?"

The question didn't sound at all rhetorical, and I could feel him looking at me again. But I stared ahead at the rocks and said nothing.

It had been dark for a while by the time we traded vehicles and got to the freeway. Jared waited a few careful minutes with the inconspicuous sedan's lights off. I counted ten cars passing by. Then there was a long darkness between the headlights, and Jared pulled onto the road.

The trip to Phoenix was very short, though Jared kept the speed scrupulously below the limit. Time was speeding up, as if the Earth were spinning faster.

We settled into the steady-moving traffic, flowing with it along the highway that circled the flat, sprawling city. I saw the hospital from the road. We followed another car up the exit ramp, moving evenly, without hurry.

Jared turned into the main parking lot.

"Where now?" he asked, tense.

"See if this road continues around the back. The tanks will be by a loading area."

Jared drove slowly. There were many souls here, going in and out of the facility, some of them in scrubs. Healers. No one paid us any particular attention.

The road hugged the sidewalk, then curved around the north side of the building complex.

"Look. Shipping trucks. Head that way."

We passed between a wing of low buildings and a parking garage. Several trucks, delivering medical supplies no doubt, were backed into receiving ports. I scanned the crates on the dock, all labeled.

"Keep going . . . though we might want to grab some of those on the way back. See — Heal . . . Cool . . . Still? I wonder what that one is."

I liked that these supplies were labeled and left unguarded. My family wouldn't go without the things they needed when I was gone. *When I was gone;* it seemed that phrase was tacked on to all of my thoughts now.

We rounded the back of another building. Jared drove a little faster and kept his eyes forward — there were people here, four of them, unloading a truck onto a dock. It was the exactness of their movements that caught my attention. They didn't handle the smallish boxes roughly; quite the contrary, they placed them with infinite care onto the waist-high lip of concrete.

I didn't really need the label for confirmation, but just then, one of the unloaders turned his box so the black letters faced me directly.

"This is the place we want. They're unloading occupied tanks right now. The empty ones won't be far . . . Ah! There, on the other side. That shed is half full of them. I'll bet the closed sheds are all the way full."

Jared kept driving at the same careful speed, turning the corner to the side of the building.

He snorted quietly.

"What?" I asked.

"Figures. See?"

He jerked his chin toward the sign on the building.

This was the maternity wing.

"Ah," I said. "Well, you'll always know where to look, won't you?"

His eyes flashed to my face when I said that, and then back to the road.

"We'll have to wait for a bit. Looked like they were almost finished."

Jared circled the hospital again, then parked at the back of the biggest lot, away from the lights.

He killed the engine and slumped against the seat. He reached over and took my hand. I knew that he was about to ask, and I tried to prepare myself.

"Wanda?"

"Yes?"

"You're going to save the Seeker, aren't you?"

"Yes, I am."

"Because it's the right thing to do?" he guessed.

"That's one reason."

He was silent for a moment.

"You know how to get the soul out without hurting the body?"

My heart thumped hard once, and I had to swallow before I could answer. "Yes. I've done it before. In an emergency. Not here."

"Where?" he asked. "What was the emergency?"

It was a story I'd never told them before, for obvious reasons. It was one of my best. Lots of action. Jamie would have loved it. I sighed and began in a low voice.

"On the Mists Planet. I was with my friend Harness Light and a guide. I don't remember the guide's name. They called me Lives in the Stars there. I already had a bit of a reputation."

Jared chuckled.

"We were making a pilgrimage across the fourth great ice field to see one of the more celebrated crystal cities. It was supposed to be a safe route — that's why there were only three of us.

"Claw beasts like to dig pits and bury themselves in the snow. Camouflage, you know. A trap.

"One moment, there was nothing but the flat, endless snow. Then, the next moment, it seemed like the entire field of white was exploding into the sky.

"An average adult Bear has about the mass of a buffalo. A full-grown claw beast is closer to the mass of a blue whale. This one was bigger than most.

"I couldn't see the guide. The claw beast had sprung up between us, facing where Harness Light and I stood. Bears are faster than claw beasts, but this one had the advantage of the ambush. Its huge stone-like pincers swooped down and sheared Harness Light in half before I'd really processed what was happening."

A car drove slowly down the side of the parking lot. We sat silent until it had passed.

"I hesitated. I should have started running, but . . . my friend was dying there on the ice. Because of that hesitation, I would have died, too, if the claw beast hadn't been distracted. I found out later that our guide — I wish I could remember his name! — had attacked the claw beast's tail, hoping to give us a chance to run. The claw beast's attack had stirred up enough snow that it was like a blizzard. The lack of visibility would help us escape. He didn't know it was already too late for Harness Light to run.

"The claw beast turned on the guide, and his second left leg kicked us, sending me flying. Harness Light's upper body landed beside me. His blood melted the snow."

I paused to shudder.

"My next action made no sense, because I had no body for Harness Light. We were midway between cities, much too far to run to either. It was probably cruel, too, to take him out with no painkillers. But I couldn't stand to let him die inside the broken half of his Bear host.

"I used the back of my hand — the ice-cutting side. It was too wide a blade . . . It caused a lot of damage. I could only hope that Harness Light was far gone enough that he wouldn't feel the extra pain.

"Using my soft inside fingers, I coaxed Harness Light from the Bear's brain.

"He was still alive. I barely paused to ascertain this. I shoved him into the egg pocket in the center of my body, between the two hottest hearts. This would keep him from dying of cold, but he would only last a few short minutes without a body. And where would I find a host body in this empty waste?

"I thought of trying to share my host, but I doubted I could stay conscious through the procedure to insert him into my own head. And then, having no healing medicine, I would die quickly. With all those hearts, Bears bled very fast.

"The claw beast roared, and I felt the ground shake as its huge paws thudded down. I didn't know where our guide was, or if he lived. I didn't know how long it would take the claw beast to find us half-buried in the snow. I was right beside the severed Bear. The bright blood would draw the monster's eyes.

"And then I got this crazy idea."

I paused to laugh quietly to myself.

"I didn't have a Bear host for Harness Light. I couldn't use my body. The guide was dead or had fled. But there was *one* other body on the ice field.

"It was insanity, but all I could think of was Harness Light. We weren't even close friends, but I knew he was slowly dying, right between my hearts. I couldn't endure that.

"I heard the angry claw beast roaring, and I ran toward the sound. Soon I could see its thick white fur. I ran straight to its third left leg and launched myself as high up the leg as I could. I was a good jumper. I used all six of my hands, the knife sides, to yank myself up the side of the beast. It roared and spun, but that didn't help. Picture a dog chasing its tail. Claw beasts have very small brains — a limited intelligence.

"I made it to the beast's back and ran up the double spine, digging in with my knives so that it couldn't shake me off.

"It only took seconds to get up to the beast's head. But that was where the greatest difficulty waited. My ice cutters were only . . . about as long as your forearm, maybe. The claw beast's hide was twice as thick. I swung my arm down as hard as I could, slashing through the first layer of fur and membrane. The claw beast screamed and reared back on its hindmost legs. I almost fell.

"I lodged four of my hands into its hide — it screamed and thrashed. With the other two, I took turns cutting at the gash I'd made. The skin was so thick and tough, I didn't know if I would be able to saw through.

"The claw beast went berserk. It shook so hard that it was all I could do to hold on for a moment. But time was running out for Harness Light. I shoved my hands into the hole and tried to rip it open.

"Then the claw beast threw itself backward onto the ice.

"If we hadn't been over its lair, the pit it had dug to hide in, that would have crushed me. As it was, though it knocked me silly, the fall actually helped. My knives were already in the beast's neck. When I hit the ground, the weight of the beast drove my cutters deep through its skin. Deeper than I needed.

"We were both stunned; I was half smothered. I knew I had to do something right away, but I couldn't remember what it was. The beast started to roll, dazed. The fresh air cleared my head, and I remembered Harness Light.

"Protecting him from the cold as well as I could in the soft side of my hands, I moved him from my egg pocket into the claw beast's neck.

"The beast got to its feet and bucked again. This time I flew off. I'd let go of my hold to insert Harness Light, you see. The claw beast was infuriated. The wound on its head wasn't nearly enough to kill it — just annoy it.

"The snow had settled enough that I was in plain sight, especially as I was painted with the beast's blood. It's a very bright color, a color you don't have here. It raised its pincers, and they swung toward me. I thought that was it, and I was comforted a little that at least I would die *trying*.

"And then the pincers hit the snow beside me. I couldn't

believe it had missed! I stared up at the huge, hideous face, and I almost had to . . . well, not laugh. Bears don't laugh. But that was the feeling. Because that ugly face was torn with confusion and surprise and chagrin. No claw beast had ever worn such an expression before.

"It had taken Harness Light a few minutes to bind himself to the claw beast — it was such a big area, he really had to extend himself. But then he was in control. He was confused and slow — he didn't have much of a brain to work with, but it was enough that he knew I was his friend.

"I had to ride him to the crystal city — to hold the wound closed on his neck until we could reach a Healer. That caused quite a stir. For a while they called me Rides the Beast. I didn't like it. I made them go back to my other name."

I'd been staring ahead, toward the lights of the hospital and the figures of the souls crossing in front of those lights, as I told the story. Now I looked at Jared for the first time. He was gaping at me, his eyes wide and his mouth hanging open.

It really *was* one of my best stories. I'd have to get Mel to promise that she'd tell it to Jamie when I was . . .

"They're probably finished unloading, don't you think?" I said quickly. "Let's finish this and get back home."

He stared at me for one more moment, and then shook his head slowly.

"Yes, let's finish this, Wanderer, Lives in the Stars, Rides the Beast. Stealing a few unguarded crates won't present much of a challenge for *you*, will it?"

# CHAPTER 52

# *Separated*

We brought our plunder in through the south vent, though this meant that the jeep would have to be moved before dawn. My main concern with using the bigger entrance was that the Seeker would hear the commotion our arrival was sure to cause. I wasn't sure if she had any idea of what I was going to do, and I didn't want to give her any reason to kill her host and herself. The story Jeb had told me about one of their captives — the man who had simply collapsed, leaving no external evidence on the outside of the havoc wreaked inside his skull — haunted my thoughts.

The hospital was not empty. As I squeezed myself through the last tight bubble of space out into the main room, I found Doc preparing for the operation. His desk was laid out; on it, a propane lantern — the brightest illumination we had available — waited to be lit. The scalpels glinted in the duller blue light of the solar lamp.

I had known that Doc would agree to my terms, but seeing him thus occupied sent a wave of nervous nausea through me. Or maybe it was just the memory of that other day that sickened me, the day I'd caught him with blood on his hands.

"You're back," he said with relief. I realized that he'd been worried about us, just as everyone worried when someone left the safety of the caves.

"We brought you a gift," Jared said as he pushed himself free behind me. He straightened up and reached back for a box. With a flourish, he held it up, displaying the label on the side.

"Heal!" Doc crowed. "How much did you get?"

"Two cases. And we've found a much better way to renew our stores than to have Wanda stabbing herself."

Doc did not laugh at Jared's joke. Instead he turned to stare at me piercingly. We both must have been thinking the same thing: *Convenient, since Wanda won't be around.*

"Did you get the cryotanks?" he asked, more subdued.

Jared noticed the look and the tension. He glanced at me, his expression impossible to read.

"Yes," I answered. "Ten of them. It was all the car could hold."

While I spoke, Jared yanked on the rope behind him. With a clatter of loose rock, the second box of Heal, followed by the tanks, tumbled onto the floor behind him. The tanks clanked like metal, though they were built of no element that existed on this planet. I'd told him it was fine to treat the empty cryotanks roughly; they were built to withstand much worse abuse than being tugged through a stone channel. They glinted on the floor now, looking shiny and pristine.

Doc picked one up, freeing it from the rope, and turned it around in his hands.

"Ten?" The number seemed to surprise him. Did he think it too many? Or not enough? "Are they difficult to use?"

"No. Extremely easy. I'll show you how."

Doc nodded, his eyes examining the alien construction. I could feel Jared watching me, but I kept my eyes on Doc.

"What did Jeb, Brandt, and Aaron say?" I asked.

Doc looked up, locked his eyes on mine. "They're . . . in agreement with your terms."

I nodded, not convinced. "I won't show you unless I believe that."

"That's fair."

Jared glared at us, confused and frustrated.

"What did you tell him?" Doc asked me, being cautious.

"Just that I was going to save the Seeker." I turned to look in Jared's general direction without meeting his gaze. "Doc has promised me that if I show him how to perform the separation, you will give the released souls safe conduct to another life on another planet. No killing."

Jared nodded thoughtfully, his eyes flickering back to Doc. "I can agree to those terms. And I can make sure the others follow through. I assume you have a plan to get them off-planet?"

"It will be no more dangerous than what we did tonight. Just the opposite — adding to the stack rather than taking from it."

"Okay."

"Did you . . . have a time schedule in mind?" Doc asked. He tried to sound nonchalant, but I could hear the eagerness behind his voice.

He just wanted the answer that had eluded him for so long, I tried to tell myself. It wasn't that he was in a hurry to kill me.

"I have to take the jeep back — can you wait? I'd like to watch this."

"Sure, Jared," Doc agreed.

"Won't take me long," Jared promised as he shoved himself back into the vent.

That I was sure of. It wouldn't take enough time at all.

Doc and I did not speak until the sound of Jared's scrambling exit had faded.

"You didn't talk about . . . Melanie?" he asked softly.

I shook my head. "I think he sees where this is going. He must guess my plan."

"But not all of it. He won't allow —"

"He won't get a say," I interrupted severely. "All or nothing, Doc."

Doc sighed. After a moment of silence, he stretched and glanced toward the main exit. "I'm going to go talk to Jeb, get things ready."

He reached for a bottle on the table. The chloroform. I was sure the souls had something better to use. I would have to try to find it for Doc, before I was gone.

"Who knows about this?"

"Still just Jeb, Aaron, and Brandt. They all want to watch."

This didn't surprise me; Aaron and Brandt would be suspicious. "Don't tell anyone else. Not tonight."

Doc nodded, then he disappeared into the black corridor.

I went to sit against the wall, as far from the prepared cot as I could get. I'd have my turn on top of it all too soon.

Trying to think of something besides that grim fact, I realized that I hadn't heard from Melanie since . . . When was the last time she'd spoken to me? When I'd made the deal with Doc? I was belatedly surprised that the sleeping arrangements by the jeep today had not elicited a reaction from her.

*Mel?*

No answer.

It wasn't like before, so I didn't panic. I could definitely feel her there in my head, but she was . . . ignoring me? What was she doing?

*Mel? What's going on?*

No answer.

*Are you mad at me? I'm sorry about before, by the jeep. I didn't* do *anything, you know, so it's not really fair —*

She interrupted me, exasperated. *Oh, stop. I'm not* mad *at you. Leave me alone.*

*Why won't you talk to me?*

No answer.

I pushed a little harder, hoping to pick up the direction of her thoughts. She tried to keep me out, to put the wall in place, but it was too weak from disuse. I saw her plan.

I tried to keep my mental tone even. *Have you lost your mind?*

*In a manner of speaking,* she teased halfheartedly.

*You think that if you can make yourself disappear, that will stop me?*

*What else can I do to stop you? If you've got a better idea, please share.*

*I don't get it, Melanie. Don't you* want *them back? Don't you want to be with Jared again? With Jamie?*

She writhed, fighting the obviousness of the answer. *Yes, but . . . I can't . . .* She took a moment to steady herself. *I find myself unable to be the death of you, Wanda. I can't stand it.*

I saw the depth of her pain, and tears formed in my eyes.

*Love you too, Mel. But there's not room for the both of us here. In this body, in this cave, in their lives . . .*

*I disagree.*

*Look, just stop trying to annihilate yourself, okay? Because if I think you can do it, I'll make Doc pull me out today. Or I'll tell Jared. Just imagine what he would do.*

I imagined it for her, smiling a little through my tears. *Remember? He said no guarantees about what he would or wouldn't do to keep you here.* I thought of those burning kisses in the hall . . . thought of other kisses and other nights in her memory. My face warmed as I blushed.

*You fight dirty.*

*You bet I do.*

*I'm not giving up.*

*You've been warned. No more silent treatment.*

We thought of other things then, things that didn't hurt. Like where we would send the Seeker. Mel was all for the Mists Planet after my story tonight, but I thought the Planet of the Flowers would be more fitting. There wasn't a mellower planet in the universe. The Seeker needed a nice long lifetime eating sunshine.

We thought of my memories, the pretty ones. The ice castles and the night music and the colored suns. They were like fairytales to her. And she told me fairytales, too. Glass slippers, poisoned apples, mermaids who wanted to have souls . . .

Of course, we didn't have time to tell many stories.

They all returned together. Jared had come back through the main entrance. It had taken so very little time — perhaps he'd just driven the jeep around to the north side and hidden it under the overhang there. In a hurry.

I heard their voices coming, subdued, serious, low, and knew from their tone that the Seeker was with them. Knew that the time had come for the first stage of my death.

*No.*

*Pay attention. You're going to have to help them do this when I'm —*

*No!*

But she wasn't protesting my instruction, just the conclusion of my thought.

Jared was the one who carried the Seeker into the room. He came first, the others behind. Aaron and Brandt both had the guns ready — in case she was only feigning unconsciousness, perhaps, and about to jump up and attack them with her tiny hands. Jeb and Doc came last, and I knew Jeb's canny eyes would be on my face. How much had he figured out already with his crazy, insightful shrewdness?

I kept myself focused on the task at hand.

Jared laid the Seeker's inert form on the cot with exceptional gentleness. This might have bothered me before, but now it touched me. I understood that he did this for me, wishing that he could have treated me this way in the beginning.

"Doc, where's the No Pain?"

"I'll get it for you," he murmured.

I stared at the Seeker's face while I waited, wondering what it would look like when her host was free. Would anything be left? Would the host be empty or would the rightful owner reassert herself? Would the face be less repugnant to me when another awareness looked out of those eyes?

"Here you go." Doc put the canister in my hand.

"Thanks."

I pulled out one thin tissue square and handed the container back to him.

I found myself reluctant to touch the Seeker, but I made my hands move swiftly and purposefully as I pulled her chin down and put the No Pain on her tongue. Her face was very small — it made my hands feel big. Her tiny size always threw me off. It seemed so inappropriate.

I closed her mouth again. It was moist — the medicine would dissolve quickly.

"Jared, could you please roll her onto her stomach?" I asked.

He did as I asked — again, gently. Just then, the propane lantern flared to life. The cave was suddenly bright, almost like daylight. I glanced up instinctively and saw that Doc had covered the big holes in the roof with tarps to keep our light from escaping. He'd done a lot of preparation in our absence.

It was very quiet. I could hear the Seeker breathing evenly in and out. I could hear the faster, tenser breathing of the men in the room with me. Someone shifted from one foot to the other, and sand ground against rock under his heel. Their stares had a physical weight on my skin.

I swallowed, hoping I could keep my voice normal. "Doc, I need Heal, Clean, Seal, and Smooth."

"Right here."

I brushed the Seeker's coarse black hair out of the way, exposing the little pink line at the base of her skull. I stared at her olive tan skin and hesitated.

"Would you cut, Doc? I don't . . . I don't want to."

"No problem, Wanda."

I saw only his hands as he came to stand across from me. He set a little row of white cylinders on the cot next to the Seeker's shoulder. The scalpel winked in the bright light, flashing across my face.

"Hold her hair out of the way."

I used both hands to clear her neck.

"Wish I could scrub up," Doc muttered to himself, obviously feeling underprepared.

"It's not really necessary. We have Clean."

"I know." He sighed. What he really wanted was the routine, the mental cleansing that the old habits had given him.

"How much room do you need?" he asked, hesitating with the point of the blade an inch from her skin.

I could feel the heat of the other bodies behind me,

squeezing in to get a better view. They were careful not to touch either of us.

"Just the length of the scar. That will be enough."

This didn't seem like enough to him. "You sure?"

"Yes. Oh, wait!"

Doc pulled back.

I realized I was doing this all backward. I was no Healer. I wasn't cut out for this. My hands were shaking. I couldn't seem to look away from the Seeker's body.

"Jared, could you get one of those tanks for me?"

"Of course."

I heard him walk the few steps away, heard the dull, metallic clunk of the tank he chose knocking against the others.

"What now?"

"There's a circle on top of the lid. Press it in."

I heard the low hum of the cryotank as it powered on. The men muttered and shuffled their feet, moving away from it.

"Okay, on the side there should be a switch . . . more like a dial, actually. Can you see it?"

"Yes."

"Spin it all the way down."

"Okay."

"What color is the light on top of the tank?"

"It's . . . it's just turning from purple to . . . bright blue. Light blue now."

I took a deep breath. At least the tanks were functional.

"Great. Pop the lid and wait for me."

"How?"

"Latch under the lip."

"Got it." I heard the click of the latch, and then the whir of the mechanism. "It's *cold!*"

"That's sort of the point."

"How does it work? What's the power source?"

I sighed. "I knew the answers when I was a Spider. I don't understand it now. Doc, you can go ahead. I'm ready."

"Here we go," Doc whispered as he slid the blade of the scalpel deftly, almost gracefully, through the skin. Blood coursed down the side of her neck, pooling on the towel Doc had placed underneath.

"A tiny bit deeper. Just under the edge —"

"Yes, I see." Doc was breathing fast, excited.

Silver glinted out from the red.

"That's good. Now you hold the hair."

Doc switched places with me in a smooth, swift movement. He was good at his Calling. He would have made quite a Healer.

I didn't try to hide what I was doing from him. The movements were too minute for him to have any chance of seeing. He would not be able to do this until I explained.

I slid one fingertip carefully along the back ridge of the tiny silver creature until my finger was almost entirely inserted into the hot opening at the base of the host body's neck. I traced my way to the anterior antennae, feeling the taut lines of the bound attachments stretched tight like harp strings into the deeper recesses of her head.

I twisted my finger around the underside of the soul's body, caressing down from the first segment along the other line of attachments, as stiff and profuse as the bristles of a brush.

I felt carefully at the juncture of these tight strings, at the tiny joints, no bigger than pinheads. I stroked my way about a third of the way down. I could have counted, but that would have taken a very long time. It would be the two hundred seventeenth connection, but there was another way to find it. There it was, the little ridge that made this joint just a bit bigger — a seed pearl rather than a pinhead. It was smooth under my fingertip.

I pressed against it with gentle pressure, tenderly massaging. Kindness was always the way of the souls. Never violence.

"Relax," I breathed.

And, though the soul could not hear me, it obeyed. The harp strings loosened, went slack. I could feel the slither as they retracted, feel the slight swelling of the body as it absorbed them. The process took no more than a few beats of my heart. I held my breath until I felt the soul undulate under my touch. Wriggling free.

I let it twist itself a little farther out, and then I curled my fingers gently around the tiny, fragile body. I lifted it, silver and gleaming, wet with blood that was quickly shed from the smooth casing, and cradled it in my hand.

It was beautiful. The soul whose name I'd never known billowed like a silver wave in my hand . . . a lovely feathered ribbon.

I couldn't hate the Seeker in this form. An almost maternal love swept through me.

"Sleep well, little one," I whispered.

I turned toward the faint hum of the cryotank, just to my left. Jared held it low and angled, so it was a simple matter for me to ease the soul into the shockingly cold air that gusted from the opening. I let it slide into the small space and then carefully relatched the lid.

I took the cryotank from Jared, easing it rather than tugging it, turning it with care until it was vertical, and then I hugged it to my chest. The outside of the tank was the same temperature as the warm room. I cradled it to my body, protective as any mother.

I looked back at the stranger on the table. Doc was already dusting Smooth over the sealed wound. We made a good team: one attending to the soul, the other to the body. Everyone was taken care of.

Doc looked up at me, his eyes full of exhilaration and wonder. "Amazing," he murmured. "That was incredible."

"Good job," I whispered back.

"When do you think she'll wake up?" Doc asked.

"That depends on how much chloroform she inhaled."

"Not much."

"And if she's still there. We'll have to wait and see."

Before I could ask, Jared lifted the nameless woman tenderly from the cot, rolled her face-up, and laid her on another, cleaner resting place. This tenderness did not move me. This tenderness was for the human, for Melanie. . . .

Doc went with him, checking her pulse, peeking under her lids. He shone a flashlight into her unconscious eyes and watched the pupils constrict. No light reflected back to blind him. He and Jared exchanged a long glance.

"She really did it," Jared said, his voice low.

"Yes," Doc agreed.

I didn't hear Jeb sidle up next to me.

"Pretty slick, kid," he murmured.

I shrugged.

"Feeling a smidge conflicted?"

I didn't answer.

"Yeah. Me, too, hon. Me, too."

Aaron and Brandt were talking behind me, their voices rising with excitement, answering each other's thoughts before the questions were spoken.

No conflict there.

"Wait till the others hear!"

"Think of the —"

"We should go get some —"

"Right now, I'm ready —"

"Hold up," Jeb cut Brandt off. "No soul snatching until that cryotank is safely on its way into outer space. Right, Wanda?"

"Right," I agreed in a firmer voice, hugging the tank tighter to my chest.

Brandt and Aaron exchanged sour glances.

I was going to need more allies. Jared and Jeb and Doc were only three, though certainly the most influential three here. Still, they would need support.

I knew what this meant.

It meant talking to Ian.

Others, too, of course, but Ian would have to be one of them. My heart seemed to slump lower in my chest, to curl limply in on itself. I'd done many things I had not wanted to do since joining the humans, but I couldn't remember any this sharply and pointedly painful. Even deciding to trade my life for the Seeker's — that was a huge, vast hurt, a wide field of ache, but it was almost manageable because it was so tied up in the bigger picture. Telling Ian goodbye was a razor-sharp piercing; it made the greater vision hard to see. I wished there was some way, any way, to save him from the same pain. There wasn't.

The only thing worse would be telling Jared goodbye. That one would burn and fester. Because he *wouldn't* feel pain. His joy would far outweigh any small regret he might feel over me.

As for Jamie, well, I wasn't planning on facing that goodbye at all.

"Wanda!" Doc's voice was sharp.

I hurried to the bed Doc was hovering over. Before I got there, I could see the tiny olive hand fisting and unfisting where it hung over the edge of the cot.

"Ah," the Seeker's familiar voice moaned from the human body. "Ah."

The room went utterly silent. Everyone looked at me, as if I were the expert on humans.

I elbowed Doc, my hands still wrapped around the tank. "Talk to her," I whispered.

"Um . . . Hello? Can you hear me . . . miss? You're safe now. Do you understand me?"

"Ah," she groaned. Her eyes fluttered open, focused quickly on Doc's face. There was no discomfort in her expression — the No Pain would be making her feel wonderful, of course. Her eyes were onyx black. They darted around the room until she found me, and recognition was quickly followed by a scowl. She looked away, back to Doc.

"Well, it feels good to have my head back," she said in a loud, clear voice. "Thanks."

# CHAPTER 53

# Condemned

T he Seeker's host body was named Lacey; a dainty, soft, feminine name. *Lacey.* As inappropriate as the size, in my opinion. Like naming a pit bull Fluffy.

Lacey was just as loud as the Seeker — and still a complainer.

"You'll have to forgive me for going on and on," she insisted, allowing us no other options. "I've been shouting away in there for years and never getting to speak for myself. I've got a lot to say all stored up."

How lucky for us. I could almost make myself glad that I was leaving.

In answer to my earlier question to myself, no, the face was not less repugnant with a different awareness behind it. Because the awareness was not so very different, in the end.

"That's why we don't like you," she told me that first

night, making no change from the present tense or the plural pronoun. "When she realized that you were hearing Melanie just the way she was hearing me, it made her frightened. She thought you might guess. I was her deep, dark secret." A grating laugh. "She couldn't make me shut up. That's why she became a Seeker, because she was hoping to figure out some way to better deal with resistant hosts. And then she requested being assigned to you, so she could watch how you did it. She was jealous of you; isn't that pathetic? She wanted to be strong like you. It gave us a real kick when we thought Melanie had won. I guess that didn't happen, though. I guess you did. So why did you come here? Why are you helping the rebels?"

I explained, unwillingly, that Melanie and I were friends. She didn't like that.

"Why?" she demanded.

"She's a good person."

"But why does she like *you?*"

*Same reason.*

"She says, for the same reason."

Lacey snorted. "Got her brainwashed, huh?"

*Wow, she's worse than the first one.*

*Yes,* I agreed. *I can see why the Seeker was so obnoxious. Can you imagine having that in your head all the time?*

I wasn't the only thing Lacey objected to.

"Do you have anywhere better to live than these caves? It's so *dirty* here. Isn't there a house somewhere, maybe? What do you mean we have to share rooms? Chore schedule? I don't understand. I have to work? I don't think *you* understand . . ."

Jeb had given her the usual tour the next day, trying to

explain, through clenched teeth, the way we all lived here. When they'd passed me — eating in the kitchen with Ian and Jamie — he threw me a look that clearly asked why I hadn't let Aaron shoot her while that was still an option.

The tour was more crowded than mine. Everyone wanted to see the miracle for themselves. It didn't even seem to matter to most of them that she was . . . difficult. She was welcome. More than welcome. Again, I felt a little of that bitter jealousy. But that was silly. She was human. She represented hope. She belonged here. She would be here long after I was gone.

*Lucky you,* Mel whispered sarcastically.

Talking to Ian and Jamie about what had happened was not as difficult and painful as I'd imagined.

This was because they were, for different reasons, entirely clueless. Neither grasped that this new knowledge meant I would be leaving.

With Jamie, I understood why. More than anyone else, he had accepted me and Mel as the package deal we were. He was able, with his young, open mind, to grasp the reality of our dual personalities. He treated us like two people rather than one. Mel was so real, so present to him. The same way she was to me. He didn't miss her, because he had her. He didn't see the necessity of our separation.

I wasn't sure why Ian didn't understand. Was he too caught up in the potential? The changes this would mean for the human society here? They were all boggled by the idea that getting caught — the end — was no longer a finality. There was a way to come back. It seemed natural to him that I had acted to save the Seeker; it was consistent with his idea of my personality. Maybe that was as far as he'd considered it.

Or maybe Ian just didn't have a chance to think it all through, to see the glaring eventuality, before he was distracted. Distracted and enraged.

"I should have killed him years ago," Ian ranted as we packed what we needed for our raid. My final raid; I tried not to dwell on that. "No, our mother should have drowned him at birth!"

"He's your brother."

"I don't know why you keep saying that. Are you trying to make me feel worse?"

Everyone was furious with Kyle. Jared's lips were welded into a tight line of rage, and Jeb stroked his gun more than usual.

Jeb had been excited, planning to join us on this landmark raid, his first since I'd come to live here. He was particularly keen to see the shuttle field up close. But now, with Kyle putting us all in danger, he felt he had to stay behind just in case. Not getting his way put Jeb in a foul mood.

"Stuck behind with that creature," he muttered to himself, rubbing the rifle barrel again — he wasn't getting any happier about the new member of his community. "Missin' all the fun." He spit on the floor.

We all knew where Kyle was. As soon as he'd grasped how the Seeker-worm had magically transformed into the Lacey-human in the night, he'd slipped out the back. I'd been expecting him to lead the party demanding the Seeker's death (I kept the cryotank always cradled in my arms; I slept lightly, my hand touching its smooth surface), but he was nowhere to be found, and Jeb had quashed the resistance easily in his absence.

Jared was the one to realize the jeep was gone. And Ian had been the one to link the two absences.

"He's gone after Jodi," Ian had groaned. "What else?"

Hope and despair. I had given them one, Kyle the other. Would he betray them all before they could even make use of the hope?

Jared and Jeb wanted to put off the raid until we knew if Kyle was successful — it would take him three days under the best circumstances, *if* his Jodi still lived in Oregon. If he could find her there.

There was another place, another cave we could evacuate to. A much smaller place, with no water, so we couldn't hide there long. They'd debated whether they should move everyone now or wait.

But I was in a hurry. I'd seen the way the others eyed the silver tank in my arms. I'd heard the whispers. The longer I kept the Seeker here, the better chance that someone would kill her. Having met Lacey, I'd begun to pity the Seeker. She deserved a mild, pleasant new life with the Flowers.

Ironically enough, Ian was the one who took my side and helped hurry the raid along. He still didn't see where this would lead.

But I was grateful that he helped me convince Jared there was time to make the raid and get back before a decision was made about Kyle. Grateful also that he was back to playing bodyguard. I knew I could trust Ian with the shiny cryotank more than anyone else. He was the only one I would let hold it when I needed my arms. He was the only one who could see, in the shape of that small container, a life to be protected. He could think of that shape as a friend, something that could be loved. He was the best ally of all. I was so grateful for Ian, and so grateful for the obliviousness that saved him, for the moment, from pain.

We had to be fast, in case Kyle ruined everything. We went to Phoenix again, to one of the many communities that spun out from the hub. There was a big shuttle field to the southeast, in a town called Mesa, with several Healing facilities nearby. That was what I wanted — I would give them as much as I could before I left. If we took a Healer, then we might be able to preserve the Healer's memory in the host body. Someone who understood all the medicines and their uses. Someone who knew the best ways to get to unattended stashes. Doc would love that. I could imagine all the questions he'd be dying to ask.

First the shuttle field.

I was sad that Jeb was missing this, but he'd have so many other chances in the future. Though it was dark, a long line of small snub-nosed shuttles drifted in to land while others took flight in an endless stream.

I drove the old van while the others rode in the back — Ian in charge of the tank, of course. I circled the field, staying clear of the busy local terminal. It was easy to spot the vast, sleek white vessels that left the planet. They did not depart with the frequency of the smaller ships. All I saw were docked, none preparing to leave immediately.

"Everything's labeled," I reported to the others, invisible in the dark back. "Now, this is important. Avoid ships to the Bats, and *especially* the See Weeds. The See Weeds are just one system over — it takes only a decade to make the round trip. That's much too short. The Flowers are the farthest, and the Dolphins, Bears, and Spiders all take at least a century to go one way. Only send tanks to those."

I drove slowly, close to the crafts.

"This will be easy. They've got all kinds of delivery vehicles out here, and we blend in. Oh! I can see a tank truck — it's just like the one we saw them unloading at the hospital, Jared. There's a man looking over the stacks . . . He's putting them onto a hover cart. He's going to load them . . ." I drove even slower, trying to get a good look. "Yes, onto *this* ship. Right into the open hatch. I'll circle back and make my move when he's in the ship." I pulled past, examining the scene in my mirrors. There was a lit sign beside the tube that connected the head of the ship to the terminal. I smiled as I read the words backward. This ship was going to the Flowers. It was meant to be.

I made a slow turn as the man disappeared into the hull of the ship.

"Get ready," I whispered as I pulled into the shadow made by the cylindrical wing of the next enormous ship over. I was only three or four yards from the tank truck. There were a few technicians working near the front of the Flower-bound vessel and others, farther away, out on the old runway. I would be just another figure in the night.

I cut the engine and hopped down from the driver's seat, trying to look casual, like I was only doing my job. I went around to the back of the van and opened the door a crack. The tank was right at the edge, the light on top glowing dull red, signifying that it was occupied. I lifted it carefully and closed the door.

I kept up an easy rolling pace as I walked to the open end of the truck. But my breathing sped up. This felt more dangerous than the hospital, and that worried me. Could I expect my humans to risk their lives this way?

*I'll be there. I'll do it myself, just like you would. On the off chance you get your way, that is.*

*Thanks, Mel.*

I had to force myself not to keep glancing over my shoulder at the open hatch where the man had disappeared. I placed the tank gently atop the closest column in the truck. The addition, one among hundreds, was not noticeable.

"Goodbye," I whispered. "Better luck with your next host."

I walked back to the van as slowly as I could stand to.

It was silent in the van as I reversed out from under the big ship. I started back the way we'd come, my heart hammering too fast. In my mirrors, the hatch remained empty. I didn't see the man emerge before the ship was out of sight.

Ian climbed into the passenger seat. "Doesn't look too hard."

"It was very good luck with the timing. You might have to wait longer for an opportunity next time."

Ian reached over to take my hand. "You're the good-luck charm."

I didn't answer.

"Do you feel better now that she's safe?"

"Yes."

I saw his head turn sharply as he heard the unexpected sound of a lie in my voice. I didn't meet his gaze.

"Let's go catch some Healers," I muttered.

Ian was silent and thoughtful as we drove the short distance to the small Healing facility.

I'd thought the second task would be the challenge, the danger. The plan was that I would — if the conditions and numbers were right — try to lead a Healer or two out of the facility under the pretext that I had an injured friend in my van. An old trick, but one that would work only too well on the unsuspecting, trusting Healers.

As it turned out, I didn't even have to go in. I pulled into the lot just as two middle-aged Healers, a man and a woman wearing purple scrubs, were getting into a car. Their shift over, they were heading home. The car was around the corner from the entrance. No one else was in sight.

Ian nodded tensely.

I stopped the van right behind their car. They looked up, surprised.

I opened my door and slid out. My voice was thick with tears, my face twisted with remorse, and that helped to fool them.

"My friend is in the back — I don't know what's wrong with him."

They responded with the instant concern I knew they would show. I hurried to open the back doors for them, and they followed right behind. Ian went around the other side. Jared was ready with the chloroform.

I didn't watch.

It took just seconds. Jared hauled the unconscious bodies into the back, and Ian slammed the doors shut. Ian stared at my tear-swollen eyes for just a second, then took the driver's seat.

I rode shotgun. He held my hand again.

"Sorry, Wanda. I know this is hard for you."

"Yes." He had no idea how hard, and for how many different reasons.

He squeezed my fingers. "But that went well, at least. You make an excellent charm."

Too well. Both missions had gone too perfectly, too fast. Fate was rushing me.

He drove back toward the freeway. After a few minutes, I saw a bright, familiar sign in the distance. I took a deep breath and wiped my eyes clear.

"Ian, could you do me a favor?"

"Anything you want."

"I want fast food."

He laughed. "No problem."

We switched seats in the parking lot, and I drove up to the ordering box.

"What do you want?" I asked Ian.

"Nothing. I'm getting a kick out of watching you do something for yourself. This has to be a first."

I didn't smile at his joke. To me, this was sort of a last meal — the final gift to the condemned. I wouldn't leave the caves again.

"Jared, how about you?"

"Two of whatever you're having."

So I ordered three cheeseburgers, three bags of fries, and three strawberry shakes.

After I got my food, Ian and I switched again so I could eat while he drove.

"Eew," he said, watching me dip a french fry into the shake.

"You should try it. It's good." I offered him a well-coated fry.

He shrugged and took it. He popped it into his mouth and chewed. "Interesting."

I laughed. "Melanie thinks it's gross, too." That's why I'd cultivated the habit in the beginning. It was funny now to think how I'd gone out of my way to annoy her.

I wasn't really hungry. I'd just wanted some of the flavors I particularly remembered, one more time. Ian finished off half my burger when I was full.

We made it home without incident. We saw no sign of the Seekers' surveillance. Perhaps they'd accepted the coincidence. Maybe they thought it inevitable — wander the desert alone long enough, and something bad would happen to you. We'd had a saying like that on the Mists Planet: Cross too many ice fields alone, and wind up a claw beast's meal. That was a rough translation. It sounded better in Bear.

There was a large reception waiting for us.

I smiled halfheartedly at my friends: Trudy, Geoffrey, Heath, and Heidi. My true friends were dwindling. No Walter, no Wes. I didn't know where Lily was. This made me sad. Maybe I didn't want to live on this sad planet with so much death. Maybe nothingness was better.

It also made me sad, petty as it was, to see Lucina standing beside Lacey, with Reid and Violetta on the other side. They were talking animatedly, asking questions, it looked like. Lacey was holding Freedom on her hip. He didn't look especially thrilled about this, but he was happy enough being part of the adults' conversation that he didn't squirm down.

I'd never been allowed near the child, but Lacey was already one of them. Trusted.

We went straight to the south tunnel, Jared and Ian laboring under the weight of the Healers. Ian had the heavier one, the man, and sweat ran down his fair face. Jeb shooed the others back at the tunnel entrance and then followed us.

Doc was waiting for us in the hospital, rubbing his hands together absently, as if washing them.

Time continued to speed up. The brighter lamp was lit. The Healers were given No Pain and laid out facedown on the cots. Jared showed Ian how to activate the tanks. They held them ready, Ian wincing at the stunning cold. Doc stood over the female, scalpel in hand and medicines laid out in a row.

"Wanda?" he asked.

My heart squeezed inward painfully. "Do you swear, Doc? *All* of my terms? Do you promise me on your own life?"

"I do. I will meet all of your terms, Wanda. I swear it."

"Jared?"

"Yes. Absolutely no killing, ever."

"Ian?"

"I'll protect them with my own life, Wanda."

"Jeb?"

"It's my house. Anyone who can't abide by this agreement will have to get out."

I nodded, tears in my eyes. "Okay, then. Let's get it over with."

Doc, excited again, cut into the Healer until he could see the silver gleam. He set the scalpel quickly aside. "Now what?"

I put my hand on his.

"Trace up the back ridge. Can you feel that? Feel the shape of the segments. They get smaller toward the anterior section. Okay, at the end you should feel three small . . . stubby things. Do you feel what I'm talking about?"

"Yes," he breathed.

"Good. Those are the anterior antennae. Start there.

Now, very gently, roll your finger under the body. Find the line of attachments. They'll feel tight, like wires."

He nodded.

I guided him a third of the way down, told him how to count if he wasn't sure. We didn't have time for counting with all the blood flowing free. I was sure the Healer's body, if she came around, would be able to help us — there must be something for that. I helped him find the biggest nodule.

"Now, rub softly in toward the body. Knead it lightly."

Doc's voice went up in pitch, turned a little panicky. "It's moving."

"That's good — it means you're doing it right. Give it time to retract. Wait till it rolls up a bit, then take it into your hand."

"Okay." His voice shook.

I reached toward Ian. "Give me your hand."

I felt Ian's hand wind around mine. I turned it over, curled his hand into a cup, and pulled it close to Doc's operation site.

"Give the soul to Ian — gently, please."

Ian would be the perfect assistant. When I was gone, who else would take such care with my little relatives?

Doc passed the soul into Ian's waiting hand, then turned at once to heal the human body.

Ian stared at the silver ribbon in his hand, his face full of wonder rather than revulsion. It felt warmer inside my chest while I watched his reaction.

"It's pretty," he whispered, surprised. No matter how he felt about me, he'd been conditioned to expect a parasite, a centipede, a monster. Cleaning up severed bodies had not prepared him for the beauty here.

"I think so, too. Let it slide into your tank."

Ian held the soul cupped in his hand for one more second, as if memorizing the sight and feel. Then, with delicate care, he let it glide into the cold.

Jared showed him how to latch the lid.

A weight fell off my shoulders.

It was done. It was too late to change my mind. This didn't feel as horrible as I'd anticipated, because I felt sure these four humans would care for the souls just as I would. When I was gone.

"Look out!" Jeb suddenly shouted. The gun came up in his hands, pointed past us.

We whirled toward the danger, and Jared's tank fell to the floor as he jumped toward the male Healer, who was on his knees on the cot, staring at us in shock. Ian had the presence of mind to hold on to his tank.

"Chloroform," Jared shouted as he tackled the Healer, pinning him back down to the cot. But it was too late.

The Healer stared straight at me, his face childlike in his bewilderment. I knew why his eyes were on me — the lantern's rays danced off both his eyes and mine, making diamond patterns on the wall.

"Why?" he asked me.

Then his face went blank, and his body slumped, unresisting, to the cot. Two trails of blood flowed from his nostrils.

*"No!"* I screamed, lurching to his inert form, knowing it was far too late. "No!"

# CHAPTER 54

# *Forgotten*

"Elizabeth?" I asked. "Anne? Karen? What's your name? C'mon. I know you know it."

The Healer's body was still limp on the cot. It had been a long time — how long, I wasn't sure. Hours and hours. I hadn't slept yet, though the sun was far up in the sky. Doc had climbed out onto the mountain to pull the tarps away, and the sun beamed brightly through the holes in the ceiling, hot on my skin. I'd moved the nameless woman so that her face would be out of the glare.

I touched her face now lightly, patting the soft brown hair, woven through with white strands, away from her face.

"Julie? Brittany? Angela? Patricia? Am I getting close? Talk to me. Please?"

Everyone but Doc — snoring quietly on a cot in the darkest corner of the hospital — had gone away hours ago. Some to bury the host body we'd lost. I cringed, thinking of his bewildered question, and the sudden way his face had gone slack.

*Why?* he'd asked me.

I so much wished that the soul had waited for an answer, so I could have tried to explain it to him. He might even have understood. After all, what was more important, in the end, than love? To a soul, wasn't that the heart of everything? And love would have been my answer.

Maybe, if he'd waited, he would have seen the truth of that. If he'd really understood, I was sure he would have let the human body live.

The request would probably have made little sense to him, though. The body was *his* body, not a separate entity. His suicide was simply that to him, not a murder, too. Only one life had ended. And perhaps he was right.

At least the souls had survived. The light on his tank glowed dull red beside hers; I couldn't ask for a greater evidence of commitment from my humans than this, the sparing of his life.

"Mary? Margaret? Susan? Jill?"

Though Doc slept and I was otherwise alone, I could feel the echo of the tension the others had left behind; it still hung in the air.

The tension lingered because the woman had not woken up when the chloroform wore off. She had not moved. She was still breathing, her heart was still beating, but she had not responded to any of Doc's efforts to revive her.

Was it too late? Was she lost? Was she already gone? Just as dead as the male body?

Were all of them? Were there only a very few, like the Seeker's host, Lacey, and Melanie — the shouters, the resisters — who could be brought back? Was everyone else gone?

Was Lacey an anomaly? Would Melanie come back the way she had . . . or was even that in question?

*I'm not lost. I'm here.* But Mel's mental voice was defensive. She worried, too.

*Yes, you are here. And you will stay here,* I promised.

With a sigh, I returned to my efforts. My doomed efforts?

"I know you have a name," I told the woman. "Is it Rebecca? Alexandra? Olivia? Something simpler, maybe . . . Jane? Jean? Joan?"

It was better than nothing, I thought glumly. At least I'd given them a way to help themselves if they were ever taken. I could help the resisters, if no one else.

It didn't seem like enough.

"You're not giving me much to work with," I murmured. I took her hand in both of mine, chafed it softly. "It would really be nice if you would make an effort. My friends are going to be depressed enough. They could use some good news. Besides, with Kyle still gone . . . It will be hard to evacuate everyone without having to carry you around, too. I know you want to help. This is your family here, you know. These are your kind. They're very nice. Most of them. You'll like them."

The gently lined face was vacant with unconsciousness. She was quite pretty in an inconspicuous way — her features very symmetrical on her oval face. Forty-five, maybe a little younger, maybe a little older. It was hard to tell with no animation in the face.

"They need you," I went on, pleading now. "You can help them. You know so much that I never knew. Doc tries so hard. He deserves some help. He's a good man. You've been a Healer for a while now; some of that care for the well-being of others must have rubbed off on you. You'll like Doc, I think.

"Is your name Sarah? Emily? Kristin?"

I stroked her soft cheek, but there was no response, so I took her limp hand in mine again. I gazed at the blue sky through the holes in the high ceiling. My mind wandered.

"I wonder what they'll do if Kyle never comes back. How long will they hide? Will they have to find a new home somewhere else? There are so many of them. . . . It won't be easy. I wish I could help them, but even if I could stay, I don't have any answers.

"Maybe they'll get to stay here . . . somehow. Maybe Kyle won't mess up." I laughed humorlessly, thinking of the odds. Kyle wasn't a careful man. However, until that situation was resolved, I was needed. Maybe, if there were Seekers looking, they would need my infallible eyes. It might take a long time, and that made me feel warmer than the sun on my skin. Made me feel grateful that Kyle was impetuous and selfish. How long until we were sure we were safe?

"I wonder what it's like here when it gets cold. I can barely remember feeling cold. And what if it rains? It has to rain here sometime, doesn't it? With all these holes in the roof, it must get really wet. Where does everyone sleep then, I wonder." I sighed. "Maybe I'll get to find out. Probably shouldn't bet on that, though. Aren't you curious at all? If you would wake up, you could get the answers. *I'm* curious. Maybe I'll ask Ian about it. It's funny to imagine

things changing here. . . . I guess summer can't last forever."

Her fingers fluttered for one second in my hand.

It took me by surprise because my mind had wandered
away from the woman on the cot, beginning to sink into
the melancholy that was always conveniently near these
days.

I stared down at her; there was no change — the hand
in mine was limp, her face still vacant. Maybe I'd imagined the movement.

"Did I say something you were interested in? What
was I talking about?" I thought quickly, watching her
face. "Was it the rain? Or was it the idea of change?
Change? You've got a lot of that ahead of you, don't you?
You have to wake up first, though."

Her face was empty, her hand motionless.

"So you don't care for change. Can't say that I blame
you. I don't want change to come, either. Are you like me?
Do you wish the summer could last?"

If I hadn't been watching her face so closely, I wouldn't
have seen the tiny flicker of her lids.

"You like summertime, do you?" I asked hopefully.

Her lips twitched.

"Summer?"

Her hand trembled.

"Is that your name — Summer? Summer? That's a
pretty name."

Her hand tightened into a fist, and her lips parted.

"Come back, Summer. I know you can do it. Summer?
Listen to me, Summer. Open your eyes, Summer."

Her eyes blinked rapidly.

"Doc!" I called over my shoulder. "Doc, wake up!"

"Huh?"

"I think she's coming around!" I turned back to the woman. "Keep it up, Summer. You can do this. I know it's hard. Summer, Summer, Summer. Open your eyes."

Her face grimaced — was she in pain?

"Bring the No Pain, Doc. Hurry."

The woman squeezed my hand, and her eyes opened. They didn't focus at first, just whirled around the bright cave. What a strange, unexpected sight this place must have been for her.

"You're going to be all right, Summer. You're going to be fine. Can you hear me, Summer?"

Her eyes wheeled back to me, the pupils constricting. She stared, absorbing my face. Then she cringed away from me, twisting on the cot to escape. A low, hoarse cry of panic broke through her lips.

"No, no, no," she cried. "No more."

"Doc!"

He was there, on the other side of the cot, like before, when we were operating.

"It's okay, ma'am," he assured her. "No one is going to hurt you here."

The woman had her eyes squeezed shut, and she recoiled into the thin mattress.

"I think her name is Summer."

He flashed a look at me and then made a face. "Eyes, Wanda," he breathed.

I blinked and realized that the sun was on my face. "Oh." I let the woman pull her hand free.

"Don't, please," the woman begged. "Not again."

"Shh," Doc murmured. "Summer? People call me

Doc. No one's going to do anything to you. You're going to be fine."

I eased away from them, into the shadows.

"Don't call me that!" the woman sobbed. "That's not my name! It's hers, it's hers! Don't say it again!"

I'd gotten the wrong name.

Mel objected to the guilt that washed through me. *It's not your fault. Summer is a human name, too.*

"Of course not," Doc promised. "What is *your* name?"

"I — I — I don't know!" she wailed. "What happened? Who was I? Don't make me be someone else again."

She tossed and thrashed on the cot.

"Calm down; it's going to be okay, I promise. No one's going to make you be anyone but you, and you'll remember your name. It's going to come back."

"Who are you?" she demanded. "Who's she? She's like . . . like I was. I saw her eyes!"

"I'm Doc. And I'm human, just like you. See?" He moved his face into the light and blinked at her. "We're both just ourselves. There are lots of humans here. They'll be so happy to meet you."

She cringed again. "Humans! I'm afraid of humans."

"No, you're not. The . . . person who used to be in your body was afraid of humans. She was a soul, remember that? And then remember before that, before she was there? You were human then, and you are again."

"I can't remember my name," she told him in a panicked voice.

"I know. It'll come back."

"Are you a doctor?"

"I am."

"I was . . . she was, too. A . . . Healer. Like a doctor. She was Summer Song. Who am I?"

"We'll find out. I promise you that."

I edged toward the exit. Trudy would be a good person to help Doc, or maybe Heidi. Someone with a calming face.

"She's not human!" the woman whispered urgently to Doc, her eye caught by my movement.

"She's a friend; don't be afraid. She helped me bring you back."

"Where is Summer Song? She was scared. There were humans. . . ."

I ducked out the door while she was distracted.

I heard Doc answer the question behind me. "She's going to a new planet. Do you remember where she was before she came here?"

I could guess what her answer would be from the name.

"She was . . . a Bat? She could fly. . . . She could sing. . . . I remember . . . but it was . . . not here. Where am I?"

I hurried down the hall to find help for Doc. I was surprised when I saw the light of the great cavern ahead — surprised because it was so quiet. Usually you could hear voices before you saw the light. It was the middle of the day. There should have been someone in the big garden room, if only crossing through.

I walked out into the bright noon light, and the giant space was empty.

The fresh tendrils of the cantaloupe vines were dark green, darker than the dry earth they sprang from. The earth was too dry — the irrigating barrel stood ready to fix that, the hoses laid out along the furrows. But no one manned the crude machine. It sat abandoned on the side of the field.

I stood very still, trying to hear something. The huge cavern was silent, and the silence was ominous. Where was everyone?

Had they evacuated without me? A pang of fear and hurt shot through me. But they wouldn't have left without Doc, of course. They would never leave Doc. I wanted to dart back through the long tunnel to make sure Doc had not disappeared, too.

*They wouldn't go without us, either, silly. Jared and Jamie and Ian wouldn't leave us behind.*

*You're right. You're right. Let's . . . check the kitchen?*

I jogged down the silent corridor, getting more anxious as the silence continued. Maybe it was my imagination, and the loud thumping of my pulse in my ears. Of course there must be something to hear. If I could calm down and slow my breathing, I'd be able to hear voices.

But I reached the kitchen and it was empty, too. Empty of people. On the tables, half-eaten lunches had been abandoned. Peanut butter on the last of the soft bread. Apples and warm cans of soda.

My stomach reminded me that I hadn't eaten at all today, but I barely noted the twist of hunger. The panic was so much stronger.

*What if . . . what if we didn't evacuate soon enough?*

*No!* Mel gasped. *No, we would have heard something! Someone would have . . . or there would be . . . They'd still be here, looking for us. They wouldn't give up until they'd checked everywhere. So that can't be it.*

*Unless they're looking for us now.*

I spun back toward the door, my eyes darting through the shadows.

I had to go warn Doc. We had to get out of here if we were the last two.

*No! They can't be gone!* Jamie, Jared . . . Their faces were so clear, as if they were etched onto the insides of my eyelids.

And Ian's face, as I added my own pictures to hers. Jeb, Trudy, Lily, Heath, Geoffrey. *We'll get them back,* I vowed. *We'll hunt them down one by one and steal them back! I won't* let *them take my family!*

If I'd had any doubts where I stood, this moment would have erased them. I'd never felt so fierce in all my lives. My teeth clenched tight, snapping together audibly.

And then the noise, the babble of voices I'd been so anxiously straining to hear, echoed down the hall to us and made my breath catch. I slid silently to the wall and pressed myself into the shadow there, listening.

*The big garden. You can hear it in the echoes.*

*Sounds like a large group.*

*Yes. But yours or mine?*

*Ours or theirs,* she corrected.

I crept down the hall, keeping to the darkest shadows. We could hear the voices more clearly now, and some of them were familiar. Did that mean anything? How long would it take trained Seekers to perform an insertion?

And then, as I reached the very mouth of the great cave, the sounds became even clearer, and relief washed through me — because the babble of voices was just the same as it had been my very first day here. Murderously angry.

They had to be human voices.

Kyle must be back.

Relief warred with pain as I hurried into the bright sunlight to see what was going on. Relief because my humans were safe. And pain because if Kyle was already safely back, then . . .

*You're still needed, Wanda. So much more than I am.*

*I'm sure I could find excuses forever, Mel. There will always be some reason.*

*Then stay.*

*With you as my prisoner?*

We stopped arguing as we assessed the commotion in the cavern.

Kyle *was* back — the easiest one to spot, the tallest in the crowd, the only one facing me. He was pinned against the far wall by the mob. Though he was the cause of the angry noise, he was not the source of it. His face was conciliatory, pleading. He held his arms out to the sides, palms back, as if there was something behind him he was trying to protect.

"Just calm down, okay?" His deep voice carried over the cacophony. "Back off, Jared, you're scaring her!"

A flash of black hair behind his elbow — an unfamiliar face, with wide, terrified black eyes, peeked around at the crowd.

Jared was closest to Kyle. I could see that the back of his neck was bright red. Jamie clung to one of his arms, holding him back. Ian was on his other side, his arms crossed in front of him, the muscles in his shoulders tight with strain. Behind them, every other human but Doc and Jeb was massed in an angry throng. They surged behind Jared and Ian, asking loud, angry questions.

"What were you thinking?"

"How dare you?"

"Why'd you come back at all?"

Jeb was in the back corner, just watching.

Sharon's brilliant hair caught my eye. I was surprised to see her, with Maggie, right in the center of the crowd. They'd both been so little a part of life here ever since Doc and I had healed Jamie. Never in the middle of things.

*It's the fight,* Mel guessed. *They weren't comfortable with happiness, but they're at home with fury.*

I thought she was probably right. How . . . disturbing.

I heard a shrill voice throwing out some of the angry questions and realized that Lacey was part of the crowd, too.

"Wanda?" Kyle's voice carried across the noise again, and I looked up to see his deep blue eyes locked on me. "*There* you are! Could you *please* come and give me a little help here?"

# CHAPTER 55

# *Attached*

Jeb cleared a path for me, pushing people aside with his rifle as though they were sheep and the gun a shepherd's staff.

"That's enough," he growled at those who complained. "You'll get a chance to dress 'im down later. We all will. Let's get this sorted out first, okay? Let me through."

From the corner of my eye, I saw Sharon and Maggie fall to the back of the crowd, melting away from the reinstatement of reason. Away from my involvement, really, more than anything else. Both with jaws locked, they continued to glare at Kyle.

Jared and Ian were the last two Jeb shoved aside. I brushed both of their arms as I passed, hoping to help calm them.

"Okay, Kyle," Jeb said, smacking the barrel of the gun against his palm. "Don't try to excuse yourself, 'cause there ain't no excuse. I'm plain torn between kickin' ya out and shootin' ya now."

The little face, pale under the deep tan of her skin, peeped around Kyle's elbow again with a swish of long, curly black hair. The girl's mouth was hanging open in horror, her dark eyes frantic. I thought I could see a faint sheen to those eyes, a hint of silver behind the black.

"But right now, let's calm everybody down." Jeb turned around, gun held low across his body, and suddenly it was as if he were guarding Kyle and the little face behind him. He glared at the mob. "Kyle's got a guest, and you're scarin' the snot out of her, people. I think you can all dig up some better manners than that. Now, all of you clear out and get to work on something useful. My cantaloupes are dying. Somebody do something about that, hear?"

He waited until the muttering crowd slowly dispersed. Now that I could see their faces, I could tell that they were already getting over it, most of them, anyway. This wasn't so bad, not after what they'd been fearing the last few days. Yes, Kyle was a self-absorbed idiot, their faces seemed to say, but at least he was back, no harm done. No evacuation, no danger of the Seekers. No more than usual, anyway. He'd brought another worm back, but then, weren't the caves full of them these days?

It just wasn't as shocking as it used to be.

Many went back toward their interrupted lunch, others returned to the irrigation barrel, others to their rooms. Soon only Jared, Ian, and Jamie were left beside me. Jeb looked at these three with a cross expression; his mouth opened, but before he could order them away again, Ian took my hand, and then Jamie grabbed the other. I felt another hand on my wrist, just above Jamie's. Jared.

Jeb rolled his eyes at the way they'd tethered themselves to me to avoid expulsion, and then turned his back on us.

"Thanks, Jeb," Kyle said.

"Shut the hell up, Kyle. Just keep your fat mouth *shut*. I'm dead serious about shooting you, you worthless maggot."

There was a weak whimper from behind Kyle.

"Okay, Jeb. But could you save the death threats till we're alone? She's terrified enough. You remember how that kind of stuff freaks Wanda out." Kyle smiled at me — I felt shock cross my face in reaction — and then he turned to the girl hiding behind him with the gentlest expression I'd ever seen on his face. "See, Sunny? This is Wanda, the one I told you about. She'll help us — she won't let anyone hurt you, just like me."

The girl — or was she a woman? She was tiny, but there was a subtle curviness to her shape that suggested more maturity than her size — stared at me, her eyes huge with fright. Kyle put his arms around her waist, and she let him pull her into his side. She clung there, as if he were an anchor, her pillar of safety.

"Kyle's right." Never thought I'd say that. "I won't let anyone hurt you. Your name is Sunny?" I asked softly.

The woman's eyes flashed up to Kyle's face.

"It's okay. You don't have to be afraid of Wanda. She's just like you." He turned to me. "Her real name is longer — something about ice."

"Sunlight Passing Through the Ice," she whispered to me.

I saw Jeb's eyes brighten with his unquenchable curiosity.

"She doesn't mind being called just Sunny, though. She said it was fine," Kyle assured me.

Sunny nodded. Her eyes flickered from my face to Kyle's and back again. The other men were totally silent and totally motionless. The little circle of calm soothed her a bit, I could see. She must have been able to feel the change in the atmosphere. There was no hostility toward her, none at all.

"I was a Bear, too, Sunny," I told her, trying to make her feel just a little more comfortable. "They called me Lives in the Stars, then. Wanderer, here."

"Lives in the Stars," she whispered, her eyes somehow, impossibly, getting wider. "Rides the Beast."

I suppressed a groan. "You lived in the second crystal city, I guess."

"Yes. I heard the story so many times . . ."

"Did you like being a Bear, Sunny?" I asked quickly. I didn't really want to get into my history right now. "Were you happy there?"

Her face crumpled at my questions; her eyes locked onto Kyle's face and filled with tears.

"I'm sorry," I apologized at once, looking to Kyle, too, for an explanation.

He patted her arm. "Don't be afraid. You won't be hurt. I promised."

I could barely hear her answering whisper. "But I like it here. I want to stay."

Her words brought a thick lump to my throat.

"I know, Sunny. I know." Kyle put his hand on the

back of her head and, in a gesture so tender it made my eyes smart, held her face against his chest.

Jeb cleared his throat, and Sunny started and cringed. It was easy to imagine the frayed state her nerves must be in. Souls were not designed to handle violence and terror.

I remembered long ago when Jared had interrogated me; he'd asked if I was like other souls. I was not, nor was the other soul they'd dealt with, my Seeker. Sunny, however, seemed to embody the essence of my gentle, timid species; we were powerful only in great numbers.

"Sorry, Sunny," Jeb said. "Didn't mean to scare you, there. Maybe we ought to get out of here, though." His eyes swept around the cave, where a few people lingered by the exits, gawking at us. He stared hard at Reid and Lucina, and they ducked down the corridor toward the kitchen. "Probably ought to git along to Doc," Jeb continued with a sigh, giving the frightened little woman a wistful glance. I guessed he was sad to be missing out on new stories.

"Right," Kyle said. He kept his arm firmly around Sunny's tiny waist and pulled her with him toward the southern tunnel.

I followed right behind, towing the others who still adhered to me.

Jeb paused, and we all stopped with him. He jabbed the butt of his gun into Jamie's hip.

"Ain't you got school, kid?"

"Aw, Uncle Jeb, *please?* Please? I don't want to miss —"

"Get your behind to class."

Jamie turned his hurt eyes on me, but Jeb was

absolutely right. This was nothing I wanted Jamie to see. I shook my head at him.

"Could you get Trudy on your way?" I asked. "Doc needs her."

Jamie's shoulders slumped, and he pulled his hand out of mine. Jared's slid down from my wrist to take its place.

"I miss *everything,*" Jamie moaned as he turned back the other way.

"Thanks, Jeb," I whispered when Jamie was out of hearing.

"Yep."

The long tunnel seemed blacker than before because I could feel the fear radiating from the woman ahead of me.

"It's okay," Kyle murmured to her. "There's nothing that's going to hurt you, and I'm here."

I wondered who this strange man was, the one who had come back in Kyle's place. Had they checked his eyes? I couldn't believe he'd carried all this gentleness around inside his big angry body.

It must have been having Jodi back, being so close to what he wanted. Even knowing that this was his Jodi's body, I was surprised that he could expend so much kindness for the soul inside it. I would have thought such compassion was beyond him.

"How's the Healer?" Jared asked me.

"She woke up, just before I came to find you," I said.

I heard more than one sigh of relief in the darkness.

"She's disoriented, though, and very frightened," I warned them all. "She can't remember her name. Doc's working with her. She's going to be even more scared when she sees all of you. Try to be quiet and move slowly, okay?"

"Yes, yes," the voices whispered in the darkness.

"And, Jeb, do you think you could lose the gun? She's a little afraid of humans still."

"Uh — okay," Jeb answered.

"Afraid of humans?" Kyle murmured.

"We're the bad guys," Ian reminded him, squeezing my hand.

I squeezed it back, glad for the warmth of his touch, the pressure of his fingers.

How much longer would I have the feeling of a hand warm around mine? When was the last time I would walk down this tunnel? Was it this time?

*No. Not yet,* Mel whispered.

I was suddenly trembling. Ian's hand tightened again, and so did Jared's.

We walked in silence for a few moments.

"Kyle?" Sunny's timid voice asked.

"Yes?"

"I don't want to go back to the Bears."

"You don't have to. You can go somewhere else."

"But I can't stay here?"

"No. I'm sorry, Sunny."

There was a little hitch in her breathing. I was glad it was dark. No one could see the tears that started rolling down my face. I had no free hand to wipe them away, so I let them fall onto my shirt.

We finally reached the end of the tunnel. The sunlight streamed from the mouth of the hospital, reflecting off the dust motes dancing in the air. I could hear Doc murmuring inside.

"That's very good," he was saying. "Keep thinking of details. You know your old address — your name can't be far behind, eh? How does this feel? Not tender?"

"Careful," I whispered.

Kyle paused at the edge of the arch, Sunny still clinging to his side, and motioned for me to go first.

I took a deep breath and walked slowly into Doc's place. I announced my presence in a low, even voice. "Hello."

The Healer's host started and gasped out a little shriek.

"Just me again," I said reassuringly.

"It's Wanda," Doc reminded her.

The woman was sitting up now, and Doc was sitting beside her with his hand on her arm.

"That's the soul," the woman whispered anxiously to Doc.

"Yes, but she's a friend."

The woman eyed me doubtfully.

"Doc? You've got a few more visitors. Is that okay?"

Doc looked at the woman. "These are all friends, all right? More of the humans who live here with me. None of them would ever dream of hurting you. Can they come in?"

The woman hesitated, then nodded cautiously. "Okay," she whispered.

"This is Ian," I said, motioning him forward. "And Jared, and Jeb." One by one, they walked into the room and stood beside me. "And this is Kyle and . . . uh, Sunny."

Doc's eyes bugged wide as Kyle, Sunny attached to his side, entered the room.

"Are there any more?" the woman whispered.

Doc cleared his throat, trying to compose himself. "Yes. There are a lot of people who live here. All . . . well, mostly humans," he added, staring at Sunny.

"Trudy is on her way," I told Doc. "Maybe Trudy could . . ." I glanced at Sunny and Kyle. ". . . find a room for . . . her to rest in?"

Doc nodded, still wide-eyed. "That might be a good idea."

"Who's Trudy?" the woman whispered.

"She's very nice. She'll take care of you."

"Is she human, or is she like that one?" She nodded toward me.

"She's human."

This seemed to ease the woman's mind.

"Oh," Sunny gasped behind me.

I turned to see her staring at the cryotanks that held the Healers. They were standing in the middle of Doc's desk, the lights on top glowing muted red. On the floor in front of the desk, the seven remaining empty tanks were piled in an untidy heap.

Tears sprang to Sunny's eyes again, and she buried her face against Kyle's chest.

"I don't want to go! I want to stay with you," she moaned to the big man she seemed to trust so completely.

"I know, Sunny. I'm sorry."

Sunny broke down into sobs.

I blinked fast, trying to keep the tears from my own eyes. I crossed the small space to where Sunny stood, and stroked her springy black hair.

"I need to talk to her for a minute, Kyle," I murmured.

He nodded, his face troubled, and pulled the clinging girl from his side.

"No, no," she begged.

"It's okay," I promised. "He's not going anywhere. I just want to ask you a few questions."

Kyle turned her to face me, and her arms locked around me. I pulled her to the far corner of the room, as far from the nameless woman as I could get. I didn't want our conversation to confuse or frighten the Healer's host any more than she already was. Kyle followed, never more than a few inches away. We sat on the floor, facing the wall.

"Jeez," Kyle murmured. "I didn't think it would be like this. This really sucks."

"How did you find her? And catch her?" I asked. The sobbing girl didn't react as I questioned him; she just kept crying on my shoulder. "What happened? Why is she like this?"

"Well, I thought she might be in Las Vegas. I went there first, before I went on to Portland. See, Jodi was really close to her mother, and that's where Doris lived. I thought, seeing how you were about Jared and the kid, that maybe she would go there, even when she wasn't Jodi. And I was right. They were all there at the same old house, Doris's house: Doris, and her husband, Warren — they had other names, but I didn't hear them clearly — and Sunny. I watched them all day, until it was nighttime. Sunny was in Jodi's old room, alone. I snuck in after they'd all been asleep for hours. I yanked Sunny up, threw her over my shoulder, and jumped out the window. I thought she was going to start screaming, so I was really booking it back to the jeep. Then I was afraid because she *didn't* start screaming. She was just so quiet! I was afraid she had . . . you know. Like that guy we caught once."

I winced — I had a more recent memory.

"So I pulled her off my shoulder, and she was alive, just staring up at me, all wide-eyed. Still not screaming. I carried her back to the jeep. I'd been planning to tie her up, but . . . she didn't look that upset. She wasn't trying to get away, at least. So I just buckled her in and started driving.

"She just stared at me for a long time, and then finally she said, 'You're Kyle,' and I said, 'Yeah, who are you?' and she told me her name. What is it again?"

"Sunlight Passing Through the Ice," Sunny whispered brokenly. "I like Sunny, though. It's nice."

"Anyway," Kyle went on after clearing his throat. "She didn't mind talking to me at all. She wasn't afraid like I'd thought she'd be. So we talked." He was quiet for a moment. "She was happy to see me."

"I used to dream about him all the time," Sunny whispered to me. "Every night. I kept hoping the Seekers would find him; I missed him so much. . . . When I saw him, I thought it was the old dream again."

I swallowed loudly.

Kyle reached across me to lay his hand on her cheek.

"She's a good kid, Wanda. Can't we send her someplace really nice?"

"That's what I wanted to ask her about. Where have you lived, Sunny?"

I was vaguely aware of the subdued voices of the others, greeting Trudy's arrival. We had our backs to them. I wanted to see what was going on, but I was also glad not to have the distraction. I tried to concentrate on the crying soul.

"Just here and with the Bears. I was there five life-terms. But I like it better here. I haven't had even a quarter of a life term here!"

"I know. Believe me, I understand. Is there anywhere else, though, that you've ever wanted to go? The Flowers, maybe? It's nice there; I've been."

"I don't want to be a plant," she mumbled into my shoulder.

"The Spiders . . ." I began, but then let my voice trail off. The Spiders were not the right place for Sunny.

"I'm tired of cold. And I like colors."

"I know." I sighed. "I haven't been a Dolphin, but I hear it's nice there. Color, mobility, family . . ."

"They're all so far away. By the time I got anywhere, Kyle would be . . . He'd be . . ." She hiccuped and then started crying again.

"Don't you have any other choices?" Kyle asked anxiously. "Aren't there a lot more places out there?"

I could hear Trudy talking to the Healer's host, but I tuned out the words. Let the humans take care of their own for the moment.

"Not that the off-world ships are going to," I told him, shaking my head. "There are lots of worlds, but only a few, mostly the newer ones, are still open for settling. And I'm sorry, Sunny, but I have to send you far away. The Seekers want to find my friends here, and they'd bring you back if they could, so you could show them the way."

"I don't even know the way," she sobbed. My shoulder was drenched with her tears. "He covered my eyes."

Kyle looked at me as if I could produce some kind of miracle to make this all work out perfectly. Like the medicine I'd provided, some kind of magic. But I knew that I was out of magic, out of happy endings — for the soul half of the equation, at least.

I stared back hopelessly at Kyle. "It's just the Bears, the Flowers, and the Dolphins," I told him. "I won't send her to the Fire Planet."

The small woman shuddered at the name.

"Don't worry, Sunny. You'll like the Dolphins. They'll be nice. Of course they'll be nice."

She sobbed harder.

I sighed and moved on.

"Sunny, I need to ask you about Jodi."

Kyle stiffened beside me.

"What about her?" Sunny mumbled.

"Is she . . . is she in there with you? Can you hear her?"

Sunny sniffed and looked up at me. "I don't understand what you mean."

"Does she ever talk to you? Are you ever aware of her thoughts?"

"My . . . body's? Her thoughts? She doesn't have any. I'm here now."

I nodded slowly.

"Is that bad?" Kyle whispered.

"I don't know enough about it to tell. It's probably not good, though."

Kyle's eyes tightened.

"How long have you been here, Sunny?"

She frowned, thinking. "How long is it, Kyle? Five years? Six? You disappeared before I came home."

"Six," he said.

"And how old are you?" I asked her.

"I'm twenty-seven."

That surprised me — she was such a little thing, so young looking. I couldn't believe she was six years older than Melanie.

"Why does that matter?" Kyle asked.

"I'm not sure. It just seems like the more time someone spent as a human before they became a soul, the better chance they might have at . . . making a recovery. The greater the percentage of their life they spent human, the more memories they have, the more connections, the more years being called by the right name . . . I don't know."

"Is twenty-one years enough?" he asked, his voice desperate.

"I guess we'll find out."

"It's not fair!" Sunny wailed. "Why do you get to stay? Why can't I stay, if you can?"

I had to swallow hard. "That *wouldn't* be fair, would it? But I don't get to stay, Sunny. I have to go, too. And soon. Maybe we'll leave together." Perhaps she'd be happier if she thought I was going to the Dolphins with her. By the time she knew otherwise, Sunny would have a different host with different emotions and no tie to this human beside me. Maybe. Anyway, it would be too late. "I have to go, Sunny, just like you. I have to give my body back, too."

And then, flat and hard from right behind us, Ian's voice broke the quiet like the crack of a whip.

"What?"

# CHAPTER 56

# Welded

Ian glared down at the three of us with such fury that Sunny shivered in terror. It was an odd thing — as if Kyle and Ian had switched faces. Except Ian's face was still perfect, unbroken. Beautiful, even though it was enraged.

"Ian?" Kyle asked, bewildered. "What's the problem?"

Ian spoke from between his locked teeth. "Wanda," he growled, and held his hand out. It looked as if he was having a hard time keeping that hand open, not clenching it into a fist.

*Uh-oh,* Mel thought.

Misery swept through me. I didn't want to say goodbye to Ian, and now I would have to. Of course I had to. I would be wrong to sneak out in the night like a thief and leave all my goodbyes to Melanie.

Ian, tired of waiting, grabbed my arm and hauled me

up from the floor. When Sunny seemed like she was coming along, too, still joined to my side, Ian shook me until she fell off.

"What is *with* you?" Kyle demanded.

Ian hauled his knee back and smashed his foot hard into Kyle's face.

"Ian!" I protested.

Sunny threw herself in front of Kyle — who was holding his hand to his nose and struggling to get to his feet — and tried to shield him with her tiny body. This knocked him off balance, back to the floor, and he groaned.

"C'mon," Ian snarled, dragging me away from them without a backward glance.

"Ian —"

He wrenched me roughly along, making it impossible for me to speak. That was fine. I had no idea what to say.

I saw everyone's startled face flash by in a blur. I was worried he was going to upset the unnamed woman. She wasn't used to anger and violence.

And then we jerked to a stop. Jared was blocking the exit.

"Have you lost your mind, Ian?" he asked, shocked and outraged. "What are you doing to her?"

"Did you know about this?" Ian shouted back, shoving me toward Jared and shaking me at him. Behind us, a whimper. He was scaring them.

"You're going to hurt her!"

"Do you know what she's planning?" Ian roared.

Jared stared at Ian, his face suddenly closed off. He didn't answer.

That was answer enough for Ian.

Ian's fist struck Jared so fast that I missed the blow —

I just felt the lurch in his body and saw Jared reel back into the dark hall.

"Ian, stop," I begged.

"*You* stop," he growled back at me.

He yanked me through the arch into the tunnel, then pulled me north. I had to almost run to keep up with his longer stride.

"O'Shea!" Jared shouted after us.

"*I'm* going to hurt her?" Ian roared back over his shoulder, not breaking pace. "*I* am? *You hypocritical swine!*"

There was nothing but silence and blackness behind us now. I stumbled in the dark, trying to keep up.

It was then that I began to feel the throbbing from Ian's grip. His hand was tight as a tourniquet around my upper arm, his long fingers making the circle easily and then overlapping. My hand was going numb.

He jerked me along faster, and my breath caught in a moan, almost a cry of pain.

The sound made Ian stumble to a stop. His breathing was hoarse in the darkness.

"Ian, Ian, I . . ." I choked, unable to finish. I didn't know what to say, picturing his furious face.

His arms caught me up abruptly, yanking my feet out from under me and then catching my shoulders before I could fall. He started running forward again, carrying me now. His hands were not rough and angry like before; he cradled me against his chest.

He ran right through the big plaza, ignoring the surprised and even suspicious faces. There was too much that was unfamiliar and uncomfortable going on in the caves right now. The humans here — Violetta, Geoffrey, Andy, Paige, Aaron, Brandt, and more I couldn't see well as we jolted past — were skittish. It disturbed them to see Ian running headlong through them, face twisted with rage, with me in his arms.

And then they were behind us. He didn't pause until we reached the doors leaning against his and Kyle's room. He kicked the red one out of the way — it hit the stone floor with an echoing boom — and dropped me onto the mattress on the floor.

Ian stood above me, his chest heaving with exertion and fury. For a second he turned away and put the door back in place with one swift wrench. And then he was glowering again.

I took a deep breath and rolled up onto my knees, holding my hands out, palms up, wishing that some magic would appear in them. Something I could give him, something I could say. But my hands were empty.

"You. Are. Not. Leaving. Me." His eyes blazed — burning brighter than I had ever seen them, blue flames.

"Ian," I whispered. "You have to see that . . . that I can't stay. You *must* see that."

*"No!"* he shouted at me.

I cringed back, and, abruptly, Ian crumpled forward, falling to his knees, falling into me. He buried his head in my stomach, and his arms locked around my waist. He was shaking, shaking hard, and loud, desperate sobs were breaking out of his chest.

"No, Ian, no," I begged. This was so much worse than his anger. "Don't, please. Please, don't."

"Wanda," he moaned.

"Ian, please. Don't feel this way. Don't. I'm so sorry. Please."

I was crying, too, shaking, too, though that might have been him shaking me.

"You can't leave."

"I have to, I have to," I sobbed.

And then we cried wordlessly for a long time.

His tears dried before mine. Eventually, he straightened up and pulled me into his arms again. He waited until I was able to speak.

"Sorry," he whispered. "I was mean."

"No, no. *I'm* sorry. I should have told you, when you didn't guess. I just . . . I couldn't. I didn't want to tell you — to hurt you — to hurt me. It was selfish."

"We need to talk about this, Wanda. It's not a done deal. It can't be."

"It is."

He shook his head, clenching his teeth. "How long? How long have you been planning this?"

"Since the Seeker," I whispered.

He nodded, seeming to expect this answer. "And you thought that you had to give up your secret to save her. I can understand that. But that doesn't mean you have to go anywhere. Just because Doc knows now . . . that doesn't *mean* anything. If I'd thought for one minute that it did, that one action equaled the other, I wouldn't have stood there and let you show him. No one is going to force you to lie down on his blasted gurney! I'll break his hands if he tries to touch you!"

"Ian, please."

"They can't make you, Wanda! Do you hear me?" He was shouting again.

"No one is making me. I didn't show Doc how to do the separation so that I could save the Seeker," I whispered.

"The Seeker's being here just made me have to decide . . . faster. I did it to save Mel, Ian."

His nostrils flared, and he said nothing.

"She's trapped in here, Ian. It's like a prison — worse than that; I can't even describe it. She's like a ghost. And I can free her. I can give her herself back."

"You deserve a life, too, Wanda. You deserve to stay."

"But I *love* her, Ian."

He closed his eyes, and his pale lips went dead white.

"But I love *you*," he whispered. "Doesn't that matter?"

"Of course it matters. So much. Can't you see? That only makes it more . . . necessary."

His eyes flashed open. "Is it so unbearable to have me love you? Is that it? I can keep my mouth shut, Wanda. I won't say it again. You can be with Jared, if that's what you want. Just stay."

"No, Ian!" I took his face between my hands — his skin felt hard, strained tight over the bones. "No. I — I love you, too. Me, the little silver worm in the back of her head. But my body doesn't love you. It can't love you. I can never love you in this body, Ian. It pulls me in two. It's unbearable."

I could have borne it. But watching *him* suffer because of my body's limitations? Not that.

He closed his eyes again. His thick black lashes were wet with tears. I could see them glisten.

*Oh, go ahead,* Mel sighed. *Do whatever you need to. I'll . . . step into the other room,* she added dryly.

*Thanks.*

I wrapped my arms around his neck and pulled myself closer to him until my lips touched his.

He curled his arms around me, pulling me tighter against his chest. Our lips moved together, fusing as if they would never divide, as if separation was not the inevitable thing it was, and I could taste the salt of our tears. His and mine.

Something began to change.

When Melanie's body touched Jared's body, it was like a wildfire — a fast burn that raced across the surface of the desert and consumed everything in its path.

With Ian it was different, so very different, because Melanie didn't love him the way I did. So when he touched me, it was deeper and slower than the wildfire, like the flow of molten rock far beneath the surface of the earth. Too deep to feel the heat of it, but it moved inexorably, changing the very foundations of the world with its advance.

My unwilling body was a fog between us — a thick curtain, but gauzy enough that I could see through it, could see what was happening.

It changed *me,* not her. It was almost a metallurgical process deep inside the core of who I was, something that had already begun, was already nearly forged. But this long, unbroken kiss finished it, searing and sharp edged — it shoved this new creation, all hissing, into the cold water that made it hard and final. Unbreakable.

And I started to cry again, realizing that it must be changing him, too, this man who was kind enough to be a soul but strong as only a human could be.

He moved his lips to my eyes, but it was too late. It was done. "Don't cry, Wanda. Don't cry. You're staying with me."

"Eight full lives," I whispered against his jaw, my voice breaking. "Eight full lives and I never found anyone

I would stay on a planet for, anyone I would follow when they left. I never found a partner. Why now? Why you? You're not of my species. How can you be my partner?"

"It's a strange universe," he murmured.

"It's not fair," I complained, echoing Sunny's words. It wasn't fair. How could I find this, find love — now, in this eleventh hour — and have to leave it? Was it fair that my soul and body couldn't reconcile? Was it fair that I had to love Melanie, too?

Was it fair that Ian would suffer? He deserved happiness if anyone did. It *wasn't* fair or right or even . . . *sane*. How could I do this to him?

"I love you," I whispered.

"Don't say that like you're saying goodbye."

But I had to. "I, the soul called Wanderer, love you, human Ian. And that will never change, no matter what I might become." I worded it carefully, so that there would be no lie in my voice. "If I were a Dolphin or a Bear or a Flower, it wouldn't matter. I would always love you, always remember you. You will be my only partner."

His arms stiffened, then constricted tighter around me, and I could feel the anger in them again. It was hard to breathe.

"You're not wandering off anywhere. You're staying here."

"Ian —"

But his voice was brusque now — angry, but also businesslike. "This isn't just for me. You're a part of this community, and you aren't getting kicked out without discussion. You are far too important to us all — even to the ones who would never admit it. We need you."

"No one's kicking me out, Ian."

"No. Not even you yourself, Wanderer."

He kissed me again, his mouth rougher with the return of the anger. His hand curled into a fist around my hair, and he pulled my face an inch away from his.

"Good or bad?" he demanded.

"Good."

"That's what I thought." And his voice was a growl.

He kissed me again. His arms were so tight around my ribs, his mouth so fierce against mine, that I was soon dizzy and gasping for air. He loosened his arms a little then and let his lips slide to my ear.

"Let's go."

"Where? Where are we going?" I wasn't going anywhere, I knew that. And yet how my heart pounded when I thought of going away, somewhere, anywhere, with Ian. My Ian. He was mine, the way Jared never would be. The way this body could never be his.

"Don't give me any trouble about this, Wanderer. I'm half out of my mind." He pulled us both to our feet.

"Where?" I insisted.

"You're going down the eastern tunnel, past the field, to the end."

"The game room?"

"Yes. And then you are going to wait there until I get the rest of them."

"Why?" His words sounded crazy to me. Did he want to play a game? To ease the tension again?

"Because this *will* be discussed. I'm calling a tribunal, Wanderer, and you are going to abide by our decision."

# CHAPTER 57

# Completed

It was a small tribunal this time, not like the trial for Kyle's life. Ian brought only Jeb, Doc, and Jared. He knew without having to be told that Jamie must not be allowed anywhere near these proceedings.

Melanie would have to give that goodbye for me. I couldn't face that, not with Jamie. I didn't care if it was cowardly of me. I wouldn't do it.

Just one blue lamp, one dim circle of light on the stone floor. We sat on the edge of the ring of light; I was alone, the four men facing me. Jeb had even brought his gun — as if it were a gavel and would make this more official.

The smell of sulfur brought back the painful days of my mourning; there were some memories that I would not regret losing when I was gone.

"How is she?" I asked Doc urgently as they settled in, before they could get started. This tribunal was a waste of my small store of time. I was worried about more important things.

"Which one?" he responded in a weary voice.

I stared at him for a few seconds, and then my eyes grew wide. "Sunny's gone? Already?"

"Kyle thought it was cruel to make her suffer longer. She was . . . unhappy."

"I wish I could have said goodbye," I murmured to myself. "And good luck. How is Jodi?"

"No response yet."

"The Healer's body?"

"Trudy took her away. I think they went to get her something to eat. They're working on finding a temporary name she likes, so we can call her something besides *the body*." He smiled wryly.

"She'll be fine. I'm sure she will," I said, trying to believe the words. "And Jodi, too. It will all work out."

No one called me on my lies. They knew I was saying this for myself.

Doc sighed. "I don't want to be away from Jodi long. She might need something."

"Right," I agreed. "Let's get this over with." The quicker the better. Because it didn't matter what was said here; Doc had agreed to my terms. And yet there was some stupid part of me that hoped . . . hoped that there was a solution that would make everything perfect and let me stay with Ian and Mel with Jared in a way that absolutely no one would suffer for. Best to crush that impossible hope quickly.

"Okay," Jeb said. "Wanda, what's your side?"

"I'm giving Melanie back." Firm, short — no reasons to argue against.

"Ian, what's yours?"

"We need Wanda here."

Firm, short — he was copying me.

Jeb nodded to himself. "That's a tricky one. Wanda, why should I agree with you?"

"If it were you, you'd want your body back. You can't deny Melanie that."

"Ian?" Jeb asked.

"We have to look at the greater good, Jeb. Wanda's already brought us more health and security than we've ever had. She's vital to the survival of our community — of the entire human race. One person can't stand in the way of that."

*He's right.*

*Nobody asked you.*

Jared spoke up. "Wanda, what does Mel say?"

*Ha,* Mel said.

I stared into Jared's eyes, and the strangest thing happened. All the melting and melding I had just been through was shoved aside, into the smallest part of my body, the little corner that I took up physically. The rest of me yearned toward Jared with the same desperate, half-crazed hunger I'd felt since the first time I'd seen him here. This body barely belonged to me or to Melanie — it belonged to him.

There really wasn't room enough for the two of us in here.

"Melanie wants her body back. She wants her life back."

*Liar. Tell them the truth.*

*No.*

"Liar," Ian said. "I can see you arguing with her. I'll

bet she agrees with me. She's a good person. She knows how much we need you."

"Mel knows everything I know. She'll be able to help you. And the Healer's host. She knows more than I ever did. You'll be fine. You were fine before I was here. You'll survive, just like before."

Jeb blew out a puff of air, frowning. "I don't know, Wanda. Ian's got a point."

I glared at the old man and saw that Jared was doing the same. I looked away from that standoff to level a grim glance at Doc.

Doc met my eyes, and his face clenched with pain. He understood the reminder I was giving him. He'd promised. This tribunal didn't overrule that.

Ian was watching Jared — he didn't see our silent exchange.

"Jeb," Jared protested. "There's only one decision here. You know that."

"Is there, kid? Seems to me there's a whole barrel of 'em."

"That's Melanie's body!"

"And Wanda's, too."

Jared choked on his response and had to start over. "You can't leave Mel trapped in there — it's like murder, Jeb."

Ian leaned forward into the light, his face suddenly furious again. "And what is it that you're doing to Wanda, Jared? And the rest of us, if you take her away?"

"You don't care about the rest of anybody! You just want to keep Wanda at Melanie's expense — nothing else matters to you."

"And you want to have Melanie at Wanda's expense —

nothing else matters to *you!* So, with those things being equal, it comes down to what's best for everyone else."

"No! It comes down to what Melanie wants! That's her body!"

They were both crouched halfway between sitting and standing now, their fists clenched and their faces twisted with rage.

"Cool it, boys! Cool it right now," Jeb ordered. "This is a tribunal, and we're going to stay calm and keep our heads. We've got to think about every side."

"Jeb —" Jared began.

"Shut up." Jeb chewed on his lip for a while. "Okay, here's how I see it. Wanda's right —"

Ian lurched to his feet.

"Hold it! Sit yourself back down. Let me finish."

Jeb waited until Ian, the tendons standing out in his taut neck, stiffly returned to a seated position.

"Wanda is right," Jeb said. "Mel needs her body back. *But,*" he added quickly when Ian tensed again, "but I don't agree with the rest, Wanda. I think we need you pretty bad, kid. We got Seekers out there lookin' for us, and you can talk right to 'em. The rest of us can't do that. You save lives. I got to think about the welfare of my household."

Jared spoke through his teeth. "So we get her another body. Obviously."

Doc's crumpled face lifted. Jeb's white caterpillar eyebrows touched his hairline. Ian's eyes widened and his lips pursed. He stared at me, considering. . . .

"No! *No!*" I shook my head frantically.

"Why not, Wanda?" Jeb asked. "Don't sound like a half-bad idea to me."

I swallowed and took a deep breath so my voice

wouldn't turn hysterical. "Jeb. Listen to me carefully, Jeb. I am *tired* of being a parasite. Can you understand that? Do you think I want to go into another body and have this start all over again? Do I have to feel guilty forever for taking someone's life away from them? Do I have to have someone else hate me? I'm barely a soul anymore — I love you brutish humans too much. It's wrong for me to be here, and I *hate* feeling that."

I took another breath and spoke through the tears that were falling now. "And what if things change? What if you put me in someone else, steal another life, and it goes wrong? What if that body pulls me after some other love, back to the souls? What if you can't trust me anymore? What if I betray you next time? I don't want to hurt you!"

The first part was the pure and unadorned truth, but I was lying wildly through the second. I hoped they wouldn't hear that. It would help that the words were barely coherent, my tears turned to sobs. I would never hurt them. What had happened to me here was permanent, a part of the very atoms that made up my small body. But maybe, if I gave them a reason to fear me, they would more easily accept what had to be.

And my lies worked, for once. I caught the worried glance Jared and Jeb exchanged. They hadn't thought of that — of my becoming untrustworthy, becoming a danger. Ian was already moving to put his arms around me. He dried my tears against his chest.

"It's okay, honey. You don't have to be anyone else. Nothing's going to change."

"Hold on, Wanda," Jeb said, his shrewd eyes suddenly sharper. "How does going to one of those other planets help you? You'll still be a parasite, kid."

Ian flinched around me at the harsh word.

And I flinched also, because Jeb was too insightful, as always.

They waited for my answer, all but Doc, who knew what the real answer was. The one I wouldn't give.

I tried to say only true things. "It's different on other planets, Jeb. There isn't any resistance. And the hosts themselves are different. They aren't as individualized as humans, their emotions are so much milder. It doesn't feel like stealing a life. Not like it feels here. No one will hate me. And I'd be too far away to hurt you. You'd be safer . . ."

The last part sounded too much like the lie it was, so I let my voice trail off.

Jeb stared at me through narrowed eyes, and I looked away.

I tried not to look at Doc, but I couldn't help one brief glance, to make sure he understood. His eyes locked on mine, clearly miserable, and I knew that he did.

As I quickly lowered my gaze, I caught Jared staring at Doc. Had he seen the silent communication?

Jeb sighed. "This is . . . a pickle." His face turned into a grimace as he concentrated on the dilemma.

"Jeb —" Ian and Jared said together. They both stopped and scowled at each other.

This was all just a waste of time, and I had only hours. Just a few more hours, I knew that for certain now.

"Jeb," I said softly, my voice barely audible over the spring's gushing murmur, and everyone turned to me. "You don't have to decide right now. Doc needs to check on Jodi, and I'd like to see her, too. Plus, I haven't eaten all day. Why don't you sleep on it? We can talk again tomorrow. We've got plenty of time to think about this."

Lies. Could they tell?

"That's a good idea, Wanda. I think everyone here could use a breather. Go get some food, and we'll all sleep on it."

I was very careful not to look at Doc now, even when I spoke to him.

"I'll be along to help with Jodi after I eat, Doc. See you later."

"Okay," Doc said warily.

Why couldn't he keep his tone casual? He was a human — he should have been a good liar.

"Hungry?" Ian murmured, and I nodded. I let him help me up. He latched on to my hand, and I knew he would be keeping a tight hold on me now. That didn't worry me. He slept deeply, like Jamie.

As we walked from the dark room, I could feel eyes on my back, but I wasn't sure whose.

Just a few more things to do. Three, to be precise. Three last deeds to be completed.

First, I ate.

It wouldn't be nice to leave Mel with her body uncomfortable from hunger. Besides, the food was better since I'd been raiding. Something to look forward to rather than endure.

I made Ian get the food and bring it to me while I hid in the field where half-grown sprouts of wheat replaced the corn. I told Ian the truth so that he would help me: I was avoiding Jamie. I didn't want Jamie frightened by this decision. It would be harder for him than for Jared or Ian — they each took one side. Jamie loved us both; he would be more evenly torn.

Ian did not argue with me. We ate in silence, his arm tight around my waist.

Second, I went to see Sunny and Jodi.

I expected to see three glowing cryotanks on top of Doc's desk, and I was surprised that there were still just the two Healers, set in the center. Doc and Kyle hovered over the cot where Jodi lay inert. I walked quickly to them, about to demand to know where Sunny was, but when I got closer, I saw that Kyle had an occupied cryotank cradled in one arm.

"You'll want to be gentle with that," I murmured.

Doc was touching Jodi's wrist, counting to himself. His lips pressed into a thin line when he heard my voice, and he had to begin over again.

"Yeah, Doc told me that," Kyle said, his gaze never leaving Jodi's face. A dark, matched set of bruises was forming under his eyes. Was his nose broken again? "I'm being careful. I just . . . didn't want to leave her alone over there. She was so sad and so . . . sweet."

"I'm sure she'd appreciate it, if she knew."

He nodded, still staring at Jodi. "Is there something I'm supposed to be doing here? Is there some way to help?"

"Talk to her, say her name, talk about things she'll remember. Talk about Sunny, even. That helped with the Healer's host."

"Mandy," Doc corrected. "She says it's not exactly right, but it's close."

"Mandy," I repeated. Not that I would need to remember. "Where is she?"

"With Trudy — that was a good call there. Trudy's exactly the right person. I think she's gotten her to sleep."

"That's good. Mandy will be okay."

"I hope so." Doc smiled, but it didn't affect his gloomy expression much. "I've got lots of questions for her."

I looked at the small woman — it was still impossible to believe that she was older than the body I wore. Her face was slack and vacant. It frightened me a little — she'd been so vibrantly alive when Sunny was inside. Would Mel . . . ?

*I'm still here.*

*I know. You'll be fine.*

*Like Lacey.* She winced, and so did I.

*Never like Lacey.*

I touched Jodi's arm softly. She was much like Lacey in some ways. Olive skinned and black haired and tiny. They could almost be sisters, except that Jodi's sweet, wan face could never look so repellent.

Kyle was tongue-tied, holding her hand.

"Like this, Kyle," I said. I brushed her arm again. "Jodi? Jodi, can you hear me? Kyle's waiting for you, Jodi. He got himself in a lot of trouble getting you here — everybody who knows him wants to beat him senseless." I grinned wryly at the big man, and his lips curled up at the corners, though he didn't look up to see my smile.

"Not that you're surprised to hear that," Ian said beside me. "When hasn't that been the case, eh, Jodi? It's good to see you again, sweetheart. Though I wonder if you feel the same way. Must have been a nice break to get rid of this idiot for so long."

Kyle hadn't noticed his brother was there, attached like a vise to my hand, until Ian spoke.

"You remember Ian, of course. Never has managed to catch up to me in anything, but he keeps trying. Hey, Ian,"

Kyle added, never moving his eyes, "you got anything you want to say to me?"

"Not really."

"I'm waiting for an apology."

"Keep waiting."

"Can you believe he kicked me in the face, Jodes? For no reason at all."

"Who needs an excuse, eh, Jodi?"

It was oddly pleasant, the banter between the brothers. Jodi's presence kept it light and teasing. Gentle and funny. I would have woken up for this. If I were her, I would have been smiling already.

"Keep it up, Kyle," I murmured. "That's just right. She'll come around."

I wished I would get to meet her, to see what she was like. I could only picture Sunny's expressions.

What would it be like for everyone here, meeting Melanie for the first time? Would it seem the same to them, as if there were no difference? Would they really grasp that I was gone, or would Melanie simply fill the role I had?

Maybe they would find her entirely different. Maybe they would have to adjust to her all over again. Maybe she would fit in the way I never had. I pictured her, which was picturing me, the center of a crowd of friendly faces. Pictured us with Freedom in our arms and all the humans who had never trusted me smiling with welcome.

Why did that bring tears to my eyes? Was I really so petty?

*No,* Mel assured me. *And they'll miss you — of course they will. All the best people here will feel your loss.*

She seemed to finally accept my decision.

*Not accept,* she disagreed. *I just can't see any way to stop you. And I can feel how close it is. I'm scared, too. Isn't that funny? I'm absolutely terrified.*

*That makes two of us.*

"Wanda?" Kyle said.

"Yes?"

"I'm sorry."

"Um . . . why?"

"For trying to kill you," he said casually. "Guess I *was* wrong."

Ian gasped. "Please tell me you have some kind of recording device available, Doc."

"Nope. Sorry, Ian."

Ian shook his head. "This moment should be preserved. I never thought I'd live to see the day that Kyle O'Shea would admit to being wrong. C'mon, Jodi. That ought to *shock* you awake."

"Jodi, baby, don't you want to defend me? Tell Ian I never *have* been wrong before." He chuckled.

That was nice. It was nice to know that I'd earned Kyle's acceptance before I left. I hadn't expected that much.

There was no more I could do here. There was no point in lingering. Jodi would either come back or she would not, but neither outcome would change my path now.

So I proceeded to my third and final deed: I lied.

I stepped away from the cot, took a deep breath, and stretched my arms.

"I'm tired, Ian," I said.

Was it really a lie? It didn't sound so false. It had been a long, long day, this, my last day. I'd been up all night, I realized. I hadn't slept since that last raid; I must have been exhausted.

Ian nodded. "I'll bet you are. Did you stay up with the Heal — with Mandy all night?"

"Yeah." I yawned.

"Have a nice night, Doc," Ian said, pulling me toward the exit. "Good luck, Kyle. We'll be back in the morning."

"Night, Kyle," I murmured. "See you, Doc."

Doc glowered at me, but Ian's back was to him, and Kyle was staring at Jodi. I returned Doc's glare with a steady gaze.

Ian walked with me through the black tunnel, saying nothing. I was glad he wasn't in the mood for conversation. I wouldn't have been able to concentrate on it. My stomach was twisting and turning, wringing itself into strange contortions.

I was done, all my tasks accomplished. I only had to wait a bit now and not fall asleep. Tired as I was, I didn't think that would be a problem. My heart was pounding like a fist hitting my ribs from the inside.

No more stalling. It had to be tonight, and Mel knew that, too. What had happened today with Ian had shown me that. The longer I stayed, the more tears and arguments and fights I would cause. The better the chance that I or someone else would slip up and Jamie would find out the truth. Let Mel explain it after the fact. It would be better that way.

*Thanks so much,* Mel thought; her words flowed fast, in a burst, her fear marring her sarcasm.

*Sorry. You don't mind too much?*

She sighed. *How can I mind? I'd do anything you asked me to, Wanda.*

*Take care of them for me.*

*I would have done that anyway.*

*Ian, too.*

*If he'll let me. I've got a feeling he might not like me so much.*

*Even if he won't let you.*

*I'll do whatever I can for him, Wanda. I promise.*

Ian paused in the hall outside the red and gray doors to his room. He raised his eyebrows, and I nodded. Let him think I was still hiding from Jamie. That was true, too.

Ian slid the red door aside, and I went straight to the mattress on the right. I balled up there, knotting my shaking hands in front of my hammering heart, trying to hide them behind my knees.

Ian curled around me, holding me close to his chest. This would have been fine — I knew that he would end up sprawled out in all directions when he was really asleep — except that he could feel my trembling.

"It's going to be fine, Wanda. I know we'll find a solution."

"I truly love you, Ian." It was the only way I could tell him goodbye. The only way he would accept. I knew he would remember later and understand. "With my whole soul, I love you."

"I truly love you, too, my Wanderer."

He nuzzled his face against mine until he found my lips, then he kissed me, slow and gentle, the flow of molten rock swelling languidly in the dark at the center of the earth, until my shaking slowed.

"Sleep, Wanda. Save it for tomorrow. It will keep for the night."

I nodded, moving my face against his, and sighed.

Ian was tired, too. I didn't have to wait long. I stared at the ceiling — the stars had moved above the cracks here. I could see three of them now, where before there had been only two. I watched them wink and pulse across the blackness of space. They did not call to me. I had no desire to join them.

One at a time, Ian's arms fell away from me. He flopped onto his back, muttering in his sleep. I didn't dare wait any longer; I wanted too badly to stay, to fall asleep with him and steal one more day.

I moved cautiously, but he was in no danger of waking. His breathing was heavy and even. He wouldn't open his eyes till morning.

I brushed his smooth forehead with my lips, then rose and slid out the door.

It was not late, and the caves were not empty. I could hear voices bouncing around, strange echoes that might have been coming from anywhere. I didn't see anyone until I was in the big cave. Geoffrey, Heath, and Lily were on their way back from the kitchen. I kept my eyes down, though I was very glad to see Lily. In the brief glimpse I allowed myself, I could see that she was at least standing upright, her shoulders straight. Lily was tough. Like Mel. She'd make it, too.

I hurried to the southern corridor, relieved when I was safe in the blackness there. Relieved and horrified. It was really over now.

*I'm so afraid,* I whimpered.

Before Mel could respond, a heavy hand dropped on my shoulder from the darkness.

"Going somewhere?"

# CHAPTER 58

# Finished

I was so tightly wound that I shrieked in terror; I was so terrified that my shriek was only a breathless little squeal.

"Sorry!" Jared's arm went around my shoulders, comforting. "I'm sorry. I didn't mean to scare you."

"What are you doing here?" I demanded, still breathless.

"Following you. I've been following you all night."

"Well, stop it now."

There was a hesitation in the dark, and his arm didn't move. I shrugged out from under it, but he caught my wrist. His grip was firm; I wouldn't be able to shake free easily.

"You're going to see Doc?" he asked, and there was no confusion in the question. It was obvious that he wasn't talking about a social visit.

"Of course I am." I hissed the words so that he wouldn't

hear the panic in my voice. "What else can I do after today? It's not going to get any better. And this isn't Jeb's
decision to make."

"I know. I'm on your side."

It made me angry that these words still had the power
to hurt me, to bring tears stinging into my eyes. I tried to
hold on to the thought of Ian — he was the anchor, as
Kyle somehow had been for Sunny — but it was hard with
Jared's hand touching me, with the smell of him in my
nose. Like trying to make out the song of one violin when
the entire percussion section was bashing away . . .

"Then let me go, Jared. Go away. I want to be alone."
The words came out fierce and fast and hard. It was easy
to hear that they weren't lies.

"I should come with you."

"You'll have Melanie back soon enough," I snapped.
"I'm only asking for a few minutes, Jared. Give me that
much."

Another pause; his hand didn't loosen.

"Wanda, I would come to be with you."

The tears spilled over. I was grateful for the darkness.

"It wouldn't feel that way," I whispered. "So there's no
point."

Of course Jared could not be allowed to be there. Only
Doc could be trusted. Only he had promised me. And I
wasn't leaving this planet. I wasn't going to go live as a
Dolphin or a Flower, always grieving for the loves I'd left
behind me, all dead by the time I opened my eyes again —
if I even had eyes. This was *my* planet, and they wouldn't
make me leave. I would stay in the dirt, in the dark grotto
with my friends. A human grave for the human I had become.

"But Wanda, I . . . There's so much that I need to say to you."

"I don't want your gratitude, Jared. Trust me on that."

"What *do* you want?" he whispered, his voice strained and choked. "I would give you anything."

"Take care of my family. Don't let the others kill them."

"Of course I'll take care of them." He dismissed my request brusquely. "I meant *you*. What can I give you?"

"I can't take anything with me, Jared."

"Not even a memory, Wanda? What do you want?"

I brushed the tears away with my free hand, but others took their place too quickly for it to matter. No, I couldn't take even a memory.

"What can I give you, Wanda?" he insisted.

I took a deep breath and tried to keep my voice steady.

"Give me a lie, Jared. Tell me you want me to stay."

There was no hesitation this time. His arms wound around me in the dark, held me securely against his chest. He pressed his lips against my forehead, and I felt his breath move my hair when he spoke.

Melanie was holding her breath in my head. She was trying to bury herself again, trying to give me *my* freedom for these last minutes. Maybe she was afraid to listen to these lies. She wouldn't want this memory when I was gone.

"Stay here, Wanda. With us. With *me*. I don't want you to go. Please. I can't imagine having you gone. I can't *see* that. I don't know how to . . . how to . . ." His voice broke.

He was a very good liar. And he must have been very, very sure of me to say those things.

I rested against him for a moment, but I could feel the time pulling me away. Time was up. Time was up.

"Thank you," I whispered, and I tried to extricate myself.

His arms tightened. "I'm not done."

Our faces were only inches apart. He closed the distance, and even here, on the edge of my last breath on this planet, I couldn't help responding. Gasoline and an open flame — we exploded again.

It wasn't the same, though. I could feel that. This was for me. It was my name that he gasped when he held this body — and he thought of it as my body, thought of it as me. I could feel the difference. For one moment, it was just us, just Wanderer and Jared, both of us burning.

No one had ever lied better than Jared lied with his body in my last minutes, and for that I was grateful. I couldn't take it with me, because I wasn't going anywhere, but it eased some of the pain of leaving. I could believe the lie. I could believe that he would miss me so much that it might even mar some of his joy. I shouldn't want that, but it felt good to believe it anyway.

I couldn't ignore the time, the seconds ticking like a countdown. Even on fire, I could feel them dragging at me, sucking me down the dark corridor. Taking me away from all this heat and feeling.

I managed to pull my lips away from his. We panted in the dark, our breath warm on each other's faces.

"Thank you," I said again.

"Wait . . ."

"I can't. I can't . . . bear any more. Okay?"

"Okay," he whispered.

"I just want one more thing. Let me do this alone. Please?"

"If . . . if you're sure that's what you want . . ." He trailed off, unsure.

"It's what I need, Jared."

"Then I'll stay here," he said hoarsely.

"I'll send Doc to get you when it's over."

His arms were still locked around me.

"You know that Ian is going to try to kill me for letting you do this? Maybe I should let him. And Jamie. He'll never forgive either of us."

"I can't think about them right now. Please. Let me go."

Slowly, with a palpable reluctance that warmed some of the cold emptiness in the center of my body, Jared let his arms slide away.

"I love you, Wanda."

I sighed. "Thanks, Jared. You know how much I love you. With my whole heart."

Heart and soul. Not the same thing, in my case. I'd been divided too long. It was time to make something whole again, make a whole person. Even if that excluded me.

The ticking seconds pulled me toward the end. It was cold when he no longer held me. It got colder every step I took away from him.

Just my imagination, of course. It was still summer here. It would always be summer here for me.

"What happens here when it rains, Jared?" I whispered. "Where do people sleep?"

It took him a moment to answer, and I could hear tears in his voice. "We . . ." He swallowed. "We all move into the game room. Everyone sleeps in there together."

I nodded to myself. I wondered what the atmosphere

would be like. Awkward, with all the conflicting personalities? Or was it fun? A change? Like a slumber party?

"Why?" he whispered.

"I just wanted to . . . imagine. How it will be." Life and love would go on. Even though it would happen without me, the idea brought me joy. "Goodbye, Jared. Mel says she'll see you soon."

*Liar.*

"Wait . . . Wanda . . ."

I hurried down the tunnel, hurried away from any chance that he might, with his grateful lies, convince me not to go. There was only silence behind me.

His pain did not hurt me the way Ian's had. For Jared, pain would be over soon. Joy was only minutes away. The happy ending.

The southern tunnel felt only a few yards long. I could see the bright lantern burning ahead, and I knew Doc was waiting for me.

I walked into the room that had always frightened me with my shoulders squared. Doc had everything prepared. In the dimmest corner, I could see two cots pushed together, Kyle snoring with his arm around Jodi's motionless form. His other arm was still curled around Sunny's tank. She would have liked that. I wished there was some way to tell her.

"Hey, Doc," I whispered.

He looked up from the table where he was setting out the medicine. There were already tears streaming down his face.

And suddenly, I was brave. My heart slowed to an even pace. My breath deepened and relaxed. The hardest parts were over.

I had done this before. Many times. I had closed my eyes and gone away. Always knowing new eyes would open again, but still. This was familiar. Nothing to fear.

I went to the cot and hopped up so that I was sitting on it. I reached for the No Pain with steady hands and screwed the lid off. I put the little tissue square on my tongue, let it dissolve.

There was no change. I wasn't in any pain this time. No physical pain.

"Tell me something, Doc. What's your real name?"

I wanted to answer all the little puzzles before the end.

Doc sniffed and wiped the back of his hand under his eyes.

"Eustace. It's a family name, and my parents were cruel people."

I laughed once. Then I sighed. "Jared's waiting, back by the big cave. I promised him you'd tell him when it was over. Just wait until I — until I . . . stop moving, okay? It will be too late for him to do anything about my decision then."

"I don't want to do this, Wanda."

"I know. Thanks for that, Doc. But I'm holding you to your promise."

"Please?"

"No. You gave me your word. I did my part, didn't I?"

"You did."

"Then do yours. Let me stay with Walt and Wes."

His thin face worked as he tried to keep back a sob.

"Will you be . . . in pain?"

"No, Doc," I lied. "I won't feel anything."

I waited for the euphoria to come, for the No Pain to

set everything glowing the way it had the last time. I still didn't feel any difference.

It must not have been the No Pain after all — it had just been being loved. I sighed again.

I stretched out on the cot, on my stomach, and turned my face toward him.

"Put me under, Doc."

The bottle opened. I heard him shake it onto the cloth in his hand.

"You are the noblest, purest creature I've ever met. The universe will be a darker place without you," he whispered.

These were his words over my grave, my epitaph, and I was glad that I got to hear them.

*Thank you, Wanda. My sister. I will never forget you.*
*Be happy, Mel. Enjoy it all. Appreciate it for me.*
*I will,* she promised.
*Bye,* we thought together.

Doc's hand pressed the cloth gently over my face. I breathed in deeply, ignoring the thick, uncomfortable scent. As I took another breath, I saw the three stars again. They were not calling to me; they were letting me go, leaving me to the black universe I had wandered for so many lifetimes. I drifted into the black, and it got brighter and brighter. It wasn't black at all — it was blue. Warm, vibrant, brilliant blue . . . I floated into it with no fear at all.

# CHAPTER 59

# *Remembered*

The beginning would feel like the end. I'd been warned.

But this time the end was a greater surprise than it had ever been. Greater than any end I'd remembered in nine lives. Greater than jumping down an elevator shaft. I had expected no more memories, no more thoughts. What end was this?

The sun is setting — the colors are all rosy, and they make me think of my friend . . . what would her name be here? Something about . . . ruffles? Ruffles and more ruffles. She was a beautiful Flower. The flowers here are so lifeless and boring. They smell wonderful, though. Smells are the best part of this place.

Footsteps behind me. Has Cloud Spinner followed me again? I don't need a jacket. It's warm here — finally! — and I want to feel the air on my skin. I won't look at her. Maybe she'll think I can't hear and she'll go home. She is so careful with me, but I'm almost grown now. She can't mother me forever.

"Excuse me?" someone says, and I don't know the voice.

I turn to look at her, and I don't know the face, either. She's pretty.

**The face in the memory jerked me back to myself. That was my face! But I didn't remember this. . . .**

"Hi," I say.

"Hello. My name is Melanie." She smiles at me. "I'm new in town and . . . I think I'm lost."

"Oh! Where are you trying to go? I'll take you. Our car is just back —"

"No, it's not far. I was going for a walk, but now I can't find my way back to Becker Street."

She's a new neighbor — how nice. I love new friends.

"You're very close," I tell her. "It's just around the second corner up that way, but you can cut right through this little alley here. It takes you straight there."

"Could you show me? I'm sorry, what's your name?"

"Of course! Come with me. I'm Petals Open to the Moon, but my family mostly calls me Pet. Where are you from, Melanie?"

She laughs. "Do you mean San Diego or the Singing World, Pet?"

"Either one." I laugh, too. I like her smile. "There are two Bats on this street. They live in that yellow house with the pine trees."

"I'll have to say hello," she murmurs, but her voice has changed, tensed. She's looking into the dusky alley as though she's expecting to see something.

And there is something there. Two people, a man and a boy. The boy drags his hand through his long black hair like he's nervous. Maybe he is worried because he's lost, too. His pretty eyes are wide and excited. The man is very still.

Jamie. Jared. My heart thumped, but the feeling was peculiar, wrong. Too small and . . . fluttery.

"These are my friends, Pet," Melanie tells me.

"Oh! Oh, hello." I stretch my hand out to the man — he's the closest.

He reaches for my hand, and his grip is so strong.

He yanks me forward, right up to his body. I don't understand. This feels wrong. I don't like it.

My heart beats faster, and I'm afraid. I've never been scared like this before. I don't understand.

His hand swings toward my face, and I gasp. I suck in the mist that comes from his hand. A silver cloud that tastes like raspberries.

"Wha —" I want to ask, but I can't see them anymore. I can't see anything. . . .

There was no more.

"Wanda? Can you hear me, Wanda?" a familiar voice asked.

That wasn't the right name . . . was it? My ears didn't react to it, but something did. Wasn't I Petals Open to the Moon? Pet? Was that it? That didn't feel right, either. My heart beat faster, an echo of the fear in my memory. A vision of a woman with white-and-red-streaked hair and kind green eyes filled my head. Where was my mother? But . . . she wasn't *my* mother, was she?

A sound, a low voice that echoed around me. "Wanda. Come back. We aren't letting you go."

The voice was familiar, and it was also not. It sounded like . . . me?

Where was Petals Open to the Moon? I couldn't find her. Just a thousand empty memories. A house full of pictures but no inhabitants.

"Use the Awake," a voice said. I didn't recognize this one.

Something brushed my face, light as the touch of fog. I knew that scent. It was the smell of grapefruit.

I took a deeper breath, and my mind suddenly cleared.

I could feel that I was lying down . . . but this felt wrong, too. There wasn't . . . enough of me. I felt shrunken.

My hands were warmer than the rest of me, and that was because they were being held. Held in big hands, hands that swallowed them right up.

It smelled odd — stuffy and a little moldy. I remembered the smell . . . but surely I'd never smelled it before in my life.

I saw nothing but dull red — the insides of my eyelids. I wanted to open them, so I went searching for the right muscles to do that.

"Wanderer? We're all waiting for you, honey. Open your eyes."

This voice, this warm breath against my ear, was even more familiar. A strange feeling tickled through my veins at the sound. A feeling I'd never, ever felt before. The sound made my breath catch and my fingers tremble.

I wanted to see the face that went with that voice.

A color washed through my mind — a color that called to me from a faraway life — a brilliant, glowing blue. The whole universe was bright blue. . . .

And finally I knew my name. Yes, that was right. Wanderer. I was Wanderer. Wanda, too. I remembered that now.

A light touch on my face — a warm pressure on my lips, on my eyelids. Ah, that's where they were. I could make them blink now that I'd found them.

"She's waking up!" someone crowed excitedly.

Jamie. Jamie was here. My heart gave another fluttery little thump.

It took a moment for my eyes to focus. The blue that stabbed my eyes was all wrong — too pale, too washed out. It wasn't the blue I wanted.

A hand touched my face. "Wanderer?"

I looked to the sound. The movement of my head on my neck felt so odd. It didn't feel like it used to, but at the same time it felt the way it had always felt.

My searching eyes found the blue I'd been looking for. Sapphire, snow, and midnight.

"Ian? Ian, where am I?" The sound of the voice coming out of my throat frightened me. So high and trilling. Familiar, but not mine. "*Who* am I?"

"You're you," Ian told me. "And you're right where you belong."

I pulled one of my hands free from the giant's hand that held it. I meant to touch my face, but someone's hand reached toward me, and I froze.

The reaching hand also froze above me.

I tried to move my hand again, to protect myself, but that moved the hand above me. I started shaking, and the hand trembled.

Oh.

I opened and closed the hand, looking at it carefully.

Was this *my* hand, this tiny thing? It was a child's hand, except for the long pink-and-white nails, filed into perfect, smooth curves. The skin was fair, with a strange silvery cast to it and, entirely incongruous, a scattering of golden freckles.

It was the odd combination of silver and gold that brought the image back: I could see a face in my head, reflected in a mirror.

The setting of the memory threw me off for a moment because I wasn't used to so much civilization — at the same time, I knew nothing *but* civilization. A pretty dresser with all kinds of frilly and delicate things on top of it. A profusion of dainty glass bottles containing the scents I loved — I loved? Or she loved? — so much. A potted orchid. A set of silver combs.

The big round mirror was framed in a wreath of metal roses. The face in the mirror was roundish, too, not quite oval. Small. The skin on the face had the same silver undertone — silver like moonlight — as the hand did, with another handful of the golden freckles across the bridge of the nose. Wide gray eyes, the silver of the soul shimmering faintly behind the soft color, framed by tangled golden lashes. Pale pink lips, full and almost round, like a baby's. Small, even white teeth behind them. A dimple in the chin. And everywhere, everywhere, golden, waving hair that stood away from my face in a bright halo and fell below where the mirror showed.

My face or her face?

It was the perfect face for a Night Flower. Like an exact translation from Flower to human.

"Where is she?" my high, reedy voice demanded. "Where is Pet?" Her absence frightened me. I'd never seen a more defenseless creature than this half-child with her moonlight face and sunlight hair.

"She's right here," Doc assured me. "Tanked and ready to go. We thought you could tell us the best place to send her."

I looked toward his voice. When I saw him standing in the sunlight, a lit cryotank in his hands, a rush of memories from my former life came back to me.

"Doc!" I gasped in the tiny, fragile voice. "Doc, you promised! You gave me your oath, *Eustace!* Why? Why did you break your word?"

A dim recollection of misery and pain touched me. This body had never felt such agony before. It shied away from the sting.

"Even an honest man sometimes caves to duress, Wanda."

"Duress," another terribly familiar voice scoffed. "I'd say a knife to the throat counts as duress, Jared."

"You knew I wouldn't really use it."

"That I did not. You were quite persuasive."

"A knife?" My body trembled.

"Shh, it's all okay," Ian murmured. His breath blew strands of golden hair across my face, and I brushed them away — a routine gesture. "Did you really think you could leave us that way? Wanda!" He sighed, but the sigh was joyful.

Ian was happy. This insight made my worry suddenly much lighter, easier to bear.

"I told you I didn't want to be a parasite," I whispered.

"Let me through," my old voice ordered. And then I could see my face, the strong one, with the sun-brown skin, the straight black line of the eyebrows over the almond-shaped, hazel eyes, the high, sharp cheekbones . . . See it backward, not as a reflection, the way I'd always seen it before.

"Listen up, Wanda. I know exactly what you don't want to be. But we're human, and we're selfish, and *we* don't always do the right thing. We aren't going to let you go. Deal with it."

The way she spoke, the cadence and the tone, not the voice, brought back all the silent conversations, the voice in my head, my sister.

"Mel? Mel, you're okay!"

She smiled then and leaned over to hug my shoulders. She was bigger than I remembered being.

"Of course I am. Wasn't that the point of all the drama? And you're going to be fine, too. We weren't stupid about it. We didn't just grab the first body we saw."

"Let me tell her, let me!" Jamie shoved in beside Mel. It was getting very crowded around the cot. It rocked, unstable.

I took his hand and squeezed it. My hands felt so feeble. Could he even feel the pressure?

"Jamie!"

"Hey, Wanda! This is cool, isn't it? You're smaller than me now!" He grinned, triumphant.

"But still older. I'm almost —" And then I stopped, changing my sentence abruptly. "My birthday is in two weeks."

I might have been disoriented and confused, but I wasn't stupid. Melanie's experiences had not gone to waste; I had learned from them. Ian was every bit as honorable as Jared, and I was not going to go through the frustration Melanie had.

So I lied, giving myself an extra year. "I'll be eighteen."

From the corner of my eye, I saw Melanie and Ian stiffen in surprise. This body looked much younger than her true age, hovering on the edge of seventeen.

It was this little deception, this preemptive claiming of my partner, that made me realize I was staying here. That I would be with Ian and the rest of my family. My throat thickened, felt oddly swollen.

Jamie patted my face, calling my attention back. I was surprised at how big his hand felt on my cheek. "They let me come on the raid to get you."

"I know," I muttered. "I remember . . . Well, Pet remembers seeing you there." I glared at Mel, who shrugged.

"We tried not to scare her," Jamie said. "She's so . . . kind of fragile-looking, you know? And nice, too. We picked her out together, but I got to decide! See, Mel said we had to get someone young — someone who had a bigger percentage of life as a soul or something. But not too young, because she knew you wouldn't want to be a child. And then Jared liked this face, because he said no one could ever dis . . . *distrust* it. You don't look dangerous at all. You look the opposite of dangerous. Jared said anyone who sees you would just naturally want to protect you, right, Jared? But then I got the final say, because I was looking for someone who looked like *you*. And I thought this looked like you. Because she sort of looks like an angel, and you're good like that. And real pretty. I knew you would be pretty." Jamie smiled hugely. "Ian didn't come. He just sat here with you — he said he didn't care what you looked like. He wouldn't let anyone else put a finger on your tank at all, not even me or Mel. But Doc let me watch this time. It was way cool, Wanda. I don't know why you wouldn't let me watch before. They wouldn't let me help, though. Ian wouldn't let anyone touch you but him."

Ian squeezed my hand and leaned in to whisper through all the hair. His voice was so low that I was the only one who could hear. "I held you in my hand, Wanderer. And you were so beautiful."

My eyes got all wet, and I had to sniff.

"You like it, don't you?" Jamie asked, his voice worried now. "You're not mad? There's nobody in there with you, is there?"

"I'm not mad, exactly," I whispered. "And I — I can't find anybody else. Just Pet's memories. Pet's been in here since . . . I can't remember when she wasn't here. I can't remember any other name."

"You're not a parasite," Melanie said firmly, touching my hair, pulling up a strand and letting the gold slide between her fingers. "This body didn't belong to Pet, but there's nobody else to claim it. We waited to make sure, Wanda. We tried to wake her up almost as long as we tried with Jodi."

"Jodi? What happened to Jodi?" I chirped, my little voice going higher, like a bird's, with anxiety. I struggled to get up, and Ian pulled me — it took no effort, no strength to move my tiny new body — into a sitting position with his arm supporting me. I could see all the faces then.

Doc, no more tears in his eyes. Jeb, peeking around Doc, his expression satisfied and burning with curiosity at the same time. Next, a woman I didn't recognize for a second because her face was more animated than I'd ever seen it, and I hadn't seen it much anyway — Mandy, the former Healer. Closer to me, Jamie, with his bright, excited smile, Melanie beside him, and Jared behind her, his hands around her waist. I knew that his hands would never feel right unless they were touching her body — my body! — now. That he would keep her as close as he could forever, hating any inch that came between them. This caused me a fierce, aching pain. The delicate heart in my thin chest shuddered. It had never been broken before, and it didn't understand this memory.

It made me sorry to realize that I still loved Jared. I wasn't free of that, wasn't free of jealousy for the body he loved. My glance flickered back to Mel. I saw the rueful twist of the mouth that used to be mine, and knew she understood.

I continued quickly around the cluster of faces circling my bed, while Doc, after a pause, answered my question.

Trudy and Geoffrey, Heath, Paige and Andy. Brandt, even . . . .

"Jodi didn't respond. We kept trying as long as we could."

Was Jodi gone, then? I wondered, my inexperienced

heart throbbing. I was giving the poor frail thing such a rough awakening.

Heidi and Lily, Lily smiling a pained little smile — none the less sincere for the pain . . .

"We were able to keep her hydrated, but we had no way to feed her. We were worried about atrophy — her muscles, her brain . . ."

While my new heart ached harder than it had ever ached — ached for a woman I'd never known — my eyes continued around the circle and then froze.

Jodi, clinging to Kyle's side, stared back at me.

She smiled tentatively, and suddenly I recognized her.

"Sunny!"

"I got to stay," she said, not quite smug but almost. "Just like you." She glanced at Kyle's face — which was more stoic than I was used to seeing it — and her voice turned sad. "I'm trying, though. I am looking for her. I will keep looking."

"Kyle had us put Sunny back when it looked like we would lose Jodi," Doc continued quietly.

I stared at Sunny and Kyle for a moment, stunned, and then finished the circle.

Ian was watching me with a strange combination of joy and nervousness. His face was higher than it should have been, bigger than it used to be. But his eyes were still the blue I remembered. The anchor that held me to this planet.

"You okay in there?" he asked.

"I . . . I don't know," I admitted. "This feels very . . . weird. Every bit as weird as switching species. So much weirder than I would have thought. I . . . I don't know."

My heart fluttered again, looking into those eyes, and

this was no memory of another lifetime's love. My mouth felt dry, and my stomach quivered. The place where his arm touched my back felt more alive than the rest of my body.

"You don't mind staying here *too* much, do you, Wanda? Do you think that maybe you could tolerate it?" he murmured.

Jamie squeezed my hand. Melanie put hers on top of his, then smiled when Jared added his to the pile. Trudy patted my foot. Geoffrey, Heath, Heidi, Andy, Paige, Brandt, and even Lily were beaming at me. Kyle had shuffled closer, a grin spreading across his face. Sunny's smile was the smile of a coconspirator.

How much No Pain had Doc given me? Everything was glowing.

Ian brushed the cloud of golden hair back from my face and laid his hand on my cheek. His hand was so big just the palm covered from my jaw to my forehead; the contact sent a jolt of electricity through my silvery skin. It tingled after that first jolt, and the pit of my stomach tingled along with it.

I could feel a warm flush pinking my cheeks. My heart had never been broken before, but it had also never flown. It made me shy; I had a hard time finding my voice.

"I suppose I could do that," I whispered. "If it makes you happy."

"That's not good enough, actually," Ian disagreed. "It has to make *you* happy, too."

I could only meet his gaze for a few seconds at a time; the shyness, so new and confusing to me, had my eyes dropping to my lap again and again.

"I . . . think it might," I agreed. "I think it might make me very, very happy."

Happy and sad, elated and miserable, secure and afraid, loved and denied, patient and angry, peaceful and wild, complete and empty . . . all of it. I would feel everything. It would all be mine.

Ian coaxed my face up until I looked him in the eyes, my cheeks flushing darker.

"Then you will stay."

He kissed me, right in front of everyone, but I forgot the audience quickly. This was easy and right, no division, no confusion, no objection, just Ian and me, the molten rock moving through this new body, melding it into the pact.

"I will stay," I agreed.

And my tenth life began.

# *Continued*

Life and love went on in the last human outpost on the planet Earth, but things did not stay exactly the same.

I was not the same.

This was my first rebirth into a body of the same species. I found the transfer much more difficult than changing planets because I had so many expectations about being human already in place. Also, I'd inherited a lot of things from Petals Open to the Moon, and not all of them were pleasant.

I'd inherited a great deal of grief for Cloud Spinner. I missed the mother I'd never known and mourned for her suffering now. Perhaps there could be no joy on this planet without an equal weight of pain to balance it out on some unknown scale.

I'd inherited unexpected limitations. I was used to a

body that was strong and fast and tall — a body that could run for miles, go without food and water, lift heavy weights, and reach high shelves. This body was weak — and not just physically. This body seized up with crippling shyness every time I was unsure of myself, which seemed to be often these days.

I'd inherited a different role in the human community. People carried things for me now and let me pass first into a room. They gave me the easiest chores and then, half the time, took the work right out of my hands anyway. Worse than that, I needed the help. My muscles were soft and not used to labor. I tired easily, and my attempts to hide that fooled no one. I probably couldn't have run a mile without stopping.

There was more to this easy treatment than just my physical weakness, though. I was used to a pretty face, but one that people were able to look at with fear, mistrust, even hatred. My new face defied such emotions.

People touched my cheeks often, or put their fingers under my chin, holding my face up to see it better. I was frequently patted on my head (which was in easy reach, since I was shorter than everyone but the children), and my hair was stroked so regularly that I stopped noticing when it happened. Those who had never accepted me before did this as often as my friends. Even Lucina put up only a token resistance when her children began following me like two adoring puppies. Freedom, in particular, crawled onto my lap at every opportunity, burrowing his face in my hair. Isaiah was too big for such displays of affection, but he liked to hold my hand — just the same size as his — while chattering excitedly with me about Spiders and Dragons, soccer and raids. The children still wouldn't go anywhere near Melanie; their mother had frightened them too thoroughly before for her reassurances to change things now.

Even Maggie and Sharon, though they still tried not to look at me, could not maintain their former rigidity in my presence.

My body was not the only change. The monsoons came late to the desert, and I was glad.

For one thing, I'd never smelled the rain on the creosotes before — I could only vaguely remember it from my memories of Melanie's memories, a very dim trail of recall indeed — and now the scent washed out the musty caves, left them smelling fresh and almost spicy. The scent clung to my hair and followed me everywhere. I smelled it in my dreams.

Also, Petals Open to the Moon had lived in Seattle all her life, and the unbroken streak of blue skies and blistering heat was as bewildering — almost *numbing* — to my system as the dark press of heavy overcast skies would have been to any of these desert dwellers. The clouds were exciting, a change from the bland, featureless pale blue. They had depth and movement. They made pictures in the sky.

There was a great deal of reshuffling to be done in Jeb's caves, and the move to the big game room — now the communal sleeping quarters — was good preparation for more permanent arrangements to follow.

Every space was needed, so rooms could not remain vacant. Still, only the newcomers, Candy — who had remembered her correct name at last — and Lacey, could bear to take Wes's old space. I pitied Candy for her future roommate, but the Healer never betrayed any discontent at the prospect.

When the rains ended, Jamie would move into a free corner in Brandt and Aaron's cave. Melanie and Jared had kicked Jamie out of their room and into Ian's before I'd been reborn in Pet's body; Jamie wasn't so young that they'd needed to give him any excuse.

Kyle was working on widening the small crevice that had been Walter's sleeping space so that it would be ready when the desert was dry again. It really wasn't big enough for more than one, and Kyle would not be staying there alone.

At night in the game room, Sunny slept curled into a ball against Kyle's chest, like a kitten who was friends with a big dog — a rottweiler whom she trusted implicitly. Sunny was *always* with Kyle. I couldn't remember ever seeing them unattached since I'd opened these silver gray eyes for the first time.

Kyle seemed constantly bemused, too distracted by this impossible relationship he couldn't quite wrap his head around to pay attention to much else. He wasn't giving up on Jodi, but as Sunny clung to him, he held her to his side with gentle hands.

Before the rain, every space was taken, so I stayed with Doc in the hospital that no longer frightened me. The cots were not comfortable, but it was a very interesting place to be. Candy remembered the details of Summer Song's life better than her own; the hospital was a place of miracles now.

After the rain, Doc would not be sleeping in the hospital anymore. The first night in the game room, Sharon had dragged her mattress right next to Doc's without a word of explanation. Perhaps it was Doc's fascination with the Healer that motivated Sharon, though I doubted

Doc had even noticed how pretty the older woman was; his fascination was with her phenomenal knowledge. Or maybe it was just that Sharon was ready to forgive and forget. I hoped that was the case. It would be nice to think that even Sharon and Maggie might be softened over time.

I would not stay in the hospital anymore, either.

The crucial conversation with Ian might never have taken place if not for Jamie. My mouth would go all dry and my palms would sweat whenever I so much as thought of bringing it up. What if those feelings in the hospital, those few perfect moments of certainty right after I'd awoken in this body, had been illusion? What if I remembered them wrong? I knew that nothing had changed for me, but how could I be certain Ian felt the same? The body he'd fallen in love with was still right here!

I expected him to be unsettled — we all were. If it was difficult for me, a soul used to such changes, how hard must it be for the humans?

I was working to put the last of the jealousy and the perplexing echoes of the love I still felt for Jared behind me. I didn't need or want them. Ian was the right partner for me. But sometimes I would catch myself staring at Jared and feel confused. I'd seen Melanie touch Ian's arm or hand and then jerk away as if she'd suddenly remembered who she was. Even Jared, who had the least reason for uncertainty, would occasionally meet my confused gaze with a searching one of his own. And Ian . . . Of course it must have been hardest for him. I understood that.

We were together nearly as much as Kyle and Sunny. Ian constantly touched my face and hair, was always holding my hands. But who did not respond to this body that way? And wasn't it platonic for everyone else? Why didn't he kiss me again, the way he had that first day?

Maybe he could never love me inside this body, as appealing as it seemed to be to all the other humans here.

That worry was heavy in my heart the night Ian had carried my cot — because it was too heavy for me — to the big, dark game room.

◆

It was raining for the first time in more than six months. There were both laughter and complaints as people shook out their damp bedding and arranged their places. I saw Sharon with Doc and smiled.

"Over here, Wanda," Jamie called, waving me toward where he'd just set his mattress next to Ian's. "There's room for all three of us now."

Jamie was the one person who treated me almost exactly the same as before. He did make allowances for my puny physique, but he never seemed surprised to see me enter a room or shocked when Wanderer's words came through these lips.

"You don't really want that cot, do you, Wanda? I'll bet we could all fit okay on the mattresses if we shoved them together." Jamie grinned at me while he kicked one mattress into the other without waiting for agreement. "You don't take up much space."

He took the cot from Ian and set it on its side, out of the way. Then Jamie stretched out on the very edge of the far mattress and turned his back to us.

"Oh, hey, Ian," he added without turning. "I talked to

Brandt and Aaron, and I think I'm going to move in with them. Well, I'm beat. Night, guys."

I stared at Jamie's unmoving form for a long moment. Ian was just as motionless. He couldn't have been having a panic attack, too, though. Was he thinking of some way to extricate himself from the situation?

"Lights out," Jeb bellowed from across the room. "Everybody shut yer trap so I can get some shut-eye."

People laughed, but took him seriously as always. One by one, the four lamps were dimmed until the room was black.

Ian's hand found mine; it was warm. Did he notice how cold and sweaty my skin was?

He sank to his knees on the mattress, tugging me gently along. I followed and lay down on the seam between the beds. He kept my hand.

"Is this okay?" Ian whispered. There were other hushed conversations going on around us, made indistinct by the rush of the sulfur spring.

"Yes, thank you," I answered.

Jamie rolled over, shaking the mattress and knocking into me. "Oops, sorry, Wanda," he murmured, and then I heard him yawn.

Automatically, I shifted out of his way. Ian was closer than I'd thought. I gasped quietly when I ran into him, then tried to give him some room. His arm was suddenly around me, holding me to his body.

It was the strangest feeling; having Ian's arm around me in this very nonplatonic way reminded me oddly of my first experience with No Pain. Like I'd been in agony without realizing it, and his touch had taken all the hurt away.

That feeling erased my shyness. I rolled so that I was facing him, and he tightened his arm around me.

"Is this okay?" I whispered, repeating his question.

He kissed my forehead. "Better than okay."

We were silent for a few minutes. Most of the other conversations had died out.

He bent down so that his lips were at my ear and whispered, quieter than before, "Wanda, do you think . . . ?" He fell silent.

"Yes?"

"Well, it looks like I have a room all to myself now. That's not right."

"No. There's not enough space for you to be alone."

"I don't want to be alone. But . . ."

Why wouldn't he ask? "But what?"

"Have you had enough time to sort things out yet? I don't want to rush you. I know it's confusing . . . with Jared . . ."

It took me a moment to process what he was saying, but then I giggled quietly. Melanie wasn't much given to giggling, but Pet had been, and her body betrayed me at this most inopportune moment.

"What?" he demanded.

"I was giving *you* time to sort things out," I explained in a whisper. "I didn't want to rush *you* — because I know it's confusing. With Melanie."

He jumped just a little in surprise. "You thought . . . ? But Melanie isn't you. I was never confused."

I was smiling in the dark now. "And Jared isn't you."

His voice was tighter when he answered. "But he's still Jared. And you love him."

Ian was jealous again? I shouldn't have been pleased

by negative emotions, but I had to admit this was encouraging.

"Jared is my past, another life. You are my present."

He was quiet for a moment. When he spoke again, his voice was rough with emotion. "And your future, if you want that."

"Yes, please."

And then he kissed me in the most unplatonic way possible under the crowded circumstances, and I was thrilled to remember that I'd been smart enough to lie about my age.

The rains would end, and when they did, Ian and I would be together, partners in the truest sense. This was a promise and an obligation I had never had in all my lives. Thinking of it made me feel joyful and anxious and shy and desperately impatient all at the same time — made me feel *human*.

◆

After all this had been settled, Ian and I were more inseparable than ever. So when it came time for me to test my new face on the other souls, of course he went with me.

This raid was a relief for me after long weeks of frustration. It was bad enough that my new body was weak and nearly useless in the caves; I couldn't believe it when the others didn't want to let me use my body for the one thing it was perfect for.

Jared had specifically approved of Jamie's choice because of this guileless, vulnerable face that no one could ever doubt, this delicate build that anyone would be motivated to protect, but even he had a hard time putting his theory into practice. I was sure raiding would be every bit as easy for me now as it had been before, but Jared, Jeb, Ian, and the others — everyone but Jamie and Mel — debated for days, trying to find a way around using me for that. It was ridiculous.

I saw them eyeing Sunny, but she was still unproven, not trusted. On top of that, Sunny had absolutely no intention of setting one foot outside. The very word *raid* had her cowering in terror. Kyle would not go out with us; Sunny had gone hysterical the one time he'd mentioned it.

In the end, practicality had won out. I was needed.

It was good to be needed.

Supplies had been dwindling; this would be a long, thorough trip. Jared was leading the raid, as usual, so it went without saying that Melanie was included. Aaron and Brandt volunteered, not that we really needed the muscle; they were tired of being cooped up.

We were going far to the north, and I was excited to see the new places — to feel the cold again.

Excitement got a bit out of hand in this body. I was bouncy and hyper the night we drove to the rock slide where the van and the big moving truck were hidden. Ian was laughing at me because I could hardly hold still as we loaded the clothes and sundries we would need into the van. He held my hand, he said, to tether me to the surface of the planet.

Was I too loud? Too oblivious to my surroundings? No, of course that was not it. There was nothing I could have done. This was a trap, and it was too late for us the minute we arrived.

We froze when the thin beams of light shot out of the darkness into Jared's and Melanie's faces. My face, my eyes, the ones that might have helped us, stayed obscured, hidden in the shadow made by Ian's wide back.

My eyes were not blinded by the glare, and the moon was bright enough for me to clearly see the Seekers that outnumbered us, eight to our six. Bright enough for me to see the way they held their hands, to see the weapons that glinted in them, raised and pointed at us. Pointed at Jared and Mel, at Brandt and Aaron — our only gun still undrawn — and one centered dead on Ian's chest.

Why had I let him come with me? Why did he have to die, too? Lily's bewildered questions echoed in my head: *Why did life and love go on? What was the point?*

My fragile little heart shattered into a million pieces, and I fumbled for the pill in my pocket.

"Steady, now, everybody just keep calm," the man in the center of the group of Seekers called out. "Wait, wait, don't be *swallowing* anything! Jeez, get a grip! No, look!"

The man turned the flashlight on his own face.

His face was sun browned and craggy, like a rock that had been eroded by the wind. His hair was dark, with white at the temples, and it curled in a bushy mess around his ears. And his eyes — his eyes were dark brown. Just dark brown, nothing more.

"See?" he said. "Okay, now, you don't shoot us, and we won't shoot you. See?" And he laid the gun he was carrying to the ground. "C'mon, guys," he said, and the others slid their guns back into holsters — on their hips, their ankles, their backs . . . so many weapons.

"We found your cache here — clever, that; we were lucky to find it — and decided we'd hang out and make your acquaintance. It's not every day you find another rebel cell." He laughed a delighted laugh that came from deep in his belly. "Look at your faces! What? Did you think you all were the only ones still kickin'?" He laughed again.

None of us had moved an inch.

"Think they're in shock, Nate," another man said.

"We scared them half to death," a woman said. "What do you expect?"

They waited, shuffling from foot to foot, while we stood frozen.

Jared was the first to recover. "Who *are* you?" he whispered.

The leader laughed again. "I'm Nate — nice to meet you, though you might not feel the same way just yet. This here's Rob, Evan, Blake, Tom, Kim, and Rachel along with me." He gestured around the group as he spoke, and the humans nodded at their names. I noticed one man, a little to the back, whom Nate did not introduce. He had bright, crinkly ginger hair that stood out — especially because he was the tallest in the group. He alone seemed to be unarmed. He was also staring intently at me, so I looked away. "There's twenty-two of us altogether, though," Nate continued.

Nate held out his hand.

Jared took a deep breath and then a step forward. When he moved, the rest of our little group silently exhaled all at once.

"I'm Jared." He shook Nate's hand, then started to smile. "This is Melanie, Aaron, Brandt, Ian, and Wanda. There are thirty-seven of us altogether."

When Jared spoke my name, Ian shifted his weight, trying to obscure me completely from the other humans' view. It was only then that I realized I was still in just as much danger as the others would have been in if these *had* been Seekers. Just like in the beginning. I tried to hold perfectly still.

Nate blinked at Jared's revelation, and then his eyes widened. "Wow. That's the first time I've ever been one-upped on *that* one."

Now Jared blinked. "You've found others?"

"There are three other cells separate from ours that we know of. Eleven with Gail, seven with Russell, and eighteen with Max. We keep in touch. Even trade now and then." Again, the belly laugh. "Gail's little Ellen decided she wanted to keep company with my Evan here, and Carlos took up with Russell's Cindy. And, of course, everyone needs Burns now and then —" He stopped talking abruptly, glancing uneasily around him, as if he'd said something he shouldn't have. His eyes rested briefly on the tall redhead in the back, who was still staring at me.

"Might as well get that out of the way," the small dark man at Nate's elbow said.

Nate shot a suspicious glance across our little line. "Okay. Rob's right. Let's get this out there." He took a deep breath. "Now, you all just take it easy and hear us out. Calmly, please. This upsets people sometimes."

"Every time," the one named Rob muttered. His hand drifted to the holster on his thigh.

"What?" Jared asked in a flat voice.

Nate sighed and then gestured to the tall man with the ginger red hair. The man stepped forward, a wry smile on his face. He had freckles, like me, only thousands more. They were scattered so thick across his face that he looked dark skinned, though he was fair. His eyes were dark — navy blue, maybe.

"This here is Burns. Now, he's with us, so don't go crazy. He's my best friend — saved my life a hundred times. He's one of our family, and we don't take kindly to it when people try to kill him."

One of the women slowly pulled her gun out and held it pointed at the ground.

The redhead spoke for the first time in a distinctly gentle tenor voice. "No, it's okay, Nate. See? They've got one of their own." He pointed straight at me, and Ian tensed. "Looks like I'm not the only one who's gone native."

Burns grinned at me, then crossed the empty space, the no-man's-land between the two tribes, with his hand stretched out toward me.

I stepped out from around Ian, ignoring his muttered warning, abruptly comfortable and sure.

I liked the way Burns had phrased it. *Gone native.*

Burns stopped in front of me, lowering his hand a bit to compensate for the considerable difference in our heights. I took his hand — it was hard and callused next to my delicate skin — and shook it.

"Burns Living Flowers," he introduced himself.

My eyes widened at his name. Fire World — how unexpected.

"Wanderer," I told him.

"It's . . . extraordinary to meet you, Wanderer. And here I thought I was one of a kind."

"Not even close," I said, thinking of Sunny back in the caves. Perhaps we were none of us as rare as we thought.

He raised an eyebrow at my answer, intrigued.

"Is that so?" he said. "Well, maybe there's some hope for this planet, after all."

"It's a strange world," I murmured, more to myself than to the other native soul.

"The strangest," he agreed.